MW00945379

# Asa Mayhew:
## *Sailor*
### *Book I*

## MARJORIE BEARSE

authorHOUSE®

*AuthorHouse*™
*1663 Liberty Drive*
*Bloomington, IN 47403*
*www.authorhouse.com*
*Phone: 1 (800) 839-8640*

*Published by AuthorHouse  01/17/2020*

*ISBN: 978-1-7283-3942-9 (sc)*
*ISBN: 978-1-7283-3941-2 (e)*

*Print information available on the last page.*

*This book is printed on acid-free paper.*

# Contents

# Book 1
# Asa Mayhew: *Sailor*

# Chapter 1

# *O Captain! My Captain*

*Off the Cape of Good Hope aboard the
SS Mary Lovejoy, October 1915.*

Heavy as slate, a slit of sky disappeared below the horizon as an ink-black sea swept over the bow. As the ship buffeted mountainous waves, a ghostly figure in a white nightshirt appeared, pitching toward the gunnel. Chief Mate Asa Mayhew, too far away, saw him from the bridge.

"Good God! It's Cap'n James!"

Asa had left two men taking care of him, but Captain James Lovejoy, delirious with fever, had slipped away from them.

"I've got him, Mr. Mayhew!" The second mate grabbed him. With one hand on the captain's shoulder and the other holding his arm, Mike struggled to steer him across the slick deck back to his stateroom. But Captain James slipped like an eel from his wet hands and tipped over the gunnel into the raging sea. With rain streaming down in cataracts, it was hard to tell whether he fell or jumped.

"Man overboard!" echoed throughout the ship. The bo's'n's pipe blasted out the same message.

Asa rang the bells to the engine room and spun the dial on the ship's telegraph. Impatient and wanting to make damned sure they responded immediately, he backed up the order through the voice pipe, "Astern, dead slow!" He bellowed at the bo's'n, "Mr. Martin, to the bridge!" The men could hear the bo's'n's pipe over the loudest gale. He grabbed a loud-hailer, clattered down the ladder, and went out onto the open deck. "Prepare to lower the stahb'd lifeboat!"

Tommy Martin's whistle echoed the command.

The men fought to remove its canvas tarpaulin as the wind snapped it at their arms and faces.

"Kelly! Throw that lifebuoy ovah! You men in the bow! Stand by to lower the anchor!" Lightning lit up the roiling sea. "I see him! You men there, abaft the stahb'd beam! Lower that lifeboat! Martin! Take the conn! Telegraph stop engine! You men in the bow! Heave the hook!" He called over the side, "Hold on, Cap'n! I'm comin'!"

The storm chose that moment to intensify its electric fury. St. Elmo's fire flared blue on the booms and derricks of the two mastheads, turning them into eerie candelabras.

"The corposants!" It seemed the disembodied voice of Starbuck, or perhaps Stubb, crying out, "The corposants! God have mercy on us!"

Drumming thunder and clapping rain drowned out the men's shouts to one another. The sea rose up and slammed down on the deck, threatening to wash them overboard. The men fought to release the wooden lifeboat from its davit, but thte wind tore it from their hands and hurled it against the steel hull, smashing it to sticks. Asa thrust the loud-hailer at the second mate, stripped off his oilskins, and wrenched off his rubber boots.

"What are you doin'?" Slocum yelled.

"Goin' aftah him!"

"You can't! It's suicide!"

"I'll not abandon him!"

"You can't abandon *us*! I'm not qualified to captain this ship!"

"Tie a line around me, Mike! Henry, get me that life vest! Double quick!"

"It's a hell of a drop! You'll kill yourself!" Slocum rigged a harness around him.

"Crissake, Mike, hurry up with those knots!"

"Done!"

Taking a deep breath, Asa knifed into the water and kicked upward. With each stroke, he stretched arm over arm, digging deep handfuls of ocean, pulling himself forward, fighting the swells that pushed him back. The sea reared up and ducked him, holding him under. He struggled to the surface. The kapok-filled life vest wasn't very good at keeping him afloat.

When a thunderbolt illuminated the scene, he caught a glimpse of Captain James. Asa had almost reached him, but then the gloom swallowed him. Unable to see the white nightshirt, Asa tread water, crying out, "James!" He got a mouthful of ocean for his effort, and spat it out. Bobbing in frantic circles, he strained for any sight of James in the dark turbulence. He had a fleeting sense of déjà vu.

"James!" he cried. "James!" But the speeding train of wind whipped his calls away. "James!" He screamed at the top of his lungs, hoping against hope for an answer. Every time he opened his mouth to yell, the sea smacked him in it. Gasping for air, he refused to give up. As loud as he could, he called out, "James!" Strained to the limit, his voice cracked. Exhaustion pulled him under, but he pushed himself to the surface, peering through the darkness for a glimmer of white against the black sea. "James!" In his broken voice, useless against the wind's roar, he sobbed out the name again, not willing to admit defeat.

His rope tightened. He heard Tommy piping out the order to haul. He rasped, "No!" He fought against the men reeling him in without Captain James in his grasp.

Suddenly he was airborne, as a gang of seamen hauled on his tether. High seas pummeled his raw-boned frame, slamming him against the side of the ship. He scrabbled for a handhold, a foothold, anything to hang onto. Where the hell was the Jacob's ladder? Waves forced water into his nose and mouth until he felt his chest would explode. Then his head whacked against something solid. Everything went black.

# Chapter 2

## *Fearful Trip*

He woke up face down on the streaming deck and felt hands pushing on his back. He coughed up water. Shivering, he struggled to his hands and knees. He retched as his lungs tried to wring themselves out. What was happening? Cap'n James… oh, God, no…

He choked out one word. "James?"

Slocum shook his head. "He's gone, Asa."

"No!" He started coughing again as he struggled to get up, and slid. Doc caught him before his face hit the deck. "We've got to—"

"It's no use, Asa. He's gone."

"*Don't* you *dare* tell me—" Asa swung at Mike, but missed as he slipped again. Doc was fast, and got a grip on his arms.

"Stop it!" Doc shook him. "Just — stop it, now."

Asa gulped air. "Mike, I didn't mean—" He shook his head. Deep within himself, he wailed, but the sound never reached his lips. His brain spun, wild as the wind; his mind cried out for James, searched for him still. He clutched his chest, coughing again. His heart, lungs, and stomach were in an uproar. Dizzy and disoriented, he doubled over and heaved up what felt like half an ocean.

*God, help me,* he prayed, *I can't break down now.* He squared his shoulders and took a few slow, deep breaths. He needed to cling to his rational mind to keep them afloat and intact. The *Mary Lovejoy* was his ship now, and she wouldn't go easy on him just because he was a newborn captain, baptized with rain and rollers.

Doc held his arm. "You need to go below and lie down."

"The hell I do!" Asa yanked his arm out of Doc's grasp. "I've got a ship to keep afloat." His voice crackled from hoarse shout to grating rasp.

They careened into each other and did a quick two-step. Doc almost tread on Asa's toes. "Where are your shoes?"

"Shoes! Who the hell cares about losing goddamn shoes when Cap'n James is lost!"

Slocum had a grip on a guy rope, and reached out a hand. "Grab on! Doc's right. You should go below."

Asa brushed their entreaties aside. "Nunno. We're into the teeth of the sto'm. The ship and men are my responsibility. I've got to guide her through!"

With the doctor following, Asa reeled his way to the bridge, grasping objects left and right. He battled the wind to open the hatch. Charts blew about before he got it closed again.

"Conklin, secure those charts! Mr. Martin, I'll take the conn, now."

"Aye, aye, Cap'n Asa," Martin said.

"Don't *ever* call me that! There was only *one* Cap'n Asa! I can't begin to fill his shoes. And this is his son's ship! I'm only *acting* as captain in his stead. *No one* is to call me Cap'n Asa!" His voice broke. "Do you hear? And you damn well make sure everybody knows it!"

"Aye, aye, Mr. Mayhew!" Tommy Martin straightened to attention. Then his shoulders fell as he changed from subordinate to friend. "I'm so sorry, Asa. 'Tis a cruel loss — terrible."

Asa nodded. "Order all the men below, Tommy, please. We don't want anybody else overboard. See to the ship. Report back any damage."

"Aye, aye, Mr. Mayhew."

"You and Doc leave together, so we don't have to chase the charts around twice."

"Aye, aye, sir."

"Mr. Mayhew, you really ought to go below and get out of those wet things. I need to look you over." The doctor wrapped a blanket around Asa's shoulders. "Your throat sounds like hell."

"No time. Sto'm's gettin' worse." He rubbed his dripping hair with the wool blanket, and then wrapped it around him, trying to sop up the sea streaming from his clothes.

"You'll catch your death…"

Asa pointed forward. "If this was any other ship, I'd be out there on an open bridge!" He offered up a silent prayer of thanks to Captain Asa Lovejoy for enclosing the bridge with the wheelhouse before anyone else was doing so. "I'm fine," he rasped. "Go back to sick bay; take care of the men who need you."

"If you'll come to sick bay with me." Doc held his eye.

Asa stared him down.

"Aye, aye, Mr. Mayhew."

Martin and Doc left together; it took both of them to struggle with the hatch. Conklin had fair warning this time, and threw himself, arms spread, over his charts.

Asa took a deep breath and got on with his job. "Jones, change course. Heading no'thwest by west, three-quahtahs no'thwest."

"No'thwest by west, three-quahtahs no'thwest, sir."

Asa turned the dial on the engine room telegraph to: Ahead slow.

"Hard right rudder!"

"Hard right rudder, sir."

He telegraphed the engine room: Ahead half.

In the time it had taken Asa to give the order, Jones to hear it and obey, they'd taken a beating from a brute of a wave on the starboard bow, but at least they hadn't taken it broadside.

Storms, Asa believed, had an animus — a governing spirit, often malevolent — which he could read. He felt the mood of the sea. He was just as glad he'd lost his boots; he felt her pulse better through his bare feet. This one screamed with increased fury as she hurled sea and sky at them.

"I'll take the helm, Jones. Quicker reaction time if I don't have to relay orders. Tell you what — you keep an eye on the barometer for me. Just sing out the changes, no matter how small."

"Aye, aye, sir."

"Don't look so crestfallen, Davy. It's not a reprimand — you haven't done anything wrong." Asa swung the wheel aport, checked his swing, and then eased back to starboard. "Easier to avoid gettin' swamped in a trough when there's no delay between thought and action." Just before a fierce gust hit them, he swung the wheel again, and faced into the mountainous swell, riding up and over it. "See what I mean? What's the pressure?"

"26.4 inches and falling, sir." Jones's face had taken on a greenish tinge.

They went on this way, battling the dirty weather for hours, hearts — and stomachs — in their mouths half the time, but never showing it. The ship heeled to starboard, and Asa steered her out of it. She rose up and slammed down, bruising the sea. The sea bruised her back, pounding her bow and rushing over her decks in torrents.

"Pressure's rising, sir — 27.5."

"Good. We'll be out of it soon, lads."

He called them 'lads,' although he was of an age with them. He'd made first mate at twenty, and wasn't quite twenty-four yet. He felt so much older, and in the past couple of hours, he felt he'd just aged another twenty years. He remembered Cap'n Asa calling him 'my lad,' almost feeling the comforting weight of the old man's hand on his shoulder. He cleared his throat and wrenched his mind back to business. *Buck up*, he told himself. *This is no time to get maudlin.*

All his senses open to storms and U-boats, Asa steadily relayed orders to the engine room and kept an eye on the compass. Jones continued to announce upward changes in the barometric pressure. At long last, the rocking and rolling subsided; the cataract became a drizzle, the wailing wind merely a stiff breeze. Where there had been no delineation between black sky and black sea, there was now a narrow strip of dark blue on the horizon.

"What's the chronometer read, Conklin?"

"0345, sir."

"Your relief should be here. All right, Jones. The helm's yours again. Heading no'thwest by no'th."

"Aye, aye, sir. Heading no'thwest by no'th."

Two men arrived to relieve Jones and Conklin.

"Helm is being relieved. Helm is in hand, heading no'thwest by no'th, rudder amidships," Jones said.

"Helm has been relieved. Heading no'thwest by no'th, rudder amidships," Yates said.

"Very well," Asa said. "Nickerson, keep an eye on the barometer and the compass."

"Aye, aye, sir."

While Asa stood watch, Jones and Conklin went to get some well-deserved sleep.

\* \* \* \*

At sunrise, Asa ordered Mr. Slocum and Mr. Martin to report to the bridge.

"How's the crew holding up, Mike?"

Slocum said, "Everyone is safe and accounted for, thank God. There were only a few minor injuries, although seasickness knocked about half the crew flat."

*Safe — not James.* Asa stared blankly at the horizon.

A ship floating into his line of sight snared his attention. He grabbed the binoculars. He thrust them at Slocum as he snapped out orders.

"Hard left rudder, Yates!"

"Hard left rudder."

Asa turned the dial to: Ahead full. When he didn't feel the increase in speed, he bellowed through the voice pipe, "Ahead full!" His voice cracked, and he turned to Slocum and rasped, "You see her, Mike? Twenty degrees off the stahb'd bow. We were headed straight for her."

"U-boat! Do you think she's spotted us?"

"Let's hope not! That's the last thing we need!"

"Why would she come to the surface?" Yates asked.

"They have to come to the surface to fire," Asa said.

"They wouldn't target us, would they?" Yates asked.

"It's possible, even though we're neutral. So right now, we're gonna keep headin' in the opposite direction, takin' a zig-zag course away from them."

"Why don't we stay closer to home, then?" Yates asked.

"Can't. Trade has to continue or the economy would collapse." Since he'd been a boy, Asa had used his intellect as a temporary escape from grief and pain.

"So it's all about the money?" Yates asked.

"That's part of it, but not all. Europeans still have to eat, and when we put food on their tables, we get paid, so we can afford to put food on our own," Asa said. "Well, I guess it is all about the money, when you come right down to it. But feeding people kinda makes it a little less cynical, don't you think?"

"Thanks for the sho'tah than usual lecture on economics, Professah Mayhew." Teasing Asa about his impromptu lectures was so habitual as to be automatic, and Mike hadn't thought before he spoke. "Um—" He quickly turned away, fiddling with the focus on the binoculars.

"Yates asked. Asa answered." Tommy glowered at Mike.

Asa put a hand on Tommy's shoulder. "Been a rough night."

Mike kept his eyes on the U-boat. "Aha! She spotted someone else. I see the torpedo wake, headed right toward that British destroyer! Now she's preparing to dive." Mike gave the binoculars to Asa. "Three points for'ard off the stahb'd bow. See her?"

"British destroyer's moving fast. Torpedo missed her! The destroyer's firing on the U-boat. They got her!" He handed the binoculars back to Slocum.

Slocum surveyed the scene. "Nothin' left of her but smoke and debris floatin' in an oil slick. The Royal Navy's all right!"

"Well, that's one disaster we managed to avoid," Asa muttered. An image of the dying German sailors flashed before him. *Trapped like sardines in a tin, poor bastids. God, what a horrible way to go.*

Asa turned the dial on the telegraph to: Ahead half. He turned to the helmsman. "Right rudder, Yates. Check your swing. Steady on a course. Heading no'thwest by no'th."

"Heading no'thwest by no'th."

"Before that U-boat so rudely interrupted us, you were making your report, Mike."

"Everyone's safe and accounted for."

Asa scowled at him.

"Well… except… of course…." Mike's face turned crimson.

"All right. Continue, please." His voice had faded to a sandpapery whisper.

"There were a few minor injuries, lots of bumps and bruises. Simmons cracked his bean on a pipe in the engine room and knocked himself out. He came around after a minute. Rivers came close to falling into a furnace, but Sampson pulled him back in time. They both have minor burns. The worst was Cooky. He damned near cut off his thumb when he tried to grab a knife rack that he hadn't secured properly." He shook his head and rolled his eyes. "Not too bright. Doc stitched him up. He'll be fine as long as he can avoid infection. Just about everybody had some seasickness, but about half the crew was really hit hard. Most have recovered, but four of them are in sickbay, getting rehydrated. Doc will give you the binnacle list."

Asa gazed out to sea. *I wish James was still on the binnacle list, tucked up safe in bed.* He sighed, closing his eyes as though the sun hurt, and fell into a reverie.

\* \* \* \*

Only hours ago, he had been sitting by James's bedside, talking to him. "Cap'n James, hang on. Don't let go. Please, don't you leave me, too."

Delirious, James had muttered, "Swim… cool… swim."

"Nunno, no swimming. Don't you go gettin' any crazy ideas in that fevered brain of yours!" Asa had wanted to wrap his arms around him, to keep him from slipping away, to pin him to the earth. Knowing that to be impossible, he had made do with putting his arm beneath James's head and helping him to sip some cold water. He had dipped a cloth in a basin of ice water, wrung it out, and placed it on James's forehead again. "I know you're burning up, but you're too weak to go swimming. Besides, there's a storm coming up, and it's too dangerous. Do you hear me? Can you even understand me? Oh, God, my poor, dear James. You've got to stay in bed."

"Father," James had mumbled. "Are you and… Uncle Alfred…. taking me… home?"

Captain Alfred and Captain Asa had died almost four years ago, six months apart. "No, James. Don't go with them. Stay with me, please. You've got to fight. For Margaret. For Mary. And for me. We love you, James; we need you." Though James was old enough to be Asa's father, he had held James's hand and kissed him on the forehead as though he were a child. "Don't leave us. Please don't leave us," Asa had whispered in his ear.

Then Mike had knocked at the door and stuck his head in. "Sorry, Mr. Mayhew, but this storm's gettin' fierce. We need you on the bridge. No one can read a storm like you do."

Asa had sat up and kept his face turned away to hide the tears. "All right, but send Doc up here first, and a couple of men to watch over Cap'n James. We can't leave him alone."

*I shouldn't have entrusted him to someone else.*

\* \* \* \*

"Mr. Mayhew? Asa! You still with us?"

"What? Oh, sorry, Mike. I must have been woolgatherin' for a moment. Long night." He yawned. Because of the storm, he had been on duty for eighteen grueling hours, and he'd been caring for James before that. Then he squared his shoulders and turned to Martin. "Tommy, is the radio workin' again?"

"Radio's still not workin'. Smitty says he thought it was electrical interference from the sto'm, but now he thinks there might be German U-boats jammin' the signal."

"Might be why we couldn't get the weathah repo't befoah the storm hit. Maybe that one we just saw was within the hundred mile radio range. Check with Smitty again aftah you finish your repo't." Asa sighed, hearing the effect exhaustion was having on his accent. Listening to Tommy's broad Down East didn't help any; but at least Mike and Tommy didn't have any trouble understanding him when he reverted to his native speech. "What's the damage?"

"Well, I got nothin' too bad to repo't. She's seawo'thy, if a mite bedraggled, as you might expect. We'll need to do a lot of cleanin' up, but theyah's no serious damage. Pumps held up pretty good — not too much watah in the hold. Cahgo's all right. Can't damage copra or gutta-percha or jute much; I mean, it's not like we're carryin' a load of fancy bone china. Anyway, you had it strapped down real good, and the men worked like blazes to make sure it didn't shift too much. They ran around like headless chickens tryin' to keep the ballast balanced. Lost a lifeboat. Couple of booms broke off. Engine's actin' up a little, but she's still runnin'."

"If you and Gunderson can't fix it, I'll take a look at it," Asa said. All at once, he felt out on his feet, nauseated and dizzy. Eyes narrowed in pain, he pressed his palm to his temple. "Tomorrow. Mr. Slocum, you're in charge."

"In that case, I'm o'derin' you to bed befoah you keel ovah. You're more bruised and battah'd than the ship. Maybe you should see Doc, get some mo'phine for that migraine." Mike had seen these headaches before. They didn't happen often, but when they did, they were of the worst kind.

"Can't abide the stuff — makes me dopey. A little sleep and a couple of aspirin's all I need."

Asa shambled off. In his berth, he stepped around his upended sea chest and over books that had escaped their stowage. He picked up his fallen pillow and crawled under his blanket. He curled up with his hands over his face, not only to shut out the eye-stabbing light, but to cover the tears that ran down his cheeks from his heart-stabbing grief. He craved oblivion, but it was hard to sleep when he felt like a vessel filled to overflowing with pain. He tried to take relaxing breaths, but it hurt even to breathe. After what seemed an eternity, he drifted into a state that was more like unconsciousness than sleep.

# Chapter 3

## *But O Heart!*

When Asa recovered from his migraine six hours later, the doctor insisted he come down to sickbay for an examination.

"I'm all right, Doc."

"You have neither listened to yourself speak nor looked in a mirror today, if you think you can get away with that. Your voice comes and goes like Smitty's radio; you look like you've gone fifteen rounds with Jack Johnson and lost, but you put up one hell of a fight. Disrobe so I can see the extent of the damage and clean your cuts and abrasions."

Asa gave in. He opened his mouth to let Doc peer into his throat. When Doc told him to gargle with warm salt water and rest his voice as much as possible, he stared straight ahead. As Doc shone a light into his eyes, he drifted into a trance-like state, sitting still on the examining table, neither seeing nor hearing. He didn't flinch as Doc applied alcohol and iodine to some raw abrasions and lacerations. He didn't wince when Doc examined his contusions.

When he was done, Doc took a step back, folded his arms, and observed Asa's absent state. "And your physical injuries are the least of it, aren't they?"

Startled, Asa blinked. The tip of his nose prickled the way it had when he was a child about to cry. He looked down. After a drawn-out silence, he spoke.

"You know how I came to be named for Cap'n Asa, Doc?"

"No, I don't think I've heard that story."

"My fathah fell ovahbo'd, and he couldn't swim. Cap'n Asa Lovejoy dove in aftah him and saved him. Mothah was expectin' me at the time, and Fathah was so grateful, he named me aftah Cap'n Asa... He saved my fathah, but I couldn't save his son. I owed him. I failed him. And my fathah. And his son. Especially his son."

"Asa, no one could have tried harder. You know James would have died anyway, despite everything we tried. In his lucid moments, he knew it as well. We had no idea what this mysterious illness *was*, let alone how to treat it. We tried quinine, aspirin, ice baths, even venipuncture to bring his temperature down. You bathed his brow, soothed him, urged him to hang on, even when he was so far gone in delirium he couldn't understand. When Mike called you to the bridge, you made sure someone kept watch over him. It wasn't your fault his minders got seasick. Perhaps if I'd kept him in sickbay rather than his cabin — but I was worried about contagion, and thought it best to isolate him. As bitter a pill as it is to swallow, neither you nor I could have saved him. You did everything you could."

"Doc, I... I can't remember."

"What do you mean? What can't you remember?"

"Well, if I knew that, then I'd be remembering, wouldn't I?" Asa's testiness was more at himself than at Doc. Abashed, he ducked his head, and then continued, "I mean, from the time the lifeboat smashed against the hull until I returned to the bridge, it's all a blank."

"I wouldn't worry too much about that. You most likely sustained a concussion when your head hit the gunnel. You refused to let me examine you, let alone to lie down, which is what you *should* have been doing. The concussion probably affected your memory, and the migraine on top of everything else didn't help any."

"How *did* my head get whacked against the gunnel? How did I get all these cuts and bruises? It… it bothers me, not remembering."

Doc gave him a long look. "I'd rather you remember it on your own. It will probably come back to you in a day or two."

Asa shrugged. "Maybe."

"Come on, get dressed and I'll take you to dinner," Doc said.

As they walked into the officer's mess, Asa overheard part of Slocum and Martin's conversation with the two engineers. It did nothing to jog his memory; moreover, he couldn't believe what they were saying.

"Heroism such as I've never seen… Jumped overboard," Slocum was saying. "Couldn't stop him. Damned near drowned, too."

Martin added his two cents, "I've always said Asa's got the courage of a dozen men."

Asa interrupted. "That's enough! No more sea stories! Not another word! I'm no hero, damn it! I didn't save him. I failed!" He turned around and walked out. Anger was acceptable. Tears were not.

They left him alone, then, and told the other men not to discuss it, at least not in Mr. Mayhew's presence. They didn't want to rub salt in the wound.

\* \* \* \*

The next day, with the ocean now calm and the ship scrubbed clean, the men gathered on the quarterdeck in the late afternoon sunlight to say a prayer for the repose of Captain James's soul. Asa read the service from the prayer book: "In the sure and certain hope of the resurrection to eternal life through our Lord Jesus Christ, we commend to Almighty God our brother, Cap'n James Lovejoy, and we commit his body to the deep…" The men joined in the Lord's Prayer as the American flag flew at half-staff from the mainmast, snapping in the breeze.

Asa went on to recite. "*O Captain! My Captain! Our fearful trip is done, / the ship has weather'd every rack...*" He continued with valor, but when he got to, "*Here Captain! dear father!*" his voice broke, his throat closed, and he stood paralyzed, looking through the sea surging in his eyes toward the blur of men floating before him.

The afternoon sunlight dimmed as clouds rolled in.

The doctor went to his side and continued, "*This arm beneath your head! / It is some dream that on the deck, / You've fallen cold and dead.*" Asa regained his voice for the last three lines, and they recited together, "*But I walk with mournful tread. / Walk the deck my Captain lies, / Fallen cold and dead.*"[1]

From the youngest ordinary seaman to the gruffest old salt, all the men stood in solemn silence, more than a few of them knuckling away a tear. A shaft of light slanted through a break in the clouds, turning the ocean to molten gold.

Though Cap'n James's body had gone beneath the waves, every man felt his presence on the deck, and sensed that he would see them safely home.

The setting sun shone red in the western sky as they sang, "Abide with me: fast falls the eventide... Help of the helpless, O abide with me." A tear leaked from the corner of his eye, but Asa's rich baritone did not falter as they reached the last line, "In life, in death, O Lord, abide with me."

## Chapter 4

## *Breaking the News*

*Wellfleet, Massachusetts, November 1915*

When Asa got back to Wellfleet on a damp and bitter November evening, he went straight to the white clapboard house crowned with a widow's walk. Subdued lamplight shone through the fanlight over the front door. Strains of classical piano music drifted out. He lingered in the shelter of the porch, listening for a moment. He was slow to lift the heavy handle of the brass door knocker. As it dropped, so did his heart.

The music stopped and Mary Lovejoy came to the door. The top of her head didn't even come up to his clavicle, but her playing suggested there was a lot of power in that petite form.

"Mr. Mayhew?" She sounded surprised.

Asa tipped his hat. "Evening, Miss Lovejoy." He stalled, trying to avoid delivering the bad news. "I liked that piece you were playing. I'm sorry to have interrupted. I wish I could have listened all night. You're very good." His smile was draped in mourning.

"Thank you," Mary said. "What is it, Mr. Mayhew?"

"Miss Lovejoy, is your mother in?"

"Yes, but Doctor Chandler has put her on bed rest, and she mustn't be disturbed. Is it—?" Her eyes opened wide. "It's Father, isn't it?" She covered her lips, as if to unsay the thought, and looked up at him. "Please tell me I'm wrong."

Asa inclined his head. He could fix broken things: clocks, engines, rudders, radios, anything. But he couldn't fix this. He couldn't restore James to his family. He wanted to help, to take her in his arms and try to comfort her, to confess this inability. But that would be taking too many liberties. So he could only reach out in tacit empathy to touch her hand.

"I'll get Doc Chandler for your mother. I should have thought to do that first."

Mary brushed a tear out of the corner of her eye, trying to cover the movement by tucking an imaginary stray hair back into her chignon. "You'd best come in out of the fog, Mr. Mayhew; you sound like you're catching cold. We can telephone him."

Wellfleet had no electricity in 1915, but they did have a rare telephone or two. On a table tucked into the curve of the staircase was a candlestick telephone.

"Hello, operator?" Mary jiggled the switch hook. "Hello?" She turned to Asa. "It's not working. I suppose the wind must have knocked down a line somewhere." She rolled her eyes, muttering to herself, "I'm uttering nonsense."

"Will you be all right while I go to get him?"

With Yankee fortitude, she stiffened her spine and said, "I shall be perfectly all right, thank you."

Her look defied him to suggest otherwise, and her tone said she'd brook no argument. He often used that same look and tone to put on a show of strength. He caught her eye and nodded in recognition, one stubborn survivor to another.

"Don't say anything to your mother just yet."

As he turned to go, Mary caught his sleeve. "Before you go, tell me."

"I don't think that's advis—"

She interrupted. "Please, until I hear you say it, I can't bring myself to believe—" Mary sucked in her breath as though she'd just pricked her finger with a sewing needle. "I need to know. I need to prepare myself to be strong for Mother. Don't you see?"

Although pale, true to her stoic New England upbringing, her voice and gaze were steady and unwavering. She was just a slip of a girl, he thought, but she'd do. Indeed, she was so insistent that he didn't know how to dissuade her without being unpleasantly rude.

"Miss Lovejoy, you'd better sit down. May we go into the parlor?"

"I'm not going to faint, if that's what you're worried about. But do hang up your coat before we go in. And put your sea bag down."

In his single-minded pursuit of carrying out his responsibility, he'd not taken the time to go home. Heavy as it was, he'd forgotten the bag slung over his shoulder. He dumped it in a corner, hung his damp reefer on the coat tree, and followed her into the parlor.

A wood fire burned low in the open fireplace. An oil painting of Captain Asa Lovejoy had pride of place over it. On the mantelpiece was a model of a clipper ship in a bottle that young Asa had made for the captain twelve years ago, when they'd sailed the original *Winged Mercury* to the Caribbean. In front of the window, there was a straight-backed mahogany settee with maroon seat cushions. A

Victorian kerosene lamp, with its rose-painted double globes and ornate brass feet, sat upon a small circular table next to this.

Mary turned up the wick on the lamp, and sat down on the settee.

Asa appreciated her beauty. He wished he hadn't noticed; he didn't know how to react. His emotional state was an agonizing muddle of grief, guilt, and desire, and he suddenly felt thrust backward into gawky adolescence, all elbows and knees. He snatched his peaked cap off his head. When he'd come into the house he'd forgotten it.

"How did…" Mary asked. "I mean, what… what happened?"

All the words he'd rehearsed fled from his mind. "I don't know how to—" Standing before her, Asa studied the rug, turning his hat in his hands. Before his nervous knees gave way, he angled himself down beside her on the settee. "Well, I guess I'd better just… spit it out. Your father was sick, delirious with a high fever. There was a bad storm. Cap'n James somehow staggered out on deck and he… he washed ovah— overboard and he… he drow—" Asa choked. His cap slipped from his fingers to the rug.

Mary didn't move a muscle; she didn't even seem to breathe. He thought that she couldn't comprehend his garbled telling of it, so he tried again.

"It was foul weather, waves washing over the deck and… well… I saw him from the bridge, too far away to grab him. Mr. Slocum almost had him, but…" Asa stiffened, digging his nails into his palm to try to stop the images flooding in. He felt his chest constrict. "We tried, but… by the time we got the lifeboat… the wind, it… broke the… broke the…"

He stared, frozen, thrust backward in time. Before his eyes, he saw the wooden lifeboat as the wind tore it from its davit to shatter it against the steel hull. Violent splintering, roaring sea, and thundering wind deafened him to all other sound. Cold rain and waves battered him as he stood on the pitching deck, wide-legged in his oilskins, fighting to stay upright, straining his eyes for a glimmer of white nightshirt in the bleak, black sea.

"Mr. Mayhew?" Mary's touch on his hand brought him back.

He blinked, at first confused by his surroundings. He bowed his head for a second, gathering his wits. Then he looked up at Mary.

"I'm afraid we couldn't… *I* couldn't… save…" His voice came out in a hoarse rasp. Clearing his throat didn't help any. "I'm so sorry, Miss Lovejoy. Your father… d-drow— The sea… took him."

"No!" Her eyes widened as she clapped a hand over her mouth. She seemed surprised, as though her shouted denial of James's death had been ripped from her throat without her consent. She turned away and sniffed, sweeping a finger under each eye. She ignored Asa's offered handkerchief. He watched her strain to rein in her emotions, straightening her back, biting her lip. As she turned to him, he saw pain in her face. "Two weeks ago?"

He nodded.

She murmured to herself, "So, it is as I feared."

It seemed almost involuntary that her hand sought his, and his natural response was to take it, conjoined to her in grief. He wanted to hold her in his arms and draw her head onto his chest. He wanted to kiss away her tears. He wanted to press his lips to her full, soft lips. *My God! How could I think such a thing at a time like this? What kind of beast am I?* He turned away as shame heated his cheeks, thankful she wasn't looking at him.

He listened to the susurrus of the sea, the ticking of the mantel clock, the hushed tap of rain on the window, and the quiet crackle of the fire in the grate, collecting himself. He wondered if Mary was doing the same, or if she had fallen into a kind of dazed shock at the news. She let go of his hand and spoke.

"You'd better go get Doctor Chandler."

"Where's Martha?" Asa referred to the Lovejoy's longtime cook and family friend.

"Her cousin Polly's children are all down with measles. She's gone to help."

"Oh, deah," Asa sighed, concerned about leaving the women alone. "Looks like she's got her hands full, but I'll drop by later and let her know. Shall I get someone for you?"

"I'm fine. I'm just worried about Mother. I'm afraid her heart—" She looked away, but Asa had seen her fear.

"I've asked Mr. Slocum to locate your Uncle George," he said.

"I don't want him! He'd just—" She heaved a sigh.

Asa nodded. George would likely show up drunk, if he showed up at all.

"*Will* you get going!" She gasped. "Oh, I beg your pardon! I didn't mean to snap at you. Just… *please*, find Doctor Chandler."

He observed her. *She won't allow herself the release of a good cry until she's alone, and she wants me to get the hell out of here.* "Right away."

He went into the hall and put on his coat. He touched the top of his head. Where was his hat? Just as he was about to go back into the parlor to look for it, Mary brought it out and handed it to him.

"Thank you, Miss Lovejoy; I couldn't think what I'd done with it," he said. "I wish there was someone to sit with you while you wait. Shall you be all right?"

"How many times must I tell you? Of course I shall!" She shook her head. "Well, perhaps I shan't, but I *will*. I have to be. Now *please, go.*"

"On my way."

His shoes crunched the wet sand as he trudged down the road toward the center of town. The fog turned into stinging needles of rain. His reefer got soaked, adding another weight to his shoulders. He turned up his collar, tugged down the peak of his cap, stuffed his hands into his pockets, and picked up his pace.

As he walked, the past dogged his footsteps: memories of Captain Asa, Captain Alfred, and Captain James, the four of them sailing the *Winged Mercury* together, when he was just a kid. James grinning at him as they dared each other before diving off those Mexican cliffs into the sea together, just last year. How honored he'd felt as an eight-year-old child, when Captain Asa had invited him to sail aboard *The Elizabeth Lovejoy* on her last journey as a ship-of-the-line. That's when James had entered his life as teacher, mentor, champion, and friend. He felt a pang of nostalgia at the flash of an older memory — climbing up the rigging after his father, when he was only six. He thought of the root of that word: *nostos*, a return home, and *algia*, pain. He was homesick for the past, a place where people he loved lived, a place to which he could never return. He found himself on Doc's doorstep, with no idea how he got there. With his handkerchief, he mopped what he told himself was rain from his face.

Asa was relieved when Doc himself came to the door rather than his housekeeper. He wouldn't have to go through Mrs. Hudson's convoluted explanations of where the doctor had gone, only to end up searching all over town.

Doc Chandler was a gray man: a disheveled thatch of gray hair, bushy gray eyebrows, a gray mustache, gray suit, gray hat, and faded black overcoat. He carried a worn black bag and drove a mud-spattered Model-T. All that gray was relieved by an eccentric bowtie. Tonight's was purple, with green polka dots.

"Doc, I'm glad you're in. I need you. What I mean is Mrs. Lovejoy needs you. You see, I, uh, have to tell her… Oh, God. James is… gone, and I fear hearing the news will have Mrs. Lovejoy following him right soon." He slumped against the doorjamb.

Doc grabbed his arm. "Get in here and sit down!" He took a flask out of his desk drawer and thrust it into Asa's hand. "Take a pull at that while I get my coat and bag."

"I merely lean against the doorpost, and you offer me whiskey?" Asa handed the flask back. "No thanks, Doc. I'm all right. Just tired, and a swallow of that'll put me right to sleep."

Doc pointed to a pitcher and glasses on his desk. "Then drink some water, and make it snappy! When's the last time you ate anything?"

"Don't remembah." Asa yawned. "Abo'd ship, I guess. Soon as we unloaded and finished the papahwork, I caught the train and came directly heah."

"You walked from the station all the way to the Lovejoy house, and then walked way over here, all on an empty stomach?" Doc shrugged into his coat, grabbed his hat and bag. "At least you don't have to walk back. Get in the motor, and let's go." After he turned the crank and got in the car, he handed Asa a chocolate bar. "Eat this — got to keep your strength up. You look like a stiff wind would blow you away. And you sound like a rusty hinge."

"If a stiff wind would blow me away, I'd have been long gone by now." Asa took a deep breath. "I'm *fine*, Doc. It's just that it was kind of a rough voyage and we didn't get much rest."

"'Kind of?'" Doc echoed. "One of your notorious understatements, I take it."

Asa shrugged. Obeying Doc's command, he chewed and choked down the chocolate bar. Over these rough roads, the Model-T's shakes and rattles made it impossible to carry on a conversation. That suited him fine. He wished he could close his eyes and sleep. When they got to the house, his mind drifted as he mounted the stairs with Doc.

*The only time I remember being upstairs was when I was a wee lad and Cap'n Asa took me up to the widow's walk to see the view. I can almost smell his pipe tobacco and feel his hand on my shoulder.*

He straightened his spine as they crossed the threshold into Mrs. Lovejoy's room.

On this grim evening, heavy blue floral-patterned draperies were closed over the large windows, spilling onto the floor to keep out the drafts. The fireplace had been fitted with a coal-burning Franklin stove.

Over the mantel was a large framed hand-colored photograph. Dressed in a morning suit, a beaming James cradled the infant Mary, nearly hidden in yards of frothy white seafoam-like lace. Margaret, in Gibson girl perfection, held up a bottle of champagne trailing ribbons, about to break it on the bow. It was the day they christened both Mary and her namesake ship.

The four-poster bed faced the photograph. Asa imagined Margaret spending hours contemplating it, dreaming of happier times before she had become so ill.

The wedding-ring quilt on the bed was shades of blue on a white background. The cedar chest at the foot of the bed likely contained more quilts and extra blankets. On its top lay a few magazines and folded newspapers. One *Boston Globe* column header was visible as a reminder of the war: "Russia Presses Rumania Hard."

The bedside table was a clutter of medicine bottles, a pitcher of water and glasses, and other sick-room paraphernalia, including a bell to summon help. Asa noticed a pile of books on the lower shelf and stacked on the floor by the table. Among the authors were Henry James, Jane Austin, Charles Dickens, Edith Wharton, and a slim volume of short stories by Willa Cather. Mary's green wing chair was at an angle for reading to or conversation with her mother. Thomas Hardy's *Jude the Obscure* lay on its seat, bookmarked about a third of the way through. These were women after his own heart — serious readers.

As he stood at the bedside with Doctor Chandler, Asa longed to escape into one of those books, rather than deliver his somber news.

Mrs. Lovejoy had been sitting up in bed, embroidering. She leaned back against several pillows, eyes closed. The embroidery hoop had slipped from her fingers.

Mary picked it up, secured the needle, and put it in the bedside table drawer with other needlework supplies. She smoothed her mother's hair. "Mother, are you awake?"

Asa could see where Mary came by petite figure and gorgeous hair, but he hoped she wouldn't have such lines of pain etched on her face as her mother did at forty.

"Oh, Mary," Mrs. Lovejoy said. "I was just resting my eyes."

"Are you awake now?" Mary plumped her mother's pillows. "Are you comfortable?"

"Yes, dear," Mrs. Lovejoy smiled at her daughter. "Good evening Doctor Chandler, Mr. Mayhew."

Asa and the doctor murmured their greetings.

"Since you're both here, I presume something has happened to James?" As a sea captain's daughter and a sea captain's wife, Mrs. Lovejoy was no stranger to the perils of the ocean.

"I'm going to monitor your pulse, all right, Mrs. Lovejoy?" Doctor Chandler took out his pocket watch.

"Certainly." She spoke to the doctor, but looked expectantly at Asa.

He thought it should get easier with the telling, but he couldn't think of the right words. No matter the gentlest way to put it, it would hit like a hard fist to her fragile, birdlike ribcage. He was terrified of killing her with the news.

"Yes, Mrs. Lovejoy, something *has* happened. James—" Asa's voice was a dry croak.

Doc nudged his arm and handed him a glass of water. Asa took a mouthful and swallowed hard, then downed the rest of the glass. He handed it back to Doc, nodding his thanks.

He cleared his throat and reassured her, "It's nothing contagious, just a slight strain of the vocal chords. Please excuse me." He tried again. "Cap'n James, though, *was* sick. He was delirious with a high fever when he wandered out on deck during a bad storm." He stopped and took a deep breath. "He washed ovahbo'd — overboard." He silently prayed, *Oh, God, please don't let her heart stop.* Then he looked her in the eye and said, "Mrs. Lovejoy, I deeply regret that I cannot restore him to you. We— I could not save him."

He bit the inside of his cheek to keep himself in the present, took another breath, and concentrated his attention on Mrs. Lovejoy and Mary. He held them in his warm gaze.

Mrs. Lovejoy looked stunned, but then she said, "Yes. I… felt something." Mary held her hand. They looked to Asa.

What could he do? How could he comfort them? "We… uh… We had a service commending him into God's hands. We prayed and sang a hymn. *Death be not proud… One short sleep past, we wake eternally, / And death shall be no more; death, thou shalt die.*"[2] He didn't know where *that* had come from; he certainly hadn't planned to quote John Donne. Now he was concerned he'd not only injured her with the news, he'd poured salt in the wound. "I am sorry."

Mrs. Lovejoy stared at him as though he had just spoken in a language she did not understand. Then her eyes overflowed. She took a handkerchief from her sleeve to try to stem the flow, to no avail. Mary sat on the edge of the bed and stroked her mother's hair.

"He read that to me once, when… we lost…" Mrs. Lovejoy's voice was faint, her speech faltering. "All these… years, I've worried… the sea would… take him from us. I keep expecting him… to walk through that door… any minute now." She gazed toward the door, as though trying to will him there.

The sound of the rote was loud in the silence of the room, as they caught themselves looking toward the door.

Mrs. Lovejoy murmured to herself, "How shall I — we — go on living without him? Ah, but soon the bell shall toll for me, as well."

Mary turned away, pressing her knuckles to her mouth. Then she took a deep breath and turned to smile at her mother. "He is — was — away so often, but he is full of joy when he comes home isn't he?" Her smile wavered. "Came home. He is — was — so vi—" She bit her lip to stop its trembling, unable to complete the word.

*Vibrant?* Asa wondered. *Vivacious? Vigorous? He was all of those. Vital. Yes, his death has diminished all of us. But she's trying too hard to be courageous and her mother knows it. They'll probably be more natural with each other when we leave.*

"Yes… every time… he entered a room… I could almost… hear a fanfare." Margaret's smile was bittersweet. Her speech was ever more halting as she became fatigued, but Asa could see she wanted — needed — to talk about him. "His smile… always that… sunlit smile." She turned toward Mary. "I wonder if that makes it… harder, or easier… to bear, my dear…. If he had been a dour… sanctimonious cuss, perhaps… we wouldn't mind it… so terribly much." Her cough was weak. She pressed her lips together and then blurted out, "*He* wasn't… supposed to… die first. Oh,

Mary… I *am* sorry. I shouldn't have… said that. It's just… I can't believe… he's not… coming back." Her eyes flooded. "I simply… *cannot*."

"Oh, Mother," Mary sniffed, "neither can I. I want to think of him as being away on a long voyage, just sailing and sailing…" She stifled a sob.

Out of the awkward silence that followed, Asa said, "*Now Voyager depart… / To port and hawser's tie no more returning, / Depart upon thy endless cruise old Sailor.*"[3] Had he really said that aloud? Hearing his own subdued baritone, without a rasp or crack, made him doubt his own ears.

"Yes, that's it," Mrs. Lovejoy's voice had faded even more. "An endless… cruise…." She closed her eyes.

"Mrs. Lovejoy, I'm going to listen to your heart, now." Doctor Chandler took out his stethoscope and leaned over the bed. "Are you in any pain?"

"My heart… is broken, Doctor."

Mary seemed lost, helplessly stroking her mother's hair again.

"My dear Margaret — Mrs. Lovejoy — of course it is. To lose your beloved… well, it feels as though a very part of yourself has been torn from you, doesn't it? I hope you know you have my deepest sympathy, and I am with you to help in any way I can." Doctor Chandler patted her hand. "But in this instance, my concern is with your corporeal heart. Are you having any chest pain?"

Asa thought Doc revealed his own emotions tonight, unusual for him. But then, he was a widower who'd lost his wife suddenly, in an accident with her pony trap, ten years ago. He must be well acquainted with this particular kind of suffering. And he must be very worried about Mrs. Lovejoy. Her heart was indeed broken, doubly so.

"That doesn't… bother me… anymore. It is… this new pain… I must… learn to bear." Mrs. Lovejoy's breathing was labored. Flagging, she closed her eyes. "James." Her husband's name upon her lips was silent.

Doc Chandler poured about half an inch of brandy into a glass, adding water and a few drops of laudanum. "Sip this; it will do you good." He handed the glass to Mary without having to ask her to assist — it had become routine over the past two weeks.

Mary's eyes filled as she held the glass to her mother's lips. "Perhaps you should rest, Mother. Don't try to talk. I'll stay right here with you."

"Mary is right, Mrs. Lovejoy. Sleep, if you can." Doc looked at Asa and tipped his head toward the door.

They moved out into the hall, conversing in low voices.

Doc shook his head. "Her heart's failing."

"Is there anything you can do for her?"

"Years ago, James took her to specialists in Boston, but they all agreed. There is a defect that she was apparently born with, but no one discovered it until she was with child. It was somewhat of a miracle that she survived giving birth to Mary. Well, I'll spare you the medical details. In short, there is really nothing we can do." Doc shrugged one shoulder. "This is taking too much of a toll on her."

"Cap'n James," Asa cleared his throat, "told me about it."

"You look like you're getting one of those headaches," Doc said. "And you keep getting hoarse. Is your throat sore? Maybe you should come see me tomorrow."

Asa looked him in the eye. "I'm fine. It's only strained vocal chords from shouting over the wind. Truly."

Doc held his eye, challenging. "You don't *look* fine. Come to my office tomorrow, two o'clock."

"I'll be all right after a night's sleep and some of Janet's good food. Besides, I've got too much to do. Have to go find George." He heaved a sigh. The last thing he wanted was to deal with George.

"I know how stubborn you can be, and I don't want to argue with you. Just make sure you *do* eat and sleep. And rest your voice," Doc Chandler ordered.

"Don't fuss, Doc," Asa countered. "Mrs. Lovejoy is our concern right now. Has she developed edema?"

"*Our* concern? Edema? You're a doctor, now, too?" Doc's eyebrows went up and down. "Well, I don't know why I should be surprised. You seem to know something of everything. Yes, I'm afraid it's dropsy of the heart."

"Would laudanum help the congestion or make it worse?"

"At this stage, it doesn't make much difference," Doc said. "I only give her small dosages at a time; it helps with the pain."

"Mary said she got worse about two weeks ago? That would be about the time, uh… She must have had some sense…" Asa tried to rub his frown away with his thumb and fingers. "Oh, I don't know."

"Was that when James drowned?"

Asa took a deep breath. "Ayuh." He studied the dark red floral pattern on the navy blue wallpaper. *Blood on the water.*

"I've heard of cases like that, when two people are very close." Doc shrugged.

Asa turned his eyes from the wallpaper to look at Doc. "Mary — Miss Lovejoy — shouldn't be alone here if Mrs. Lovejoy were to— God forbid. Poor Mary. It would be too cruel for her to lose both—" He looked at the floor.

"You would know what that's like." Doc said.

Asa pretended not to hear him. "I'm going over to the Packard's. If they're home, maybe Mrs. Packard or Miss Shirley Packard will come and stay with her for a while."

"Good — just what's needed. I'll stay until you get back."

When Asa returned from the Packard's' house, Doc met him in the hall.

"Mrs. Packard will be over soon, and Shirley will come later to stay overnight, if Mary agrees," Asa said.

"I'll run along, then," Doc said. "I've got another patient who is gravely ill, and may not last the night — old Mrs. Stedman. Tell Mrs. Packard she can most likely find me there, if need be."

"Captain Hookset's aunt? He's kinda looked after her since husband died. About twenty years ago, wasn't it? Is he here with her? Cap'n Hookset, I mean."

"Twenty years sounds about right. I was afraid he might not get here in time, but he came from New Bedford yesterday — Cap'n Hookset. Although, who knows? Maybe Mr. Stedman has come back to escort his wife to her heavenly home."

"Glad he got here." Asa shook his head and tut-tutted in unconscious imitation of Captain Hookset. "What a pity. He'll miss her. What is she — ninety?"

"She'll be ninety-two tomorrow, if she lasts the night. Up until last week, hale and hearty, too. Caught a cold that turned into pneumonia." Doc shook his head. "Well, it's too bad, but she's had a good, long life. Most people are lucky to live past sixty. Well, I'll say good night, then." Doc turned to go down the stairs, but then turned back. "I am sorry about James. I know how much he meant to you." He patted Asa's shoulder on his way out.

Asa stood in the hall for a moment, thinking James hadn't had the chance of a good, long life; neither would Mrs. Lovejoy. They should've had at least another twenty years.

Without warning, his land legs seemed to desert him. He reached out to touch the wall to steady himself. How long had it been since he'd slept? Before going back into the bedroom, he cleared his throat, attempted to smooth back his unruly curls, straightened up, and took a deep breath. He tapped at the door.

"Come in," Mary said.

"Mary — Miss Lovejoy — Mrs. Packard is coming over to help in a little while, and Miss Shirley Packard will come later. She'll stay the night, if you agree. You and your mother shouldn't be alone, especially with the telephone not working."

"I suppose you're right."

"Oh, Doc Chandler's gone over to old Mrs. Stedman's. I'll stay until Mrs. Packard comes."

"You are very considerate, Mr. Mayhew," Mary said.

"Nunno; not at all. I mean… it's nothing… ah, the least I can do," Asa stammered. "Gettin' cold out. It's important to keep this room warm. I'll bring up some more coal."

Passing through the kitchen on the way to the cellar, he decided to stir up the fire in the coal range and put on the kettle. Then he brought a hod of coal up to the bedroom and stoked the Franklin stove while he spoke to Mary. "I've put the kettle on, and I'll bring you up a pot of tea when it's ready. Is there anything else I can do for you?"

"Thank you, but you needn't feel obligated to stay. I'd just like to sit here quietly with Mother for a while."

"By all means; I won't intrude. I'll stay, just the same. I'll go down to the parlor and read. You call out if you need anything. All right?"

"It's very kind of you, Mr. Mayhew."

"Please call me Asa. I only wish I could do more." Such as bring James back, he thought.

In the parlor, he took a copy of *Poetry* magazine out of his pocket, but he couldn't fix his attention on it. Ezra Pound's words were an incomprehensible blur on the page.

He reproached himself: *If only we hadn't spent so much time ashore in India, maybe he wouldn't have drunk bad water or been bitten by that insect, or whatever else could have caused that deadly illness. If only I'd tied him to his bed the minute I heard his delirious mutterings about going for a swim. If only we'd been able to get his fever down. If I hadn't left him in someone else's care. If, if, if! Hell, it's all pointless, now. I failed him.* He looked up at Captain Asa Lovejoy's portrait over the fireplace. *Can you ever forgive me?*

He stared at the painting. Had the captain moved? *Nunno. Must be a trick of the light.* But he could have sworn he heard Captain Asa telling him he must go on a journey to search for something. *Oh, Cap'n Asa, I'd love to go on a journey with you, Cap'n Alfred, and Cap'n James. How I wish the four of us could sail into eternity on the Winged Mercury!* He rubbed his eyes and looked at the painting again. It was perfectly still. *Must be goin' crazy. Damn! I'm so tired I'm seein' things.*

His head jerked up at Mrs. Packard's arrival, and he realized he'd begun to nod off. They went upstairs to look in on Mary and her mother.

"I'm here, dear. You just let me know if you need anything," Mrs. Packard said.

"I guess I'll say goodnight now, unless you want me for anything?" Asa said.

"Thank you, but we're all right," Mary said. "Good night, Mr. Mayhew."

Asa nodded. "Good night."

\* \* \* \*

On his way home, he stopped to tell Martha the news. He went around to the back door. Knowing Martha, she would be in the kitchen.

"I won't come in, Mahtha; I know you've got moah than enough to do, with the children sick." His accent came out when he was tired, disturbed, or in the company of fellow Cape Codders. All three factors being present, it was stronger than ever.

"Oh, that's all right, Asa. Most of the children ah gettin' bettah, except for little Petey; he's still in a parlous condition. All we can do for him now is pray." She sighed. "Eben's back from sea, so Polly doesn't need me as much now. He's a good help, for a man." She rolled her eyes heavenward, but then got a good look at Asa as he shifted into the light coming through the doorway. "What's the mattah, Asa? You look like you've got the weight of the world on your shouldahs."

"Good thing Ebenezer's back, because Mrs. Lovejoy and Mary need you. I've, uh, got sad news." He steeled himself and took a deep breath. "Cap'n James drow—" He faltered, unable to say it.

"Oh, deah Lawd." She seemed to sag.

Martha understood. She was so comfortable, so homely and motherly that all of Asa's defenses started to crumble. He wished he were a child again, so she could hug him and give him solace. They stood on the back porch, blinking at each other. Both looked away at the same time. Martha sniffed.

"You bettah go now, Asa, befoah we both staht bawlin' like those children inside."

He nodded, patting her shoulder. He couldn't speak. He felt like shaking his fist at the sky, howling his sorrow and rage.

*Nunno, Mahtha's right. I'm too old to behave like a child, and even when I was a child, I didn't cry. Not even at Mother and Dad's funeral. Didn't everybody say I was such a little soldier, such a little man? Huh! I was stunned. I couldn't take it in. Cry? I couldn't utter a sound.*

He hefted his sea bag and tried to walk off his grief, taking the long way home, glad of the dark. When he got there, Silas and Janet were already in bed. Fishermen had to rise before the sun. Although he knew they would condole with him, he was just as glad. He could not go through telling it one more time tonight.

Thoroughly worn out, Asa tumbled into his own bed and fell asleep. But the nightmare repeatedly awoke him, just as he was about to drown.

## Chapter 5

# *Hunting George*

*Boston, November 1915*

Asa met Slocum for lunch — 'dinnah,' in their vernacular — at Durgin & Park. Most of the customers were sailors and working men. It certainly wasn't the place to go if you wanted a private conversation, but it wasn't pricey and the food was plentiful.

No sooner had they squeezed into a loud crowd at the end of a long table, than an ill-mannered waitress demanded their orders. "We got pot roast, baked beans, chowdah. Whaddya want? Hurry up! I haven't got all day."

"Baked beans, black tea," Slocum said. "I don't mean just the colah of the tea leaves. I mean no milk and no sugah. Last time, they got it wrong."

"Wrong! Well, pahdon *us* all to blazes, mistah." The waitress glared at him.

"Chowdah, black coffee," Asa said. "Please."

"Huh! *Please* is it? Ain't *you* the polite one!" She went off with their orders.

Asa snorted. "Is bein' rude a prerequisite for the job, or does all their politeness just get wo'n away aftah workin' heah for a while? So, any luck?"

"I've been lookin' all ovah town, but I haven't been able to find him. From the evasive answers I got at the office, I figure he's probably out on a toot. I've been traipsing from one bah to another like some old sot, but I've eithah just missed him or he hasn't been there yet. From what I can gathah, he stahted befoah we even got into po't. He's tryin' to drown sorrows he doesn't yet know he has," Slocum said.

Asa heaved a sigh. "Oh, hell's bells. It's gonna be awful, breakin' somethin' like this to him when he's already drunk and he already hates me. I wish I could leave him in ignorance, but if he hears it from someone else, he'll be after my head on a pike."

"Do you want me to tell him, Asa? I could keep lookin', and—"

"Nunno, Mike. You've done enough. It's my responsibility. I've got to be the one to do it. Where've you looked?"

"I made a list." Mike took it out of his pocket and handed it to Asa.

"Thanks. No sense coverin' old ground."

"Most of the likely ones said they'd let me know if he turns up, but by the time the messenger boy finds me, he'll probably have moved on again."

"Well, if all else fails, I suppose I could just go to his house and sit on the doorstep until he turns up." Asa shook his head. "Damn it."

The waitress slammed their food down on the table, snarling at Asa, "Watch your damn language."

Slocum laughed.

Asa exhibited one of his more Gallic shrugs, shoulders, eyebrows and palms upward. The bowl of chowder came with common crackers. After crumbling a handful into his chowder, he took a spoonful. "Mm, they do make a good chowdah — not quite as good as Janet's, of coss, but wo'th puttin' up with surly waitresses."

"Baked beans are even bettah than Mothah's," Slocum said. "Brown bread's not as good, although my brothah disagrees. But then, he's accustomed to Navy rations."

"Hahd tack and monkey-meat — yummy." Asa deadpanned.

"It's not as bad as that," Mike said.

"Ayup, I know my onions — navy beans, too." Asa sighed. "I was *tryin'* to make a joke, Mike, but I can see it fell flat. So, how is yah brothah?"

"He's been promoted to Commandah."

"Good for him," Asa said. "You evah think about joinin' the regulah Navy?"

"Too much regimentation," Mike said. "Much moah than the mercantile marine."

"Perfectly logical and necessary to have a chain of command, so orders get obeyed instantly in battle or emergencies; however, all those rigid rules and kowtowin' to officers has always seemed kinda like revertin' to feudal society to me. Guess I'm just too egalitarian. Even aboard our ships, I have trouble with everybody callin' me 'Mistah.' I'd rathah be called by my given name, 'specially given who I was named aftah." Asa's smile fell.

"Cap'n Asa was a grand old man, wasn't he?"

"Like a grandfathah to me."

"Tough, losing both of them," Slocum said.

"Ayup." Asa pushed his half-finished chowder away.

After saying goodbye to Slocum, he took the trolley to Brookline, and went to George's house, a bleak Victorian

Gothic. Perhaps it would have looked more inviting in spring, with leaves on the trees and flowers softening the stone structure, but there was nothing to relieve its grimness now.

Mrs. Lovejoy herself came to the door, wearing a severe brown dress that covered her from chin to ankles. Her hair was scraped back into a tight gray bun. She gave Asa an arctic look.

He doffed his cap. "Good afternoon, Mrs. Lovejoy. Is Mr. Lovejoy at home?"

Mrs. George Lovejoy, drawn up to her full, narrow height and looking down her long, narrow nose, said, "I shall *not* allow Mr. Lovejoy into the house until he signs a temperance pledge and abides by it."

"Do you know where I might find him?"

"I neither know nor care where that old reprobate could be." Mrs. Lovejoy folded her arms and stuck her nose higher in the air.

"Please, can you think of *anywhere* he may have gone? I must find him. I have sad news. Cap'n James," Asa cleared his throat. "Cap'n James Lovejoy was lost at sea."

"Well," she said, "it's a pity that Mr. George Lovejoy's brother has passed away, but I fail to see how it is any concern of mine. Good day, Mr. Mayhew."

"Good day, Mrs. Lovejoy. Thanks for all your help."

She slammed the door in his face as he slapped his cap back on his head.

*Why'd she damn near smash my nose? I was* not *sarcastic. Dry, that's the word.*

On his walk down the drive, he rubbed his arms for warmth, though the weather was fine. If he hadn't known George drank before he met her, he might have thought she drove him to it. He wondered why they'd ever married. Well, George had married her for her money; that was no secret. Maybe she'd thought she could reform him, but her puritanical rigidity had likely made matters worse.

He went to George's club. The major factotum informed him that Mr. Lovejoy was no longer welcomed there. Neither were any further questions from Asa.

Then he went to the offices of the Lovejoy Shipping Line. George should have been the one to tell them, but it could wait no longer. He informed the triumvirate who ran the Lovejoy Line in James's absence, Messrs. Fisher, Bennett, and Parker, of Captain James Lovejoy's death. Never had he seen three businessmen look so stricken. They did not hesitate to tell him where George might be.

When Asa went to the address, he found a rundown residential hotel not far from the waterfront. The desk clerk was reluctant to give him Mr. Lovejoy's room number.

"In that case, would you be so kind as to inform Mr. Lovejoy that his brother has been lost at sea?"

"No, sir, I would not. He's in room 213."

"I suppose I ought to thank you, but…" Asa shrugged.

"Hmm, yes, quite. Heaven knows in what condition you'll find him, sir."

"Thanks for the warning," Asa said. "Oh, would you have someone deliver about a gallon of black coffee?" He gave the clerk almost enough money to buy all the coffee in Suffolk County and a tip to ensure delivery. "He's liable to throw it at me. What's left should cover the stain removal bill."

Asa knocked and got no answer. He knocked again and called out, "Mr. Lovejoy?" Still no answer. The desk clerk had told him George was in, so he pounded on the door. "Mr. Lovejoy! Please open the door!" He paused and then pounded some more. "George Lovejoy! It's Asa Mayhew! Open up!" He waited and then banged on the door again. "George! Open the door! I *must* speak with you! It's about James. Let me in!" He put his ear to the door and listened. Then he hammered on the door and bellowed, "George, I *know* you're in there! I can hear you moving around! If you don't open the damned door, I'll knock it down!"

"Hold your horses! I'm coming." George took his time getting to the door. It was obvious he had not spent that time tidying up. The bed was a rumpled mess, as was he. He was unshaven, uncombed, wearing nothing but a collarless, cuff-less, half-buttoned, stained shirt and wrinkled trousers. Jacket and vest lay in a crumpled heap on the only chair. Empty bottles lay on the floor. The room reeked of whiskey.

"Whaddaya want? Can't you shee I'm busy?" George flopped onto the bed.

"Busy doing what? Drinking yourself into a coma?" Yelling through the door had turned his voice to sandpaper again, just when he'd thought it was getting better. "Mr. Lovejoy, please try to sober up for a minute. I've got some serious news to tell you."

A waiter arrived with a squeaky-wheeled cart bearing an urn of coffee and thick ceramic cups.

"Thank you." Asa tipped him.

He poured two cups and tried handing one to George. "Sit up and drink some coffee."

George pushed the cup away. "Get that away from me."

Asa drank his in a few gulps. The warm liquid helped raise the volume of his speech. He put a hand behind George's head and held the cup to his lips. "Drink it."

"*Coffee*? You gotta be kidding!" He grabbed the cup and threw the contents at Asa, who quickly stepped out of the line of fire. Then he reached under the bed and brought out a half-empty fifth of Old Overholt.

"No more!" Asa knocked the bottle out of his hand. It hit the floor and broke.

"No! What the hell you do that for? My last bottle!" George was almost in tears.

"George! Control yourself! You *must* sober up! I don't want to tell you what I have to tell you while you're blind drunk."

Asa poured another cup and forced George to drink. George spluttered, spat, and sprayed him with coffee.

"Shoulda worn my oilskins," Asa muttered. An image flashed across his mind of the last time he'd worn them. He could not go back there. He gritted his teeth. As he thought of James while looking at this sorry excuse for a brother, his sorrow turned to rage.

"God damn it, George! Drink it!" He pulled George's head back by his hair and poured coffee down his throat.

George coughed, choking it down. When he caught his breath, he let loose a stream of invective, his voice like a taut violin string about to snap. "How dare you! You low-class son-of-a-bitch, weaseling your way in! You've no background, no family, so you had to steal mine! You son of an Irish whore and a lowbred bastard of a deck monkey!"

Before he could stop himself, Asa's fist shot out and smashed at the vile insults to his parents coming out of that foul mouth. He grabbed George by the shirtfront and shook him. "Damn you, George! James is dead!"

He hadn't intended to punch George in the mouth. He certainly hadn't wanted to break James's death to him with such abrupt anger. Before he had a chance to apologize, George was on him, roaring at him, swinging wildly.

"*You* killed him! You did it on purpose, so you'd get the ship for yourself! You always wanted to take over! Father's fair-haired boy! You'll never work for Lovejoy Lines again! I'll have you arrested for murder!"

"George! For God's sake, stop imitating a windmill, and stop yelling! Do you want me to beat the tar out of you? Because, believe me, that's what I feel like doing. The only reason I haven't is that it wouldn't be gentlemanly to take advantage of a falling down drunk. But if you keep this up, I might not be able to restrain myself much longer."

George kept flailing at Asa, continuing to denounce him at the top of his voice. Asa blocked him, averting the blows he didn't duck with his forearms. George's inability to connect further enraged him.

"Murderer! You'll never get your captain's certificate, you bastard! I'll see to it! No other ship owners will ever hire you, ever again! You son-of-a-bitch, I'll see you hanged! You murderous fucking usurper!"

"Enough!" Asa pinned George's arms to his sides, restraining him. "Damn it! Don't you know I loved him like a brother?"

"Brother! *I'm* his brother — *not you*!" George shoved him off. "Fuck you! You killed him! Get out, you fucking murderer! Get the hell out! I'll see you in goddamned court!"

"I'll go, with pleasure! Trying to get through to you is maddening. But you've *got* to sober up and be responsible, damn it! You've got a memorial service to arrange, and a company to run." As he went out the door, he said, "We both know I was a far better brother to him than you ever were." He neither knew nor cared whether George heard him.

As he trudged down the sidewalk, heading to South Station, Asa fumed. *That low-down, beslubbering, rat-hearted lout! That craven, crook-pated, calumnious, drunken knave! Sodden-witted sea-hating landlubber! Changeling! He could not possibly be James's brother! Belly-crawling, liquor-swilling snake. Hah! He doesn't know I already have my captain's papers. He can't take them from me now.*

Captain James had planned to promote Asa to captain of one of the Lovejoy Line's Atlantic coast ships after they had returned from that voyage. A few more years' experience and he'd have his Master Mariner's Certificate, qualified to captain ships of any tonnage, anywhere in the world. But he didn't care now. His dreams had died with James.

He sighed. *Not that I'll ever use them. But maybe I should — just to show that filthy, hard-hearted, money-grubbing, mean, disgusting... Damn! Even when he sobers up — if he sobers up — he* will *accuse me of murder, maybe even manage to get me arrested.*

By the time he reached South Station, he'd walked off most of his anger. Weary in body and soul, he sank down on a bench to await his train. He unbuttoned his coat to get at his pocket watch. It was earlier than he'd thought.

Despite his disgust with George, Asa felt sorry for him. Even after all these years, George had never outgrown his unreasonable jealousy. *Even when I was only a little eight-year-old orphan, and he was a thirty-year-old man, he blamed me for stealing his father's love away from him, and he still does. He could never see that Captain Asa did love him; he only objected to his behavior. And he still can't see that his actions have anything to do with his loveless existence. Trouble is, he not only blames, but punishes everyone else for his misery, and now he's got me in his sights. He'll probably go through with his threat. And God knows I'm in no mood to fight a legal battle with him.*

# Chapter 6

## *Josiah Mayo*

A sa thought he might need some advice from a lawyer, so he went to see his friend, Josiah. No one was home. He kept a sailboat in Josiah's boathouse. It made sense, since Asa was so often at sea that his friend got more use out of it. The breeze was chilly and the sun setting, but he felt keyed up and wanted some hard physical labor. When he let himself into the boathouse, he lit a lantern, got out his kit, got down on his knees on the deck, and started scouring, pausing for a drink now and then.

It may have been the subliminal suggestion of George's bottle, but more likely it was simply that he was in a blue funk. Whatever the reason, he had impulsively purchased a half-pint of rum on the way home from Boston. He thought His Majesty's Royal Navy might have the right idea: a wee tot of grog made the life of a sailor more bearable. Besides, he told himself, it was good for his larynx. Indeed, after a few slugs, it did seem to help him sing. To hell with resting his voice. How could a man work without singing?

Putting some muscle into scrubbing the deck with a holystone, Asa belted out a sea shanty. "And we'll take a rope and we'll lower him down. And we say so. And we know so. And we'll take a rope and we'll lower him down. O poor old man." *Poor Old Man (or The Dead Horse)*[4] had a good rhythm for holystoning, but something about the lyrics bothered him. His pitch wobbled as he puzzled over it.

When Josiah returned, he was surprised to hear a familiar baritone resounding from the boathouse. "Hey, Choirboy!" Josiah called as he entered. When they'd been children, he and Asa had sung in a boys' choir together. "Never heard *you* sing off-key before. What's up?"

"Josiah! My ol' buddy, my pal. Want some rum?" Asa waved the bottle. He knew Josiah didn't drink, but seemed to be having a temporary lapse of memory.

"What on earth are you doing drinking rum?" Josiah frowned at him.

"Just practicin' to join the Royal Navy." Asa's smile was lopsided. "American Navy's dry, so I was just thinkin' I might give the British a try. Help them fight the bloody Boche. Do you know they give the sailors a ration of rum a day?"

"Very funny." From his tone, Josiah thought it was anything but. "Haven't seen you for some time. Why don't we chew the fat for a while? So put your gear — *and* the rum — away and come in for some coffee."

"Sure, Josiah. But forget the coffee. I'll stick with this."

"You know very well you can't drink *that* in my house." Josiah was firm. He was teetotal, not because of any political or moral beliefs, but because he had been devastated by his brother's death from addiction to alcohol and laudanum. He made no objection to social drinking by his friends, but he would have no alcohol in his house.

"Oh, damn." Asa grimaced. "I'm sorry, Josiah, I shouldn't have brought it here. I dunno how I forgot. Maybe we should leave this visit for some othah time. I'll just clean up and go on home."

"Don't go yet, Asa. Best not let Janet catch you three sheets to the wind."

"Don't exaggerate. I'm not that fah gone! Not even two sheets — possibly, now just *maybe*, mind you — *one* sheet to the wind. Only one little sheet flappin'."

"Well, you're not reeling, I'll grant you, but you're not sober, and it shows. I promise not to give you a temperance lecture," Josiah smiled. "It's tea time in the Royal Navy, you know. Why not practice *that* British custom? Come on in the house. I only want to give you a cup of coffee and a bite to eat, and find out what's eating *you*."

Asa turned his face away as grief came flooding back. He busied himself clearing up, clattering the cleaning devices into their storage box as though they had offended him.

Josiah watched him for a moment. "You look like thunder, but I trust you've manners enough not to walk off without a word." He went toward the house, calling over his shoulder, "Come into the kitchen when you're done."

Feeling somewhat like a rebellious schoolboy, Asa took another pull on the bottle, smacking the cork in with the heel of his hand before stowing the half-pint in his reefer pocket. At first, the alcohol had worked as a pleasant anesthetic for his pain, but it didn't last. His mood had turned black as a sudden thunderstorm,. He felt like breaking things, and had all he could do not to start smashing up his sailboat. He threw the holystone into the kit and slammed the lid, giving it a hard bash with his fist for good measure. Between George and the barnacles, his knuckles were already scraped and bruised, but he didn't care. He growled, restraining the howl of rage that was trying to get out. He tugged at his hair, swearing.

"What the hell," he muttered to himself. "Maybe I *should* join the Royal Navy. Do somethin' useful with all this violence — kill a few Boche." He swore again, in French this time, with a few choice words about revenge for the rape of the countryside. In truth, he knew it wasn't the Germans he was fighting against.

He couldn't understand it. He thought his anger with George had abated, at least for the time being. He wasn't annoyed with Josiah, only somewhat chagrined to be caught listing a bit to starboard. It dawned on him that he resented James for leaving him. It made no sense. After all, it's not as if James had abandoned him on purpose. It wasn't James's choice; it wasn't James's fault. It was whatever caused that illness. It was the vicious storm. It was his own fault for failing to protect James. For failing to save him. To feel such anger was selfish of him, disgraceful. He was infuriated with the world in general and with himself in particular.

He couldn't go into Josiah's kitchen in such a wild, savage frame of mind. Imagining himself smashing Josiah's dishes against the walls like a crazy man, he snorted and rolled his eyes. "Buck up, you mad bastid," he told himself. He fished in his pocket for cigarettes and lit one, giving himself time to get his feet on the ground.

\* \* \* \*

"Asa, I didn't know about James." Josiah poured them each a cup of coffee. "I was out of town. I just got a call from Doc Chandler about something else, and he told me. I don't know what to say. All I can do is offer feeble condolences that don't come anywhere near expressing what I feel for you. Now I know why you were seeking solace in the bottle."

"Humph! If I *that's* what I was doin' I should've known bettah." Asa paused. "I went to see George today. He was on a bendah, wringing the last drops from a bottle of Old Overcoat, and there were plenty of dead soldiers on the floor. He should've been negative example enough, but I guess... Well, I dunno." He made a dismissive gesture, as though shooing a fly.

Josiah waited in silence for Asa to say more. When it appeared that more was not forthcoming, he pushed a plate of small triangular sandwiches across the kitchen table towards Asa. "You might feel better if you eat something — sop up the alcohol."

Asa ignored the sandwiches, but drank his coffee, and started talking. "He blames me — claims I *murdered* James! Can you believe it? I'm ashamed to say I gave him a good sock in the mouth. In my own defense, it was only after he called my mother an Irish whore."

"God almighty! If he'd said such a scurrilous thing about my mother, I'm afraid I'd have given him a great deal more than one punch. You'd probably be bailing me out of jail about now."

"Believe me, I wanted to, but was afraid I'd find killin' him all too easy, and I'd go stahk, starin' mad if I was locked up in a cell. He stahted swingin' at me, though, and I had to get him in a clinch to make him stop. Felt so bizarre, huggin' him while we both yelled at each other — crazy." Asa shook his head. "He gave me the sack; said I'd never sail another Lovejoy ship. Well, I wouldn't work for him, even if he'd have me. But he says he's gonna bring *chahges* against me — for *murdah*."

"I wouldn't worry about that. He's all bluff and bluster, always crying that he's been wronged when he's the one who wrongs others."

"Ayup, but he's got the Lovejoy name and the Lovejoy money. I'm nobody. If he wants to make trouble for me, he can. Could be he's got a case for negligence, at least. I keep thinkin' of all the things I should've done differently. Oh, hellfire and damnation! I *feel* guilty. If I'd only—" Asa flung up his hands in frustration. "Damn me all to hell!"

"For heaven's sake, Asa! Cut out that kind of talk," Josiah ordered.

"Please forgive my lack of restraint." Asa felt himself blushing, thinking it was the second time today, or maybe the third, he'd made himself look like a loon.

"Nothing to forgive, except that you're showing a marked lack of confidence in my legal skills. You know I could argue your case against the devil himself and get you off the hook. If you *had* killed George, for instance, I could make a very eloquent, unquestionable defense of justifiable homicide." Josiah smiled. "Under the circumstances, I'd say you've shown admirable restraint. George is an unmitigated ass. And he cheats at poker."

"Not only at poker, at everything. That's why he got kicked out of Hahvahd. How he could come from the Lovejoy family and act like that," Asa shook his head. "It's beyond me."

"It's certainly a mystery. Do you suppose he could have been a changeling?"

"Called him that earlier today, among other things," Asa said. "But only in my head."

"They say great minds think alike." Josiah smiled at him.

"*They* say. *I'd* say great minds think original thoughts, not clichés." Asa smiled back. "Proves neither one of us has a great mind."

"Hmm. I'd say you've got me there," Josiah said. "But getting back to our discussion: you said George has got the name, but as far as names go, so do you. You know we're distant cousins, don't you? Fifth, or sixth, or something — I can never keep that straight. We might not spell our names the same, but we Mayos and Mayhews come from the same root, and our roots go very deep around here. Did you know our history on the Cape goes back further than the Lovejoy's? But genealogy aside, you're hardly what I'd call *nobody*. Everyone knows you and respects you, and they know you'd never hurt a fly."

"Waell, I dunno about that," Asa said. On rare occasion, it had been his duty to use physical force to maintain discipline on deck. He could hold his own in a donnybrook. And he'd just given George a fat lip, hadn't he?

Misunderstanding Asa's demurral, Josiah said, "Admittedly, *everyone* is a sweeping generalization; however, to my knowledge, everyone I know in Wellfleet and everyone who has ever sailed with you holds you in high regard. As to your ruminations on, 'I should have done thus,' and 'maybe if I'd done so,' *stop* it. No one is to blame, least of all you."

"But I was *responsible* for that ship and the safety of every man aboard her. Cap'n James had such a high fever. I *should* have known, or at least been alert to the possibility that—"

"How?" Josiah interrupted. "Do you have a crystal ball? Don't torture yourself. You're getting close to despondent self-pity here. I blame it on the drink."

Asa heaved a sigh. "You're right. I've been making a goddamned fool of myself all afternoon. George and I with our bottles — talk about unmitigated asses."

"In *no* way can you place yourself anywhere *near* the same category with him. I'm warning you, my friend, one more self-deprecatory comment, and I'm going to…" Josiah frowned. "I don't know what — maybe slap you in the face or something. I'm getting damned tired of it. Do you hear me?"

Asa opened his mouth, then closed it and stared at Josiah. "Well, uh… *tarnation*, Josiah, I hear you all right. But do you have to sound so peeved and threatening about it? I really ticked you off about the rum, didn't I? And you're lookin' for any excuse to hit me, aren't you?"

"The way you've been talking sounds to me like you're looking for a little help in punishing yourself by egging someone on to smack you in the eye." Josiah gave him an arch glance. "Thought maybe if I offered, you'd stop doing it to yourself."

"Uh-huh. Now that's real friendship. Mighty considerate of you," Asa said.

"Any time, my friend," Josiah smiled. "Listen, if George tries to give you any legal trouble, you know I'll take care of it. But I very much doubt anyone will listen to his spurious, concocted complaints."

"Thanks, Josiah — for the legal advice, and for metaphorically slapping me into shape," Asa looked at his pocket watch. "Oh, my, look at the time. I'm afraid I've intruded upon your evening."

"Not at all. If I'd had any plans I'd have kicked you out long ago. Why don't you stay and have supper with me? I'm afraid you'll have to take pot luck. I didn't know whether I'd be back this afternoon, and I gave Mrs. Hodges the day off," Josiah said. "Or were Janet and Silas expecting you?"

"Nunno. I told Janet I didn't know when or if I'd get back from town, so not to wait supper for me. Good thing, too, or she'd be ready to tan my hide by now." He reached for a sandwich.

"Those must be pretty stale," Josiah said.

"They're fine." Asa washed it down with more coffee.

"Well, I don't know about you, but I want more than a couple of dried-up little triangles of thinly sliced bread surrounding an even thinner layer of devilled ham for my supper."

"What are you complainin' about? You made them," Asa said. "You want somethin' else? I'll cook. What've you got in the lahdah, uh, larder?"

"Haven't the foggiest. Let's go look," Josiah said. "You must be sobering up, to be working on your accent. But drunk or sober, you're a much better cook than I am."

Asa responded with a derisive snort. "Among my many talents."

"You laugh, but it's true. You could turn your hand to just about anything." As they gathered ingredients and began putting the meal together, he asked, "Have you any ideas about what you might like to do now?"

"Haven't really thought about it yet." Asa sifted flour, baking powder, and a little sugar into a bowl, cut in shortening, added milk, and began mixing. "I'll probably look for another shipping line, but I won't work for any of those companies that treat the men like galley slaves. I hear Bay State Lines is all right. Mr. Wass won't stand for mistreatment, and he has spoken out against the crimp, calling it enslavement, pure and simple. Too many companies are corrupt, and these syndicates are the worst, breaking the law and the men's backs just to get a buck. There are not enough owners like Mr. Wass and the Lovejoys." Asa looked grim. "Lovejoys that *were*, that is. If George doesn't immediately drive the company into the ground, I suspect he'll take the criminal, money-grubbing tack. What a sorry fate for what was once one of the best, most humane companies in New England shipping. I tell you, Josiah, it breaks my heart to think what George will do to it." He looked down at the biscuit batter he'd been stirring. "Oh, damn it. I'll have to throw this out and start ovah."

"Why? What's wrong with it?" Josiah asked.

"Supposed to stir it gently, just until the dry ingredients are moistened. I beat the hell out of it. These biscuits will be hahd as shot put — break your teeth," Asa said. "Although, I suppose you could bake up this dough and use the resulting cannonball as a doorstop."

"Yankee thrift. I might just do that. The library door always seems to swing shut when I want it to stay open," Josiah said. "Tell you what — in order to ruin neither the preparation nor the digestion of supper, I promise not to ask you any more probing questions. You don't have to talk about James until you want to, when you're ready. For the duration of the meal, we should ban the subjects of George, the war, how President Wilson thinks he can keep us out of it, and other grim topics. We'll exchange gossip, talk about books we've read recently, and try damned hard to think of an amusing anecdote or two. If all else fails, we can always reminisce about the innocent days of our childhood, that is *if* we can go back far enough into the past to *remember* any innocence!"

"It's a deal," Asa said. "Be nice to get through a whole meal without one thing or another ruinin' my appetite."

# Chapter 7

# *Janet*

Awakened by the smell of coffee, Asa yawned and stretched. He huddled under the blankets, reluctant to leave their warmth. *Lazybones*, he called himself, threw off the covers and got up. Shivering, he poured water into the washbasin, washed, brushed his teeth, and then threw on a pair of corduroy trousers and a turtleneck fisherman's sweater. He'd shave after he got some hot water from the cast iron kettle on the kitchen stove. After pouring the washwater into the slop bucket, he took it to the outhouse to empty it. When he took it back to his room, he washed his hands, and then dumped the soapy water into it. In a house without plumbing, it was a never-ending job.

Yawning some more, he went down to the warmest room in the house — the kitchen with its big coal stove. "Mo'nin' Janet." He looked around. "Where's Si?"

"Mo'nin', Sleepyhead. He's been out makin' a livin' for hours." Her eyes smiled at him as she looked up from frying bacon in a cast iron spider.

"Why didn't you wake me?"

Janet poured him a cup of coffee from an enamelware coffeepot. "You needed your sleep, after that rough night you had. Do you want toast or griddle cakes with your eggs?"

"Toast — just one slice, please, and only two eggs. You always make enough to feed a ship's crew." Asa winked.

"You're a growin' boy." As she placed a thick slice of homemade bread in a long-handled wire toaster, Asa got up, slotted the lifter into the iron plate of one of the stove's burners, and moved it aside for her. Janet placed the toaster over the open fire, watching to flip it before it burned. "You need your food."

"Not that *much* food. I'm not a growin' boy anymoah, leastwise, not vertically. You'll only be makin' more work for yourself — lettin' out the seams on all my clothes." Asa smiled as he sat down again. Then he frowned. "Rough night? What are you talkin' about?"

"Asa, don't you remembah? You were tossin' and turnin' so much, you fell out of bed. We heard a loud thump, and Si went in and found you on the floah. He said you sat up and looked at him for a minute as if you didn't know wheyah you were or who he was. He gave you a hand up, and got you back into bed again," Janet said. "I heard you walkin' around downstaiahs latah, pacin' back and fo'th. You didn't get much sleep."

"Sounds like you and Si didn't eithah. I'm sorry," Asa said. "I don't remember any of it. Could I have been sleepwalkin'? Nevah done that befoah, far as I know."

"You did once or twice, aftah… well," Janet dropped her voice, "when you were orphaned."

"Hmm." Asa frowned. "Si must've been pretty tiahed when he had to get up befoah the crack of dawn this mo'nin'. Listen, I can't be keepin' you up at night like this. I'll go sleep in one of Si's cottages."

Janet put a plate of toast, bacon, and fried eggs in front of Asa. "Now, Asa, this is your home. Don't be actin' like an unwanted guest. We want to help."

"Si needs his sleep. There are so many ways he could get hurt on that seiner if he wasn't payin' attention. I can't have him walkin' around half asleep because of me," Asa insisted. "I'll just sleep there; I won't live there, and I'll make it ship-shape for the summah people before I close it up again."

"Theyah's no need of that. You stay heah." Janet was just as stubborn.

Buttering his toast, Asa pretended not to hear her. "Speakin' of work, I've got to go out and find some. Once I get a berth, I'll be out of your haiah. No more of *me* goin' bump in the night."

"*Why* do you—" Janet sighed. "You know you're like a son to us." She put her hand on his shoulder — the equivalent of a bear hug from anyone else. "Eat your eggs befoah they get cold."

"Sit down and have coffee with me," Asa said. "And then I'll do the dishes."

For Janet, taking a mid-morning break was unheard of, but she topped up his cup, poured one for herself, and sat down.

She looked at him. "You need a shave."

"Ayup, soon's I bring some hot watah upstaiahs. That all right with you?"

"Just wondered if you forgot, that's all."

"Just wanted my coffee first, that's all." He smiled. "Janet, I want to ask your advice." He took a bite of toast, chewed, and swallowed. "Um... uh..."

"Waell? Are you goin' to get around to askin' or do I have to guess?"

"Waell, I... ah... Do you think it would be all right if I go around to the Lovejoy's to see if they need anythin', or would I be intrudin'?"

"Why, Asa Mayhew! You're blushin'!" Janet teased.

"Am not. What do you take me for?"

"A no'mal young man. And Mary Lovejoy's a very attractive young woman. But this is no time to go courtin'."

"Who said anythin' about courtin'!?" Asa felt his face get warmer.

"You *could* bring some flowahs of condolence, and since Geo'ge is not likely to be of any use, you could offah to talk to the ministah and such," Janet suggested. "Of coss they won't be needin' the undahtakah's services, but mebbe you could offah to go see Mr. Ritchie, the stonecuttah, about a mahkah in the family plot. You could also contact Mr. Ives about the readin' of the will. They'll be dazed with grief, and likely unable to think straight. Might be a load off Mary's mind to have someone do these practical things for her."

"Janet, you're a genius. It's what George *should* be doin', and he'll certainly not thank me for it. But why should I care what he thinks? They need help, and if *he's* not gonna do it, *I* will." Asa ended his sentence with a brisk nod, and then resumed eating his breakfast. After a couple of bites, another thought occurred to him. "Oh, but we don't have a florist in town. Where can I get flowers this time of year?"

"What about that greenhouse you built me last yeah?" Janet smiled. "It's not just for tomatoes, you know. We need somethin' pretty to get us through the gray wintah months, don't we? And that's why people give flowahs for bereavement — it helps to be reminded that life still holds beauty."

"You've got a solution to everythin'. I don't know how Si and I could get along without you," Asa said. "I thought the tradition of flowers came about to covah the smell, but you know? The beauty of nature *can* bring solace." He

nding on the bluff at sunrise yesterday before
rain into town, watching the wind ruffle the
as the sky turned pink. The tide foamed up
_led, and bubbled forth again as he listened to
uie breakers crash on the jetty. To his chagrin, his eyes filled.

"Let it out, deah boy." Janet reached across the table and touched his arm. "I know how much yaw grievin' for him, but yaw tryin' like the devil not to show it. Think 't ain't manly to cry, I suspect. Well, nobody heah but us, and I won't tell a soul, not even Si. Let it out. It'll eat away at you like a cancer if you don't." She got up and went into the other room, coming back with a stack of handkerchiefs. She'd embroidered an anchor in one corner. "Made these for you out of wo'n out sheets."

Janet's kindness and generosity moved him. All the tears he'd dammed up came rolling down his cheeks. He bowed his head and pressed a handkerchief to his face. When the tears let up, Janet stood behind him — good heavens! — massaging his shoulders.

"Feel any bettah?" she asked.

"I would, if only I could breathe through my nose." Smiling through his tears, he reached back and patted her hand.

"Complain, complain, complain," Janet said. "It's always somethin'."

When she leaned over and kissed the top of his head, he almost fell off the chair, and his eyes filled up again. Janet never showed physical affection.

He'd been raised aboard ship, by men. It struck him how much he had missed his mother. He was touched to the core that Janet thought of him as a son and wanted to console him as a mother would. He'd always known that she and his cousin Si would have adopted him if they could, but they were only sixteen and eighteen when his parents died, just married, poor, and living in a shanty until Si saved enough for his own fishing boat. Although Janet was only eight years older than he, she'd always been older and more discerning than her years.

"There, there, my lad," Janet said. "'Tis all right. All right. Si and I will never leave you."

Though he knew she could never promise such a thing, it comforted him. But now it was time to gather himself together and leave childhood behind.

He got up and pumped some cold water into the soapstone sink, added enough boiling water to heat it up, and washed the dishes.

\* \* \* \*

Later that morning, when Asa came into the kitchen wearing his best navy blue suit, Janet inspected him from head to toe.

"Shined your shoes and everything," she said.

"Mm-hm," Asa said. "What smells so good? Dinnah?"

"Ayup, but not for us. It's a nice pot of chicken soup for Mrs. Lovejoy and Mary. They won't feel like much, but they have to eat," Janet said. "It'll be a bit awkwa'd to carry all that way, so see if you can get Si's old machine stahted."

"Should've told me that before I put my suit on," Asa said.

"You can always take it off again," Janet said.

With a smile, Asa shook his head, and then turned to go upstairs to change.

The double shed doors might have been green once, but they were so weather-beaten it was hard to tell. The hinges screeched as he opened them, revealing Si's 1906 Model N. He had purchased it used from a traveling salesman for a pittance; it had seen a lot of use. The motor wouldn't crank over, so Asa removed the hood cover and went to work.

After barking his beat up knuckles a few more times and turning the air blue — not with engine exhaust but with curses — he tried adjusting the throttle and turning the crank again. A crank handle could kick back and break one's thumb or wrist, if one didn't know to hold it with thumb and fingers on the same side. It kicked back the first time. Swearing, Asa jerked his hand out of the way and tried again. After three more tries, it ticked over, sounding like a sewing machine. He got in and drove it around to the back door. Trusting to luck, he shut it off.

Taking hot water with him to wash and scrub the grease from under his nails, he went upstairs. After putting on his suit again, he tried to slick back his sun-streaked curls, to no avail, so he jammed a navy blue cap over them. There — he snorted at the mirror — sartorial splendor. Well, at least his collar and cuffs were clean and starched, four-in-hand knot perfect in his blue tie.

On the kitchen table, he saw a bouquet of pink roses and soft green ferns with a mauve satin ribbon tied around it, arranged with Janet's characteristic artistry.

"Come with me." Asa held her eye, beseeching.

"Though you may not believe it, you're just as good at comfortin' people as I am." Janet smiled. "But I'll come. I can hold the soup, keep it from spillin'. Be a shame to waste any of it, after I spent all mo'nin' slavin' over a hot stove to make it." She took off her apron and put on her coat and hat.

Asa helped Janet up into the car, and handed her the soup pot. They sat high in the narrow seat, faces burnished by the chill breeze as they set off down the dirt road. As he pulled into the drive, Janet said, "Let's go around back, to the kitchen doah. Mahtha can tell us whethah they're up to receivin' visitahs."

"Makes sense," Asa said. As he took the pot of soup from her and helped her down, his eyes upon her were as blue and warm as a summer morning. "You're so wi—"

"Don't go getting' all soft, now. I'm not 'so wise,' and you and Si could get along just fine without me, if you'd only use your common sense."

He goggled at her, and then he laughed. "I guess I must overdo it, if I'm so predictable. But I can't exaggerate my appreciation of you, you know."

Janet sighed. "You don't need to keep sayin' it. You're an open book, deah. Now close your mouth befoah Mahtha opens the doah."

Just as the door opened, Asa looked at Janet in a panic. "The flowahs! What did I do with the flowahs?"

"Aftahnoon, Mahtha," Janet said. "Excuse me just a moment. The flowahs," she turned to Asa, holding up the bouquet, "are right heah."

"Oh." He gave her a sheepish look. "Pahdon my lapse of mannahs, Mahtha. How are you this aftahnoon?"

Martha smiled at him. "Come in; come in. Standin' heah with the doah open, all the heat's getting' out. What've you got theyah, Asa?"

"Janet made chicken soup for the ladies. Shall I put it on the stove?"

"Please do. Mrs. Lovejoy likes your soup, Janet. Let's hope this will be just the thing to coax her to eat a little."

"I didn't think either one of them would feel like much, but just a little somethin' warm and light might be comfortin', and I imagine you've got your hands full. How are they doin'?" Janet asked.

"Much as you might expect. I finally got Mary to let me sit with Margaret for a while so she could get some rest. She won't leave her side. I don't think she slept much at all last night."

Asa nodded. "We suspected Mary might not be up to dealing with the practical things, and I wondered if I might be able to help. If she's too distressed to see me, maybe you could just ask her if that would be all right. You know — talking to the minister, Mr. Ives, and such, to see that things are attended to properly."

"That would be good of you. Mr. Geo'ge Lovejoy won't be of any help. We haven't seen hide nor hair of him. Not so much as a lettah. Humph." When speaking of George, Martha looked as though she'd just opened the icebox door and smelled rotten fish.

"Oh, but if she's sleeping, don't disturb her," Asa said. "I can always come back latah." His back was to Mary as she entered the kitchen.

"She's not sleeping, and she's not too distressed to see you, Mr. Mayhew."

He spun around, whisking his cap off. "Ah, Mary," he breathed, gazing at her with rapt attention. "Excuse me, I mean, Miss Lovejoy." As he offered her the roses, he felt his cheeks flame. "I, um, we… that is… Janet and I brought you these that you might find some beauty… I mean, some solace in the nature of beauty — the beauty of nature." Looking at the floor, he ran a hand down his face and muttered, "Oh, Lord." He heard a sound he thought was a sob and was about to sink to his knees begging her forgiveness when he looked up.

Pressing two fingers to her smile, she tried to suppress little laugh that kept forcing its way out in delicate puffs from her nose. It brought a shine to her eyes and a little color to her cheeks.

Relieved, chagrined, enchanted, confused, his eyes widened as he watched her. Stunned. That was the word. He felt hit over the head.

"Sit down, deah." Martha guided Mary to a seat at the kitchen table. "How about a nice cup of tea?"

"Tea. Yes, please." Mary agreed. She giggled. "Oh, I suppose this is most inappropriate behavior."

"I am sorry, Miss Lovejoy," Asa began, but she cut him off.

"No, no, don't be. Please. I… I'm glad you… well…gave me a reason to smile." Her smile wavered, and then swiped a tear from the corner of her eye. "Oh, no. I'm afraid I…" She sniffed. And then she couldn't stem the tears.

All of a sudden he found himself down on one knee, offering her a handkerchief, holding her hand, murmuring soothing sounds, and then drawing a chair close to her, stroking her hair as he cradled her head on his shoulder. "There, there," he heard himself saying. "Oh, my deah. There, there, my deah girl."

As though she were a living hummingbird, vibrant and fragile in his hands, he held her. She leaned into him, and he felt her fluttering begin to still. Patting her back with a feather touch, he sighed. She sighed with him.

Touching her — this level of intimacy was not gentlemanly, but his instinct to comfort her had overcome propriety. He had a vague awareness of Martha bustling around, making tea. Out of the corner of his eye, he saw Janet arranging the flowers in a vase. Nevertheless, he would shelter Mary in his arms for as long as she wished to remain there. "Oh, my deah, deah girl," he whispered.

Mary exhaled on a long, shuddering sigh, and then pushed herself upright. She tucked a few loose strands of hair back into her bun and straightened her clothing. "So, um, Mr. Mayhew, what did you wish to see me about?"

"See you about?" Darts from one thing to the next like a hummingbird, too, he thought, taking a second to catch up. "Oh, yes. It's uh… not really my place, but… I don't think George will… Well, I wondered if there was anything I could do to make things easier for you, practical things, like talkin' to the minister and Mr. Ives. You just tell me what you'd like, and then I could make the arrangements. If you want."

"Oh, that would be such a help! I didn't know where to begin. But… it's too much. I should—"

"Of coss it's not too much. I wouldn't have asked if—" Asa steadied his nerves with a breath. "I'd *like* to do it for you, please."

"Thank you." Her nose and eyes turned pink as she blinked at him, biting the corner of her lip.

He nodded and patted her hand, blinking back.

\* \* \* \*

The following day, Asa went to Boston to see Mr. Ives, to inform him of Captain James Lovejoy's death and to arrange a date and time for the reading of the will.

Distinguished in manner and looks, with his wavy snow-white hair and tailored suit, Mr. Ives beckoned Asa to sit.

"You can't imagine how sorry I am to hear that," the lawyer said. "Captain James Lovejoy was an extraordinary man. His passing is a great loss to us all."

Asa gazed at the top of Mr. Ives's desk. "Yes. A very great loss." A cloud seemed to pass over him before he raised his eyes. "We've arranged the memorial service for the day after tomorrow, at the house. I imagine the family — well, at least Mary and Mrs. Lovejoy — shall be in a kind of dazed state, so it might be best to wait for a day or two before the reading."

"Quite right, Mr. Mayhew. Let me check my diary. Since my wife has been ill, I've been trying to spend more time with her, less at the office, so I'm sure I can find an opening. Oh, yes, here." He pointed to a date. "I shall come out in the afternoon, say around two o'clock? If that is inconvenient for the family, let me know, and we shall arrange another time."

"I'm sure that will be fine. Mrs. Lovejoy's precarious health keeps them confined to the house, and since James… well, Mary won't leave her side… I, uh… I'm sorry to hear your wife hasn't been well. That must be quite worrying for you."

"Yes." Mr. Ives stared off into space. Then he took an audible breath and looked at Asa. "I should very much like to attend the service, but I'm afraid my wife's health shall prevent my being away for such an extended period of time twice within one week."

"Is there someone to look after her when you come out for the will reading?"

"There shall be. I'm interviewing nurses this afternoon."

"I might know of—"

At that moment, George burst into the office. His face, already florid from whiskey, turned livid.

As Asa stood up to face him, George grabbed him by the lapels, shouting, "What are *you* doing here? You… you son of a bitch! You fake heir! Stealer of birthrights!"

With a stony look, Asa commanded, "Let go of my coat."

"You bastard! You… you cuckoo in the nest! Thief!" Continuing to hurl epithets at him, George let go with a shove, but Asa had braced himself and stood rock solid.

"I'd tell you I'm not heir to anything, but I don't suppose it would do any good," Asa said. As George continued to rant and rave, he sighed, "No, I didn't think so."

Mr. Ives had risen, saying, "Mr. Lovejoy, stop this nonsense at once!"

George gave him no notice, screaming at Asa, "What are you doing here, then?"

Composed, Asa answered. "What you should have been doing two days ago, George. I'm informing James's lawyer of his death. By the way, you should know that the Reverend Mr. Nickerson has agreed to hold the memorial service at the house. Mrs. Lovejoy isn't—"

George stepped closer and yelled into his face. "You think you can just take over, you bastard? You had *no right*, you murderer! Get out!" He tried to shove Asa in the chest, but it had about as much effect as shoving one of those well-established maple trees in the Public Gardens, visible from the second-story window, blazing with fall color.

Asa maintained his self-restraint. "I had every right to assist two grieving women in performing these practical chores, since *you* weren't helping them."

Mr. Ives's usually fair coloring burned with outrage. He glared at George, saying, "How *dare* you behave in such a rude and aggressive manner! Leave my office immediately, and don't come back until you've learned some manners!"

Shouting over both of them, George continued to rail at Asa. "And don't dare show your face at the memorial, or I'll have you arrested, you... you... Get out! Get out!"

"I shall leave now, but only to spare Mr. Ives any further distress." Asa stood straight, hoping it looked more like dignity than rigid fury. "My apologies, Mr. Ives. We shall speak at another time."

Mr. Ives glared at George as he pointed toward the door. "Out! *Now*, Mr. Lovejoy!"

Asa hesitated by the door, in case Mr. Ives should need protection against George or a hand in booting him out.

George turned on the lawyer. "How *dare* you take sides with this... this... usurper! This presumptuous arrogator *killed my brother* to take over the ship, and *you're* in cahoots with him. You're conspiring against me! Well, if you think you can do me out of what's rightfully mine, think again. I have my own lawyers, and I'll bring suit!"

After this outburst, he turned on his heel and stormed out, slamming the door. His feet pounded down the stairs, and then the bang of the outer door reverberated through the hallway.

Mr. Ives's and Asa's eyes met as they mirrored each other, mouths slightly open.

Reaching into the bottom drawer of his desk, the lawyer removed a bottle of brandy and two glasses. "I know it's rather early in the day, Mr. Mayhew, but I feel the need of a little something to restrain my heart from galloping like a racehorse on the stretch. Won't you join me?"

"George tends to have that effect on people." Asa exhaled forcefully. "Thank you, Mr. Ives, I believe I shall. Although it is early — early enough for George to still be able to pronounce 'usurper' and 'presumptuous.' I certainly don't want to fall into any of his bad habits, so just a wee dram, please, to calm the nerves." He held his thumb and forefinger about a half-inch apart. "If you don't mind, I'll tarry awhile, to prevent me going after him to tear him limb from limb." His even tone belied the violence of his words.

"Surely you don't mean that," Mr. Ives said, pouring an inch of brandy into each glass.

"I never knew a man who creates such savage urges within me. But I hope I would never act on them. I've often imagined he deserves to be drawn and quartered, but that's rather too medieval and a bit rash; don't you think? Nevertheless, he should be cast out from society in some way. He lies; he cheats; he ruins everything he touches and then blames everyone else."

"Not to mention his public displays of drunken offenses against the decency of every citizen of our fine city, most especially the ladies," Mr. Ives said. "For that alone, since he's incorrigible, he should be imprisoned for public lewdness, or at least institutionalized until he dries out."

"Captain Asa Lovejoy and James tried to get him into a drying-out place, but he wouldn't stay. I tried to get him to see reason, but of course that fell flat. He has hated me since Captain Asa took me in. There never was any reason for such jealousy, but he could not believe his family loved him even more than they loved me. He was blood. The thing they couldn't love was his behavior — the lying, the cheating, the drinking, and then the stealing from his own family. He could benefit from some psychiatric help, but it won't work unless he's sober and willing. Ah, well, I'm afraid he's too far gone by now."

"You have great forbearance, Mr. Mayhew," Mr. Ives said.

"I don't know about that. My patience has been worn as thin as a hand-me-down shirt; if you hold it up to the light, you can see right through it.

"Now, about your need of a nurse — and once again, I regret that terrible fracas intruded upon your careworn state."

"Kind of you to offer apologies for him, but he should be offering them himself," Mr. Ives said.

"That'll be a cold day in hell," Asa said. "Begging your pardon, sir."

Mr. Ives smiled. "Before you interrupted yourself, what were you saying?"

"You were telling me about looking for a nurse for Mrs. Ives," Asa said. "I might know someone. She's Martha's… brother's sister-in-law's cousin's… um… something-or-other," Asa shook his head. "I can never follow the convoluted trail of Martha's many relatives. Anyway, she was a nurse before she got married, but her husband has mysteriously disappeared, so she's looking for work."

"Just how did he 'mysteriously disappear,' and is this woman reliable?"

"He went out to the tobacconist one day, and nobody's seen him since. It's a mystery. As far as anyone knew, he wasn't a philanderer, he didn't gamble, and he didn't drink. He and Mrs. Potts seemed to get along well. No one — well, no one in Wellfleet, anyway — can figure out where he went or whether he's still alive," Asa said. "Is she reliable? By all accounts, Mrs. Potts was a very good nurse, dependable as the sunrise, strong as a stevedore, and willing to work hard."

"You say 'was,'" Mr. Ives said. "What about now?"

"I only used the past tense because she hasn't been working as a nurse for six months. Susan and Albert Potts were only married four-and-a-half months before he disappeared," Asa said.

"Where is she living now?"

"Mrs. Bird's boarding house."

"I know Mrs. Bird," Mr. Ives said. "Very respectable. If you can get in touch with Mrs. Potts, have her come see me this afternoon." He took out his watch. "Let's see… about three o'clock. No, make that one o'clock. I'll interview her first, and if she suits, I'll cancel all the others. I'd like to give the job to someone who needs it and may have trouble finding other employment in her, er, *uncertain* circumstances. If she proves to be as competent as you say she is, you'll have my eternal gratitude, Mr. Mayhew."

\* \* \* \*

After he stopped by Mrs. Bird's, Asa went down to the waterfront, and ran into Captain Hookset.

"I understand Mrs. Stedman has been seriously ill. How is she faring?" Asa asked.

"She made it to ninety-two, and then passed on to her heavenly home early yesterday morning, about 0300," the captain said.

"You have my deepest sympathy."

"Well, you know how independent she was, and she would have needed someone living in the house to care for her. That would have greatly displeased her. Still, I shall miss her." Captain Hookset was silent for a moment. "May I offer my condolences to you on the terrible loss of Cap'n James? He would have had many good years to come, were it not for the tragedy. How are you holding up?"

"I... uh..." Asa studied the bricks of the sidewalk searching for a socially acceptable answer that wasn't an outright lie. "As well as can be expected, I guess. I've been runnin' around, tryin' to arrange things for Mrs. Lovejoy and Mary, because George is not helping them at all. Matter of fact, I just came from Mr. Ives's office, where George barged in, shoutin' accusations that I murdered James. Accused poor Mr. Ives, too. Says we're conspiring against him."

"Tsk, tsk! Has he lost his wits? Why, you risked your own life trying to save James!"

Asa narrowed his eyes. "Who told you *that*?"

"I've just been talking with Mr. Slocum, and he relayed the whole story to me. You behaved in a heroic manner!"

"Well, I'd take that with a grain of salt, if I were you. Mr. Slocum tends to exaggerate," Asa said. "He's a great one for yarns."

"Nunno, Mr. Mayhew. After all my years as a captain, I can tell when a man's stretching it too far. He told the truth. But far be it from me to question your modesty, for does not the Lord teach us that whosoever shall exalt himself shall be abased; and he that shall humble himself shall be exalted?"

"Well... ah... you would know your scripture better than I, sir."

Captain Hookset raised an eyebrow. "I doubt that. I've heard you quote the Bible as well as your favorite poets. You've a phenomenal memory for such things."

Asa didn't know what to say. Where were all those famous poets when you needed one? It didn't help that Captain Hookset was taller than he, and with his powerful build and flowing beard, he looked much as one would picture an Old Testament prophet, that is, if a Jeremiah or an Isaiah were to wear a sea captain's uniform. He felt awed in the captain's presence.

"You need to go back to sea again, son," Captain Hookset said.

"Sort of like getting back up on the horse after you've been thrown?" Asa asked. "I don't imagine it'll come as any surprise to you that George Lovejoy has fired me."

"Tomorrow is my aunt's funeral, but the day after, we're putting out to sea. I need a chief mate. How about it?"

"That's the day of James's memorial service, but…" Asa sighed. "Perhaps I'd best not attend. George has threatened to cause a ruckus if I do, and I fear poor Mrs. Lovejoy's heart could very well give out on the spot. Whose company? Bay State Lines?"

"You know I don't sail for anyone but Bay State and Lovejoy Lines, but I won't be sailing for Lovejoy anymore. Not with George at the helm."

"May I think on it and give you my answer tomorrow?"

"Of course you may. Are you coming to the funeral? It's at the Methodist Church, ten o'clock."

"Janet'll probably be making something for the collation in the church hall. I got Si's old motor running, so I'll give her a ride." Asa sighed. "There'll be a lot of black worn around Wellfleet in the next couple of days."

"We'll meet again tomorrow, then," Captain Hookset extended his hand.

Asa shook it. "And perhaps we'll ship out together the day after. I appreciate you offering me the job."

\* \* \* \*

The bells were clanging and the conductor shouting, "All aboard!" as Asa dashed onto the train. In summer, a seat would have been difficult to find, but in bleak November, he had the carriage almost to himself. He flopped down in a seat by the window, took his hat off, and ran his fingers through his hair. A curl flopped onto his forehead. He had a fleeting thought about a visit to the barber, but a myriad of other concerns crowded it out. He gazed out the window without seeing any of his favorite sights.

What had Slocum meant about him risking his life? He shivered as he remembered being flat on the deck like a landed fish, wet, freezing, gasping, coughing… but he shook it off. This was not the time to try to piece it all together, not while riding in a public conveyance. Did he really want to go to sea again? But what choice did he have? He needed to work, to occupy his mind and body, and it seemed his best bet.

But Mary… what about Mary? He didn't want to leave her. On the other hand, if he stayed, George's hatred of him could boil over onto Mary. George could cause real harm, especially with Mrs. Lovejoy in such a fragile state. Perhaps he should stay away, at least until George had time to simmer down. Maybe if he was out of sight, he'd be out of George's mind.

He hoped he'd done the right thing in recommending Mrs. Potts to Mr. Ives. Although he didn't know her well, he trusted Martha's judgement. He'd never known her to be mistaken in her assessment of people. If Mrs. Ives didn't recover, he feared poor Mr. Ives wouldn't either. He sent a prayer, or more accurately, a wordless plea, heavenward.

While he was at it, he prayed that Mary and her mother would be safe from George's rage, and that their grief wouldn't be too much to bear.

Mary… ah, Mary. Picturing them together, a year or two hence, walking hand-in-hand along the beach, watching the seagulls dip and soar… or sailing, her auburn hair aflame in the sun, both of them laughing as they tacked into the wind… stealing a kiss now and then, his arm around her… spreading a blanket on some verdant, velvet grass, unpacking a picnic basket… Well, it was a pleasant daydream, but what could she see in him? He'd probably always be a painful reminder of her father's death. Perhaps she'd start to resent him, blame him for it. And why not? He blamed himself.

No, he must stop thinking like that, he lectured himself. It would only lead to a black mood that made him unfit to be around people. He didn't want to sit morose at the table with Janet and Si, making them blue, too. He didn't want to be old stone face around Mary. He didn't want to snap and snarl at the ship's crew. No. He would put that darkness out of his mind. Put a good face on it.

Mary was most important now. What was best for her? Should he stay, and risk George's wrath spilling over onto her? That could very well kill Margaret, and where would that leave Mary? An orphan, and he knew what that was like, to lose both parents at once. Probably best not to take that chance. Surely Mr. Ives, Martha, and Doc Chandler would look out for them.

Distracted, he almost missed his stop and had to scramble to get off before the train moved on. He went straight to Mary's.

She came to the door, putting her finger to her lips. "Sh. Uncle George is finally here, and he's sleeping it off." They stood at the foot of the curved staircase in the hall, talking in low voices.

"Miss Lovejoy — Mary, I… uh," Asa ducked his head. "I'm sorry, but I don't think I'll be able to come to the service."

"Oh, I was hoping… well…" She turned away, seeming to droop.

"You know I *want* to be there; to say my last…" He closed his eyes, swallowing the lump in his throat.

"Then why?"

"It's George. I ran into him when I went to see Mr. Ives, and he threatened to… well, let's just say there's likely to be a very unpleasant scene if I'm there, and I don't want to subject either you or your mother to that. I fear it may be too much of a strain on her heart."

"I'd far rather ban George. But I suppose we couldn't do that… his own brother… But you were closer to Father and have every right…" She sighed. "I realize that you're trying to protect us."

"If I were you, I wouldn't mention my name around him. Anyone he thinks is my friend he views as an enemy. He even accused Mr. *Ives* of… well…" Asa shook his head. "Cap'n Hookset has offered me a position as Chief Mate on the *Eastern Trader*. I think it's best if I ship out with him. If I'm out of George's sight, maybe I'll be out of mind, too. Give him a chance to calm down a little."

"How I wish you didn't have to go! You've done so much for us, and I'm afraid I've become rather dependent. Whatever shall I do without you?" Mary's eyes filled as she looked up at him.

He took her hands in his. "Oh, Mary, I don't want to go! I wish I could stay, but… it could make things so much worse for you… I know it's hard to think that anything could be worse than the way you're feeling now, but… George could hurt you in terrible ways."

Their eyes locked as they stood solemnly facing each other, holding hands perhaps a little longer than was strictly proper.

"I understand." Mary tried to blink her tears away. Then she turned and fled up the stairs.

"Mary—" Asa stood helplessly looking after her, holding out a clean handkerchief with an anchor embroidered in the corner.

Martha came into the hall. "Anything I can do, Asa?"

"I just— I just wanted to give her this." Asa thrust the handkerchief into Martha's hand, biting his lip. He just managed to mumble, "G'bye, Mahtha," before he, too, turned and fled — out the front door.

"Oh, hell." He ground his teeth as he marched off at a good clip. *Goddamned George! Who is going to protect that poor, sweet girl from him? It should be me, but he'd— Damn him!*

He felt like yelling in anger or sobbing with grief. Instead, he muttered a string of curses in a dozen languages, under his breath.

# Chapter 8

# *The Eastern Trader*

*The Atlantic Ocean, November 1915*

The first night they were underway, Captain Hookset invited Asa, Mike Slocum, and Doc to join him at supper. When they were seated, he said grace: "Dear Lord, bless this food to our use and us to thy service. Trusting in thy mercy, we pray that thou shall forgive us our sins, and help us to become worthy of thy many blessings. Protect us, oh God, from the perils of the sea and the hazards of war. We beseech thee to see us safely to our destinations and home again. Grant us the strength to fulfill our duties, and make us ever mindful of the needs of others. This we ask in thy name, Jesus Christ our Lord. Amen." Long-winded prayers and extemporaneous sermons had given him the nickname of Preacher Hookset.

He shook out his napkin and placed it on his lap. Then he looked across the table and began the conversation. "Doctor Coffin, how did you come to be a ship's doctor?"

Doc smiled. "I know ship's doctors are always suspected to be running away from something — a bad marriage, a botched operation followed by a lawsuit, or some other dark scandal. Well, I'm not married, I've never maltreated a patient, and I have lived a very ordinary life, except for a few hair-raising perils at sea. But I suppose I am running away from something — my unfortunate name."

Captain Hookset raised his eyebrows. Asa and Mike smiled. They knew the story.

"Oh, I have no shame in it. I'm a Coffin from Nantucket, a good family, for the most part. But it's not a fortuitous name for a doctor, is it? When I first set up practice, just how many patients do you think came to me, with a name like that? One — my mother. And she only came to measure my office windows for curtains."

His table companions laughed.

"On board ship, the men have no choice but to come to me, so I get to practice my craft. I suppose doctors named Graves or dentists named Payne have the same trouble. Still, I prefer not to advertise my name. The men feel more comfortable if I'm known simply as 'Doc.'"

"I don't hold with such superstitious belief; it's unchristian. Nevertheless, I know how difficult it can be to persuade men out of such foolish notions, and I don't want them avoiding necessary medical care because of it. Therefore, on this ship you shall be called 'Doc,' as you wish."

"I appreciate it, Captain."

Captain Hookset addressed Asa. "Did you know that every one of the men who sailed aboard the *Mary Lovejoy* with you has vowed never to sail for Lovejoy Lines again, as long as George is in charge?"

Asa looked up. "All of them? I hope none of them has limited his chance of employment because of that."

"You needn't worry. Mr. Wass of Bay State Lines is happy to have them. Hearing you were to be Chief Mate led every one of them to sign on for this voyage. They're very devoted to you. Tsk, tsk! Mr. George Lovejoy is good for nothing except stirring up a lot of trouble. Don't let him get under your skin, Mr. Mayhew. No one who knows either one of you would believe his wild talk."

"Aye, sir." Without his presence to rile him, he hoped George would leave Mary in peace. In his concern for Mary, it took him a while to question the timing of his signing on as chief mate, and the crew signing on out of loyalty. Had the captain conned *him* or the *crew*? *Preacher Hookset*? Impossible. And yet…

The captain sighed. "I pray for the sake of his soul that he will repent one day, and become a better man."

While Asa stared at his plate, considering the unlikelihood of this, Mike rolled his eyes. Captain Hookset looked at him. "I don't believe in giving up hope until a man is in his grave, Mr. Slocum."

"Aye, sir." Mike blushed.

Asa bit his lip to restrain the words that had leapt to his tongue — words Captain Hookset wouldn't hold with. He should have stayed ashore to protect Mary. But Mr. Ives would look out for her interests. Wouldn't he?

Doc leaned toward Asa and spoke sotto voce. "Eat your stew, Asa. You've got to keep up your strength."

Asa scowled at Doc as he took a piece of meat, chewed it, and chewed it, and chewed it. It was nothing but gristle. He couldn't very well spit it out at the captain's table; he swallowed it with a grimace and a large gulp of water. "Call this beef stew? More like gum eraser stew," he muttered to Doc.

Captain Hookset changed the subject. "Mr. Slocum, I understand your brother has been promoted to Commander. What does he think about our chances of staying out of this war?"

"Well, sir, he doesn't want war, but he is frustrated by the Navy's lack of preparedness. He agrees with Admiral Knight that the Navy is woefully understaffed, and Congress should allocate more money for men and ships…"

Lost in thought, Asa listened with half an ear, picking up names and random words: "Secretary Daniels… Naval Attaché Boy-Ed recalled… Justice department… picked up Albert's attaché case when he fell asleep on the elevated… spy ring, but they still can't prove anything… What's-his-name? The Military Attaché…"

"Von Papen," Asa contributed.

"Wasn't there talk of him hiring saboteurs? I understand some people want him out of the country," Captain Hookset said.

"Yes, there's talk of having him recalled to Germany, quite soon, as I understand it," Mike said.

Asa drifted in and out of the conversation, trying to look more interested than he felt. His unease about Mary increased, and the knowledge that it was too late to change his decision added to his guilt.

Doc spoke into Asa's ear, "Are you feeling all right? You look a bit flushed." He reached out to touch Asa's forehead.

Asa pulled away. "For Christ's sake, Doc!"

"Mr. Mayhew!" Captain Hookset said. "You know very well I don't hold with swearing, and I will not tolerate having the Lord's name taken in vain on my ship!"

Asa sat up straight. "Aye, aye, Cap'n. It won't happen again." He gave Doc a sidelong look.

Though the ship's cat might tolerate him, Asa thought his discontent was beginning to make him unfit for human companionship. When they had moved on to coffee and tobacco, he made his escape. "May I be dismissed, Captain? I told Mr. Martin he'd only need to spell me for half an hour or so."

"You're dismissed, Mr. Mayhew."

* * * *

Their first destination was Liverpool, bringing a cargo of grains and other foodstuffs. With the danger of U-boats and mined harbors, the *Eastern Trader* would rendezvous, a hundred nautical miles offshore, with a Royal Navy minesweeper to escort her into port.

Slocum had midwatch, from midnight to 0400, but he wasn't feeling well, so Asa took his watch as well as his own four-to-eight watch. Just before sunrise, still about ninety nautical miles west of the rendezvous point, he saw a tiny glimmer of light in the distance.

He grabbed the binoculars. "Conklin, you see that distress signal?"

"Where? Oh! Aye, sir! I see it now."

"Go see if the Captain's up and then get Doc and Mr. Martin. There might be survivors."

"Aye, aye, sir."

"Yates, standard left rudder, heading east by no'th," Asa ordered.

"Standard left rudder, heading east by no'th," Yates repeated.

Asa peered through the foredawn's nebulous light. As they got closer, he could just make out the silhouette of a lifeboat, crowded with men.

"Can you see survivors?" Captain Hookset spoke as he entered the bridge.

"Looks like an overcrowded lifeboat, sir. There may be more men clingin' to debris. Can't see much in this fog — not until we get closer." Asa pointed, giving the captain the binoculars.

"Hmm, quite far off. We can go a little faster without fear of running them over."

"Aye, Cap'n." Asa telegraphed the engine room: Ahead two-thirds. "Would you care to take the conn, sir?"

"Not yet. It's still your watch." He handed the glasses back to Asa. "Your eyes are younger than mine."

Leaning forward, binoculars pressed close to his eyes, Asa muttered to himself, "Like tryin' to see through a thick curtain of old, gray cobwebs hangin' in some dahk cellah. Wish that sun would try a mite hahdah to rise up and poke its head through the clouds."

Captain Hookset's ears hadn't lost any of their acuity. "Let us pray." Before Asa got a chance to say a word, the captain had launched into his prayer. "Dear Lord, you have told us that whenever two or three are gathered in your name, our prayers would be answered. We pray now that we may see through the morning fog to rescue those men and bring them to safety, before they are exposed to further danger and suffering. All this we ask in your name. Amen." At his pointed look, Asa said, "Oh! Amen."

The sky lightened as the sun made a watery appearance. It wasn't much, but it was enough for Asa to see the men a bit clearer.

Tommy arrived. Asa turned to him. "Blow general quarters. We've got a wreck." Even before Asa had finished the order, Tommy's piercing whistle penetrated the ship.

The captain and Tommy spoke at the same time: "How many?"

"Looks like fifteen or more, still alive, but a few of them are just clinging to their flimsy flotsam rafts. The fellahs in the lifeboat seem to be faring better. We'll need a lot of helping hands to get those men aboard. Conklin, did you see Doc?"

"Aye, sir. I asked him to come to the bridge."

"Well, go back and tell him to shake a leg. Then see if Mr. Slocum's feeling better. Tell them to report to the bridge, pronto."

"Aye, aye, Mr. Mayhew." Conklin hastened off.

Asa lowered the glasses to judge the distance better with his naked eye. He telegraphed the engine room: Ahead half. "We're comin' up too fast. Don't want to drown them in our wake when we come alongside them."

"How soon?" Captain Hookset asked.

"Fifteen, twenty minutes. Tommy, blow general quarters again, and then go roust anyone who's somehow managed to sleep through that."

Men swarmed on deck, taking their positions. Doc and Slocum arrived at the bridge.

"Took you long enough. Next time, leave preparing sick bay to the mates." Asa handed Doc the binoculars. "How bad are they?"

"Still alive; can't tell much more from here."

"Slocum, how are you feeling?" Asa asked.

"Bettah. It seems to have run its course."

"Good. Get a gang of big, strong men — Mac, Joe, and a couple of stokers to row out and bring them in. Get a breeches buoy set up."

"Aye, Aye, Mr. Mayhew."

"Tommy, get another gang to round up all the blankets they can find, and dry clothing in various sizes. Pajamas, union suits, anything the crew can spare. And socks, thick, heavy socks; we can use them for mittens, too. When you're done with that, go help Mr. Slocum on deck."

"Aye, aye, Mr. Mayhew."

"Doc, you know what to do."

"On my way." Doc went out and began setting up a triage area on deck.

Asa rang the bells to the engine room and turned the dial on the telegraph to "Ahead Slow." When he could see the wreck without binoculars, he spoke through the voice tube, "Ahead dead slow, prepare to stop." He turned to the helmsman. "Yates, right handsomely." As they came up alongside the wreck, Asa spoke through the tube, "Engine stop." Then he hailed the men standing by the davits. "Prepare to lower lifeboats." He hailed the men on the foredeck, "Lay anchor."

The anchor chain rattled through the hawse pipe. When the men were sure she was secure, they called, "Anchor laid."

"Lower lifeboats." Asa watched through the binoculars, pleased to see the men doing a fine job on their own. Then he turned his attention from his men to the men clinging to floating hatches and other bits of debris, blue with cold, so exhausted as to seem lifeless, and the men huddled in the sole remaining lifeboat, shivering.

"I wonder how long the poah bas—" Asa stopped short and cleared his throat. "I wondah how long they've been out there."

"I pray we're not too late. What was wrong with Mr. Slocum?"

"Case of the trots."

"You took his watch, as well as your own?"

"Well, he wouldn't have been very effective, runnin' to the head every fifteen minutes. I was up, anyway." Asa watched the rescue preparations. "Good, they're picking up the men from the makeshift rafts first, just as they were trained to do. Look at Mac; he's lifting them into the lifeboat singlehandedly. And Joe's just about as strong." He picked up the loud-hailer. "Joe! Leanin' too far to stahb'd! Watch it! Don't capsize your own lifeboat! Sidney, balance him to po't! Keep your eye on them, Tommy, and use your pipe!"

Tommy's whistle issued commands by arrangements of short, sharp blasts and trills keeping the men coordinated.

"They're a good crew. They do their jobs without needing much direction," Captain Hookset said.

"Most of them were apprentices under Cap'n James. He never had a man punished for doing something wrong. Instead, he taught him how to do it right, or he had me teach him. They're a good team, very loyal to him. It wasn't their fault that lifeboat—" Asa turned away, biting the inside of his cheek to stop the scene from running through his interior vision.

Captain Hookset placed a hand on Asa's shoulder. "This is the first time you've mentioned him. I know you don't like to talk about it, Asa, but I've been talking to some of the men. You—"

Asa held up a hand, shaking his head. "Please, sir, I need to concentrate on this rescue mission."

"All right. I'll just say this. Stop punishing yourself. There's no reason for it."

"*Punishing* my—" Asa stopped himself. Arguing with the captain — especially Captain Hookset — was simply not done. He turned his binoculars back to the rescue. "Mike! Looks like a man in the watah, off the stahb'd beam! See him? Get that breeches buoy and get him up!"

The men in one of the rescue boats rowed to the drowning man and pulled him aboard. Two muscular stokers, Peterson and Sampson, grabbed the ring buoy and put him into the canvas pants attached to it. They gave Mike the thumbs up, and the men on deck hoisted the half-drowned man aboard with the pulley apparatus.

Doc rushed to him and immediately began the Schafer method of respiration, pushing rhythmically on the man's back. Asa stared, transfixed, as the man began coughing up water.

"Good thing you spotted him," Captain Hookset said. "I don't think anyone else did."

Awakening to the present, Asa said, "Sir?"

"That man," the captain said. "Looks like he's going to recover, due to your good eyes, Mr. Mayhew."

"Excuse me, sir. If you would care to take over the conn, now, I could help out over there." He tipped his head in the direction of activity around the port beam. "I can perform triage for Doc."

"Triage?" Captain Hookset asked.

"Sorting out who needs care first. It's a French term."

"It certainly makes sense. You know how to do that — to judge their conditions?"

"Aye, Cap'n. Doc taught me."

"All right, I've got the conn. Go help those poor men," the captain said. "Oh, Mr. Mayhew, before you go — there won't be enough room in sickbay for all of them. Use the fo'c's'le, but put the officers in your quarters and have men set up cots in my stateroom for you and Mr. Slocum."

"Aye, aye, sir."

Asa grabbed an armload of blankets and a couple of canteens from the emergency locker in the wheel house. He ran into Bo's'n's Mate Don Henry on his way out. "Henry! Round up anything that can be used as warming pans, and go down to the galley to get embers to put in them. It'll help if we warm up the beds. Get some men to help you. Have Cooky heat up a good, rich broth and make an urn of strong, sweet, piping hot tea."

As he went from man to man, wrapping each in a warm blanket, taking pulses and checking respirations, giving sips of water, he tried to reassure them. "You're safe, now. We'll take care of you." When he found a man unconscious, in shock, or nearly so, he called out, "Doc! Over here!"

Doc had those men transported to sickbay as soon as he had attended to them, giving care instructions to his assistants.

Davy Jones, the youngest, smallest crew member came on deck, carrying an arm-stretching mass of donated clothing. He craned to see over the top. "That's the lot. What can I do next?"

Doc answered. "You can take those down to sickbay, help the men to get dried off and into them, and then start taking care of their feet. Make sure you get this right, Davy, or you'll do more harm than good. Soak them in warm water — *warm*, not hot. About 100° to 104°. Use a thermometer. Hands, too, if they show signs of frostbite — whiteness or mottling of the skin, swelling, loss of sensation. Got it?"

Davy repeated the instructions, finishing up with, "Aye, aye, Doc, I got it." He nodded, and then hurried off to sick bay.

"Asa, have we been through them all?" Doc asked. "Any others needing my immediate attention?"

"We've looked over all the men aboard. Still searchin' for any others."

"Some of the men need care for serious wounds and burns. I'm going below to attend to them now." Doc shook his head. "It's a wonder they didn't all die of exposure."

At first, the men were too parched to talk and too exhausted to move, except for incessant shivering. As Doc, Asa, and their helpers got them warmed up, rehydrated, and fed, they began to be able to tell what had happened.

"Can you tell me your name?" Asa asked the sailor who was tucked into Asa's bed.

"Angus Ross, chief mate."

"Pleased to meet you Mr. Ross. I'm Asa Mayhew, chief mate." Asa examined Ross's hands. "They don't look too bad. How do they feel? Can you move them?"

"Cold, a little painful, but I *can* still feel them, thank God, and I can move them a bit, though quite clumsily."

"Well, let's bathe them in a little warm water, all right?"

"That would be just the ticket."

After bathing and drying them, Asa took a pair of thick socks from a drawer and slipped them over Ross's hands. "These should help. I'd suggest keeping them snugged into your armpits for a while. Has anyone treated your feet for frostbite yet?"

"Feet? No."

"Do you mind if I do that now?"

"Please, go ahead. I'd like to keep as many toes as possible. But I don't think they can be too bad. I was one of the lucky ones in the lifeboat." He looked away.

"I'm sure the men wanted you to be there." Asa prepared a basin of warm water and pulled the blankets from the foot of the bed. "Can you swing your legs over the side a little? Here, I'll help you." While Ross's feet soaked, Asa engaged him in conversation. "How many men were you?"

"Twenty, including Captain Menzies. I believe he... went down with the ship."

"Well, we've picked up seventeen of you, so far. We're still looking. By the maple leaf insignias I see all around, I take it you're Canadian?"

"The Maple Leaf Line, the *Annie Laurie*, out of Halifax, Nova Scotia. We were bringing wheat, oats, and barley to Liverpool, when a U-boat got us. Sometimes they come back and shoot the survivors, but we were lucky. Some luck, eh?" Ross laughed bitterly and started coughing.

"Try a little water." Asa held the canteen to his lips. "Perhaps you should rest a while. We can talk later."

After he drank, Ross put his sock-mittened hand on Asa's sleeve. "No, I must warn you. I debated over lighting the lantern, afraid they'd see it and come after us again, but I didn't want another ship to run over us in the fog, or miss a chance at rescue. Thank God it was you saw it. We've got to get out of here before they come back to finish us off."

"We will, soon as we're sure we've got all your crew aboard," Asa said. "You know, I heard they used to take the crew off before they sank the ship."

"When some merchantmen began arming themselves, the Jerries likely reckoned it was more expeditious to scuttle her, crew and all. Then some of them started shooting survivors."

"Why, I wonder? What danger could the survivors possibly pose to them?"

"'*Why*?' What difference does it make? They themselves probably don't know. It's war," Ross said. "All a merchantman can do is to try to get the hell away from them."

"Well, we'll get you to Liverpool, anyway. How long have you been out there?"

"What day is it?"

"Wednesday morning."

"Since yesterday afternoon, then. It seemed longer. You must speak to your captain, man! Neutral or not, if you stay in one place, you make yourself a sitting duck."

"Take a deep breath to calm yourself, Mr. Ross, and let it out slowly. Again… keep breathing. I assure you, we are aware of the danger, and we're keeping a sharp lookout. Soon, we're to rendezvous with a Royal Navy minesweeper, and she'll escort us in. Your U-boat is most likely off hunting other prey by now. Besides, I don't think the Germans want America to enter war just yet. Sinkin' our ships on purpose would be to their disadvantage."

As they talked, Asa dried Ross's feet, applied petroleum jelly, loose gauze bandages, socks, and then tucked them under the blankets again.

With Asa's care, Mr. Ross slept, exhaustion overruling his vigilance against U-boats.

# Chapter 9

# *Caring for the Rescued*

Asa went below to help Doc in sickbay, treating frostbite with warm water, loose dressings, and shots of whiskey. Whiskey was on the list of things Preacher Hookset didn't hold with, but he made an exception for medicinal purposes. When all their patients were asleep, they walked toward the hatch, talking in low voices.

"It's a wonder any of them survived, out here in the North Atlantic, late November…" Doc shook his head. "A few of them will probably lose toes to frostbite."

"Captain Hookset's been offering up some powerful prayers," Asa said. "Mr. Ross told me there were twenty souls aboard. We've found seventeen?"

"Yes. There's no hope for the other three. Not a trace of them."

"Their captain's gone, then."

Doc squeezed Asa's shoulder.

Asa turned and walked away. *Damn it all to hell, Doc! Leave me be! I've got a job to do.* He wasn't angry; he just didn't know how to keep a stiff upper lip with Doc and the captain oozing sympathy all over him. Without turning his head, he waved at Doc as he stepped through the hatch. He took a few calming breaths on his way to the galley.

"Something smells good."

"Roast in the oven for dinner," Cooky said.

"Got any coffee? I missed breakfast."

The cook handed Asa a cup. "I could fry you up an egg, if you'd like. I sent one of the lads down to sick bay with a tray for Doc a little while ago."

"Nunno, this's fine." Asa raised his cup to Cooky.

"Toast? How about some toast?"

Asa smiled and raised his cup again. "Here's a toast to you, Cooky! Coffee's fine, thanks."

Cooky grinned. "It'll be dinnertime in about half an hour, anyway."

"Would you please make a big pot of some nutritious soup for the men we just fished out of the deep? After they've slept a while, they'll be able to handle something a little heartier than the broth they had earlier."

"Aye, Mr. Mayhew. I've already started a fresh broth with some marrow bones. I'll add meat, vegetables, and barley to it — oh, and potatoes and beans, too — and have something ready for them when they wake. Poor fellahs."

"Maybe add a little butter in it, too, to make it richer, and some herbs and warming spices. Just a suggestion."

"Good idea. It'll make it tastier, too," Cooky smiled.

"How's your thumb?"

"Oh, it's fine, now. Doc did a real good job." He flexed his thumb for Asa to see.

"Good God! I mean, ah, good *heavens*! Gotta practice mindin' my tongue if I don't want to slip up around Cap'n Hookset. He doesn't 'hold with taking the Lord's name in vain.'" Asa winked. "That's some scar. I'm amazed it's still attached and workin'."

"Me, too. Doc says the scar will fade. He's real good at his job, ain't he?"

"Top-notch. See ya, Cooky."

He walked around checking on the rescued men not in sickbay. Most were in the deep sleep of exhaustion, emitting snuffling snores. When he entered the fo'c's'le, he heard a muffled cry of fear. He followed the sound to a lower rack, where a boy lay moaning in his sleep. He put his hand on the boy's brow and murmured to him, "Sh, sh. It's just a nightmare."

The boy awoke with a scream, grabbing Asa's wrist in both hands. To keep from toppling over onto him, Asa sat on the edge of the rack. After the trauma of being torpedoed and the hours on a freezing lifeboat, this slight boy's strength amazed him.

"Hush, hush, lad. It's all right now. Sh, sh. You don't want to wake the other men. Do you think you can let go of me, now?"

"*Les sous-marins!*" [5]

"*Je comprends. Vous êtes sauf maintenant. Êtes-vous de Québec? Parlez-vous anglais?*"

"*Oui, pardon.*" The boy calmed down a little, and let go of Asa's wrist. "Yes, pardon me. I forget myself."

"Completely understandable. I awakened you out of a nightmare, and you have just been through a terrifying experience. *Je m'appelle Asa Mayhew, et vous?*"[6]

"I am called Jean-Claude Bilodeau."

"I'd like you to call me Asa. May I call you Jean-Claude?"

"*Oui, mais bien sûr.*[7] It is my name."

Asa smiled. "If you don't mind my asking, how old are you, Jean-Claude?"

"I 'ave — I am sixteen years."

"Is this your first voyage?"

Jean-Claude blushed. "*Oui.* Is it so evident? I am a… 'ow to say… a frightened shild — child?" There was a defensive edge to his tone.

"Nunno, not at all. You are the right age to be just starting out; that's all I meant. If it had been my ship attacked by a U-boat, I'd have been frightened out of my wits, and I'm a tough old salt with a lot of experience… It must have been horrifying for you — your first voyage, getting blown up, and fighting to survive in that frigid water. Show me a man who isn't afraid in a situation like that, and I'll show you a man who has something wrong with his mind."

"Perhaps, but… they do not show it so much."

"You can bet they did when they were first starting out. It takes practice to hide your fear, and to persevere despite it. In certain situations, you have to do that to survive; but it's not a good idea for the long run. Talking might help you to feel a little better. You can tell me anything you want. It will be just between us."

*Hypocrite*, Asa called himself. *Why don't you take your own advice? Because getting swept back there makes me feel crazy, and I need to stay sane. I have responsibilities. And the most important one right now is this frightened boy.*

"*D'accord.*" [8] Jean-Claude hesitated. "I 'ave desire to be a sailor *depuis* — ah, *since* I am a child. But now… I do not know. I want to go 'ome, but I must sail across the *Atlantique* to get there. I do not know if I am able. I despair."

"I see." Asa patted the boy's hand. "It will be difficult, but if your desire to go home is strong enough, you will be able to do it. And maybe once you get through that journey, the sea won't hold such terror for you. But a little fear isn't a bad thing, you know. As long as it doesn't overwhelm you, it can sharpen your senses to what's going on around you — make you vigilant. That may give you a chance to avoid disaster. Do you see?"

"What does 'overwhelm' mean?"

"*Submerger.* Sometimes things like fear, desperation, hopelessness, or grief—" Asa looked away and cleared his throat. "*Pardonnez-moi*, Jean-Claude — frog in my throat."

"A frog?" Jean-Claude looked puzzled.

Asa translated. "*Un chat dans la gorge.* Where was I? Oh! Sometimes emotions can sweep over us like an enormous wave, and push us under. We have to struggle against that, or we can drow—" Asa attempted to clear his throat, but when he tried to talk, nothing came out but a hoarse croak. He stood up and turned away, willing himself not to become plunged into cold confusion and dark despair. He would not go back there. A frightened young lad needed him now. He closed his eyes and took a few deep breaths. After a moment, he turned and perched on the edge of the rack again.

Jean-Claude's expression was a mixture of puzzlement and concern. "'Ave you a sore troat? Throat. I 'ave trouble to remember *t-h* sound."

"I am quite well. It just seems quite difficult to evict this family of frogs who have taken up residence in my throat." Asa smiled. "How do *you* feel? Have you warmed up any?"

"I am more comfortable in my body, but my mind is still confused. *La mer*, she calls to me, but she frightens me. 'Ow can I be a sailor now?"

"I understand your dilemma. You see, I *have* been a sailor since I was a little boy. I love her, but *la mer* can be a cruel mistress. Something has happened, and I, too—" Asa stopped. "I am sorry, Jean-Claude. I should not have allowed my own troubles to intrude."

"*Monsieur,* do not apologize. You make me see I am not alone, and I am less afraid. You treat me as your equal, not as a child. You honor me to tell me of your personal trouble. As you say to me, it is *entre nous.*"

"Thank you for your kind understanding, Jean-Claude. If it somehow helped you, then I suppose it was all right. All the same, you have difficulties enough of your own without mine coming into it." Asa smiled. "What's it like at home in Quebec?"

"Ah, we 'ave a small farm. We grow vegetables and fruits, and 'ave shickens — *chickens*, pigs, cows, and goats. We make sheese. I 'ave… *have* four brothers and tree — *three* sisters. I am the eldest. Papa wants me to stay 'ome and work with 'im, and take over the farm someday."

"Do you think you might like that?"

"Perhaps… but I want to go to sea like my Grand-père. Maman says if I want to go to sea like her father, Papa should let me go for a few years. Papa says Grand-père fills my 'ead with all sorts of wild tales. I know most of his stories are exaggerated *récits* — 'ow you call them — yarns. But now I go to sea, I know *some* of his stories are true. It is the great adventure. But with the war, it is *de trop* — too great, too much."

Asa nodded.

"Maybe I go 'ome until the war is over. But if it does not end soon, maybe the Army will conscript me. I prefer to join the Navy, but I am afraid to do either one. Maybe I die before I 'ave a shance to live. Am I a coward?"

Jean-Claude's brow wrinkled and his eyes glittered with unshed tears. His dashed hopes touched Asa's heart.

"Nunno. You've gone through a terrible experience, so you know better than those boys who go rushing off to join up, thinking it's all glory. If they stopped to think about the reality of it, they probably wouldn't be so anxious to go." He paused, but Jean-Claude didn't seem convinced, so he went on. "Having a drive for self-preservation isn't cowardice. We all have that. Everyone's afraid at one time or another, even if they won't admit it. Bravery is going forward despite being scared, still persevering even when your legs feel like rubber. Do you see?"

Jean-Claude thought about it. "Everyone is afraid? Even those who seem brave?"

"Pretty much," Asa said. "Right now, you are looking fear in the eye and wondering what to do about it, aren't you?"

"Ah... *oui*. I do not know what to do. 'Ow... *How* do I advance in despite of fear? Can I embark upon a ship without trembling and sweating and *maladie*? How do you say it?"

"Illness?"

"Not quite ill..."

"Feeling nauseated?"

"*Oui* — I mean — *yes*, feeling nausea. How do I do that?"

"The question is: can you board ship *even though* you're trembling, sweating, and feeling queasy? By the way, you *do* know you're aboard ship right now."

Jean-Claude's mouth and eyes formed three large *O's*. "*Oui, bien sûr! Comment pourrais j'ai oublié?* Oh! I— Ze sheep *américain*! You rescue us! Oh, I— I—"[9]

"That's all right, Jean-Claude. You've had a very trying time. It's bound to affect your thought processes."

"I do not understand. Thought processes?"

"When we have suffered a terrible shock, sometimes it can take a little time for our brains to work as they normally do. Things like not being fully aware of your surroundings are quite common. *Voyez-vous?*"[10]

"Ah, *oui*. I see. Asa?"

"Yes?"

"I am aboard ship, but I have no fear. Not right now. Not with you."

Asa reached out and patted Jean-Claude's shoulder. "You're making progress already."

An orange tabby came padding in, tail aloft. She went directly to Asa, purring and rubbing up against his legs.

"Ah, here's a friend. Do you like cats?"

"*Mais oui*. We 'ave two cats in the barn, and one in the 'ouse. They keep the mice and rats away, and they make good companions."

Asa picked up the cat, placing her beside Jean-Claude. "This is Leo. She'll keep you company, and help keep you warm, too."

Leo washed her face and ears, then butted her head against Jean-Claude's arm, begging for attention. He scratched under her chin, and she stretched her neck out, leaning into him, purring.

"Leo is a girl's name?"

"Well, no, but by the time we discovered he was a she, she already answered to the name. She's hell on rats, but she's a sweetheart to sailors."

Jean-Claude patted the cat, yawning.

"Do you think you can go back to sleep, now? A little rest might be restorative."

"I am afraid of the dream, *le cauchemar*. 'Ow... *H*ow do you call it?"

"Nightmare. Yes, that can make it very hard to sleep. But you may be able to get a little sleep before the dream comes. And if it does, maybe you can tell yourself you're safe now; it was only a dream. You might even be able to go back to sleep again. Even a little sleep is better than none, and you do need it to recover, you know." *Right, do as I say, not as I do.* "Would it help if I stay with you until you fall asleep?"

"*Je vous en prie, ne partez pas encore,*"[11] Jean-Claude pleaded.

"All right, I'll stay. Eventually, however, I shall have to get back to my duties."

"*Merci,*" Jean-Claude sighed.

"Leo seems to know when a fellah needs a little comfort. She'll stay, at least until something else catches her attention."

Jean-Claude scratched behind the cat's ears, whispering to her. "*Tu es une bonne chatte.*"[12] Leo purred louder. After a moment, the boy said, "I tink pair'aps I can cross ze *Atlantique* again. Even if it is only to go 'ome to Maman as a frightened boy." He yawned again.

"I'll bet you're braver than you think. No more talking, now. Just breathe. Deep breaths, that's right."

Afraid he may put himself to sleep, Asa did not engage in the breathing exercise with the boy. Instead, in his warm baritone, he sang a French lullaby until Jean-Claude's eyes closed, and his breathing took on the rhythms of sleep.

Leo stood up, stretched, yawned, turned around, and then curled up as she had been, nestled into Jean-Claude's side.

\* \* \* \*

Asa's eyelids felt weighted down with lead. Before going on watch at midnight, he had only managed to catch a few hours of interrupted sleep. But that had grown to be a matter of course. He would awaken from the drowning nightmare, coughing, spluttering, and as drenched in sweat as though he had actually been underwater, and go back to sleep only to dream of cruel Mr. Murdstone, Clara dying, and David Copperfield being left a penniless orphan. Only little Davy had somehow turned into a beautiful young woman with glowing auburn hair.

*Hope the cold air on deck will wake me up.* He yawned. *Now where did I leave my reefer? Oh, in my quarters, when I was talking to Mr. Ross.*

He slipped in and picked up his coat. Ross was snoring. Another man was sleeping in Slocum's bed, and a cot had been set up, holding yet another soul deep in slumber. Asa looked at his bed for a minute, longing to crawl into it. But it would be another day or two before they reached Liverpool and discharged their passengers.

When he went out onto the weather deck, he glanced up to see Slocum on the bridge, looking through a pair of binoculars for the minesweeper they should be meeting up with soon. Captain Hookset was on the foredeck, scanning the horizon with a telescope. Asa joined him.

"No sign of her yet?"

"No, and I don't like it. We're almost to the coordinates. Despite stopping to pick up those poor men, we're well within the general timeframe. I should think we'd catch some sight of her."

Asa stifled a yawn. "Have we tried to radio her?"

"All Smitty can get right now is static. I don't like that, either. That U-boat could be close by, interfering with the wireless signal."

"When we meet up with her, we'll have to communicate with semaphore, then. Maybe I should take a look at the radio," Asa said. "May I borrow your spyglass?"

"Here. Maybe you can see something my old eyes have missed."

"You're not old, Cap'n," Asa smiled as he adjusted the glass.

"Be sixty-five, come April."

"No! You must be pulling my leg. You never look it."

"Well, I'm beginning to feel it."

"Aha! There she is." Asa handed the glass back. "Dead ahead."

"That fishing trawler?"

"Ayup. They've converted civilian trawlers to minesweepers."

"I know that!" Captain Hookset bristled. "I just didn't expect her to look so *much* like an ordinary fisherman's craft. I suppose it's good camouflage."

"In the beginning, maybe, but I'd say the Germans have caught on by now." Asa cast a sideways glance at the captain, hoping he hadn't insulted him by telling him yet another thing he already knew.

"Fishing trawler or minesweeper — it probably wouldn't make any difference to them. Tsk-tsk. Attacking an unarmed merchantman! Isn't that against the Hague Convention?"

"Wouldn't make any difference one way or t'other. They've already broken the rules by using poison gas," Asa said.

"Unconscionable! But I understand the British have started fighting back with the same methods. 'The other side used it first,' is no excuse, to my mind. Sin is sin."

In silence, they looked out to sea.

Then Captain Hookset turned to Asa. "You've been taking care of the patients?"

"Helped Doc for a while, and then went around checking on the ones not in sick bay. Spent some time with a scared young kid. Sixteen years old, first trip out, and he meets up with a torpedo." Asa shook his head.

Captain Hookset tsk-tsked. "Poor lad. What's his name?"

"Jean-Claude Bilodeau."

"I'll add him to my prayers. How is he?"

"He was asleep when I left him. Leo's keeping him company, for now. I hope the nightmares don't disturb him too much, after our talk." Asa tried to stifle another yawn.

"You haven't been getting much sleep yourself, have you?"

Asa shrugged.

Captain Hookset looked at him the way his cousin Janet looked at him when he put his elbow on the table.

"Oh! I, uh, beg your pardon, sir. I didn't mean to be rude," Asa said. "It's true, I've had some insomnia lately, but it will pass. I'm fine, sir."

"You're not eating enough, either."

As Asa opened his mouth to protest, Captain Hookset stopped him with a look.

"Don't try to lie to me, young man," the captain said. "You need to eat and sleep properly if you are to be able to carry on with your duties. Do you hear me?"

"Aye, aye, sir." Abashed, Asa looked at the deck. "I hope I have not been remiss in my duties, Cap'n."

"No, by gum, you haven't! If anything, you take on extra duties, such as taking Mr. Slocum's watch and helping the doctor. Not only that, you are schooling Mr. Martin to pass his test for becoming a licensed third mate, aren't you?"

"Well—"

Without giving Asa a chance to answer, Captain Hookset went on, "You don't slack off on drilling the men in emergency procedures, either, and you keep a pretty cool head. That's why the rescue went so smoothly this morning."

"But that's just—"

"You can sense a storm coming long before there are any signs of it, and you always seem to know when there's a U-boat around. I could go on, but I don't want you getting a swelled head." The captain smiled. "That's why I want you to take better care of yourself, Asa. You're too valuable to go down sick."

"Um… well… I'm just doing my job, sir. I, uh, don't know what to say."

Captain Hookset took out his watch. "Say you'll go eat dinner now, and take a nap afterwards. I've ordered cots set up in my quarters for you and Slocum. Use one of them."

"Aye, aye, sir."

*I don't know how I'll ever be able to sleep in the captain's cabin. What if I wake him up at night with one of my nightmares? Feel like I'm nine years old again, when Cap'n Asa took care of me after that bugger— No, I won't think about that.* Yet, an image flashed through Asa's mind of Captain Asa Lovejoy, setting up a hammock in his cabin for him, and getting out of bed to comfort him when the nightmares came.

"And leave the radio to Smith and Martin," Captain Hookset said. You don't have to do every job on this ship. The other men are perfectly capable of performing their duties."

"Aye, sir."

# Chapter 10

# *Liverpool*

The longshoremen's foreman supervised as the crane dipped down into the hold, where the men below attached netted bundles of sacks to the hook. The winch drew these up to the deck, where dockers formed a line to carry sacks down the gangway, load them on drays, and then return to repeat the process. Standing at the rail, Asa watched over the men unloading the cargo. Mike stood beside him with a clipboard and pencil, writing down the count as Asa gave it to him. The buyer was in Captain Hookset's office, while his agent stood at the foot of the gangway, taking his own count.

"You there! Watch what you're doing!" Asa called to one of the longshoremen, or dockers, as the British called them. "Don't tear that sack with your cargo hook! You'll be trailing grain all over the place!"

The docker grumbled, but shifted his big hook from his neck to his belt so it wouldn't snag the sacks of grain he was hauling on his back with his smaller sack hook.

"That's ten more sacks of wheat," Asa said.

"Got it," Mike answered.

They were a motley group, middle-aged and older, with a few younger ones who were none-too-healthy looking. The young and fit were entrenched in the mud of France, dying in the bloodbath of Gallipoli, and suffering untold horrors throughout the world. With the men left to take their places, unloading was going to be a longer, more arduous process than usual. They were just as slow going up the gangplank unburdened as coming down it bearing a heavy sack.

"Mike, did you notice that one of those fellahs goin' in hasn't come back out again?"

"Tell the truth, they all look alike to me — like a trail of ants carrying crumbs back home to the mound."

"Dark hair, baggy jacket with suspiciously bulging pockets," Asa said. "You keep count, and keep a sharp eye here. I'm goin' below to look for him. Either something's happened to him, or he's up to no good."

"Think he's stealing?"

"Or worse. I'll find out."

"Who had the tenth sack of wheat?" Mike asked.

"Guy with the red neckerchief. See him?"

"Got it." Mike went back to his tally.

Just as his foot hit the bottom rung of the ladder, Asa saw the man disappearing through the hatch to the engine room. He dashed down the passageway after him.

The engine room was a crowded maze of vertical and horizontal pipes sprouting dozens of green levers and red wheels. The bulkhead was full of gleaming dials and gauges, and there were two polished bronze engine telegraphs, currently reading full stop. Three bulbous white-plastered boilers pushed steam into shining copper pipes. The steam drove the big triple-expansion engine with its green triangular columns, steel pistons, and enormous wheels that turned the crankshaft that drove the propeller.

Most of the crew had liberty, but Gunderson had remained behind, finishing up some maintenance. He lay unconscious, his thick blond hair matted with blood. The stranger stood over him, a length of pipe in his raised hand, about to land another blow. Asa leapt at him, slamming his wrist against one of the engine's columns. The pipe clanged to the deck. Grunting, they wrestled in the tight space. "Damn!" Asa cursed as he banged his elbow against a pipe for the second time. Twisting to avoid a kick to his groin, his knee met up with a stopcock. "Son of a bitch! You fight dirty!" Fury revitalized him. He grabbed the bastard by the neck, slammed him up against a cold boiler and pinned him tightly between two copper pipes in the cramped space.

"All right, where is it?"

The man gave him a blank look.

Asa tried again, "*Wo ist es?*"[13]

The man responded with a sneer.

Asa applied pressure to his windpipe. "*Sagen Sie mir oder ich werde dich töten!*"[14]

The man struggled in vain. His lips were turning blue when he gave up and pointed at the base of the triple-expansion engine.

In a tick, Asa snagged a nearby rope and lashed him to the pipes. The saboteur struggled against his bonds, only succeeding in making them tighter.

Asa went to Gunderson. "Sorry, Sven," he murmured as he slid him away from the engine. "Emergency. I'll get to you in a minute."

*It* was jammed halfway under the crankshaft — eight sticks of dynamite secured together and connected by two wires to a ticking alarm clock. There was one minute left.

Okay, he thought, I've seen this before. I can do this. Have to — no choice. As he took out his multi-tool knife, he heard the saboteur suck in a breath. He chose a blade.

The only sound in the engine room was the ticking clock as the relentless second hand marched on.

Asa slowed his breathing to steady his trembling hands. He lifted the first wire, sure it was the correct one. Well, pretty sure. He closed his eyes, visualizing the illustration. He opened them and picked up his knife. He stopped breathing. He cut the wire. He heaved a sigh of relief.

Calmer now, he cut the second wire. Then he removed the detonator fuse, detached the clock, and stopped it. He wiped the sweat off his forehead with the back of his hand and suppressed a wave of nausea.

The saboteur let out his breath in a whoosh and then resumed his fruitless struggle against Asa's knots, muttering curses in German.

Looming over him and squeezing the saboteur's cheeks with one hand, harsh and threatening, Asa demanded, "*Mehr Bomben en Bord?*"[15]

"*Nein, nein.*"[16] The man shrank away from him.

"Humph." Asa stuffed the clock in one reefer pocket and the dynamite in the other. Then he attended to Gunderson.

"Sven! Sven Gunderson, can you hear me? Wake up!" He slapped Gunderson's face. "Wake up, Sven!" Open palm to each cheek, once more. "Gunderson! Open your eyes!"

Gunderson groaned.

"Open your eyes, Sven!"

Gunderson obeyed.

"Good man. Keep them open," Asa said. "How do you feel?"

"Oooh, my head!" Gunderson moaned and gave Asa an unfocused look. "What the hell?"

"That fellah tied to the pipe tried to knock you into the next world. Good thing you've got such a thick thatch to cushion the blow."

"Bomb! There's a bomb!" Gunderson struggled to sit up.

"I got it, Sven. Lie down." Asa pointed to the dynamite sticking out of his pocket. "It's defused. Clock's in the other pocket." He held his index finger up. "How many fingers do you see?"

"Hold still."

"I'm not movin'. Take a guess. How many fingers?"

"Uh, two?"

"Will you be all right here until I get rid of this gink? I'll send Doc down," Asa said.

"'M aw ri'."

"You most definitely are not! You stay right there and don't you move! Keep your head still. Doc'll be down in a minute. Try to stay awake, okay?"

"Yah." Gunderson closed his eyes.

"Uh-uh. Keep those eyes open. Don't want you driftin' off into a coma. Can you stay awake?"

"Yah, all right."

Before Asa freed the saboteur from the pipe, he tied him hand and foot, leaving just enough slack to allow him to climb the ladder. A rope tied around his waist acted as a tether. "All right, up you go." He pointed to the ladder.

The fellow snarled something in German at him. Asa snarled back, repeating his order in German and prodding him up the ladder. Feeling slightly revived, Gunderson hurled a couple of Swedish curses after the saboteur.

"That's tellin' him, Sven. You keep up that spirit, and stay awake now, mind."

"I'm awake."

On the weather deck, Asa spotted Mr. Martin. "Tommy, thank God you haven't left yet! Go get Doc, and send him down to the engine room. This guy knocked Sven on the head with a pipe. He's conscious now, but he's in bad shape." He pushed his struggling captive toward the captain's office.

"Cripes! What the—?"

"Saboteur. Get Doc. Step lively, now."

Tommy hurried off to sickbay.

"What's going on, here?" Captain Hookset demanded, striding across the deck.

"This guy was attemptin' to blow us all to kingdom come, Cap'n. We need the police, the army, Scotland Yard, or *whoever* the he— uh, heck handles this kind of thing."

"Mr. Jarvis!" Captain Hookset called to the buyer. A monocled, ruddy-faced gent in striped trousers, a black frock coat and black bowler hat bustled out of the captain's office.

"We've got a saboteur, here. Will you please get the proper authorities?"

"I say! Right ho, Captain!" Jarvis scurried down the gangplank, elbowing dockers out of the way.

"Pretty spry, for a stout old fellah," Captain Hookset said.

"Amazing how much pep the threat of a bomb can give a man," Asa said.

"Until they get here, I suggest we tie *him* to a chair in my office." Captain Hookset gave the would-be bomber a thunderous look.

Asa gave their captive a none-too-gentle nudge in the right direction. In the office, he ordered the man to bend over and put his hands on the desk, in sharp, clipped German. When the fellow was uncooperative, Asa muttered in exasperation, "Don't be such a stupid mule." Then he pushed him forward and kicked his feet apart. He checked for a gun in his belt, pockets, or a shoulder holster. Nothing. He patted down his pants legs, and found a wicked-looking knife in a sheath, strapped to his right calf. "Hmm. Glad he didn't pull that on me. Probably couldn't get at it. Tight squeeze down in the engine room." He checked both sleeves and the back of the man's neck, in case he'd hidden another knife, and found none. He searched the guy's pockets, coming up with a handkerchief, a half-empty cigarette case, a brass match safe containing nothing but wooden matches, a crown, a few shillings and pence, a couple of pound notes, two keys, a penknife, and the stub of a pencil. "No billfold, no identification papers, but I didn't expect to find any. No tiny secret messages tucked away in the match safe. Too bad."

Asa plunked him in a chair, and secured him to it. After a few attempts to free himself, the fellow stopped struggling against his bonds, seeming to realize that a sailor's knots would never give. He sat glowering at them.

Asa took the dismantled pieces of the bomb out of his pockets and spread them on the captain's desk with the other items.

"Good heavens! Less than one minute to go on that clock!" Captain Hookset said. "Thought you'd have us all standing before the pearly gates, did you?"

"He doesn't seem to speak English, Cap'n. Would you like me to translate?" Asa asked.

"That won't be necessary. I suspect he may understand more than he lets on."

"He hit Mr. Gunderson over the head with a pipe," Asa said.

"Dear Lord! I pray he shall be all right. Is he unconscious?"

"He was, but he came around. He had double vision, but he seemed to be perking up a bit when I left him. He uttered a few Swedish imprecations at this fellah, here." Asa jerked his thumb in the saboteur's direction. "Doc should be tending to him by now."

"Normally, I don't hold with cursing, but in his case, I'd say it was a good sign." The captain smiled, and then tipped his head toward the fellow in the chair, asking, "How did you catch him?"

"Noticed one of the dockers didn't come back, so I left Mr. Slocum in charge and went to find him. Caught sight of him goin' into the engine room, so I hied myself down there and discovered him about to take another swing at Mr. Gunderson with a lead pipe." Asa shrugged. "Grabbed him, knocked him down, and found the bomb. Hmm. I believed him when he said there were no more bombs, but perhaps I should take a look, anyway."

Asa's jaw dropped as Captain Hookset stood over the man, leaning close to his face and booming at him, "*Gott wird dich bestrafen, wenn du lügst!*"[17]

The man's eyes popped open in fearful awe as though an Old Testament prophet had just burst forth from the sky, thundering dire predictions of hell at him. He pushed back in the chair, trying to distance himself from the captain. "*Gott ist mein Zeuge, gibt es nicht mehr!*"[18]

"Cap'n Hookset, I think you've just put the fear of God into him."

"That was my intent. Do you still believe him?"

"I very much doubt he had time to hide another one. If he had, most likely we'd have been nothing but a few splinters drifting down the River Mersey by now."

"I'll have men standing by to evacuate the ship, but I don't believe it will be necessary. He's not in a panic, or making much of an effort to get away, and he doesn't strike me as the suicidal type — more the type who would murder a ship full of men just to make a quick buck," the captain said. "The last thing those poor men from the *Annie Laurie* need is mention of a bomb, and I don't wish to delay the unloading. Nevertheless, we should be prepared, if it becomes necessary. Slocum's busy. Send Martin to me. I'll have him round up whoever hasn't left the ship."

"Aye, aye, sir," Asa said. "Just to be on the safe side, I'll check all the likely places."

"What are you waiting for?"

"Will you be all right alone with him?"

Captain Hookset withdrew a Colt .45 "Peacemaker" from his desk drawer, smiling. "I don't believe in killing, and I won't captain a ship with armaments in the cargo; however, I wouldn't be averse to shooting him in the foot, if he tries anything. I'm a *very* good shot."

Asa's eyes widened, riveted to the gun. "A gun! You? Cap'n Hookset, you... you leave me speechless!"

"You must remember, I've been around a good many years, and my nickname hasn't always been 'Preacher.'"

His wicked grin was so out-of-place that Asa stared at him, dumbfounded.

"Come, come, Asa. I never thought *you* would be so easily shocked."

"It's just that… Well, I… I never thought that *you* would speak German so menacingly, pack a… a *cannon*, and grin like a… like a *rogue*. Sir."

The captain chuckled. "Get a move on, now. Go take a look, just in case, but in all likelihood, you won't find anything."

"Aye, aye, sir."

"*Nicht mehr! Gibt es nicht mehr!*"[19] The prisoner insisted.

"Methinks thou does protest too much," Asa muttered. "Nevertheless, I believe you." He called to Slocum as he crossed the deck.

"You seen Tommy?"

"He went below with Doc. Haven't seen them since then."

"Keep your eyes peeled, Mike. Look at their faces, not just the cargo. That fellah was a saboteur, trying to blow us up." Asa kept walking as he talked.

Mike gaped at him. "You mean *that* guy—? Holy mackerel!" He quickly turned his attention back to the dockers. "If I'd been in charge, we'd all be blown to smithereens! So *that's* why Mr. Jarvis was running hell-bent-for-leather down the gangplank!" He made another mark on his clipboard.

"Gone to get the proper authorities. Look sharp, now. I'm going to search the ship."

"All by yourself? It's a hell of a lot of ground to cover." Mike kept his eyes on the dockers.

"He didn't have time to go far. Engine room, stokehold, cargo holds. But the dockers are all over the cargo holds, emptying them out, so that wouldn't do. And if he'd set more than one bomb, we'd *already* be smithereens." Asa walked backwards toward the hatch, facing Mike. "He swears there are no more, and I believe him. Cap'n Hookset about scared him to death with his Hosea impersonation, or maybe it was Jeremiah. Scared me, too." As he opened the hatch, Asa shook his fist in the air. "Woe be unto thee if thou liest!"

Mike laughed as Asa disappeared down the companionway.

Asa came across Tommy and Doc walking Gunderson to sickbay. They squeezed by each other in the passageway.

"Tommy, go report to the captain. He's in his office."

"Right away, Asa."

"He wants you to round up all the men still aboard, so if you see anybody leavin', stop him." Asa called after him.

Tommy waved, nodding.

"How you doing, Sven? Can you make it all right with only Doc's support?"

"Oh, yah, I'm not too bad. Just a li'l dizzy."

"After I clean and bandage your wound, we'll get you into bed. You'll feel better tomorrow," Doc said.

Gunderson stopped walking and turned to speak to Asa. "I knew I should've left with the other guys, instead of sticking around to grease the engine. Now I've missed liberty. I could kill *den lilla skiten*!"[20]

Asa laughed as he walked off in the direction of the engine room. "Don't let Cap'n Hookset hear you. He just said he doesn't hold with cursing, and surprised me by speaking very fluent German. He's been around long enough to know a few Swedish swear words, too."

"Yah, yah."

"Enough talk," Doc said. "Let's get you fixed up."

Asa stripped off his coat, sweater, and shirt before descending the ladder to the engine room. He reached into ventilation shafts and other dark recesses, climbed up, crouched down, and lay on his back to look up into potential hiding places. He stifled a shiver of revulsion and fear at having to crawl into small, hidden spaces, and got on with it. He went into the stokehold. Being a stoker had to be the worst job on the ship. It was still hot in there, even with only one boiler still operating. He didn't know how they could stand it when it got to be over 120° with the furnaces blazing. There wasn't a lot of coal left. They'd be coaling tomorrow and scrubbing everything down the day after. He took a shovel and shifted the remaining coal around. He found nothing.

After his search, he concluded the fellow had been telling the truth. Before going back to the captain's office, he stopped to scrub off the dust, grease, and coal grime.

He was dead tired, but the way things were going, he had a feeling it wasn't going to be smooth sailing from here on.

# Chapter 11

## *Questioning*

By the time he got back, two Special Branch agents had come to arrest Herr Schmidt, saboteur. Mr. Jarvis, nervous about bombs and Special Branch agents, had gone.

"Johann Schmidt, eh?" Asa said. "A likely story."

With a clipped military moustache to match his clipped British speech, one of the Special Branch agents turned on him. "What, precisely, is your meaning? Do you know this man?"

"I didn't bother askin' his name because I was sure he'd come up with some such alias. You'd think these guys could be a little more imaginative than John Smith," Asa said. "As to your second question, I met him for the first time in our engine room, about half an hour, forty-five minutes ago. He was bashin' one of our engineers over the head with a pipe at the time, so believe you me, he's no friend of mine."

"How did you know where to find the bomb?"

"I made him tell me."

"You speak German?" The agent's eyes narrowed suspiciously.

"Would you like me to translate when you question him?" Asa tried to be helpful.

"That shall not be necessary. How do you know German? Do you have dealings with the Germans?"

Asa sighed. "I'm not the enemy, Mistah… what did you say your name was?"

"Detective Inspector Smythe-Jones."

Asa tried to restrain it, but snort of laughter escaped him. "Let me guess. Your first name is John?"

The agent reddened.

"All right. I apologize for my remarks about the name. I assure you, Detective Inspector Smythe-Jones, I hold no sympathy for would-be murderers such as this fellah, here. Yes, I speak German. I also speak French, Flemish, Spanish, Italian, Portuguese, Dutch, Russian, Polish, Greek, Japanese, Mandarin, Cantonese, Hindustani, Afrikaans, Arabic, Swedish, Norwegian…" Asa rattled off the list at a rapid clip, and paused to suck in some air.

"That will do, Mr. Mayhew. You have *quite* made your point."

"Danish, Finnish, Gaelic, Welsh, Hungarian, some Croatian, a little Zulu, and a little Swahili. Phew! Sorry, once I got goin', I just couldn't stop." Asa grinned.

Smythe-Jones glared at him, while the other agent hid his smile behind his hand. Captain Hookset gave Asa a warning look.

Asa felt his face get hot. *I bettah watch my tongue. I'm gettin' silly with fatigue, but I sound arrogant. Well, I guess I am a smart aleck. I have to admit, I do not tolerate pompous fools with any manner of grace.* "I beg your pardon. That was… foolish of me."

"Quite," Smythe-Jones said.

Asa tried to smooth things over. "It's not at all unusual for ship's captains and mates to speak a variety of languages, at least enough to conduct business in various ports of the world."

Smythe-Jones ignored Asa's explanation. He proceeded to interrogate Asa as though *he* were the criminal, not giving him enough time to answer before he was on to the next question.

"Why did you go after him?"

"He didn't come back with the other dockers."

"Had you seen this man before?"

"No."

"How did you know he was a saboteur?"

"I didn't."

"How did you manage to find the bomb so quickly?"

"I made him tell me where—"

"You dragged your wounded engineer away from the engine without attending to his wounds?" Smythe-Jones made it sound as though Asa were guilty of the severest breach of conduct — letting the side down.

"Time was of the essence." Asa had all he could do not to roll his eyes.

"How did you know how to disarm the bomb?"

"It was a simple de— "

"Weren't you taking an awful risk?"

"If I hadn't disarmed it, we wouldn't be—"

"Now, Mr. Mayhew, tell me again how you knew Schmidt was a saboteur." He would not be deterred, but doggedly gnawed away.

Asa took a deep breath. *Ain't I the lucky one to be this pit-bull's chosen bone. I will not let him get my goat. I will* not *let him get my goat. I shall remain calm. I* will *be calm.* He exhaled on a sigh, and answered in a monotone. "I have told you — three times already. I did not know. I suspected something was up when he went below decks and didn't come back with—"

"How did you know where to find the bomb?"

"Again, I did not know. I made him show me. I threatened—"

"How did you know how to disarm it? Are you an explosives expert?"

Asa caught himself grinding his teeth, and took another deep breath. "Mr. Smythe-Jones, if you had been paying attention, you would have heard me say that I am not. I read a description of such a time bomb in a book, once, and have some familiarity with mechanical and electrical engineering. As I said, it was a simple device. I could see just by looking at it how to disarm it. With only a minute to go, I didn't have time to go find an explosives expert to ask his advice. I just did it."

Asa persevered in answering the detective inspector's maddening questions. *Oh, God, give me strength. This guy seems determined to tear my patience to shreds — or my nerves — whichever breaks first.* He took a deep breath and held on to the arms of his chair as though they were his equanimity.

Captain Hookset intervened. "Mr. Smythe-Jones, you seem to be somewhat confused as to who the enemy is."

"Humph! I am not in the least *confused*, as you put it." Persistent, he turned to Asa. "You risked setting it off?"

Speaking in a slow, clear voice, as though trying to teach something to a backward child, Asa said, "To repeat: had I not disarmed it, we would all be smithereens by now, as Mr.

Slocum put it. Smithereens, in case you have never heard the term, are little, tiny, splintered pieces." He illustrated, holding his thumb and forefinger a hair's breadth apart. "A good part of this dock may have gone up with us. At the very least, the cargo awaiting transport would have caught fire. The intense heat may well have set off whatever ammunition nearby ships have in their holds." His equanimity slipped from his grasp as he dripped sarcasm. "Perhaps you would have preferred that outcome. At least you would have got rid of *me*."

Smythe-Jones ignored that comment.

"Who is Mr. Slocum?"

Asa rolled his eyes. "Second mate. You saw him when you came aboard. Fellah with the clipboard. He took ovah my duties ovahseein' the unloadin' when I went aftah this guy." He jerked his thumb in Schmidt's direction.

"You were derelict in your duties?"

Asa hung in the balance between sliding to the floor, exhausted, and leaping up to strangle D.I. Smythe-Jones with his bare hands. He slouched in his chair, long legs stretched out in front of him, ankles crossed, widespread steepled fingers on his lips, jaw clenched, eyes hooded, as he looked daggers at Smythe-Jones. *God, help me. I don't even need TNT or a clock. One more so-called question and I'm gonna go off! Tick, tick, tick.*

Captain Hookset interceded. "He most definitely was not! You should be *thanking* Mr. Mayhew, rather than badgering him! He has answered your questions. No matter how many times you ask, his answers shall be the same. He does not lie. Enough, gentlemen! We have survivors from the torpedoed ship, *Annie Laurie*, aboard, awaiting transport to the hospital, and the last thing they need is the slightest suggestion of further explosions. Therefore, I would appreciate it if you would take this prisoner away at once, along with all this evidence cluttering up my desk, and allow us to get on with things."

Smythe-Jones reacted. "Torpedoed ship? When? What did you have to do with it? Is this ship armed?"

"Absolutely not! Whose side are you on, Mr. Smythe-Jones? First, you attack Mr. Mayhew, and now you seem to be confusing *me* with the U-boat captain. Firmly holding to the commandment, 'Thou shalt not kill,' I will neither captain an armed ship nor transport armaments! We *rescued* those men. My full report has already gone to the proper authorities. If you wish to read it, consult His Majesty's Royal Navy." Captain Hookset rose. "Now, with everything that has gone on in the past few days, we are all rather tired, and still have many other duties to perform. I remind you that *we* are not the enemy. No more questions, gentlemen. Take your prisoner and go."

As his colleague was stowing the evidence in an attaché case, Smythe-Jones said, "I'd like to question some of those men from the torpedoed ship."

"In the name of all that's holy!" Captain Hookset erupted. "Those men are ill! Do you not understand that? They are suffering from injuries, exposure, dehydration, frostbite, and hunger! Not to mention the shock to their systems! They are Canadians — your compatriots! They have absolutely nothing to do with this— *this* miserable sinner." As though shooing a fly, he flapped his hand at Herr Schmidt. "They'd be *appalled* by his presence. If you do not leave immediately, I shall speak to your superior about your rude, inconsiderate treatment. Nay! I shall lodge a *formal complaint* as to your *harassment* of innocent citizens of a neutral country! Mr. Mayhew has caught a German saboteur for you! Take him and go! I bid you good day, gentlemen!"

Elbows still resting on the arms of the chair, Asa pointed his steepled fingers at Smythe-Jones. "You bettah go. Cap'n Hookset might just call down the wrath of God upon you, and he can do it, too. He's a powahful preachah. If we're still here on Sunday, you should come to the mo'nin' service. You might learn a thing or two." He didn't bother to stifle a yawn. "Oh, and apologize to the captain before you go."

Smythe-Jones stood up, red-faced, and took a step toward Asa. His fellow agent had not said a word. Now he grasped Smythe-Jones's elbow, and steered him toward the exit.

"I didn't hear an apology," Asa said. He did not rise to say goodbye. He had not stirred from his slouched position, even when Smythe-Jones had looked about to strike him.

Captain Hookset raised a speculative eyebrow at him.

"We *do* apologize, don't we?" The younger agent applied pressure to Smythe-Jones's elbow.

"Very well, if you insist!" Smythe-Jones snapped, yanking his arm away from his colleague's hand.

"Don't forget to take your prisoner." Asa's voice was weary; his eyelids drooped.

"You… you!" Smythe-Jones glared at Asa.

"Not me — him." Asa jerked his thumb toward Schmidt.

When they had finally gone, and Captain Hookset had resumed his seat, Asa looked at him. "Both. Rude *and* tired."

"So you can read minds, too?"

"Not minds. Faces."

Captain Hookset asked dryly, "So, you think a mere man, such as I, has the power to call down the wrath of God? Were you mocking God, or me?"

Asa sat up straight and met his gaze. He could feel his face turning hot, and his nose stung. "No, sir! I would *never* do such a thing. Perhaps you don't call down God's wrath, but you certainly have the power to make men fear it. Yet, at the same time, you remind us to love our brothers, not only by your words, buy by your example. Yes, you are a man, but not a *mere* man. You are a *good* man, a *great* man. It is an honor to serve you, sir." His voice had grown thick. He bowed his head, mortified.

Surprised, Captain Hookset said, "I believe you are sincere." He contemplated Asa for a moment. "Young man, you are overtired and overwrought. Perhaps you ought to go into my cabin and lie down. Rest for a while."

Asa cleared his throat. "I beg your pardon, sir. I didn't mean to be so… um… uh… well… I don't know what to call it. Excessive." Taking a deep breath, he squared his shoulders. "I was hoping to say goodbye to some of the men from the *Annie Laurie*, sir."

"The young boy from Quebec?"

"Yes, and Mr. Ross, as well as one or two others, if time allows."

"Before you do that, I suggest you take the time to get yourself in order."

Asa hung his head and tried to suppress the confusion of emotion that surged up within him. *Why is he being so kind to me? If only he would chastise me! What the hell is wrong with me? If I don't get out of here, I'm liable to make an absolute fool of myself. Something about him makes me want to fall to my knees and repent, weeping. But, God help me, we'd both be horrified if I did that!* He swallowed and cleared his throat, but his voice was still hoarse. "Yes, sir. Perhaps I ought." He stood up and embarrassed himself further by tripping over the chair leg.

Captain Hookset steadied him. "You're out on your feet, man! What did I tell you about taking better care of yourself? Do a better job of it! That's an order!"

Asa breathed a sigh of relief. Brisk talk. That's what he needed. "Aye, aye, sir."

He went into the captain's cabin, took off his shoes, sat cross-legged on the deck, and did some deep breathing exercises until he felt calmer. Then he fell asleep, still seated in the half-lotus position.

# Chapter 12

# *Saying Goodbye*

Slocum entered the captain's cabin and began gathering his pajamas, toothbrush, and shaving things. "I just saw the ambulances coming down the street toward the dock. I thought you wanted to say goodbye to the *Annie Laurie* crew."

He got no answer.

"Asa?" He stepped closer and snapped his fingers in Asa's face. "Asa! Wake up!"

"Uh…. Huh?" Asa blinked and knuckled the sleep from his eyes.

"Criminy! How can you sleep, sitting with your legs all twisted like a pretzel? The ambulances are coming. If you want say goodbye to your kid, you better hurry."

Asa tried to uncross his legs and stand up. He could usually do this in one fluid motion; but this time, he had to grasp his ankle with both hands to pry his foot off his thigh. "Ugh. Good thing I didn't attempt the full lotus." When he stood up, he had to clutch at the dresser to steady himself.

"What's the mattah with you?"

"Feet are asleep." Asa got his balance and stumped around in his stockinged feet until the feeling came back.

"I can see that, but what's all this about lotus flowers? Don't tell me you've been eating them!"

Asa grinned. "Well, I might try it if they worked the way Odysseus thought they did; but no, I haven't been eating them. It's the name of a yoga position, for meditation. What time is it?" He took a tinfoil roll of Pep-O-Mint Lifesavers out of his pocket and offered them to Slocum.

Slocum stared at Asa, shaking his head.

Asa shrugged and popped a mint into his mouth.

"Almost suppertime, so don't take too long saying goodbye. Cap'n Hookset won't be any too happy if you don't eat."

"What! Why didn't you wake me to relieve you? I'm supposed to be on watch! Jeez, no wonder my feet fell asleep."

"Relax, Asa. We're in dock, remember? Kelly's on security watch and Henry's on fire watch."

"Mind like a steel — colander," Asa muttered.

"Go say goodbye to your kid."

"Mike, he's not *my* kid. I'd have had to be able to father a child at the age of eight, minus a couple of weeks. And I've never even met his mother!" Asa grinned as he headed to the fo'c's'le.

"Asa!"

Asa stopped and turned around.

"Aren't you going to put on your shoes?"

Asa looked down at his feet. "Oh, geez, what a scatterbrain! And Captain Hookset thinks I notice everything. Hah!" As he tied his shoes, something else he'd forgotten occurred to him. "Unloading can't *possibly* be finished! Who's overseeing that?"

"They knocked off for four o'clock tea. Bombs and saboteurs and rationing be damned. There will always be four o'clock tea."

Asa laughed.

"When they come back, Cap'n Hookset himself will take over, so I can grab a bite to eat. He told me to let you rest. He's worried about you," Slocum said. "Night shift's comin' on soon. You can take over then. I'll stay on, so we can keep each other awake."

"*Worried* about me?" Asa exclaimed. "Oh, nevah mind. I've got to get goin' to say my goodbyes."

He rushed off. *I've been sleeping away the afternoon, and the captain, instead of telling me to pull up my socks, is treating me like some poor little invalid.* Worried *about me! I can't allow this to go on. I feel like some malingering sham Abram, not pulling my weight. I have to admit, though, I do feel better for that good long nap. I wonder— Nah, if I slept like that all night, I'd never be able to get unstuck, especially if I got into the full lotus.*

"*Bonjour*, Jean-Claude."

"*Bonsoir*, Asa," Jean-Claude corrected. "It is evening, already dark."

"So it is; you're absolutely right." *Third thing in a row I've missed — no, fourth! I've got to wake up!* "I see you're all dressed and ready to go. I'm sorry I didn't get a chance to come and see you sooner, but we've been busy unloading the cargo." *And sleeping, when I should have been here to reassure you.*

"Yes, and I 'ear some of ze crew talking. Is it true you catch a saboteur? 'E pretend to be a dockair? 'E try to blow up zees sheep? Right 'ere, at ze dock?" Wide-eyed, his voice climbing the scale, Jean-Claude reached out to grasp Asa's hand.

Asa tried to comfort the boy, patting his hand. He sighed. "I was hopin' you wouldn't hear about that. But don't you worry. The police have taken him away, and he can't do any more damage here."

"Did 'e explode somezing?" Though it seemed impossible, Jean-Claude's eyes opened wider.

"Nunno. We caught him before he could get that far. The damage he did was to the poor engineer's head. Doc's taking good care of him — Mr. Gunderson, that is — the engineer. When I last saw him, he was complaining about missing liberty because of *cette petite merde*,[21] only he said it in Swedish." Asa winked. "Want to learn how to swear in Swedish?"

He achieved the effect he'd hoped for when Jean-Claude giggled.

"'Ow you say it in Swedish?"

"*Den lilla skiten*, but don't say it in front of Captain Hookset. He doesn't like swearing, and if he hears I've been teaching you, he'll have my hide."

"*Den lilla skiten*," Jean-Claude repeated, grinning. "What does it mean, 'have your hide'?"

"It means to punish someone severely, but he'd probably just give me a stern talking-to, a reprimand." Asa smiled. "You know, the captain only had to speak to him in a harsh voice, and that *petit merde* was cowering in his chair. Believe me, Jean-Claude, you don't have to worry about him."

"Are you sure there are no bombs?"

"Absolutely. I searched for them myself. If we had any doubts, we'd have evacuated you fellahs, *tout de suit*,[22] but it wasn't necessary. We're safe. Anyway, in a few minutes, you'll be going in an ambulance to the hospital. And when you've recovered enough, you'll be going home. All right?"

"Yes, I want very much to go 'ome, but I am still afraid of the torpedoes. I will cross the ocean, though, because it is not safe 'ere — in England, I mean — with the Zeppelins dropping bombs. I wish only—" Jean-Claude broke off, looking away.

"It's all right, Jean-Claude. You can tell me. What do you wish?"

Asa waited, but when Jean-Claude didn't continue, he said, "I'll tell you what I wish. I wish there was no war. I wish we could end it right now, today. I wish young lads like you didn't have to go through such terror, when you should be safe at home, on your farm, with your family. If only human beings could be as peaceful as your chickens, goats, cows, and cats. They may squabble, but they don't wage war."

"I wish you could come with me, or I could go 'ome on your ship," Jean-Claude blurted out. "You make me feel safe."

"Well, I wish I *could* watch over you. But I'm afraid that's not possible, my lad. And you wouldn't want to come with us. We're going to another hazardous spot next — the Mediterranean. And then we're going on to India before we go home. It will take a long time, and who knows what might happen? No, you'd be safer to go straight back to Canada from here. And you won't be conscripted until you're eighteen. Maybe the war will be over by then. I certainly hope so."

"Yes, I knew you could not come with me, and I could not go with you. It was only…"

"It was reassuring to think so, for a little while. Is that right?"

Jean-Claude nodded.

"Tell you what. Whenever you're afraid, you think of me. Think hard, and then I'll be with you. Not in my body, but in your mind. You just remember that you once met an American sailor who told you this: you are *brave*, braver than you think. And remember this, too. Bravery is not the lack of fear. It is *persevering* despite fear. Perhaps you will be able to find some comfort in that, and after a while, you will come to recognize your own strength. All right?"

Jean-Claude smiled. "You make me feel like I could be brave, but I know I am not."

"Yes, you are. Look at all you have survived so far, on your very first voyage. I know you must be in some pain, but you never complain."

"The pain is not too bad. Other men are hurt more bad than me. Mr. Ross, he take me in the lifeboat and hold me close. He try to keep me warm. Where is he?"

"He's in my bed, actually. Kind of appropriate, don't you think? The chief mate in the chief mate's bed?"

"You are chief mate? And I have been talking to you as if you are an ordinary seaman! Oh, forgive me, *s'il vous plaît. Je suis désolé.*"[23]

"Jean-Claude, there is nothing to forgive. I didn't tell you because I didn't want my rank to… well, because I wanted you to be comfortable talking to me. I didn't mean to tell you just now, but I don't seem to be too bright this afternoon. Besides, how could you know? I've been wearing a sweater instead of my uniform blouse, so you had no insignia to go by. Anyway, I prefer to be called 'Asa' to 'Mr. Mayhew.' Remember when we talked about how we are alike? Well, that hasn't changed."

"I do not tink — *th*ink we are alike. You are brave. You catch the saboteur."

"I think you *are* brave. When you overheard those seamen talking about the saboteur, you did not cry out for me, but waited. You knew I would come, and even if I did not, you could bear up. You know that when you are well enough, you will get on a ship bound for home."

Jean-Claude sniffed, trying not to cry. "You 'ave such kindness and patience with this frightened boy."

Leo sauntered in and jumped up on the rack. She stood on Jean-Claude's chest and looked into his face, nose to nose.

"Well, look who's come to say goodbye," Asa grinned.

The cat's whiskers tickled, and Jean-Claude giggled. He rubbed the cat's head. "Leo, she come to take the sadness out of goodbye." The stretcher bearers were coming. "I will always remember you, Asa Mayhew."

Asa brushed the boy's hair off his forehead. "I'll never forget you, Jean-Claude." He handed the boy a piece of paper. "That's my home address. Will you write to me, when you get home? I don't know when I'll be home again, so it might be a while before I answer, but I'd like to know you made it home safely."

"Yes, I would like to write to you." He looked past Asa's shoulder. "Ah, these men are impatient for me to go with them. *Au revoir*, Asa. *Je vous remercie*."[24]

"*Bonne chance*,[25] Jean-Claude. Don't forget — you are braver than you think."

When the bearers had left with Jean-Claude, Asa hurried to his quarters, hoping Angus Ross was still there.

"Oh, good. I was afraid I might have missed you. I wanted to say goodbye and wish you luck."

"I sincerely thank you for all you've done."

"Nunno, I haven't done anything. I'm just glad we happened to come across you, and that you're alive. I… ah, I'm very sorry about your captain."

Ross's eyes slid away from Asa's face. After a pause, he went on: "How can you say you've done nothing? Mr. Mayhew, you *saved* us. You took care of my crew, and I hear you took young Jean-Claude under your wing. What's more, I heard you caught a saboteur and prevented him from blowing us all to blue blazes. It seems as though Jerry is bound and determined to blow us out of the water, but you're not letting him. I wish we could keep you with us as a good luck charm."

"Scuttlebutt sure travels fast. The captain and I were hoping to spare you fellahs any knowledge of him." Asa smiled. "Perhaps I should join the Canadian merchant marine. Young Jean-Claude expressed a similar wish. I heard what you did for him."

"I don't recall doing anything."

"You held him close, kept him from freezing to death. He's slight-built, not an ounce of fat to insulate him against the cold. He wouldn't have been able to hold out long, but for you."

"Poor lad, his first time out."

"How are you feeling?"

"Oh, I think I'll keep all my toes," Ross laughed.

"And otherwise?"

"The questions you ask! You sure you're not a doctor?"

"I'm not a doctor, but I am concerned about you." Asa held Ross's gaze.

"Those eyes of yours! By God! You see right through me, don't you? All right, I admit it. I feel bad about Captain Menzies. I tried to get him to come away, but he insisted upon trying to save the engineer and his mate. There wasn't a chance! The engine room took a direct hit from that death-dealing torpedo. He *ordered* me to board the lifeboat." Ross sighed, shaking his head. "I should have knocked him out and dragged him with me. Stubborn fool!"

Asa reached out to him, but Ross pushed his hand away.

"It hurts. I know." Asa's voice was so low, Ross almost didn't hear him. "And it's easier to hide from it, if people aren't kind and solicitous."

Ross was silent for a minute, and then spoke as if to himself.

"I shouldn't have been on that lifeboat. I should've given my place to another man."

"And then who would've kept wee Jean-Claude alive?" Asa asked.

Ross's eyes focused only on the near past. "Right after we got everybody on the lifeboats, the boiler blew up. The other lifeboat was too close to the ship. It didn't kill the men, thank God, but the lifeboat had too much damage to stay afloat. We got as many as we could aboard, but... one more and we would've capsized." He shook his head. "That's why some of them were clinging to pieces of deck, hatches...."

"Mr. Ross, you did what you could do. It's a miracle that seventeen out of twenty survived. And they're all going to pull through, Doc says. It was your job to survive. The men needed a leader, and you were that. You kept them from panicking, and you kept their hope alive, even if you couldn't feel it yourself. You made them cling to life."

"What do you know? You weren't there." Ross sounded more defeated than challenging.

"Your men have told me. I've been helping Doc, when I can, and I've seen every one of them at least once. They respect you. They know you did everything you could for them. Remember that."

"Mr. Mayhew, I… I'm sorry I said that. You do know, don't you?"

"My ship has never been torpedoed, but I suppose you could say I know a little bit about guilt and grief, and about having your men stand by you. Don't blame yourself, Mr. Ross. Your men don't."

*Why don't I take my own advice? But it's different. I only had one man to save, and I failed. He had a whole boatload, and he mostly succeeded. As for the three that didn't make it, it was a German torpedo that caused their demise, not any negligence on the part of the chief mate.*

"You said I kept their hope alive. *You*'ve given *me* hope. Thank you."

"Don't thank me. That hope comes from within yourself," Asa said. "Well, here come the fellahs with the stretchers. I wish you good luck, Mr. Ross, and may your journey home be a safe one. Oh, and keep an eye on Jean-Claude for me, will you?"

"You bet. Good luck to you as well, Mr. Mayhew. I'm glad to have met you."

"I hope we meet again someday."

Asa went to join the captain.

Captain Hookset halted the unloading of cargo until the crew of the *Annie Laurie* was all aboard the waiting horse-drawn ambulances. Cooky made the dockers happy when he provided them with a large urn of tea and trays of sandwiches and sugar cookies. Sandwiches with real meat, and biscuits, as they call cookies, were a rare treat in England, due to food rationing.

The captain looked over the side at the horses pulling the ambulances. "Look at those poor beasts."

"Looks as if they've been commandeered from a dozen hard-scrabble farms. I suppose all the big, strong horses have gone to France to pull artillery and supply wagons, and ambulances. I hope those poor nags last long enough to get these fellahs to hospital," Asa said.

"It would seem most of the motor lorries, along with the gasoline to run them, have gone over to France, too."

"I read that even some London double-decker buses have gone over to transport men. It must be strange to see them in France, still displaying advertisements for English cigarettes or furniture stores."

As the bearers began to carry one stretcher at a time down the gangway, the officers of the *Eastern Trader* wished each man of the *Annie Laurie* goodbye and good luck. Captain Hookset added, "God bless you." As the last ambulance clattered away over the cobblestones, Asa said, "Well, I'll take over doing my job now. Thank you for filling in for me, Captain."

"You will not take over until you've eaten supper. And don't tell me you've already eaten, because I know you haven't."

"Would I lie to you, sir? I distinctly remember you telling the gentlemen from Special Branch that I do not lie." Asa grinned.

"Smart aleck! It's a good thing I like you, Asa, or I'd have to discipline you for not showing the proper respect due my rank."

Asa humbly bowed his head. "I assure you, sir, I meant no disrespect."

Captain Hookset sighed. "I know you didn't; I was joshing you, son."

"Well, you didn't smile when you said it, sir."

"Get some supper, and then get back here to keep an eye on the cargo — and these dockers. Not only do we have to make sure no cargo goes astray, now we have to make sure the dockers are truly dockers! Tut-tut! What this world has come to! We shall have to pray, Asa. Pray that men will come to their senses and end this bloody slaughter."

"Amen to that, sir."

Captain Hookset nodded. "Go get — or should I be more specific and say *eat* — your supper. Dismissed."

# Chapter 13

# *Letters Home*

*Liverpool*

*November 30, 1915*

Dear Mary,

*This ought not to be a letter of profuse apology, according to the etiquette guides; neither should it be of great intimacy, since our close acquaintance is recent. Even if we were intimate friends, it should not be overly emotional, lest some third party for whom it was not intended should be so impolite as to read it. But I must break all those rules of etiquette for this letter to have any meaning.*

*To begin with, I hope you do not mind my taking the liberty of addressing you as Mary, for that is how I think of you. Although we have only known one another in the conventional sense for a very short time, "Miss Lovejoy" seems too formal. Do you feel, as I do, that we are somehow bound together through our love of James and our grieving over him? And drawn to each other by something more?*

*Too late, I regret not staying to support you and your mother through the memorial service and the days and weeks afterwards, despite George. Concern for you occupies my mind often, and I can only trust that Mr. Ives and Dr. Chandler will serve as your protectors in my absence.*

*Wishing to serve as your protector sounds rather grandiose, as though I were casting myself as a chivalrous knight to my lady. I have certainly failed in that role. Mixing my metaphors and centuries, I fear I have abandoned you to the machinations of some Dickensian dastardly uncle. I pray that is not the case, but confess my doubts.*

*Martha is a strong woman who loves you, but may not be strong enough to stand against the wealth and name that give George power, regardless of his personal disrepute, and I dread the effect he may have on your mother. Please call upon Janet and Si should you need help. You know how openhearted they are, and they would do everything they could for you and your mother.*

*Mary, can you ever forgive me for doing such a terrible job at showing how much I care for you? And for stepping over the bounds of propriety by admitting that it is not simply for your father, but for you alone?*

*Though I am thousands of miles away from you, at sea in more than the literal sense, know that you are very close to me in thought. Wishing to be closer, I remain*

*Devotedly yours,*
*Asa*

\* \* \* \*

*Brest, France*
*December 8, 1915*

*Dear Si and Janet,*

*I hope this letter finds you hale and hearty, happy and healthy.*

*We are in Brest only long enough to unload a cargo of coal, scrub everything down, and load a cargo of wine, so I'm hoping to get this finished and in the mail before we leave.*

*Quite obviously we are not a collier, but since German troops are occupying French coal mining country, the French are suffering in this cold winter. The English are sparing what coal they can, so rather than sail empty to France, we loaded up with coal. We are taking the wine to Bombay, where it shall probably be consumed by Englishmen staying at fancy hotels. Then we shall take on cargo of gutta-percha, jute, and tea. From there, we shall stop in Portuguese East Africa to top off the holds with copra, cashew nuts, and spices, and then we'll head for home.*

*From what we've heard so far, the war hasn't got too hot in Mozambique, so we should be all right. Although, farther north, between German East Africa and British East Africa, it's another story. I hope we won't have any difficulty obtaining enough coal for the journey home. If we do, we'll have to stop in yet another port to fill up the coal holds, and that shall delay my getting home to you. (Pray for enough coal, calm seas, and a following breeze, please.)*

*On the way to Liverpool, we came across the wreck of a Canadian merchantman, the "Annie Laurie," and took seventeen men aboard. Sadly, their captain and two of their crew perished in the attack. We got the survivors to Liverpool, where they were taken to the hospital.*

*It was in Liverpool that we discovered a saboteur, before he could do any damage, lucky for us. A couple of Special Branch agents carted him off to who knows what fate.*

*Later, we caught a docker trying to make off with a side of beef. This poor guy must have been desperate for food. He was so skinny he could hardly lift it, let alone run down the dock with it to his accomplice's horse and wagon. I don't know how he ever thought he'd get away with it. Instead of turning him in, we just took the beef back. His apologies were so abject and his gratitude so pronounced that Cooky took pity on him and, with the captain's permission, brought him a carton of groceries from our own kitchen to take home. Then Captain Hookset thought it would look like a reward for stealing, so we ended up giving almost half of our own food away to the rest of the dockers. You could see they needed it, though. A lot of these fellows are too old or too devitalized to be doing such heavy work, but most of the healthy young men have gone overseas to fight in France, so the hiring bosses have to take whomever they can get.*

*A week ago, Cooky made me a chocolate cake for my birthday, with a regular conflagration of twenty-four candles on it. The men sang "Happy Birthday" and "For He's a Jolly Good Fellow." I was quite touched by it all. Later, Doc and Mike snuck me down to sickbay for a celebratory slug of medicinal whiskey, but don't let on to the captain! Alcohol is Number 1 on the list of things he "doesn't hold with," and this is a dry ship.*

*Janet, I'm sure you've looked in on Mrs. Lovejoy and Mary from time to time, but would you and Si try to keep an eye on them, please? I'm worried about George harassing them, trying to take whatever James has left them and otherwise making their lives miserable. I wish I were there to do it myself, but it's too late now.*

*Must close now in order to get this in the mail before we sail. If we don't get out in the nick of time, we'll have to delay again because of weather. Sky's beginning to look grim.*

> *With much love and affection,*
> *Asa*

\* \* \* \*

*Gibraltar*
*December 25, 1915*
*Christmas morning*

*Dear Mary,*

*With all you have on your heart just now, I know it cannot be a merry Christmas, but I hope you are finding some consolation in your memories of James, bittersweet though those memories may be.*

*Walking the deck, especially in the quiet of the night, I often think of him. Last night, as I stood in the bow and gazed at the stars, the memory of him teaching me the constellations came to me, and for a moment I was a child again, and could almost feel his hand on my shoulder, as my eyes followed his other hand pointing at the sky. And then I pictured you, standing in your back yard, looking up at all those glittering cosmic jewels on their black velvet bed, your father's hand on your shoulder, telling you their names. When I come home, we shall have to go out one evening and look at the stars together.*

*Alas, the low reverberations of artillery from France broke the quiet of last night, and the constellations along the horizon were confused with the Very lights high above the battlefields. At midnight, though, it stopped, and it's quiet today. A one day truce for Christmas. If only* we could see the senselessness of it all, the waste, and extend that truce forever.

Oh, dear, I am sorry. I didn't mean for this letter to have such a solemn, mournful tone. On the other hand, when one is in mourning, nothing seems more annoying than having someone try to cheer one up. Don't you find it so? Still, perhaps I shouldn't write in this mood. It may add to your pain, and that is certainly not my intent.

Later
Christmas afternoon

Mary, dear, I do hope you are well and being looked after by Janet and Si. I have written to them to ask them to make sure you were all right, but the letter most likely won't have reached them yet, if it ever does. With the U-boats prowling the waters, a lot of letters are ending up on the ocean floor, especially from Royal Mail ships or French ships. I don't mean to alarm you — we're still neutral, and I don't think the Central Powers want us to get into the war, so the U-boats tend to avoid us.

I am impatient to get home to you, but we have been held up in Gibraltar for a week. We were stopped by the British blockade, and then held up again because of a naval battle in which we definitely did not want to get embroiled. After that, we had to wait in line for clearance. At long last, the Royal Navy has finished searching our ship, and we're free to *move on, so I must close now if I want to get this in the mail. It's just as well — I can't seem to write anything that isn't gloomy today, and perhaps this is one letter that should end up on the ocean floor. Nevertheless, I haven't time to write another and don't want you to think I've forgotten you, so I'm sending it.*

*Oh, but Cooky made us a nice Christmas dinner and we did sing carols. Forgive the hasty scribble, but I just couldn't end with all that darkness.*

*Affectionately yours,*
*Asa*

\* \* \* \*

*Port Said*
*January 1, 1916*
*Morning*

*Dear Si and Janet,*

*Happy New Year! I wanted to let you know I'm safe and well. I hope you are the same.*

*You may not wish to hear it, freezing your tootsies and sitting by the stove trying to get warm, but it's quite hot here in Egypt, and we've had to get out our summer duds. In a way, I regret having to put away the soft, warm comfort of the sweater you knit for me, Janet,* but I suppose this way, it won't wear out as fast, as long as I keep the moths away.

I imagined you busy making Christmas cookies, and then you and Si going around delivering them to everyone in town on Christmas Eve. Did you take the train into Boston this year, to see the stores all decked out in Christmas lights? I wish I could have been with you.

Cooky did his best, providing us with a turkey dinner and mince pies. We decorated the mess with red and green ribbons for Christmas, and a couple of the men are pretty good at origami, the Japanese art of paper folding. So we had a green paper tree about a foot tall, tiny paper candles with red foil for flames, and decorations of birds and other animals festooned about the place. We had a good time making them while eating Cooky's cookies and drinking coffee. It was a welcome break from normal routine for the men. The captain doesn't hold with strong drink, but he unbent enough to allow us some mulled wine on Christmas Eve. He even went ashore in Brest to buy the wine and spices himself, and made just enough to provide one cup apiece. Cooky's Christmas cookies are nowhere near as good as yours, but they'll do. Captain Hookset held a service. He preached a rousing sermon, and we enjoyed singing carols.

*Have you seen or heard anything of Mrs. Lovejoy and Mary Lovejoy? I was wondering how they're doing. This Christmas must have been particularly hard for them. I hope George hasn't been playing the part of Ebenezer Scrooge.*

*Must go on watch now. I'll pick this up later.*

*Jan. 1, 1916*
*Evening*

*Sailing the Atlantic and the Mediterranean has become a mite tricky lately, but our captain and crew are equal to it. We've been delayed in every port so far. We hadn't planned on stopping in Gibraltar, but the Royal Navy, with their blockade, had other ideas. They detained us so a convoy of battleships could go through the Straits of Gibraltar, and yet again because of a battle. We had to wait while the British searched our ship, but they could see we're not smuggling weapons because the wine is in bottles, not casks. At least they didn't break any. Still, we had to repack them in straw and nail the crates closed again. Thus, we are far behind schedule, which exasperates me no end, because I am itching to get home. So far, we've encountered shipwrecks, saboteurs, and thieves. Not to mention storms. To see out the old year, there was a storm last night, and very high seas are seeing in the new year today. We are fortunate to be safely in port.*

*It may not have made the papers back home yet, but two days ago, a British passenger ship, the SS Persia, was sunk off Crete. We were quite far off, but began steaming toward them, preparing to lower lifeboats. A British minesweeper, the HMS Mallow, signaled us. She was closer, and could accommodate more than a hundred passengers and crew. We only had room for about twenty or so, and it would have been a tight squeeze. So the Mallow rescued most of the survivors. A Chinese ship, the Ning Chow, rescued the remainder. We heard there were over 500 souls aboard, but only 176 survived. The crew were all heartsick. We felt helpless in the face of such tragedy, and arrived too late to be of any use. The investigation is still going on, of course, but scuttlebutt has it that witnesses saw the track of the torpedo. How can human beings be so inhumane? How can men slaughter innocent civilians like that? I shall never understand it.*

*We've had a little excitement here in Port Said, too. It was nothing to do with the war. A fistfight that grew into a donnybrook broke out on the dock. I'm still not entirely sure what it was about. It was one of those things where somebody said something to which somebody else took offense. Then another fellow poked his nose in and got it bashed, and it escalated from there. A few of our men were involved. Thinking I should get them out of it, I stepped in to break it up. It was not one of my better decisions. I'm embarrassed to say the police came along and arrested me along with everyone else! Captain Hookset got me cleared of all charges and out of jail. Thanks to him, I won't be going stir crazy in an Egyptian prison. Unfortunately, our three crew members have got to spend 24 hours in jail. Ah well, perhaps that will make them think twice before they get involved in another brawl.*

*Thank goodness the battles and raids that took place on the canal over the last year have ceased — for now, at least. The atmosphere is tense, but the Allied defenses seem quite formidable. There are French, British, and Japanese ships, all bristling with guns. Huge cannons defend the port, which is swarming with English, Australian, and New Zealand forces. There are Egyptian Camel Corps on the western bank, and Indian Camel Corps on the eastern. ANZAC encampments all down the western side of the canal do a good job of protecting it, but the Ottomans still occupy the Sinai Peninsula. British troops have made inroads there, and now have forces in addition to the Indian Camel Corps along the eastern banks as well, but the Central Powers have by no means given up the fight over the canal. If they could close it down, it would not only hurt the British militarily, but would also be a severe economic blow. Having to revert to the ancient route around the Cape of Good Hope to get to India would take too much time and too much coal, not only for England, but for everyone who uses the Suez Canal, neutral countries — and by that I mean us — included. The cost of shipping would skyrocket. There have been rumors of it closing, but there are always rumors. There are no battles right now, so it remains open. We would all like to leave this place as soon as possible. The weather isn't the only thing that's hot. Well, enough war news, for now.*

*I know you have met Captain Hookset, old Mrs. Stedman's nephew, but how well do you know him? He's quite a character. His nickname is Preacher, because he is prone to extemporaneous sermons and prayers. Although he holds a worship service every Sunday, he doesn't order the crew to attend. Most do, not only out of respect for him, but because he preaches a rousing sermon and we enjoy the hymn-singing. At the risk of sounding sacrilegious, it's quite entertaining.*

*If only more companies and captains would understand what the old Lovejoys (George excepted), Mr. Wass, and men like Captain Hookset do. When you treat the men as men, and not as galley slaves, you get a good crew with fewer fights, less grumbling, and more willing workers. You get young men who want to learn and older men who are willing to teach them, and who take pride in a job well done. The atmosphere on the ship is agreeable. But when you treat the men as mere beasts of burden, as all too often happens, you get resentment, sloppy work and surly workers who mistrust not only their officers, but each other. I fear that under George's control, Lovejoy Lines will slide toward the latter category. But I digress.*

*Captain Hookset genuinely cares about the men, and he has been very good to me. I think you'd get along splendidly with him, Si. Your principles and philosophy of life are so similar. He's just more outspoken about it. I am glad I've had the opportunity to sail with him before he retires. He told me he will be sixty-five in the spring, but you'd never know it. He's taller than I am, very erect in posture, and powerfully built. With his flowing beard and bushy eyebrows, it's easy to imagine him as an Old Testament prophet. He can use that to advantage when need be. He thundered at that saboteur we caught, scaring the truth out of him. It even works with those of us who know what a warm heart beats beneath that fearsome exterior, at least until the initial shock has worn off!*

*If not for the war, Captain Hookset would probably never want to retire, but he told me that he is considering making this his last voyage. Although well versed in storms, shoals, and reefs, he is unaccustomed to war and torpedoes. He seems to think that his vision and reflexes may have dulled with age, and fears he may not be quick enough to keep his men and his ship out of danger. I see no signs of* age slowing him down at all, but I suppose he knows himself far better than I do. At first, I couldn't imagine him happy ashore, but then I thought about him behind a pulpit. I could see him as a somewhat saner Father Mapple. (You remember the character from Moby Dick?) I think he'd like being a minister.

I haven't had a chance to go ashore in any port we've been to so far, except for my brief stint in jail. We'll be here at least two days, possibly three, coaling, scrubbing everything down, painting, polishing, and replenishing our supplies, while awaiting our turn through the canal. I was going to go ashore, but after my encounter with the police, I thought it best to stay aboard. So I've no exotic travelogue, this time. I may go to visit a friend in Bombay, if things quiet down by then.

The collier has just come alongside. Coaling is a filthy job. Coal dust gets in through every vent and crack. It gets into your eyes and nose. It covers everything and everyone. With the derricks and cranes working, the swing of a load could knock a man into the hold. At night, with clouds of coal dust dimming the lights and a crowd of men wielding shovels, the ship looks like one of Dante's circles of hell. I must put on my oldest, shabbiest clothes and pitch in, so I'll say goodnight for now.

Keep well and keep warm.

>      With all my love and good wishes for the
>      new year,
>      Asa

## Chapter 14

## *A Sea of Troubles*

Captain Hookset called to Asa, who was busy directing the coaling, keeping an eye on the winch and the swing of the derrick as well as the crew. An inattentive winch operator could easily knock a man into the hold; likewise, an inattentive man could walk into the path of the load hoisted on the cable and be struck. Distraction could kill a man.

"Mr. Slocum, take over here, will you?"

"Aye, aye, Mr. Mayhew. Mac! Watch where you're goin'! You wanna get flattened?"

"You want me, Captain?"

The captain coughed. "Let's step into my office, get out of the worst of this." He coughed again, trying to wave a cloud of coal dust away. His gray beard and eyebrows were black, and his office wasn't much better.

"I want to know why the police haven't released Sampson and Rivers," the captain said. "With Peterson hurt, we're short three stokers. Yates said when he asked why they weren't releasing his shipmates along with him, they threatened to lock *him* up again if he didn't stop asking questions. Why the delay?"

Peterson had been down in the hold with the hazardous job of shoveling coal into the corners as it was loaded. When a load had nearly landed on him, he jumped out of the way, and was lucky to sustain only a sprained wrist when it wrenched the shovel out of his hands. With high seas rocking both collier and ship, and the loss of manpower, coaling was proving to be an even tougher job than usual.

"Well, sir, I can't say for sure, but I'd hazard a guess." Asa frowned.

"Well? What *is* your guess?"

"Yates is white," Asa said.

"They would hold two of my men because of the color of their skin? Pah! Are we in Egypt or the deep south? That is outrageous!"

Asa shrugged. "We're not the only country with prejudice, sir. Look how the British and all the other imperialist countries treat the indigenous people of their colonies."

"We supposedly Christian countries don't behave in a very Christian manner, do we?" the captain grumbled.

"Humph. Under the condescending guise of what we call 'civilizing' people who happen to have different cultures, we tyrannize them with soldiers, governors, missionaries, and businessmen who make off with their natural resources. And look at our own country — how we tried, and are still trying, to wipe out all the people who were already living there..." Asa threw up his hands. "How's *that* for teaching democracy and Christianity?"

"Indeed. But we don't have time to get into that discussion right now. We've got to get our men back."

"As chief mate, the crew's wellbeing is my responsibility, so of course I'll go, sir."

"I'm a bit concerned that those stubborn, officious, idiots at the police station might lock you up again, too." The captain tut-tutted, shaking his head. "But we can't just sit here and wait, hoping for the best. Take Mr. Martin to second you. Mr. Slocum and I can take over the direct supervision of operations up here, while Mr. Olafson and Mr. Gunderson keep an eye out below. I'll finish up the business end with the captain of the collier later."

"Well, I'd better get cleaned up as much as possible with all this going on." Asa swept his hand through the coal dust circulating in the air, and coughed. "If I wear my fancy duds with all the braid and everything, maybe they'll treat me with a little more respect. I intend to come back with both men in tow, Cap'n."

"I don't doubt you will. Get Mr. Martin, scrub off that coal grime, and get going."

"Aye, aye, Cap'n."

Asa let out a piercing whistle that carried over the noise on deck. "Tommy!"

"Aye, sir!"

"Come with me to get Sampson and Rivers released. Cap'n's worried if I go alone I might get locked up again."

Tommy's eyes roved up and down Asa's stubble-faced, hollow-eyed, rangy, coal-begrimed frame. Then he grinned. "The way you look, they probably will."

"Hah!" Asa socked him on the arm. "Come on, let's get washed up and changed to lessen that likelihood a mite."

Clean-shaven, bright-faced, and crisply dressed, they mounted the steps to the police station. Tommy said, "You'll do the talking?"

"Ayup, but if that pig-headed sergeant is behind this, I might want to haul off and belt him. Don't let me. You know he insisted to Captain Hookset that I did *not* step in to break up that brawl. On the contrary, I'm the one who started it! Despite the fact that all the men who were involved — Yanks *and* Brits — were telling him I tried to stop them."

"I'll likely want to belt him one, too, but I'll try to keep the peace."

"Thanks, Tommy."

The police sergeant was a block-shaped, thick-featured, ruddy-faced Englishman with a toothbrush moustache and a gap between his front teeth. Asa suspected his physical dimensions were not the only things thick and blocky about him. There was nary a glimmer of intelligence in his piggish eyes.

"Sergeant, I'm Chief Mate Asa Mayhew, of the *Eastern Trader*, and I'm here to collect Able Seamen Paul Sampson and Sidney Rivers."

"Haven't any idea what you're on about, Jack."

"Well, if your memory is so bad, why don't you check your records," Asa said. "They were picked up last night along with a dozen other men involved in a fight. They were supposed to be released this morning."

"The men involved in that were released. P'r'aps your man simply wandered off to 'ave a bit of an 'oliday before going back to the ship," the sergeant said.

"'My man' — *one* of them — did come back. Yates couldn't understand why you didn't release his shipmates along with him this morning, and I hear you threatened to put *him* back in a cell if he persisted in asking for an explanation. I will *not* put up with that kind of bigotry. Do you understand? Release my men now, sergeant— what is your name?"

"It's not on. Blacks can't get away with inciting a riot round 'ere, Jack."

"So you *do* remember." Asa's jaw tightened. *Hitting him,* he thought, *while it might bring momentary satisfaction, will only make things worse.* His eyes flamed like blue gas jets. His voice carried the firm weight of command. "I am no simple Jack Tar, and you would do well to remember that." He pinned the sergeant with his gaze.

The sergeant glared back, but failed to stare him down, and shifted in discomfort.

Asa dragged out the silence until the sergeant opened his mouth, and then cut him off and continued, "Wasn't it only last night you were accusing someone *else* of starting that brawl?" He waited until the light of recognition dawned in the sergeant's eyes. "Ayup, and we both know *that* wasn't true either. Bring them to me. Here." He jabbed his finger at the floor in front of him.

The sergeant dug in his heels. "You're not in charge, 'ere, Jack—"

Asa's eyes narrowed and he spoke through clenched teeth. "My name. Is not. Jack. You will address me as *Mister* Mayhew. Bring my men *here*. Now!"

The sergeant stalled, with a lot of angry posturing.

Asa's fist rose up and at the last minute opened to slap the desk, leaning forward as he repeated, "Now! Or do I have to go get them myself?" He reached for the sergeant's ring of keys.

The sergeant snatched the keys away and set off, his face sullen.

"You're pretty quiet, there, Tommy."

"I was just thinkin.' I might feel a little moah confident about becomin' third mate if you could teach me how to do that," Tommy said.

"Do what?"

"Get pig-headed idiots to do what you command, despite themselves."

"Hah! I think he was afraid of my barely controlled rage, which is all too visible beneath the thin veneer of my trying to behave like a somewhat civilized human being. Phew! I'm out of breath."

Tommy laughed. "No wondah! That was some sentence! Asa, you've got moah civility than most of us. On the othah hand, I *was* gettin' ready to grab your right ahm if need be. Would've been hahd, though. I wanted to pound the bastid, myself."

"If I had any such civility, you wouldn't *need* to keep me out of trouble. But thanks, Tommy."

"No need." Tommy shrugged off Asa's thanks, and then grinned. "But gettin' back to that veneah thing — did I heah you *growl* a minute ago?"

"Maybe," Asa smiled back. "Sure felt like it."

The rattle of keys and the tramp of several sets of feet announced the return of the sergeant. A couple of guards escorted their prisoners with viselike grips on their arms.

Sampson looked beat up. He had a bump on his forehead and a black eye. Rivers looked worse, with a smashed nose and eyes so swollen Asa wondered how he could see. They moved slowly, in obvious pain. The guards shoved them.

Rivers gasped, putting a hand to tender ribs as he pitched forward. Asa caught him, trying to be gentle. But the stoker was heavier, and he staggered back a bit, having to hold him more firmly than he had intended. Rivers stifled a cry of pain.

Tommy went to help Sampson, who was doubled over, arms wrapped around his stomach.

Asa's anger flared. "Who did this to them?"

"Who? They were, after all, arrested for brawling." The sergeant sneered.

"Nunno. I saw them when they were brought in. They didn't sustain these injuries in that little donnybrook. They were beaten in these cells. Either you did it or you ordered it, and *that's* 'not on,' sergeant."

"Perhaps some of them carried on with their fisticuffs after they were in the cells," the sergeant shrugged. "You cannot prove otherwise."

"You haven't heard the end of this."

"Asa, let's go," Tommy said.

"Not so fast, there, Jack. Should you wish further inquiry, we shall have to detain these men for questioning."

"Oh, no you don't! We're taking Sampson and Rivers with us. Come on, lads, you heard Mr. Martin, let's go."

The sergeant's complexion got redder. "Who are *you* to tell *me*—?"

They had begun making slow progress toward the door when Asa turned to answer. "Who am I? I am a *man* — a *human being*. And what kind of *monster* are you that you can treat men like this?"

"How *dare* you—"

"How dare I what? Tell the truth?" Asa opened the door.

"You come back here! You can't talk to me like—"

Asa closed the heavy door. Sampson and Rivers needed help getting down the stairs.

"Big bully! Poutin' like a ten-year-old who's been told to clean his room," Tommy said. "Except most ten-year-olds ain't so willfully ignorant — and mean with it."

"Sharp as a button," Asa muttered.

Sampson and Martin grinned.

"Don' dey say 'bright as a button'?" Rivers asked.

"Ayup. He's bright as a completely oxidized razor."

Sampson grinned at Rivers. "Rusty."

Rivers laughed, and then drew in a sharp breath, holding his ribs.

"Tommy, see if you can find us a taxicab, please." They all winced in the bright sunlight, but it was too much for Rivers's poor eyes to take. Asa took off his officer's cap and put it on Rivers's head, pulling the peak low over his eyes.

"Sir, I cannot wear your hat," Rivers protested.

"Why not? Doesn't it fit?"

"It's not dat, sir—"

"Sidney," Sampson said, "just say 'thank you, sir,' and shut up."

Rivers's smile looked as though it hurt his bruised face. "T'ank you sir."

Just as a horse-drawn carriage drew up, the sergeant came steaming out the door, his face scarlet.

"You can't— You can't— You're all under arrest!"

"Everyone in the carriage," Asa ordered. "Tommy, please help the men while I deal with this idiot. If violence breaks out, get the driver to go hell-bent-for-leather back to the ship."

He walked toward the sergeant, speaking in a soothing tone of voice. "This tropical sun is too much for you. You really ought to go lie down in the shade for a while."

"You— You—"

"What are you trying to say, sergeant? Come on, spit it out; I haven't got all day." Smiling, Asa kept his tone less testy than his words.

"You can't just come in here and tell me what to do! I'm in charge here; *not you!*"

"What's your name, sergeant?" Asa asked. "You never did tell me."

"What? What! What's my *name*? Why do you want to know that? Who the hell do you think you are, Jack?"

"Nunno. I told you, I'm not Jack. I'm Chief Mate Asa Mayhew." Asa stepped forward, extending his hand. "I'd like to address you as something other than 'sergeant' all the time, that's all. I told you my name, what's yours?"

"Withers," the sergeant started to extend his hand, too, but then jerked it back. "No, no, you're not going to fool me with your slick charm. You can't get away with just breaking these men out of jail right from under my very nose! Who the hell do you think you are?"

"I'm Mayhew, Chief Mate of the *Eastern Trader*. Have you forgotten so soon? Sergeant Withers, I'm rather worried about you. Your color is far too high; you look quite apoplectic. You need to go inside, out of the sun, and lie down. You must have someone send for a doctor."

"Doctor! I don't need a bloody doctor. Get out of my sight!" Withers screamed.

"With pleasure," Asa turned and bounded down the stairs. "Go. Go," he said to the driver. "The man's *mad*. He's going to give himself a stroke." He shook his head as Withers continued to scream unintelligible words after them.

"Should he not be in 'ospital, Mr. Mayhew?" Rivers asked, his Jamaican lilt a pleasing melody to Asa's ear. "Or maybe in a cell, 'imself, so he cannot 'urt men the way 'e do?"

"How could they let such a mean, insensible idiot—?" Tommy gave up, throwing his hands in the air.

"You should see the way he and his toughs treat the natives," Sampson said. "Couple fellahs in the cell with us got beat real bad."

"Real bad, mon," Rivers agreed. "Stomped on dere poor, bare feet wit' dere big policemon boots. Even if dey was tieves, no call for dat kind of beatin'. Said dey would cut dere hands off for tievin'. Me, I t'ought dat kind of eye for an eye and toot' for a toot' t'ing belong in Old Testamont times."

"That's horrible, Sid," Asa said. "Thank God you're out of there."

When they got back to the ship, the collier was leaving, and a gang of men was swabbing the deck. Black water sluiced down the scuppers into the sea.

Asa thanked the driver and gave him a generous tip. The leathery, wizened man gave him a broad, toothless smile. Asa couldn't help but grin back. That smile was worth far more than the tip had cost him. It shone through the dark clouds Sergeant Withers had spread in his sky.

Captain Hookset, freshly scrubbed, came down the gangway to greet them. "Praise the Lord! I rejoice that our lost sheep have been found and am relieved to have you all returned to the fold. I'll get your report later, Mr. Mayhew. First, let's get these men to sickbay."

Sampson and Rivers spoke at once:

"I'm all right, sir, but Sidney's ribs—"

"When de swellin' go down round my eyes, I be fine, but Paul's stomach—"

"Paul, Sidney, Doc will examine both of you. I don't want you doing any heavy labor — or any labor at all — until he pronounces you fit," Asa said.

"I agree," Captain Hookset said. "Neither of you is fit for work."

"Aye, sirs." Looking abashed, Sampson and Rivers spoke in unison.

"Captain, we should also have Doc thoroughly document every injury. Paul and Sidney were attacked by policemen, not just brawlers. They had far fewer injuries when we were being booked last night," Asa said.

"Good heavens, Asa! Do you mean to say the *police* beat them? Whatever for?"

"For no good reason. That blockheaded sergeant kept calling me 'Jack.' Perhaps he just doesn't like sailors. But his bigotry was blatant."

"They beat us as well as the thieves. Because of the color of our skin. Good thing they don't come aboard when we're coalin'." With bitter sarcasm, Sampson put on an exaggerated accent. "We *all* de same color, den. Look like a damn minstrel show. Dat sho'nuf keep 'em busy. Sorry, Cap'n, I know you don't like cussin'."

"That's quite all right, Mr. Sampson. In this case, 'damned' is an accurate adjective. Did the policemen use obscenities against you?"

"De sergeant, he make it plain, de t'ings he call us," Rivers said.

"Did the sergeant himself beat you, or did he order his men to do so?" Asa asked.

"De sergeant, he beat de t'ieves and stamp on dere bare feet so dey cannot walk, mon!" Rivers shuddered. "Had mon to hold dem, so dey could not dance away or hide dere feet."

"When we tried to intervene, he beat us, too. But we're twice the size of those poor little guys, and we fought back. And then he called in more men." Sampson looked disgusted. "They held our arms so we couldn't fight back."

"Took *five* mon to 'old us, plus de mon 'e already 'ad in dere." Rivers showed a touch of pride. "An' den 'e smack us one, two times wit' his stick before 'e go, to remind us what 'e do if we don' keep our mout' shut."

"Sadistic little rat," Asa muttered.

"So, the sergeant *himself* hit you and insulted you? He used worse than curse words —words I do not allow on my ship?" Captain Hookset couldn't hide his anger.

"Words Cap'n James and Mr. Mayhew wouldn't tolerate, either," Sampson said. "Even some I never heard before, but we got the picture."

"Some words de British in Jamaica use, Paul not familiar wit', but I know dere meanin'."

"He asked me how come I don't talk like a black. I asked him what he meant by that."

"What did he say?" Captain Hookset asked.

"He said, 'You know bloody well what I mean.' I said, 'No, I don't. I have dark-complexioned friends from all over the world, and they all have different accents. I come from generations of sailors going back to the 1770's, from Connecticut, but I don't suppose you've ever heard of the place.' He didn't like that, thought I was sassing him. He slapped me in the mouth."

"Was it that kind of talk started the fight?" Asa asked.

"No, not that," Sampson said. "I was included with all the other Americans, for a change. They were using anti-American slurs, not racial ones."

"But... why?" Captain Hookset said. "The war of 1812 was over a century ago. Don't tell me they're still holding a grudge!"

"Not about that war, about this one." Sampson smiled, then winced. "Because we don't declare ourselves on the side of the Allies. They say we're cowards, afraid to fight. We would have walked away, but Yates, he's not used to that kind of baiting. He had to show them different. We couldn't leave him to bear the brunt, could we? He was outnumbered."

"I don't hold with fighting, but in your case, I'd say it was admirable to support your shipmate. Moreover, you suffered quite enough in that cruel jail. Tsk, tsk. I won't discipline you any further. Just don't get into any more fights."

"Oh, no, sir. We've learned our lesson. Haven't we, Sidney?"

"We don' do dat again; no way, sir."

"Do you know, I didn't see any of those English boys we were fighting in the cells. Did you, Sid?"

"Maybe dey put de whites someplace else."

"You're right, Paul. They weren't in the cells," Asa said. "While I was waiting to be booked, the police took their names and then released them. You're right, too, Sidney. They do have segregated cells, but Yates and I were the only whites from that fight thrown into one."

Captain Hookset tut-tutted. "British Protectorate. Just whom are they protecting?"

"Not the Egyptians, it seems. I would guess themselves and their own business interests, sir," Asa said.

Conklin and Nickerson were helping Doc scour the sickbay. Doc dropped his cleaning rag back in the bucket of soapy water and rushed to attend to his patients.

"What happened?" Doc asked. "Asa, help Rivers onto the examining table first. Where does it hurt most, Sidney?"

"Sometime my face; but when I breathe, is my ribs, Doc."

"How did this happen?" Doc asked.

Paul, Asa, and Tommy started explaining all at once.

"All right, everyone pipe down! Let me attend to my patient," Doc said. "Oh, I beg your pardon, Captain. I didn't see you there."

"Doctor, I want you to provide a detailed account of these men's wounds. Pay particular attention to any wounds that may have been caused by a truncheon, or similar weapon. It is obvious that they shall not be able to return to their duties for some time, and before they do so, they must have medical clearance. We'll leave you to get on with it. Mr. Mayhew, I'll hear your report now. Let's go to my office."

Asa sniffed. "Do you smell smoke, sir?"

Captain Hookset sniffed the air. "*Man is born to trouble as the sparks fly upward.*[26] Where is it coming from?"

"We better find out in a hurry." Asa stripped off his jacket. "Seems to be coming from the starboard quarter. Yes! There's smoke! Blow the fire horn, Tommy! Let's go!" He called over his shoulder, "Conklin, Nickerson, you stay and help Doc. If we need to evacuate, he'll need help. In the meantime, close the hatch to keep the smoke out. And keep cleaning."

"I'll have Smitty radio for the fire brigade." Captain Hookset headed to the radio room.

Oily smoke billowed from the engine room, where fires were notoriously difficult to put out. Asa prayed they could keep the ship from burning to the water line. Gunderson and Olafson were already using fire extinguishers.

"Henry, Yates, man the pumps! Keep those flames from getting to the boilers, lads. Abel, direct that hose over there! Joe, throw that bucket of sand on the deck, right there!" Eyes everywhere, Asa grabbed another extinguisher and went to work, quelling sparks and directing men to hot spots at which to aim their hoses. With the fire's rapid discovery and their coordinated hard work, they put it out in short order.

"Good job, everybody," Asa said. "Now you see why all those fire drills are necessary. We'll have to keep a close eye on it to make sure it doesn't start up again. All right, let's check the damage."

There was only minor damage to the engine room and to the engineer's sleeping quarters above it. The engine would have to be overhauled, the boilers and entire system checked for damage. Repairs and cleaning would take some time.

"Could have been a hell of a lot worse, but still— Damn it all to hell! We'll never get this fixed before nightfall. And here I was, hoping to leave this godforsaken port with the next convoy down the canal." Asa ran a hand through his hair, leaving a sooty streak. "Tommy, help me figure out how it started, will you?" He examined the burn marks, following the pattern until he came to the most likely origin of the fire. He got down on his hands and knees and sniffed, frowning. "Gasoline."

"How can you smell gasoline in this fug?" Tommy asked. "Anyway, wouldn't it have bu'nt off by now?"

"Try it yourself. Get down here and put your nose to the test," Asa said.

Tommy took Asa's place. "I see what you mean. Kinda suspicious on a coal-fiahed ship, ain't it? Ah you thinkin' ahson?"

"Ayup. This was deliberately set. Who's been on watch?" Asa squatted down and pointed to a blackened object. "Well, look at this. Burnt up match safe. Cardboard, not metal. See how it's open a little on the end, with just the burnt stub of a wooden match stickin' out? Definitely arson. Somebody struck this match and tucked it into the end of the box so they'd all flare up after a brief delay, then threw it near the gasoline, but not right into it, givin' him just enough time to get away. He must've done it while we were all down in sickbay, or it would have got goin' a lot soonah. Lucky we got back when we did. Whole ship could've burnt to the watah line."

When Tommy tried to fish the object out with his pencil, it disintegrated into a little pile of soggy ash. "Sorry, Asa. Looks like I've just destroyed the evidence."

"Nevah mind, Tommy. I don't know how it retained enough of its shape to identify it at all." He raised his voice. "Wheyah the hell was everybody?"

Several voices answered. "Dinner break."

"Ayup, okay." Asa turned back to Tommy. "Let's see, when we left, who was on watch? Jones was on security and Kelly was on fiah — *fire* watch. Right?"

"We bettah find out where they are now," Tommy said.

"I'll do that. I want you, Gunderson, and Olafson to get a gang together and start cleaning up this mess and fixing that engine. Check the boilers and — well, you know what to do. I want to get out of this port as soon as possible. Somebody here, be it human or the god of luck, doesn't like us one bit."

"You got that right. Sven! Oly! Pick your crew, and let's get started," Tommy said.

# Chapter 15

# *More Trouble*

Asa found Jones lying under the ladder to the bridge, his eyelids just beginning to flutter as he came to. He had a livid egg on his temple, along with scrapes and bruises.

"Davy! Davy, can you hear me? Wake up! Come on, Davy. Open those eyes!"

"Ungh, wha—? Ooh, my head. Mr. Mayhew, I don't know what happened. I was…" Jones tried to sit up.

Asa stopped him. "Just stay down until you get your bearings, lad. Don't want you smacking your head on the ladder and knocking yourself out again."

"I didn't—"

"Nunno, that's not what I meant. Seems there's more than one fellah handy with a cosh hereabouts. Now, you just lie still for a minute, and see if you can remember what happened."

Jones thought. "Um… I… uh… heard somebody coming up the ladder behind me. I started to turn to see who it was. All-of-a-sudden I was falling down the ladder, and this thing came flying at my face. Well, not all by itself. Somebody swung it at me. Next thing I know, here I am with you waking me up. I'm sorry, Mr. Mayhew. It all happened so fast, I didn't get a good look at him. He was big, and strong enough to yank my feet out from under me."

A lot of men might look big to Davy, who was five feet, three inches tall.

"My height?" Asa was six feet tall.

"Yeah, but he weighed a heck of a lot more. He was fatter than Cooky."

"Could you see how he was dressed?"

"Not really." Davy closed his eyes, trying to visualize the man. "Hmm, I get the impression of some loose kind of suit, grayish — no — white, but grimy. Sorry, I can't remember any more."

"Maybe one of those baggy tropical suits. That's good, considering you only saw him for a second before he knocked you out. How ya feelin'? Think you can sit up now? Wait; let's get you away from the ladder a bit more. Don't want you hittin' your head." Asa pulled him away from the ladder and helped him sit up.

Davy blanched as he put a hand to his head.

"We've got to get you to sickbay. Come on; I'll carry you piggy back," Asa said.

"I can walk." Davy's head drooped like the heavy blossom of a fritillary.

"Walk! You can't even hold your head up. Put your arms around my shoulders and rest your head against mine. No arguments, now; that's a good lad." Asa lifted Davy on his back and carried him to sickbay. "Got another one for you, Doc."

"What in God's name is going on around here? Put him on the—"

"Doc! Doc! He's not breathing!" Mac came rushing in with Kelly slung over his shoulder. He dumped him on the examining table.

Doc began mouth-to-mouth while Asa helped Jones to lie down on a rack. "All right, Davy?"

"Yah. Help Kel'."

"We found him stuffed in a gear locker, with all the buckets and swabs," Mac said. "Don't you think he's kinda blue? Is he still alive, Doc?"

Asa took Kelly's pulse. "He's still alive, Mac. You found him in the nick of time. The locker just off the engine room?"

"Yeah. He musta got a lotta smoke. Can Doc save him?"

Just then, Kelly took a breath. "Kelly! Open your eyes!" Doc commanded. "Keep breathing, Johnny. Johnny Kelly! Open your eyes!" Doc slapped his face. Kelly took in a wheezing breath, opened his eyes, and started coughing. Doc sat him up and thumped him on the back.

Asa held an emesis basin under Kelly's chin. "That's it; get that black stuff off your lungs."

"Mac, open up all the vents and turn that fan on. He needs plenty of fresh air." Doc looked at the back of Kelly's head. "Looks like your fellow with the cosh struck again."

"He's not *my* fellah," Asa said. "If I catch him, I'll take away his cosh and use it on *him*. See how he likes it! Keepin' our men in jail for no reason is one thing; tryin' to kill them and stahtin' fires on the ship is somethin' else. You know, I could see that German saboteur tryin' to wreak havoc on the Liverpool docks and stop us deliverin' food to England, but why would anyone want to stop us deliverin' wine to Bombay? None of this is makin' any sense to me, Doc."

"Don't look at me; I'm just as baffled as you are. How are you doing, Kelly? Breathing any better?"

"Least I'm… breathin'." Kelly wheezed.

"Where are Conklin and Nickerson?" Asa asked.

"Cap'n sent them on an errand."

"I can help out for a while," Asa said. "You need anyone else?"

"Not as long as you can stay; Frank and Seth finished the cleaning."

"Okay, Mac, you can go back to helping in the engine room," Asa said.

"Aye, sir." At the hatch, he turned around to address Kelly and Jones. "You fellahs take it easy and do what Doc says. You don't wanna end up stupid, like me."

"Now, Mac, we'll have none of that. Didn't affect your kind heart any, and in my book, that's more important. You're a good man with a strong back. Time to put it to use," Asa smiled.

"Aye, aye, sir!"

"What did he mean?" Kelly asked when Mac had gone.

"Used to be a boxer. One more blow to the head would've killed him," Asa said.

"But he was going to go back in the ring anyway, because he didn't know any other way to make a living, and the promoter was pressuring him. So Asa dragged him aboard and convinced him to try other employment," Doc said. "Let me take care of your head, and wash some of this soot off."

"Kelly's not the only one with soot to wash off," Asa said.

"Yes, I can see you've been fighting fires, too."

Asa made a circular motion around his mouth.

"What?" Doc frowned.

"You've got soot around your mouth."

"In that case, I'd better clean myself up as well." Doc started rolling up his sleeves. "We'll fix up a bed for you topside, get plenty of fresh air into you. Okay, Johnny?"

Kelly looked a little wary.

"We won't leave you alone," Asa said. "You'll need care, and I'll see to it your caregiver has some defensive weapon."

Kelly began coughing again. Asa tended to him.

Doc washed the soot off his face and scrubbed up before gathering a basin of water, carbolic soap, iodine, and bandages.

"Asa, you can help by seeing to Jones's head. Scrub first."

Asa started to unbutton his cuffs.

"That shirt looks like it's been down in the bottom of a coal bin. Take it off. You can borrow one of mine to go topside," Doc said.

"Aye, aye, Doc."

"Sorry, I meant to make it a request, not order," Doc said.

"That's all right. I know *you* know I outrank you." Asa washed the top half of his body. Then he lathered up to his elbows with carbolic soap and vigorously scrubbed his hands and nails with a brush.

"Not by much, and certainly not medically," Doc grinned.

"How are your other patients?" Asa dried off with a towel that smelled faintly of bleach.

"Sampson's just shaken up and bruised. He's got a knot on his forehead, but he says he never lost consciousness, and he's not dizzy, nauseated, or uncoordinated, so I don't think he has a concussion. I gave him aspirin and an ice bag for his headache and black eye. I suspect Rivers has a cracked rib or two, a broken nose, as well as quite a collection of contusions and abrasions. After taping up his ribs and nose, I gave him aspirin for the pain. Then I gave him an ice bag, too, to bring down the swelling around his eyes. They're both sound asleep. They've had one hell of a night in that place."

"It is a hellish place," Asa said. "Davy, let's check you over. Davy, wake up. Davy!"

"Ooh," Davy groaned and opened his eyes. "Ooh, I don't feel so good."

Asa grabbed a basin, just in time. "Doc, what do you do for a concussion?"

"Is he bleeding from the ears, nose, or mouth?"

"Just a little from the bash on his head," Asa said.

"Pale, or flushed?"

"Pale."

"Keep him lying down. Turn him on his side to prevent aspiration if he vomits again. He'll need bed rest and observation for twenty-four hours. We'll see how he's progressing after that. In the meantime, you can clean his wounds. As soon as I'm finished here, I'll examine him."

"Not Davy, too!" Kelly started coughing again.

"Relax, Johnny. He's a little banged up, just like you, but we'll take care of you both. Easy, now." Doc rubbed Kelly's back until he stopped coughing and gasping for breath.

"We'll be a'right, Kel'. Don't worry about me. You jus' keep breathin'." Davy winced, gingerly touching his head. "Tell him, Mr. Mayhew."

"Davy's right, Johnny. Just as Doc said, we'll take care of you both."

Yates, his jaw looking like a ripe eggplant, his knuckles cut and bruised, came in. "How are Sampson and Rivers— Oh, my God! Davy! Kelly, too!? What the hell is going on around here?"

"Sampson and Rivers are sleeping, or trying to, so keep it down to a soft bellow, okay?" Asa said. "And watch your mouth, Yates. I know it's a shock, but you're lucky the captain isn't standing behind you. You're also lucky we've been too busy for me to discipline you. You *do* know your shipmates only stepped into that fight to back you, don't you? So I'm afraid I don't have as much sympathy for your injuries as I have for theirs. Yours are your own fault. Theirs came at the hands of a brutal, bigoted police sergeant. They never would have been arrested if they hadn't stepped in to save your skin."

Yates looked over his shoulder, breathing a sigh of relief that Captain Hookset hadn't just walked in the door. Then he looked at the deck. "I'm sorry; I didn't mean to cause trouble. I never thought—"

"You never thought; that's the problem," Asa said. Then he smiled. "As far as what the hell is goin' on, that's what we all want to know. Glad you stopped by, though, Bob. You can make yourself useful by setting up a cot on deck for Kelly. He needs as much fresh air as he can pump into his poor lungs. He also needs someone to be his nurse and bodyguard. You're elected. Get a move on."

"Aye, aye, sir."

"Yates," Doc called to him.

"Sir?"

"Before you do that, wash your hands and face again, and I mean scrub." Doc pointed at the sink. "With carbolic soap. It might sting, but that's better than an infection. Understood?"

"Aye, sir." With a hangdog look, Yates obeyed.

\* \* \* \*

Asa helped Kelly up the companionway and opened the hatch to the weather deck.

"He's the one!" Kelly clutched Asa's arm and doubled over, coughing again.

About twenty feet from where Yates had set up a cot for Kelly, Captain Hookset stood on deck. He had his Colt .45 pointed at a large, sloppy man wearing a dirty white suit and a battered Panama hat. The captain appeared to be exhorting him to confess his sins.

Yates was riveted to the scene.

"All right, Johnny. I've got you — and the captain's got *him*." Asa helped him to the cot. "Sit down; here, let me help you put your feet up. Got enough pillows? Easier to breathe if you're—"

Kelly coughed. "Sir, you shouldn't be—" He interrupted himself with more coughing.

"Of course I should. Easy, now." Asa rubbed his back. "We'll get rid of *him* as soon as we can, so you'll be able to rest. Yates will watch over you. Won't you, Bob?"

With the ease of youth, Yates had bounced back from his humiliation. He was fit; he was muscular; he was armed. Squinting at the Panama hat, he took a few practice swings with his ersatz bat — a sturdy wooden oar taken from one of the lifeboats.

"Don't worry, Kel'; I'll protect you. Mr. Mayhew, what's going on?"

"Unless I miss my guess, that's the guy who hit Jones and Kelly over the head, and then started the fire." Asa walked over to the captain, "You get anything out of him, Captain?"

Yates and Kelly peered at them, straining their ears.

"I found him in my office, trying to open the safe. It seems he started the fire as a diversion. It also seems he is an unbeliever, and the prospect of eternal damnation has so far failed to elicit a confession. See what you can get out of him," Captain Hookset said.

Asa addressed the man. "Just what did you expect to find? This is a cahgo ship. We don't get paid until *aftah* we delivah the goods, genius."

"You are taking the Maharajah to Bombay," the man said.

"Maharajah! This is *strictly* a cahgo — a *cargo* ship. We don't have any fancy accommodations for royal passengers."

"Is this not the *Eastern Star*?"

"You mean you just about killed two of our men and set fire to the ship without checking her *name* first? She is *not* the *Eastern Star*; she's the *Eastern Trader*! Even if you can't read, surely you can see the American flag! The *Eastern Star* is of Indian registry. Or can't you tell the difference between the Ensign of the Royal Indian Marine and the Stars and Stripes?" Asa stared at the man, incredulity and indignation fighting to be the uppermost expression on his face. "You're just as bright as Sergeant Witless. What is it with you guys? Spendin' too much time in the noonday sun? Broiled your brains?"

Yates grinned at Kelly. Kelly tentatively smiled back.

"I went to all this trouble, and there are no diamonds?" The inept brigand gaped at Asa.

"Sorry to disappoint you, Mr. — what *is* your name? John Smith, I suppose."

"Not Smith — Greenstreet."

"Could be right. I don't credit you with having that much imagination. To dispel any remaining doubt in your gnat-sized intellect, let me make it perfectly plain. There are no diamonds, nary a single carat. Captain, did you have any opportunity to contact the police?"

"Mr. Greenstreet, here, yanked a wire or two out of the ship-to-shore radio. That's why we couldn't get the fire brigade. Thank the Lord you men put it out so quickly. Smitty is repairing the radio now. I've sent Conklin and Nickerson to get the police — anyone but that obnoxious sergeant. Is his name is really Witless?"

"Withers. Can you imagine the balled-up mess that would result from the meeting of *two* corrupt witless wonders?" Asa asked.

"Perish the thought! Ah, here they come now. Good. I have a few words to say to that police captain."

Asa nodded to a sailor approaching him.

"Excuse me, Mr. Mayhew. May I speak with you?"

"Of course, Don. What is it?" He took a few steps toward the bo's'n's mate.

"I think I know how he got aboard."

"Well? If you *saw* somethin' and didn't *tell* someone, Henry, I'll—" Asa shook his head. "Nevah mind, just tell me."

"I didn't see *him*, sir, or I sure *would* have got you or the captain! I saw a rope ladder over the side when we were coaling. I didn't think anything of it. But now I wonder why it was there to begin with."

"Where? And when did you see it?"

"Broad on the starboard bow, not far from the collier. And there was a dinghy tied up to her. Before they took off, I saw the men on the collier looking at her — the dingy, that is — and making gestures to one another, like they didn't know where she came from. Then they just cut her loose. Wasn't that odd?"

"When?"

"Just after we came back from dinner break."

"So that's how he got aboard without anybody seeing him. Everybody was either at dinner or down in sickbay. The crew of the collier must've been too busy eating to notice him, too. Got anything else to tell me?"

"No, sir. That's all."

"Thanks, Don. You solved one mystery for me. Okay, get back to supervising clean-up. Be careful around Kelly; stirrin' up clouds of coal dust is the last thing he needs on top of lungs full of smoke."

"Aye, aye, Mr. Mayhew. Most of it has been pretty well sluiced down the scuppers, sir."

"Good."

Asa turned back to Captain Hookset as the police captain arrived with two constables. They immediately handcuffed Mr. Greenstreet and searched his pockets for weapons. Captain Hookset handed them the cosh.

"I took this from him. He used it on two of my men. Almost killed one of them." He gestured toward Kelly. "Let us go into my office, gentlemen, where Mr. Mayhew and I can tell you what we know. Captain, ah…"

"Withers," the captain supplied.

Captain Hookset raised an eyebrow at Asa. Asa nodded.

"Captain Withers, there are one or two other items I wish to discuss with you, as well." Captain Hookset opened the hatch to his office and showed them in.

"I would suggest we deal with Mr. Greenstreet first. After the constables take him away, you and I shall be able to talk," Captain Withers said.

"I want Mr. Mayhew in on the discussion."

"Very well. As I understand it, Captain Hookset, you caught this man in your office attempting to break into your safe?"

"Yes. He seems to have confused us with the *Eastern Star*, a passenger ship out of India. When we questioned him, he said he was looking for the Maharajah's diamonds."

Captain Withers looked at Greenstreet and shook his head. "And you said he hit two of your men over the head with a cosh?"

"David Jones and John Kelly, the men on security and fire watch," Captain Hookset said. "And then he set fire to the engine room."

"Where was the rest of the crew?"

"We were coaling at the time, and the crew had gone to the mess for dinner break, as had the crew of the collier. Mr. Mayhew and Mr. Martin had gone ashore to retrieve two crew members the police picked up along with about a dozen other men for engaging in a brawl last night. They were supposed to have been released from your jail this morning, but were not. When we got them back, we were in sickbay attending to them; they had suffered abuse at the hands of *your* men."

"Yes. We shall get to that later. Do you mean to tell me that this man simply walked aboard without anyone being the wiser?"

"I believe I can answer that, Captain," Asa said. "Bo's'n's Mate Donald Henry just told me he saw a rope laddah broad on the stahb'd bow and a dinghy tied up to the colliah when they came back from dinnah. He didn't think anything of it at the time, but when he saw the crew of the colliah — *collier* — cutting the dinghy adrift before they left, he thought it seemed rather odd. It would seem Greenstreet rowed over and flung up the ladder while the crews of both ships were below decks in the mess." Asa's smoke-reddened eyes flashed fire as he glared at Greenstreet, "Is that about right?"

With Captain Withers' gaze like swords running him through, and Captain Hookset's furrowed eyebrows threatening thunder, Greenstreet capitulated. "Oh, what the hell. You've got me. I confess."

"And it's not as if nobody noticed him," Asa went on. "Jones and Kelly both noticed him all right, and got knocked unconscious because of it. Jones is in sickbay with a bad concussion. The young man in the bed on deck is Kelly. He has to get plenty of fresh air to help him recover from smoke inhalation. Greenstreet, here, nearly killed him when he bashed him over the head and then crammed him into a storage locker before setting the fire. As soon as Kelly saw this mug," he jerked his thumb in Greenstreet's direction, "he grabbed my arm and said, 'He's the one!'"

"I wasn't trying to kill him; I swear it! I only wanted him out of the way," Greenstreet said.

"A spontaneous, unsolicited identification, as well as an admission of guilt. Well, it looks as though you gentlemen have done all my work for me." Captain Withers turned a grim face to the constables. "Lock him in a cell. Don't let the sergeant near him."

"Yes, sir. May I ask, sir, how do you suggest we keep Sergeant Withers away from him?"

"Tell him you are relaying my orders. Take his keys, even if you have to do so by force. Let him know I shall speak with him upon my return, and he is to wait at his desk. If he gives you any trouble, throw him in a cell," Captain Withers said. "Take this bungling would-be thief away."

"Yes, sir!"

"Come on, you!" The second constable grabbed Greenstreet by the arm and marched him out.

"Captain Hookset, I rather suspect I know, but suppose you tell me what you wish to discuss with me," Captain Withers said.

"Mr. Mayhew, tell him about your visit to the police station this morning."

Asa related his encounter with Sergeant Withers, and the condition in which he found his men. "And another thing — I was arrested yesterday. The sergeant refused to listen to witnesses who told him that I was not engaged in the fight, but was trying to put a stop to it, or at least get my men out of it. He went so far as to accuse me of starting it. Captain Hookset had to leave the ship and go to the police station to intercede on my behalf. And by the way, one of our men was released this morning, and when he asked why his shipmates were not, Sergeant Withers threatened to lock him up again if he asked any more questions. Just when we needed all hands, Mr. Martin and I had to take time out from coaling to go and get them released."

"They should have been allowed to contact you."

"Of course they should. Moreover, your men beat them. Remember, I saw them after that donnybrook; therefore, I know that they did not sustain such injuries as a result of it."

"That is most definitely unacceptable. I shall see to it whoever did this is severely punished."

"'Whoever did this'? Our men were in the cells with those little fellahs accused of stealing, and they can tell you that Sergeant Withers had constables hold them down as he beat them and stomped on their bare feet with his hobnailed boots. When our big stokers tried to protect the smaller men, the sergeant called in more constables to hold *them* back while he turned his fists on *them*. Before he left, he gave our fellahs a couple of extra bruises with his nightstick, for good measure, and told them to keep their mouths shut. But you can't cow big American stokers so easily. They told me in the presence of Tommy Martin, our bo's'n. When we got back, they told it again to Captain Hookset."

Captain Withers nodded. "I see. Will they tell it again? Are they well enough to speak to me?"

"You might want to see Doc's records of his examinations of their injuries, too."

"Yes, of course." As they walked to sickbay, Captain Withers dispassionate demeanor crumbled. "He'll pay for this, by God! Family notwithstanding, he's out!"

"What is he, your cousin?"

"Nephew, so he says. My eldest brother has been in India for many years. I haven't seen this chap since he was an infant and I was a child. Either there is something rotten in the family tree, or he's a fraud. He simply showed up one day and presented me with a letter. It looked like my brother's handwriting, but... I really can't say. We weren't close, and he died several months ago. Perhaps this... this person is my nephew, but I sincerely hope not. Naturally, I have tried to check his story. The war has made that rather difficult, what with the slowness and unreliability of non-military communications, and the Central Powers targeting Royal Mail Ships all too frequently. He's been nothing but trouble. Claims he was a policeman, but I suspect his experience of the law has been from the other side. He has the heart and soul of a vicious criminal."

"And the brain of an ant," Asa said.

"That would be maligning ants. They are at least honest and hard-working. If you must compare him to a biological species, a parasitic worm would be more apt."

"I stand corrected, offering apologies to the family Formicidae. I should have known better. Ants are social creatures."

"Yes, and my so-called nephew is about as antisocial as they come. If I don't succeed in throwing him in prison for the rest of his life, I shall see to it he gets sent to the front, where he can apply his vicious streak to the Central Powers."

"As long as he doesn't apply it to his trench-mates," Asa said.

"Right. Prison is the place for him, but neither you nor your men will be here to testify in a court case against him."

"If it would help, we'd be willing to give depositions, if you can get a lawyer down here before we leave. Because of the fire, we've been delayed, but I'm hoping to get the engine fixed by tomorrow afternoon — morning, if we're lucky."

"Quite. I wish to see the damage Greenstreet did, as well. I mustn't forget my sergeant isn't the only criminal here."

"Right this way, Captain Withers," Asa said.

# Chapter 16

# *Too Full of Woe*

Asa stood on the weather deck with Tommy, looking around. The ship was spic and span again, scrubbed free of coal dust and soot. Gunderson and Olafson had repaired the engine, while some of Tommy's crew had aired out and repainted their cabin. The brightwork glittered in the sun. They restocked food and water supplies. Lines of washing hung in the bright afternoon sunlight, flapping in the ocean breeze.

Captain Withers and the prosecutor had just left with a sheaf of papers they would give in evidence to the magistrate. The *Eastern Trader* had only to await her departure time.

Asa took a deep breath. "Ah! Clean, bright, and shipshape. The men have worked hard. Tell them what a good job they've done, Tommy. I'm sorry we can't approve shore leave, but… well, with the way things have been going here… Besides, we've got to be ready to raise anchor at a moment's notice. Don't want to spend one second more than necessary in this place. You've got some kind of entertainment planned?"

"We've got up a little band with Bob on guitah, Don on clarinet, Jack on co'net, and Seth on violin."

"I didn't know Seth played the violin," Asa said. "How did I miss that?"

"Ayup. This is the first time he's brought his violin aboard. Says the damp isn't good for it. Cooky has loaned them a couple of pots for an improvised drum section. He's also providin' refreshments," Martin said. "The captain and officers are invited, of course."

"Thanks; you've got some good musicians there, and some other time I'd like to hear them, but I think our presence might have an inhibiting effect," Asa smiled. "The men deserve to let their hair down a bit. Let them play ragtime, sing bawdy songs, and swear to their heart's content. We'll keep the captain occupied. Just make sure everyone's careful with their cigarettes and pipes — last thing we need is another fire. Enjoy yourselves. See you later."

Asa joined Captain Hookset, Doc, and Mike, who were sitting under a tarpaulin the crew had erected to provide shade, sipping iced tea. "Gunderson and Olafson not coming?"

"They decided to accept the men's invitation," Mike said. "Said they'd have more fun."

Blotting the sweat from his forehead with his handkerchief, Asa said, "Phew! It's hot. Left your patients all alone, Doc?"

Doc smiled. "They're doing so well, I gave them permission to attend the entertainment Tommy and Don have arranged. That doesn't mean you can put them back to work yet, though. They're to check in with me at least once a day. It will take some time for Sidney's ribs to heal, and I still need to monitor Paul for possible internal injuries. But there's no reason they can't sleep in their own racks. Davy and Johnny should be more or less back to normal in a day or two, barring any complications."

"I'm glad they're doing well," Captain Hookset said. "Still, we mustn't undo all the good care you've given them by rushing things."

"Even when you give the okay, Doc, they'll be on light duty for a while," Asa said.

"After that so-called music, they'll probably all be back in sickbay with headaches," Slocum said. "I hear Cooky given the, um, *band* some pots and pans for drums, and wooden spoons for drumsticks." He rolled his eyes. "All I know is when my sister's kiddies start in with the kitchen tympani, I generally remember a pressing appointment elsewhere."

The other men laughed.

"Captain Withers was smart to send that photographer aboard yesterday, before we cleaned up all the damage. And to take pictures of the injuries the men sustained. I hope they come out well enough to be useful in court," Asa said. "So, Cap'n, what do you think his chances are of sending Greenstreet and that phony sergeant to prison? Do you think Captain Withers can do more than just sack him? The sergeant, I mean."

"I believe with the photographs, medical records, and the depositions the prosecutor has in hand, they'll be able to get guilty verdicts on both of those scoundrels. They may be able to charge that sergeant with stealing the real nephew's identity papers, if they ever hear from India."

"If not worse — one can't help but wonder what happened to the real nephew, since this fellah seems so obviously an impostor. He's like a virulent infection. They should lock him up and throw away the key to prevent his vileness from spreading. He made it plain he hates sailors — kept calling

me 'Jack,' with a sneer. He seemed proud of his bigotry —
*proud*. Bad enough what he did to Paul and Sid, but from
what they said about those poor little fellahs — they were
thieves for a reason — they were starving. How can they *walk*
again? His hobnail boots stomping their poor bare feet—"
Asa shook his head. He reached for his iced tea, but instead
of taking a sip, he held the cold glass to his forehead.

"How could one man contain so much hatred?" Captain
Hookset shook his head. "I pray he may see the error of his
ways before it is too late to save his soul."

"Waell, forgive me, Cap'n, but I wouldn't hold my breath
waitin' for *him* to see any kind of light. I suspect he may be
mad in both senses of the word." Asa sighed, and then an
impish look came over his face. "Forsooth, I should have
smelt the sulfurous corruption on that base, beetle-headed
bugbear; that churlish, clay-brained cur; that villainous,
venomous varlet; that decayed, dissembling dew-worm; that
loggerheaded, lumpish lout; that—"

Mike's chuckles became guffaws. Captain Hookset
looked startled at first, but soon began to smile, emitting
little huffs of laughter from his nose.

Doc succumbed to a real belly laugh. "Stop!" He gasped,
holding his sides.

"Pumpkin-headed, pig-eyed pustule," Asa finished.

"Hah! I do love a good Shakes—ha-ha—pearian style of
h-h-insult, Asa, and I uh-ha-ha — marvel at how rap-rapidly
you can string them together, with alliteration, no less; but
— *please* — no more! Ow!" Doc hugged his sides as he tried
to stop laughing and catch his breath.

"Sorry, Doc." He finally took a sip of tea.

"Don't apologize. It's good to hear you joke again."

"It's either that or cry. I tell you, I can't wait to get out of this port." He coughed and cleared his throat. "So far, this journey has been one bloody damned thing after anoth— Oh! I beg your pahdon, Cap'n."

"Well, your curses weren't blasphemous, and I can't say you're wrong, so I'll let it go — this time," Captain Hookset said. "Since you've been the one wearing yourself thin straightening out one mess after another, I'd say you're entitled to complain."

"But I haven't been—" Asa looked down, feeling his face grow even warmer. "Cap'n, *you've* straightened out just as much — *more* — I mean, um—" He lapsed into an awkward silence. The air felt oppressive — too heavy and hot to breathe. He leaned back and closed his eyes against a dizzying feeling of nausea.

"Mr. Mayhew, are you quite all right?" the captain asked.

"Fine." He tried to convince himself, but that spinning, sick feeling was getting worse, and he was afraid he might embarrass himself and everyone else by vomiting in front of the captain, fainting — or worse — both. "Um, not fine. Please excuse—"

He stumbled to his feet, pressing his handkerchief over his mouth, dashed to the head in his nearby quarters, and threw up. Sweating and shaking, he leaned against the bulkhead as he scrubbed his teeth with Dr. Lyon's tooth powder. Splashing cold water on his face didn't help much. He staggered to his bed and lay down in an attempt to stop the compartment spinning. Not taking his shoes off didn't matter; his feet always hung off the end of the bed. One foot dropped to the deck. It didn't steady him any.

Doc had followed him in, but Asa only vaguely registered his presence, let alone his questions.

A wave of nausea engulfed him. Lurching to his feet, he stumbled to the head, crashed to his knees, and was sick again.

Then Doc was at his side, helping him. "Come on; let's get you to sick bay."

"Lemme... stay here..." Asa mumbled. He absolutely had to lie down, on the deck if he couldn't get to the bed.

"Can't do that; you're too sick. I have to keep an eye on you."

Doc half walked, half dragged him to sick bay, where he collapsed onto a rack with his head hanging over the side, his stomach wracked with painful spasms as he vomited into a bucket.

Doc held his head. "You're burning up. How long have you been feeling ill?"

"Ungh. Wasn't." He was sick again.

"It just hit you out of the blue while we were relaxing out on deck?" Doc asked.

"Uh-huh." His abdomen went into another spasm; this time he only brought up a thin stream of bile. He was trying to wipe his nose and mouth with a handkerchief when gray spots began to cloud his sight, and he hadn't even the strength to hold onto his handkerchief anymore. He drifted off as it fluttered to the deck.

He was next aware of something cool and wet on his face. It took him a minute to realize it was damp cloth, and that Doc was speaking to him.

"Asa. Asa, can you hear me?"

He struggled to answer. "Uh."

"Can you open your eyes for me?"

Asa got one eye half open, and then made an effort to jack up the other lid.

"That's it," Doc said. "Stay with me, now. I need to take your temperature. Can you open your mouth and keep this thermometer under your tongue for a few minutes?"

"Uh."

"Good man," Doc said. "While we're waiting for that to register, I'm going to take a little blood from your arm, all right? I need to look at it under the microscope to see what's wrong with you." He swabbed Asa's arm with alcohol, tied a rubber tube around it, and then drew some blood.

It seemed to take an eternity. Asa felt his nostrils flare in an attempt to get enough air while Doc made him keep his mouth closed to get an accurate reading.

Doc secured a square of gauze on Asa's arm with tape. "Are you having difficulty breathing?"

Asa tried to point to his stuffy nose, but it took too much effort.

Doc removed the thermometer and frowned as he read it.

"Let me listen to your chest." He took out his stethoscope and listened to Asa's lungs. "Hm. Sounds a bit croupy."

"Croupy?"

"In a manner of speaking," Doc said.

Asa coughed. Everything started turning gray and fuzzy again, and his eyelids weighed far too much. He vaguely felt hands turning him on his side and heard a muffled buzz, as of distant voices, and then everything slipped away.

He tried to cling fast to the present, but dizzying images crowded his mind. Insistent, they pried his fingers off the here-and-now and dragged him down into a whirlpool of then as he fell into a fevered dream.

*The wind tears the lifeboat from its davits and hurls it against the hull. It flies apart in splinters.*

*Gone. No! James! Don't leave me!*

*Waves smash over the side of the ship and fling me to the deck, battering me, forcing water into my nose and mouth.*

*Drowning, drowning.*

*How did I get to the wheelhouse, hair and clothes streaming? So cold. Am I drowned and shrouded in seaweed?*

*No, no, not yet. I must save the ship! I must save the men! I must save James! "Save me, O God; for the waters have come unto my soul."[27]*

*A white flag! No, it's James! Don't surrender, James! Hang on! I'm coming! I'm—*

*Knocked backwards in time and space, topsy-turvy in a churning vortex of surging sea and torrential sky.*

*The sea has seized him in her grip.*

*No! Take me in his stead! Take me, Oh, Sea, and give Jamie back!*

The pages in his picture book flip back to the beginning. His dreaming voice is reedy, piping.

*Help! Someone help us!*

*Look! There is man up on the dunes. He will never get here in time.*

*I'm coming, Jamie! Hang on! Where are you? Why can't I hear you?*

*Diving, searching, frantic, searching.*

*Where are you? Oh, Sea! Give him back! Take me instead. Oh, Jamie, don't leave me!*

*Can't breathe. Kick! Kick! Surface; gulp deep breaths. Twisting, turning, where are you? Jamie! Raw throat screaming: Jamie!*

*I'm too young to drown. But he's only five. It's all my fault. He's too little. Jamie! Come back! I love you, baby brother; don't go.*

*Dive down again. Find him.*

*Fight, Jamie, fight! Don't let her take you. Hang on! I'm coming to get you!*

*So cold and dark and deep. Jamie, where are you? Why can't I see you? Has the light gone out of your bright blue eyes? Jamie, don't go! Please!*

*Please, dear Lord Jesus, send your angels to protect him. Please, please don't let him drown. I am afraid to drown, but please take me instead. Tell the sea to give him back. I'm to blame. I should have said no; it's too dangerous. He tugged my sleeve and said, "Please, I want to see the big waves," and I wanted to see the big waves, too. Please, give him back. Take me. I was supposed to protect him and I didn't. I deserve to drown. Please don't take him! Please-please-please!*

The pages flip forward.

*So tired.*

Sinking down, down, heavier, aging with each fathom deep.

*In this pitch black, who can tell which way is up? Let go, give up, and drown.*

His body is too heavy-boned to rise. Still, he kicks and claws at the sea's net, fighting to get free.

*Why can't I just let her take me? Surrender; stop fighting. Drowning, I am drowning in her cold, black, briny deep, deaf, blind, numb. So tired. Why can't I stop fighting? How will I know when I am dead?*

*Oh, James why did you stop fighting? Why did you let go? James, where are you? Come back! Let me fight for you. Let me wrest you from her clutches. 'Too late,' she says; she will not let you go. I am weary and alone. If only I could let go, too, and be with you. But I can't. I have to save the ship; I am responsible.*

A page flips back, and he is on the bridge, shouting through the voice pipe.

*Engine astern, dead slow!*

And then he is at the gunnel, screaming into the wind.

*James! James! Hang on! I'm coming!*

A tiny voice echoes from deep within his subconscious: *Jamie! Hang on! I'm coming!*

*The wind tears the lifeboat off its davit and hurls it against the hull. It flies apart in splinters.*

Strong hands grip his arms. Someone shakes him like a rag doll. His cheeks sting, first one side, then the other.

"Asa! Wake up! Come on, Asa, wake up!"

*What…? Lemme be. Wake up. God, it's like trying to swim up from the bottom of a sea of black gelatin. Wake up. I'm trying. Who…? Where…?*

"Asa Mayhew! Wake up! Open your eyes and look at me!"

He came awake with a gasp, coughed, and peered at the face looming over him. "Unh… Doc?"

"Can you see me?"

"Well, ayuh." Asa coughed. "I'm lookin'… straight at you." Well, that took care of who. Yawning, Asa remembered where: Oh, yah, the Eastern Trader. "What's wrong? The lads all right?"

He felt like a turtle flipped onto its back as he struggled to sit up. What's the matter with me? Why won't my body obey my brain? My head feels stuffed with cotton wool. Am I sick? Oh, damn. I am.

"Easy, now. Lie still. They're all as well as can be expected. It's you I'm worried about."

"Me?" Asa was panting from the exertion of trying to sit up. He coughed again. "I'll be… all right. It's just… a little… tummy upset."

"'Just a little tummy upset,' eh? You seem to have forgotten that I'm your doctor. Aside from turning your stomach inside-out, you're alternately burning up and shaking with chills, and then you're coughing and spluttering like an old engine." Doc's tone softened. "You were mumbling and choking, with tears streaming down your cheeks. Can you tell me what you were dreaming about?"

It was the drowning dream, but there was something different about it this time. Some frightening shadow swam around the edges of Asa's consciousness, but he couldn't quite pin it down. He didn't want to pin it down; he wanted it to swim clear away. He feared that it could drag him overboard into a sea of insanity.

"Dunno. Can't… remember."

"Can't or don't want to?"

Asa was fading, but he made an effort to keep his eyes open. "So ti—" His eyes closed. He forced them open. "Latah, Doc… can't keep… eyes op—" He was asleep before he could finish the word.

A few minutes later, he moaned in his sleep, seeing it all over again. "Jamie," he mumbled. "No!" He began to sob and choked on his tears, waking himself up, coughing and crying.

"Asa, sh, sh, it's all right." Stroking his forehead, Doc tried to soothe him. "Can you tell me?"

Asa began choking again. Drowning, drowning. No. Wake up.

Doc pulled him into a sitting position and thumped him on the back. "Breathe through your nose." He handed Asa a handkerchief. "Here, this might help."

Asa blew his nose and then took a deep, shuddering breath. Doc pulled an extra pillow down from the top rack, and plumped up the pillows behind him.

"Try a little sip of water," Doc held the glass to his lips.

After taking a sip, Asa pushed it away and leaned over the side of the bed, retching.

Doc rubbed his back, murmuring, "It's all right. All right. Easy, now." He helped Asa to sit back against the pillows again and sponged his damp brow with a cool cloth. "It might help if you can tell me."

Asa whispered, "Oh, God, please, forgive me. Please. I didn't mean to. Oh, Jamie. I nevah should have…" He broke down weeping.

"Jamie? Do you mean James?"

"No, *no*." Asa sobbed. "Jamie! Jamie… little… brother. Oh, God… It's all… my… fault." He tried to stop crying, taking in gasping breaths, but broke down again. His mouth opened in a soundless wail, and he stopped it with his fist, biting his knuckles. Tears streamed down his cheeks as his chest heaved.

Doc pulled his fist away. "Don't. Don't hurt yourself." Muttering something that sounded like, "Screw clinical distance," he put his arms around Asa. "There, there." He rubbed Asa's sweating back. "Sh. Sh. It's all right now. It was a dream. Just a dream."

"No!" Asa pushed Doc away. His normal baritone had climbed to a high-pitched woodwind, reedy and child-like. "No, it wasn't! I... I *killed* my... little... brothah! Oh-God-oh-God-oh-God. I should have... drowned, too! Oh, God!" He folded his arms across his stomach and rocked back and forth. Sweat matted his hair and dripped from his forehead.

Although Dr. Freud was very much alive, Doc muttered a prayer to him. "Oh, Sigmund Freud, help me. I'm in way over my head, here."

"You're praying to the wrong deity," Captain Hookset said.

Doc jumped. "Jesus!" He clapped a hand over his mouth. "Oh! I beg your pardon, Captain Hookset. I didn't hear you come in. You scared the be— daylights out of me."

His eyes gentle, Captain Hookset held Doc's gaze. "Jesus *is* the right deity for your prayers. Allow me to help."

He took Doc's place on the edge of the bed. Placing his hand on Asa's head, he prayed. "Dear Lord Jesus Christ, comfort and restore our brother, Asa, and grant your power of healing to Doctor Coffin. May they have confidence in your loving care and be strengthened thereby. Amen." Making a cross on Asa's forehead with his thumb, he prayed, "May God the Father bless you, God the Son heal you, and God the Holy Spirit give you strength. Amen."

Asa wept as Captain Hookset enfolded him in his arms, saying, "My son, you are forgiven. You were forgiven a long, long time ago. You were a *child*. You were *not* responsible. Do you hear me?"

"But… but I… I nevah should have taken him there! It was too dangerous! The waves were too strong for such a little boy." His voice was still that of a teary seven-year-old — one who was spent, weary, and ill. "He was so little! He was only five! I should have saved him!" He wailed. "It's my fault he drowned!"

Captain Hookset took Asa by the upper arms and looked him in the eye. "No. No, lad. You didn't know any better. The wind and rain had let up, and no one told you it was still dangerous. You *tried* to save him. Do you remember?"

"The sea, she *wouldn't* give him back. She tried to take me, too. But she *wouldn't* give him back!" His spine curled over, he hung his heavy head in defeat, failure, and shame.

"Yes, and you tried to make a bargain with her, didn't you? You offered yourself in exchange for Jamie, didn't you?"

Asa tried to stop crying with sharp little aspirations. "How… how do you know?"

"Do you remember the man on the dunes?"

Asa stared at the captain, agape. "*You?*"

Captain Hookset nodded. "I barely managed to snatch you from the sea's grasp. I tried to get to Jamie, too, but — he was already gone. I'm terribly sorry, Asa. You were unconscious when I took you from the water. When you came around, you didn't remember anything, and within hours, you became very sick with the croup. You almost died, dear boy. The doctor stayed with you day and night."

Asa ran a knuckle under his eye and sniffed. "Ma — she blames me. I thought it was because I gave Jamie the croup and that's why he died." His face crumpled.

"No. No, she didn't blame you, son. She had just suffered a miscarriage, and then she lost a son. It was grief, not blame.

Only grief." Captain Hookset drew him into his arms again. "We erred on the side of kindness, but it wasn't right to let you forget. I see that now."

Asa suddenly shook with a teeth-rattling chill.

The captain wrapped him in a bear hug and held him until he fell into a fevered half-sleep.

Asa felt himself being laid down on the pillows and a sheet being pulled up around his shoulders. He felt the bunk creak as the captain rose, and heard a distant conversation that seemed in some strange way to have both something and nothing to do with him. He felt detached from it, as though it were a part of someone else's dream.

"All these years…" It was Doc's voice.

"Yes." The captain said. "How sick is he, Doc? Is it the fever that's causing this return to child— ahem, the past?"

"He's very sick, I'm afraid. With his high fever and debilitated state, as well as all the grief he's been shoving away, this — this—" There was a pause. "I wouldn't call it a breakdown, not yet. Let's just say I think his fevered dreams have leaked into his waking state, causing a temporary regression to a very painful childhood event he had repressed. Physically, he's had some slight difficulty breathing at times, which could be partly due to his emotional state, but I wouldn't rule out an upper respiratory infection. He's had a couple of bouts of coughing. More worrying, it's a struggle for him to keep down even a sip of water. He's diaphoretic and dehydrated, and that can be very dangerous if we can't get him to keep fluids down. With the respiratory symptoms, nausea, fever, dizziness, and extreme fatigue, it could be any one of a half-dozen different diseases from influenza to malaria. I haven't had a chance to make a slide and examine his blood yet. I couldn't leave him."

"I'll sit with him while you do that," Captain Hookset said.

Doc nodded his thanks and went to prepare a slide. Peering into the microscope, he said, "Malaria, definitely. I'll start him on quinine, but it may be difficult, since he can't even keep down a sip of water."

"Are there similarities to what James suffered?"

"With James, I found the inflamed mark of an insect bite on the back of his neck, directly over the cervical spine. Even so, there was no clear connection between the insect bite and James's illness. There were no malarial parasites in his blood. I tried a course of quinine anyway. It didn't help."

"You did all you could, Doctor," the captain said.

Doc stood looking sadly down at Asa, and then reached out to brush a lock of sweaty hair back from his brow. "I'd like to bathe him in cool water to bring his temperature down."

"Can I help you?"

"Captain, you would handle a very sick man? I'm not sure you ought to risk—"

"Doctor Coffin, wouldn't you say it's rather too late to be worrying about risk? Now look here, Sampson and Rivers are bruised and in pain. That leaves me the largest man on the ship, with the exception of Mac and Joe. I'd prefer to keep them out of this; they have never heard of such a thing as discretion. I simply can't see one of your usual assistants handling him with the ease I can employ. Can you?"

As his consciousness waxed and waned, Asa heard their voices fading in and out.

"Very well, Captain. It would be a great help. It is difficult to get his clothing off without help when he keeps drifting off into unconsciousness."

Asa felt hands on him, moving him, undressing him. He thought perhaps he should help in some way, but his limbs seemed to be made of cast iron, too heavy to move. The voices went quiet. He felt cooler, and vaguely wondered if he was floating in the ocean. *Swim… cool… swim.* Then all sensory awareness left him.

\* \* \* \*

When Asa awoke, there were clean white sheets, a clean white nightshirt. He smelt of soap and water, not sickly sweat. He took a deep breath and looked up to see Doc's face.

"How are you feeling?"

Asa took another breath. "Bettah." He tried to sit up.

"Whoa, not so fast," Doc smiled, put out his hand to keep him lying down.

"What happened? How long have I—"

"First, let's try to get this down you."

"What is it?"

"Quinine."

Doc handed Asa a pill and helped him drink some water. Asa choked it down.

"Good." Doc took out his pocket watch and made an entry in Asa's chart. "How much do you remember?"

"About what?"

"Stop fighting it, Asa."

The shadow of memory swam closer. Why can't I stop fighting?

Much to Asa's chagrin, he felt a tear trickle into his ear. He tried to clamp down on his emotions, but they had suddenly become as slippery as a wet bar of soap. The tighter he tried to hold onto them, the faster they escaped his grasp. He turned his face away.

"Did you say something?" Doc asked. "I can't hear you if you talk to the bulkhead."

He redirected his eyes to the watery-looking blur that was Doc. "Can't."

"Why not?"

"If I stop fighting, I'll drow—" Asa bit his lips.

Doc frowned in puzzlement. "Do you mean you'll drown?"

"I mean, I'll die. No. I won't know if I'm still alive. Nunno, that's not—" Asa heaved a sigh. "I don't know what I mean! I'm… It's… Oh, just…" He shook his head. "Nevah mind. Jeez, Doc, I'm so tired and muddled, I'm not makin' any sense. Half the time, I think I'm losin' my mind."

"Asa, you've slept hard for several hours. Something happened before that. If I'm to help you, it's important that you tell me everything you remember. Start wherever you can."

Asa frowned in concentration. "Hmm. Bits and pieces. We were just sitting talking when this thing came along and slammed me galley-west. I got sick as a dog. Things get kind of fuzzy after that. Um… did you and the captain… Oh, God." Plucking at the clean nightshirt, he felt his face get hot.

"You have some kind of history with him, don't you? He's very… well, almost fatherly toward you."

Closing his eyes in embarrassment and confusion, Asa tried to calm himself by becoming utterly still.

"Asa?" Doc fumbled in his pocket for his stethoscope, and then leaned over Asa, listening to his heartbeat.

"Hmm?"

"For heaven's sake, don't scare me like that. What else do you remember?"

His face burning, Asa couldn't meet Doc's eyes.

"Captain Hookset, much younger, striding across the dunes like a colossus. And then here, holding me in his arms. Was I, uh… was I a… a child again? In more than just, ah, memory?"

"Well, your voice and your demeanor—" Doc shrugged. "I'd have to say yes."

"Oh, God, no," Asa muttered to himself. "Have I completely lost my mind?"

"No, Asa. It was… I think the memory was so powerful, it swept you back in time for a bit."

Asa's gaze slipped off to the side. He could barely speak above a whisper. "Jamie — I remember Jamie — drow— drow—" He bit his lip as his eyes filled up and overflowed. "I failed him, just as I failed Cap'n James."

"That's not what Captain Hookset said. You almost lost your life trying to save him, just as you almost lost your life trying to save Cap'n James. What more can you ask of yourself?"

"Maybe I should have," Asa muttered.

"Should have what?"

He turned his face to the bulkhead. "Lost my life."

"Is that the thanks you give to Captain Hookset for saving you when you were a child? To the men who hoisted you aboard the *Mary Lovejoy*? 'Thanks, anyway, but I'd rather drown'?"

Struggling to push himself up, Asa protested. "No, Doc! That's not it at all! It's just— What? What do you mean, the men hoisted me aboard?"

"You don't remember?"

Silent, staring into space, Asa tried to catch hold of shadows. "I remember the lifeboat smashed and then... ah, no, that's not quite... um." He flopped back against the pillows. "There's some vague... something. I just can't seem to get it to come into focus."

"Hmm. I would have thought... Don't you have any sense of it at all?"

Asa groped around in dark recesses of his memory. He sighed and shook his head. "I don't know. It's just a... a blur of... confused... images. It's not real; it's a dream."

"Can you tell me about some of those images?"

"Then you'll *know* I've lost my mind. They don't make any sense."

"That doesn't matter, and it *doesn't* mean you've lost your mind. Tell me, anyway."

"Well, uh... In one of them, we're diving off the cliffs in Acapulco, Cap'n James and I." Asa's voice was dry and cracked. Clearing his throat was fruitless.

"Try a little sip of water," Doc held the glass to Asa's lips.

Asa drank, and for once, his stomach didn't revolt. "Ah. Thanks."

"Can you go on?"

"Um, we're swimming, and suddenly it's blowing a gale. What was a sunny day is now night and I can't see him anymore. I'm looking for something white." He frowned in puzzlement. "But that can't be right, because his bathing suit was gray and black stripes, up to his neck and down to his knees, so there wasn't even much skin showing." He shook his head. "Anyway, I can't find him. The seas are so high they're washing over the tops of the cliffs. But that's impossible." He sighed. "I told you it doesn't make sense."

"Little drink… that's good." Whenever Asa paused, Doc fed him another sip of water.

"Dream images often don't seem to make sense, until we examine them. There's more, isn't there? Tell me."

"Well… uh, this is screwy. Now you'll *know* I'm bats." Asa paused.

"You think that's news to me?" Doc smiled. "This is just between us."

Asa sighed. "Well… all right. I… uh… this is nuts. But I get this notion that the sea has kidnapped him, and I offer myself for ransom, but she refuses to release him. Just as she's about to take me, too, a giant plucks me from her grasp. It's like some kind of weird fairy tale. Then I'm face down on a ship's deck… but I'm drowning — on the deck. And then I'm standing at the helm, wearing a dripping seaweed shroud." He shook his head. "I told you it didn't make any sense. It's more hallucinatory dream than memory. Did you give me any drugs? Laudanum? Morphine?"

"No opiates — just quinine. Are you so sure it makes no sense? Replace the cliffs with a ship's deck," Doc suggested.

Asa's jaw dropped as he stared at Doc.

"Is it becoming any clearer?"

Asa blinked and closed his mouth. "And… and replace the bathing suit… with… with a white nightshirt. Then it's true? Mike and Tommy weren't making up yarns?"

"You tell me."

"I… I still feel all at sea, floundering around in circles. Why is my memory of it so muddled?"

"Perhaps your psyche is trying to make it less painful by substituting the good memory of cliff diving, but it's not succeeding. Perhaps it was so much like your experience trying to save Jamie, you have confounded the two in your mind. You tried to make a bargain with the sea for Jamie's life, Captain Hookset said. You described him as striding across the dunes like a colossus; he would seem to be the giant that plucked you from the sea."

"You're saying it hurt too much to remember Jamie…" Asa looked away. "Jamie… drow—" He slipped his hand under his pillow, taking out a handkerchief. He dried his eyes, blew his nose, and turned back to Doc. "So my mind cloaked it in the garb of a fairy tale? I suppose that's plausible, in a way."

"Perhaps it's too painful to come at directly, all at once. I honestly don't know, Asa. Nevertheless, these images do have meaning. When you can piece them together in the correct order and figure out what the symbolism means to you, I think the whole picture shall reveal itself. Talking about it may help you to sort it out."

"You've already sorted out one thing for me. I couldn't figure out why I should remember a storm in Acapulco, when it was a beautiful day." Asa's eyes reflected a far off summer sky. "It truly was, Doc. The sky and the ocean were such gorgeous shades of blue; it took my breath away. We were watching the cliff divers, graceful, athletic, fearless. I said I'd like to be able to do that. Cap'n James suggested we go ask them about it. We offered to pay them for lessons, and they agreed. After we'd jumped a few times from a lower promontory, we dared each other to go higher. It was wonderful. We soared off that cliff like birds. We sure had some good times together." His eyes filled as he whispered, "Oh, God, I miss him."

Doc nodded. He observed Asa quietly for a moment. "You were so close and so much alike; you may as well have been blood brothers."

"But Cap'n James was twenty years older, old enough to be my fathah. So how could it be like losing Jamie?"

"Was it?"

Small sounds deepened the silence: the muffled clattering rhythm and hissing steam of the engine, water lapping against the hull, the distant voices of the crew, the ticking of Doc's pocket watch.

When Asa spoke, his voice was low and full of wonder. "I was only two when Jamie was born, but I remember it. I remember the first time I held him. I was sitting on the settee beside Father. He was holding Jamie, and he showed me how to hold him, being careful to support his head. Then he put the baby in my arms, and Jamie opened his eyes, looked up at me, and smiled. It was probably just gas, but I was enchanted. I loved my little brother from that moment on. He was so tiny and fragile. It was my job to protect him." Asa struggled not to cry. "But I didn't protect him; did I? I let the sea snatch him right out of my hands. He was so little."

"You were only a child yourself. Someone older should have protected both of you."

With tears trickling down his cheeks, Asa's breath came in sharp, shallow inhalations every few words. "But Father was at sea. Mother was sick. Aunt Tillie came by every day to tidy up and feed us, but she had her own brood to care for, and there wasn't room in their little house for Jamie and me to stay with them. There was… no one. It wasn't their fault. It was up to me… to look after him."

Doc sponged the sweat and tears from Asa's face with a cool, damp cloth. "I know it wasn't their fault. But it wasn't yours, either. Do you hear me? It was *not* your fault. It's only natural for boys to want adventure. You didn't have the experience to know it might be dangerous. You only wanted to see nature putting on a show. Who could blame you? Not Captain Hookset, and certainly not I."

Asa turned his face away. *Mother did. I do.*

"When I was about that age, maybe a little older, I remember going down to the beach with some other boys to see the waves during a blizzard. Well, *toward* the beach. The blinding snow and wind battled us all the way across the dunes. When we got to the top, we couldn't even *see* the beach, but we could see the waves all right. They were crashing over the seawall, washing away the beach road, and beginning to take large bites out of the base of the dune we were standing on. Before the storm got a chance to open up its maw and swallow us, we skedaddled. We were lucky," Doc said. "What happened to Jamie was an *accident,* Asa. It wasn't your fault."

Asa wept.

*I need to get control of myself. I wish I could stop, but the waters that have flooded my soul keep overflowing through my eyes. I wish I could feel forgiven. Cap'n Hookset and Doc are trying so hard to help me, but… I feel so alone.*

"You are not losing your mind, Asa. You are grieving — not only for James, but for Jamie, and for all the other losses you didn't allow yourself to grieve fully," Doc said.

Asa sniffed, fumbling for his handkerchief with shaking hands. "Shouldn't I have got over it by now?"

"No," Doc said. "You can't get over it without going through it, and it takes time. Besides, I don't know if we can ever truly be said to 'get over it.' Rather, we learn to live with it."

A wave of fatigue slammed into Asa. "Sorry," he slurred. "Too tired to—" As sleep defeated him, he thought he heard someone at a great distance say, "Grief is exhausting."

# Chapter 17

# *Venting a Heavy Heart*

Asa was asleep when Davy came in to ask Doc for a couple of aspirin tablets.

"How often have you been getting these headaches?" Doc asked.

"I haven't had one for a few days, so I don't think this is from being hit over the head, Doc. It's just squinting into the sunlight reflecting off the water, especially when I've got the helm, and this heat doesn't help any."

"Let me take a look at your eyes." Doc got out an ophthalmoscope and was just about to begin his examination when a sharp cry startled them. "Here, Davy, take this packet and come back tomorrow for an examination. And keep quiet about this."

He dashed to Asa's bedside to find him curled up in the corner of the rack, against the bulkhead, trembling.

"What is it? Asa, what's wrong? Talk to me."

Asa was still asleep, his eyes darting beneath closed lids. He mumbled, "Cap'n Alfred, help me." Groaning, he muttered, "It was Gunn."

On his way out, Davy stopped short, taut as a brace, and then spun around. His mouth opened and closed; his Adam's apple went up and down before any words came out. "Um, Doc, I, um, think… I know what his nightmare is about."

"How could you—" Doc glanced up to see a haunted look in Davy's eyes as the color drained from his face. "Sit down, quick, and put your head down before you faint." Wishing he could divide himself in two, Doc hastily covered Asa's shivering form with a blanket, and then went to Davy.

"I'm all right; stay with—"

"You most certainly are *not* all right. Now lie down!" Pulling the blanket up over Davy, Doc said, "This close to the equator and you're both shivering. Is this something that happened to both of you?"

"In a way." Davy said. "Do you remember when… that time in Marseilles… when… when I was… um… attacked?"

"Of course. We were very worried about you." Doc frowned. "Asa helped you in some way I could not. Is this something to do with that?"

Taking a deep breath, Davy nodded. "He… I wouldn't ever tell anybody… I wouldn't tell you now, but… it's only to help him, and you mustn't ever say anything—"

"It's all right, Davy. I think I know what you're getting at. Something like it happened to him, and he told you about it to let you know you weren't alone. Is that it?"

Davy nodded. "He was only a kid, his first year aboard ship. He wanted me to know I… I didn't do anything wrong; that I'm… I'm still a man… that I *could* survive it… that only a *monster* would do… that… to… to… to…"

"Sh… easy, lad. You don't have to talk about it," Doc said.

"No, I… I'm trying to tell you he helped me. He only told me so I'd know *he* knew… what it was like. I wanted to kill my— I wanted to die. He saved my life. He said I should talk to him any time I started to feel bad. And that it might take a long time to feel safe again. You know he taught me that jiu-jitsu? He said an Asian sailor aboard ship taught him when he... when it happened to him. For confidence as much as for self-defense. But they didn't talk about... no one talked about... what happened to him. When he just said 'Cap'n Alfred,' and then he said, 'Gunn,' I recognized... what he told me. He... he must still have nightmares about it, too." A tremor ran through Davy's body as his eyes filled up.

Doc handed Davy a handkerchief. "This has been very painful for you. Thank you for telling me, lad. It helps to know what his suffering is about." He observed Davy for a moment. "Speaking of suffering, I'll bet you really need that aspirin, now. As soon as I check on him, I'll bring you a glass of water. Just lie there and rest, all right?"

Asa was on his side with his knees drawn up, the blanket clutched in his fists under his chin, still asleep. Shivering had given way to an occasional twitch. Although his face was wet with tears and sweat, he had quieted.

Doc brought a glass of water and two aspirin to Davy. After drinking it down, Davy was about to hand back the packet Doc had given him earlier. "Keep it," Doc said. "If your pain comes back, you can take another dose in four hours. Why don't you rest here until the headache goes away?"

Davy looked over at Asa. "If it's all the same to you, Doc, I'd rather go back to my own rack. I don't want him to be... embarrassed... if he thinks I was here when... um... you know."

"Well... if you prefer. But if your pain doesn't go away, come back. And if you're having chills and fever, or even feel like you might be coming down with something, get yourself in here pronto; don't wait." Doc gave Davy a long look. "Or if you feel bad in any way at all — *any* way, Davy — come see me. Do you understand?"

"Aye, aye, Doc." Davy looked toward Asa again. "Take care of him, please? He means a lot to us."

"To me, too." Doc nodded. "Goodnight, now. And remember — I'm here if you need me."

"Thanks. G'night, sir."

Tidying up, Doc dropped his ring of keys on the deck. As he bent to pick them up, Asa moaned.

* * * *

*Panic-struck, Asa heard something hit the deck with a clunk.*

*A hand the size of a garden spade was clamped over his mouth and nose so he couldn't cry out, and the man bore down on him. He couldn't breathe.*

*He tried to fight, to wriggle away, to scream, but any sound he made was muffled by that beast's paw. He couldn't move, jammed into this small, dark space in the back corner of a hold, thrust down hard on all fours, knees bruised, trapped.*

Make a sound and I'll kill you, *the man growled. Asa felt cold steel against his neck and froze. He heard cloth rip as that hard hand split his breeches, and then the man rammed him, grunting like an animal.*

*He'd never felt such harrowing pain. He couldn't stop the scream that tore through his throat.*

*Let him kill me. Anything to make it stop.*

*The man's knife nicked his neck, and a trickle of warm blood dampened his collar.*

"You li'l sumbitch! Say a word, and I'll cut you up and feed you to the fish."

*A hiss of hot sour breath in his ear and then that big hand yanked his hair back and banged his head against the corner of a crate. Everything faded to gray spots and then went black.*

*He awoke to confusion, and then... pain that left him gasping brought memory back.*

*He tried to get up, to run away. The pain was so bad, he felt nearly torn in two. His knee slipped in the blood. His ankles were tangled in his pants, and he fell flat on his face. Muscles weak and shaking, he couldn't move. At a sound, he froze, holding his breath, but his heart was beating so loudly, he was sure the man would hear it.*

*Has he come back to cut me up in chunks... to feed me to the fish?*

*He exhaled in relief at the familiar tap-step, tap-step of Captain Alfred's peg leg. He could barely raise his voice loud enough to be heard.*

*"Oooooh, Cap'n Alfred, help me."*

*"My God! Oh, my dear boy, who did this to you?" Captain Alfred bent over him.*

*"He said he'd kill me, but I don't care. Gunn. It was Gunn."*

*Captain Alfred helped him to pull up his torn and bloody trousers, but his legs gave out when he tried to stand. Cradling him in his arms, Captain Alfred carried him to sick bay.*

*Blood. Pain. Shame. Let me die, oh, God, please let me die. Now.*

Asa sat bolt upright. "Cap'n Asa! He's back! Gunn's back!"

"Asa! Asa, wake up, now. Can you hear me?"

His breathing rapid and shallow, Asa began shaking again. "Oh, God, it hurts."

"Breeeeathe, Asa. Slow down your breathing." Doc took Asa's wrist, feeling his pulse. "Breathe with me. In… and out… in… and out… That's right. Easy, now. Once more. In… and out…"

Asa looked around, bewildered. "Doc," he croaked. "I thought…"

"It's all right, now. It was a dream, only a dream. Will you be all right if I leave you for a moment to get you some water? The pitcher is over there, only a few steps away. You can keep your eyes on me."

Asa nodded.

When he returned, Asa reached out for the water, but his hands trembled so much, Doc held the glass to his lips. As the water began to soothe his throat, swallowing got easier.

"Can you take another quinine tablet now? It's time," Doc said.

"Ayuh." Asa took the tablet with more water. A sip at a time, he drank half the glass.

"Better?" Doc asked.

He panted, nodding. Sweat and tears glazed his face.

"Can you tell me about the dream?" Doc asked.

Sitting hunched over, he stared at the blanket. "Another trip to childhood… only this one I… never forgot. I thought… I thought these dreams were… over and done with… a long time ago. Cap'n Asa… Cap'n Asa set up a hammock in his cabin for me, so he could… comfort me when the nightmares came."

Doc nodded and waited for more. When Asa didn't continue, he prompted, "Who was Gunn?"

Asa's head jerked up, and he peered at Doc suspiciously.

"In your sleep, you said his name — and Captain Alfred's," Doc said. "You seemed very threatened by this Gunn."

"Cap'n Alfred saved me… and then… then he almost lost his own life… when Gunn… turned on him with a carving knife." He twisted the blanket in his hands. "In the galley. Later. Took 50 stitches. If Cap'n Asa hadn't come along and brained that… that… brained him with a cast-iron spidah…" Asa shook his head and immediately regretted it. He closed his eyes to stop the spinning and lay down.

Doc reached out and put his hand on Asa's forehead. "Feverish. Are you feeling sick?"

"Dizzy," Asa said. "Bettah… lyin' down."

As he spoke, Doc poured some cool water into a basin, and dipped a cloth into it. He wrung it out and bathed Asa's face. "Do you have the strength to continue? To tell me what happened?"

While concentrating on his breathing, Asa thought about it. "Where… was I?"

"Captain Asa hit Gunn on the head with a spider."

"Yah… Cap'n Asa only wanted to… to save his brothah… He grabbed the first… thing that came to hand. He didn't mean to… to kill that… *him*… But I'm glad he did… I think. Sometimes."

"Was he a seaman aboard a Lovejoy ship?"

"He was… cook… aboard *The Sarah Lovejoy*… I was his… his apprentice. He's the reason… tight, dahk co'nahs… hidden places… in the holds… still give me… the creeps."

Doc waited, but again, Asa had stopped talking.

"Can you tell me what you're feeling right now?"

"I don't... don't know, Doc. Sick... hurt... angry... shaken... scared. Isn't that... ridiculous? Still... scared, after all these... years. And the bastid is... long dead."

"How many years?"

"Fifteen." Asa didn't have to stop and think.

"Not at all ridiculous. That nine-year-old boy who was brutally attacked by a pederast still lives inside you, Asa, just as the eight-year-old who lost his parents, and the seven-year-old who lost his beloved baby brother and almost died himself."

"Wait," Asa said. "Did I tell you? I don't remember... telling you... what he did to me."

"I... deduced it from your story," Doc said.

"Oh, no." Asa flung the blanket away, turning on his side. "No. I... vaguely heard... voices. Was Davy here? He's the only one... who knows, unless... Captain Hookset... No... Neither Cap'n Asa nor Cap'n Alfred... would tell... anyone... The only way Davy would... tell you... Oh, damn. It was... one of those... feverish... nightmares, wasn't it? And he was here... he was... trying to... He wanted to... Oh, God, poor Davy."

"Are you having difficulty breathing?"

"Hot. Headaches. Everything aches. How's... Davy?"

"He never would have said a word, Asa, and it was very hard for him to do so. It was only... he thought if I knew, I could help you."

"Oh, hell! And it... it brought back... all his own... pain. Damn!" Tears sprang to Asa's eyes. "Damn!"

He leaned over the side of the bunk, dragged the bucket out from underneath it, and vomited. Every muscle and joint ached as his fever spiked again. Pain wracked his body and mind; sweat streamed from every pore. He pressed his palms over his temples to keep his head from exploding. Trapped in the center of a storm, he was turning inside out, breaking apart. Unable to regain control, he sobbed in frustration. A wild howling sound horrrified him, and when he realized it was coming from him, it mortified him. He had a vague sense that Doc was holding him, before leaving him for a minute. Asa felt a sting in his right buttock, and then the whirlwind seemed to slow down to a blurry turmoil. He felt hands on him, washing him, drawing a sheet up to his shoulders, and then nothing.

\* \* \* \*

"Wha… go 'way." His eyes still closed, Asa tried to brush away whatever was disturbing his sleep.

"Come on, Asa. Just for a minute. Take your medicine, drink some of this, and then you can go back to sleep."

"Ugh." Trying to pry his eyelids up was such a strain, he wondered if lead weights really were holding them down. He raised an unsteady hand and rubbed his eyes with thumb and forefinger. No sinker, no plumb.

"Let me help you sit up." Doc put another pillow behind Asa's back. He slipped a pill into Asa's mouth and held a cup to his lips. "Take a mouthful… swallow. That's good. Keep going… little sips."

After drinking a quarter of it, Asa turned his face away. "No… more."

"Rest for a while, and we'll try some more later," Doc said.

Four hours later, Doc woke him again. Another pill, another glass of water, another cup of sweet tea. It went on this way, increasing his fluid intake every four hours, and when that stayed down, adding milk to the tea.

\* \* \* \*

When Asa opened his eyes to daylight streaming through the porthole, he lay rocked by the motion of the ship, listening to the comforting thrum of the engine, the lap of waves against the hull. After a while, he yawned, stretched, and looked around. "Say, Doc, when did we leave Port Said? And why don't I remember it?"

"We left two days ago. You don't remember because you were too sick." Doc sat on the edge of the bed and patted the back of Asa's hand.

Asa looked askance at Doc's hand on his. "Just *how* sick?"

"Asa, don't tell me you can't recall all that agony you— Well, perhaps that's for the best. You were shivering and sweating, either asleep, having nightmares, unconscious, delirious, or heaving. At least you can hold down liquids now, and your temperature has gone down a bit." Doc sighed. "I admit to being quite worried about you, especially when you were having such a hard time keeping the quinine down. You're not out of the woods yet, so don't be thinking you're going to get out of bed and go back to work anytime soon."

"Oh." Feeling his face get hot, Asa looked away. Then he turned back, grinning and brazening it out. "Now I remember, to my eternal chagrin. Well, except for the unconscious parts. But I do feel better. At least I'm conscious without being nauseated, and I can sit up. It shouldn't take too long, should it?"

"Should what?"

"Before I can go back to work."

Doc heaved a sigh. "Every time you wake up, you say, 'I feel better.' And after the least exertion, such as trying to drink a cup of tea, you conk out again. Just be patient, will you? For once? Please?"

Asa heaved a sigh of his own. "Well, when can I get out of bed, at least to go to the head, and then maybe walk up and down a bit? Just enough to staht workin' on gettin' my strength back a little, you know."

"Not today. Soon. But that's the least of your problems. You've got a ways to go. Let me help you. Talk to me."

"Hmm." Asa thought about it. "I must admit, letting some of those bats out of my belfry has cut the terror of being locked in the looney bin down to mere anxiety." He ducked his head with an embarrassed smile.

"Well, I suppose that's some progress." Doc's eyes were gentle as he smiled back. "Are you truly feeling a little better, now?"

"You've helped, Doc. Thanks." Asa yawned.

Doc smiled. "Go back to sleep for a while. I'm going down to the galley to have Cooky make you a little broth and some tea. Maybe we can go so far as to try a little hardtack today. You know it's better for your stomach if you can eat something before taking the quinine." As Doc opened the hatch, Leo hopped in. "Well, look who's here! She must have sensed your need of a little comfort. I'll be back soon."

"Hello, sweetie." Leo jumped up on the bed. Asa rubbed under her chin and behind her ears. "What've you been up to? Catching rats? Cap'n Hookset and I caught a few, too — two-legged ones. Well, before I ended up an invalid. How's that for a word, eh? Get sick and I'm no longer valid, as though I haven't paid my dues to the human club and they've cancelled my membership. Declared null and void. In-valid. Think your species might accept me as an honorary member?"

Leo purred louder, as if in affirmation, and made herself comfortable on his abdomen as he patted her. She was like a furry hot water bottle, soothing his sore belly. For a moment, he wished he led the simple life of a cat. As she rode up and down on the tide of his breath, they both fell asleep.

After a while, he vaguely heard Doc come in and put the tray down on a table, and then felt a whisper in his ear.

"I hate to disturb you two sleeping beauties, but if you don't wake up in a minute, your broth and tea will be stone cold."

Asa brushed the back of his fingers against his ear and rolled his head to one side.

Doc picked up Leo in his arms and tickled Asa's ear with her tail.

Asa flapped his hand at his ear.

"Okay, Leo," Doc tipped the cat onto the bed. "Wake him up."

Asa came awake with a smile as Leo gave him a cat-style face wash, her rough tongue rasping against the beard stubble on his jaw and cheek. "Time for my morning facial, eh, precious?" He rubbed behind her ears and she purred, leaning her head against his hand.

"Except that it's afternoon," Doc said.

"Oh, when is my internal chronometer gonna staht workin' again?" Asa groused. "When can I get out and see the sun?"

"When you can walk without falling over," Doc said. "I'll grant you human assistance. Leo isn't tall enough."

"Aw, shucks! She'd let me get away with all sorts of stuff *you'd* never let me do," Asa grinned.

"Leo!"

The cat stopped begging attention from Asa long enough to give Doc an enquiring look.

"Now, Leo, you know you're supposed to watch him better than that!"

Leo squinted at him, opened her eyes wide, and blinked twice. Then she went back to rubbing her chin against Asa's knuckles.

"See that? She's tellin' you she loves you," Asa said. "Cat semaphore."

"I don't know. It looks more like she's telling me I bore her silly." Doc looked pleased. "Nice to see you smile. Now let's see you eat."

When Asa sat up, Leo jumped down. Doc put the tray table over his legs and whisked the oversized dome off the tray, revealing a bowl of broth and a cup of tea, along with five saltines on a plate.

"Dome that size," Asa said, "thought it was gonna be a Thanksgiving turkey."

"It was the only thing I could find to keep it hot, or at least lukewarm. How is it?"

Asa gave it a doubtful look.

"You need to replenish your fluids, and you're not going to get better if you refuse to eat and drink," Doc lectured.

"All right. All right. I know." With a spoon, Asa pushed aside a few small areas of thin scum that had formed on the surface of the cooling broth. He made a disgusted face.

Doc made an impatient sound. "Does your lordship wish me to fetch a cheesecloth-covered strainer and a clean cup?

Come on, Asa, it's just a little fat. It won't kill you. If anything, you can use all the fat you can get. I could stand you up at the front of anatomy class naked, to teach all the bones in the human body. A living skeleton! Take a damned spoonful!"

Feeling his face burn, Asa took a deep breath and brought the spoon to his mouth. Instead of putting the whole spoon in his mouth, he choked down four tiny sips from it. The next two spoonfuls were the same painful process. After the fourth, he gagged, but clamped his teeth together and forced himself to swallow.

Watching Asa struggle, Doc's face went from impatience to concern. "Take a rest, and then try the tea. All right?"

Asa nodded. The tea went better. The saltines caused him to cough and sneeze as though he were trying to eat feathers.

"Why don't you try crumbling those into the broth, and give them both another try?" Doc suggested.

"I'll eat… the crackers… but that broth… is foul," Asa said.

"Maybe that's what's wrong with it. Cooky used an old fowl instead of a chicken."

Asa looked up at him from under frowning eyebrows.

Doc shrugged. "You know, the quinine won't upset your stomach so much if you take it after eating something." He handed Asa the pill. "So it would help if you eat something."

Asa choked it down with obvious difficulty. The remainder of the tea helped, little sips at a time.

"I'm exhausted just watching you. Relax for a while, but don't lie flat." Doc plumped up the pillows behind Asa's back again. "We've got to get more nourishment into you. Physical depletion will only drive you into an emotional breakdown quicker, you know."

"Sounds like you're sayin' it's inevitable."

Doc softened. "Not if you let me help you, Asa."

"But—" Asa rubbed his eyes with thumb and forefinger, and then ran his hand down his face. From under drooping eyelids, he gave Doc a weary, skeptical glance.

"But first, you look exhausted. I think another nap is in order. Close your eyes now. Deep breaths; relax. Sleep."

After what Doc had just seen him through, Asa told himself his reluctance and embarrassment were foolish. But he'd been brought up to keep his inner turmoil hidden, and talking about it made him feel… well, peculiar. Although he didn't like it, he had to admit that he needed help.

He took deep breaths and relaxed, not enough to sleep, but enough to be revelatory. "I keep thinking of this verse to a poem, Doc. Do you know Walt Whitman's *Prayer of Columbus?*"

"Can't say that I do."

"It starts out talking about Columbus as a battered, wrecked old man, alone on an island, far from home. I don't remember it exactly, but the last line of the first stanza is: *Venting a heavy heart.* The part I remember is the second stanza:

> *I am too full of woe!*
> *Haply I may not live another day;*
> *I cannot rest, O God, I cannot eat or drink*
>     *or sleep,*
> *Till I put forth myself, my prayer, once*
>     *more to Thee,*
> *Breathe, bathe myself once more in Thee,*
>     *commune with Thee,*
> *Report myself once more to Thee.*"

"Do you see yourself in that?"

"Well… I don't think God hears my prayers. He's angry with me. I've been wondering if all this bad luck we've had is my fault, as though I'm some kind of Jonah. You should throw me ovahbo'd."

"My dear Asa, I'm quite sure he's *not* angry with you, and you are *not* a Jonah. Why do you persist in blaming yourself? As Captain Hookset would tell you, God loves you. Bad luck just happens. It's not your fault."

"My head knows that, but… my heart… I, uh… I dunno, Doc. I just feel… guilty."

"Because you survived and James didn't? We've talked about this, but you can't seem to accept it, can you? You did *everything* you could. It was *not* your fault."

"Nunno, that's not it. I dunno… It's just this… this sense of something… *My brain feels rack'd, bewildered* — another line from that poem." Asa sighed. "I don't know why I said that. Oh, God, when *is* my brain gonna staht workin'?" Damn, there was that water in his eyes again.

Doc observed him. "You are in no condition to pursue this further right now, but I think we should revisit it when you're not so depleted. There is one thing I must know, though. That second line: *Happily—*"

"Not happily, *haply* — perchance."

"*Haply*, yes. *Haply I may not live another day…* Well, either way, it raises the question, Asa… Do you want to die?"

Asa considered the question. "No. Ah… no. I don't think so. There are times when it seems *a consummation devoutly to be wished*, but that's just a… a passing darkness of my soul. I wouldn't do anything to bring it about, if that's what you're worried about."

"What about starving yourself? I'm talking about before you got sick. Why do you find it so hard to eat?"

"You think… you think I'm trying to kill myself? Nunno, Doc. It's hard to eat when I feel like…. Oh, what the hell." Asa heaved a sigh. "It's hard to get food past this lump in my throat."

Doc nodded. "And you are too full already — full of woe. That's why you need to talk. You need to vent that heavy heart. Will you continue to do that?"

"I don't know what to say, but… if you think it'll help, I'll try." Asa's eyelids felt swollen, hot, and heavy.

"You've just made a very good start. But I think you've had enough for now. You need to rest. Just breathe…. That's right…. Relax…. Close your eyes… and sleep."

Leaning back, Asa nodded off.

* * * *

After putting a cool cloth over Asa's eyes, Doc went to his desk to catch up on his record keeping. When Captain Hookset came in, he looked up from his log book, put down his pen, and applied a piece of green blotting paper to the page. He capped the ink bottle with its black rubber stopper. Glancing toward Asa, he spoke in a low voice. "What can I do for you, Captain?"

After gazing at Asa's sleeping form for a moment, the captain sat down in the chair beside the desk. "I admit to being worried about him. More than once, I have urged him to take better care of himself. He seems to find it quite difficult to do so, though I do believe he tries. Since he performs all of his duties well — and half of everybody else's into the bargain — I cannot call him to task. All I can do is pray for him. Doctor," Captain Hookset paused. "Is he very ill?"

"After a nap, he seems to rally a bit, but it doesn't last long. The acute nausea he was experiencing has let up, but even attempting to eat exhausts him. To be frank, if he can't get more nourishment into him, I fear for the outcome," Doc said. "But I'm not without hope. Though still occurring, his chills and fever have diminished. He can talk without becoming breathless, and his lungs sound better. But his liver and spleen are still somewhat tender. I believe a longer course of quinine should help, now that he is more able to keep it down."

"Do you think it is entirely physical?"

"He has been afflicted with malaria; this much is clear. But I think we both know that is not the sole cause of his anguish."

"He's been carrying around a heavy burden of guilt, and there's been no reason for it." Captain Hookset shook his head. "Tsk tsk."

"I know his parents both died when he was eight. Just a year after Jamie?"

"That's right, poor child."

"What happened? I don't believe I've ever heard."

"It was botulism from home canned lobster. Asa didn't eat any, so he was spared."

"What a horrible way to die." Doc grimaced.

"His Uncle Nathan's fishing trawler had gone down in a storm the year before. Come to think of it, it must have been the same storm that took Jamie. At the time Asa's parents died, his widowed aunt was busy taking care of five children with scarlet fever. Of course, the doctor had to quarantine them. He was run ragged with that outbreak. Asa ran to get him, but he couldn't do much of anything for Mr. and Mrs. Samuel Mayhew. Young as he was, Asa tried to keep them as clean and comfortable as possible. Tsk, tsk. Can you imagine an eight-year-old child's fear and helplessness, watching the terror in his parents' eyes as the paralysis reached their respiratory apparatus?"

"Oh, dear God. After all he'd been through the year before, it's a wonder he didn't go staring mad." Doc shook his head. "Were there no adults to help him?"

"I was at sea, but heard about it later. The Lovejoys were in Boston at the time, taking Mrs. James Lovejoy to another specialist, I believe. Mrs. Silas Mayhew was only sixteen then, but she did what she could. The scarlet fever outbreak affected every household with children. Because of the quarantine, they could not leave their homes. Those who *were* free to go out were afraid of catching the fever, and many didn't understand that what Mr. and Mrs. Mayhew had wasn't contagious. Mercifully, if such a thing can be said of so terrible a death, the course of the disease did not last over long. They both died within three days, Sarah first, and Sam'l about an hour later. When Captain Asa Lovejoy came back from Boston and heard what had happened, he adopted Asa, although I don't know as there was any legal formality about it."

"Where was Silas?"

"Stellwagen bank, on Phineas Bertram's fishing schooner. He got back the day Asa's folks died," Captain Hookset said. "Just in time to arrange the funeral."

"Why didn't Si and Janet take him in?"

"They had just married; Silas was only eighteen and, as I said, Janet was sixteen. They lived in a little place that wasn't much more than a fishing shack. They tried to help Asa, but they were too young and too poor to be able to raise, feed, and clothe a growing boy. Captain Asa Lovejoy supported him and saw to his education, but he did stay with Silas and Janet Mayhew when he wasn't at sea." Captain Hookset tut-tutted. "The three of them are all that's left of what started out as a large family."

"He's been through such a lot of grief, hasn't he? It's terrible to contemplate what all this must have done to him." Doc stared at the top of his desk. He was silent for a moment before he looked up and met the captain's eyes.

"Seeing him like that… I'm not sure I know how to treat him, Captain. I wish I had a psychiatry text aboard."

"He doesn't need a lot of fancy jargon and poppycock about Greek myths and complexes. Don't look so surprised, Doctor. I may be old, but I *do* read about the latest things, you know."

"Yes, sir."

The captain continued, "I know you're the doctor, but my prescription would be prayer, love, listening, understanding, rest, and nourishment. Would you concur?"

"That's just what I would prescribe, Captain," Doc said. "Let's hope it works."

\* \* \* \*

Doc continued waking Asa every four hours for medication and nutrition, alternating sugary, milky tea with hardtack softened in broth. When Asa was able to eat and drink with less difficulty, Doc added rice to the broth. Next, he added a few teaspoons of applesauce to Asa's diet. When he was able to drink an entire cup of tea, accompanied by toast, they alternated this with small bowls of broth with rice, followed by nearly a quarter-cup of applesauce. After three days, Asa could drink a glass of milk to coat his stomach before taking the quinine. Doc continued to add one more thing at a time.

"Eggnog," he said. "I'm hoping to add a little padding of flesh to protect those bones that stick out with such vulnerability."

Asa drank. "Be bettah if you'd put a slug of brandy in it, Doc."

Doc smiled. "Drink a little more, so I can fit it in. We'll try one tot of brandy in your bedtime eggnog."

Asa smiled up at Doc when he had enough strength to sit on the edge of the bed without help. Then they took the next step, with Doc holding Asa upright as they shuffled from one end of the bunk to the other.

"You're making progress," Doc said. "Good job."

"I feel… bettah," Asa panted. Then he flopped down onto the rack and caulked off.

# Chapter 18

## *Passage to India*

Asa dreamed of Walt Whitman:

*Reckoning ahead O soul, when thou, the time*
*    achiev'd,*
*The seas all cross'd, weather'd the capes, the*
*    voyage done,*
*Surrounded, copest, frontest God, yieldest, the aim*
*    attain'd,*
*As fill'd with friendship, love complete, the Elder*
*    Brother found,*
*The Younger melts in fondness in his arms.*[28]

He saw James, whole and healthy again, with a child on his knee — Jamie. He heard James's voice, "We shall all be together again, someday. But your time has not yet come." Then he saw his mother and father, aunts and uncles, cousins, Captain Asa and Captain Alfred, all standing behind James and Jamie, as though posing for a photograph, smiling at him. James repeated, "Your time has not yet come, and you can do nothing to hasten it. Be patient, dear brother, and you shall see us all again. We love you."

The dream enfolded him as one of his grandmother's quilts. The motion of the ship rocked him as a cradle, lulling him into a deeper and more peaceful sleep.

The smell of coffee woke him up. He stretched and yawned.

Doc appeared by his bedside. "How do you feel?"

"Mmm, give me a chance to get my eyes open." Asa knuckled his eyes and yawned again. "Do I smell coffee?"

"Will you eat some breakfast?"

"Breakfast? Have I slept that long?"

Doc smiled. "Twelve whole hours, without being awakened by a nightmare."

Asa sat up fast, bumping his head on the upper rack. "Twelve hours!"

"Ouch!" Doc said. "Let me look at your head."

"It's fine, Doc. I didn't hit it that hard. What time is it?"

Doc checked for a lump, anyway. "Relax, Asa. You don't have to go on watch. You're still on the binnacle list, remember? Let's get some breakfast into you."

"You know, I'm actually hungry! But, after twelve hours without a piss, my first priority is the head."

Asa swung his legs over the side of the rack and started to stand up, but sank back down again. He put a hand to his forehead and blew out a breath, leaning forward.

"Maybe you hit your head harder than you thought," Doc said.

"Nunno, just a li'l dizzy. Must have got up too fast," Asa said.

"You're trying to do too much, too soon. Let me help you."

"Oh, Jeez, Doc. I don't have to be taken to the head like a toddler." He swayed when he stood up.

Doc steadied him. "Maybe you'd rather to crawl to the head like an infant?"

"Oh, all right. I admit defeat." Asa allowed Doc to walk him to the door. "Okay, this is as far as you go."

"Don't latch it. If I hear a thud, I'll come in and pick you up," Doc said.

Asa heaved a sigh of exasperation.

The sigh when he had attended to his bladder was one of relief. He washed his hands and face and came out shoving a damp lock of curls off his forehead with his fingers, but it flopped back again. His sigh this time was one of frustration.

"Better?" Doc asked.

"Ayup," Asa said. "I guess I really needed that sleep. I had the most wonderful dream."

"Let's get some food into you, and you can tell me all about it. What would you like?"

"Mm... I have a craving for bacon and eggs, toast with butter, and coffee. Lots of coffee."

"You shall have rashers of bacon and dozens of eggs!" Doc grinned. "And *one* cup of coffee."

"Don't get carried away, Doc. Two eggs, two strips of crisp bacon, and one slice of buttered toast will do. But I need at least two cups of coffee to get my brain started." Asa smiled, trying to look the picture of happy, healthy, red-blooded American male. He spoiled the effect by reeling into the bulkhead.

Doc took hold of his arm. "You'll feel better once you've eaten."

"Hope so. Can't be staggerin' around the deck. The men will think I'm drunk."

"You need to take a little more time to recover before you go back on duty."

"I can't be lyin' around in bed like some sham Abram. I'll be fine after I eat."

"After you eat, we'll talk." They had reached Asa's bed. "Lie down," Doc ordered. "I'll get Cooky to cook you up some eggs and bacon. Fried or scrambled?"

"Fried, over easy," Asa said. "Thanks Doc. If you ever wash out as a doctah, you could always get a job as a waitah."

Doc shook his head. "You should wait until after breakfast before you try to make jokes. Your brain needs fuel."

Asa smiled. "It was pretty feeble, wasn't it?"

Doc smiled back. "Rest, you feeble fellow. I'll be right back."

"Aren't you gonna finish dressing?"

"You don't think I'm going to put on cuffs, collar, tie, and coat just to go visit a hot galley, do you?"

"My mistake. You are perfectly dressed for the occasion."

Twenty minutes later, Asa dug into his eggs with relish. "Mm... oh, man, I never realized how hungry I was! Mm, mm, mm. This is like ambrosia of the gods."

Doc laughed. "Hunger makes even humble bacon and eggs taste like *haute cuisine*. It's wonderful to see you eat like this. I was beginning to be afraid you'd fade away to nothing."

Asa grinned. "Well, it'd save the cost of a funeral, wouldn't it? Well, Ma'am, we don't rightly know what happened. He started gettin' pale and thin, and one day, he just vanished. Poof! Just blew away like the fog." He waved his toast around and then took a bite.

Doc chuckled. "Still needs work. Doubt they get much fog in Dusty Gulch. You've either got to drop the western accent or the fog."

"Is that so? What about San Francisco?" Asa countered.

"Okay, you've got me there," Doc laughed. Then his smile faded. "I hope you *are* feeling better, and this isn't just another smoke screen."

"I am really feeling better, Doc. I had this dream, but it was more like a message from James. I saw him holding Jamie, and Cap'n Asa, Cap'n Alfred, Mother and Father, and all my aunts, uncles, and cousins were there. James told me we'd all be reunited again, but I'd have to be patient, because it wasn't my time yet."

"Well, I'm glad to hear *that*," Doc said. "Maybe I can exhale now."

"Don't worry. I'm gonna live, thanks to you. But this dream… It was so… reassuring. They were all smiling at me. James said, 'We love you.' I felt forgiven. I felt hopeful. It was as if… as if I wasn't alone anymore. I could feel James, and Jamie, and all of them, still with me. They haven't left me. They're all right here." He put his hand over his heart.

"I'm glad, Asa. I hope that good feeling will stay with you."

"Why wouldn't it?" Asa asked.

"I'm not saying it won't. It was a wonderful dream, and you should take comfort from it. But grief isn't predictable. You may begin to feel better, and then feel worse again. I don't want you to lose hope if that happens."

Asa sighed. "You mean I have to be prepared for when it comes along and knocks me down again?"

"It might not. I only issue this warning so you won't be… well, inclined to punish yourself. There may be some ups and downs before you settle on an even keel."

"But James *is* here." Asa put his palm to his chest. "He… I don't think he blames me."

"I *know* he doesn't blame you. You were the only one who ever did," Doc said.

"George—"

"For heaven's sake! George's brain is pickled in whiskey; he's irrational." Doc sighed. "I only want to remind you that grief isn't straightforward. Do you understand?"

"Yah, it can't be so easily overcome by a dream. I might feel good now, but… it may not last any longer than the dream lasted. It's a step in the right direction, though, isn't it? A step toward getting over, or rather through it?"

"It's a start. As long as you continue to eat and sleep enough. When you're physically depleted, it can be much more difficult to weather the emotional storms."

"*Mens sana in corpore sano.* Sure. A sound ship can withstand heavy weather better than a leaky old tub. I'll eat, I'll sleep, and I'll do whatever you tell me to do, without complaint. I want to be strong again."

Doc snorted. "If you start following my orders *without complaint, then* I'll start to worry."

"What do you mean?" Asa frowned.

"For you to lose that fiercely independent streak, my dear fellow, would not be a good sign. It would tell me that you'd become utterly dispirited, that you'd stopped fighting to get better."

"Oh, I see," Asa said. "Sorry to be such a difficult patient, Doc. Why would you want to keep me on the binnacle list? I should think you'd be glad to get rid of me!"

Doc burst out laughing. "You're funnier when you're not trying to be."

"What did I say?"

"First you tell me you'll follow my orders without complaint; then you apologize for being a difficult patient, and in the same breath, you complain about my recommendation that you take some time to recover!"

"I wasn't complaining!" Asa paused to think about it. Then he ducked his head and grinned. "Well, I guess maybe I was, in a round-about sort of way. But I can't just lie here, Doc. I need something to do."

"Asa, you went through a complete physical and emotional collapse. You may feel better today, but you are not yet well. I need to keep an eye on you, and to do that, I need you to stay here. Then we'll see how you're feeling tomorrow. We'll take it one day at a time."

Asa sighed. "Will you, at the very least, let me get dressed so I can go get my toothbrush, shaving kit, a clean shirt and underclothes? If I look like a hobo, you'll say I look sick, and never let me out of here. I'd also like to pick up a book or two."

Doc went to a cupboard and tossed Asa a small yellow cardboard box containing a new Prophylactic toothbrush. "I always carry a good supply of these. You'd be surprised at the number of men who don't have them, and have never learned how to brush their teeth. You can use my shaving soap and safety razor; just put a fresh blade in. You can even use my hairbrushes. I've examined you; I know you don't have galloping dandruff."

"Galloping dandruff! Jeez, thanks a lot, Doc. I don't even have the regular kind. Do I?

"No, you're one of the few who don't."

"What about clean clothes?"

"Tomorrow."

"You don't trust me enough to just go to my quarters for a few minutes?"

"I'm just saving myself the necessity of bandaging up some part of your anatomy. You're liable to get dizzy halfway up the companionway and fall down."

"I'm not that—"

"That bad," Doc joined in. "What were you just saying about following my orders without complaint? While you're shaving, take a good look in—"

"The mirror," Asa said with him. "Think we should add a dance number to this routine, Mr. Bones?"

Doc smiled. "You got the roles reversed. You, being more skeletal, are Mr. Bones. I'm the other guy. And a dance routine would be too much trouble. I'd only have to hold you up."

"Oh, all right, if that's the way you feel about it! No dancing! Humph, what a killjoy." Asa sighed. "I shall stay here, as you wish. May I go shave now?"

"Hold out your hands, palms down."

Asa complied. "See? Steady as a rock."

"Well, I guess you won't accidentally slit your throat. Go ahead." Doc started to walk with him.

"I don't need a minder," Asa snapped.

"I was just going to show you where everything is."

"Oh. Um, sorry, Doc. I guess being a tottering wreck has made me a little tetchy."

"You're used to standing on your own two feet. It's understandable that you find my vigilance somewhat galling."

"So you *are* watching over me like a mother hen."

"Well, the type of injuries you've suffered require much more complex care than disinfection, stitches, and a clean bandage. Frankly, I admit to being a little out of my depth, so perhaps I am keeping too sharp a weather eye on you. I'd much rather risk annoying you than risk taking chances with your health," Doc said.

Asa held Doc's eye for a moment. "I'm going to shave now, and when I come out, I want to hear a little more of this frank talk from you. So start thinking about your diagnosis, prognosis, and precisely *why* you feel a little out of your depth."

"Asa, it's not—" Doc sighed. "Very well. It's nothing you haven't heard before, but perhaps you deserve a more concise, straightforward explanation." He took his shaving kit from a drawer and handed it to Asa. "Here — razor, blades, hairbrushes, toothpowder. Shaving mug's beside the sink. Oh, wait a minute." Doc went to a cupboard. "Clean towel and washcloth."

"Thanks, Doc."

First, Asa stripped off his nightshirt, filled the sink with hot water, and soaped up the washcloth. It felt good to wash off all that stale sweat. As he whipped up lather with the shaving brush, he worried. *He keeps telling me I'm not losing my mind, but he's treating me like an invalid. He says he's out of his depth, so it's not just the malaria, is it? Unless it's something rare or serious, but I'd know if I had something that bad. Wouldn't I? Well, I guess I was sick enough to concern him, but I am better now... almost. No, it's got to be mental. He told me psychiatry is not his forte.* He slathered lather on his face and began shaving. *That... whatever it was — when I regressed to being a seven-year-old kid again — that was bizarre, scary. So, he* does *think I'm losing my mind, or on the verge of it, and that's why he's watching me like a hawk.* He nicked himself. *Damn! Wonder if Doc's got any styptic in this bag.*

He couldn't find any styptic, so he stuck a piece of toilet paper on the cut, but it fell off when he brushed his teeth. He stuck another piece on, but it soon became wet with blood and fell off when he was brushing his hair. He tried again, applying pressure, but the damned thing just wouldn't stop bleeding.

"Hey, Doc, you got any styptic?"

"Nick yourself? Try toilet paper."

Asa came out and handed Doc his bag. He pressed a wad of paper to his neck. "Tried it. It's not working."

"And here I thought I could trust you not to slit your throat. Let me see." Doc washed his hands and examined the cut. "Just a little nick. It should have let up by now. There's nothing in your records to indicate a bleeding disorder. Have you ever had trouble like this before?"

"Styptic usually helps, but I couldn't find any in your bag. Oh, by the way, thanks for letting me use your kit."

Doc rummaged in a drawer and found a new alum block. He tried it, without much success. "Hmm. Little sting." He swabbed the cut with alcohol, and then folded a piece of gauze and applied it to the cut, holding it in place with surgical tape. "Does it usually take such a long time for cuts to stop bleeding?"

"I dunno. How long is it supposed to take?"

"Well, we'll keep an eye on it."

"This is a wrinkled mess, and it's not very clean." With disdain, Asa plucked the nightshirt away from his body. "If you won't let me get clean clothes, may I at least have a clean nightshirt?"

Doc got a fresh nightshirt from a cupboard. "Here. You're very particular. I'd say some woman taught you well, if I didn't know you'd been raised by a bunch of men."

"Cap'n Asa taught me. He said if I wanted to be respected, first I had to respect others; second, I had to behave respectably; and third, I had to look respectable. He said it wasn't vain to take care about one's cleanliness and appearance. On the contrary, it showed respect for other people not to offend their sensibilities by one's slovenly appearance or odor." He turned his back and slipped off the old nightshirt.

"And you learned your lesson very well."

Asa pulled on the fresh nightshirt. "I wanted to grow up to be a fine man, just like he was. I wanted to be worthy to bear his name."

"You did, and you are."

Asa turned to face him. "Well, I dunno about that. But if that's what you think, why are you treating me as though I'm made of glass? Why won't you take your eyes off me? It's as if you're afraid I'm going to shatter at the slightest touch. You *do* think I might be losing my mind, don't you? Is that why you feel over your head?"

"Whoa, slow down. One question at a time. Come sit down by my desk."

Asa sat. "All right, Doc, give it to me straight from the shoulder."

"You make it sound like a boxing match. I assure you, Asa, it is not my intention to land any blows. Quite the contrary."

"I didn't mean it that way." Asa looked down. "It's just… a way of… I dunno… pretending to be tougher than I feel, I guess."

"Yes, I see. But did you ever think I'm the one who feels challenged?" Doc held up a hand. "Not by you. By this illness. It has tested all my skill as a doctor."

"On top of it, I've tested your patience. At the risk of testing it further, though, Doc, I need some answers."

"Of course. What you wanted to know, as I recall, were my diagnosis, prognosis, and why I feel over my head. Well, first, you don't recover from malaria overnight. You're feeling better now, but you shall more than likely have recurrences, perhaps spread out over years. Quinine can help to control that. You were thin as a rail to begin with, and then for days you couldn't keep anything down. You could have died of severe fever and dehydration, and I had a hell of a time getting fluids and medicine into you. Right now, you're malnourished, and although you're not a complete wreck anymore, you are still tottering."

Asa nodded.

"I think you'll find yourself getting very tired within an hour or so. You'll need frequent naps and frequent small meals to regain your strength."

"But I am going to recover from this thing, right?"

"It certainly looks that way now, but you gave us quite a scare."

"So, on top of... everything else, did these high fevers affect my mind? I mean... I've been feeling so... going back into childhood, and all these awful memories that should be in the past, but keep intruding into the present and making me feel so... crazy. Doc, am I... um, headed for the looney bin? And is that why you feel 'over your head'?"

"You're not crazy. You are rational — well, with the possible exception of setting impossible standards for yourself and your propensity to blame yourself for things that are beyond your control. You *are* sane, and I don't believe you are in any danger of losing your mind."

Asa raised a skeptical eyebrow.

"Having said that, you have been through so much grief and pain in your life that it's bound to take its toll. Heaven knows what would have happened to you if it hadn't been for Captain Asa, Captain Alfred, and Captain James. After your parents died, they raised you and cared for you as their own. Their love for you and the depth of your love for them kept you on an even keel. When Captain Asa and Captain Alfred died within a year of each other, you were only nineteen. It rocked you, but you had James. You went through that grief together, steadying and comforting each other."

Asa nodded.

"His death has been a severe blow, and you've been trying to weather it alone."

Asa bit his lip.

"As if that wasn't enough," Doc continued, "the similarity of James's drowning to Jamie's brought that grief to the surface. Jamie's death was such a shock to your child's mind that you had to bury it deep in your subconscious simply to survive with your mind intact. Perhaps you'll be more able as an adult than you were then to understand and to work your way through to some peace. Still, you are not going to recover from such psychological injury without time and work."

Asa's eyes filled.

"Captain Hookset and I are here to help you, but it isn't like having Captains Asa, Alfred, and James, is it? We haven't that long-standing knowledge of one another that comes over so many years spent in close familial relationship. No one can make up for the loss — for all the losses — you have suffered."

Asa bit his lip.

"I have no doubt that you *will* recover, and you will be stronger for it. But in the meantime, you are vulnerable. You need somewhere safe to lick your wounds, so to speak. I think the best place for you is with Janet and Si, in the shelter of your family. You know and love each other. You won't have to explain yourself to them or pretend to be strong when you're feeling utterly beat up by life. You won't have to take on the added burden of responsibility for everything and everyone around you, and you won't have to worry what they think of you."

"But—"

"Yes, but. But it will take us a long time to get home, and in the meantime, as Chief Mate, you *are* responsible for everyone, and you *do* worry what people think of you. But you don't have to carry that responsibility alone. The ultimate responsibility belongs to Captain Hookset, and Mike and Tommy are capable of taking on most of your duties. You've trained them well. You needn't worry so much about what the men think of you. Every one of us aboard this ship knows you're grieving for Cap'n James. We are, too, though ours is not as deep, not as severe a wound as yours is. You need to ease up on yourself, Asa. Don't try so hard to be perfect."

"But doesn't Jesus command us to be perfect? *Be ye therefore perfect, even as your Father which is in heaven is perfect.*"[29]

"I'm sure you must be taking that out of context. God knows we can't be perfect. Otherwise, why would we need forgiveness? Captain Hookset can most likely explain it to you better than I can."

Asa sat in silence, hands folded on his lap, eyes cast down.

Doc observed him. "Is this why you're so hard on yourself? Why you're so obsessed with what you perceive to be your failures? You've been trying to be *perfect* because you see it as some kind of commandment?"

Asa felt his face flush. "Pretty stupid, huh?"

Doc sighed. "Well, did you think you *could* achieve perfection?"

"No, of course not, Doc. It's not possible. I just thought we were supposed to *try*, that we were supposed to aim for it."

"All I can say is, thank God you don't hold the rest of us to the standards you set for yourself. Asa, you try harder than anyone I know, and *still* you lambaste yourself when you don't succeed. You truly do *not* have to try so hard. For heaven's sake, give yourself some slack!"

Doc's advice prompted a memory. "When I was a little kid, about four years old, I learned to lace up and tie my shoes without help. My father was so happy with me; I decided to learn how to tie sailors' knots. While he was away at sea, I studied that book, and I could tie a bowline, a clove hitch, a half hitch, and even a Carrick bend. I had a little trouble with the eye splice, but I got that one down just before he came back. Yet, no matter how hard I tried, I could *not* get the monkey's paw. Well, I sat on the floor tying knots, and I showed him all the knots I had learned. But when I got to the monkey's paw, I cried in frustration that I couldn't get it to come out right. I wanted so much to learn all the knots my father knew, to be like him. He picked me up in his arms and hugged me. He told me it was wonderful that I could do all those knots. 'But,' he said, 'you know you don't have to be able to tie a single knot for me to love you. I love you more than words can say, simply because you're my little boy. I'm proud of you, son. You don't have to try so hard.'" Asa's smile wavered.

Doc nodded.

"And then we sat in the big rocking chair and he sang to me." Asa sniffed, knuckling away a tear. His voice dropped to a whisper. "I loved him so much, Doc. I feel like that little kid again, trying so hard to please, but I'd got it wrong. I didn't need to do all that. He was already pleased with me."

"If Captain Hookset was here, I'm sure he'd say your heavenly father is much like your earthly father in that respect. He doesn't expect you to be perfect. He loves you anyway. Your father sounds like a good man who loved you very much. So, just where do you come by this perfectionist streak?"

"I dunno. I guess I've always been like that." Asa frowned. "Maybe my mother. She was a perfectionist, but she didn't— well, she never demanded anything of me that she didn't demand of herself." With his elbow on Doc's desk, Asa leaned his head in his hand.

"Maybe we should talk about her some more — another time. You've had enough for now; this has taken a lot out of you. I want you to listen to your father, and listen to me: stop pushing yourself. Rest for a little while."

"Doc…"

"Yes? What is it?"

"Why do I keep going back to childhood memories? Why do I… Why do I feel so much like… like a child? I mean, since I got sick. Tell me I'm going to get over this, please."

"You're a Whitman aficionado, aren't you? Remember when he talks about

*The Past — the dark unfathom'd retrospect!*
*The teeming gulf — the sleepers and the shadows!*
.............................................

*For what is the present after all but a growth out of the past?*[30]

"Perhaps you have to revisit your past in order to repair that foundation, so that the future shall have a firm footing upon which to build."

"You've helped put things into perspective. Thank you."

"Do you think you can rest, now? Lie down and take a nap."

Asa yawned. "Hmm… yah." He shambled over to his bunk and fell onto it, asleep before his head hit the pillow.

# Chapter 19

# *Harmony*

Doc looked up from his logbook. "Want to talk, Asa? Sit down." He finished an entry, put the pen in its holder and capped the ink bottle, then looked at Asa expectantly.

Asa sat in the chair beside the desk. "Doc, except for our ten-minute promenades on the deck twice a day, I've been sleeping and eating every couple of hours like an infant, or lying around here reading. Oh, by the way, thanks for lending me your Shakespeare. Been a while since I've read all the Henries — fourth, fifth, and sixth."

"All six of them?"

"Waell, it's not as if I had anything else to do. I thought about writing letters, but... I just can't think of anything to say... I mean, I can't talk about this... especially to Mary... and—" Asa shrugged.

"Mary?" Doc raised his eyebrows.

"Miss Lovejoy. I'm afraid I— Well, I thought George would give her more trouble if I was there, but now I think maybe I should have stayed to protect her. I don't know. Why would she want me, anyway? I'd be just a painful reminder of how I let her father d-d—"

Doc sighed, reaching out to touch Asa's arm. "Will you *please*, stop blaming yourself?"

Asa looked down, embarrassed.

"Do you like her? Have you written to her?" Doc asked.

"Well, yes, but…"

"But what?" Doc persisted.

"I can't… I don't want to talk about her right now. It's too… um, soon." Asa felt his cheeks flame.

"Of course. I don't mean to pry into your love life," Doc said.

"It's not exactly what one could call a 'love life,'" Asa protested. "We hardly know each other. Just… drop it, all right? I shouldn't have said anything."

As he sat back and folded his arms, Doc studied Asa. Asa looked off to the left, studying the eye chart, avoiding Doc's eyes.

"Um." Doc's grunt sounded vaguely affirmative. "What about Janet and Si?"

Asa turned to face him. "What about them?"

"Don't you think they'd want to know how you are? Have you tried writing to them?"

"Nunno. I'll write later, maybe when we get to Bombay. If we have time to go ashore, I can tell them about our adventures."

"Adventures?" Doc's eyebrows traveled upward again.

"Waell," Asa drawled, "p'haps just a bit of colorful travelogue."

Doc gave him a wry look. "But will you tell them about being sick?"

"What would be the point? They can't do anything, and it would only worry them. By the time we get home, I'll be fine."

"Well, I certainly hope you'll be *better*, but I don't know as I'd go so far as to say 'fine,'" Doc said. "You might want to warn them, so they won't be shocked by your appearance."

"Oh, don't be so pessimistic. I'll fill out by then. Anyway, I'm not dizzy and sleepy anymore, and I want to go back on duty tomorrow." Before Doc could protest, Asa quickly offered a compromise. "If you want, I'll sleep here at night, and you can pour eggnogs down my throat as often as you deem necessary. But I just can't lie around doing nothing, or I *will* go crazy. So, will you take me off the binnacle list?"

"We'll see how you're feeling tomorrow morning."

"You want to get up at 0330 just to see how I'm doing? My watch starts at 0400, you know. I'll be all right. If I start to feel bad, I'll send one of the lads to get Mr. Martin or Mr. Gunderson to take over for me, and I'll come back here. How about that?"

"If you sleep well tonight, maybe, but not for morning watch. We'll see how you feel by 1600. If you're plagued by nightmares, no. Any more night sweats and chills, or if your temperature rises again, no."

"But I feel so much bettah. I know there will be ups and downs, but I'm prepared for that. I can ride the swells."

"We'll see. If I do let you go back, you're to start out with first dog watch *only*. You may feel better now, but you still have a long way to go."

"You're a hard man to convince, Doc." Asa sighed. "All right. You let me do my four-to-eight, and I'll rest in between, do light things like keeping the log, checking the cargo, making sure the—"

Doc held up a hand. "Belay there! *If* I agree to take you off the binnacle list, you may go on watch from 1600 to 1800 and keep the log, but *nothing else*. No fixing things, solving everyone else's problems, or even *helping* to perform heavy labor like shifting cargo. You've been training Tommy to be a mate. Let him test his mettle, and let Slocum step up. They've been doing fine, so far."

"But—"

"Have faith in your men, Asa. Trust them to do as you've taught them. Believe me when I tell you, you've *got* to take it easy. We'll see how you are tomorrow afternoon. If you're well enough to partially resume your duties, you're to come back here immediately afterwards, so I can see how you're doing."

"Damn! All right!" Asa sighed and shook his head. "I didn't mean to snap at you, Doc. I'm just fed up with lying around."

Doc smiled. "I was wondering how long it would take."

"Before I started fighting you again? I know I promised to do everything you say, but… It's so hard to just… to just…" Asa circled his hand in the air, searching for the word, but failing to grasp it.

"Yah," Doc said. "I think I'd make a pretty poor patient, myself. It's very hard, when you're used to a lot of activity, and you're used to being the fellow in charge. Suddenly you find yourself flat on your back, forced to be passive, having to take orders, rather than issue them."

"It's not so much that you order me around. It's more that I'm not used to needing someone to… uh… take care of me. I'm grateful, but… well… at the same time…" Asa shrugged.

"I think it was Aristotle who said gratitude soon grows old. It can lead to resentment, especially if one were to be ostentatious in one's generosity, rubbing it in, so to speak."

Doc snickered. "'After *all* I've *done* for *you*.' Someone said that me once, and it set my teeth on edge. He continued to press unwanted gifts and favors upon me, refusing to accept reciprocal gifts. Then he became angry when he learned he couldn't buy me, keep me under his thumb, or use me to get into my mother's good graces." He huffed, and then took a calming breath. "Remembering him makes me irritable all over again. You didn't ask for this. Don't be grateful. Whether you fight me, resent me, or are passively compliant, it doesn't matter. I'll still do my job. I wouldn't have gone to medical school if I didn't want to take care of people. I want to take care of you." Doc smiled. "Whether you want me to or not."

"All right, already! I get it!" Asa shook his head, grinning. "It's a good thing I like you, Doc — forcing all your healing arts and tender care upon me." He sighed. "I do trust you. You know what you're doing. It's just... Well, I guess my pride gets in the way."

"Is it pride, or is it just that you're more comfortable doing for others than you are having others do for you?"

"Are you talking about me or yourself, Doc?"

Doc laughed. "What is it they say? 'It takes one to know one?'" He paused, giving Asa a questioning look. "I get the feeling something else is bothering you."

"Um... Ah, there's one thing worries me... about going back on duty," Asa said.

"What's that?" Doc asked.

"Well..." Asa studied his hands. "How can the men still... um... will they still... respect me... after... after all this?"

Doc reached out and covered Asa's hands with his own. "Asa, have you no idea how much the men on this ship care about you? It's more than loyalty. They have genuine affection for you. You've taken the time to know each one of them. You know the names of their wives and children, girlfriends, mothers and fathers. You know what their families are like, what problems they have. You try to help out, when you can."

Asa was shaking his head. "And I forget they're grieving, too. Just when they might need my help, I crawl into my own little shell and snap shut, like a clam."

Sitting back, Doc seemed to veer off the subject. "Except for Captain Hookset, did you ever sail with anybody other than Captain Asa or Captain James?"

"Once — tramp steamer out of Marseilles. Why?"

Doc looked puzzled. "Marseilles? Never mind; tell me later, if you'd like. I don't want to get off track.

"Do you know the kind of treatment some of these men have received from brutal masters and mates? The first time I ever went to sea, I saw men beaten and whipped from stem to stern for the most minor infractions of the rules, and sometimes for nothing but the mate's bad temper. And they couldn't just quit, as I could. They were victims of the crimp, signing away their lives to the shipping companies. They had to pay exorbitant rent bills to the boarding houses at which the shipping companies forced them to stay. Even with the passage of La Follette's Seaman's Act last year, making that illegal, most companies are still tyrannical and corrupt. There are exceptions, like Bay State and Lovejoy Lines, but with George at the helm, Lovejoy may well follow suit. Given the alternative, is it any wonder some of these men practically worshipped Captain James *and* you?"

Asa sighed. "Although I haven't had to experience much of it, thank heavens, I *do* know about that kind of inhumanity. I supported Senator La Follette's Seaman's Act, and wrote to my senators and congressman to urge them to vote for it. Doesn't go far enough, but it's a start. All the same, Doc, I didn't *do* anything to earn the men's affection and loyalty. It just came to me sort of by default, because some of the men used to work for brutes."

"*Why* must you always diminish—" Doc rolled his eyes. "Damn it, Asa! Of course you earned it! You treat these men like *men*, not as though they were some kind of lower species. Moreover, you see every man as your equal. From the stokers to the captain, you give them all the same respect. You don't think that counts for anything, because it comes so naturally to you. Far too many ship's officers are *not* respectful of their men, and even among the good ones, who try to treat them fairly, there is a definite air of… well, smug superiority. You don't have that; you don't look down your nose at anybody."

Asa snorted. "Oh, yes I do. I do not suffer fools gladly, and all too often, I let it show. I can have a sharp, sarcastic tongue. On this voyage alone, I can think of four men I could have cheerfully strangled with my bare hands. I'm no paragon, Doc."

"Oh, well, if you're talking about that saboteur, that officious Special Branch dimwit, Sergeant Witless, and that Greenstreet thug — I can safely say every man aboard this ship would have been happy to help you. And that's including Captain Hookset."

Asa grinned. "Nunno, he wouldn't stoop to the level of fisticuffs. He'd more likely draw himself up to his full, considerable height and thunder righteous jeremiads at them.

Prob'ly be more effective, too. He's pretty impressive when he does that — downright frightening."

"Of that, I have no doubt." Doc's lips quirked up in a wry smile. "The only trouble is, when you're dealing with such nincompoops, a jeremiad would most likely go right over their heads. They wouldn't understand it as anything to do with them."

"Hah! You're right." Asa said. "Thanks, Doc."

"For what?"

"For being such a stalwart friend, for making my embarrassment easier to bear, and for generally making me feel bettah."

"Do you truly feel better?"

"Would I lie to you?"

"Hah! About your health?" Doc chuckled.

"Is it a lie if I really believe it?"

"Well, I suppose one could call that a delusion. But if you're delusional, then I'd have to keep you here until you come to your senses," Doc countered.

Asa sighed. "I can't win."

"It's not a contest." He leaned forward and patted the back of Asa's hand. "Don't worry. The men are just as anxious to have you back on duty as you are to be there, but they don't want you overdoing it and collapsing again. Neither do I."

"Well, as Captain Hookset said, a little humility is good for the soul. I guess I shouldn't worry so much what the men think of me."

"You were young when you were promoted, but you've proven yourself time and time again. You don't have to keep on proving yourself. The men trust in your competence. You've seen them through many a tough scrape. I think they'd like to reciprocate. How many times have I told you? You don't have to weather this storm alone."

"I guess I… well… I thought I should be able to…." Asa shook his head and turned away, feeling his face burn.

"Remember when you sang in the children's choir you told me about, with Josiah?"

Asa cleared his throat. "What's that got to do with anything?"

"Did you think you had to sing all the parts yourself?"

"No, but when called upon to sing a solo, I did it alone."

"Look at the music; listen to the choirmaster. Your solo's over. This part calls for harmony."

Asa ducked his head, then looked up and smiled. "Okay, I get the message."

"If you doubt me, why don't you try it out?"

"How?"

"Well, if you want me to trust you to keep watch for a couple of hours on your own tomorrow, then perhaps you should try going above for a little stroll, get some sunlight and fresh air. I'll bet the men will approach you, happy to see you up and around without me acting as nursemaid. If you find yourself getting wobbly, either physically or emotionally, you've got the perfect excuse to hightail it back down here. What do you say?"

Asa grinned. "I feel like I've just passed some kind of test. You bet, Doc. I'll just go brush my teeth, comb my hair, and make sure I look squared away. Best foot forward, and all that."

Doc laughed. "I'll meet you in an hour for our afternoon tea, all right? Cooky promised he'd make you something he was sure would tempt your palate."

"Well, that'll get me back, just out of curiosity to see what he's come up with," Asa said. "See ya latah, Doc."

* * * *

The first to greet him with a broad grin was Slocum, walking the deck on his afternoon watch. "Asa! Good to see you up and about! I don't mind tellin' you I missed you. Feelin' bettah?"

"Thanks, Mike. I'm feeling much bettah than I was, and I missed you, too. I'm hopin' to go back on duty tomorrow, at least for a couple of hours." Asa smiled. "Anything been happenin'?"

"Nah. Since we left Port Said, everything's been just fine. Not even a U-boat to contend with. It seems if we're left to ourselves, we do quite well. We'll be getting into Bombay soon — two, three days — so we'll see what that brings."

"That soon? Man, I've really lost track of time." Asa shook his head. "But I don't think we'll run into any trouble. I have at least one friend there."

"Only one?" Slocum said. "You've got friends all over the globe, Asa, and you've even got one in Port Said, now."

Asa snorted. "Port Said? I doubt that, Mike."

"Captain Withers," Mike said. "Just before we left, he came to see you. Too bad you were too sick to hear what he had to say. It seems his so-called nephew was wanted in India, Great Britain, and Arabia for fraud, impersonating British officers, and even murder! Captain Withers's real nephew, thank heavens, is still alive and well in India. The real identity of 'Sergeant Withers' is yet to be determined, but he is also known as Corporal Bittersby-Grimes, Sir John Ratcliffe, Ensign Byrd-Pitts, and God knows what else.

Captain Withers got a commendation for capturing him. He said it was your complaint that prodded him into action sooner rather than later."

"Is that so?" Asa smiled. "Well, I'm glad Captain Withers is finally free of him, and that his real nephew is all right."

"Ayup," Slocum answered. "The important thing, though, is that you're on the road to recovery, well enough to be walking around without Doc hovering over you. It sure is good to see you."

"I can't tell you how good it is to see you, Mike, and to be standing here on my own two legs, talking to you," Asa grinned, shook his head, and sighed.

Mike reached out and patted Asa's upper arm. "Afraid if I give you a slap on the back, I'd knock you over. Man, we gotta get some meat on those bones. When you coming back to our quarters?"

"Dunno. Doc wants me to sleep in sick bay for a while, so he can keep wakin' me up to pour eggnogs down my throat every couple of hours, to fatten me up like a Christmas goose. I guess I'll be back when I gain whatever amount of weight he judges essential before freeing me. Good to see you, Mike. I won't keep you from your duties; you'd best get on."

"Aye, aye, Mr. Mayhew," Slocum grinned. "Drink gallons of eggnog and whatever else Doc wants, you hear? We need you, my friend." He touched his cap and walked away.

Asa took a deep breath and continued his promenade toward the bow.

"Mr. Mayhew! Mr. Mayhew, how are you?" Davy ran to catch up. "I was so worried, and it's so good to see you out here in the sunshine."

Asa smiled and put his hand on Davy's shoulder. "Ah, Davy. How are *you*? I'm so sorry you had to witness... well..." He looked around. No one was within earshot.

"Doc shouldn't have... I left because I didn't want you to be... well..." Davy faltered. "I'm sorry if I did anything wrong."

"You didn't do anything wrong, and he didn't tell me you were there until I guessed it. You were trying to help, and I thank you for that. But... oh, my lad, I only wish you hadn't had to go through all that pain again."

"No, it's all right. I'm only sorry that you," Davy lowered his voice, "still have the dreams, too."

"Hardly at all, anymore." Asa said. "I wish they didn't still torment you. Is there anything I can do?"

"Mr. Mayhew, just seeing you... just knowing there's a chance... maybe I could..." Davy blushed. "Well, I know I'll never be tall, but maybe I could be like you someday... Don't you see? You give me hope, sir."

"Davy, I..." Asa looked at him, dumbstruck. He cleared his throat. "Davy, don't be like me. Be like *you*. Because you are kind, brave, good, and honorable. Be the best David Jones that you know how to be, all right? *That* shall make you an extraordinary man."

"But I'm not—"

Asa looked him in the eye.

"Aye, sir. I shall certainly try," Davy said.

"And so shall I," Asa said. "I must at least *try* to live up to your elevated opinion of me. And remember, in private conversation, when we're not on duty, you don't have to be so formal as to call me 'sir.' 'Asa' will do."

Their eyes held compassion for each other.

In the distance, a bell rang: three double chimes, and one single. It was 1530.

"I must go and relieve Yates at the helm in fifteen minutes, sir… um, Asa," Davy said.

"Of course," Asa said. "And, Davy… thanks."

"But, sir…"

"No buts," Asa raised an eyebrow.

After a pause, Davy said, "You're welcome. And you know what, um… Asa?"

"What's that?"

"You can talk to me about it, anytime it bothers you, too, okay?"

Asa blinked away a sudden blurriness in his vision. "Okay." He sniffed and tied to smile. "Bettah get yourself on duty, kiddo. I don't want you to get written up for bein' late on my account."

"Aye, sir." Davy hurried off.

Asa ducked quickly into his own nearby quarters, dried his eyes and blew his nose, and then checked his face in the mirror. He shook his head. *Damn. Turnin' into a real weak sistah. This'll nevah do.* He bathed his face in cold water before venturing out again. He told himself he'd get over this, as soon as he was well again. He would. He'd damn well better.

As he exited his cabin, he bumped into Tommy Martin, quite literally.

"Whoa, theyah." Tommy grasped him by the upper arms, and then gave him a quick hug. "Asa! Man alive, is it evah good to see you! Alive, too!"

"Ayup, I'm alive, all right," Asa forced a grin. "Thanks to Doc's hard work. Good to see you, too."

"How yah doin'? I mean, I can see you've been through hell and the devil took a strip off yah, but ah you feelin' bettah now?"

"Hah! He sure did. I am feelin' bettah, Tommy," Asa said. "Well, as you can see, at least well enough to be up and around, which is a heck of a lot bettah than a couple of weeks ago. Gettin' there. Gonna try to go back on duty for a couple hours tomorrow."

It was beginning to dawn on him that Doc was right to limit him to two hours. He'd only been out talking to people for half an hour, and he was already exhausted. But he also realized that talking to Davy about… Well, that was different, and bound to be more taxing.

"How's the ship?" Asa asked. "Everythin' workin' all right?"

"Once we got her engines all fixed up aftah that fiah, she's runnin' like a top. Knock wood," Tommy reached out and tapped on the oak hatch to Asa's cabin. "Don't you go thinkin' we don't need you, though. One reason she looks so clean and shiny is that Don and I keep tellin' the men that hahd wo'k will take their minds off worryin' about you. Tell the truth, it didn't stop us worryin', but it kept the brightwo'k bright."

Asa laughed. "Sure did. Smoked glasses would come in handy to keep us all from bein' blinded by it! You're doin' a great job. Listen, Doc's bein' pretty strict about my not engagin' in too much physical activity too soon, but whenever you've got the time, we can go back to studyin' up on the questions for the examination. That certainly doesn't take much strength. What do you say?"

"Not much strength for *you* mebbe, but my brain doesn't seem to be quite as nimble," Tommy laughed.

"Oh, come on, Tommy. To listen to you, one would think you're some kind of a dolt, and we both know that's not true. You'll pass that test with flyin' colahs. You just need a little confidence, that's all."

"All right. If Doc'll let me past the gates to his sanctum sanctorum, I'll show up sometime tomorrow, othah than between 1600 to 1800, that is."

"'Sanctum sanctorum' eh? My deah Mistah Mahtin, you just gave yourself away. No longah can you masquerade as a country bumpkin without the requisite smahts to pass this examination."

They laughed together and hugged each other, then drew hastily apart, embarrassed that their emotions had shown so plainly.

"We've been friends a long time," Asa said.

"Ten years. You were bo's'n when you were just fo'teen," Tommy said. "I was your mate at sixteen."

"Hey, at sixteen, you're lucky you weren't still an ordinary seaman, just starting out. Cap'n James saw your potential even then," Asa said.

They looked at one another and quickly stepped back into Asa's cabin.

"Jesus, Asa. I know it's nothing like… I mean, you lost so much more… but… Oh, God. I miss him."

Asa couldn't speak. He tried to turn away, but Tommy was quicker, putting his arms around him. Asa bit the inside of his cheek, struggling to control his emotions. But when he felt, more than heard, a sob escape Tommy, he broke down. He no longer felt quite so alone in his grief. He had known, intellectually, that Doc and the men had grieved with him, but this was the first time it had felt real. Tommy wept with him. Someone else knew; someone else showed that he felt something akin to what he was feeling.

When they began to pull themselves together, Asa stammered, "Tommy... I... I don't know how to thank you." He sniffed.

"For what?" Tommy ran a knuckle under his eye.

"For... for... You're the first one who has shown me honest emotion." Asa couldn't stop the tears trickling down his face. "You... you were brave enough... Oh, God, Tommy..."

Tommy quickly hugged him again, thumped him on the back, and then they both took out their handkerchiefs to mop their faces.

"I can't believe no one... no one has... Well, I guess we're all afraid to show how much... how much it hurt to lose him. And now... how much we feared we may lose you, too," Tommy said.

Asa stepped back. "What? Me, too? Did you think... But he was worth ten of me! How could—"

"Did you evah stop to think mebbe we don't see it that way?" Tommy demanded. "You weren't bo'n with a silvah spoon in your mouth. You came up the hahd way... the real hahd way. Dammit, Asa! A lot of us think..."

"Think what?"

Tommy calmed down, saying quietly, "We just think you're wo'th moah than all the Lovejoys put togethah. I know you don't think so, but we're entitled to our opinion."

"But James was more than... more than I could ever hope to..."

"I shouldn't have said that," Tommy said. "I wasn't thinkin'. You're really pale. Let me help you back to sick bay."

"Leave me be, Tommy, please." Asa brushed past him, his abruptness more out of a need to get away than out of anger. He had never considered that the men might not worship his idols as he did, or that they may feel anything of the sort toward him. Suddenly, he felt like he couldn't catch his breath, and his internal gyroscope seemed to go awry.

Rushing down the companionway, he slipped, clutching the rail just in time to prevent a headlong fall, but not in time to prevent a sprained ankle.

"Ow! *Merde!* Oh, for Christ's sake!"

Limping down the passageway, he reached up as he went through the hatch to sick bay, reminding himself to duck, but as he stepped through, his ankle gave out, and he sprawled to the deck in a heap.

Doc looked at him, shaking his head. "Good heavens, Asa! *Must* you keep punishing yourself?"

"Ugh," Asa replied, pushing himself up to his knees. "I don't *have* to, but somehow, it just happens. I dunno. Guess I'll nevah make it in the *Ballets Russes*. Two left feet."

"Come on, Twinkle Toes," Doc helped Asa up and onto the bed. "Can't trust you alone for a minute. What happened?" He proceeded to take off Asa's shoe to examine his ankle.

"Slipped goin' down the laddah, that's all. Could happen to anybody." Asa was defensive. He winced as Doc palpated and rotated the ankle.

"Uh-huh," Doc said. "Sprained it pretty good, but it's not broken. I'll wrap it up and put some ice on it. You'll have to keep it elevated until the swelling goes down. No going back on duty tomorrow." He proceeded to bandage the ankle as he talked.

"Oh, come on, Doc. It's not that bad."

Doc looked Asa in the eye. "You're putting a good face on it, but you're pale and shaking, and your eyes are red."

Asa's gaze slipped away. "It was... hahdah than I thought."

"Yes?" Doc prompted.

"I can't... talk... not right now... I, uh... need to be alone for a while. Please?"

Doc observed Asa for a minute. "All right. Just let me get an ice bag for that ankle."

He went out and came back with a tray bearing an ice bag, a pitcher of water and a glass, a twist of paper containing two aspirin, a stack of handkerchiefs, a towel and facecloth. He had a cane over his arm. He put the tray down on a table at the foot of the bed, and hung the cane over the ladder to the upper bunk.

"Now I don't want you getting out of that bed unless it's absolutely necessary." Doc elevated Asa's foot on a pillow and arranged the ice bag on it. "If you truly *must* get up, say if we get hit by a torpedo or something, use that cane. Understood?"

"Doc," Asa said through gritted teeth. "Just go. All right?"

"For an hour," Doc agreed. "I'll bring you back some supper. Try to be kind to yourself. All right?"

Biting his lip, Asa nodded stiffly, making little shooing motions with his hand. As soon as Doc was gone, he broke down weeping. Rattled and exhausted, he was aware of other disconcerting feelings roiling beneath the surface. Right now, he simply didn't have the energy to sort out what they were. After going through three handkerchiefs, he sat up and took the aspirin, and then lay down again with a damp facecloth folded over his eyes and fell into a deep sleep.

# Chapter 20

## *Seeker*

The British, Indian, and Australian forces were keeping the Turks and Germans at bay for the moment, so the Red Sea was tranquil, as was the Arabian Sea. *The Eastern Trader* encountered no further difficulties on her voyage to Bombay. After they had put into port, Captain Hookset called Asa and Doc to his office.

"Asa, I want you to go visit your yogi friend, and Doc, I want you to go with him. You can keep an eye on each other."

"Excuse me, Cap'n. Did you say you wanted us to go visit Mr. Sharma?" Asa asked.

"You heard me correctly," Captain Hookset said.

"You don't mind that Sharmaji isn't Christian?" Asa asked.

"As far as I can see, the practice of yoga doesn't conflict at all with Christianity," the captain said. "In fact, learning how to meditate deeply may enhance it. You've got five days leave."

Asa gaped at him, astonished that the captain should profess such a liberal view, and then gathered his wits to ask, "Five days? Are you sure Captain?"

"I don't think we'll be here much longer than that; do you?"

"It's only that… well, I thought you wanted to leave in three, sir."

"That would be rushing it a bit. Pack your bags and get going," the captain said.

Asa protested, "But, sir, there's the cargo to unload, and the coaling, and—"

"Cargo? Coaling? My dear young man—" Captain Hookset placed his large hand on Asa's shoulder, seeming at a momentary loss for words. "Heaven help you, since you seem so intent upon driving yourself into an early grave. And heaven help *you*, Doc, for having to deal with such a recalcitrant patient. You are both exempt from duty, effective immediately. Get yourselves underway, now."

"Aye, aye, sir," Doc said.

Feeling stupid and useless, Asa looked at feet. When Doc nudged him, he came to attention, belatedly answering, "Aye, sir."

Again, Captain Hookset shook his head. "Most men would be delighted by five days leave, but you look like you've been condemned to a firing squad. Try to enjoy your time off, will you?"

Shamefaced, Asa answered. "Aye, Cap'n. Thank you."

"Godspeed, son," the captain said.

Before they left, although Asa claimed his ankle was fine, Doc insisted upon wrapping it up tightly and that Asa use his cane.

As they headed down the gangplank, Doc said, "Five days — that was generous of him."

"You don't have to stay with me the whole time if you want to go sightseeing or something," Asa said.

"The captain wants us to keep an eye on each other, meaning he wants *me* to keep an eye on *you*."

"Humph! I don't need a—" Asa broke off, shaking his head. "Dunno why I'm bein' so touchy." His irritation vanished as he looked thoughtfully at Doc. "Prob'ly because I'm afraid I *do* need a nursemaid, and I hate that idea with a passion. No reflection on you, Doc."

"Don't fret, Asa. You *are* progressing, but it's only natural to have some ups and downs."

"Yah, yah, you keep tellin' me that," Asa grumbled.

As though Asa hadn't spoken, Doc continued, "Besides, I'm interested in meeting this friend of yours."

Chagrined by his irritability, Asa ordered himself to behave with more courtesy. "You might find him a little, um... unsettling at first, but I think you'll like him."

"'Unsettling?'" Doc asked. "How so?"

"Sharmaji is... hmm, different than the fellahs we usually meet. How shall I put it? He can be kind of... mystical, I guess you could call it." Asa shrugged. "You'll have to judge for yourself."

Walking through the crowded streets of the waterfront, where construction was beginning on the Gateway of India and the Marine Drive, they watched a dozen turbaned Sikh cavalrymen ride by on their trotting horses, with their backs bolt upright and their lances pointing skyward.

Asa coughed. Catching Doc's worried glance, he said, "Just dust. Horses," he sneezed, "stirred it up. Either that, or it's my dusty brain."

"Didn't make me cough," Doc said, "so it must be your desiccated brain. I warned you about not getting enough fluid into you."

"Is that what they call dry wit?"

"Or dried wits," Doc retorted. "Depending upon whether the subject is you or me."

"Dunno if I can fully appreciate your sun baked wits. Make that 'half-baked humor.'"

Doc laughed. "Imbalanced humors. Too much yellow bile makes me choleric. Too much black bile makes you melancholic. They're both dry humors, by the way."

"Mercy! I put my trust in a modern doctor, only to find out you've gone back to the practices of the ancient Greeks!" Asa coughed again.

Doc patted him on the back. "Need some water?" He nodded toward a standpipe across the street.

Asa shook his head. "Wait until we get there." Another cough. "That water might not be safe to drink."

After the soldiers had passed, Asa and Doc crossed the street, turned the corner, and stumbled upon a happy hubbub of haggling.

The market street was brilliant with tropical flora, mounds of brightly hued fresh fruit and spices, the women's saris in all the shades of the spectrum. Underlying the sweet scents of flowers and fruit, along with the sharp tang of spices, was the unmistakable odor of animal dung. Oblivious to the traffic and pedestrians milling around it, a humped, dirty white Brahman cow rested in the street. A small boy herded a few goats to market. Chattering, a monkey swooped down from a banyan tree to steal a banana from a fruit stall.

"I've never seen so many brilliant colors all in one place!" Doc exclaimed.

"Mm-hmm, like a rainbow fell from the sky and landed here." Asa sounded flat, as though he'd seen it all before and was just repeating a well-worn phrase.

Doc's delighted face sobered as he looked at Asa.

"What's *that* look for?" Asa challenged.

"Well, your words are okay, but you sound like my Uncle Percy when out-of-state company was gushing over a New England autumn: 'Trees. You've seen one tree, you've seen them all,'" Doc quoted. "You look exhausted. Did you get any sleep last night?"

Asa snorted at the Uncle Percy imitation. "Sorry if my enthusiasm level doesn't match yours, Doc. It *is* beautiful, but I *have* seen it before. I'm all right."

Doc raised his eyebrows.

"There's no call to look at me like that. I'm *fine*. Truly. Don't be such a mother hen."

"Let's look for a rickshaw," Doc said. "Walking puts too much stress on your ankle, and in all this crush, you might injure it again."

Asa glared at Doc, and then rolled his eyes at himself. "You're right, Doc. I'm grumpy because my ankle aches, and I shouldn't be takin' it out on you." Raising his arm, he whistled and called to a rickshaw-puller.

Sinewy and barefoot, the man seated them and then jogged along through the noisy throng until they got to the quieter outskirts of the city, and stopped before a gate in a high stucco wall. Thanking him, Asa paid, adding a generous tip.

"What is this place?" Doc's voice was hushed as they went through the open gate.

Through an overabundance of green grasses, fern-like fronds, flowering bushes, and palm trees, they ambled down a wide path toward a yellow bungalow with a porch that ran the length of it. It appeared to be the main house among several smaller buildings.

"An ashram," Asa said. "It's a kind of retreat and center for spiritual study. It's self-supporting, with a small farm.

They grow their own vegetables and keep a few goats and chickens for milk and eggs."

A man wearing loose white cotton pajamas came out to meet them. After greeting each other with "Namaste," bowing over steepled hands, Asa made introductions.

"Doc, I'd like you to meet Guru Ramachandra Sharma. Sharmaji, this is my friend, Doctor Simon Coffin."

"It is a pleasure to meet you, Dr. Coffin."

"Please, call me 'Doc.' My surname, I am afraid, makes men fear the undertaker, which is not a very good thing for a man of my profession. I am delighted to meet you, sir."

Mr. Sharma smiled. "Doc, yes, I see. I feel you are indeed a friend to Asa Mayhew, helping him to bear his sufferings."

"Well… I… um," Doc stammered, taken aback.

"Teacher, as usual, you see far more than I have told you," Asa said.

"Your face and body reveal much, my friend. May I offer my sympathy for Captain James's passing?"

Asa gasped and stood staring at him. "Um… I… uh… thank you. But how—"

"He would have been here with you, otherwise."

"Ah." Asa slumped, leaning heavily on his cane. Doc put a hand under his elbow.

"He begs your forgiveness. He simply could not bear such a protracted, inevitable death. He hopes you will understand," Mr. Sharma said.

"How do you…? How is it possible that…? Oh, God. James." Feeling dizzy, Asa bowed his head, biting the corner of his lip.

Murmuring, "It's all right. I've got you; lean on me," Doc put an arm around him.

"Let us go into the garden where it is quiet." Mr. Sharma led the way through the house to an inner courtyard surrounded on three sides by cloister-like verandas, with cushions scattered about. A purple bougainvillea climbed one wall. Borders of golden marigolds perfumed the air. Pink lotus flowers floated on a formal pool in the center of a verdant lawn, ringed by colorful flowerbeds. Delicate butterflies flitted from flower to flower, their wings of every shade: sunrise blue, moonlight green, lemonade yellow, tiger-striped orange. Beyond that, the vista opened upon a lake partly surrounded by green woods.

Indicating a group of cushions, Mr. Sharma said, "Please, sit. You shall be more comfortable if you take your shoes off."

After lowering Asa to the ground, Doc sat tailor-fashion. As he couldn't bend his ankle with all that supportive bandaging on it, Asa sat in a sort of modified half-lotus, one leg straight, the other knee bent, foot on the straight leg's thigh. In his homespun garments, Sharmaji easily sat in the full lotus position, facing Asa. It was impossible to tell how old he was, for though his face was lined and wrinkled as a walnut, he moved with the supple grace of youth.

He placed his fingertips on Asa's forehead. "Breathe, my friend. Breathe through the pain. Breathe in; expanding your lungs… Wait a moment, holding the breath in your body… Now breathe out, slowly squeezing all the air out of your lungs… Wait again, holding the emptiness… Now breathe in and repeat the process. Concentrate on nothing but your breath. Deep… and slow… In… and out… Let other thoughts drift away as you return to your breathing… in… and out… Calm and peaceful… in… and out…" He kept his fingertips on Asa's head, breathing with him to maintain the rhythm, until Asa was relaxed, sitting absolutely still, with eyes half closed.

Doc watched intently.

Mr. Sharma turned to him and spoke sotto voce. "Doctor Coffin, how long is it you shall be in port?"

Keeping his voice equally low, Doc shot covert glances at Asa. "Several days, probably, until they've finished unloading, coaling, and loading the new cargo. The captain has exempted us from duty and given us five days leave."

"I should like you both to stay here with me. I feel you have suffered much, as well. Have you not?"

Doc admitted nothing. "Asa has suffered much bereavement and pain in his life. It is difficult for him."

"I wish to be of help to you both." Mr. Sharma placed a hand on each of them, as light and swift as a butterfly's blessing. "Shall you stay?"

"Yes, thank you. He is — well, as you can see — quite depleted."

"Life is pain, Doctor Coffin. There is much suffering in the world, as you well know. But there is a path to the release from suffering, if one chooses to follow it." His accent and inflection alone seemed to lighten the darkness and weight of his words.

Doc looked toward Asa, who appeared to be in a daze, and then back at Mr. Sharma. "I'm not sure I understand."

"Perhaps Mr. Mayhew is now ready to set foot upon that path. When he awakens, we shall see."

"'When he awakens?' Did you mesmerize him? Is he in a trance?"

"The path of the seeker is the way of awakening." Mr. Sharma smiled. "Oh dear. Rather than enlightening you, I seem to have perplexed you further. It is quite all right,

Doctor Coffin. He is merely finding his center, regaining his balance, one might say. We shall not disturb him. When he is ready, he shall rejoin us. Would you care for some tea?"

Doc goggled at him for a moment and then suddenly seemed to realize Sharmaji had asked him a question. "Tea? Oh! Um, yes. Please."

Mr. Sharma gestured toward the house, and a young man came out. "Rahul, would you have tea prepared for us on the veranda, please?"

Rahul bowed his head in acknowledgment and went away in silence.

Doc looked at Asa.

"I am sure that by the time the tea is ready for us, Asa shall be ready for it," Mr. Sharma smiled.

They sat in silence for a few moments, until Asa took a deep breath and sighed. "Ah, that's better. Don't look so worried, Doc. I was just… uh… sort of… hmm… getting myself on an even keel… ah… more or less. I'm all right now. Sharmaji, I'm sorry I reacted so strongly. It's just that you took me by surprise, and I still cannot comprehend it."

"You have no need to apologize. I must admit that I cannot explain it, but perhaps we are not meant to understand — merely to accept. I was given a message. I passed it on to you. That is all. Let us leave off discussing it for the moment. I have no wish to distress you further. Come, we shall take some tea."

As Doc handed Asa his cane and helped him up, Asa said to him, "You all right? You look a bit flummoxed."

"That's because I'm *completely* flummoxed. As a man of science, I simply cannot account for something so outside the realm of substantiality."

Mr. Sharma smiled. "Admitting that is perhaps the first step towards enlightenment. You must continue in your scientific pursuits; however, for you may find much that could be of help to mankind there, as well. Should you care to learn more of spiritual enlightenment, I shall attempt a rather superficial explanation of what it means to be an awakening being, over tea. For me to teach you fully, your stay would have to be far longer than five days; your study and practice deep. Nevertheless, you may continually teach yourselves beyond that. Indeed, traveling the path to the perfection of awakened awareness is a lifelong process, but it brings much joy along the way."

\* \* \* \*

They talked during tea and after it, Mr. Sharma teaching, answering questions, and engaging them in lively discussion. Doc was intrigued and Asa rapt as he made an effort to recall past lessons and to learn more. Their discourse continued throughout supper and beyond, until Asa's fatigue began to show.

Rahul showed them to adjoining rooms in an airy wing overlooking the lake. There were identical spaces, each containing a white-sheeted bed, a small writing table, and an intricately carved wood privacy screen in the corner, behind which was a washstand with a plain white bowl and pitcher, soap, and white towels on the towel racks. Floor-length sheer white curtains drifted in a breeze coming through the open French doors.

The decor was more western than eastern in its simplicity, and Asa supposed they had been given these rooms to make Doc feel comfortable in otherwise unfamiliar surroundings.

When he and James had stayed, they had been in a different wing, altogether more ornate and colorful. He admitted to himself that, in his current mood, he found this unadorned style more easeful. He took a deep breath and stretched.

"It's all so peaceful," Doc said. "I could just drift off to sleep."

"It is perhaps best that you retire early after your strenuous journey, so you may be refreshed for a new day," Rahul said. "Should you need anything, I shall be nearby."

"Thank you, Rahul. I believe I shall follow your advice," Asa said, stifling a yawn.

"Good night, then. Namaste." Rahul smiled, bowed over his steepled hands, and left them.

"You were right, Asa. I do like Sharmaji, very much, but I must admit that his way of speaking and the things he says are all so new to me, I'm having trouble taking it all in," Doc said. "Still, I can see the potential benefits of the practices of mindfulness and meditation to medicine. And when all else fails, there's always patient forbearance."

"That one always trips me up. I try, but I fear I'm the type that always wants to rush ahead; and right now, I'm very impatient to be fully recovered, so I can do everything I used to do." Asa yawned. "Which room do you want?"

"It's too bad you can't be as patient toward yourself as you are toward the men when you're teaching them something. I know how hard it is for you, though, and I'm sorry I haven't got a magic cure in my bag. But you *are* making progress," Doc said. "Doesn't matter which room. Why don't you take this one? The bed's closer; you can just fall into it. Oh, but first, let me unwrap that ankle."

Asa lay down on the bed. The next thing he knew, Doc was shaking his shoulder.

"Asa! Wake up!"

"Ungh, wha—"

"I hate to wake you, but you'll sleep more comfortably if you get undressed," Doc said. "Here, sit up. Let me help you."

"I can do it." Asa mumbled, fumbling with the buttons of his blouse.

"You can barely open your eyes. If you'll cooperate, we can get you into bed faster, all right?"

"Mm-hmm."

Doc helped Asa out of his summer whites and into his nightshirt, and then under the covers.

"Sleep well. I'll be next door if you need me."

"Yes, mothah," Asa muttered. "Sleep well, yourself. G'night."

\* \* \* \*

Rather than sleeping, though, Doc took out his writing case and began composing a letter:

*Bombay, India*
*January 29, 1916*

*Dear Mr. and Mrs. Mayhew,*

*Please allow me to introduce myself. I am Dr. Simon Coffin, medical officer aboard the Eastern Trader. Although we have never been formally introduced, Asa speaks of you so often, I feel I know you. From what he has said, I believe you care for him as deeply as he does for you. Please do not be alarmed at my writing to you out of the blue, but the reason for my presumption shall soon become clear.*

*Knowing Asa as you do, I am sure you are aware of his propensity for stoicism and reticence when it comes to any problems he may have. Frankly, this is a breach of confidentiality on my part, but I think it is important that you know what I am about to divulge, because I doubt that he shall tell you.*

*Approximately three weeks ago, while we were still in Port Said, Asa became seriously ill with malaria. I shan't go into all the details, but suffice it to say his fever was prolonged, high, and very worrisome, and as a consequence of being unable to keep food down, he lost a great deal of weight. Grief for Captain James had already placed him at a low ebb, although he tried to hide his pain from us. With his physical strength depleted, however, and the fever affecting his mind, he has also been suffering psychological distress. All the loss he has been through in his life has seemed to come back to haunt him.*

*Although he is still quite frail, he is getting better, slowly gaining weight, and not having as many nightmares unless he is overtired or under some type of additional stress; but he still suffers frequent fatigue, insomnia, lack of appetite, and depression. I would, at times, go so far as to call it melancholia, but that, too, is slowly improving. Two days ago, he went back on light duty for two hours a day, and so far, he is handling that well (although it can be quite a task for the rest of us to prevent him from overdoing it).*

*Right now, we are in port, and Captain Hookset has given us five days leave. We are staying with Asa's friend, Mr. Sharma, and I hope that we may build up his strength with fresh food, rest, and the peaceful atmosphere here. Still, it shall take quite some time for him to return to full health.*

*When he arrives at home, he shall need your understanding and support, however much he may deny that. I would imagine you are well acquainted with his stubborn independence. It is important that he can continue to feel — and to be — independent, so please don't hover over him or be solicitous to the point of angering him. What I ask is that you simply be aware of any problems that may arise, be a support for him, and step in to help him if necessary.*

*In the meantime, I shall of course continue to do everything I possibly can for him. I have advised him to take sufficient time off to recover fully, but he has been considering the idea of leaving the merchant marine. Without Captain James, his heart seems to have gone out of it. Most of our crew have been together for quite a few years, unusual in such a transient industry,*

*but the men repeatedly sign on because they
wish to serve under Asa. It is not mere loyalty.
He is well and truly beloved by all of us. If he
decides not to come back, we shall sorely miss
him. He shall not take kindly to my having
written this, but, you see, I overstep the bounds
of propriety because of concern and affection
for him.*

*Sincerely,*
*Doc*
*Simon Coffin, M.D.*

He sealed the letter in its envelope, and stepped out to look for Rahul, who took it, saying he would place the letter in the mailbag to be picked up in the morning.

Then he lay on his bed, staring at the ceiling, wondering how best to help Asa. He hoped he had done the right thing by writing to Si and Janet, as he thought of them, having heard so much about them through the years.

A few days ago, when he'd returned to sick bay after granting Asa an hour alone, he had looked at the pile of sodden handkerchiefs and the cool cloth over Asa's eyes, and had sat watching him sleep, feeling unutterably sad. He'd leaned over to brush a lock of hair from Asa's forehead.

Asa had stirred and removed the facecloth, opening his eyes.

"Sorry, I didn't mean to wake you," Doc had said. "How are you?"

Asa had blinked a few times and had run his tongue over his teeth. "Hmm. I'll let you know after I get my eyes open."

After a moment, he had asked, "What day is it? What time is it?"

Doc had smiled. "You've forgotten so soon? You've only been napping for about an hour."

"Oh." Asa had frowned in concentration. "Ah, I remember now. I was so confused, Doc, but I think… I think I know why it was so… um… I mean… Mike, Davy, Tommy, you… yah, even you, earliah today… you're all tellin' me things… how the men feel, how you feel… and I just can't live up to all that. It's too much. I'm not… what you all seem to think I am. I can't… measure up."

"Asa," Doc had sighed. "Don't you understand? For God's sake, man. You've nothing to measure up *to*. We've all been telling you what you *already are*."

"No! No, Doc. I'm not. I'll just let you down."

"You still don't get it, do you? We know you're not perfect. You can be grumpy and abrupt; you can close yourself off. But you've got a unique — some might say eccentric — sense of humor; you make us laugh. You are a patient teacher and you are generous to a fault — not only with your wallet, but more importantly, with yourself. On the other hand, you can be… well, shall we say a little blunt at times? We don't put you up on some pedestal. We like you as you are, warts and all," Doc said. "The men are not demanding anything of you. Can't you see that?"

Asa had shaken his head and muttered, "I'm not… what you think."

Now, in the quiet night of the ashram, Doc searched for an answer. Was there anything he could do to help restore Asa's confidence in himself? No matter how long he stared at it, the ceiling offered no help. He yawned. Though by no means certain there was any such being as God, a vague notion of Pascal's wager and being at his wit's end prompted about the closest thing Doc had come to extemporaneous prayer in his adult life: "Help me to help him." On that note, he drifted off to sleep.

\* \* \* \*

Perhaps it was simply his ingrained hypervigilance toward threats, or the sound of the door clicking open, but, in the middle of the night, something startled Asa instantly awake. Listening intently in the dark, he opened his eyes. There was just enough light for him to see a shadow at the foot of the bed beginning to descend on him. Roaring, he reflexively pulled his knees up and planted his feet in the figure's chest. As Asa kicked, the attacker grabbed his hair; they rolled to the floor and struggled against each other. Asa saw a glint of steel, grabbed his adversary's wrist and slammed it against the floor, forcing him to drop the knife.

Then there was light and shouting. Doc rushed in from next door and Rahul from outside. Rahul yanked the assailant off Asa. The fellow continued to flail in Rahul's grasp as Doc helped Asa up.

"Wait, Rahul," Asa panted. "Don't… take him away… yet." He paused, his chest heaving. "I want to… question…" While catching his breath, Asa peered at the fellow struggling to get free of Rahul's impassive grip. The light revealed him to be young, probably no more than sixteen or seventeen. He was unkempt, not only disheveled from the fight, but perhaps from living rough. "Who… are you? Why would… you want to… attack me?"

"You! You killed my mother!"

Still struggling to get control of his breathing and heart rate, Asa stared at the boy, aghast. After a moment, he said, "I don't even… know you, but I… assure you, I've never purposely… killed anyone… in my entire life, especially not… a woman! Who do you… think I am?"

"You are my father! You murdered my mother so she would not reveal your shame!"

"Father!" Asa almost laughed, but realized the lad was serious, and in psychic pain. "Um, just how old… do you think I am? I'll admit, I have been… sick, but I don't look… *that* old, do I? Look again — I'm twenty-four. What are you — about sixteen, seventeen?"

Appearing confused, the young man nodded. "You are not Asa Lovejoy?"

"Asa Mayhew. I was named for Asa Lovejoy." He hoped this sick feeling was merely the aftereffects of too much exertion in the fight. "And you are?"

The boy glared at Asa, and shouted, "I have *no* name! My *father* denied me and *murdered* my mother!"

Asa suspected the boy's anger may have been more a cover for despair. The lad had worked himself up to seek revenge, only to find his target was not who he thought he was. It must have been a hell of a letdown.

"Now, wait just a minute, there," Asa said. "Who told you Asa Lovejoy was your father? Was it your mother?"

The boy spoke in a rapid-fire Indian accent. "No, I was a baby when she was killed. But I have asked many people and have searched him out at last. You were named for this… this… defiler! You carry his shame! Where is he? I must kill him to avenge my mother!"

Asa sighed. "What made you think I was him? And how did you know I was here?"

"A woman I know at the marketplace saw your ship, and then she saw you! Arrogant Americans, striding around like you own the place," the boy spat. "Almost as bad as our British overlords."

"Well, leaving the British and Americans in general out of it for now, I haven't been able to stride around since I sprained my ankle, and I do not to wish to own anyplace whatsoever." A picture of a rose-trellised cottage down the Cape, where a small auburn-haired woman smiled at him from the doorway flashed through his mind so quickly, he almost missed it. Asa shook his head. "Look, kid, I don't for one minute believe Cap'n Asa was your father or that he killed your mother. Cap'n Asa Lovejoy died five years ago. And at his age, I rather doubt… well… Anyway, the man I knew didn't have it in his character to be a rapist or a murderer. He was no libertine. He was a *good* man, and generous. If, by some distantly remote possibility, he had fathered a child out of wedlock, he'd have taken responsibility. He'd have provided for you and your mother — a house to live in, money for food, clothes, school. The man I knew would have been likely to visit as often as he could, bringing presents. He would have cared for you. He certainly would *not* have killed her. Whoever told you that is lying. So, you see, your revenge is not only too late, but misguided."

"How do I know *you* are not the one lying to me?"

"You don't. But, I tell you, I knew him. When I was orphaned, he took me in. He raised me as though I was his own, and he had no reason to be so good to me. He had nothing to gain. It was only out of the goodness of his heart.

Other than my own knowledge of the man, I admit I can offer you no proof," Asa said. "But I *do* know that revenge is never a solution to anything. It only brings more suffering, most often to generations who had nothing to do with… with whatever the supposed original offense was. I'm sorry you've suffered so much. As an orphan myself, I know it's hard." Asa coughed, putting one hand to his chest and another to his aching temple, in a momentary attempt to quell the pain. He needed to concentrate on this boy. "But my advice to you would be to give yourself a name — whatever name you like — and get on with making a life for yourself."

"Make a life for myself? How? I am untouchable, and a bastard." The boy glowered.

"It won't be easy, but it's not impossible. You're in a port city; you speak English, and you're young enough to sign on as an apprentice seaman aboard any ship — be it American, Australian, Canadian, any nation that doesn't care about your caste — should you so choose. You could learn another language. Go somewhere, anywhere you're not known. Use your imagination. Invent yourself anew." Asa began to shiver, rubbing his arms. "And now, if you'll excuse me, I'm not feeling very well. I should very much like to go back to bed."

Doc took the blanket from the foot of the bed and wrapped it around him.

"What shall I do with him, sahib?" Rahul asked.

"Ask Sharmaji. As far as I'm concerned, you can let him go. I don't think he'll attack me again." Asa turned to the boy. "Will you?"

Downcast, the boy said, "No, sahib." But then he gave Asa a defiant look. "At least, not tonight."

"Gee, thanks." Asa's teeth were beginning to chatter. "Hey, k-kid. You want to t-talk, come see me. Not t-tomorrow... day after, maybe... when I'm feelin' bettah."

The boy snarled, "Why would I want to talk to *you*?"

"Then don't. Up t-to you." Asa's shivering worsened.

"Come on, let's get you into bed," Doc said. He turned to Rahul. "Thank you for all your help. Could you please keep Mr. Mayhew from being disturbed any further tonight, if possible?"

"I beg your forgiveness, sahib. It was a... a... how do you say it? A calling of nature?" Rahul asked. "Otherwise, I would have been here to stop that boy."

"I quite understand," Doc said. "I doubt he shall trouble us further. Good night."

"Good night, sahib."

Asa called to him, "Rahul."

"Yes, sahib?"

"Where do you sleep?"

Rahul smiled. "I sit and meditate outside your door. To serve you is my choice. Sharmaji said he would allow it."

"But — why?" Despite feeling dreadful, Asa had to satisfy his curiosity.

"I am practicing the transcendental gift of generosity, sahib. Please, will you allow me to continue?"

Asa's sharp blue eyes softened as he looked at Rahul. "How could I... possibly... deny such a request? But, please... do not call me 'sahib.' C-call me... Asa. Thank you, Rahul." He put his shaking hands together, closed his eyes, and bowed his head. "Namaste."

"Namaste," Rahul bowed. "Rest now, Asa Mayhew."

Sitting beside him, Doc rubbed Asa's arms, trying to warm him.

"Damn… I'd thought these… chills and fevers were… over and done with."

"Patient forbearance, dear friend. I know it's just about the hardest thing for you to practice, but you know malarial fevers can be recurrent, and they may come and go for a while, until the disease burns itself out. And as ill as you have been, you just successfully fought off an attacker whose sole purpose was to kill you!" Doc said. "What do you expect of yourself? Superhuman perfection?"

Pulling the blanket tighter, Asa half smiled. Violent shivering impeded his speech. "I d-did, d-didn't I? Even with a t-twisted ankle, I ki-kicked him off me, and then disarmed him. Not t-too bad, after all, eh?"

"Jeez, here I've been, wracking my brains about how to restore your self-confidence." Doc wrapped his arms around Asa to try to ease his shaking. "And along comes this guy… Well, if I'd known it was going to be that easy, I'd have attacked you myself, a long time ago!"

"Hah!" As Asa's shivers abated and as he began to sweat, he said, "You know, it might have been George."

Doc got up to prepare a cool, damp cloth to help bring down the fever that followed the chills. "What might have been George?"

"It could have been… 1898 or '99, when that… kid was born. Cap'n Asa was still… trying to make George get accustomed… to the sea…. I was only seven, but I remembah… hearin' my fathah… talkin' to some othah men… about a… a disastah involvin' Geo'ge that had to be… hushed up. There was… a lot of money changin' hands… It was… to do… with India. Dad was real… angry; said Geo'ge should've been… prosecuted."

"You're panting. Slow down and take a deep breath," Doc said.

Asa's attempt at a deep breath turned into a coughing fit. Doc patted his back and handed him a glass of water.

"Thanks. Of coss, I didn't… undahstand it… and I might've got it all wrong. And I am biased. Still… aftah that, Geo'ge nevah went back… to sea." Asa gasped. "Doc… ah!"

"What is it?"

"Oh, God… it hurts."

"Easy, now." Doc helped Asa to lie back. "Where does it hurt? Show me."

Asa put one hand over his midriff and one on his head. "Here… and I've got… one hell of a… headache."

"In the fight, did he hit you here?" Doc began to examine him.

"Happened too fast." Asa sucked in a breath as Doc touched a tender spot. "Don't remembah."

Doc lightly palpated his liver and spleen. "Hmm. With malaria, the liver and spleen can become enlarged, but—"

Asa flinched. "But what?"

"Did you have any symptoms before you got so sick? Anything you brushed off as unimportant? Any chills or fever?"

"Nunno… Nothing like that," Asa said. "Doc, could I… please… have a couple of… aspirin… for this… headache?"

"Of course! I'll just get my bag," his voice faded as he walked away. When he came back, he handed Asa the aspirin and a glass of water. "Damn it, where is my mind? You *finally* confess, of your own free will, to being in pain and ask for my help. And where am I? Off in the clouds, wondering if— Oh, hell."

After swallowing the aspirin, Asa took pity on him. "Wondering if you… might have caught this… sooner…" He took a few breaths, holding up a hand to preclude any interruption. "Well, you… didn't miss anything because… there wasn't anything to miss."

"Asa…"

"Wait," Asa took a few more breaths. "And if you… examine my middle in the… full light of day, I'm sure you'll see… some bruises there… from that fellah's fists… all right? Stop… doubting yourself."

"Humph! I might offer you the same advice," Doc said.

"What do you—" Asa cut himself off as understanding dawned. "Oh."

"And stop doubting the men's opinion of you. They're not suckers, and you're no P.T. Barnum. All right?"

"Ayuh," Asa took another breath. "Ah, my head… worse than… migraine… both sides…" Sweat poured off him. "Doc?"

"I'm here, Asa." Doc put his hand over Asa's. "What is it?"

"Don't… leave me."

"I'm staying right by your side." He took out his stethoscope. "I'm just going to check your heart and lungs, all right?"

"Yah." Asa didn't understand why this sudden terror had come over him. Maybe because he'd been too sick to care before. Maybe after a few days of feeling better, he'd begun to believe Doc had cured him, and this recurrence blindsided him.

"Mm hmm, good. Your heart and lungs are strong enough. I can give you some morphine for the pain."

"I don't want to… be knocked out. Much as I… hate… to admit it, I'm… scared. I need to… ah… stay conscious."

"Your pallor, diaphoresis, and tremor, along with that distressed look on your face, tell me that you're in agony. You truly do not need to suffer so much. I'll stay with you."

Although Asa tried to suppress it, a low moan escaped him. "Remembah… when you asked about… 'Haply I may not live another day'?"

"You're not dying," Doc said. "I won't let you."

"Good… because… I don't… want to." Asa gasped. "Strangely… enough."

"You do *not* have to go through such torment," Doc said. "Let me give you some morphine. It won't hurt you."

"You'll keep me… alive? You promise? Ah!" He clutched his head with both hands, eyes narrowed against the lamplight.

"Do you doubt me, Asa? For Christ's sake, I promise."

"No, Doc… I trust… All right."

Doc gave Asa a shot and then sat beside him. "Close your eyes and sleep, now. When you wake, you'll feel better."

## Chapter 21

## *The Boy With No Name*

Although Asa had asked him to return in two days, the boy came back the next day. Hearing Rahul tell him to go away, Asa called out, "Rahul, let him come in." Taking no chances, Rahul accompanied the boy.

Sitting up in bed, Asa addressed Rahul, "I'm feeling better than I was last night. I'll talk to the lad for a short while. I don't believe he still means to hurt me, but you may stay if you wish."

Patting the edge of the bed, he turned to the boy. "Come and sit down, so we don't have to shout across the room. All right?"

The boy hesitated; but then, head down, he inched across the room. He sat at the foot of the bed, angled to face Asa, but looked at his hands and began to fidget.

Asa copied the boy's movements. "'This is the church; this is the steeple; open the doors and see all the people.' I remember playing that, when I was a child in Sunday school. Were you in a Christian orphanage?"

The boy nodded.

The complete reversal from the angry fellow of last night to this shy child who seemed to want to curl up and disappear perplexed Asa. Had he come only to sit, withdrawn and mute?

"Is there something I can do for you?" Asa asked.

The boy shook his head.

"Why did you come?"

The boy shrugged.

Asa sighed. "They must have given you a name at the orphanage. Will you tell me what it was?"

After a long silence, he said, "David."

"May I call you David?" Asa asked.

No answer.

"It's a good name," Asa said. "Do you know what it means?"

David shook his head.

"It means 'beloved,'" Asa said.

"What does 'Asa' mean?" David challenged.

Asa smiled. "It means 'healer.' Kind of ironic, considering my condition, wouldn't you say?"

"Wouldn't you say that 'beloved' is ironic also, given that I'm an untouchable and an orphan?" Anger flashed in the boy's eyes.

"Ah, there's the lad I recognize from last night," Asa said. "Perhaps now you'll tell me why you wanted to see me?"

"I know now you are *not* my father." David ducked his head. "I apologize for attacking you and beg your forgiveness."

"Well, even though you knocked me for a loop, I understand that you were feeling quite... hmm, aggrieved. Why don't we start all over again with a clean slate?"

"What does it mean, 'knocked for a loop,'" the boy asked. "And what is 'a clean slate'?"

Asa smiled. "It means to upset someone, either physically or mentally — or both. So I guess we were both quite upset. A 'clean slate' is to erase what went on between us before now, and start fresh. David — do you mind my calling you David?"

"It is the name *they* gave me." His resentment came to the fore in rapid, emphatic speech. "The name my *mother* gave me I *cannot* remember. I was only *two* years of age when she was killed."

"I am sorry that you were so young to be without a mother," Asa spoke with deliberate calm. "Far too young. But will David do for now? At least until you choose a name for yourself, or find out what your mother named you? I would like to call you something, and 'hey, you!' seems a bit rude."

"I suppose it will have to do. I cannot choose another name until I know who I am."

"Ah. It has to fit," Asa said. "Is that right?"

"Yes. But I do not know how… how to…" The boy threw his hands in the air in a gesture of frustration and confusion.

"Maybe when I'm feeling better, we can go out exploring, to see if we can find out who you are," Asa said. "Would you like to do that?"

For the first time, the boy looked directly at Asa, and the darkness that had clouded his countenance seemed to lift. "Perhaps." He paused. "Perhaps *that* is why I came here today. I was not entirely sure."

Asa smiled. "In that case, come back tomorrow. I'm afraid I don't have the energy to go exploring today. All right?"

"Yes, I shall return tomorrow," the boy said. "In the morning?"

"After breakfast," Asa said. "Are you staying here?"

"Sharmaji has asked me to stay, but I am not sure about this kind of study — for myself."

"Why not give it a try? If nothing else, you might learn how to overcome the pain of all that anger." Asa shrugged. "And at least you'll have a roof over your head and food to eat until you decide what *is* right for you."

The boy sighed. "Perhaps."

"See you tomorrow."

The boy nodded and went out.

\* \* \* \*

Doc came in with a tray. "Brought you some dinner. They said it was something called dal, but it looks like a kind of lentil stew, rice, and this flatbread they call roti. It's very good — spicy. I think you'll like it. And it doesn't take much chewing, so eating it shouldn't exhaust you."

Asa laughed. "Doc, 'dal' is the word for lentils, but I agree, the way they prepare them is quite tasty. Thank you." After a few bites, he said, "You missed my visitor."

"Visitor?" Doc raised his eyebrows.

"David, the boy from last night," Asa said.

"Oh, so he *does* have a name," Doc said.

"Well, it's the name they gave him in the orphanage. He doesn't seem to like it very much, even after I told him its meaning. To him, it's something that was forced upon him, something that took away the name his mother gave him," Asa said.

"What does it mean?" Doc asked.

"Beloved — you didn't know that?"

"Oh, yes. I recall hearing something like that about an eon ago, when I was a child, and forced to learn my religious lessons," Doc said.

Asa grinned. "Thirty years constitutes an eon, now? My, how quickly *tempus fugit.*"

"Oh, I'm *much* older than that. I went to school with Methuselah."

Asa snapped his fingers. "Thirty-three."

"You got it. Actually, my classmate's full name was Geoffrey Methuselah. Said he was descended from the old man, but I rather think he was pulling our legs," Doc winked.

Asa laughed. "Man, you can spin them."

"Well, I try my best, but I could never top you, and Mike Slocum's got me beat by a mile. At least I got a laugh out of you," Doc said. "On a more serious note, David didn't try to attack you again?"

"Nunno. He was quite diffident and had trouble saying anything at all, at first. Rahul was here, though I didn't need protection. You'll get to meet him for yourself, in a different light. He's coming back tomorrow. Maybe we'll go for a walk," Asa said.

Doc sighed. "*If* you have no further setbacks and your stamina has increased. And I'll accompany you, whether he likes it or not."

"Well, I don't know what face he'll present tomorrow," Asa said, "but today, he just seemed like a vulnerable child. He's had a hard life, Doc. And he apologized. Let's give him the benefit of the doubt, all right?"

"All right. Finish your dal before it's stone cold."

"Aye, aye, Doc." He proceeded to eat, enjoying his food, much to Doc's expressed delight.

A few minutes later, Sharmaji arrived. "Please, do not let me interrupt your meal. You must eat if you are to get well, my friend."

Asa chewed and swallowed, then dabbed his mouth with the napkin. "You're not interrupting, Sharmaji. That was my last bite. Please give the current batch of students working in the kitchen my compliments. It was delicious." He put his plate aside.

Doc beamed. "You don't know how high a compliment that is, Sharmaji. You've no idea how long I've been trying to force food down his throat, and this is the first time I've seen him eat with unfeigned pleasure."

Asa said, "Aside from fatigue, I do feel a great deal better today, Doc. Do you think last night might have been the crisis that finally turned things around?"

Doc shrugged. "One can always hope."

Asa turned to Sharmaji and said, "Doc isn't being gloomy. He doesn't want me to get my hopes up only to feel crushed with disappointment if the fevers and chills recur. All the same, he knows that *I* know that malaria can't be so easily predicted."

Doc gave Asa a wry look. "You read me so easily."

"I am sorry I did not attend to you last evening, when you were so ill," Sharmaji said. "I knew, however, that Doc and Rahul were with you, and I thought perhaps the boy needed me more. I understand he came to see you this morning? I requested he wait until you had time to recover. I regret that I was not more persuasive in restraining him."

"Nunno, it's quite all right. I'm glad he came. Perhaps together we may discover the mystery behind his birth and in the process of searching, he may discover who he is," Asa said.

Sharmaji sighed. "As it is, he believes his father to be a killer, so he tried to be a killer. And you, my dear Asa, will persist in the active route, like a police detective, when it is looking within that teaches us who we are. You do know that who the father is — or was — has not terribly much to do with who the boy is, unless he chooses to believe it so."

"Did I say that?" Asa grinned. "It is *in the process of searching* that he may discover who he is. We may have to cloak it in the activity of an investigation in order to get him to agree to begin that process, but eventually, I believe he'll come to find himself. And then he shall be able to give himself a name that he feels 'fits' what we have — *he* has — discovered. I can only hope to get him started on the quest, as I'll only be here for a few more days, but I was hoping…" He gave Sharmaji an inquisitive look.

Sharmaji laughed. "You are feeling much improved, I see." Then he looked seriously at Asa and said, "It is well you seek to help the boy to discover himself, but I must caution you not to do so as an escape from your own inner journey. You do understand this, do you not? Your health depends upon it."

Asa contemplated this for a moment, and then answered, "I wish I could stay longer with you for the benefit of your guidance, Sharmaji. It is so much easier to help another to navigate the path than to light one's own way in the dark, is it not?"

Sharmaji held Asa's gaze for a few moments, and then nodded. "If you are feeling up to it, I am giving a lecture on mindfulness at two o'clock in the main hall. I invite you both to attend. And now, please forgive me for this short visit, but I must go and prepare for it."

# Chapter 22

# *The Search*

"How do you feel today, Mayhew sahib?" The boy had bathed and dressed in clean, homespun clothes. Asa thought Sharmaji must have given them to him.

"Much better, thank you, David-for-now. I hope you are feeling as well as you look. Have you eaten breakfast?" Asa took the last sip of his coffee.

"Yes, sahib. I feel well and I have eaten breakfast. And you? Would you like more tea?"

Asa smiled. "Thank you, no. I prefer coffee, but the coffee here… well, let's just say it leaves a lot to be desired, if you know what I mean."

"I do *not* know what you mean, sahib."

Asa laughed. "It means it's not very good. Call me 'Asa', or if that name bothers you, how about just 'Mayhew?' I don't particularly care for 'sahib.' It makes me feel like some kind of imperialist with a superiority complex." Seeing the boy's puzzled expression, he attempted to explain. "I'm not your better, lad. There's no caste system in my world. We're equal, all right?"

"Equal? I do not understand. There is no caste system? Do you not think Brahmins are better? Do you not think untouchables are the lowest of the low? Do you not think whites are better? Do you not think the English have a right to rule by virtue of their superiority?" Curiosity tempered the boy's sarcastic bite. "What kind of world is your world?"

"Is that what you were taught in that so-called 'Christian' orphanage?" Asa shook his head and sighed. "Well, *I* was taught that we are all the same in God's sight. My world? I'm an American. But that doesn't really explain it, does it? There are Americans who believe whites are better. *I* believe they're wrong. There are Americans who believe people with money are better than people without. I believe *they're* wrong. There are American men who believe they are better than women, so women shouldn't have the right to vote. I believe they are wrong. In *my* world, *all* people are equal — men, women, every color of the rainbow, rich, poor, and everyone in between. Someday, perhaps everyone shall know that as the truth, especially those who profess to believe in God — but that's another argument for another day. So, in the world according to me, we're *equal*, okay?"

The boy looked skeptical. "What is 'okay'?"

"Sorry," Asa grinned. "It's American slang. In this context, it means 'all right.'"

The boy smiled. "Perhaps you are doolally, but it is oh-kay with me. Oh, 'doolally' is the new English slang from this war. It comes from the military mental institution at Deolali—"

Asa grinned. "Ayup, the hospital down the road a piece. And despite not being in this war yet, perhaps I am doolally. But because such a war exists, so is most of the world, far as I can tell. The point is, I'm on your side. So don't call me 'sahib,' okay?"

"Oh-kay, Mayhew," the boy said. "What do we do today?"

"Because he's worried about me, Doc's coming with us. He's just in the next room, makin' sure he has prepared his medical bag for every conceivable sort of emergency, and then we'll go find the woman who told you about my ship — and me — coming into port. Do you know where she is?"

The boy suddenly became anxious. "No, I... I do not want to get her into trouble."

"No trouble," Asa said. "Why would I want to get her into trouble? All I want is to trace back these rumors as to who your father might be, and we need to start somewhere. You *do* want to find out — don't you?"

"I... yes. She was in the market yesterday, selling spices. It is near the construction of the Gateway of India."

"Ah, yes. Doc and I walked through there. Is it one market day a week, or is it still going on?"

"They may have moved to another place today. I do not know," the boy said.

"Well, we can try going back there. If they've moved on, we'll see if anyone can tell us where," Asa said.

Doc came in, carrying his medical bag. "Ready, men? Don't forget your cane, Asa."

"You must use a cane?" the boy asked.

"Didn't I tell you? Sprained my ankle aboard ship. Didn't help it any, kicking you in the ribs," Asa smiled. "How are they, by the way?"

"My ribs are fine, thank you."

"Humph! That's more than I can say for mine," Asa said.

"Please forgive me, sahib," the boy hung his head.

"Hey, chin up, and no more 'sahib.'" Asa lifted the boy's chin with his finger. "We've got work to do. Okay?"

"Oh-kay, Mayhew," the boy grinned.

\* \* \* \*

At first, they thought they were in luck. The market was still going on, and the woman was still there selling spices. Her reaction to the boy showing up with his American companions was anything but fortuitous, however; she seemed to draw back from the boy, and looked upon them with suspicion.

"What do *you* want?" she demanded of Asa.

"I was wondering if you could help this lad—"

Asa got no further. A wild-looking woman shoved between him and Doc. She screamed at the spice-seller in a dialect that was difficult for Asa to follow at such a rapid clip.

"Oh, God," Asa muttered. "She thinks the spice-seller killed her son. I think he's—"

"Bai," Asa addressed her in her own dialect. "Your son—"

The woman flared up at the spice-seller with violent gestures, deaf to Asa's words.

"Your son—" he tried again.

But she couldn't hear him, too wrapped up in her own anger.

"Doc, get the boy away from here, quick!"

Doc tried to pull David away, but he was too late. The boy had heard and understood. His mother was not dead at all. She was the mad woman, shrieking at the spice-seller, hitting her, pulling her hair, and threatening to kill her.

The boy pulled on her arm. "Mother, Mother, I am here! I am not dead! I thought *you* were dead, and have sought to avenge you!"

The spice-seller was yelling back, "What else could I do? You took him with you to wander about in the woods. You would have let the boy starve! I could not take care of him; I had nothing. The orphanage was the only place he could go to survive! You were so crazed; you'd have killed him and yourself!"

"You! You turned me over to the police! You put me in the worst prison for the lowest of the low — an untouchable woman like me! The horrors I had to endure! I will kill you!"

The woman's arm rose. Metal glinted in the sunlight.

"Doc, knife!"

While Asa tried to shield David, Doc tried to get the knife, but in the woman's frenzy, she moved too fast for Doc to catch hold of her.

The woman flew at the spice-seller. The spice-seller grabbed her wrist with both hands and tried to knock the knife away. They yelled and kicked one another. Still, the woman did not let go of the knife.

Asa grabbed David's arm, but couldn't hold him. The boy leapt into the fray, screaming, "No, Mother!"

She didn't hear him.

"Mother! I am not dead! Look at me!" He dodged in front of her and into the path of her slashing knife. Blood sprayed from his neck as he crashed to the ground like a felled tree.

"Asa, compress!" Doc dropped to his knees beside the boy, applying pressure with one hand. He searched for a pulse with the other, and put his ear to the boy's chest to listen for a heartbeat.

Asa grabbed a wad of bandaging from Doc's bag and pressed it to the spurting wound.

The spice-seller bent over them, fright and sorrow chasing each other across her features.

The other woman screamed and jumped on her back. "My son! What have you done?"

"What have *I* done? *You* have just cut him!" the spice-seller yelled.

The knife flashed again. The spice-seller let out an aborted cry and fell. She lay dead, stabbed through the heart.

"Oh, my God," Asa gasped. The world spun, and he thought he would vomit, but he swallowed and kept his hands firmly on the compress.

The woman stood, hand clutched around the bloody knife. She looked at the bodies on the ground, uncertain. Appearing to notice the boy for the first time, she said hesitantly, "Aahva?"

Asa nodded.

"Aahva!" she cried, stricken. She threw herself across the boy.

"Get out of the way, woman! I am a doctor. Let me try…" Doc shoved her aside and resumed his ministrations. He pounded on the boy's chest once, twice, trying to start the heart. He listened, and tried again.

Asa tried to hold back the hysterical woman with one arm while maintaining pressure on the wound. Blood leaked around the compress, pooling in the dirt.

"Doc, is he alive?" Asa was desperate, close to tears.

Doc checked for a pulse at wrist and neck. He put his ear to the boy's chest once more, and then gave Asa a hopeless look and shook his head.

Asa got up. His vision swam before his eyes as a heat shimmer on a scorching summer road. A jostling, cacophonous crowd surged forward to see what had happened, and then back in horror. Whistles blew, horses parted the crowd, and policemen surrounded them.

In all the pandemonium, with all the blood, Asa stood paralyzed, dazed, as sight and sound began to recede. His grasp on the woman slackened, and she slipped away from him.

A scream rent the air. "Aieee! Aahva!" The boy's mother's knife flashed once more as she plunged it into her own breast.

"No, no," Asa agonized. "No, no, no."

Doc could do nothing. As with the spice-seller, the knife had slipped between the ribs and directly through the heart, stopping it instantly. He held Asa up; perhaps more accurately, they leaned into each other, blood-spattered, pale, and shaken to the core.

Despite their condition, they were roughly hustled off to the station to "help the police with their enquiries" in separate interrogation rooms.

* * * *

Doc, in his cell, answered the interrogator: No, we didn't know the women at all, had never met them before. We only met the boy the other night when he barged into Mr. Mayhew's room believing Asa to be his father, but when we lit the lamps, he could see that was impossible. He came back the next day and apologized. We were only trying to help him trace his parentage. I thought it was too much for my friend, because he has been so ill, but he is soft-hearted that way. What? Oh, malaria. He only wanted to help the boy, certainly not to harm him. No, we had never seen the women before, didn't even get to know their names. We were trying to trace the rumor to its source, and perhaps discover the truth. Apparently, we blindly stumbled into a situation that had been brewing since this boy was an infant — since he was born.

\* \* \* \*

In another grim cube, Asa told his story: No, I hadn't seen either one of the women until this morning. The boy came to me the other night, thinking I was his father. As you can see — perhaps you can't, though — I admit to having aged ten years in the last ten minutes. At any rate, he was mistaken. I'm not nearly old enough. I only wanted to help him find out who his family was. Obviously, I failed the poor lad. His name? He said they called him David, at the orphanage. The woman — you heard her? Called him Aahva, just before… just before she… We tried to stop her. But it happened so fast. Oh, God. Oh— Pardon me, I didn't quite hear— Steady on, indeed. No, I'm fine. Just a little rocky. Could you please repeat that? Oh, yes, I've had malaria… No, please don't touch me. I'm all… covered in… Oh, God.

\* \* \* \*

Their answers corroborated each other's, and when the officers who had been sent to question Rahul and Sharmaji at the ashram returned, and further attested to their truth, Asa and Doc were at last released.

Asa was taut, his jaw clamped shut, when Doc met him outside.

Doc whistled for a taxi, a rickshaw, for any conveyance that might answer. It seemed they had suddenly become pariahs, at least as far as the hackneys were concerned.

"We've got to move… away…" Asa swayed, and managed to stagger a few steps to a clump of bushes before his breakfast came up. He fumbled for his handkerchief. "Oh, damn. Sorry."

"Well, at least you missed getting any on either of us. Not that it matters." Doc looked at their bloodstained uniforms. "Were you trying to say no one will pick us up from in front of the police station?"

"Yah. Got to… sit down." Asa's knees began to buckle.

Doc quickly supported him. "Not here. I've got you. There's a bench across the street. Can you make it that far?"

Asa nodded.

"Put your arm around my shoulder," Doc said. "Hang on. Here we go." He steered them through a break in the human, animal, and motor traffic and zigzagged them safely across to the bench. "All right, now, lean forward. Head between your knees. Lower. I won't let you fall." After a minute, he said, "Your color's coming back a little. Still dizzy?"

"Not as much," Asa started to sit up.

"Stay down just a minute longer." Doc put his hand on Asa's back. "And then sit up very slowly."

"I'm such an arrogant bastard," Asa said.

"Um… I'm not following you," Doc said. "Why?"

"Because I thought I could fix that poor boy's… life, and look what… happened. Oh, God — it's my fault! I should have—"

"What?" Doc said. "Should have been able to foretell the future? Christ, Asa! Haven't we talked about this kind of thing before? There's no way you're to blame. You're just making yourself sick with guilt that doesn't belong to you. Stop it. Just *stop* it, now."

A single sob escaped Asa, and then he grit his teeth. Doc rubbed his back. "I know you cared about the boy, and you were trying to help. What happened was gruesome, horrendous. But you have *nothing* for which to reproach yourself. It was *not* your fault. This course of events was set in motion long before you ever came on the scene. Do you understand?"

"I need... to go... home," Asa whispered.

"We'll get a taxicab soon." Doc craned his neck to look for one.

"Taxi... won't take me... to Wellfleet," Asa said.

Doc rubbed Asa's back as his eyes filled with sympathy.

\* \* \* \*

When they got back to the ashram, Asa insisted he'd be fine after a bath and a short rest, but Doc insisted the rest be a long one.

Sharmaji agreed with Doc, and went on to suggest that Doc claim the bath next, and take a nap for himself. "A warm bath shall help to relax those tight muscles, and I should think a rest is in order after all you've been through."

After he had scrubbed his body, hair, and teeth a few times over, and once more for good measure, Asa got into bed. Still, he kept seeing the blood on his own futile hands after he'd tried to stop the boy from bleeding out in the street.

Sharmaji came in to sit with him. "How are you, my son?"

"I've never... Sharmaji, I've seen a lot of sights in my sixteen years at sea, but..." Asa shook his head, at a loss for words. "It was… I can't… describe… I can't… can't… comprehend…" He gestured, palms upward, and stared at his hands for a moment. "It was all… too fast… and yet… somehow… it's still… happening. It was over like…" Asa snapped his fingers. "No time to react… Three people dead, in… in… in minutes." As though to shake off the sight, he shook his head again. "Not… not men at the front… just… two women and a boy. The… the senselessness!" Asa's eyebrows came together over eyes like a turbulent sea. "I couldn't… couldn't save the boy. Couldn't have saved any of them. What a… What a… Oh, God."

"Yes," Sharmaji said. "I'm sorry you had to witness such a thing."

"If I hadn't interfered in that boy's life—"

"No, Asa. Do *not* take that on yourself. It was terrible, but such things are not unheard of. We have the stress of living under a colonial power, the strict division among classes that oppresses some people unbearably, so many people fighting over scraps, and now — war on top of it all. This poor woman was made a pariah, her son taken away; she was jailed and abused. She did not know how to live with any of these things, and her mind became deranged. If she had not come into the marketplace today, perhaps we could have saved her son, but," Sharmaji spread his hands in a shrug, "perhaps not. You feel very bad, my friend, but think of this: you gave him hope, for at least a day, and that is more than he had felt for his entire life. And in the end, although he did not discover who his father was, he found his mother — alive, for a short while, at least."

"I am sorry, Sharmaji; I can take no comfort in that. That poor boy. His death was so… so… meaningless. It never should have happened. Neither one of the women should have died. It just… it just…"

"The men fighting in this senseless war now… do their deaths have meaning? We wrap them up in the various flags of the opposing countries and make heroes out of them all, but that is, as I think we both know, window dressing to cover up the ugliness and waste of it all," Sharmaji said. "On the other hand, we all have to die. And none of us — or at least not many of us — can choose when, how, or why. Death, my dear friend, is simply a fact of life. A transition. Sometimes, it can be dreadful. At other times, it is peaceful, a blessed release. It is harder for those of us left behind to lose a loved one, or for those, such as you and Doc, who witness such a terrible thing. But for the dead — they are no longer beset by the troubles of this world. It is even possible that their next life may be a better one."

"Sometimes, I envy them," Asa blurted out. "I didn't mean—"

Sharmaji put his hand on Asa's arm. "It is completely understandable, especially with the world in such dire straits right now. And I know you don't mean to be ungrateful for life, and you would never hurt your friends by taking your own life. But after a day such as this… indeed, after all you've been through… it does not surprise me that you should have occasional feelings such as this."

"Thank you, Sharmaji, for your kind understanding," Asa said.

Sharmaji shook his head indulgently. "My dear Asa, have I not known you since you were not much older than that poor boy? Did you not stumble across my doorstep when you were out exploring and got lost, and did not Captain James come looking for you and stay with us for a while? And did you not both come back, year after year, to seek learning? What kind of friend would I be, had I not garnered some understanding of you in all that time?"

Tears began to flow down Asa's cheeks. He could not stop them. Embarrassed, he turned away.

"You miss James, and would particularly wish him to be by your side now. There is no shame in those tears," Sharmaji said. "Breathe. Simply breathe. Do you recall what one of your English saints said? *It behooved that there should be sin; but all shall be well, and all shall be well, and all manner of thing shall be well.*[31] All shall be well. Breathe."

Asa wheezed out an attempt at a laugh. "Oh, sure. Leave it to you to quote a fourteenth century English saint, of all things. And may I remind you," he coughed, "I'm not English, but American. What the hell did Juliana of Norwich know, anyway? Another saint with delusions. I'm sorry, Sharmaji. I simply cannot believe that all shall be well. Neither shall all be evil, at least I hope not. It's more likely to be a mixture of both."

Sharmaji smiled. "You are quite correct. But you do know that Juliana was not talking of earthly life. She had been through a terrible illness and nearly died. She believed she saw Jesus, and felt great ecstasy, and thereafter lived with joy in her soul, no matter how great her suffering. Who are we to say her experience was delusional?"

"Well, all right, but sightings of otherworldly beings, especially at the height of a fever, are quite suspect to me. Back then, they believed these things because they had no real medical or scientific knowledge."

"The Buddha, having been brought up as a pampered prince, protected from the world, was very disturbed when he first went out and discovered such great suffering everywhere. He then spent a good deal of his life in self-sacrifice and suffering in an attempt to find holiness. After many years of searching, he finally discovered that we each hold within ourselves the capacity to overcome suffering and become a force for good, not through fasting or excoriating oneself, but through selfless love and compassion. You *tried* to be a force for good, Asa, and that is *enough*. You cannot control the outcome, especially when you are dealing with the frailty of human nature."

"The outcome was that three people *died* suddenly, violently, horribly. That is *not* all right. I feel as though I caused it by blundering into a situation I didn't understand. I didn't question the lad further when he was at first hesitant. I pushed him to go and meet the spice-seller." Asa gestured with his hands, ending with his palms upwards, as if in supplication.

"You could not foresee the outcome. Put *down* this burden of guilt, my friend. It is *not* yours to carry," Sharmaji said.

"Then whose is it?" Asa demanded. "The mysterious father who abandoned him? The societal pressures that helped to drive his mother mad? The woman who only wanted to save the child, but perhaps put him in the wrong orphanage? The orphanage for instilling in the boy that he would never be good enough, no matter how hard he tried? In the end, I was the last straw that broke that camel's back; wasn't I?"

"Fault is not the issue; nevertheless, you are not to blame. Life, as you well know, is cyclical. Whether it is our collective life in society or the life of the cosmos, there is birth in innocence, a gradual decline into corruption and death, and then rebirth, when everything is made new again. It was simply time; nothing to do with you," Sharmaji said firmly. "And as I said previously, you perhaps gave the boy a day or so of hope that he had never known before."

"What? Are you saying that because of the cosmogonic cycle, I escape any responsibility? I don't buy that. Just because there may be massive events beyond our control, that doesn't preclude our individual obligation to be our brother's keepers. I failed him," Asa said. "He's dead because of it."

"Yes, we are responsible for our own actions and must do our best to help others. But no, Asa, you did not fail him. You are not a god, that you could control the circumstances or the outcome. You are a man who did the best you know how to do," Sharmaji said. "That is enough. You are distraught. Some deep breathing may help to calm you. Shall we breathe together for a while?"

Asa broke down weeping, and Sharmaji held him. "Let it go, my son. It is all right. It is all right."

Dressed in a robe over his nightshirt, Doc came in with a glass containing an ounce of medicinal brandy for Asa, into which he placed a few drops of laudanum. "Sorry to interrupt, but this may help, especially if he is unable to calm himself by breathing."

Sharmaji hesitated. "It will not harm him?"

"Not if he doesn't get habituated, and I'll see to it he doesn't," Doc said.

"Asa," Sharmaji said. "Perhaps you should drink what Doc has brought you. I hate to see you in such needless pain."

Asa pulled away from Sharmaji and shook his head. "No… no laudanum." He dried his eyes and blew his nose, but kept drawing in his breath in rapid gasps, trying to stop crying. He looked down at the blanket. He wished he could disappear or, failing that, that they'd go away and leave him to bury his head under the covers in misery and mortification.

"Come on, just a drop in a little brandy," Doc said. "It will help you to get the rest you need."

Asa gave in and allowed Doc to give him the drink. After a few minutes, he was able to take some deep breaths to calm himself.

"Better?" Doc asked.

Asa nodded. "I apologize."

"For what?" Doc said. "I was there, remember? I damn near went to pieces, and I'm a doctor, used to blood and gore. I cried, too, in the bath."

Asa shook his head.

"Asa, I meant to ask you, what did she mean, when she called out, 'Aahva'?"

"His name," Asa said. "It means 'beloved.'"

# Chapter 23

# *Long, Too Long*

*Bombay, India*
*February 1, 1916*

*Dear Si,*

*I would rather you not read this aloud or share it with Janet until you have read it yourself. Several times, I have begun a letter to you, only to abort the attempt in despair of finding anything good to say. I do not wish to worry you unnecessarily; yet, I feel that I owe you some explanation of my long silence.*

*First, I confess that I have been very ill with malaria, and although I have had some recurrence of the fever, I do hope the worst is over and I am recovering. Doc, bless him, is taking good care of me.*

*Perhaps my illness and depleted state has contributed in making the second half of this voyage so difficult. During this trip, I have seen so many instances of man's inhumanity to man on such a grand scale that it has severely damaged, if not destroyed, any optimistic opinion I may have had about people eventually doing the right thing. I have seen such horrors. There is the war, of course, but not only that. I have seen the senseless, violent death of two women and a boy happen before my eyes, which I could do nothing to stop. Moreover, I fear I may have inadvertently been the cause of it.*

*Si, although I am here at a center for spiritual study, I have failed to find any comfort. I know you to be a man of great faith, and all I can ask is that you pray for the state of the world, for Doc and me, and that I may soon find my way home to you. I feel so lost.*

Again, Asa crumpled up the letter and threw it in the wastebasket in disgust. He thought himself weak, and wished he could have Sharmaji's equanimity in the face of the world's horrors. But no matter how hard he tried, he could not overcome his personal reaction to things, could not fully attain that sense of selflessness… but then, that was the problem.

He *sensed* too much. He could not help but feel things. Colors were too bright; sounds were too sharp; touch was too acute; taste and smell altogether too insistent of notice. His very being got in the way of his spiritual ascension to a higher plane.

He had a body; he had a soul; he could not very well divorce himself from them and become purely an atom in the oceanic existence of all life, could he? And even if he *was* merely a drop, could he abdicate his responsibility to all the other drops that comprise the ocean with him? It seemed obvious to him that he could not.

Perhaps he had not advanced enough to understand the concept, but Sharmaji's lectures offered him no comfort.

Moreover, they offered him no direction to action, no opportunity to improve things. The world was in dire straits. He couldn't simply gaze at his navel and chant about peace. What was he to do?

> *Dear Si,*
>
> *I am sorry to be so long in writing, but things have been rather hectic of late. When I last wrote, I believe we were in Port Said. Well, we got stuck there for much longer than I would have wished, due to*

Due to... due to what? Damn, so many things… so much… crap. Again, he crumpled and tossed the missive.

> *Dear Si,*
>
> *Please do not read this aloud or share it with Janet unless you absolutely have to do so. This is my umpteenth attempt at writing. I am sorry to be so remiss, but things have simply been too horrible to write about. I want to come home so badly. I miss you and Janet. Yes, that makes me sound and feel like a child again, and I admit it. I confess to having been very ill lately with malaria, but that's no excuse. Doc has taken very good care of me.*
>
> *I've seen such terrible things. It is not only the horror of the war, with U-Boat attacks on civilian ships and the deaths of innocent people. It is the senseless murder in the street of women and children. Well, perhaps that's exaggerated to*

*a certain extent, but I've been told that the ones I witnessed were not completely out of the ordinary.*

*We are so cruel to each other. We stigmatize people because of poverty, illness, things that are beyond their control. We punish them for not being wealthy or strong or able to stand up for themselves (and by themselves) in a world that stacks the deck against them. We push people beyond their limits. Is it any wonder that they crack?*

*Dear God, what have we come to? Where is the humanity in the human race?*

*Si, I keep trying to write about something else. I keep trying to write a letter that is not so bleak and miserable, but I have wasted so much paper in the attempt... I can either send this or not write anything at all.*

*Well, at least we said a prayer and floated some marigolds on the lake for them. As if that could do any good.*

*We're leaving Bombay tomorrow, and after one more port of call in Mozambique, we will begin our journey home across the Atlantic.*

*I cannot wait to get home to you and Janet. I cannot stand alone, and I need you. There, I've said it. I no longer care if I sound weak or unmanly.*

*Pray for me.*

*Asa*

He skimmed the letter and disgustedly crumpled it up, tossing it in the wastepaper bin to join the others. Sitting with his head in his hands, he stared, unseeing, at the desktop.

# Chapter 24

# *Going Home*

Asa kept an eye peeled for U-boats through the long watch of the night, as they zigzagged across the Atlantic to avoid them.

"West by no'th, Jack," he said to the helmsman.

"West by no'th, sir."

The night sky was moonless, studded with stars so numerous and brilliant, Asa felt as though he could almost reach out and touch them. Where was the awe he usually felt at such a sight? Where was the thrill? As far as spirituality went, he felt bereft.

Why did this horror seem worse than the all the others? They'd been too close — close enough to drown in death's bloody trough. Finding nothing that could erase the stains, he and Doc had had to burn their uniforms. He could not begin to comprehend the madness he'd witnessed, let alone come to grips with it. Lighting some incense and throwing marigolds on the lake while chanting prayers — how utterly useless. Their brief stay with Sharmaji had helped neither Doc nor him find peace. They could only look at one another, hollow eyed and arid.

How he wished Cap'n Asa, Cap'n Alfred, and Cap'n James were still alive to talk with him. What use are the stars in plotting a course? Where do I go without my captains? They've sailed beyond the horizon, and all I desire is to follow their wake.

Maybe sixteen years at sea is enough. The age of *The Winged Mercury* has passed; steamers are dirty with coal, and diesel engines aren't much cleaner. Nothing has the romance of that old clipper ship Cap'n Asa had loved. Perhaps those days weren't as hopeful as I remember them, but the world seems to have become so dark and hopeless now that I feel powerless to do anything about it.

*The Winged Mercury* — now, there was a beauty. I can see her now, feel her wooden deck under my feet, and hear the crack of the sails. Cap'n James had loved her, too, refusing to sell or scrap her, though she was too old-fashioned to be of any use to the fleet anymore. I remember scrambling up the rigging, breathing in the salt smell of the ocean, the scents of spices on the wind when we got close. Never again shall I sail to the West Indies with Cap'n Asa and Cap'n Alfred, her holds filled with green and gold bananas, along with a tarantula or two.

I remember those days as idyllic, though I suppose they weren't. Now that Cap'n James is gone, I share those memories only with ghosts.

God damn him to hell, George will probably scuttle her, out of spite. Our beloved ship. It's just too much to contemplate.

Rubbing his forehead with his thumb and fingers, he gazed toward the horizon, not really seeing it. *I think this will be my last voyage. Unless we get involved in this war. Then maybe I'll join the Navy. But… maybe not. Maybe… oh, hell, I don't know. Right now, it's time for me to get home to Janet and Si. Thank God I have them.*

*Family — poor Mary, with James gone and Margaret not long for this world. And George is no kind of family. I wonder how she's doing. Where does she go to lick her wounds?*

*What with all the to-do George stirred up, I didn't get to stay home long enough to see her again. She seems steady, and smart, too. Different from most girls I've met. Well, it's more than that, isn't it? I guess if I'm honest with myself, I'm a little in love with her.*

He pictured her in that blue dress, petite, delicate but strong, with her beautiful auburn hair.

*I wouldn't have minded kissing those soft lips.* Pacing back and forth, he mentally slapped his temple with the palm of his hand. *Jeez, what the hell is wrong with me? How could I think of her in that way at a time like that? What a base, shallow knave. Next to her grace, I'm just some big, gangling galoot. Why ever would she want to see me again? I'd just be a painful reminder of James's death.* He stopped pacing and stared into the distance.

God, I miss him.

The sad melody of an old sea shanty, "Tom's Gone to Hilo," ran through his mind, though he heard a different name in the lyrics. *James is gone, what shall I do? He's gone to Hilo. Oh James is gone, and I'll go too. He's gone to Hilo.*

"All right, Mistah Mayhew?" Tommy Martin stepped into the pilot house, surprising Asa out of his reverie. "You seem to be in kind of a brown study."

Blinking absently, Asa wrenched his mind back into the present. "Oh! I'm fine, Tommy. Just contemplatin' life, such as it is. Eight bells already?" He turned to the helmsman. "Who's supposed to replace you, Jack? Is it Joe? I'll take the helm while you go turn him out. Time for you to hit the rack."

"Helm is being relieved…" Jack began the formulaic phrases.

Asa smiled. "No need to go through all that with me. We're steady on a course, west by no'th. The helm is relieved, all right? Now go tell Joe to get a hump on."

"Aye, aye, Mister Mayhew," Jack said.

"Only 'bout anothah day and we'll be puttin' into po't. Be good to get back home again for a while, won't it?" Tommy's vowels were sometimes so drawn out as to go up and down the scale.

"Ayup. Think maybe I'll swallow the anchor, make it permanent," Asa said.

"Retire!" Tommy was surprised. "But you're only, what, twenty-four? What'll you do for the rest of your life? And besides, you ain't got near enough money to retire on, if what we make at sea's all you got."

"Got enough to tide me ovah for a time," Asa said. He played his cards close to the vest, and only Si and his banker had an inkling that he'd made more than enough, through wise investments, to see him through quite a few years. "Maybe I'll go fishin' with Si. Maybe do some tinkerin' around with engines. There are plenty ways to make a livin' if you put your mind to it, and are willin' to work hahd."

"But *why*, Asa?" Tommy implored. "I thought ya loved the sea."

"Well, the last couple of voyages have pretty much put the kibosh on *that* love affair." Leaving a lover who had hurt him came to mind. The longing was still there, but the pain had made it impossible to stay.

"Ayuh, I can see how ya might think that. But ya might change yah mind in a while."

"Lovejoys ran a good company, bein' sailahs themselves. But that'll change, now Geo'ge is in chahge. Anyway, I sure as hell won't be workin' for *him* anymoah." Asa's voice was deep and subdued. "Even *if* he'd have me."

"Why not stay with the Bay State Line? You know they'd keep you on, 'specially now you've got your captain's papers."

"I dunno, Tommy." Asa sighed. "Besides, havin' to stop for all the British blockades, and those damn U-boats torpedoin' anythin' that moves, sailin' the Atlantic's becomin' mighty tricky. If I'm gonna endangah my life, might's well be for my country instead of for some rich bastid only interested in linin' his pockets. I don't mean Wass — he isn't like that."

"Thinkin' of goin' into the Navy? I've been thinkin' about that, too. They ah goin' ta need single, fit fellahs like us to fight the Kaisah if we get into this thing."

Asa noted Tommy's eyes traveling up and down his spare frame as he'd said 'fit.' "Workin' on it," he smiled. "They'll need a few men who know lahb'd from stahb'd, at least." He turned to the sailor hurrying in, still doing up his buttons. "'Bout time, Joe. Tell me: what time does mo'nin' watch staht?"

"It starts at 0400, sir."

"And what time are you supposed to be here?" Asa asked.

Joe blushed. "I should have been here at 0345, Mr. Mayhew, but I—"

"Ovahslept? Try to get here by 0400 at least. Late for watch again, and I'll have to write you up, much as I don't want to. Undahstood?" Asa said.

"Aye, aye, sir."

"All right, Joe. Change course. Heading west-no'thwest, one-half west."

"Aye, aye, sir. West-no'thwest, one-half west."

"Keep an eye out for U-boats," Asa said.

"Ayup, and keep zigzaggin' to avoid 'em," Tommy said. "Waell, sun'll be up soon. Why don't you get some shuteye? It's my watch, now."

Asa yawned, covering his mouth with his fist. He stretched his arms over his head, then out to the side. Placing his hands on the small of his back, he bent backward, stretching his spine. He yawned again, giving his facial muscles and jaw a workout.

Tommy grinned. "You remind me of Leo, when you stretch like that."

Asa gave Tommy a weary smile. "G'night, Tommy. Or should I say good mo'nin'?"

Instead of going to his berth, he turned up his collar, packed his pipe with tobacco and walked to the bow, smoking and watching until the stars faded and the sky turned that particular shade of blue he loved, just before the sun came up. Then he walked toward the stern and watched the pastel pinks, lighter hues of violet, and one thin streak of pure gold on the horizon as the sun began to rise. As Leo wove herself around his ankles, he tapped out his pipe and put it in his pocket. Then he picked up the cat and carried her to his berth. He had the compartment all to himself, since Slocum was down in sick bay after Doc had pulled an abscessed molar.

When he undressed and lay down on his back under the covers, the cat settled herself on his stomach, purring. He scratched behind her ears and rubbed her chin for a while. He sighed.

Why was it that when you were in a hurry, things always took twice as long? They'd got stuck in Mozambique until some fighting between the British and the German colonies in East Africa had died down. They had begun to round the Cape of Good Hope when the engine broke down, and they'd limped into Cape Town for repairs. Except to get engine parts, Asa hadn't left the ship in either port, feeling thoroughly sick of the world and all its ills. Finally, they were almost home, but it had taken almost another month after leaving India. It would be March before they got back to Boston.

He'd try to catch a few hours sleep before meeting Doc for breakfast.

# Chapter 25

# *Calling George's Bluff*

A t long last, the *Eastern Trader* docked at Eastern Wharf in Boston. The men slipped the camel between the ship and the wharf and secured the lines around the bollards. Asa and Captain Hookset stood at the rail as the crew lowered the gangplank. Captain Hookset spotted George Lovejoy waiting with the harbormaster and a policeman. He put his hand on Asa's shoulder and extended his other arm, pointing. George's bulbous, broken-veined nose glowed like a beacon through the harbor mist.

The big policeman looked familiar. No, it couldn't be, Asa thought. Last he knew, Hanson had a bushy beard, and was still dredging for oysters. Although, that was a few years ago. Despite his attempt to ignore George, George's eyes had honed in on him. Asa couldn't help but look at that choleric, fuming face and feel disgust.

"So, he really went through with it," Asa said. "Well, we'll just see how far he gets with this."

"Tsk, tsk. Wait just one moment," Captain Hookset said. He stepped into the office and returned with a thick folder. "I was afraid he might pull something like this, so I had the men write down their own recollections of the night that

Captain James Lovejoy went overboard. George won't get anywhere. We've got your back."

"That was very prescient of you," Asa said. "Thank you, sir."

Captain Hookset called, "Slocum, Martin! See to the unloading. I'll be back when we've cleared up this little matter," he nodded in the direction of the three men standing near the gangplank, "but by then you might be done. If the buyer wants me, send him to the harbormaster's office."

"Aye, sir," Slocum said. As the captain turned to leave, Mike looked at Tommy and muttered, "Can you believe the gall of that… that—"

"Son of a bitch." Tommy hardly moved his lips, leaning close so that only Slocum could hear him.

As they disembarked, Asa caught himself grinding his teeth and clenching his fists. He shot a quick sideways glance at the captain, to see if he'd noticed.

Looking straight ahead, and seemingly apropos of nothing, Captain Hookset said, "Even Jesus got angry from time to time."

"Aye, sir," Asa suppressed a grin. "But I shall try to refrain from throwing him out, as Jesus did with the money changers."

Captain Hookset smiled and walked forward, extending his hand to the harbormaster. "Mr. Perry, how good to see you again."

"Good to see you, too, Captain Hookset," Perry shook his hand. "Sorry to say the circumstances aren't so good, though." Perry shot George a look of barely disguised venom.

"Well? Aren't you gonna arrest him?" George demanded. "He murdered my brother!"

Asa narrowed his eyes as he looked at George. He took a step forward as his fist began to rise, seemingly of its own volition.

Captain Hookset placed his hand on Asa's forearm, with a slight shake of his head.

That touch brought Asa back to his senses. Unclenching his teeth, he shook out his hands, nodded, and took a step back. He kept his mouth shut. Fury was making it hard for him to think, but it wasn't helping to keep him warm in the frigid temperature on the docks. He turned his collar up and jammed his hands into his reefer pockets.

Captain Hookset drew himself up to his full height and thundered down at George, "Woe be unto you, sinner, for bearing false witness against this good man. Fear the Lord and repent!" he lowered his voice, but spoke firmly, "If you cannot speak the truth, you would do well to keep quiet, and remember, the Lord God is the final judge."

Asa looked at Captain Hookset, agog. *Well, blow me down!* The harbormaster had folded his hands, and the policeman had placed his hand on his heart. They both looked ready to fall to their knees and beg forgiveness for all their sins, lest they end up in perdition. Glancing at each other, they looked away, blushing. Then they shook off this momentary reaction and resumed their business-like demeanor.

Captain Hookset's sermonette had no such effect on George, and he immediately started bleating his one-note complaint about Asa. "He murdered—"

Perry glared at George. "Let's take a walk to my office and discuss this out of the cold, in private. The Assistant District Attorney will meet us there."

George opened his mouth to say something, but Perry turned his back and began walking down Commercial Street, towards Battery. Captain Hookset and Asa followed. Glancing back, Asa saw George sneaking a swig from a silver-plated hip flask. The policeman straggled along, seeming somewhat baffled at his purpose there. Looking skyward and sighing, he gave the appearance of a man who wished to be anyplace else.

After they entered the office, there was a knock at the door and a sleek, well-dressed man swept into the room. As he was carrying a briefcase, Asa assumed that it was one of the Assistants to the District Attorney.

"Ah, Mr. Fielding," the harbormaster said. "This is Captain Hookset, Mr. Asa Mayhew, Mr. George Lovejoy, and Mr. er…"

"Hanson," the policeman supplied.

"So it *is* you," Asa smiled. "It's been such a long time, I didn't recognize you."

"Had to shave off my beard to get into the police force," Hanson smiled back.

"Well, Hanson, why haven' you arrested 'im yet?" George swayed toward him, his aspirated *h* spreading the smell of whiskey like an atomizer.

"Not my purview, Mistah Lovejoy," the state policeman said. "I don't know why you wanted *me* here. The ocean sure isn't in my jurisdiction. It's probably the jurisdiction of the U.S. Revenue Cuttah Se'vice. Ah, no, it's not called that anymoah. I keep fo'gettin' it's the Coast Gahd, now they've combined with the Life Savin' Se'vice. At any rate, I have no authority in this mattah. Even if I did, from what I've heard, looks to me that Mistah Mayhew did everythin' right and nothin' wrong. Mattah of fact, I only agreed to come along because I suspected Asa, heah, might need protectin' from *you*."

Asa shot him a grateful look.

"Well," Mr. Perry said, trying to regain control of the meeting, "Are we all properly introduced? Take a seat here, Mr. Fielding," he offered his own desk chair.

All the men nodded politely at one another, except for George, whose countenance grew darker. "Enough of that! What is this, a goddamned business meeting? Arrest that man!" He pointed his finger in Asa's face.

Asa snapped his head back as his eyes nearly crossed looking at that stubby digit that had come all too close to his nose. Restraining a wild impulse to bite it off, he stared incredulously at George. Couldn't he even maintain some semblance of propriety among men whose positions, at least, deserved his respect? Moreover, men from whom he wanted something — namely, my arrest. Mr. Fielding's question saved him from voicing that thought.

"What's this all about?"

Again, George started pointing and sputtering. "That— That— He—"

"Tsk, tsk." Captain Hookset intervened, shaking his head at George. Addressing Mr. Fielding, he said, "Mr. Lovejoy, here, is operating under a delusion that Mr. Mayhew is somehow responsible for his brother's death. I assure you, nothing could be further from the truth. Mr. Mayhew nearly lost his own life in his attempt to rescue Captain James Lovejoy from drowning. I have here twenty-two signed and witnessed statements from every man aboard *The Mary Lovejoy* at the time of the accident."

It was a relief to allow Captain Hookset to take the lead, but Asa was still taut with fury and foreboding. Taking a deep breath, he tried to relax his muscles.

Captain Hookset placed his sheaf of documents on the harbormaster's desk in front of the Assistant District Attorney. "I was afraid that George, here, would try some harebrained scheme like this, so I had the men write down their own recollections of that voyage. They're not strictly legal depositions, since we didn't have an attorney aboard, but they are all in the men's own handwriting, signed and witnessed by me; Mr. Michael Slocum, the second mate; and Dr. Simon Coffin, the ship's doctor."

"Bunch a' lies!" George shouted. "He's got those men… they'll say wha'evah he wants… Can't trusht a word! Don' believe 'em."

Mr. Perry narrowed his eyes at George, who continued his heated and incoherent bluster about murder and arrest. "How would *you* know what's in these documents, Lovejoy? This is the first we've seen of them. I'd suggest you just shut up, or I'll ask Hansen, here, to lock you up on drunk and disorderly."

"Why you…" George leaned toward Mr. Perry.

Hanson put his huge hand on George's chest and glowered at him. "One more word out of you, and I'll do it. Now, step back." He moved to stand beside George, placing one heavy paw on his shoulder to restrain him.

For the moment, George stopped talking, his face flushed, his breathing heavy as he glared around the room, his pugnacious jaw thrust forward.

Fielding picked up the first sheet in the stack and said, "Well, this could be a sticky situation as far as jurisdiction is concerned, since the incident happened on the high seas, but as it was a United States ship registered in Massachusetts from a Boston shipping company, I'll take a look. Jurisdiction may be a moot point if no crime has been committed."

Hanson abruptly cut off George's squawk with a grip close to his neck.

Fielding ignored him and began to look over the documents.

After a cursory examination, the attorney gave George a disgusted look. "Mr. Lovejoy, were you aboard?" He didn't give George a chance to answer. "No? Not at any time before, during, or after the incident, were you? Well then where did you get this outlandish idea of yours? Far from having broken any laws, it seems to me Mr. Mayhew behaved in a heroic manner in his attempts to save your brother's life. You have no case, and I do *not* appreciate having my time wasted simply because you bear some kind of ancient grudge."

George continued to sputter his protests. "But he… you can't believe those men! He's got them—"

Hansen applied visible pressure as he squeezed George's shoulder. George winced.

Mr. Fielding read from one of the documents, 'He sat with Captain James day and night, nursing him in his fever,'" he turned a page, "'…and when wind smashed the lifeboat against the ship, breaking it, he dove in,'" turned another page, "'If it wasn't for Mr. Slocum insisting we tie a line around him, we'd have lost him, too.'" He continued turning pages as he read the testimony of man after man: "'He was distraught, insisting we go back and look again.'"

Asa was beginning to feel sick as the memories came flooding back. His face felt odd — somehow hot and cold at once. Looking at the floor, he appreciated Captain Hookset's unexpected arm around his back, supporting him. Raising his eyes, he saw Mr. Perry watching him with what seemed to be a thoughtful glance. He quickly looked away, only to catch George's visage turning violent colors as he sputtered under Hanson's confining grip. He returned his gaze to the floor, trying not to listen as Mr. Fielding went on.

Without a break, Mr. Fielding pointed to another passage, "Look here: 'suffered a concussion,' and here: 'When we hauled him up, he was near drowned…' Another says, 'Snatched him from the jaws of death…'" With the flourish of a trial lawyer, he slapped the pile of papers with the palm of his hand. "Page after page of such statements, all agreeing that Mr. Mayhew risked his own life trying to save Captain James Lovejoy. What more do you want, Mr. Lovejoy? *You have no case*, and I ought to arrest *you* for knowingly bringing false charges against this man. Now, look, I am a very busy man, and I have no patience for this kind of nonsense. Go home, sleep it off, and do not bother my office again, or you'll find *yourself* behind bars."

George wrenched himself from Hanson's grasp. "You haven't heard the end of this!" he shouted at Asa. His face purple with rage, he stomped off.

"What on earth is the matter with that man?" Mr. Fielding wondered aloud as he shrugged into his coat.

As he was looking at Asa, Asa felt compelled to answer. "Well… ahem… well. I think he's finally lost… um… all that drinking… has affected his mind," Asa sighed. "And he's… ah, always hated me. Thinks I stole his father's… affection, or something. I'm sorry you were dragged out for this." Overcome with a welter of emotions — embarrassment, anger, and grief among them — he wanted to go home and crawl into bed, to go to sleep for a year or two, and wake up to discover the past six months had all been just a nightmare. "Mr. Fielding, do you need me for anything else?"

"No, not at all." Fielding buttoned his coat and picked up his briefcase. "You certainly needn't worry about being charged with anything, but I would suggest you place these papers in the hands of your attorney, in case *he* tries to make trouble again." He tipped his head in the direction George had taken. "Good day to you, gentlemen."

"Mr. Perry, are we all set here?" Captain Hookset asked.

Perry shrugged. "Sure, you can go. And Mr. Mayhew, you can be sure I won't be in any hurry to waste your time with complaints from *that* drunken idiot again. Humph! Lovejoy's isn't what it used to be, is it?"

"Sadly, no," Captain Hookset said.

Asa bit his lip. He feared he was going to swear a blue streak in front of the Captain, or worse, break down crying. Their walk back to the ship was silent until they reached the gangway.

"I'm sorry he put you through that," Captain Hookset said.

"Mm-hm. Me too," Asa said.

The captain gave him a long look. "You look done in. Slocum, Martin, and I can finish up here. Why don't you grab your sea bag and head on home."

For once, Asa didn't argue. "Thank you, Cap'n, and thanks for all your help back there. I'll just say goodbye to Doc."

Slocum overheard Asa's last sentence. "Sorry, Asa, you just missed him."

"Oh." He suddenly felt desperate to get away. "Well, I'll see ya, Mike, Tommy."

"You goin' out to sea with us again, Asa?" Tommy asked.

"No," Asa said. "Not for a while, anyway. But we'll keep in touch."

# Chapter 26

# *Home At Last*

Asa hurried to South Station and just made the Cape train. As he sat down and removed his cap, his sandy, sun-streaked hair fell into loose, unruly curls. He brushed a lock back from his forehead, but it flopped forward again when he dropped his hand. He'd have to remember to get a haircut.

Or maybe he'd just let his hair and beard grow, and go live in a little hut in the woods somewhere, and be a hermit. Seemed like a good idea at the moment. *The world is too much with us; late and soon, / Getting and spending, we lay waste our powers; / Little we see in nature that is ours; / We have given our hearts away, a sordid boon.*[32] And for everything, *I* am out of tune, he thought. How does the rest of it go? I should have been a Pagan in a creed outworn… hm, something about hearing old Triton blowing his horn. Oh, why didn't I just throw myself on Neptune's mercies and be done with it?

He sighed, feeling drained. Although he'd been well enough to resume his duties a couple of weeks ago, he hadn't yet recovered. Fatigue and depression dogged his footsteps. He unbuttoned his reefer and tried to find a comfortable position, not easy in these cramped seats. Still, he was glad it wasn't summer when the train would be crowded, allowing him a certain amount of solitude. He couldn't have mustered up any polite conversation if his life depended on it.

Seeking escape in a good story, he pulled a new book out of his sea bag. When he found himself reading the same sentence over and over, he gave up on *A Far Country*. He yawned.

He tugged at his constricting collar and loosened his tie. He wished he dared take the stiff collar off, but he'd gone pretty far already. There were no ladies in the carriage now, but there were many stops between Boston and Wellfleet. He wouldn't want to embarrass anyone by being in dishabille. Leaning his head back, he listlessly gazed out the window. The wheels on the track lulled him with their rhythm: home again, home again, home again, home. He drifted into a cat nap.

As they neared a crossing, the whistle woke him and he looked around, disconcerted to have fallen asleep like an old man. Oh, well, no matter. The only other person in the carriage was a long-legged, wiry, white-haired old man whose moustache fluttered with each sleeping breath. For a fleeting moment, Asa wondered if he was witnessing himself, some fifty years hence. Then he blinked and shook his head, hoping he hadn't been snoring like this fellow. He rubbed his clean-shaven face and ran his fingers through his hair.

In Brockton, a stout woman juggling several shopping bags got on. She looked something like Martha's cousin's sister-in-law, Jenny Sylvester. When she appeared to be making a beeline for him, he panicked, put his hat on, grabbed his sea bag, and got up, heading to the exit at the other end of the carriage, as though about to miss his stop. After she sat down, he chose a distant seat. A long chat about who was related to whom, and did you know so-and-so was the last thing he needed now, although Josiah, had he been there, would have been in his element. They clattered past the coal bins at Keith's Coal and Coke, and headed on through West Bridgewater, East Bridgewater, and Bridgewater. When the woman got off in Middleborough, he knew he had been mistaken about her being Mrs. Sylvester, and felt foolish. He dozed off again and awoke to see the old man getting off in Hyannis. Damn, he'd seen the filthy coal bins but slept through the two-year-old wonder of the Cape Cod Canal. This trip was taking forever.

When they finally reached the tiny Wellfleet station, he was hoping Eldon from the garage might be around with his taxi, but there was not a soul in the place. He thought about visiting Mary, but he was too tired and travel-worn. Maybe tomorrow.

As he hefted his sea bag and set off on the long walk home, he hoped some kind soul would come along and offer him a lift. His back and shoulders ached; his sea bag had never been so heavy. Although it was cloudy, the light started bothering his eyes, a warning sign of an incipient headache. He couldn't recall ever having felt so dragged down. Walking in soft sand was harder work than striding across a solid deck. He was having trouble getting his land legs back; they felt rubbery, unreliable. Doc Chandler came along about then, in his Model-T, doing his rounds of house calls.

"Good Lord, Asa, you're even skinnier than the last time I saw you. Don't they feed you in the Merchant Marine? Hop in."

Asa forced a chuckle and resorted to the old joke, "Don't know as you could rightly call it food."

Doc gave him a piercing look. "Come see me once you get settled in. I'd like to take a look at you."

Asa changed the subject. "How are Mrs. Lovejoy and Miss Lovejoy, Doc?"

"Sad to say, Mrs. Lovejoy passed away a couple of weeks after you left," Doc answered. "After James died, she seemed to have lost the will to live. She simply didn't wake up one morning; went as quiet as that. Wasn't too long after, Mary packed up and moved into Boston."

Boston? Asa felt as though he'd just been sucker-punched. Two weeks, three weeks after he'd left? He'd done a lousy job of protecting her, hadn't he? Perhaps she hadn't even received any of his letters. His last bit of strength drained away so quickly that if he hadn't already been sitting down, he'd have collapsed. He didn't know what to say.

After a moment, he gathered his wits and came up with, "I'm sorry to hear that. Poor Mary."

They sat in silence for the rest of the ride.

When Doc stopped the car at the end of the lane, Asa got out. As he reached in for his sea bag, he said, "Thanks for the lift, Doc."

Doc nodded. "Come see me."

Asa pretended not to hear him. He slung his sea bag over his shoulder and set off down the rutted, sandy lane toward a two-story cottage, its cedar shakes aged silvery gray. He crunched up the oyster-shell drive and went in the back door.

"Si? Janet?" No answer. "Humph. Some homecoming," Asa grumbled. Working the pump at the kitchen sink, he washed his hands and face in frigid water. He shivered. Despite his grumbling, the peace and quiet suited him fine. He was too damned tired to talk. He trudged up the stairs and dropped his sea bag onto the bedroom floor. He draped his jacket over the back of a chair, yanked off collar and tie, and toed off his shoes. He stretched and yawned, flopped down on the bed, and fell asleep.

*Dark rain on a sea lashed deck. Cold wet screeching wind. The world spinning upside down. Slipping, sliding, sinking, plummeting to the depths. Slammed against the hull. Scraping fingernails can't hold on. Scrabbling around blind in the drowned black night, seeking a handhold, a foothold, anything to grab on to, to pull himself up, as unbearable pressure crushed his chest.*

Just as he got to the part where he inhaled a lungful of ocean, he heard himself moaning and awoke with a start.

He found himself tangled in the counterpane, drenched in sweat, still fully dressed. He dragged the back of his hand across his brow. Oh, hell, he'd thought these dreams were a thing of the past.

The sun was more than half way toward the western horizon. How could he have slept that long? He took in a deep breath and let it flow out. He pushed himself to sit up, and swung his feet over the side of the bed. "Oh, God." Feeling slightly sick, he sat resting his elbows on his knees, hanging his head.

*What's going on? Why am I having that dream again?* He saw the stack of papers on the harbormaster's desk. George, bringing it all up again. Must be.

After a moment, he got up. He thought he'd have to make another trip downstairs to the pump, but discovered his water pitcher was full. He poured about half of it into the basin, stripped, and washed from head to foot. There were fresh towels and soap. The water wasn't as cold as if it had just come from the well. Janet must have brought it up this morning, and it had sat in the sun coming in the window for hours. Still, it was cool enough to revive him. Wanting comfort, he dressed in worn corduroy trousers and a soft-collared blue work shirt, pulled a navy blue sweater over his head, and slid his bare feet into moccasins. He ran a comb through his hair before going downstairs.

Janet was in the kitchen, beginning preparations for supper. "Oh! You're home!"

"Of coss I'm home — or do you lug a pitcher of water up the stairs every day, just in case? You haven't been out and about today? Didn't hear about all the excitement when we docked in Boston?"

"You get outta bed on the wrong side this mo'nin'? What excitement?"

"Sorry, Janet. I didn't mean to be so grouchy. It's just —" He heaved a sigh. "Mr. George Lovejoy was gettin' ready to drag me off to jail, but the prosecutor wouldn't hear of it." Asa dropped into a chair at the kitchen table. "I shouldn't be takin' out my anger with him on you."

"Jail! Whatevah faw?" Janet exclaimed.

"Don't you remembah, he said I was responsible — no, that I *murdahed* James?" Asa shook his head. "He hasn't given up on that notion, and the hahbahmastah, Hanson — who's a policeman, now, by the way — and George met Cap'n Hookset and me at the dock. One of the Assistant District Attorneys met us in the hahbahmastah's office. When Cap'n Hookset showed him some statements he'd got from the men, the attorney gave George what for, and sent him packin'."

"Oh, that man! The way he treated his niece! Why, it just doesn't bear repeatin'!"

Asa straightened up, alert. "What did he do to her? Janet, what did he do to Mary?"

"He turned her out of James's house. Throwin' an eighteen-year-old girl out of her own home! What kind of family does that?"

"How could he *do* that!?"

"Said it wasn't hers; it belonged to the comp'ny."

"That can't be right! Cap'n Asa left that house to James — *only* to James. And James left it to Margaret and Mary. I know, because he told me, when he made his will. George has no claim on it!"

"Mary told Mistah Lovejoy how you stayed on after the doctah left, just to make sure they didn't need anythin', and how you asked the Packahds next doah to look in on them. Mistah Lovejoy hit the roof, said she was no kin of his!" Janet stood with her fists on her hips, outrage on her face. "Mahtha told me. She was standin' right theyah. He turned around and said to her, 'We won't be needin' you anymoah! Pack yah bags and get out!'"

"Damn and blast him! Excuse me, Janet. I shouldn't use such language in front of you. But he's just taken this thing too fah!" Asa dragged in a deep breath, exhaling with force. He muttered under his breath, "Poah Mary. It's all my fault."

"Of coss it's not!" Janet gave Asa a stern look, then softened and patted his hand. She brought a bowl of early peas to the table, and began shelling them. "Don't worry about Mary. She got a job as secretary to young Mistah Chase at the Chase Impo't Comp'ny in Boston. She bo'ds with Mrs. Bird on Beacon Hill. By all accounts it's a comf'table house and respectable. Sarah Cook says she's doin' fine."

"You know he's always resented me. Now she's cast out of her own family, just because she stood up for me. Not that George is much of a family, but still… he's all she's got left." Asa sat with one elbow on the table, leaning his forehead on his palm.

"Now, now. You know how he is. I don't want to hear anothah word about this bein' yaw fault. Nothin' to do with you. It's all ovah now — time to put it behind you. You'll find anothah ship and be back at sea again in no time." Janet frowned at Asa's elbow on the table.

He took the hint. Weary, he slumped against the back of the chair. "Not goin' back, at least not now. Think I'll stay around here, maybe go out fishin' with Si, if he'll have me. I'll get myself a little place, so you won't have to have me underfoot all the time."

"Yaw not undahfoot, Asa. This is yaw home."

Asa, surprised and embarrassed to be so moved by Janet's gentle tone, couldn't speak. He started shelling the peas, giving them far more attention than necessary.

Janet turned to peeling potatoes at the sink, allowing Asa his silence. After a while, she spoke again. "You got your captain's license. I thought yaw dream was to captain your own ship. Are you sure you want to give it all up?"

"George Lovejoy won't have me at all, let alone as captain. And I wouldn't work for him, even if he would. Cap'n Hookset would put in a good word for me with the Bay State Line, but I dunno how much longer Mr. Wass can hold out against that conglomerate that's trying to buy him out. Things've changed." Asa sighed. "I've changed. I'm tired of flittin' from port to port. Without James…" He lapsed into silence again.

He stared at the tabletop, seeing a blurry image of James's face there.

Asa was vaguely aware of Janet turning to look at him and shaking her head. She lifted a cast iron stove lid to check the fire. Adding a pinch of salt to the potatoes, she put them on to boil. She put her hand in to check the oven temperature and then opened another door to poke up the fire. A pot of chowder was slowly cooking on a cooler spot on the back of the stove; she lifted the lid and gave it a stir. It was too soon to cook the peas, so she put them aside. As she gathered ingredients for biscuits, her movements around the kitchen aroused Asa from his reverie.

"Maybe I'm just gettin' older, had enough adventure. What with the war, and even passenger ships like the Lusitania being sunk…" Once more, he let the sentence hang. He didn't want to tell Janet that they'd picked up survivors from a wreck, another time arriving too late. He didn't want to tell her about all the brutality and criminality he'd seen, the hardship and cruelty, the insanity and murder. He shook his head slowly. "Too much death." He didn't realize he had spoken that thought aloud.

Janet raised her head and looked at him, but she kept quiet, waiting for him to speak.

"The sea's kinda lost its romance for me. No place in the world is better than right here on the Cape. This's home. Guess I just want to stay for a while."

"For as long as you want, Asa," Janet said. "You stay right heah with us."

She frowned over her biscuit batter.

Outside, the sound of rubber boots crunching up the drive, the splash of the outdoor pump, followed by the shed door banging, announced that Silas was home. He'd wash off the fish scales before he came into the house.

"Here's Si, right on time for suppah! Won't he be su'prised to see you!"

"Don't know as he'd be surprised. He must've read we were due in today in the shippin' news." Asa was puzzled at Janet's sudden false cheer, so unlike her usual staid demeanor. At the sound of Silas's boots clunking to the floor of the shed, Asa pushed back his chair and stood, ready to greet his cousin with a firm handshake when he came in the kitchen door.

"Hey, Si. Good to see ya."

"Great to see you, Asa!" Silas grinned, clapping him on the shoulder. "Glad yah back, safe and sound. Heard that district attorney put Mistah Geo'ge Lovejoy in his place this mo'nin'! Guess he'll think twice befoah he decides to go aftah you again!"

"Scuttlebutt sure travels fast around these parts. Let's just forget about George Lovejoy, for now, okay? I'm gettin' sick of hearin' his name," Asa said.

"Ayup," Si said. "Can't say as I blame you."

"Suppah's ready. Sit down at the table," Janet ordered.

"Sure smells good!" Si said as he pulled out his chair and sat down.

They all bowed their heads as Silas said grace. "Bless, oh Lawd, thy gifts to our use and us to thy service. Amen."

In honor of Asa's homecoming, Janet had made a thick clam chowder, baked cod, potatoes smothered in butter and fresh parsley, fresh early peas from the greenhouse, light and airy biscuits. There was chocolate cake for dessert.

"My, my, Janet, you've outdone yourself! This is mighty tasty!" Asa smiled. He took a small amount of everything, to be polite. Out of the corner of his eye, he saw Janet watching him pretend to eat, pushing the food around on his plate. He felt guilty, but it was hard to swallow past an Adam's apple that suddenly felt the size of a large Gravenstein.

He tried to hide his discomfiture by asking Si about the fishing industry, the catch, the prices, some new rules and regulations that had the fishermen complaining.

"Is there enough work for me to help out on your seiner?"

"You really wanna stick around here and try fishin'?" Silas seemed incredulous.

Asa had thought about staying for Mary, but she wasn't here anymore. Maybe I should go to Boston? Sure. Maybe I should go to the moon. I'm the last person she'd want after the disaster with George. What the hell is the mattah with me? There is no cryin' at the suppah table! Or anywhere else, for that mattah, he lectured himself. He blinked and cleared his throat.

"Sure, why not? Maybe workin' on a seiner'll make me saner."

"Well, I dunno about *that*," Si grinned. "But if yah serious, sure I can take you on. I know Tony would agree to it. But yah know you'll nevah get rich fishin'. Whatevah we get f' the fish, we shayah — aftah expenses. Trouble is, when the fish ah plentiful, the price drops. Most fellahs have gone ovah to shellfishin' from the public beds, or even payin' to lease beds," Si said. "Tony and I are 'bout the only ones still fishin' for mackerel, but we gotta go way out beyond Provincetown to catch any. Fishin' f' mackerel's best in the fall. Even then, the profit tends to get et up in fuel expenses and pay f' the crew. When the summah people come, we can always hiah out as fishin' guides — take the tourists out deep sea fishin', or row 'em out on one of the ponds f' fresh watah fish. We usually do that when the catch is low, supplement our income that way. Of coss, those two summah cottages make a little rent, and then theyah's always odd jobs heah and theyah."

"Sounds like yah tryin' to scare me away." Asa was kidding, but he couldn't muster up a laugh.

"Nunno, not 't all." Silas protested. "Just makin' sure yah know the lay of the land — or the sea. It's a tough way to make a livin'."

"Can I go out with you tomorrow?" Asa asked.

Si gave him an appraising look. "Why don't ya just take it easy for a couple days. Ya just got back, and it's been a heck of a yeah fo' ya. Nunno, don't shake ya head. Ya need rest, Asa. And food. Yaw skinny as a beanpole."

Asa shrugged. There was that damned mist in front of his eyes again.

"Tell yah what, today's Wednesday. Why don't ya staht out with me on Monday? That'll give ya time to get all squayahed away and build up those muscles some. Ya might find fishin' to be hahdah work than ya think." Si winked.

"Build up those muscles some! What do you think of that?" Grinning, Asa flexed his biceps, showing off lean, hard muscles. "And when have I evah been afraid of a little hahd work? But, all right. I'll wait 'til Monday to staht if you say so. You're the boss."

"Asa, you know I'm just joshin' you," Si said.

"I'm joshin' you right back, Si," Asa said. "Didn't you see my grin?"

Si raised his eyebrows. "Looked t'me moah like a grimace."

Asa raised one shoulder in a dispirited shrug. "Guess I need a little practice."

"Have some cake, Asa," Janet said.

"Nunno, thanks, Janet. Just coffee, please."

"It's chocolate, with mocha frostin' — yaw favorite."

Asa smiled. "Maybe latah. I'm too full right now. A cup of coffee'll do me fine."

Janet gave him a sharp look, and he knew she saw right through him. He studied his coffee cup.

After dinner, Si said, "I'm goin' to get the mail and the papahs, Asa. Want to come?"

"Nunno, Si. I think I'll just stay here and help Janet with the dishes, if that's all right." Asa stifled a yawn. "Excuse me. Don't feel like hobnobbin' with all that crowd tonight."

"'Coss it's all right. I'll be quick as I can." Si put on his coat and left. A minute later, Asa heard the car ticking over.

The mail came in daily on the evening train. One could wait until the next day and go to the postmaster, who was currently the proprietor of the Little Store, but collecting the mail when the train came in was a social occasion, and most people didn't like to miss it. Besides, Si went off early in the morning, before the store was open.

Si was quiet when he came back. He and Asa went into the parlor while Janet was busy in the kitchen.

"Anything wrong, Si?" Asa asked.

"Nunno. Why do you ask?"

"You seem kind of… I dunno… preoccupied."

"Just thinkin'," Si said. "Anything wrong with that?"

Asa frowned, puzzled. "'Coss not."

Asa sat in the old Boston rocker and stretched out his long legs, every once in a while giving a push to set the chair in motion. Silas took the threadbare but comfortable easy chair. They lit their pipes, and sat reading the newspapers.

Although President Wilson had kept the United States out of the war with a policy of non-intervention, some young American men had gone north to enlist in the Canadian Army. Others had gone to France as pilots — enough to have an American flying corps within the French Army. More had volunteered for the American Field Ambulance. Adventurous young men weren't the only ones heading to France. One hundred and ten surgeons and nurses, organized by Harvard University, had set up hospitals serving with the British Expeditionary Force. Other hospital units from across the country followed. Americans were already involved. It was only a matter of time before their government followed suit. Meanwhile, the small American army was involved in the Mexican civil war, fighting skirmishes along the Mexican border with Pancho Villa.

"This war is a terrible thing," Si said. "So many young men slaughtahed — and f' what? Why can't we learn to live peaceably togethah?"

"Mm-hm. As if we didn't already have enough trouble with this war in Mexico spillin' over our bo'dahs. You know," Asa kept his voice low to keep Janet from hearing, "if we do get involved in Europe, I've decided to go into the Navy. So you might not have to put up with me for very long."

"'Put up with you?'" Si echoed. "F' heaven's sake, Asa!" He shook his head.

Asa shrugged.

"Think it'll really come to that?" Silas asked.

"Ayup. Sailin' around Europe and a lot of the colonial ports in Asia and Africa requires some pretty slick tactics to keep from gettin' torpedoed. All this sinkin' of merchant and civilian ships, especially with all those American passengers on the Lusitania — people's attitudes are changin'. We'll be in it before long, I'll bet."

"Killin' innocent civilians — it's beyond the pale!" Si was silent for a moment, looking grim. He sighed. "Dunno why people can't be happy with what they've got, instead of tryin' to go around annexin' other people's countries. How come human bein's have such a hahd time just livin' and lettin' live? And why do men so willin'ly march to their death?"

"Well, that's a question for the ages," Asa said. "*Theirs not to make reply, / Theirs not to reason why, / Theirs but to do, or die.*" There was more than a hint of sarcasm in his voice.

"Who said that?"

"Tennyson. *Charge of the Light Brigade.* A bunch of criminally stupid officers in the Crimean War got their men slaughtered. Haven't learned a thing since then, it appears." Asa sighed.

"Well, we *should* ask questions. Othahwise, how'd we know whethah 'tis right or wrong to do a thing? But if yah country is in dangah, then I guess ya have to fight." Si paused. "Still, I don't believe in fightin' — not unless you're attacked and have to defend yahself or die. Didn't Jesus tell us to love our enemies, bless those who curse us, do good to those who hate us, and pray for those who persecute us? The Germans and Austrians are Christians, ain't they? So ah the French, Belgians, English, and Russians. So why ah they killin' each othah? Didn't they read that paht of the Bible?"

Asa shrugged. "I suspect it has somethin' to do with insecurity, jealousy, weakness, and incompetence among the royal cousins, and not much of anythin' to do with their religious beliefs, if they have any. The Ottomans are Muslim; it has nothing to do with their religion, either. It's more to do with alliances and empires. They all want to expand, or at least keep, their empires. And there's this web of treaties and sworn allegiances that goes back to Queen Victoria. She thought marryin' her offspring off to the crown heads of Europe would preserve the peace and expand Britain's influence, but it looks as if that's pretty much backfired since King Edward VII died. Who knows? Mebbe it comes down to the Kaisah feelin' snubbed at the funeral, and he's been nursin' a grudge evah since. Sorta like George."

"To think that a family squabble could get the whole world into a war. But you know it's more complex than that," Si said.

"'Coss it is," Asa said. "But I can't help feelin' these foolish men playin' 'Mine's biggah' is a paht of it. Too bad we can't put all the royal babies in a ring and let them fight it out on their own without their subjects havin' to get involved. But no, they've got to drag the rest of the world into it. Austria didn't have to be so hahd-nosed with Serbia. After all, the Serbian government caught the assassin and the group he was in, and they made all kinds of concessions. But no, nothing would do for the Austrians but that Serbia give up its sovereignty to them. No mediation, no nothing. So here we are, because one fat royal was murdered by a handful of anarchists in a little Balkan country, the whole damned world has to get embroiled."

"Is that the only reason?" Si asked.

"Well, no. It's not that simple. That was just the match dropped in the tinderbox," Asa said. "But it's too late now to go back and change things, and I'm afraid we'll be in for it before long."

"What would I do, I wondah, if we get into it and my country wants me to fight?" Si said. "I can't see myself with a rifle in my hand. I couldn't kill anothah human bein'. It goes against everythin' I believe. If I'm not too old for conscription, guess mebbe I'd have to be a conscientious objectah. Mebbe they'd send me to jail. But I'd rathah my body be imprisoned than my soul."

"You're waxin' philosophical tonight." Asa drew in his long legs and sat forward, watching Silas. "What's got into you? I nevah heard you talk like this befoah."

"Well, we ain't nevah had a great wah befoah," Si said.

"You got me there. I don't know, Si. It's a hell of a mess." In Asa's vision, black thunderclouds piled up on the horizon. "This war sometimes seems like a senseless farce and a deadly tragedy all rolled into one. Only thing we humans seem to be good at — gettin' ourselves into deep, dahk trouble. Bein' powah hungry, pigheaded, and willfully ignorant. And endin' up killin' each othah. Stupid, stupid, stupid!" Asa thumped the arm of his chair.

"Take it easy, Asa." Si leaned over to touch Asa's arm. "Not all of us are like that, as you well know. Mebbe 'twas a mistake to talk about the wah tonight. Yaw still grievin' ovah Cap'n James, and yaw plumb wo'n out. I'm sorry I brought it up."

"Wasn't you brought it up. We can't very well avoid it, can we?" Asa slapped the front page of the newspaper. "Blazin' headlines in great big type screamin' the news. Besides, it's nevah wise to avoid the truth, howevah horrible it may be."

"As long as it *is* the truth, and not just yaw jaundiced view," Si said.

"'My jaundiced view?'" Asa echoed. "Si, I've seen things, terrible things, real horrah— " He shook his head. "I can't even begin—" He looked down at the floor.

"Can you tell me?" Si asked.

"Can't—" Asa muttered, shaking his head again. "No."

Si waited, watching Asa, and then said quietly, "You must gahd against despaiah, Asa, despite what's goin' on in the world. Try to put yaw faith in God."

Asa sighed, sitting back in his chair. "Can't say as I've got much faith lately, Si." He looked away, biting his lip, clamping a lid on his emotions. A wave of fatigue crashed over him.

"Nevah mind," Si said. "Janet and I will pray for you."

Asa pushed down on the arms of the chair, levering himself to his feet, yawning. "Well, time for me to hit the rack. Been a long day. See you in the mo'nin'. G'night, Si."

"'Night, Asa. Sleep well."

If only I could, Asa thought, as he dragged himself up the stairs. Exhausted as he was, he felt nervy, too keyed up to sleep well. He sometimes thought the upheaval and chaos in the world had invaded his brain and warring camps had made it a battleground. If only he could broker a peace treaty within himself.

\* \* \* \*

Janet, finished with the evening's chores, joined Silas in the sitting room, taking the chair Asa had just vacated. "It's good he's gone to bed early. He looks so washed out. He was awful upset about the way Mistah Lovejoy treated poah Mary. I'm worried about him."

"Mm," Si reached into his pocket and took out a letter. "This is addressed to us. Took a while gettin' heah. I took the libahty of readin' it at the station. It's from the ship's doctah."

"What's it say?" Janet reached for the letter. "Is he sick? He hardly ate a bite."

"Read it for yourself. Dunno whethah we should let Asa know... Doc says he prob'ly wouldn't like it, and he... Well, you read it."

As Janet read, she murmured, "My, my... oh, deah." Folding the letter again, she handed it back to Si. "Well, no wondah he looks so thin and wo'n out, poah lad. Thank God he made it home to us. I'm glad the doctah let us know. Why do you suppose it's so hahd f' Asa to tell us such things?"

"Doesn't want to worry us, I suspect," Si said. "I guess we should tell him we know. Be awkwahd tryin' to take cayah of him otahwise. Wish he wasn't so stubbin when he needs help and won't admit it. But the doctah says to let him be independent."

"Mebbe goin' to wo'k with you is too hahd f' him right now. He needs rest."

"Well, a month ago, he'd been back on partial duty, so maybe it's not that bad. And if he comes in with me, I can keep an eye on him, see that he doesn't ovahdo," Si said. "He is recoverin', Doc says, so mebbe he'll feel a little bettah aftah a few days' rest. We'll see."

"Well, mebbe." Janet didn't sound so sure. "It's his mental state I'm worried about, as much as anythin'. He seems so downhahted. Melancholy, as the doctah says."

"Ayup. Angry, too. The wah's got him upset, and Geo'ge, of coss. But theyah's no place for that angah to go. Theyah's somethin' else eatin' at him, but it's too hahd f' him to talk about. Somethin' horrible." Si paused, thinking. "We'll just have to keep lettin' him get it off his chest, and keep prayin' for him." He yawned. "Prob'ly time we were gettin' up to bed, too. Gotta get up befoah the sun tomorrow, to catch those elusive fish."

He lit a candle before extinguishing the oil lamp. He took his wife's long fingers in his callused ones for a moment, patted the back of her hand, and then let go. In the dim candlelight of the stairwell, she could just make out the soft look his eyes held for her.

## Chapter 27

# *Catharsis*

A sa was up early enough to eat breakfast with Si and Janet the next morning.

"How are you feelin' this mo'nin'?" Janet asked. "Sleep all right?"

"Feelin' fine, thanks. Slept like a log. And you?" Asa replied.

Janet and Si exchanged a significant glance.

Asa looked from one to the other of them. "What's goin' on?"

Si took a deep breath. "We got a letter yesterday, from Doctah Coffin. He told us—"

"He had *no right*!"

"Well, were *you* evah goin' to get around to tellin' us?" Janet said. "Malaria isn't the common cold, you know. How can we take propah cayah of you if we don't know these things?"

"Janet, I'm sorry. I—" Asa took a deep breath and let it out slowly.

"You didn't want t' worry us," Si said. "Mebbe Doc ovahstepped, but if he did, he did it f' yaw own *good*. You can be too damned stubbin sometimes, Asa. You want to do everythin' for everybody *else*, but *nobody* can do a *thing* f' you. *Pride*, that's what it is. And *pride*, young man, goeth before a fall! We ah goin' to help you! Would you expect us to do anything else?"

Asa opened his mouth to respond, but stared at Si, speechless.

Si seemed nearly as surprised. "Um. Mebbe I came on a little too strong, theyah." He took a gulp of his coffee. "What I mean to say is, we love you, and we want you to get well. So yaw gonna rest up, eat, and get yaw strength back befoah you come out fishin' with me, all right? We'll take it day by day, see how it goes."

Asa closed his mouth, humbled. He smiled at Si to show there were no hard feelings. "Well, uh, *gosh*, Si. I guess so. You're the boss."

"Bettah believe it," Si smiled back.

Janet put a plate of eggs, bacon, and toast in front of Asa. "Now you *eat* that. Don't just push it around on the plate. We can't affo'd to waste good food."

"Yes, ma'am!" Asa said. "Phew! I guess I've got *my* marching orders, clear enough." He picked up his fork and had a bite of egg and toast. Janet and Si watched him. "All right, you don't have to watch me like a hawk. I'm not gonna keel ovah, and I'm not mad. In a way, I'm glad you know. I don't have to pretend, and I don't have to explain." He had a sip of coffee. "Kind of a relief."

Janet reached out and patted his arm. He smiled at her, embarrassed.

"Phew! Glad we got that straight." Si spooned up the last of his oatmeal, and Janet placed a plate of scrambled eggs, bacon, and toast in front of him.

Poor Si, Asa thought. Mornings were usually quiet, not fraught with emotion.

Janet sat down with her own plate, and their breakfast returned to its normal preparation for the day. Asa got up and refilled everybody's coffee cups.

\* \* \* \*

He spent the morning helping Janet with some gardening. She was starting some new seeds, and Asa was watering the plants already growing. Despite the March chill, a small potbellied stove and bright sunlight made the greenhouse seem tropical.

With the back of her wrist, Janet wiped the perspiration off her brow. She pushed back some of the tendrils that had escaped the bun at the back of her neck. Asa noticed that her light brown hair was beginning to be streaked with gray. She works too hard, he thought; she worries too much.

"Shall I pick a mess of peas for supper tonight?"

"Ayup," Janet said. "Might use the leftovah fish from yestahday in a casserole, and have peas on the side. Think you'd like that?"

"Anything you make is bound to be good. I apologize for not havin' much appetite yestahday. You know I love your cooking, and you really outdid yourself."

"Well, theyah's leftovah chowdah and chocolate cake f' dinnah," Janet said. "How's that?"

"Sounds good, but didn't we just finish breakfast?"

"Hours ago," Janet said. "Don't tell me yaw still full."

"Well, it's still too early to be thinkin' about dinnah," Asa said. "Not even nine o'clock."

"What about a mo'nin' coffee break?" Janet asked.

"Now you're talkin'," Asa said. "You know I seldom say 'no' to anothah cup of coffee. As long as you sit down and have a cup with me."

"All right," Janet said. "Oh, look, Asa! The tomato plants I stahted a few days ago are already stahtin' to poke up some little green shoots. And pretty soon we'll have some Boston lettuce ovah heah. I'll just pick some of this pahsley, and I'll be right along. Put the kettle on, will you?"

"Will do." He picked up his pail of early peas, and headed into the house to wash up.

When Janet came in, he had already started the coffee. She put the parsley in a glass of water to keep fresh, and then got out the leftover biscuits, split a couple, and buttered them. After sprinkling them with cinnamon and sugar, she popped them under the broiler for a minute.

When they sat down at the table, she asked him, "How are you feelin', and don't just say, 'fine.'"

"Well, what do you want me to say, Janet? I am a lot bettah than I was. I was back to full duty a couple of weeks befoah we came home, so you don't have to treat me with kid gloves, all right? I get tired, that's all." Asa sighed. "I need to work. I need to keep busy."

"As long as you don't ovahdo it, and end up sick again," Janet said.

"Wasn't ovahwork that made me sick," Asa grumbled. "Was a mosquito bite. I don't think I have to worry about that in Ma'ch in New England. It's still cold enough to freeze a witch's— Oh! Sorry, Janet. I wasn't thinkin'."

"You think I'm that innocent?" Janet laughed. "You know, you give yourself away when you get grumpy. Yaw tiahed. How about a nap befoah dinnah?"

"I'm not that tiahed. Just… I dunno… out of sorts. I was hopin' to see…" He shrugged. "Oh, I dunno."

"Hopin' to see Mary again?" Janet asked.

Asa sighed. "Am I that transparent?"

"Do you think I'm that blind?" Janet asked. "I saw you two togethah befoah you left. Why don't you write her a lettah, see if you can visit next time you go to town?"

"I wrote her lettahs, but she nevah wrote back. Maybe she never got them. It's been so long now, she must think I don't cayah. What can I say?"

"Waell, say what you said in the lettahs you think she nevah got. And then ask if you can visit," Janet said. "You could've figahed that out f' y'self."

Asa ducked his head, smiling. "Aw, but then I still would've been wonderin' if it was proper. Maybe I needed your approval."

"Pshaw! When was the last time you needed *my* approval for anything?" Janet smiled. "Oh, speakin' of lettahs, I fo'got to give you yaw mail that came while you were gone. It's in the desk in the pahlah, second cubbyhole from the left. You can look it ovah befoah you staht writin', in case theyah's anythin' you need to respond to."

When he sat down and thumbed through the letters, one caught his eye. Mailed from Liverpool a couple of weeks after they'd left, it was from Angus Ross. "When he was so very ill, Jean-Claude Bilodeau gave me your address and asked if I would write to you if anything should happen to him. I regret to inform you that he has died of pneumonia." There was more, but none of the rest of it mattered. The letter fell from Asa's fingers as he slipped back in time. As though looking through a rain-streaked window, images floated through his mind.

*Men crammed into a lifeboat, floating on debris from a wreck.*

*The boy gripped his wrist in terror. Young... so young, so innocent and eager until war smashed his dreams. So young, until death took him away.*

*Monstrous Death, breaking apart, severing, tearing love from his bleeding heart, leaving him unrigged, adrift.*

*Swept further back, thrust into a cold, gray sea, buffeted by savage waves. Rain sheeting down from a slate-colored sky. Howling wind and...*

"Asa!" Janet was shaking his arm.

"Where..." He blinked, confused. "What?"

"Asa, you were... you were stock-still, starin' at nothin'. What's wrong?"

"Wrong?" His glance fell on the letter, and he let out a shuddering breath. "Oh. It's just... just... a young lad I used to know... I... I suddenly feel very tired. I think I will take that nap now, Janet. Excuse me."

He stumbled up the stairs and fell onto his bed, feeling as though some supernatural winch operator had swung some heavy cargo into him, knocking him into the deepest of holds. And then kept dropping load after heavy load on top of him. He closed his eyes, but the oblivion of sleep evaded him.

Then he remembered that back when they were in India, Doc had given him an envelope with a few packets of a powder to take if he couldn't sleep. He had put it in his toiletries bag and forgotten about it. There was the bag, on top of the dresser. But it was such an effort to get up when his limbs felt like lead. He closed his eyes again.

Sometimes one by one, sometimes in groups, the faces of the dead appeared to him, vision after vision: childhood friends who had died of scarlet fever, croup, measles, whooping cough; Uncle Nathan, Aunt Tillie, and his cousins; Jean-Claude; Aahva and the two women; Mrs. Lovejoy, James, Captain Asa, Captain Alfred, even the monster Gunn; his Mother and Father and Jamie; and then they'd start again. He could not wash the gory scene in India from his mind. He could not forgive himself for failing to save Jamie and James.

His eyes popped open and he pushed himself out of bed to the dresser, opened his kit and found the envelope. He took out one of the packets and dumped it in his tooth mug, poured some water over it, stirred it with the handle of his toothbrush, and then gulped it down. He couldn't remember what was in it, but right now, he didn't care. All he wanted was for it to work — fast. Anything to dissipate these ghosts that sapped his strength and wouldn't let him sleep. Shaking, he put the tin mug down too close to the edge of the washstand, and it fell onto the braided rug. He stumbled back to bed.

He knew the ghosts weren't real; they wouldn't hurt him. Still, he lay rigid, staring at the ceiling; unwilling to see them again. After a while, the powders took effect. He closed his eyes and slept.

\* \* \* \*

When Janet woke him at noon, he felt fuzzy and befuddled.

"Come and have some dinnah," she said.

"Huh?" Asa rubbed his eyes and blinked at her. "What time is it?"

"Dinnah time," Janet smiled. She bent to pick up the fallen mug. "Oh, you knocked your mug ovah. What's this powdery stuff? Asa, did you take somethin'?"

"Huh? Oh, that. It's just somethin' Doc gave me."

"What's in it?"

"Dunno. Can't remembah."

Janet shook her head. "Look at you. Whatevah it is, I don't think you should take it again. You look like you've been out on a three-day bendah. Now sit up and get yaw bearin's."

Asa pushed himself up and swung his feet to the floor. A wave of dizziness assaulted him and he put his head between his knees.

"What's the mattah?" Janet sounded worried. "Are you sick? Should I get Doc Chandlah?"

"Nunno, Janet." He slowly raised his head. "I'm all right. Just a little dizzy. Sat up too fast, that's all."

"You need somethin' to eat. That's what's wrong with you. Now, I'm gonna wash this out, and by the time I bring it back up heah, I want you to have washed yaw face and combed yaw haiah. And then we'll go down and have some dinnah."

All he wanted was to lie down and go back to sleep again, but he said, "Yah. Wash face. Comb haiah. Dinnah."

Janet frowned and shook her head again. "And no moah of whatevah that was Doc gave you, you heah? It's got you all muddled up."

"No moah," Asa said. "I don't like bein' muddled up anymoah than you like seein' me this way."

He obediently followed Janet's orders and managed to eat a bowl of chowder for dinner. After a cup of coffee, he felt more revived, and agreed to a piece of cake. "Mm. Good cake. Still moist even a day latah. You know, I might have anothah slivah with my second cup of coffee." He smiled.

"Theyah, see? All you needed was some food in yaw stomach." Janet beamed at him. "You had me worried theyah for a minute, but you look much bettah now."

"I think it was just those powdahs. I probably took too much. I thought the packet was a single dose, but that was meant for nighttime, not just a nap."

"Why'd you take it, anyway?" Janet asked.

"Well… I was… I dunno." He looked down at the table. How could he possibly tell her he was seeing ghosts?

"Hmm. Exhausted but too nervy to sleep, huh? Well, next time that happens, I'll make you a cup of chamomile tea."

Asa blinked rapidly. "Okay. Thanks." He sniffed.

"What are you gonna do this aftahnoon? Write lettahs?" Janet asked.

"I thought I'd take a walk, get some fresh ayah," Asa said. "Mebbe go by the Little Stoah, send a message to Josiah to set up a time to go see him."

"Well, fresh ayah might do you some good, but dress wahm, and don't stay out too long," Janet said. "It's cold out."

* * * *

Asa pulled on a sweater over his flannel shirt and wrapped a scarf around his neck before putting on his heavy reefer. He put on his watch cap and turned his collar up. He thought of strolling down to the beach, but even before spring arrived, there were too many people — digging clams or harvesting oysters, surf fishing, seaweed raking; there were dogs cavorting, and the high-pitched voices of kids playing. Today, he wanted solitude.

There weren't nearly as many as there were when the town was first settled, but the old whalers hadn't taken *all* the trees for masts and ships. He headed off into a wood of white cedar, scrub pine, and oak, where he knew of paths traveled only by rabbits, squirrels, and skunks. He hoped he wouldn't run into the latter.

*Just what in hell's the matter with me?* He was impatient with his endless fatigue, his lack of appetite, his depression. He could be gregarious, but lately his fellow human beings irritated him, and he'd catch himself grinding his teeth at their superficial heartiness. Besides, the fear that he might burst into tears at any moment mortified him.

All too soon, he found himself flagging. When he had to fight his way through some tangled brambles, he became confused by his surroundings. *Lost! I've never once got lost in these woods!* To his utter chagrin, he felt tears on his cheeks. *God, I feel like a five-year-old! No! A two-year-old. I was never this much of a crybaby when I was five!*

His tears turned into weeping. He sniffed. Feeling weary and defeated, he stretched out his arm and leaned against a tree to hold himself up. Wave after wave of overwhelming grief washed over him. He hung his head and sobbed. Desperately trying to stop, he gagged, and felt his dinner rising in the back of his throat. He swallowed and tried to keep it down, but his sobbing lead to retching until his stomach was empty. Staggering away from the spot, he wiped beads of perspiration from his forehead with his sleeve.

Careening into another tree, he wrapped his arms around it to keep from falling. *Weak, you're just weak! Come on, pull yourself up! Stand up! Stand up and be a man!* Berating himself only made his exhaustion and depression worse. He clung to the tree and cried. He couldn't help himself. *What has happened to my manhood? Jeez! Cryin' like a child in the arms of a tree! I should be strong enough to bear my grief alone. Instead, I've turned into a weak-kneed, lily-livered little kid. Mary, that poor slip of a girl, is stronger than I am.* Utterly undone and deeply ashamed, he pounded his fists against the trunk, insensitive to the injuries he was inflicting on his hands. He pushed himself away from the tree, and shambled toward a clearing.

*Damn it, James! I prayed to God to spare you! Why did you have to die? Why?*

Asa threw his cap to the ground, grabbed fistfuls of hair, and tugged, howling in frustration. He threw his head back and shook his fist at the sky, crying aloud. "God! Why must you take the people I love?" He tried to stop sobbing, dragging in gasping, shuddering breaths. "If you must have any more Lovejoys or Mayhews, take me! Spare Mary! Spare Janet and Si! Strike *me* down. Please. It would be a mercy."

He fell to his knees and wept. *I've gone mad, out here in the woods, screaming at God. Stark, raving mad! Seein' ghosts when I close my eyes. God help me! Oh, no he won't. He didn't help James, when I pleaded with him. He didn't help Mother and Father, not listening to my artless child's prayers. He didn't help Jamie — innocent little Jamie. He has never answered a single one of my prayers — or the answer was always no. Why would he help me, when they deserved his help, and I don't?*

He wept not only over the loss of Cap'n James, Jamie, and all the other people he loved, but over the loss of his faith.

His rational side often saved him from becoming swamped in emotions. He tried to summon it, to reason his way back to sanity, but his thoughts were as ungovernable as his feelings. The tears poured down his cheeks and dripped off his jaw.

*Loss, loss, loss. Each loss seems to multiply and compound the others, like a debt owed to some celestial loan shark; and in the end, the only way to pay is with my own life. Nunno, I mustn't get carried away. People die, and it hurts like hell, but offering my own life won't stop death. It's wildly hubristic to think so — as if I were a lesser god in some kind of Greek myth, making a deal with a greater god to make mortals immortal.*

*James is dead. I must accept that. I'm not the only one wracked by grief. Poor Mary, to lose both mother and father within weeks of each other. I wonder if she can bear up under the weight of it.*

*Maybe I need to face this grief head-on. Tryin' to ignore it sure isn't workin' very well, is it? I can't think my way out of it; emotions aren't necessarily amenable to reason. Maybe it's all right to let it out, to purge all of that anger, grief, and bitterness. What bitter losses! But I cannot let them sink me. Maybe I've got to let the bilge pumps work; get it all out before I founder.*

It was frightening to stop struggling to regain control, but he had to admit that he had already lost it. *What if I can't stop? What if I become utterly lost, swept downstream into a sea of insanity?* But he couldn't fight it any longer, and gave himself over to wailing out his pain, letting it pour out of him in a flood, letting go of his fear that he would be washed away with it.

He lost all sense of time, of his surroundings, even of his own senses. He neither knew nor cared whether he was hot or cold, kneeling on an anthill, or scratched by brambles. He wept until the fountain of his tears ran dry. When he came back to himself, he was unsure whether he felt better or worse. But he had a sense that something had changed.

*All right, so I cried, and screamed, and yelled at God. Maybe I am crazy. Maybe I'm just human, with all the failings and frailties inherent to all of us. In any case, now it's time to get myself shipshape and face the world.*

Searching in his pockets, he found his handkerchief, dried his eyes and blew his nose. He picked up his cap, stood on wobbly legs, and looked around, taking a few deep breaths. As though a fog had lifted, he recognized where he was. He wasn't lost anymore. Certain he would be alone at this time of year, he went to a small, hidden pond. Squatting on its bank, he cracked its thin coating of ice with his fist, cupped his trembling hands in its clear water and bathed his face. The icy water numbed the cuts and bruises on his hands and lessened the swelling of his knuckles. He rinsed his mouth, drank some water, and sat back on his heels. He felt drained.

When he stood up, he had such a spinning sensation that he thought he might faint. He sat down on a rocky outcrop in the sun to rest and breathe. Breathing in through his nose, he filled his lungs and counted to five. Slowly exhaling through his mouth, he pushed all the air out, and counted to five. When he slipped into a rhythm, he didn't need to count anymore. Without trying, he opened his hands and let go of thought, fear, anger, and grief. He drifted into a trance-like state. When at last he roused himself, the sun was beginning to cast long shadows.

He stood and stretched, sucking in air, expanding his lungs. Kneeling by the pond's edge, he cupped his hands and drank again. He used his cap to beat off the pine needles and sand from his trousers and jacket, shook it out, folded its cuff, and pulled it down over his ears. Taking a few deep breaths of salty, pine-scented air, he headed for home.

That dragged-down feeling was gone. He had a newfound sense of peace.

This was what he had been searching for with Sharmaji, but had been unable to achieve. *Achieve, attain*, he thought. *That was the problem. The key is in letting go, not in grabbing on; in accepting, not in fighting; in relaxing, not in striving. Sharmaji tried to teach me that, but I guess I just wasn't ready to open my mind or my clenched fists.*

He hunted in his pockets, found a roll of peppermint Lifesavers, and popped one in his mouth to freshen his breath.

*Well, that was strange. Think I went truly bats for a while — had some kind of a breakdown. Hope I got it all out of my system. Good thing nobody saw me. I'm glad that's over. At least, I sure hope it's over.*

He put his hand on his stomach, aware of a vaguely familiar sensation, something he hadn't felt for a long time. *Hunger — that's what it is! Hope I'm not late for suppah.* He quickened his pace.

# Chapter 28

## *Visiting Josiah*

When Asa awakened the next morning, his eye fell upon the thick folder he had left on top of the chest of drawers. It took a minute to clear the sleep from his eyes and from his brain; then he remembered.

*Oh, yah. It's the statements from the men. I ought to get that file over to Josiah, so he can put it in his safe. Just in case…*

After breakfast, as Asa was finishing his second cup of coffee, he told Janet he was going to Josiah's with some papers.

"How do you know he'll be theyah? Did you call? Might be a long walk for nothin'," Janet said.

"No, I haven't made an appointment. I thought I'd walk over there on the off chance that he would be home. His office is just next door, you know. If he's not home, I'll check there."

"Well, heah." Janet handed him an orange. "Take this to keep your strength up. Good if you get thi'sty, too."

"Janet, it's only a half-hour walk, not a mountain hike. Besides, I've got enough to carry with that thick file of papers."

Holding up one finger, Janet said, "Wait a minute. I've got just the thing."

Asa shook his head as she left the room. He could hear the hall closet door opening. Then he heard Janet moving things around and muttering.

"Now, whayah… Aha! Gotcha."

He wondered what she had unearthed.

She came in with a triumphant smile and placed a canvas messenger bag in front of him.

"Thanks, Janet. That's perfect," Asa said.

"If yah don't mind my askin', what ah they?"

"It's only that—" Asa sighed. He didn't want to talk about it, but he didn't want to be secretive with Janet. "Captain Hookset got each man on the ship to write down his recollection of the day… the night that… the sto'm when we were aboahd the *Mary Lovejoy*." Asa took in a deep breath and let it out slowly. "They prove that Geo'ge has no case against me. The lawyah from the D.A.'s office told me to give them to my lawyah, just in case Geo'ge tries anything else."

Looking somber, Janet asked, "Have you read them?"

"Nunno." Asa shook his head. "Couldn't bring myself to even glance at them. Too… Well." All at once, he saw mountainous waves washing over the deck, heard the rumble of thunder and the men's voices shouting over the roaring wind, smelled the ozone of lightning, and felt the cold black sea pulling him down.

Janet nodded, placing her hand on top of his.

Taking another deep breath, but letting it out quickly, Asa shook off the nightmare and awakened to his surroundings. He was sitting on a wooden chair in *this* kitchen, at *this* time, with Janet *right now*.

He checked his pocket watch. "Look at the time! I'd bettah get goin' if I hope to catch Josiah still at home." He stuffed the papers into the bag, accepted the orange Janet insisted he take, grabbed his coat, and headed out the door. "Bye, Janet! Thanks again."

* * * *

When he knocked, Josiah opened the door with a piece of toast in his hand.

"Oh, good! You're home." Asa said. "Did I interrupt your breakfast?"

"Asa! I could offer you the same greeting — well, except for the breakfast part. It's good to see you!" Josiah said. "Come in, come in. Have a cup of coffee with me, and we can talk for a while." He looked at the grandfather clock in the hall. "I have to head out in about an hour, but that gives us some time."

In the kitchen, when Josiah had put down his toast, and Asa had slipped his bag off his shoulder, they hugged, thumping each other on the back.

Josiah stood back and looked at Asa. "You're even thinner than the last time I saw you. Are you all right?"

"Waell… I hate to admit it, but I *was* sick for a while. I'm bettah now," Asa said. "With Janet's cookin', I'll put the weight back on in no time."

"What was it? Did they know?" Josiah asked.

"Malaria," Asa said.

"Bad?" Josiah asked.

"Let's just say I wouldn't wish it on my worst enemy — even George."

"Oh, Lord, that *is* bad. I'm glad you survived," Josiah said. "Sit, sit," he pulled out a chair. "Let me just get an extra cup."

Though Asa had already had almost three cups of coffee, he wouldn't say no. "Thanks, Josiah." He took a sip. "Good coffee."

"I'm no kind of cook, but coffee is the one thing I know how to make," Josiah grinned.

"Mrs. um… What's her name? Heaven's sake, I know it as well as I know my own, but it just escapes me. Hm. Higgins… Hodgkins… Hodges! That right?"

Josiah nodded. "You got it in three guesses."

"You give her time off again?" Asa asked.

Josiah struck a silent movie pose of despair, with the back of his wrist on his forehead and the other hand on his heart. "She *left* me! Can you believe it? She left me here to *starve*." He grinned.

"Finally got sick of your tyrannical demands, eh?" Asa grinned back.

"Tyrannical? My friend, you hurt me to the quick. You know I'm not a tyrant — just your ordinary, run-of-the-mill despot."

They laughed together.

"In actuality, she had to go to New Hampshire to tend to a sick relative — an aunt, I believe. Apparently, the old auntie has some kind of chronic illness, so Mrs. Hodges said I would be without a cook for a very long time, and I should hire someone else," Josiah said. "I'm devastated," he returned to his joking plaint. "I don't know *what* I shall do without her. I've been living on *crackers* and *cheese*."

Asa laughed. "No luck finding a replacement?"

"Who could ever replace Mrs. Hodges?" Josiah said. "No luck. No one has even applied for the position."

"I'll ask Janet if she knows someone," Asa said. "She usually does."

"She seems to know everyone," Josiah said. "If she can't suggest anyone, I'm sunk."

"Well, I'm goin' to work for Si, but I could always moonlight as cook for you — suppers only, you understand."

"You're going to work for Si?" Josiah's jocular tone vanished. "So, you've made a firm decision about not going back to sea?"

"Except for Captain Hookset, I've sailed under Lovejoys. It's… too many memories. Captain Hookset is… he's great, and I don't mean that as we use it in the vernacular; he's formidable, but fair, compassionate — a truly good man. I could go on, but we don't have time. Suffice it to say, he's one of a kind. I'd sail with him any day, but he feels he's getting too old; said that would be his last voyage. He's retiring. Do you know he tracked down every man I sailed with on the *Mary Lovejoy*, and they all signed on to sail with us on the *Eastern Trader*?"

"I hadn't heard that, no," Josiah said.

"I came to see you as a friend, but I also came to ask a favor," Asa said. "Captain Hookset had every one of those men write down what they remembered about the night… the night James…" Tears came to his eyes, and words couldn't get past the lump in his throat.

After a brief silence, Josiah asked, "Depositions?"

"No, they weren't notarized," Asa said. "But they were signed and witnessed by Captain Hookset and either Doc or Mike Slocum, so I think they could pass as such." He paused. "When the *Eastern Trader* docked in Boston, George was waiting with the harbormaster and a policeman. Hanson — did you know Hanson had joined the police?"

"Yes. Stop stalling, and tell me what happened," Josiah said. "Please."

"Well, George — no surprise there — wanted to charge me with murder. At his demand, an assistant from the D.A.'s office came to the harbormaster's office. He thought he didn't have any jurisdiction over the high seas, but said he'd listen to us, anyway, to see if he could determine who should handle it. Captain Hookset had come with me, thank God, and he showed the men's statements to Mr. Fielding, the D.A.'s man. After reading portions of each one, he glared at George and said that contrary to… Well, he said George had no case."

"Of course he hadn't," Josiah said. "I told you that last fall."

"Anyway, he — Mr. Fielding — said that I should take these statements to my lawyer for safekeeping, in case George should try anything else." Asa blew out a breath and took the thick file from the messenger bag. "So, will you put these in your safe?"

Taking the folder from Asa, Josiah said, "Of course I will, Asa. Moreover, if George gives you any more trouble, come to me. Let me handle it. No matter the time, day or night; come by or send me a message."

Asa's eyes filled up. "Thank you, Josiah. You're such a good friend to me, and I'm afraid I neglect you terribly. But that doesn't mean I don't love you like a brother, you know."

"You don't neglect me any more than I neglect you. We're busy or have to contend with other things," Josiah said. "Let's take these to the office and put them in the safe."

Asa used the few minutes it took to walk next door to breathe in the fresh air and collect himself.

"There," Josiah said, spinning the dial on the safe after depositing the papers. "That safe is fireproof, too, so your defense is secure."

"Thank you so much, Josiah," Asa said.

"I'm more than happy to help in any way I can. You know that."

"Yah, I do. And if you ever need me for anything, just ask," Asa said. "I don't know what good I'd be, but I'd try like hell." He grinned.

"Thanks, pal," Josiah lightly punched him on the arm. "I think you'd move heaven and earth, if you had to." Pulling his watch from his waistcoat pocket, he said, "Speaking of busy with other things, I've got to dash if I'm going to pick up that surveyor and meet my client at the site. Property dispute," he explained. "Let's get together for dinner some night."

"Oh, speakin' of food," Asa tossed the orange to Josiah, who reached out and caught it. "A little somethin' besides cheese and crackers."

Josiah laughed.

"About that dinner," Asa said. "I'll cook. Just let me know what you'd like to eat."

"That'd be grand. Sometime next week?"

"Let's do it."

"Well, sorry to rush off like this, but—"

"You've got clients to see and work to do. Thanks again, Josiah. See ya latah."

On the walk home, Asa felt better than he'd felt in a long time. He'd hardly been aware of the tension he was holding in the muscles of his neck and shoulders until it lifted. Taking a deep breath, he relished the smell of salt sea air and pine trees. Home.

He remembered the first time he'd met Josiah and smiled.

Walking down to a small pond to look for tadpoles, Asa had come across a boy throwing stones at the frogs on their lily pads.

He walked up to the boy, and stopped about three feet away. He tipped his head to the side and asked, "Why are you doin' that?"

"Because I'm mad at my brother, not that it's any of your business."

"But what did those poah frogs evah do to you?" Asa scolded but he never raised his voice. "It's wrong to kill a livin' thing, unless you're gonna eat it."

"What do you know? How old are you, kid?"

"Four. How old are you?"

"Ten," Josiah had stood tall and puffed out his chest. "So who are you to tell me anything?"

Asa held firm. "Just because I'm youngah, doesn't mean I don't know right from wrong." He swung his arm out and pointed at the frogs. "And those frogs are God's creatures, just like you and me. How would *you* like it if somebody stahted throwin' stones at you because they were mad at somebody else?" Hands on hips, he looked at Josiah with reproach.

Josiah dropped the stone he had in his hand, and turned to Asa with a puzzled look. "You sure you're only four? You're tall for your age."

"Well, I'm four-and-a-half, but yaw changin' the subject."

"I don't believe it," Josiah said. "No little kid talks like you."

"Cap'n Lovejoy says I'm precocious; that means I'm smahtah than my years. Are you gonna keep throwin' stones at those frogs?" Asa persisted.

"No," Josiah said. "Your reasonable argument has convinced me."

"You should apologize to them," Asa said.

"What!? Are you nuts? Apologize to a pond full of frogs?"

"You were mean to them, and you did wrong," Asa lectured. "What do you do when you are wrong, and you know it? Didn't your parents teach you *anything*?"

"Well, all right!" Josiah faced the pond and shouted, "I apologize for being mean to you, frogs. I won't do it again, I promise." He burst out laughing. "I have never met a kid like you. Here you are, just a little four-year-old, and you've got me apologizing to a pond full of frogs! What's your name?"

"Asa Mayhew. What's yours?"

"Josiah Mayo," Josiah stuck out his hand and Asa shook it. "Pleased to meet you, Asa. You know, I came out here, mad as blue blazes. I meet you, and now I'm happy and laughing. You're the funniest kid I ever met."

"Do you mean funny ha-ha or funny strange?" Asa was sober-faced.

"Both!" Josiah laughed. "You talk like a little old man — no — a Sunday school teacher!" Josiah squinted at him. "I don't know — you're awfully tall for four."

"Well, yaw pretty smaht for a ten-year old and you know a lot of big words. But I believe *you* when you say yaw ten." Asa grinned. "Would a Sunday school teachah tell a lie?"

Josiah laughed. "Come on, let's go look at the tadpoles."

And we've been fast friends ever since, Asa thought. The age difference never mattered. And he's had me laughing plenty of times when I've come to him blue and downhearted, or angry with George. With Josiah at my side, I don't have to worry about George.

Asa felt as though a burden had been lifted off his back. There was a tune running through his head that he couldn't quite place. As soon as he started whistling it, he remembered that it was something he had sung with Josiah in the children's choir: *All things bright and beautiful, all creatures great and small.* In this brief moment, all things did seem bright. He smiled into the sunlight and took a deep breath, savoring it.

## Chapter 29

# *Bill Porter*

Si's only suit, worn in summer's heat and winter's cold, was black wool. Every Saturday afternoon, Janet brushed and pressed it, steaming it with a damp towel. The iron was cast iron, heated on the stove. Wielding it required strong muscles and pot holder. Si was in charge of polishing their shoes.

"If you'll bring down yah suit, Asa, I'll press it." Janet moved the towel down the leg of the trousers, careful to keep the crease straight.

"Nunno, Janet. You've got too much to do already. I'll do it. Just let me know when you're finished with the iron. Can I help you with anything, like makin' suppah?"

"Beans are already bakin' in the oven."

"I'll make Sunday dinnah tomorrow, then."

"Ahn't you goin' to church?"

"I'll put the roast in befoah church, and I'll come back aftah the service to cook the rest of the meal. The time it takes you and Si to say goodbye to everybody, it'll be ready for you by the time you get home. All right?"

Janet smiled. "All right. Thank you, Asa."

"No need to thank me. Long as I'm livin' heah, I got to keep up my paht."

"You already help, and you always wash and wax the kitchen floah aftah we take ah baths on Sat'dy night."

"Well, truth be told, I just can't seem to empty the tub without spillin' watah all ovah the floah. Have to clean it up anyway; might's well do a thorough job." Asa grinned.

Every Saturday night, Asa and Si brought the big galvanized tub into the kitchen and sat it on the floor in front of the coal stove, where large pots and kettles of water had been heating for hours.

The fourth week they did this chore together, Si looked at Asa. "I'm real pleased to see you healthy and strong again, but yah know? The only time I saw you come alive in the last couple o' weeks was when you picked us through that fog bank usin' yaw eahs and nose. Yaw bo'd with fishin', ain't ya?"

"Oh, it's all right. I guess I'd just like somethin' a little less routine, somethin' that makes me use my wits more." Asa hastily added, "That's not to say you don't need smahts to be a fishaman. You know I don't mean it that way, Si."

"I'm not *that* touchy, Asa. Yaw not just smaht, yaw quick. Takes most guys moah than a day to memahrize all the different sounds of the bell buoys and fog ho'ns, and most of 'em nevah learn how to sniff out theyah location — don't have noses sensitive as yaws. And a lot of 'em don't realize how fog can disto't sound. Watch it! Don't burn yahself — use that potholdah. Hah! Too bright t' be satisfied with fishin' every day, but not bright enough to use a potholdah to pick up a hot kettle!" Si grinned as they poured the water into the tub.

Asa laughed. "Not as bright as you thought, and senseless to boot, eh Si?"

"Nunno, yah not senseless. I dunno how you do it, with those callused hands, but you got the most sensitive fingahs of anybody I know."

Asa raised his eyebrows. "You all right, Si? What do fingahs have to do with anythin'?"

"I'm talkin about yaw senses."

"I didn't mean senseless in its literal sense, you know."

"Ya meant foolish, but ya also meant ya wouldn't feel it if ya touched that hot kettle. I know how ya like to use words that have two meanin's. Yaw sense of touch is just as keen as yaw senses of hearin' and smell. And I nevah seen anybody as eagle-eyed."

"Si, dogs have a fah bettah sense of smell than any of us. Does that make them smahter than us?"

"I've known some pretty smaht dogs, but let's leave them out of it. I'm tryin to talk about you."

Asa shook his head. "Let's leave me out of it, too."

Si ignored him. "Remembah when my thumb stahted to get all red and swollen? You examined it evah so gentle and found a splintah buried so deep we couldn't see it. I couldn't even feel it when you took it out. I felt it when you cleaned it with alcohol, though. And then you made me soak it in that watahed down cahbolic acid solution every night."

"Well, I wanted to stop the infection. You wouldn't want to have your thumb amputated because of a little splintah, would you?"

"The point is, Asa, ya got sensitive hands. Janet! Tub's ready — you first."

Asa and Si left the kitchen, closing the door to insure Janet's privacy.

"So, let me get this straight. I'm some monstrous kind of a chimera? With the nose of a hound, eyes of an eagle, hearing of an owl, and part — what's known for its sense of touch? Maybe the whiskers of a cat, or the antennae of some kind of insect. What a beauteous mug I'd have!" Asa chortled.

Si laughed. "I hate to disappoint ya, but yaw not quite *that* unique."

"Befoah we digressed, weren't we talkin' about fishin'? Oh, yah! I was gonna say, you and Tony are the brains of the operation. You only need me and the rest of the crew for brawn."

"I like havin' you abo'd, so don't get the idea I'm pushin' you out. But I undahstand if ya want t' look fo' somethin' a little moah challengin'."

"I like spendin' the day with you, Si. But, you're right. The only time I feel like I'm doin' somethin' useful is when we have to deal with some trouble, like dirty weather or a broken-down engine," Asa said. "And since I overhauled her, the engine's been runnin' all right, but that's not sayin' much. That Fraser make-and-brake engine is not very reliable. There's no clutch, no idle, and you have to stop and start again just to turn around."

"Well, we've still got the sails."

"Have to. If these engines are to be any real use, designers and manufacturers have got to make an awful lot of improvements. They help you go fahthah, but that's about it."

"Ayup, we still have to rely on sail. You're a good sailmakah, too. I'll miss havin' you abo'd."

"I ain't gone yet, Si. I'm not leavin' 'til I get a bettah offah."

When Janet went up to bed, and Si took his turn in the tub, Asa started sketching ideas for fishing boat engines. He didn't have any means of manufacturing and testing a prototype, but it was fun to try to come up with something better than the existing models. *Almost anything would be bettah than what we've got now,* he thought. *Be hahd not to improve on it.*

*Could I scale down a ship's engine?* he wondered. *Nah, too impractical. Have to make so many modifications, might's well come up with something entirely new. Hmm, I wondah how I could fix up an automobile engine to fit in that engine compartment.*

Si came out of the kitchen in his bathrobe. "Yaw turn, Asa."

"Huh?" Asa looked up. "Oh, thanks." He put down his paper and pencil, and went into the kitchen for his turn in the tub, after which, he'd only work up a sweat again, washing and polishing the kitchen floor. After the first time, he'd learned to save enough warm water for a sponge bath afterward.

That night, he dreamt of engine designs. In the morning, he awoke with a sense of having solved a knotty problem, but the ephemeral dream had drifted away with the morning mist. *Ah, well, maybe it will come back to me. Maybe it wouldn't have worked, anyway.*

\* \* \* \*

On Sunday morning, they dressed in the clothes they'd prepared on Saturday. Si wore a white shirt, a stiffly starched white wing collar, and a tie. He brushed off his black derby hat. Everything had to be spic and span for Sunday.

Janet's Sunday best was a dark blue shirtwaist dress, with a high, stiff lace collar and cuffs. Its skirt covered her ankles. It had been old-fashioned when she had first made it ten years ago, from sturdy homespun and a borrowed pattern. Hot weather or cold, she wore a chemise, waist-cinching corset, over-corset, and at least two petticoats. In summer, she wore a broad-brimmed straw hat with a blue ribbon, fastened with a long hat pin. The rest of the year, she wore a narrow-brimmed navy blue felt hat she had made herself. She had found blue jay's feather in the yard and stuck it in the hatband. Asa smiled whenever he saw it; it reminded him of Janet's whimsical side. She wasn't as staid as she pretended to be. This May Sunday was warm enough for her to leave her winter coat at home and wear a wool shawl.

"Why don't I buy you both some new clothes for Sunday best?" Asa asked.

"What's wrong with *this* suit?" Si asked.

"Nothin's wrong with it, but wouldn't you like a light-weight one for summah and a wahmah one for wintah? Somethin' a little less Vic— uh, moah comf'table? I don't see how you can stand that wing collah, Si." Asa tugged at his own collar in sympathy. "Janet, wouldn't you be moah comf'table in some material that's not so heavy?"

Janet flat out refused. "This is good wool broadcloth, lasts a long time. Yaw not wastin' money on a new dress when this one is pe'fectly se'viceable. And Si's suit still has a few good yeahs left in it."

"Oh, I fo'got," Asa said. "The eleventh commandment of New Englandahs: 'Use it up; wear it out. Make it do; or do without.'"

"No call to be sahcastic, Asa," Janet said. "It makes pe'fect sense not to waste money on unnecessary things."

"You're right, Janet. I apologize."

"And you give us too much as it is," Si said.

"I give up," Asa raised his hands in surrender. "No new clothes — at any rate, not yet."

At least they still fit well, Asa thought. Sometime when they're not home, I'll sneak in and take measurements from these clothes. And then, maybe for Christmas, I'll surprise them.

Asa was dressed in his navy blue suit, crisp white round collar and a navy and red striped four-in-hand tie. He switched the grosgrain band on his straw boater to navy blue and white, to match his suit.

"You wearin' that hat to church?" Si asked.

"Why not? It must be respectable enough if President Wilson wears one," Asa said. "I'll be takin' it off indoors, anyway."

As they walked to church, Asa noticed a few other men wearing straw boaters.

He enjoyed the singing, and said a silent prayer of thanks that this new minister didn't preach for an entire hour, as had the last one. It seemed he trusted his congregation was bright enough to comprehend the message in twenty minutes, as long as he had the Old Testament lesson, the epistle, and the gospel backing him up.

Asa approved; if they couldn't get it then, they weren't likely ever to get it. After all, how many times had they already heard it? And if they read their Bibles as they said, wasn't the sermon just an exegesis of the text?

Asa didn't have much patience with being repeatedly beat over the head with something he had intuitively understood as a child. When one came right down to it, it was all about the two greatest commandments, wasn't it? Love the Lord your God with all your heart, and all your soul, and all your mind; and love your neighbor as yourself. Who is your neighbor? Every living being, as it turns out. And in Jesus, there is neither Jew nor Gentile, nor slave nor free, nor male nor female, for we are all one in Christ. He told us God is love. If only Christians actually believed as they professed, and acted that way.

Si and Janet were always the last to leave after the service. Though he exchanged greetings with his beloved neighbors, Asa didn't feel any compunction to speak at length to every person there. He strode home ahead of them, to check the roast and put on the vegetables.

\* \* \* \*

Just as Janet and Si were never in any hurry to leave church, they were never in any hurry to walk home. Sunday, after all, was a day of rest. As they strolled along, Si said to Janet, "I am content, on sea o' land, to enjoy the beauty of naychah, and to live quietly heah with you, my deah. I am happy to walk, but Asa needs to so-ah." He swept off his hat, and pointed with it to the gulls wheeling, dipping, and soaring high in the sky.

Janet looked at him and smiled, to all appearances as in love as she'd been at sixteen. Si smiled back and offered his arm; she took it.

\* \* \* \*

Asa still went out seining for mackerel with Si. Spring was the slow season, with low catches of skinny fish; fall was usually much better, with fatter, more plentiful fish. He didn't think he could feign enough interest to stay on until fall. Si already knew he was bored. It wouldn't be long before Tony and the crew caught on.

One Friday, as they came into dock with their day's catch, Asa noticed the *Emily*, a Bermuda rigged sloop, tied up. She was a fine looking craft, with a spotless teak deck, gleaming paintwork and shining brass. Like some modern sailing craft, she had an engine for ease in getting into and out of crowded ports, and in case of becoming becalmed. Her owner was engaged in attempting to repair this engine, with many a barked knuckle and a sprinkling of colorful language.

"Give you a hand, Mistah Pawtah?" Asa asked. Silas and Tony had joined a group of men swapping tales while awaiting their turn with the fish buyer.

"Aren't you Asa Mayhew?"

"Ayup, that's me."

"Haven't seen you in a dog's age. I see you've gone from callow youth to seasoned mariner in the interim," Porter said. "Welcome aboard. I thought I'd found the problem, but just when I think I've got her fixed, she goes and dies on me again. I swear she's taken against me!"

"Well, let's see." Asa swung himself aboard. "Hmm, you've made some interesting modifications here. Looks more like an automobile engine than those things they're laughably passing off as engines to the fishing fleet. Oh, this is a good idea for achieving more speed, but it could be that you've... hmm, let's see, here..."

He trailed off as his deft fingers and sharp eyes examined this and that. "Aha! I believe I've found the trouble. You see…" He explained the problem as he fixed it. When he was done and started her up, she ran smoothly. "Shall we take her for a spin around the harbor, try her out?"

"Well, I'll be damned! I thought I knew everything about that engine; after all, I *did* design it. But here I've been working on that thing for hours, to no avail. Then you come along, spot the problem, and fix her up in nothing flat! Right, let's take her out and see what she can do. You take the helm."

Asa grinned to be at the helm of such a beauty. It sure beat an old seiner. As they got away from the other traffic in the harbor, he opened the throttle. The engine nearly sang to him.

"Well, Mr. Pawtah, she looks like she'll do," he beamed at Porter, happy with the yacht and happy with his work.

"Call me Bill. Did I see you come in on that fishing boat with Silas Mayhew? How's the catch these days?" Bill asked.

"Waell," Asa drawled, "not as good as one might hope. Enough to keep Si and Tony busy, but I feel about as useful as a fifth wheel."

"Thinking about looking for something a bit more challenging?" Bill rubbed his hands together. "How would you like to work for me? Skipper the *Emily*, and maybe tinker around with a few other kinds of engines?"

"Pawtah engines?" Asa smiled, interested.

"I've been looking for a fellow who's as gifted with machinery as you seem to be. Do you know anything about automobile engines?"

"Waell, if you can count gettin' Silas's rickety old flivvah runnin', but anybody can fix a Ford." Asa didn't mention that he knew all kinds of marine engines inside out. "But isn't this a bit sudden? I mean, you don't really know me, and here you're offerin' me a job right off the bat. How do you know I'm not some lazy lout, or worse?"

"I must confess I overheard some men talking about you when you were coming into the harbor. They were saying how surprised they were when you didn't ship out again. There was some dispute about whether you'd made chief mate at the age of nineteen or twenty. One fellow said you'd got your captain's license, while others said they hadn't heard that, but they all agreed they didn't think you'd be happy with puttering around home for long."

"Waell, I got my license, all right." As soon as he'd said it, Asa wished he hadn't.

Bill looked at him for a moment, but didn't pursue it.

"I thought how rare it was not to hear a negative word about someone who wasn't even within earshot. I shouldn't have been eavesdropping, I know, but I couldn't help but hear them; they were so close to where I was busy barking my knuckles on that motor." Bill sucked on a scraped knuckle.

"Now, I just can't believe you didn't hear one negative word, knowing how the folks around here like to gossip. Are you sure they didn't tell any tales about my being almost arrested for murder, or how the Lovejoy Line won't have me on one of their ships again?" Asa laughed.

"Mr. Mayhew," Bill began.

"Asa," Asa interrupted. "If I'm to call you Bill, you sure can't be calling me *Mister* Mayhew!"

"Very well. Asa, the closest thing to a negative word those fellows said was that they couldn't understand why you didn't beat the tar out of George Lovejoy. I've heard talk, of course, but all I've heard paints you in a good light, and casts Lovejoy in a pretty bleak one. He was at Harvard when I was, and I never thought much of him. Got himself expelled for cheating, among other things."

Asa sped up as he pulled the boat around, casting a large arc of spray, which caught the sunlight and threw fleeting rainbows over them. He'd created that brief colorful display to free himself from the darkness he felt at the mention of George's name. The speed of the boat exhilarated him, and he turned to Bill and grinned.

"She runs smoother and faster than she ever did! You're a wizard!" Bill said. "Come to work for me, Asa. I pride myself on knowing engines, but I swear this thing had me licked. Nearly all you had to do was look at her, and here she is purring like cat!"

Asa laughed. He hoped his tanned face hid the blush he felt warming his cheeks. He slowed the boat as they headed back into the harbor. "I must say it's a tempting offer. I'll think about it and let you know. How long you gonna be around?"

"My family and I are here for the summer at our place up on the hill near Gull Pond," Bill said. "You know the place?"

"The old Newcomb place?" Asa asked. "I heard somebody had bought it and was fixin' it up."

"Yes, that's the place. I might not be here the whole time if I'm needed back at the plant, but I'll be back and forth. Come see me when you've made up your mind." Bill grinned. "Come see us anyway. I'd like you to meet my family. Maybe seeing us in our natural habitat would help you to decide."

They pulled up to the dock, and Asa threw the bow lines to Si, who had been watching the sloop. As he made the stern lines fast, Asa introduced his cousin to his prospective new boss.

"Oh, I know Mistah Bill Pawtah, Asa," Si said. "We're old fishin' buddies."

"Silas is the best guide around," Bill grinned. "He can always find the fish, salt water or fresh."

"Nevah spent the day sittin' waitin' for a bite with a bettah companion." Si nodded to Bill. He turned to Asa with mock resignation. "I suppose he's been tryin' to hiah you away from me."

"Ayup. Says I'm some kind of wizard with machinery." Asa rolled his eyes. "Don't know as I should listen to half what he says. My hats might get too tight."

"Silas, you've given me an idea. Asa, if you want to get to know me better, why don't we go fishing on Gull Pond tomorrow? It's Saturday. Surely this slave-driver doesn't make you work on Saturday."

"Well, he usually does, but we decided to give the fish a day off, seein' as how they've been so sluggish about bein' caught." Asa grinned. "Six o'clock too early for you?"

"Make it seven. Meet me up at my house. We'll have a cup of coffee before we go."

"Seven it is," Asa said.

* * * *

When Asa and Si got home, Janet had supper ready. "What took you so long? Suppah's nearly all dried up!"

"Oh, Asa was just lahkin' around the hahbah on Mistah Bill Pawtah's yacht. Took her for a pretty good spin, too," Silas said, pulling out a chair.

"Asa, you nevah!"

"But, Janet, I put her right back where I found her, all nice and tied up to the dock." He winked and grinned at her. "You think I stole her?"

"Coss not!" Janet said. "But I never knew him to let anyone else but himself at the helm."

"Seems Bill was havin' a bit o' trouble with that priceless engine of his, and Asa fixed it for him in a jiffy. He was so grateful that he not only let Asa take the helm, he offered him a job!" Si beamed at Asa.

"Coss, I haven't accepted it, yet. Though it's mighty temptin'. Gonna go fishin' with him tomorrow; get to know him a little. Then I'll decide. On the othah hand, could be that after a day of fishin' with me, he might take back the offah."

"Oh, go on with you!" Janet said. "After a day of fishin' with you, *he'll* prob'ly want to adopt you as well!"

Flustered, Asa dropped his napkin on the floor, and ducked under the table to retrieve it. "Go on with yourself, Janet!" He came up laughing. "Anyone would think you were my dotin' mothah, to hear you talk!"

"Janet, you're embarrassin' the boy. Besides, I'm beginnin' to wonder if I shouldn't be jealous!" Si winked at her.

It was Janet's turn to blush. "Well, sometimes I *feel* like yaw mothah the way *both* of ya need lookin' aftah!" She got up and brought the coffee pot to the table.

"Asa, you want ta take the flivvah tomorrow, or shall I drop you off at Pawtah's in the mo'nin'?"

Before Asa got a chance to answer, Janet said, "Si'll drop you off, Asa. We need to go to the Little Stoah for kerosene, lamp wicks, stove black, and all kinds of othah things. I don't want to have to lug it all home."

Asa reached into his pocket for his wallet. "Before I fo'get, here's my share of the food bill." He thrust a generous amount of money into her hand, folded so Janet wouldn't see and protest that it was too much. "Oh, and since you're goin' to the stoah, would you be so kind as to pick me up some shoelaces, a can of 3-in-1 oil, and some peppahmint Lifesavahs?"

"Let me write that down on my list, befoah I fo'get." Janet took paper and a stub of pencil from her apron pocket. "Black shoelaces?"

"Ayup. Thanks, Janet."

They continued talking and laughing all through supper. Asa insisted on cleaning up the kitchen afterward.

\* \* \* \*

As Si was lighting his pipe in the sitting room, Janet spoke to him in a low voice, "I'm so glad to see Asa back to his old self again."

"So am I," Si said. "But there are times when a bleak look seems to pass across his face, still. Ah, well, we all grow oldah and learn some hahd lessons along the way. I think Asa's not so much his old self as a new self, with some ballast added to deepen his lightah side."

"Waell, he's always had that, but it seems deepah now."

"Ya right," Si looked toward the kitchen and lowered his voice further. "I dunno what I was thinkin'. He's had those hahd lessons since he was a child. He keeps gettin' knocked down, but he always gets back up again. Just seems to have taken longah this time."

"Ya know, he's written to Mary Lovejoy, and I think he's disappointed she hasn't ansahed."

"Too bad," Si said. "Seems like they'd make a good couple."

"Ayup," Janet said.

"I'm glad Mistah Pawtah offahed him this job," Si went on. "Fishin's not what it used to be. We'ah gettin' squeezed out by the big comme'cial fleets operatin' outa Glo'stah, Boston, and New Bedfo'd. 'Sides that, the catch is gettin' smallah and smallah. I hate to say it, Janet, but I dunno how much longah I'll be able to make a livin' fishin'."

"You mustn't get too discouraged. Ya know there ah good yeahs and bad yeahs; it'll pick up again," Janet said.

Si shrugged. "I can always make a livin' doin' othah jobs. I'll miss Asa, but I hope he takes this job. At least he'll have a fewchah in manufacturin' automobiles."

He opened the evening paper to the war news. "How long befoah we get into the wah? Will they take Asa to fight? Will he come back, if they do?"

"No sense worryin' until we're in it." Rummaging through her sewing basket, Janet said, "Dahnin' egg's not heah. Must've dropped it somewheyah." She got up and left the room.

* * * *

Finished with the dishes, Asa joined Si. He lit his pipe and opened up yesterday's *Boston Globe.* Si was reading the *Barnstable Patriot.* The *Boston Post* and the *Boston Journal* lay on the table.

"Can't see wastin' money on any moah than two newspapahs. We nevah get to finish them all on the day they come out, and they all say the same thing," Si said.

"Well, not exactly. They all have a different slant, and I want to get a well-rounded view."

"Well, it's yaw money. I guess you can spend it any way you want."

Asa read that on the Eastern front, the Russians were being overrun with the slaughter of a million men. In France, the Battle of Verdun dragged on and on, and the Battle of the Somme continued in a stalemate, with devastating loss of life on both sides. U-boats continued to torpedo merchant ships, and although Germany had agreed not to target ships from neutral countries, their "mistakes" in torpedoing hospital ships and unarmed, neutral merchant ships were a little too numerous to be believed.

"Right," Asa said aloud. "You were aimin' for that British destroyah, and hit that Canadian hospital ship by mistake. Only trouble is, the destroyah was a hundred *miles* away at the time."

"I was talkin' to Bert Billings t'other day. You know, his cousin, Tom Eliot's a fishahman out of New Bedfo'd. He says Tom and all the men on his boat thought they saw a German U-boat headin' towa'd the Nantucket shoals last week," Si said.

"They've been spotted around Newpo't, so I've heard," Asa said.

Si turned back to his paper. "Look at this. Anothah suspicious fiah at a chemical plant."

They looked at each other glumly.

Asa picked up another paper and pointed to the headlines. "How long can this go on? So many men just mowin' each othah down in the mud, neithah side gainin' an inch. And for what? What makes men so belligerent?"

"It's a wondah to me how we've managed to stay out of it so fah. How much longah will be, do you think?" Si said.

"Dunno, but when it comes to it, I'll be signin' up for battleships, instead of merchant ones," Asa said.

"Don't go unless you have to," Si said. "I don't want to lose you."

"Why Si! I didn't know you cared!" Asa tried to joke about it, but he knew Si was serious. They were all that remained of their family.

"I mean it, Asa. I know you. Always lookin' f' the next great advenchah. But wah's no advenchah — it's deadly. Don't go volunteerin' to die for somebody else's cause."

"Well, it may not come to that. We might stay out of it, though somehow, I doubt it," Asa said.

The clock on the mantle struck eight.

"Time to get the mail. You comin' tonight, Asa?"

"Think I'll skip it tonight, Si. Speaking of mail, I've got a few letters to answer."

# Chapter 30

## *Fishing and Motors*

On Saturday morning, the sky was a bright blue backdrop to a few scudding white clouds and wheeling seagulls. As Silas pulled up in front of the Porter's cottage, Bill came around the side of the house, smiling.

"Thought I heard a motor. Morning, Asa, Silas." Bill nodded in greeting. "Say, I was forgetting my manners yesterday. Should have asked if you wanted to come along. How about it? Join us for a spot of fishing?"

"Thanks anyway, Mr. Pawtah, but m' wife's already got m' day planned out. Besides, the two of ya got a lot to talk about. Hope the fish'll be bitin' fo' ya! Well, got to go along now; mustn't keep Janet waitin'. See ya latah!"

As Si drove off, Bill remarked. "I always thought those old Model N's had an awful tinny sound, but that one hums right along. Do I detect your magic touch?"

"Took me one whole morning just to get her to start up. Had to jury rig all kinds of thingamajigs to replace parts that were plumb worn out. Fellah Si bought her from was a travelin' salesman, so she's got a heck of a lot of miles on her. Guess she'll hang on for a few more. Maybe last the day out, at least 'til Si gets all Janet's errands done."

"Sounds to me like it'll last a good sight longer than that." Bill smiled and shook his head. "I'm curious. Why do you call it 'she?' Do you equate automobiles with ships?"

"Oh, I dunno. You work on motors long enough, you kinda get to know them. That one just seems to have feminine qualities. Perhaps it's because *l'auto* is a feminine noun in French. Although, *le moteur* is masculine. In Spanish, *el automóvile* and *el motor* are both masculine, so that can't be it. Must just be my own peculiar whimsy." Asa shrugged, gave Bill a sheepish grin, and drawled, "Waell, you did ask, and I hadn't thought it through befoah."

Bill laughed. "So, I got the added benefit of listening to your thought process."

Asa rolled his eyes. "Muddled as it is. My only excuse is that I haven't had my second cup of coffee yet."

Bill chuckled. "Well, come on in and meet my family, Emily's got coffee ready for us in the sunroom, and little Billy's up early today in anticipation of meeting you."

The coat of white paint on the exterior was so fresh that traces of its oily smell lingered beneath the scent of salt air and scrub pine. The sunroom was a large screened porch added onto the back of the house, overlooking a pond on one side and a bluff, with the ocean beyond, on the other. Wicker chairs surrounded a low table displaying a silver coffee service and an assortment of muffins in a linen napkin-lined basket.

Emily was a slender blonde who appeared to be in her early thirties, younger than her husband by perhaps ten years. She was clad in a light blue summer dress, loose-fitting and falling just to the ankle in the latest style. She wore her hair in a soft chignon, with a few loose curls at the sides of her face. She smiled at Asa, and offered her well-manicured hand as Bill introduced them. "Mr. Mayhew."

"Very pleased to meet you, Mrs. Porter."

Little Billy, about six years old, came bounding into the room with great enthusiasm to show Mr. Mayhew his brand new toy truck.

Asa squatted down to the boy's level. "Oh, a fire truck! Is that a steering wheel in the back? Well, isn't that the latest thing. What kind is it?" Asa asked.

"An American La France, type 33. It *is* a steering wheel — it's so long it needs another man to steer the back! Look, it has hoses and ladders that come off! I have a Ford, but I like this one better."

"That's a *real* good one, Billy. I bet it goes faster than the Ford, too," Asa said.

"Daddy says the American La France Company makes racing cars, so *I* bet the engine is faster, too!"

"Have you ever seen a Seagraves truck?" Asa asked.

"No, I never heard of them. Do they make fire trucks?"

"Ayup, they do. I don't know if there are any toy models, though. I'll have to keep my eye peeled for one."

"I've seen a *real* one of these. At the fire station across the Charles River, in Allston. It's *brand new*."

"Wow, I'd like to see that," Asa said. "I wonder if they'd let me look at the engine. What do you think?"

"Well, they *might*," Billy shrugged.

"Maybe if you bring me over some day and introduce me." As Asa rose, he ruffled the child's soft blond hair and winked at him.

When he sat down, little Billy leaned over the arm of the rattan chair, chattering away. Asa engaged with him in a discussion about cars, trucks, and fire engines.

Bill and Emily looked on fondly, and then Bill said, "Okay, Billy, that's enough for now. You don't want to monopolize all of Mr. Mayhew's attention, do you?"

"What's monopolize?" Billy asked.

"To keep him all to yourself," his father replied.

Little Billy replied with a six-year-old's candor. "Yes, I do." The adults laughed.

"All right, Billy. I'm sure Martha's got your breakfast ready in the kitchen. You can see Mr. Mayhew again when he and your father come back from fishing," Emily said.

"But, Mama—" Billy began to protest.

"You do as your mother says, and I'll see you latah, Billy," Asa said.

"You promise?" Billy asked.

"I promise," Asa said. "Maybe I'll even have a fish story to tell you. You know what a fish story is?"

"What?" Billy asked.

"It's usually an exaggeration about the one that got away, describin' him about this big," Asa held his hands about a yard apart, "when he was really only about this big." He brought his hands closer together by two feet. He grinned and winked at Billy. "You go eat your breakfast, now, and I'll see ya latah, kiddo."

"Okay," Billy agreed, skipping off in the direction of the kitchen.

"You're very good with children, Mr. Mayhew," Emily said. "Do you have any of your own?"

"No ma'am. I'm not married." He smiled. "Please call me Asa, if you feel comfortable doing so."

"Very well, Asa. How do you take your coffee?"

"Just the way it comes, please — black." Asa was glad to see that the cups were of the everyday sort, not those fine bone china ones that you could almost see through. He was always afraid one of those would burst like a bubble the minute he touched it.

"Bill has told me he wants you to come to work for him," Emily said, as she poured his coffee. "You should, you know. Admittedly, I am biased, but Bill is an excellent boss. He treats everyone with respect, and he appreciates creativity. I think you'd like working for him."

"Thank you," Asa said as he accepted the cup. He was somewhat taken aback by her directness. "Oh, I don't doubt that Mr. Porter's a wonderful boss, ma'am, but how do you know I'd be a good worker for him?"

"Please call me Emily. 'Ma'am' makes me feel like an old fuddy-duddy." She smiled briefly, and then spoke seriously. "Asa, I knew James and Margaret Lovejoy. They always spoke very highly of you, and so does Martha. As for George, well, the less said, the better. His opinion is not worth the smallest bubble emitted from the mouth of the tiniest minnow. You know that fish you were telling Billy about? Well, I suspect you are much bigger — a royal sturgeon filled with ideas as rich as caviar, and we don't want to let you get away. It would seem Bill has made an excellent catch, if only he can hang onto you."

"I'm not all that… uh… that is… ah," Asa looked down, feeling the heat rise in his face. He cleared his throat. He looked at Emily and opened his mouth to speak, then closed it again, dumbfounded.

She smiled. "Besides, if you go to work for Bill, little Billy and I shall see a lot more of you. We'd enjoy that. Please, do say yes."

Asa smiled. "Bill, you ought to hire Emily here as a salesman. Seems to me she'd be real good at it."

"Why do you think I invited you for coffee?" Bill grinned.

Asa's smile faded. "I, uh… have this idea I'd like to settle down, but…to tell the truth, I'm used to roaming. I might turn out to be as slippery as a fish — hard to pin down."

"I don't want to pin you down. I want to see what you can do. If I wanted a sure thing, I never would have gone into business," Bill said. "It may turn out to benefit both of us. If in the end you swim away, so be it."

"At least give us a try for a while." Emily finished her coffee.

Asa reached for his cup, still ambivalent. He liked Bill and his family, and the job was tempting, but… what if he was chained to a desk? What if it turned out to be uninteresting and tedious? Then, there was the sea. True, he was on the outs with her right now, but what if she called him back and he couldn't resist? And what about the threat of war? Would he be taking this job just to turn around and join the Navy? Bill seemed to be saying that he wouldn't mind, but Asa didn't feel right, committing to something he may not be able to carry out. He took a sip from the nearly empty cup.

"Well, I've said my piece. I'll let you gentlemen get on with it. It has been a pleasure to meet you, Asa Mayhew," Emily said as she rose. The men rose with her. She once again extended her hand to Asa.

"It has been my great pleasure to meet you and your son. I shall keep my promise to come back and tell him a story, if it's all right." Asa smiled warmly as he took her hand.

She smiled back. "Yes, of course. He'd be delighted." She floated into the house.

"I want you to know that I didn't put her up to that," Bill said to Asa. "That's just Emily. She's always very straightforward, says what she thinks. It's one of the things that attracted me to her."

"Ayup. She is direct. Smart, too. I liked that metaphor she came up with," Asa said. "Although, I'm not sure it applies to me. Caviar, indeed. My ideas are probably more like the scraps you'd feed to the cat."

Bill laughed. "You've made a good impression on all of us. I hope you'll decide to come aboard, Asa."

Asa smiled.

"What do you say we go fishing, and I'll drop the recruiting speeches for now, eh? If we don't get to it, the fish'll all be taking their afternoon siestas," Bill said.

They walked out to the garage, and piled their gear into the back of Bill's Porter Twelve. "We could walk, but I didn't feel like lugging a picnic basket along with our fishing rods and tackle. Besides, I want to show you the latest Porter," Bill said.

Before getting in, Asa stroked its hood as though it were a living thing. It was a beautiful open car, gleaming racing green with sleek lines. As they got underway, he thought the engine was so quiet you'd be able to carry on a conversation in whispers and still be heard. With Silas's old rattletrap, you had to shout at each other to be heard over rough back roads and bumpy lanes such as these.

"Great suspension," Asa commented. "Mind if I look over the engine later?"

"Nothing could please me more," Bill said. "We've got some new designs on the drawing board. I'd be interested to hear your opinions."

"Sure, I'd like to take a look at them," Asa said.

There was a wooden dock on the pond, a new-looking dory tied up to it. As herring gulls circled overhead crying and calling, they loaded their gear and cast off. For a time, the only other sound was the rattle of the oarlocks and the ripple of water as Asa rowed out to the center of the pond. He shipped the oars and picked up a rod.

"Any trout in here this year?" Asa asked, choosing a fly from his tackle box.

"Tell the truth, I haven't had time to find out. We've been so busy at the plant that I just got down three days ago," Bill replied. "I'm working on a new model, but some of my ideas haven't worked out quite as I'd envisioned. I was hoping you could help me with that."

"Thought you said you'd drop the recruiting speeches," Asa smiled.

Bill smiled back. "Do you tie your own flies?"

"These are Si's, hand tied by him," Asa said. "You?"

"Used to — haven't had time, lately," Bill answered.

They cast off and waited. Asa took a deep breath, enjoying the quiet sounds of the gulls, of water lapping against the hull, and the feeling of sun on his face.

Bill broke the silence. "I heard that you overhauled the engine on Si's seiner so it runs like new. I also heard the engine stopped dead on the *Eastern Trader* in the middle of the Atlantic and you fixed it, single-handedly, in the middle of a storm. Fellow told a pretty hair-raising story. He also told me there wasn't anything you didn't know about marine engines."

"Oh, come on. Bill," Asa said. "You know sailors spin some pretty good yarns. You can't believe everything you hear."

"But this one was true, wasn't it?" Bill persisted.

Asa shook his head. "Wasn't much dirty weather, just some high seas, and it wasn't the middle of the Atlantic. We were close enough to Cape Town to get her into port for more permanent repairs. Who told you? Mike Slocum? He likes to make his sea stories wild and hairy. Engine kicked up a little bit, that's all. Nothin' of any great consequence." He shrugged. "We keep talkin', we'll scare all the fish away."

Bill asked, "That wasn't quite all, was it?"

Asa frowned. "Nothin' more to it."

Bill looked at him. "If you say so."

They sat in silence for a while, waiting for the fish to bite. Asa was the first to catch a trout, but it was a small one. "Swim back to mama, baby, 'til you're big enough to leave home," he said as he released it.

Bill got a tug on his line, and reeled in one not much bigger. "Looks like nothing but small fry."

"Have patience," Asa said. "Maybe mama and papa trout'll swim by before long."

No sooner were the words out of his mouth than they both got strikes at the same time.

"These are no youngsters!" Bill exclaimed.

They rocked the boat in their struggles to bring the fish aboard. Alternately swearing and laughing as they drenched each other with fishy splashes, they each landed a trout substantial enough for supper for four.

"Whew!" Bill said, as he patted his pockets looking for cigarettes. He drew out a damp pack. "Well, I think these have had it." He laughed. "I wonder how they'd taste if I spread them out in the sun to dry."

"Like smoked fish?" Asa took a dry cigarette case from an inner pocket, offered them to Bill, and then took one for himself. "Now if only I can find a dry enough match." He began searching his pockets.

Bill took out a silver-plated lighter, engraved with the Porter Motorcar logo, and managed to get it lit after a few tries. "Teamwork," he said as they both inhaled.

"Well," Asa said. "I dunno as I've ever seen a less graceful way of landing a couple of fish! I only hope nobody was watching from the shore. They'd think we were a couple of landlubbers!" Both men went into gales of laughter again. "What say we paddle back over to the dock and bring out that picnic basket? Worked up a mighty appetite with all that splashing. How about you?"

"I'm hungry," Bill replied. "I'm sure Martha put up a good lunch for us."

Asa turned the dory around and rowed back. "Thanks, Bill. This's been real fun. Haven't laughed so much in a long time."

"I'm glad I could amuse you!" Bill replied.

"Oh, I think we amused each other." Asa grinned. He poured them each a cup of coffee.

"These thermos flasks are the greatest invention. Keeps the coffee nice and hot," Bill said as he accepted his cup.

"Ayup, it ranks right up there," Asa said. "As far as the greatest goes, though, I'd say electricity, the telephone, the automobile, and the airplane — in that order."

"Well, of course," Bill said. "I should have said '*a* great invention.' I didn't think you'd take me quite so literally."

Asa laughed. "I'm just teasin' — guess I was too sober faced. Si would have said I can be mighty picky about language for a fellah who abuses it the way I do."

Bill laughed. "Why do I get the feeling you abuse it on purpose, to catch people off guard?"

"I bettah watch it — you're gettin' to know all my little tricks already." Asa winked.

They sat in the sun to dry off while eating their thick ham sandwiches. When they had finished eating and were having their postprandial coffee and cigarettes, they began talking about the Great War encompassing the world. Americans didn't want it to affect their lives, but could no longer hide their heads in the sand and pretend it didn't exist.

"You've been back from your last voyage — what — two or three months?" Bill asked.

"'Bout that," Asa said.

"Encounter any U-boats?"

"Ayup." Asa sighed. "Encountered some of their victims, too. Unarmed merchant ships. Did our best to save the ones we could, but…" He shook his head.

"Yes; it's unconscionable. Even hospital ships — I simply can't fathom that kind of cruelty." Bill turned his hands palm up, at a loss for words. "I'm sure you've been reading the increasingly bad news in the papers."

"As have we all," Asa agreed. Had a cloud just covered the sun, or was it simply his dark vision?

"Wilson's campaign slogan—" Bill began.

"He kept us out of the war," Asa joined in. Had he caught something of his own sarcastic tone in Bill's voice?

"You'll note that's in the past tense," Bill said.

"Ayup; I had noticed that. Do you think it's inevitable that we're gonna get involved in this?" Asa asked.

"I'm afraid so," replied Bill. "There've been some feelers put out by one of our senators about possibly using the Porter plant to make some sort of armored vehicle. This is for your ears only, you understand."

"Senator Cabot Lodge? He's for preparedness, isn't he?" Asa asked.

"I can't tell you that at this point. At any rate, we haven't talked anything over in any detail, you understand. It's all very preliminary — as I said, 'feelers,' nothing more."

"Well, now," Asa crossed his arms. "You wouldn't have told me this much unless you knew I'd already decided to come to work for you. What gave me away?"

Bill nodded toward the car. "Well, you're itching to get your hands on that engine. We've been getting along well, and I don't think you've had any better offers. The only thing that might appeal to you more is going back to sea, but..." He paused, contemplating Asa for a moment. He lowered his voice and raised his eyebrows. "I don't think you want to do that right now."

Asa shook his head. There was that damned cloud covering the sun again.

"I can't see any barriers to your accepting the job. Can you?"

"The only thing might be if we do get into this war. Do you think Congress is going to pass the Naval Act?"

"There are still quite a few who are against preparedness. Majority Leader Kitchin thinks we can only remain neutral if we commit to remaining demilitarized. I think those who agree are getting to be more and more in the minority, though. What do you think?" Bill asked.

"I'd hate to see us get into it, but it seems to me less and less likely that we'll be able to remain neutral. Isn't it better to prepare, even if we somehow manage to stay out of it, than not to prepare and get dragged into it anyway? We'd be sending our boys over there without training or equipment. Be like asking them to fight a house fire without watah, sand, axes, or know-how." Asa cleared his throat. "I'd say that's pretty irresponsible."

"I think the only sensible course is to prepare ourselves. The handwriting is on the wall."

"How long, do you think, before we succumb to the inevitable?" Asa asked.

"Oh, perhaps six months to a year, tops — unless something happens to break the stalemate in France and the allies start winning. That, I'm afraid, would take a miracle."

"Well, if the Naval Act passes and they create a Naval Reserve, as a sort of retired sea captain, I could join it. I might's well tell you now that I've decided to join the Navy if we do get into it," Asa said. "Still want me to come aboard?"

"You bet. If we start making armored vehicles. I'm going to need all the help I can get," Bill said. "Even if you're off fighting, we'll still have mail. We'll be able to exchange ideas."

"It'd have to be in code," Asa said. "Si says he doesn't want me to go, but I think he'll change his mind if it comes down to it. Besides, might not have a choice, and I'd rather be in the Navy than get drafted into the Army." A brief vision of Jean-Claude flashed across his mind and he steeled himself against an onrush of grief.

"I heard you speak languages from nearly every port in the world. Maybe the Office of Naval Intelligence can use you," Bill suggested.

"Where'd you hear that?"

"Word gets around. Remember, we knew James and Margaret Lovejoy. And of course, I've met up with Josiah Mayo and a few of the other men you've sailed with, like Captain Hookset and Mike Slocum," Bill explained.

"I swear, livin' in a small town with all the gossips around, a man can't keep a single secret. That being the case," Asa veered sharply off the subject, "how come your wife asked me if I had any children of my own? Wouldn't she have known?"

"Well, you know what they say about you sailors — a woman in every port." Bill winked.

"Ayuh, so they say, but… your *wife*!" Asa goggled at Bill.

"I'm sure she didn't mean it that way," Bill laughed. "We haven't been out for the past couple of summers while Porter Motors was getting going, and she didn't know if you'd got married and settled down in the interim. When people said you'd stopped going out to sea, some of them assumed it was because you had in mind some girl with whom to settle down. Do you?"

"Nunno, not yet." Asa flashed on an image of Mary.

His mind's eye gazed upon the beautiful color of her hair, her lovely oval face, her perfect, petite form. He hadn't seen her in seven months, he told himself. For all he knew, she was already engaged. Nunno, he'd have heard that. But she hadn't answered his letters, so he she probably didn't want to have anything to do with him. He would very much like to meet her again, though. He wondered if he could come up with some plausible reason to call on her in Boston. Then again, maybe not. He might only serve as a reminder to her of loss and grief. Maybe that's why she hadn't written back. Yet, he was drawn to her, to her beauty and her grace, as the tides are drawn by the magnetic pull of the moon.

"Asa?" Bill said.

"Hmm?" Asa coaxed his mind back from thoughts of Mary. His eyes were slow to turn toward Bill, blinking.

"Thought you drifted off, there." Bill looked questioningly at him.

"Oh! Ah, nunno. Just woolgatherin'." Asa ducked his head with a sheepish smile.

"No special girl in mind, eh?" Bill raised his eyebrows.

Asa grinned and shook his head, even as he felt his face get warm.

* * * *

The two men spent the rest of the day in the old carriage house, converted into a garage and workshop, looking over the Porter engine and reviewing the plans for new models. While offering suggestions for improvements and small changes here and there, Asa told Bill he was impressed with many of the new plans. He began to think of a new design for a carburetor, but he wanted to do some tinkering on his own to see if his idea was feasible before he mentioned it. The men spent the afternoon happily engrossed in engine parts and motor oil.

Billy came skipping in, beaming at Asa. "Mr. Mayhew, will you tell me a story about the sea?"

"Billy, where are your manners?" his father asked. "First, you don't interrupt when people are talking. Second, you say 'hello' before you start asking for favors, and then you say 'please.'"

"Hello, Mr. Mayhew," Billy said. "Please?"

"Hello, Billy," Asa grinned. "I'd be happy to tell you a story, but right now, your father and I are busy. I'll tell you a sea story later, all right?"

"Oh, goody! I can hardly wait!" Billy clapped his hands.

"What do you say to Mr. Mayhew, Billy?" Bill asked.

"Thank you, Mr. Mayhew," Billy said. He was about to run off, but then turned around. "Oh! I almost forgot!" With furrowed brow, he stood thinking for a moment, and then recited: "Father, Mother's says to tell you not to forget dinner at the Packard's tonight. She says you have to get ready, and to bring Mr. Mayhew in for a drink."

"Oh, she does, does she?" Bill gave his son an indulgent smile. "Tell her we'll be right along, as soon as we get this grease cleaned off."

"Okay!" Billy ran off with the message.

The men entered the house via the sunroom, talking and laughing as they passed through the kitchen, where Martha was preparing supper for little Billy. "Oh, Asa," she said. "Don't fo'get to take yaw fish with ya, out of the ice box, when you go."

"Maaahtha," Asa drew out the name, breaking into a smile. "Haven't seen you in a long time! Looks like we're workin' for the same family again. How've yah been?" Asa stayed behind to talk to her.

"Oh, you comin' to work for Mr. Pawtah? I'm so glad. They're an awful nice family."

Little Billy danced into the kitchen. "Martha, can I have a cookie? I mean, *may* I have a cookie?" He smiled up at Asa. "Please?"

"Not now. You'll spoil your suppah. I'll let you have one aftah if you eat everythin' on yaw plate. Billy, ya know bettah than to interrupt when folks are talkin'. Now, apologize to Mr. Mayhew, and then run along and get washed up."

"I'm sorry for interrupting, Mr. Mayhew. Say, is it true you sailed *all* the seven seas? Did you see pirates? Are there really such things as sea monsters?"

Asa chuckled. "I'll tell you all about it sometime. Next time I come, I'll tell you about the first time I went to sea, when I wasn't much biggah than you. For now, you just do as Martha tells you."

"Did you really? Go to sea when you were little, I mean? Could *I* go to sea?" Billy asked.

"Nunno. I don't think it would be such a good idea for you to be runnin' away to sea. Your folks wouldn't like it one bit, and they'd probably have my hide for puttin' ideas into your head." Asa laughed, and ruffled Billy's hair. "Besides, the law says you have to wait until you're at least sixteen. Now, run along and get washed up. Mahtha's about got your suppah ready."

As Billy ran off, Martha laughed. "He apologizes for interruptin', then continues right on. But he's such a deah little chap, you can't help but love him."

"You been tellin' him stories about me, Mahtha?" Asa asked.

"Waell, I told him I knew you from befoah, when we both wo'ked for Cap'n James. He had all kinds of questions. I just ansahed the best I could." Martha shrugged.

"Heard anythin' about… the old family we worked for?" Asa asked.

"Waell, now you mention it. I did heah somethin' about Mistah Geo'ge Lovejoy. Seems he's been runnin' the business into the ground, and has taken up drinkin' moah than evah. 'Twas Cap'n James kept things runnin' smooth aftah old Cap'n Asa Lovejoy died. Waell, yah don't need me to tell yah. Without him, things ah just goin' downhill. 'Tis a shame."

Asa scowled and nodded. "I wondahed how long it would take him to completely ruin everythin'. And Mary? How's she doin', do you know?"

"Waell," Martha drawled, "you know that Mrs. Bird up on Beacon Hill? She runs a kind of bo'din' house f' genteel ladies, except 't ain't really a bo'din' house. 'Tis her own home and she takes in two or three ladies to abide with her. You prob'ly heard. Mary's livin' theyah. Well, my Cousin John's wife's sistah's the cook theyah. She says Mary's been sick and is undah the doctah's cayah. That Jack Chase she works for has just run her ragged, and she come home from work one day and just collapsed. One of t' othah bo'dahs had to get the doctah for her."

"Is it serious?" Asa felt his heart beating faster and his breathing stop. Martha's sentences inched along at such a slow pace that he wished he could haul them from her mouth, hand-over-hand.

"Just exhaustion, from what I heah. Few moah days bed rest, she should be all right. But I don't know as I like the idear of her goin' back to work f' that young Mistah Chase. Wondah wheyah his fathah's been in all this? You'd think he'd a put a stop to it. And Sally, that's my cousin John's wife's sistah, she says that doctah's a right handsome lad. And he seems to know what he's about, for all he's so young."

"My, my. I had no idea all this was goin' on. Hope she'll be all right."

He felt a twinge of jealousy toward this young doctor. Could he get away for a trip to Boston? Would it be proper for him to look in on Mary?

"Could I visit her? Or would seein' me just bring back painful memories for her?"

"I don't think the doctah's allowin' visitahs just yet, from what I heah," Martha replied. "But when he does, I'd say it's been long enough. She might like to talk about her fathah with someone who knew him as well as you."

"Hmm." Asa nodded.

Bill stuck his head in the kitchen door. "Asa, thought you'd got lost. How about that drink?"

"Comin'," Asa said. "Be seein' you, Mahtha. Thanks for the news, and the advice."

"Didn't mean to keep you waitin', Bill. I, uh, was just catchin' up with my old friend," Asa smiled as he joined Bill in the library. A silver tray of cut glass decanters was set out on a polished side table; the stoppers were topped with crystal rhombohedra that caught Asa's eye.

"What'll you have?" Bill asked.

"Mm… I like the way those act as prisms, catching and separating the light into all the beautiful colors of the spectrum," Asa murmured, gazing at the play of light and color. He looked down and shook his head, laughing at himself. Then he cleared his throat and turned to Bill. "To tell the truth. I'm not much of a drinker. But I'll have a glass of beah, if you've got any."

"Certainly," replied Bill. "Emily, didn't I see a bottle of beer around here someplace? Did you put one in the icebox?" He turned to Asa. "I like it cold. You know, I think I'll join you, instead of having a whiskey. Cold beer sounds good after all our labors on a warm day."

Emily asked Martha if there was any beer on ice, and she came back bearing a tray with two glasses. Asa thanked her.

"I've got to go and get ready for our engagement this evening, so I'll leave you," Emily said. "Don't be too long, Bill, will you?"

"Perhaps I'd best be runnin' along," Asa said. "Let you folks get ready for your evenin'."

"No need to rush off. Emily takes hours to fix herself up — not that she needs any fixing up, in my opinion. But she thinks otherwise. You know how women are!" He laughed.

"Um… well, not, uh… really," Asa said.

Bill didn't seem to notice Asa's stammering demurral. "Whereas, I can be ready in two shakes. We've got plenty of time. Say, Asa, if you haven't any plans for tomorrow, how'd you like to go on the payroll? I know it's Sunday, and short notice, but I've got some people coming out for a sail, and I'd like you to skipper the *Emily*. It'll be Senator Cabot Lodge and Mr. Nathan Bradford with their wives, along with Emily and me. I think the Senator wants to talk to me about the possibility of making those vehicles we talked about, if we get into this war. Of course if you have other plans…"

"Nunno. I've nothin' planned, except church, and, well, to be frank, I'd just as soon have an excuse to skip it. I'd be happy to take the helm on that little beauty." Asa grinned. "About what time do you want me down t' the dock?"

"Oh, it'll be afternoon, after church. The Senator has to be seen to be a good and Godly man, you know." Bill chuckled. "Say one o'clock or so. Look, I want you to take the other Porter out in the garage, last year's model, to use for yourself. Call it a perquisite for working for me," he said.

"Well, I'm just *de*lighted!" Asa mimicked Teddy Roosevelt, beaming. "Thank you."

The men chatted about improvements to the engine of the prototype model before they finished their beer and stood up.

"I know you've got to get ready for your dinner party, so I'll say goodbye now. If it's all right with you, though, I'll stay just long enough to tell little Billy a story. I did promise him one."

"Oh, you don't have to—" Bill started, but Asa interrupted.

"No, I'd like to — he's quite a kid." Asa grinned. "And I don't want to break my promise."

"I must admit, I'm rather proud of him," Bill said. "But don't let him keep you too long. Only one story, even if he begs for more. We're trying not to spoil him too much. It can be all too easy with an only child."

"All right. See you tomorrow, one o'clock down to the dock, then," Asa said. He extended his hand and the men shook. "Good to be workin' for you."

"We'll take some more time to go over just what we'd like your job description to be, and then I'll have a contract drawn up next week sometime," Bill said. "Suit you?"

"Handshake's good enough for me, but you're the boss. If you need a contract, I'll sign it," Asa said. "See you tomorrow. Enjoy your dinner party."

# Chapter 31

# *Mary*

"That prissy old bat!" Jack said. "You talk to him, Mary. You've got such a way with him. He likes you."

"You know, Jack, sooner or later, you'll have to learn how to deal with difficult customers," Mary said.

"But we just rub one another the wrong way. And you've already been working with him on this problem. You talk to him, please? Just this once?"

"All right, I'll speak with him." *Just this once for the twenty-seventh time.*

At first, Mary considered herself fortunate to have a job as secretary to young Mr. Chase at the Chase Import Company. Since she had no experience, she thought Mr. John Chase, Sr., who had known James, had only given her the job out of pity after her after her father's death and her uncle's bitter intemperance had left her with nothing.

Mr. John Chase, Jr., called Jack, had recently graduated from Harvard, with gentleman's C's, and joined the family firm. Though he had worked, to use the term loosely, during summer breaks in various departments, he still had much to learn. Because of her excellent work habits and quick mind, Mary was learning the ropes faster than he was. She was well aware that Jack took advantage of this state of affairs to get her to do most of his job for him. If something went wrong, he blamed Mary. If something went right, he took the credit. It rankled, but she said nothing. She needed this job to survive. Besides, who would believe a woman over a man — especially a rich man with a Harvard degree?

Jack had always used his charm to get what he wanted. When Mary began to feel overburdened with his responsibilities piled upon her own, he beguiled and cajoled, teased and flirted, and went on his merry way. He asked her to cover for him when he went off gambling and partying with his old college friends; he told her his troubles; he sent her for aspirin and coffee to nurse his hangovers. He seemed to sense when she was just about to get fed up with him, and would then bring her little bribes: a lacy handkerchief, a nosegay of violets, a bar of perfumed French-milled soap. He was a shameless manipulator, and Mary knew it, but she reminded herself she needed the job.

After one particularly trying day, she wondered how she managed to drag herself along the cobblestones in her white high buttoned shoes. She could hardly breathe in her corset. She regretted her choice of clothing. Though it had seemed all right at 7:30 this morning, by 5:30 in the afternoon, her fitted suit was too hot. Why on earth had she chosen to buy yards of apple green linen? She liked the color, and linen was supposed to be cool; but it wasn't, and it soon turned into a mass of wrinkles.

She wondered how women could move at all back when corsets were so tight at the waist that they twisted women's bodies into unnatural shapes. Thank goodness she'd been a child then, and spared the torment of wearing such a tight corset. Of course, hobble skirts had been in fashion only a few years ago, their very name giving away what they did to women. She wouldn't be caught dead in one, mincing along with tiny little steps, having to jump up to get onto a streetcar. A woman very well *could* get caught dead wearing such a thing — killed because she couldn't run to get out of the way of a careening motor, or a runaway horse. She thought about the long, heavy skirts and myriads of petticoats her grandmother, and even her mother, used to wear. At least her skirt hem was above the ankle, and didn't drag along the ground collecting all kinds of filth, as they did twenty years ago. Imagine having to clean those, especially when *every* conveyance was horse-drawn. The very thought made her nose wrinkle.

Convincing herself that she had it so much easier than women of the past got her down the sidewalk. Then she remembered that women still had a long way to go — a very long way. And she no longer had the time or energy to devote to women's suffrage, as she wished. She dragged herself up the steps, clutching the handrail. She just wanted to crawl up to her room, take off her corset, and fall into bed. But Mrs. Bird met her in the hallway as she came in the door.

"Oh, my dear, you look absolutely exhausted," plump Mrs. Bird exclaimed. "That young Mr. Chase works you too hard!"

Mary hung on to the newel post to keep herself upright. "You may be right, Mrs. Bird, but what can I do? Somebody has to be the responsible one, and Jack's not going to do it. I need this job, and I'm grateful to Jack's father for hiring me when I'd had no previous experience."

"Yes, dear, I understand, but you simply can't go on like this. You're wearing yourself out! Just look at you, so weary you can hardly stand. Take your jacket off, dear; you look a little overheated." Mrs. Bird proceeded to tug Mary's jacket off as she kept talking. "You ought to be able to enjoy yourself with other young people of an evening. But whenever Miss Dickinson and Miss Brooks ask you to accompany them to a lecture, or even a picture show, you're too tired to go."

"Not always — I did go and hear Alice Paul speak," Mary said.

"Yes, well," Mrs. Bird said. "I'm not altogether sure I approve of Miss Alice Paul or those suffrage women; one can hardly call them ladies with some of the things they get up to. On the other hand, they are right about some things. Men are certainly not all they're cracked up to be. I've managed very well without Mr. Bird. You see, after he died, I decided on the conversion of the coal range in the kitchen to gas, and I came up with the idea of making this little tea room at the same time. All on my own. Humph, I didn't need a man to oversee the workmen, either. Come, my dear, you need a bit of a pick-me-up. I'll make you a cup of tea myself. Sally's down in the kitchen, making supper." Mrs. Bird bustled Mary into the little kitchenette, of which she was inordinately proud. "Don't you like this room? I think it's nice to look out on a bit of green, and watch the birds playing in the birdbath. Admittedly, the garden is very small, but so are all the gardens on this street."

"Mm-hmm." Mary had only heard the first sentence, but it didn't matter. She could have recited the rest of it by heart.

"Of course, Mr. Bird had the modern plumbing installed before we were married — in 1895 that was. He turned the smallest bedroom into the bath, and took half the cloakroom downstairs for the little comfort room, so guests wouldn't be traipsing up and down the stairs. He replaced the pump in the kitchen with taps, too. I'm afraid that's about the last useful thing he did, although he did live for ten more years," Mrs. Bird chattered on. "Aren't you feeling any better, dear? You're not drinking your tea."

Mrs. Bird had fussed over Mary since she had come to live there. "Poor girl, to lose both parents nearly at once, and then to be treated so badly by her uncle," she had said.

The attention and excessive concern embarrassed Mary, but she appreciated Mrs. Bird's kindness, and didn't want to be rude. So she allowed herself to be ushered to a chair and ministered to with tea and sympathy. She was so very tired. She was almost unaware of her surroundings or of Mrs. Bird's chit-chat. Her eggshell-thin china cup suddenly weighed ten pounds. She replaced it in its saucer with great care. Gray spots danced before her eyes. She was desperate to get to her room and lie down. The next thing she knew she was lying on the floor, with Mrs. Bird chirping, fluttering, and fanning her with a dish towel.

"Oh, dear! Oh, dear!" Mrs. Bird twittered. Another boarder came in the front door. "Oh, Miss Dickinson, come here, please! Oh, do hurry! Look, she's fainted. Oh, what should we do? Beryl, will you call the doctor?"

"I'm all right." Mary tried to sit up, but then the room began to spin and she found herself drifting off again. Distantly, she could hear the voices of Beryl and Mrs. Bird, then nothing.

She regained consciousness in her own bed. The doctor sat in a chair at the bedside, leaning over her with his thumb gently holding her eyelid open, shining a light in her eye. He turned it off and dropped it into his bag.

Mrs. Bird was standing near the doorway, eyes darting from Mary to the doctor, and then out the door, edging closer to it. She was silent — a rarity.

"How do you feel, young lady?" Doctor Stone wasn't all that much older than she. It hadn't been long since he had finished his residency and gone into private practice. Tall, with wavy black hair and a fair complexion, he sported a neatly trimmed black mustache. His self-confidence seemed as genetic a trait as his green eyes. His doctor's bag and shoes were of the finest black leather, his gray summer suit finely tailored. His accent was pure Boston Brahmin.

"Embarrassed," she said. "I've never fainted in my life!" To her further embarrassment, she began to cry, and then made it worse by trying desperately to stop, with big, gulping breaths. She hid her face in her hands. Realizing someone had unbuttoned her blouse and loosened her stays, she hoped it had been Mrs. Bird. At least the sheet preserved her modesty.

"There, there. Easy, now. Just relax. Miss Lovejoy, please take your hands away from your face and look at me." When Mary complied, he said, "Good. Now, take a slow, deep breath, like this." He demonstrated. "That's right — nice and slow. Now exhale. Again — deep breath in, and then out. There you go. That's it. Keep breathing slowly," he encouraged. "From what Mrs. Bird has been telling me, I'm surprised you haven't collapsed sooner. I understand that about seven months ago, you lost both parents, and your remaining family was far from helpful." He patted her hand. "Breathe normally now. She tells me your boss is very demanding and has run you ragged. Is that correct?"

Mary nodded, wishing she could vanish in a puff of smoke as had the magician's assistant she'd seen in a music hall show. She'd gone with Miss Dickinson and Miss Brooks when she'd first moved here, before Jack had started overburdening her. Mrs. Bird had said it was rather naughty of them to have gone to such a place, even though they'd explained to her that it *wasn't* a burlesque show, but a family matinee.

"There, now. I'm going to prescribe strict bed rest for at least a few days." He firmly precluded Mary's burgeoning protest. "No going into work! I don't care how indispensable you are! You're terribly run down. Your pallor suggests anemia. Would you please roll up your sleeve? I'm going to need a blood sample."

He kept talking as he drew the blood, to distract as well as to instruct her. "Mrs. Bird has offered to look after you, and you'll let her, won't you? You need rest and good food. You're too thin and too pale. You haven't been eating properly, have you?" He withdrew the needle, and pressed a wad of cotton batting to the spot, bending her elbow. "Hold this tightly for a moment."

"Oh, my, no, she doesn't eat enough to keep a bird alive!" Mrs. Bird said as Mary glared at her. "Oh, Mary, don't look that way. You know it's true. I'm only trying to help you."

"I'm sorry, Mrs. Bird. It's just that I hate to be made such a fuss over. I feel awful to be putting you to so much bother."

"You can take this off in a couple of hours." Doctor Stone applied a strip of surgical tape to hold the cotton in place, and went on with his examination. "When was your last menses?"

Mary lowered her eyes. "It started yesterday."

"Is your menstrual cycle regular?"

Mary blushed. "Um, pretty much."

"And how many days does it usually last?"

"Um, seven," Mary mumbled, clutching the sheet up to her chin. She wished she could draw it up over her head.

"Miss Lovejoy, I'm sorry to embarrass you, but you understand I must ask these questions. Any problems with cramps or excessive bleeding?"

"Some, yes, but I'm not sure what's excessive." In her embarrassment, Mary looked to Mrs. Bird. She could see she'd get no help there. Mrs. Bird, scarlet as the geraniums in the window box, had one foot out the door.

"Mrs. Bird, perhaps Miss Dickinson would be so kind as to come in," Doctor Stone suggested. "I can see you are uncomfortable with this, but I cannot examine Miss Lovejoy without a woman present."

Mrs. Bird scooted out of the room, and Miss Dickinson entered.

"Thank you, Miss Dickinson. I hope you are not as discomfited by this as Mrs. Bird seems to be," Doctor Stone said.

"I am a teacher at a girl's high school, Doctor. I have had experience in dealing with such feminine difficulties," Miss Dickinson smiled.

"Ah, thank heaven. I shall step out while you disrobe — down to your chemise, please, Miss Lovejoy."

"Let me help you," Beryl said. "I suggest you do away with that corset altogether, even when you're feeling well enough to come downstairs. After all, it's just us girls together. And you're certainly thin enough not to need one."

"You're right, Beryl. It's far too hot to be wearing it." Mary yawned. "Oh, excuse me."

"Oh, dear, I'm afraid this skirt is ruined. Right through the pad, chemise, and two petticoats. No wonder you're so weak."

"Oh, no, has it gone right through to Mrs. Bird's sheets?"

"No, not yet. Lie still. I'll get a towel and a fresh pad," Beryl said.

When she finished helping Mary, she said, "There, all set. Oh, don't cry, dear. Are you in pain?"

"It's not that… It's just… I'm so…" Mary blushed. "With Mrs. Bird, and you… and him… knowing… Oh…"

"You've no need for shame, Mary. It's not our bodies that are unnatural. It's the shame we've been taught to feel about them that's unnatural."

Mary looked at Beryl. "I never thought about it that way."

"I'll just let Doctor Stone know we're ready." Beryl stepped out into the hall and spoke to the doctor in low tones. He nodded, frowning.

"Miss Lovejoy, you needn't be embarrassed or frightened. As a doctor, it's my job to try to help you feel better, all right?" Doctor Stone smiled gently. "And Miss Dickinson is right here beside you. May I examine you now?"

"Yes, Doctor." Mary submitted, still miserable, though she tried to tell herself Beryl was right.

"Tell me if you feel any pain." Doctor Stone palpated her abdomen. When Mary winced, he asked, "Does that hurt?"

"Only a little," Mary said.

When he had finished his examination and questions, he prescribed some capsules. "I don't have any with me right now, but I also want to prescribe a tonic for your anemia. I shall go back to my laboratory and perform the blood tests, and come back with your medication a little later today, all right?"

"All right."

"In the meantime, you are to stay in bed. Take a nap, and then you're to have your supper on a tray. Rest."

\* \* \* \*

A few hours later, he was back.

"I've run the blood tests. They confirm you do have anemia. I'm leaving this tonic for you to take, one teaspoonful with every meal. It will help build you up. Take one of these capsules every four hours. That should reduce the flow within a day. If it does not, we shall have to try other measures. You must have complete bed rest until the bleeding has stopped."

"For a day?"

"Longer. It should slow down in a day, but you must remain in bed for another three or four days. If the capsules work, you'll keep taking them for a total of five days. Then, in twenty-eight days, you shall take them again for five days to prevent this from happening again," Doctor Stone said. "Do you understand?"

"Am I going to have to take these for the rest of my life?" Mary was appalled. "And take to my bed every month like some nervous Victorian lady? Well, until... um... I get old."

Doctor Stone smiled. "No. I think once we build you up a bit that may take care of things."

"I certainly hope so! I have too much to do to spend half my life in bed."

"I'm sure it won't come to that," Doctor Stone smiled. "Now, Mary — Miss Lovejoy — for a few days, you're to let Mrs. Bird and Miss Dickinson take care of you. I suspect a little pampering is just what you need. I'll be back tomorrow to see how you're faring. Mind Mrs. Bird, now, do you hear me?"

"Yes, all right, doctor," Mary said. "Oh, and thank you."

\* \* \* \*

The next day, Mrs. Bird telephoned the Chase Import Company to tell them that Mary would not be in to work until the doctor gave his approval. She was put through to Jack.

"Mary sick! Oh, how awful," Jack said. "What am I going to do? I simply can't get along without her!"

"Well, you're just going to have to!" Mrs. Bird surprised herself with this sharp retort. "Oh, but I'm sure it won't be for too long."

The following morning, a florist delivered a huge floral arrangement more suited to a funeral with a note addressed to Mary, *"Please hurry and get well. I'm lost without you. Affectionately, Jack."*

In the afternoon mail, another note arrived:

*Dear Mary,*

*Terribly sorry you are indisposed. We all miss you. Please hurry and get well.*

*Sincerely,*

*Jack*

*P.S. What should I do about the Simpson account? They are claiming their latest delivery of Chinese ginger jars was incomplete.*

That evening, Jack himself, blond, gleaming smile, deceptive baby blue eyes, wearing an expensive tailor-made white summer suit, with his straw boater in hand, showed up. Mrs. Bird wouldn't let him in, telling him Mary was asleep and couldn't be disturbed. He tried charming her, but it didn't work. She smiled at him and closed the door in his face. She was abashed to know she could be capable of such rudeness, but at the same time, she felt oddly proud of herself.

As for Mary, she had barely glanced at the flowers or the note, letting it slip from her fingers onto the floor as she fell asleep again.

\* \* \* \*

When the doctor came by, he determined that the capsules seemed to be helping; however, he was concerned. Mary seemed paler and more listless than she had the day before.

Mrs. Bird told him, "She hardly touches her food."

"Mary — Miss Lovejoy, if you are to get over your anemia, you must try to eat more, especially red meat. Remember to take your tonic. Stay in bed and rest."

Weary, she nodded. She hardly spoke at all, except to answer his questions in monosyllables. Her eyelids drooped.

He noticed a piece of paper on the floor, and bent to pick it up. He read the note, raised his eyebrows, and handed it to Mrs. Bird. She looked at Mary, who seemed to be asleep, and led Dr. Stone out into the hall.

"He tried to get in to visit her earlier this evening, but I told him she couldn't be disturbed. I had to close the door in his face," she whispered.

"Well, keep him away. Make sure he knows she needs to have absolute rest, and she can't have that if he's pestering her with work problems. For now, let her sleep as much as she wants, but try to get her to eat more. Give her red meat

— liver, if she'll eat it. Make sure she takes her tonic. I'll come by again tomorrow."

\* \* \* \*

Jack wasn't about to give up. He was used to getting his own way, and never bothered to think that anyone else's needs might have precedence over his wants. He sent a fruit basket, with another note containing a post script about work. He sent delicacies from S. S. Pierce, along with more queries about work. He telephoned, but whoever answered told him that Mary was too ill to come to the telephone. He was turned away from the door again and again.

Mrs. Bird's was a narrow, three-story brick row house fronting directly on the sidewalk. Gas street lamps alternated with flowering trees, their roots buckling the red bricks. Window boxes sprouting geraniums softened the uniform lines of the flat-fronted nineteenth century houses. Wrought iron railings led up several steps to recessed front doorways. Across the cobblestoned street, Jack paced up and down, watching the front door.

After a while, Mrs. Bird came out. She carried a wicker shopping basket, so Jack assumed she would be gone for some time. The door was unlocked, and he slipped in. After some searching, he found Mary's room.

"Hello, my poor dear girl!" he exclaimed as he entered.

"Jack." Mary's voice was weak. "What are you doing here?"

"Thought I'd pop in for a visit, try to cheer you up a bit. Absolutely no fun being sick, is it? I remember once having the measles and feeling so blue 'cause no one could visit me, in case they caught it, you know. It got so boring having no one to play with day after day."

"Jack, it was nice of you to try to cheer me up, but I'm simply too tired for company."

"Oh, and after all that trouble I went through getting past that Bird woman, too!" Jack put on a joking pout. "It seems to me you really do need a bit of brightening up. You've got an awfully long face." Running his fingers down his jaw, he pulled a mock long face. He was trying to think how to ask her about the problem with Ace Shipping before she threw him out, when the doctor came in.

"What is the meaning of this? How dare you barge into a lady's bedroom?" Doctor Stone exclaimed. "Especially as she is too ill to receive visitors."

"Hello. You must be the doctor. I'm Jack Chase, Mary's boss." He stuck his hand out for a shake.

Doctor Stone ignored it. "Mr. Chase, you were informed that Miss Lovejoy was to have no visitors — especially not you bringing work problems. If you had the slightest bit of common sense, you'd realize that the more she's pestered, the longer it will take for her to regain her strength; thus, the longer it will be before she is able to return to work. Let me show you to the door." He swept his arm in its direction.

Jack's face flushed. "I'll show myself out, thank you very much!" He paused in the doorway. "By the way, Mary, if you're going to be out for too long, we'll have to train someone to replace you." He turned on his heel and exited, slamming the front door.

* * * *

Mary burst into tears.

Doctor Stone rushed to her side. "Oh, dear. He's upset you terribly. The cad! I'd like to punch him in the nose!"

Mary started laughing and crying at the same time. "I ca-can't st-stop."

"Take a deep breath," Doctor Stone suggested.

Mary tried, but couldn't stop laughing and crying long enough to breathe. Her eyes pleaded for help.

"I'm sorry to have to do this," Doctor Stone said, and slapped her face.

Mary's eyes flew open; she hiccupped a couple of times, and then stopped. The doctor poured her a glass of water. She took a drink, and said, "Thank you. I thought I was going crazy."

"No, not crazy," Doctor Stone smiled. "Simply overwrought. Feel better now?"

"Yes. Yes, I think so." Mary's brown eyes looked into his green ones, and she blushed. "You must think I'm one of those hysterical women!"

He wanted to hug her. This will never do, he told himself. She's my patient. I mustn't let myself fall for her. "Good," he said gruffly, passing over her last statement. "Now, let's take a look at you." He pulled out his stethoscope and checked her heart and breathing. "Okay, cough for me. That's good. Again. Mm-hmm. Deep breath. Hmm. Again." He took her wrist and pulled out his pocket watch. He made a note. Tongue depressor in hand, he said, "Okay, now, open wide and say 'Aah.'" He felt her neck, under her jaw. Then he checked her eyes with his little light, pulling down her lower lid. "Pale. Have you felt feverish? Any chills?" He stuck a thermometer in her mouth. She shook her head. He checked her ears. "Any stuffy nose, sneezing, coughing?"

Thermometer still in her mouth, Mary shook her head again. Doctor Stone took it out and checked her temperature. "A tad elevated, but it is quite warm in here with the sun pouring in that window. You need some air." He went to the window and opened it. "How's the bleeding?"

"Um, not as bad." She mumbled, looking away.

"When it stops, you may want to spend more time downstairs, or outside in that postage stamp of a garden. Get some fresh air and sunshine. Make sure you drink plenty: water, fruit juice, lemonade, tea. I usually recommend just water, but you need to gain a little weight. Has your appetite improved any?"

"A little. Well, not much," Mary admitted.

"I want you to try a tablespoon of brandy before meals, see if that helps any. Here." He took a half-pint bottle out of his bag. "I know Mrs. Bird doesn't allow spirits in the house, except for those tiny glasses of sherry she offers to guests, but this is for medicinal purposes. She won't mind, and if it does increase your appetite, she'll be downright delighted."

The front door opened and closed. "Hello-o!" Mrs. Bird sang. "Is that you, Doctor?" she asked as she climbed the stairs. She came into the room. "Well, how is our patient today?"

"Hello, Mrs. Bird. I've just been telling Mary — Miss Lovejoy — that I want her to take a tablespoon of brandy before meals to improve her appetite. I've left it on the bedside table, but when she's feeling up to it, she might start to take her meals in the dining room again. Perhaps tomorrow or the day after, when she — well, begins to feel a bit better, she could begin spending more time downstairs and out-of-doors.

It can be become quite stuffy upstairs at this time of day when the sun shines directly on that window."

"My dear," Mrs. Bird said to Mary, "You know, I think you actually look a bit better than you did before I went out. Has the doctor cheered you up a little?"

"Well, I thought it was pretty funny when he said he wanted to punch Jack in the nose," Mary giggled, blushing.

"Jack? Oh, no, was he…?"

"Oh, yes," the doctor said. "He was here when I came in, bothering Mary, upsetting her. I chased him away with a flea in his ear. Let me know if you have any more trouble with him. If you ask me, he's nothing but a spoiled brat, thinks of no one but himself. I'm afraid I did say I wanted to punch him in the nose, but not until after he'd left."

He saw no reason to mention Mary's brief bout of hysteria. He turned to Mary and gave her a warm smile.

She blushed.

"Oh, look!" chirped Mrs. Bird. "Mary, your color's getting better!"

# Chapter 32

## *Young Jack Chase*

"What the hell is going on, Jack?" Mr. John Chase, senior, had called Mr. John Chase, junior, into his office.

"What do you mean?" Jack put on his innocent face.

"You know damn well what I mean! There have been numerous problems in your department of late," Mr. Chase snapped. "Some of our customers are very dissatisfied. What has happened with the Simpson account? And did you straighten out that mess with the Ace Trucking Company?"

Jack hemmed and hawed. "Well, ah, Mary usually dealt with Simpson's. That prissy old clerk over there always got under my skin, complaining about every petty little thing, but Mary had such a way with him, smoothing things over, and taking care of whatever he was griping about. And, um, that Ace thing just came to my attention. I didn't even know about it until Mary was gone, and then I didn't know just where things stood. I mean, did they lose the whole shipment, or just part of it? I can't find anything in the office."

"How could you not know about it! What do you mean, you can't find anything in the office!?"

"Mary had her own system, and since she's been gone, it's all been in such disarray. I tried asking her, but between her landlady and that doctor of hers, I can't get in to see her, and she won't answer my letters. They won't even allow her to accept telephone calls! It's not *my* fault Mary's sick! I don't know what to do without her!"

"Do you mean to tell me that Mary's been doing *your* job all along, as well as her own?" Mr. Chase jabbed an irate finger at his son. "She's supposed to be your *secretary*, not the head of your department. *You* are supposed to be that! No wonder she's ill. This situation changes right now! It's about time you got down to brass tacks, young man, and get these problems straightened out in a damned hurry!"

"But, father, I need some help! Can't you at least give me another secretary to take Mary's place?"

"Not on your life! You've got a clerk and any number of other people you should have been supervising. You say they will only cooperate with Mary. Well, that's just so much codswallop! It's *your* job, they're *your* responsibility. What have you been doing all this time? Sitting on your backside and twiddling your thumbs? Meandering about with your useless friends when you should be at work? You don't seem to have the slightest inkling of what's going on in your *own* department!"

"But father…"

"How *could* I have spawned such a feckless *idiot*?" Mr. Chase, senior, raised his eyes and his hands, palms upward. One hand came crashing down on his desk. "'*But*' nothing! Get to work!"

The two continued to argue, voices raised, while the secretaries and clerks in the outer office looked toward the door, and glanced at each other with a raised eyebrow here and there. New Englanders, especially of the upper crust variety, did not express their emotions — at least, not in the presence of others. On the other hand, it was about time young Jack was getting his comeuppance.

It went on this way, and the air turned fairly blue with cursing, not all of it euphemistic. The outer office was perfectly still as all ears turned toward the heir apparent's dressing down.

"I'll give you *one week*, do you hear me?"

One secretary leaned toward another and murmured that they could probably hear Mr. Chase in Siberia.

"One week! And you'd damn well better have these problems solved, or you're out on your ear, my boy!"

Jack, muttering something about "unfair," slammed the office door so hard that the sound echoed throughout the corridor. Everyone hurriedly turned their eyes to the papers on their desks as he passed.

* * * *

Mary began to feel well enough to get up and dressed, usually by late morning. She was able to join the other women in the dining room for luncheon and supper, though she continued to have her breakfast in bed on a tray. She spent most of her time in her room, either reading or writing at the small desk by the window. She still had to take frequent naps, and felt quite sad at odd moments, as she thought of her mother and father. She wished that she had someone close to her to care for her as she had cared for her mother. Then she felt her face turn hot with shame over her self-pity.

She felt well enough one day to venture down to the sitting room across from the more formal, fussy, Victorian front parlor. Languidly turning the pages of a *Collier's* magazine, she heard the front doorbell as it seemed to take on a demanding life of its own as it rang and rang and rang.

Sally came in and asked if she was up to receiving visitors. "It's that young Mr. Chase," she said. "I would have sent him away, but he seems in an awful state."

"Oh, all right." Mary sighed. "I can't stand that bell. Let him come in."

"Mary, Mary!" Jack rushed into the room, frantic. "Thanks for seeing me. The old man just gave me the most terrible hiding! He says I've got to straighten out the Simpson's problem and the Ace Trucking mess in one week or he'll fire me! Please, Mary, tell me what to do!"

"Jack, for heaven's sake! Haven't you dealt with that yet?" She gazed ceiling-ward, muttering a brief prayer, "Please, God, give me patience."

"But, Mary, I can't find anything in the office. Without you, everything's all gone to hell. Oh, I'm sorry, I know I shouldn't use such language, but I'm just so... so..." Jack looked at her helplessly.

"Yes, so I see. What do you mean you can't find anything? You can find the Ace Trucking file under 'A' in the first file cabinet on the left. Everything should be in that: bills of lading, invoices, duplicate packing slips, and all the letters and records of all the phone calls that've been made trying to track down that shipment. Part of it has already been found and delivered."

"Wait a minute. Let me write this down." Jack searched his pockets for something to write with, coming up with nothing.

Mary sighed, went to the desk in the corner, and got Jack paper and pencil. "When I left, Mr. Roberts was helping me to track down the rest. If it's not in the file cabinet, he's got the file. I suggest you check with him and see if he's made any further progress. As far as Simpson's goes, it's a paperwork problem. The invoice was changed when there weren't enough jars available to fulfill their order, and the altered billing statement reflects that. Simply bring the corrected paperwork to Mr. Crabbe's attention, and assure him they were not overbilled. If he wishes, we can look for additional jars elsewhere. Remind him that things take twice as long due to the war, and in the end, it may not be possible."

Mary paused and took a deep breath. Looking Jack straight in the eye, she went on, "I can't believe you've let them go on complaining for nearly a whole week without even looking at the account for yourself! What on earth have you been doing?"

"But I couldn't find the account!" Jack whined like a chastised child. "It wasn't where I thought it should be."

"So, you looked in one place and then gave up?" Mary was incredulous. He *was* a child.

Jack shrugged. "I didn't know where else to look."

*Idiot,* Mary thought. She sighed. "I remember I was working on it that afternoon. I put it in the top drawer of my desk. Did it never occur to you to look there? I had placed a call to Mr. Crabbe, but he was out at the time, and I'd intended to call him back in the morning. I suggest you take the file over to Simpson's yourself, and show it to him. Perhaps he'll be appeased by a personal visit. Have Toby make copies of the revised invoice and billing statement to leave with him and make sure they're stamped 'copy.'"

Jack scribbled a few more notes. "Thank you, Mary. I don't know what I'd do without you."

"Any child with the ability to read and reason could have solved this problem." Mary's voice was dragged low with fatigue.

"Why, Mary!" Jack was taken aback. "I'll overlook it this time, since you've been such a help, and since you've been sick. But just remember in future that I *am* your boss, and you should show proper respect!"

"Yes, Mr. Chase." Mary's hint of sarcasm was obscured by her weariness. "It must be the exhaustion speaking. Please forgive me."

"Sure." Jack beamed at her, charm restored, happy that she'd solved his problems once again. "When are you coming back? You look much better than the last time I saw you. I've missed you so much, you know, and they wouldn't even let me visit you!"

"You mean you've missed me doing your job for you." Mary felt reckless. She supposed she really shouldn't talk to Jack like this. Despite his dependence, he was her boss and could fire her. She just couldn't bring herself to care. She was tired of Jack's selfish behavior, and vowed to herself that when she went back to work, she would not continue doing his job for him. It was unfair to her, and was no real favor to him. Just look at the mess he'd got himself into without her. She yawned.

As if he'd intuited her thoughts, Jack said, "I guess I've been letting you carry the ball too long. I realize that now. I didn't know how much you'd been running the department until you were gone, and I didn't have the first clue as to how to fix things. That'll all change. I promise."

"Well, all right, Jack. I suppose I'll give you another chance." Mary smiled at reversing the roles on him. "But I won't be back right away. The doctor hasn't given me a clean bill of health, and I still get very tired. In fact, I need to go up and rest now." She stifled another yawn. "Look, until I come back, do try to keep the accounts in order, and don't let problems go unanswered. You've got to keep the customers happy, or they'll go elsewhere. You can see yourself out. Good afternoon."

Mary rose and dragged herself up the stairs. Jack's visit had drained her. Doctor Stone was right. He was a spoiled brat. She felt she had to take him in hand and teach him a few things, as a mother would. Too bad his own mother hadn't done so. Poor Jack — rich, spoiled, and such an incompetent, disorganized, muddled excuse for a man. Even sadder, he thinks he's just dandy.

Mary lay down on the bed, but did not sleep. It was her birthday, but she hadn't told anyone. She wondered how to chart a course for her life, when she didn't know where she wanted to go.

She felt older than her nineteen years, having had responsibility thrust upon her at an early age, with her mother's illness and her father away at sea. She had run the household from the age of fifteen, when Margaret's heart problems had begun to get worse. Though her mother was the titular hostess at dinner parties thrown for friends and business acquaintances, Mary was the one who did the planning, made all the arrangements, sent out the invitations, and oversaw the hiring of extra help for these events. She devised the menus, dealt with the tradesmen, saw to the household accounts, and paid the bills when her father was away at sea.

They'd only had Martha who lived in as cook and companion. Letitia came in three times a week for laundry on Monday, ironing on Tuesday, and scrubbing floors on Thursday. Mary did the rest of the cleaning, with Martha's help. She also did all the sewing and mending. Brooks came at the crack of dawn, before he went out oyster dredging, to tend to the kerosene water pump, and he did the gardening on Saturday afternoons. He could be called upon to do a bit of maintenance as necessary.

Whenever her mother had bad spells, Mary sent for the doctor and then acted as nurse. She'd had a decent education. After leaving school to care for her mother, she'd been tutored at home until the age of seventeen. She'd had lessons in both piano and voice. Then she'd purchased a typewriter and sent away to correspondence school for a secretarial course. When she finished that, she took courses in bookkeeping.

She had accepted her responsibilities gladly, and had never resented being unable to spend time gadding about with girls her own age, nor did she miss the round of parties and social gaiety engaged upon by others of her acquaintance. She had gone to one such party and left early, finding it frivolous, shallow, and boring.

For all her mother's fragility, she was a much more interesting companion. Mother's heart may have been failing, but her brain still worked. She read good books and kept up with what was going on in the world by reading the newspapers. She could talk about things that had some weight and depth to them. These were quiet discussions, though, because it did not take long for her to tire, and Mary was careful not to get into any lively debate with her, for fear of stimulating her heart too much. Content at home, she found her entertainment in reading, both aloud to her mother and quietly to herself, in playing the piano, and in listening to music, after Father had bought a Victrola. When her mother felt well enough, they had occasionally attended summer concerts at the band shell on the town common.

As she stretched out, allowing her mind to drift through memory, she thought of her father. On a number of occasions, when he'd been home from sea, he had hired a nurse to care for her mother while he took Mary to Boston. They would stay at either the Copley or the Parker House for a few days, attend the opera, symphony, or ballet. They visited historic sites, the art museums, the Athenaeum, and the Boston Public Library. She had particularly liked Mrs. Gardiner's museum, with its small scale and lovely garden. Most of all, she had enjoyed her father's company.

On these trips, he gave her his undivided attention. He always had something novel and interesting to show her. He told her about all the countries he'd been to, their cultures and customs, the various landscapes, flora and fauna. He said the world was a place of endless variety. He taught her about world politics. Because of rising tensions in Europe, he predicted there would be a war two years before it began. He introduced her to new ideas, over which they would have great, incisive, intense discussions. Sometimes, they would attend a lecture by some controversial figure. When James thought Mary agreed with him too much, he would switch sides and play the devil's advocate, training her to be more precise in her reasoning, logic, and language. When she was with him, she felt he sharpened her mind, taught her how to think critically. Without him, she felt her mind beginning to dull. Then she would force herself to wake up and shake the dust off her wits, but what had seemed so effortless with him now seemed laborious. She sighed.

After all the quiet days of moving gently through life, caring for her invalid mother, her father came back from sea carrying the brisk ocean winds with him, filling her sails. She could soar with him, just as she had when she'd been a little child, and he'd lifted her high into the air over his head, both of them laughing. He was — what? He was electric! Yes, that's what it was to be with him — all shimmering light and electricity. The world suddenly took on brighter colors, clearer sounds, sharper scents, spicier flavors. Even her fingertips were more sensitive. It was as though she could feel the difference between a few grains of sugar and a few grains of salt simply by touching them, with her eyes closed, without tasting them. Part of that, she admitted, was going from sleepy town to bustling city. Still, they would pack so much into those few days, it was as if James wanted to make up for all that she may have missed while he was at sea, to give her everything the world had to offer.

He showered her with gifts of the mind, the soul, the senses. Ah, the delight of afternoon tea at the Copley! He taught her how to taste the subtle differences in a variety of teas, how to savor her food, its presentation, texture, aroma, as well as flavor. At the symphony, he taught her how to hear music with her heart as well as her ears, how to open herself up to it, submerge herself in it. At the museum, he taught her to view art in much the same way. "Don't simply look at it," he had said to her. "As with music, open up your very pores and let it enter you."

But most of all, he gave her his heart. Despite his long absences, she knew he loved her. She knew he loved her mother very much, but since Mother's illness, Father had treated her as though she were made of exquisitely fine porcelain, very valuable and exceedingly fragile. Her mother could no longer take these whirlwind trips into the city. So Mary became the recipient of all the nimble energy her father felt he had to keep bottled up around her mother. He was like quicksilver. Mercury, yes, that's fitting, Mary thought. The Roman god of trade, commerce, gain, luck, travel, and good gifts. The messenger of the gods, with his winged heels. Father was anything but mercurial, though, she thought. Though he could be intense, his temperament was steady, reliable. Like all of us, he was sometimes sad, sometimes happy, but he had no wild mood swings or unpredictable changes. One could depend upon him. Ah, but one could always depend upon him to go back to sea. Mary sighed.

She had sometimes wished he would leave his mistress, the sea, and come home to stay with his family, for good. She understood, though, that he needed the sea, in the way all living things need food. It sustained him, gave him life. Perhaps a more accurate analogy would be the need of an opium addict for his drug, for in the end, the drug kills, the way the sea had killed her father. Yes, perhaps the sea was his addiction, the way alcohol is Uncle George's. No. No, that wouldn't be accurate at all, for the sea had made her father healthy and whole, happy and lively. The drugs of opium and alcohol make people sick. Their integrity is destroyed; they become miserable. Their souls shrivel and die. What's more, drugs lead to poverty, not only materially, but in more destructive ways. Paucity of friendship, lack of love, ever dwindling mental capacity, to name a few.

But the sea had made her father rich. He had material things, yes, but those weren't the riches that mattered. He shared a love of the sea with Grandfather and Uncle Alfred;

it was an unbreakable bond. And now, they are bonded in death, she thought, but the love survives. The sea had expanded his mind, his spirit, and his heart. The sea had given him friends — great friends like Asa Mayhew.

I wonder where Mr. Mayhew is now, she thought. I wouldn't mind seeing him again. What a kind man: gentle, intuitive, trying so hard to help and comfort us. What a depth of soul he had, like Father.

Father had such broad horizons as to flood his mind with a great light that swept the corners clean of the tiniest scrap of prejudice, intolerance, or meanness. He had a wealth of experience, a deep understanding, a wide knowledge of the world — and of himself — that he was at home wherever he went. Wherever he is now, she thought, he is at home.

Her eyes filled with tears of longing for him. She wondered if Father could still feel the love she bore for him. She wondered if he could hear her thoughts. Was he with Mother? Were they in heaven, if there was such a place? She cried herself to sleep.

* * * *

Jack had begun to look at Mary in a new light. Perhaps some deeply buried recognition of his own superficiality attracted him to some force to give him ballast, to keep him from drifting off on a breeze of triviality. Maybe something in his father's tirade had jarred loose the idea that he'd have to grow up sometime, that he'd have to think of his future. For a man of his social position this meant a wife, someone to be a help-mate, a counterweight to keep him on an even keel. He'd be expected to take over the family business in time, if he didn't get himself booted out first for his incompetence.

Mary had the additional appeal of someone who could be of invaluable assistance in the business. His thoughts of her became more romantic. True, he had flirted with her and given her little gifts before, but it had merely been a way to wrap her around his little finger, to get her to do his bidding. Possibly, this was simply more of the same, but on a grander scale.

At any rate, Jack, with his father as goad and Mary as guide, began to pay more attention to his job and to develop a modicum of competence. As she continued her convalescence, his visits became more social, with fewer desperate pleas to solve problems for him. As he was practiced in conviviality and charm, if not much else, he could be good company when he chose. He won over Mrs. Bird and even managed to soothe the doctor's ruffled feathers. Thus, he was allowed to continue these social calls. He usually brought along a gift, some small token, a flower, some candy or fruit, a little book of popular sentimental verse. Too sugary for Mary's taste, she gave the latter to Mrs. Bird.

On a particularly sweltering July afternoon in the city, Jack arrived with a pint of ice cream. Mary, Beryl, and Mrs. Bird were sitting in the parlor, and Jack offered ice cream all around. "Oh, what a treat!" exclaimed Mrs. Bird. She sent Sally to get some bowls and spoons. Sally dished up and passed around the ice cream, as Jack chatted amiably with all the women, sharing the gossip of the day. He talked about what was playing at Mr. Keith's theater and at the Colonial, who was seen dining with whom at the Parker House, who had just sailed into some port on the Cape with a brand new ketch, and sundry topics. Though he appeared his usual effervescent self, he resented the other women intruding upon his time with Mary. He wanted to be alone with her.

Mary felt drained by the heat and superficial conversation. After a spoonful or two, she left the ice cream to melt in the dish. Tiring of his company, she barely heard Jack's chitchat. She leaned back in her chair and closed her eyes. Jack didn't notice, but Mrs. Bird did. "Oh, Mary," she said when she could get a word in edgewise, "poor dear, you look awfully pale. Perhaps you should go up and rest awhile. Although, heaven knows, it's even hotter upstairs."

Jack jumped on this. "Mary, would you like to go out in the garden? A bit of a breeze seemed to be stirring up when I came in. I can take out that chaise for you, if you'd like."

Mary just wanted to go to sleep, but he was trying so hard that she hadn't the heart to say no. So they went out into tiny back yard, and Mary lay down on the chaise lounge in the shade of a maple tree. "I'm afraid I'm not a very good company this afternoon, Jack. This humidity is simply draining."

"My dear girl, no wonder you're tired. Hasn't the weather been beastly! I was saying to Father today that perhaps we should join Mother on the Cape." He sat down on the chaise by her knees, facing her. "Would you like to go? Mother would be there, of course, so it isn't as if you'd be without a chaperone. And I'm sure Doctor Stone would think the Cape air just the ticket to perk you up a bit."

"It's nice of you to offer, Jack, but I'm not very well acquainted with your mother. It would be such an imposition on her. I appreciate the thought, but honestly, I couldn't." What Mary would like most right now was for Jack to leave her alone.

"Mary, I'd like you to get to know Mother better. Don't you know how much I care about you? I'd like to… well… would you … I mean… Mary, what I'm trying to say is that I'd like to court you!"

Mary looked up at him, stunned. Slick Jack, at a loss for words? She stared at him, agog. Finally, she found her voice. "Why Jack! I never dreamed… I mean, I had no idea… I … I simply… Oh! I'm sure I don't know *what* to say!"

"Oh, darling, don't say anything!" Jack breathed as he leaned forward, grabbed her shoulders and kissed her on the lips.

She was so shocked that for a split second, she froze. Then she came to her senses and pushed him away, revolted. "No, Jack, don't! I'm sorry, but I don't… I don't… feel that way about you at all."

"Give me a chance to change your mind, darling," Jack said, leaning over her again.

Tiredness was the least of her worries at the moment. She needed to escape, but she was trapped. Her heart started to palpitate like the wings of a frightened bird, beating against the cage of her ribs. She couldn't breathe. She didn't want to hurt his feelings; she didn't want to be rude, but panic overrode polite behavior. She pushed him away and stumbled to her feet as her stomach rebelled. "Oh," she gasped, "Excuse—" With her hand over her mouth, she fled into the house. She made it to the downstairs toilet just in time.

"Miss Lovejoy," Sally said from the other side of the door. "Are you all right? Should I get someone?"

Shaking, Mary splashed water on her face and rinsed her mouth. She opened the door to Sally and stood leaning against the doorjamb, clutching the doorknob. She was as white as the vanilla ice cream she'd left melting in the dish. "Sally, please make my apologies to Mr. Chase. I'm going up to bed now." Clinging to the banister, she dragged herself up the stairs.

\* \* \* \*

Jack was nonplussed. Insulted, embarrassed, outraged, he brushed past as Sally approached him with Mary's message, dashed down the hall, and slammed the front door as he left. On the sidewalk, he caromed into Doctor Stone.

"You're certainly…" Doctor Stone began. Jack pushed past him without apology, without even seeming to see him. "In a hurry," the doctor finished, but Jack was already halfway down the street.

As the doctor entered, Mrs. Bird was standing in the foyer, looking from the stairs to the door and back again. "Well," she was muttering, "I surely don't know what…. Oh! Doctor Stone, I'm glad you've come. Sally says Mary's just been sick. Young Mr. Chase brought us some ice cream, but I don't see how it could have been that. Beryl and I had some, too, and we're all right. And she was doing so much better. I hope this isn't too much of a setback," she chattered on as she preceded him up the stairs.

Doctor Stone knocked. Hearing a muffled, "Come in," he followed Mrs. Bird into the room. "Mary, what's happened?" he asked gently. "Mrs. Bird says you've been sick." He took her hand, noting its clamminess, and examined her face with its sweaty pallor. "Mrs. Bird, would you get a cool, damp cloth, please?"

"Oh, yes, of course, Doctor."

He placed his hand on Mary's forehead. "I must say, you don't look well, and you feel a bit feverish. You're trembling! Tell me truthfully, now, did something just happen between you and Jack?"

"Oh, it's not his fault, really it isn't! He… he just took me by surprise. I didn't see it coming, and I… I'm afraid I panicked. I've been so miserable with the heat, and he brought ice cream, and he was talking on and on, and I just wanted to go lie down, and he took me out to the garden, and… um… he… uh… It's only that… oh, I was simply… well, taken aback… Oh, don't look so dark! I was already feeling sick, and he just… uh, tipped the balance." She turned her face away, disconcerted. "Poor Jack. It must have been pretty awful for him."

"Here you are, Doctor." Mrs. Bird handed him the cloth.

Doctor Stone placed it on Mary's forehead. "Poor Jack, nothing! Why, you're still shaking! He must have behaved like a bounder to have upset you like this." He wished he could take her in his arms and comfort her, but even if he'd been able to overcome his professional ethics, he felt she'd have fled from him as she'd fled from Jack. For by observing her, Jack, Mrs. Bird, and Sally, he thought he had a fair idea of what had taken place. "Take a deep breath, then let it out slowly. Keep doing that until you feel relaxed."

After three breaths, Mary stopped shaking. She took two more and then said, "I feel such a fool!" She wiped her eyes and blew her nose. She pressed the cool cloth over her eyes for a moment before putting it aside. She sat up, straightened her dress, and then attempted to repair her disarranged chignon.

Doctor Stone could see the effort she was making. "It's not foolish to become upset when you're ill and suffering from this oppressive heat and humidity. And then some cad goes and forces his unwanted attentions on you on top of it. That's what happened, isn't it?"

She nodded, looking down at her lap. "He wanted me to go to the Cape with him. Oh, with his mother and father, too! You mustn't think there was anything... um, indecent about it. I thanked him for the invitation, but said no. And then he said he wanted to court me. I was so surprised I just stared at him. And then he *kissed* me. I was shocked. I stammered something at him and pushed him away. I felt like I couldn't breathe. Then I ran away and got sick. Oh dear! He must be so upset. It's worse than if I'd slapped him in the face."

"I wouldn't worry about him," said Dr. Stone. "From what I've seen, his vanity could do with a little deflating. What I'm concerned about is you and your health. He was right in one thing, though. This unbearable heat is bad for you. It takes the starch out of the most hale and hearty of us. Although I've seen some improvement over the past week, you're far from well. The Cape would be a good place for you to recuperate during the worst of the heat. Is there anyone you can stay with, any old friends in Wellfleet who'd be willing to put you up for a week or two?"

"I had a letter from my friend Shirley yesterday. She mentioned that if I could get any time off, she'd like me to visit. I haven't responded yet. I would like to go, but I wasn't sure if I could. Perhaps I ought to accept her invitation. Do you think I'd be all right to travel by train?"

"Tell you what, I'll be going to Truro this coming weekend for my sister's wedding. We could travel down together, if you wish. Then you wouldn't be alone if you began to feel unwell.

What could be better than to have a doctor on hand in case of emergencies?" He smiled.

"Thank you, Doctor." Mary returned his smile. "I'll write to Shirley tomorrow and ask if it would be convenient for her. It would be so good to get out of the city."

"Tonight, I want you to take a tepid bath to cool down. Not too cold, mind you, as that will only make you feel worse later on. I'm going to give you a mild sedative to take before bed, to help you sleep. Drink plenty of water to prevent dehydration, but just sip it, or you may become nauseated again. How is the nausea, by the way? Have you had any other upsets before this afternoon's bout? Feel like there might be any more this evening?"

"My stomach still feels rather unsettled, but not like I'm going to be sick anymore," Mary said. "Perhaps the ice cream was too cold, or something. After a couple of spoonfuls, I began to feel a bit queasy. I left it melting in the dish."

"For some people, dairy products can be hard to digest. Did you ever have any trouble with milk or cheese?"

"I've always hated milk, but I don't know if that's quite the same thing," Mary said. "My mother used to try to make me drink it when I was a child, and it would take me hours to get down the smallest glass of it. After a while, she just gave up."

"Was it the taste you hated, or something else?" Doctor Stone asked.

"I didn't like the way it made my stomach feel," Mary said. "All cold and fluttery."

"Well, there you have it. You hated it because it didn't agree with you. Perhaps you should avoid dairy products for a while, and then you can try adding them back gradually.

Perhaps you'll be able to tolerate them, but if not, you'll know not to eat them. If you have any more nausea and vomiting tonight, I want Mrs. Bird to call me. Otherwise, I'll check in on you tomorrow." Doctor Stone closed his bag, and then opened it again. "Oh, I almost forgot. Here's that packet of sleeping powders. It's one dosage. Pour the whole thing into a full glass of water and stir it up, about a half-hour before you wish to go to sleep."

"Thank you, Doctor Stone. I'll see you tomorrow."

# Chapter 33

## *Thunderstorm at Sea*

S unday dawned bright and clear. Asa rowed out to the mooring early and finished his preparations long before he was to meet Bill. He stretched out on the deck and watched wispy clouds float by on a blue, blue sky. *What is so rare as a day in June?* He remained on his back and began to breathe in the deep, cleansing way Sharmaji had taught him. After a while, serenity flowed through him.

Shortly before one o'clock, he stood up, put on his chief mate's jacket and peaked cap, and then brought the sloop around to the dock. She was large enough to accommodate all seven of them comfortably, but small enough to be crewed by one or two. Asa had her tied up, ready and waiting for her passengers, when at last he saw Bill's Porter arriving.

"Looks like a beautiful day for it!" Bill said as they approached.

"Sure does." Asa nodded toward a basket Bill was carrying. "Give you a hand with that?"

"Let's give our guests a hand, first." Bill put the large picnic basket down on the dock, and offered the women a steadying hand as Asa helped them aboard. Asa gave the men a hand in boarding, as well, and then Bill handed Asa the basket before swinging himself aboard. "We've brought some provisions along for a meal. I don't know about you, but the minister's sermons make me mighty hungry."

"I'm always starving when I come home from church, too. Could be something about the sermons that works up an appetite, or maybe it's belting out all those hymns!" His sunny smile startled the scowl from Senator Henry Cabot Lodge's face.

Before they got underway, Bill made introductions all around. Emily said she was going below to put on a pot of coffee. Mrs. Bradford and Mrs. Cabot Lodge went with her. As Asa motored away from the dock, Bill, Senator Cabot Lodge, and Mr. Bradford walked forward to the bow, talking. Asa wasn't sure exactly what Mr. Bradford did for the government, and neither Bill nor Bradford ever made it clear to him. He had the idea it was something to do with the War Department, left purposely vague lest any secrets slip out in the mere title of the job.

As they passed the breakwater, Bill helped Asa hoist the sails. Asa manned the helm, while Bill crewed. Tacking close to the wind, Asa raised his voice so Bill could hear him over the luffing sail. "We headed anywhere in particular, or just out for a good run?"

Bill returned to join Asa at the helm. "Why don't you head toward Monomoy Island? If nobody's feeling seasick by then, we can head toward Nantucket." Between the good breeze that had picked up and the secondary wind from the sails, they were flying.

"She's yare — handles like a dream," Asa grinned. "You know, you don't have to crew, unless you want to. She'll do fine if you want to go talk to your guests."

"I enjoy sailing her. I don't usually hire any crew, as Emily's a good sailor. But I suppose I do have to pay attention to my guests. When I notice the senator starting to get impatient for our little talk, I'll turn her over to you. For now, I just want to enjoy the wind, the ocean, and the speed!" Bill said. "Asa, I don't think I've ever got her to go so fast. Your technique is far more advanced than mine."

"Oh, I dunno. We're just lucky in the wind today." Asa brought her around in another tack. For some time, they enjoyed the quiet of being under sail, comfortable with each other's silence. Bill seemed to anticipate Asa's every move as if they'd been sailing together for years.

They rounded Race Point at Provincetown and turned east southeastward, headed around the elbow of the Cape. She was running fast and free when there was a change in the air and the light began to dim.

Asa reefed the mainsail.

"Why are you reefing?" Bill asked.

"Looks like a squall comin' up."

"Where? I don't see anything."

"Thunderclouds. See? Over there to the west." Asa pointed over his shoulder with his thumb.

"You have eyes in the back of your head?" Bill laughed. "Oh, they're miles away! We won't be bothered by them. Will we?"

Suddenly, the wind picked up and changed direction. The boat heeled to starboard. Asa steered her out of it. "You'd better trim the jib. Tell everyone to go below and put on life vests. Then batten down that hatch so your guests don't get wet."

Bill did as he was told. Before he returned to the cockpit, thunder rolled and rain began to fall. "Shouldn't we switch to engines?" He yelled above the wind.

"We're headed toward Nauset Hahbah. We'll get there fastah under sail with this wind. The engine doesn't have that much hosspowah," Asa yelled back. His deepening accent was his only sign of stress. "I'd rathah not to be stuck out heah when it really hits." Suddenly, the rain was sheeting down, and he was very busy. Occasionally, he barked an order at Bill, but mostly he was handling things fine on his own. Just as they reached the breakwater, lightning flashed with a loud clap of thunder. Asa quickly lowered the sail and opened up the throttle on the engine. They swung into the harbor, and made for the wharf. It was rough going, as the wind picked up and the skies opened, sending down a blinding, deafening torrent of rain. Asa slowed down and searched for a place to dock. Just as Bill began to fear they wouldn't make the wharf before lightning struck, he found that Asa had pulled her up, turned off the engine, and was already leaping onto the dock with the lines in hand. He made her fast, and rejoined Bill in the cockpit. They were both soaked to the skin, having been too busy to don their foul weather gear. The harbormaster and a group of men wearing yellow oilskins and sou'westers appeared on the wharf.

"Are you all right? Any damage? Does anyone need a doctor?" A cacophony of questions greeted them.

"Waell," Asa drawled. "Things seem to be just fine, now. Bill, why don't you check on the folks below?"

Bill had already headed off in that direction. He poked his head up from the hatch and said, "Everyone's fine. You handled her so well, they're not concerned in the slightest."

"How's the galley? Is the food still there, or did it all end up on the deck? I could use a cup of coffee," Asa said as he went below.

Everything was tight and cozy below, and there were sandwiches and coffee. Bill took Asa off to one of the cabins to see if they could find some clothes. They dressed in an odd looking assortment of ill-fitting items (at least for Asa, whose wrists and ankles stuck out in naked vulnerability), but at least they were dry.

As they ate, Bill described what had happened.

"I didn't think we were in any danger," Mr. Bradford said.

"The weather seemed fine. I couldn't see why you wanted all of us to go below." The senator folded his arms and gave Asa a critical up-and-down look. "And what kind of a sailor are you? Why the hell didn't you put on your foul weather gear?"

Asa smiled, folding his arms. "Well, I suppose 'twas because the weather seemed fi—"

"A squall can seem to come up out of nowhere," Emily interrupted, "but I'm sure I wouldn't have noticed it as quickly as you did, Asa."

"Good thing he did see it," said Bill. "I didn't notice anything at all until he pointed it out to me. If I'd been skipper today, I probably would've drowned all of us."

"Waell, not that bad," Asa drawled. "I'm sure you would've only been a mite damp."

As they all sat down with coffee and sandwiches, Bill asked if he'd missed anything interesting.

"Mr. Bradford and I were discussing immigration. I say they should be able to speak and read the language before we so much as let them set foot in the country. If they want to come here, they should learn to be Americans — none of these hyphenated Americans," Senator Cabot Lodge said. "And they ought to be able to read and write. There is too much foreign riffraff here already."

"Ain't we all foreign, though?" Asa looked at the senator as though he were an unsophisticated bumpkin seeking education. "'Cept the injuns, of coss."

"Nonsense, young man. The English civilized this country, as you would know if you'd studied any history."

"Hmm, givin' 'em the blankets of smallpox victims had a real civilizin' influence." Asa mused as he rubbed his jaw. "You study the classics at Hahvahd?"

"What has that got to do with our discussion?" the senator snapped.

In Italian, Asa asked if he'd ever wanted to visit the antiquities of ancient Greece and Rome. The senator frowned. Asa asked again, in Greek.

"What kind of jabbering is this? Speak English!"

"Waell, that's too bad. The Greeks and the Italians prob'ly shouldn't let you in to tour their antiquities, since you speak neither language," Asa smiled. "Probably don't read them, either."

"I studied the classical versions of Latin and Greek, the languages of Pliny and Aristotle, not the vulgar Italian and Greek. At any rate, I toured Europe long before you were born, young man, and for your information, one needn't speak—"

Asa cut him off. Drawing himself up to his full height and looking down his nose, he asked, in the crustiest of upper-crust accents, "The Europeans should all speak English, since we are quite obviously superior. That is your view, I take it?"

The senator stared at him, opening and closing his mouth. Then he gathered himself together and glared at Asa. "What nonsense you spout, young man! You've no idea of the issues facing this country. Young whippersnapper!"

Asa shrugged. "Waell, I read the papahs enough t' know how t' vote."

"How dare you speak to me with such effrontery?" the senator exclaimed.

Asa tried to assume a sober face, but he simply could not suppress his grin. "Senator Cabot Lodge, please don't think my effrontery has anything whatsoever to do with Bill. I suspect my political leanings and his may differ widely. I was ribbing you, sir. I didn't think you would take me seriously. I apologize. My apologies to you, too, Bill. Must be the thunderstorm. Electrical storms seem to generate a kind of whimsy in my brain."

Emily, who had been not very successfully striving to hide her amusement, burst out laughing. "Oh, you're a gem, Asa."

The senator ignored Emily. He frowned at Asa, shaking his head. "You dare call your employer by his Christian name?" He turned to Bill and growled, "Mr. Porter, where do you find these… these *people*?" He spat the word as though it was distasteful to him.

Bill grinned. "Cape Cod is just full of odd characters." He winked at Asa.

"Peppery sort of fellah, isn't he?" Asa muttered in an aside to Bill.

Eventually, Asa got the senator to accept him as a kind of harmless court jester. With his ill-fitting, mismatched clothes and accent that came and went, he certainly seemed more clown than threat. He finally won the senator over by quoting passages of Homer's *Odyssey* in the original Greek, revealing that it was one of his favorite poems. He was drawn to the adventures of the roaming sailor. They went on to talk a little about Ovid's *Metamorphoses*, and Senator Cabot Lodge in the end developed a grudging respect for this quirky young whippersnapper who had somehow managed to learn classical Latin and Greek, despite never having been to Harvard, Yale, or indeed, any college.

By the time they'd finished eating, the rain had let up, and they went up on deck. Asa pointed out a breathtaking rainbow in the sky. The storm vanished as quickly as it had arisen. They headed south, but nobody wanted to go on to Nantucket, so they sailed around Monomoy, back to Provincetown, and then home to Wellfleet Harbor. Asa manned the helm, and sailed her alone, as Bill, the senator, and Mr. Bradford went forward and spoke together in low tones. He took it gently on the return trip, not trying for any great speed. The dirty weather had blown over, but the exhilaration he'd felt on the trip out was gone.

After he dropped the passengers off at the wharf, he brought the sloop back to her mooring. First he made sure everything was clean and shipshape, and then he rowed back. He took the sails, with their coverings, to the sail loft and spread them out to dry. Bill joined him there.

"Asa, I want to thank you."

"For what?"

"For that damned fine sailing, and saving us from injury or worse. I never even saw that squall coming," Bill said.

"No need to thank me for doin' my job," Asa said. The day had started so pleasantly, but his happiness had suddenly given way to a vague depression.

Bill squeezed Asa's shoulder. "All right?"

"Fine. You?"

"Oh, just a little tired. Been a long day," Bill smiled.

"Ayup." Asa quirked his mouth into a grin. "The storm and Senator Cabot Lodge kept us on our toes, eh?"

Bill laughed. "See you tomorrow."

That night, Asa was drowning in the cold black sea as his storm dream recurred. Waking tangled in the covers, sweating, his heart pounding, he couldn't understand it. It hadn't been much of a storm that afternoon, and they had all come through it perfectly fine. Why did this dream keep coming back?

\* \* \* \*

While Bill Porter's summer vacation lasted, Asa did odd jobs for him, some days skippering the boat and keeping her shipshape, scraping off barnacles, cleaning, polishing, maintaining the engine, and caring for the sails. Other days he worked around the property doing maintenance, still others working with Bill on engine designs, crafting and trying out various components. He had time to pursue his carburetor idea, and when he was satisfied that it would work, he showed it to Bill.

"Yes," Bill said. "I see what you've done here. It's ingenious! With this design, we'll be able to achieve more miles to the gallon than we've been able to get before. It'll run cleaner, too. I knew you were a wizard. Let's go up to the plant tomorrow, so we can install this in the prototype, try it out."

From then on, Asa spent a great deal of time traveling back and forth to the plant in Cambridge, working on the prototype of the new model, fixing glitches and making improvements until it was finally in production.

He disembarked from the train one Friday evening and ran into the crowd waiting for their mail. He was tired and hoped he'd run into Si, so he wouldn't have to walk home clear to the outskirts of town. Half the roads were no more than rutted dirt lanes, so bad that it was faster to take the train to Boston and the subway to Cambridge than to drive back and forth. Si wouldn't be expecting him, since Asa hadn't let him know when or if he'd be arriving. Weaving his way through the throng on the platform, he nearly bumped into Mary, his arm brushing hers.

"I beg your pardon," Asa said. "Oh! It's Miss Mary Lovejoy, isn't it? And Miss Shirley Packard. What a pleasure it is to see you both!" Asa's tiredness vanished. He forgot about looking for Si.

"How nice to see you again, Mr. Mayhew." Mary smiled. "I see you're carrying a valise. Going on a trip?"

"Please call me Asa." He beamed at her. "Nunno, no trip. Been working at the Porter plant in Cambridge, but I'm taking the weekend off. Say, I was sorry to hear you'd not been well. Are you feeling better now?"

"Oh, yes, much better since I've been visiting Shirley. The air out here is such a healthful change from the sweltering heat of the city. Why, in just a week I feel almost like a new person! And how have you been?" Without waiting for an answer, Mary went on, "I am so sorry about that trouble with Uncle George. I hope it wasn't he who drove you away from the sea."

"Oh, that's all water under the bridge, or over the dam, or something. Don't even think of it. Nunno, he didn't drive me away. I was ready for a change, I think." Asa gave Mary a thousand watt smile.

"Well," she laughed. "You don't sound altogether sure of that."

He was drinking Mary in with his eyes. Even though he could tell she'd been ill by her paleness, she was beautiful. What really set her apart from the ordinary was her thick auburn hair, which shone like a flame in the sunlight. He wanted to prolong the conversation, but it was getting awkward, standing here with a crowd milling around them.

"Say, how would you two like to come over to the drugstore for an ice cream soda? My treat."

Shirley looked from Asa to Mary and back again. "Oh, Mr. Mayhew, that sounds lovely. We'd be delighted, wouldn't we Mary?" She stood on tiptoe, looking around. "Oh, there he is. Father, would you get the mail? Mary and I are going to the drugstore for a soda. We'll see you at home later."

"Evening, Mr. Packard." Asa tipped his straw boater.

"Why, if it isn't Asa Mayhew!" Mr. Packard shook Asa's hand. "I hear you're working with Bill Porter. He simply raves about that new carburetor you invented."

"Well, I wouldn't say 'invented.' It's just a few modifications here and there." Asa smiled. "Well, I uh… don't wish to dash off rudely, but I promised to treat these young ladies to ice cream sodas before the drugstore closes. You understand, sir."

"Of course. You young people run along and enjoy yourselves." Mr. Packard smiled as he patted his daughter's arm.

Mary's eyes glowed. "I'm afraid it will have to be something other than ice cream for me, though. I've discovered that ice cream and I do not get along very well."

"What a shame, to have to do without the pleasures of ice cream! Well, I'm sure there are many other items from which to choose." He offered his arm to Mary, and she took it as they crossed the street.

They took seats at the new soda fountain. Asa tucked his grip out of the way. "What would you like?" he asked.

"Well," Shirley said, "I don't have any problems with ice cream, so I'd like a strawberry soda."

"Coca Cola, please," Mary said.

"Black coffee for me, Pete," Asa addressed the boy behind the counter. He took out his wallet and paid.

"Say, Asa," Pete said, as he was serving them, "I heard that new model Pawtah's comin' out with is really somethin' special. Is it true you designed the cahburetah?"

"Waell, 'twas just a few modifications. But these young ladies don't want to talk about motah cahs, do you?" He turned to Mary and smiled.

"Oh, I don't mind at all," Mary beamed up at him.

He gazed at her. Had she had just fluttered those dark, curly eyelashes at him? Wake up and stop mooning like a fool, he told himself. He cleared his throat. "You just down to get the mail, or did you do anything else this evening?"

"Oh, yes, we're just off the train. We've been to the motion pictures in Orleans."

"Father didn't go. He was collecting the mail, and would have collected us, had we not had better things to do," Shirley said. "Have you been there? To the new theater?"

"Twice," Asa said. "Si and Janet and I went when it first opened. Then I took little Billy Porter and his mother. Billy was enthralled."

"How old is he?" Mary asked.

"Six — he's a great kid. Well, I'm sorry we didn't run into each other on the train — must've been on separate cars." Nothin' like statin' the obvious, Asa said to himself. "What'd you see at the pictures? Was it any good?"

"Oh, yes. It was Charlie Chaplin. He doesn't even have to do anything to be funny. He can just stand there, with that baggy suit and funny mustache. Then there's the way he walks and twirls his cane, and that sad-sack face!" Mary laughed.

Asa thought her eyes just lit up when she laughed. He found himself in danger of just sitting and staring at her, agape, like a love-struck fourteen-year-old. He closed his mouth and blinked. "Was it a double feature?"

"Yes, but the other picture was pretty awful. One of those badly made westerns, with mobs of cowboys and Indians running around shooting at each other. The story didn't make any sense. Of course, that could be because the film broke three times, and the projector once!"

Shirley had turned to chat with an acquaintance seated on her other side, easing herself out of Asa and Mary's conversation.

"Who was playing the organ? Was it old Mrs. Hatch?" Asa feared he was grinning like an idiot, and Mary would think he was touched in the head. But he just couldn't stop. "She can unintentionally add comedy to any picture!"

"I know what you mean, the way she turns around and grimaces at the audience every once in a while when the lights

474

come up. I think it's meant to be a smile!" Mary laughed. "And those wrong notes! It makes one almost feel sorry for the organ, it seems to groan so!"

Asa laughed. "Say, I saw a notice at the station advertising a band concert on the town common tomorrow, and I think there's another one Sunday afternoon. Would you like to go?"

"Why thank you, I'd love to! Mother and I used to go to those concerts when she was feeling up to it."

Asa saw the sadness she tried to hide with her smile. "I was sorry to hear about your mother. Did you get my letter?"

"No, I'm afraid I didn't," Mary said. "Perhaps it got lost in the mail."

"I sent several letters when I was at sea, but then I heard you'd, uh… moved. Still, I've written two or three times to Mrs. Bird's. It's strange… well, perhaps I got the street number wrong or something," Asa said.

"I assure you that if I'd received any letters, I would have written in reply," Mary said. "You mustn't think I've been snubbing you!"

"Oh, no, I don't think that at all. Your manners are far too good," Asa said. "But now, what about that concert? What day would be the best for you?"

"Oh, tomorrow would be fine," Mary said. "I hope this weather holds. If we have another day like this one, it will be beautiful!"

"And if it rains tomorrow, we can always go Sunday, unless you've other plans," Asa offered.

"Oh, no I haven't any. We've just been taking each day as it comes," Mary said. "But I'm sure I'll be fine for the concert tomorrow. I'm looking forward to it tremendously!"

Pete announced he was closing up in five minutes. They had finished their drinks by then, and much as neither Asa nor Mary wanted to part, it was time to go. They'd almost forgotten Shirley.

When they went out to the sidewalk, Asa discovered he *had* forgotten his grip. Embarrassed, he had to knock on the door and get Pete to let him back in for it. He came out wearing a sheepish grin.

"Forget my head if it wasn't attached," he said.

Mary and Shirley laughed.

"Allow me to escort you ladies home," Asa said.

Smiling down at her, he offered Mary his arm. Beaming up at him, she took it.

His mind suddenly went blank, and he couldn't think of a thing to say. And then he and Mary spoke at once: "Did you…" "Well, I…"

They stopped abruptly.

"You go first," Asa said.

"No, you," Mary insisted, "please."

"Well, I, uh, I'm sorry you never received any of the letters I sent," Asa said. "I can't figure out what happened."

"How many did you send?" Mary asked.

"Hmm. Six? No, seven," Asa said.

"That many?" Mary sounded surprised. "I wonder what could have happened to all of them."

"I wonder, too," Asa said. "Seems too much to be just… well, on the other hand, I don't see how anybody could've… um, interfered with the mail."

"You mean George," Mary said. "He's the most likely culprit, but I don't see how he could have done it, either. Unless Mrs. Bird has been keeping my mail from me…"

"Nunno, why would she do that?" Asa asked. "I must've got the address wrong or something. That's all. I'm sorry."

"So, what did you say?" Mary asked.

"What, in all those letters?" Asa felt his face get warm. "Too much to go into now. We're almost there. Suppose I just write it all down again in seven more letters, and you can answer each one, or not, as you choose."

"All right. If you send one to Shirley's address and I get it, then… well, I don't know exactly what that proves, but it does seem like someone's been keeping my mail from me, doesn't it?"

"Well, the ones I sent from overseas may be lost at the bottom of the Atlantic, or maybe you never got them because I sent them to your old house. Wish I hadn't left. Maybe I could have done something to… well, it's too late now. Oh, by the way, have you heard from Mr. Ives? I wrote to him about George kicking you out, but he hasn't answered me, either. Hmm. I wonder…"

"No, I haven't heard from him. What do you wonder?" Mary asked.

"I'll let you know when I figure it out," Asa said. "Oh, look, we're already to the big maple tree your great-grandfather planted, Shirley."

"Did he?" Shirley asked. "I believe you may be right, but how did you know?"

"Cap'n Alfred told me. He said your grandfather sawed a limb off it, and another off one of the oaks down the side of your house, too, to make wooden legs for him."

"Oh, is that so?" Shirley's voice was surprised and delighted. "Wasn't that kind of him? I never knew."

"I think they went whaling together, if I remember correctly," Asa said. "Obadiah Packard may have been with him on the voyage when Cap'n Alfred… um, had his accident."

"When the harpoon went through his leg, you mean," Mary said. "No need to be so fastidious with us. We both come from seafaring families, you know."

"I stand corrected," Asa said. "And abashed. Forgive me, Mary. I know perfectly well what a strong woman you are. I've seen evidence of that with my own eyes."

"Oh, go on with you!" Mary laughed. "Strong woman, indeed. If I were that strong, I'd still be working, and not lazing away my summer as a guest of Shirley's parents."

"Mary, you know that's not true," Shirley said. "Anemia may be physically debilitating, but it has nothing whatsoever to do with mental fortitude. You've been through enough to break anyone, but you're still standing."

Mary blushed. "I… um… thank you both, but I think you're giving me too much credit."

"Not at all," Asa patted her hand. "Not at all. Believe me; I know."

Mary looked at him. "I believe you do know," she said quietly.

They had reached the front porch, and could see Mr. Packard looking out the parlor window.

"Looks like father hen is hovering," Shirley said. "We'd better go in, Mary."

"Well, I'll pick you up at thirteen-forty-five — that is, quarter of two," Asa said to Mary. "That'll give us plenty of time to find a good spot. All right?"

"Yes, that's fine. I'll see you tomorrow, then," Mary said.

"Tomorrow — I'm looking forward to it. Good night, Mary." Asa beamed at her as he took her hand. He wanted to kiss it, but no, it was too soon. He didn't want to scare her away.

"Good night, Asa." Mary smiled shyly.

He was walking on air as he picked up his valise and headed home, whistling *Let Me Call You Sweetheart*.

\* \* \* \*

When they'd gone upstairs and were in Mary's room, she turned to Shirley and giggled.

"Oh, Shirley, I suddenly feel this strange mix of excitement and trepidation. Isn't he wonderful?"

"The way you were looking at each other, I'd say he thinks you're wonderful, too."

"I'd be happy to talk about carburetors or anything at all with Asa Mayhew. He's so tall and handsome, and those eyes! Blue as the ocean, as though reflecting all those years at sea. I could just drown in them. And when he took off his hat — oh, those curls." Mary looked — and felt — as though she were about to float up to the ceiling like a balloon.

"Steady on, now," Shirley laughed. "You don't want to expend all your energy raving about him, and be too tired to make your date tomorrow."

"You're right," Mary said. "Oh, but I don't know how I'm going to be able to sleep tonight."

# Chapter 34

## *A Concert*

Asa was ransacking the house for stray collar studs, asking Janet where on earth Si had hidden the shoe polish, and attempting to tame his unruly curls with brilliantine. All the while, he was singing snippets of *Moonlight Bay*.

"What ah you so dressed up for on a Satahday?" Janet asked. "You've been fussin' ovah your appearance like a young girl!"

He wore a beige summer suit with a needle-thin brown pin-stripe, matching vest, and a stiff celluloid collar on his crisp white shirt. He had put a wide brown grosgrain band on his straw boater. In front of the hall mirror, he muttered curses in French while he attempted to execute a perfect four-in-hand knot in his dark chocolate silk tie. He'd somehow got it backwards the first time, with the shorter length in the front. It wouldn't show, tucked into his high-gorged vest, but for heaven's sake, he'd been tying his own ties perfectly for half his life. What was the matter with him?

He turned to her, arms akimbo, front suit coat panels thrust to each side. "I will have you know that I am escorting a *fine* young woman to the band concert today. I want to look my best, so as not to put her to shame to be seen with me."

"Why, Asa Mayhew, I believe you're blushin'!" Janet teased. "Just who is this 'fine young woman' that's got you in such a tizzy?"

"I am *not* blushing, nor am I in a 'tizzy,' as you call it," Asa said. "If you must know, it's Miss Mary Lovejoy. I bumped into her at the station last evening, and I just thought I'd ask her, that's all."

\* \* \* \*

Meanwhile, Shirley was in Mary's room helping her to choose an outfit. "Oh, what shall I wear? Do you think this white dress makes me look too washed-out?" she asked, holding up a voile dress with a middy-style collar. The skirt was two tiers of ruffles over a lawn underskirt. "Perhaps if I took off this navy blue bow at the collar and used a colored ribbon instead?"

"You could always wear a little rouge," Shirley said.

"I don't know," Mary hesitated. "I've never worn makeup before. I'm afraid it would make me look cheap."

"Not if you apply it properly. I wear it sometimes. Will you let me put it on for you?" Shirley asked.

"All right, show me how," Mary conceded. "I can always wash it off if I don't like it."

She stood in the full sunlight coming in the window, critically checking her reflection in the hand mirror as Shirley smoothed a dab of rouge over her cheekbones.

"Now take a little bit and rub it into your lips, like this," Shirley demonstrated on her own lips. "And then blot it with this blotting paper."

Mary followed Shirley's instructions and examined the results again.

"You see? You can't tell, can you? It just makes you look healthier. A light touch, that's the trick. Oh! I know! You can borrow that pink bow from my blouse. Let's try it. Put on the dress."

Shirley went off to her own room to unearth the blouse in question. She came back and held the strip of material up to the dress. "Oh, yes, that brings a little color to your face." She slid it under the collar, and tied it in a floppy bow. "Perfect," she said.

"I don't know what I'd do without you, Shirley. I don't know anything about all this."

"Of course you do," Shirley said. "You've got a great sense of style with the clothes you make."

Mary blushed. "I don't create the styles, you know. I use store-bought patterns."

"You're too modest. You give them your own flair with the materials, colors, and embellishments you choose. That shawl you're crocheting for mother is simply magnificent." Shirley's happiness in seeing Mary enjoy herself, after the ordeals of grief and illness she'd been through, was plain to see. "What about hats? I think that wide-brimmed straw hat would be ideal, and it will keep the sun off your face. Those pink silk roses on it will add a little more color, and I like the bow in the back. Oh, have I got a pair of shoes for you!"

Although Shirley was two inches taller than Mary, they wore the same small shoe size. She dashed off to her room again, coming back with a pair of fashionable shoes with very high heels, in white leather, with pale pink crisscrossed straps that buttoned across the instep. The buttons were tiny rosebuds fashioned out of leather.

"Wear these tango shoes! They'll give you a little height so you'll at least come up to Asa's shoulder, and he won't have to bend over like a hunchback just to look at you!" She laughed. "Try them on."

"Tango shoes! Oh, how risqué! Does your father know you have these?" Mary giggled as she practiced walking around in the high-heeled shoes. "They're great, as long as I don't twist an ankle."

"Let me fix your hair."

Mary hadn't experienced this kind of female camaraderie, getting ready for tea parties and balls with other girls, growing up. She was thoroughly enjoying this time with Shirley. After months of darkness, the sun was beginning to come out. "Shirley, where are all the young men who used to come flocking around your door like bees to honey, as I recall? I feel a little guilty going off on an outing and leaving you at home. In the week I've been here, you've hardly spoken of any young men."

"There *is* one particular young man, and while you are at the concert this afternoon with Asa, I'll be going rowing with him. We're bringing along a picnic for afternoon tea." She blushed. "You know him — Edward Bellamy. He's been away for two weeks on a business matter, and he just got back yesterday."

"Oh, yes I remember the Bellamy family. Don't they own woolen mills down in Fall River? And isn't Edward that rather handsome fellow who played football at Harvard?"

"He's the one. I didn't want to say anything, because I'm not sure, but I think he may... well... pop the question this afternoon." Shirley looked down, blushing.

"Why, Shirley, you've been keeping secrets!" Mary grinned. "I'm so happy for you!" They hugged.

"I'm not sure. It may not happen, so please don't mention it to anyone else." Shirley's blush deepened. "It's just, well, there have been little signs, and his mother has been awfully attentive to me lately. Just before he went away, Edward had a private talk with Father. Father hasn't said anything, but I've caught him smiling at me oddly a couple of times, as if he had a secret. I think Edward may have asked his permission to ask for my hand. Why *Father* shouldn't tell me, I don't know, unless Edward wants to surprise me. But I mustn't get carried away. This is all just supposition, and I may be wrong about the whole thing."

"I hope you're not wrong, and I hope he asks you today. It would be such a crushing disappointment if he didn't," Mary said sympathetically.

"Anyway, there's no need for you to be feeling guilty on my account! And I'm sure I'll survive if he doesn't ask — well, almost sure." Shirley laughed.

Fastening her hat with a pin, Mary was just ready when the maid tapped on the door to tell her Mr. Mayhew was waiting in the parlor. Before going out onto the landing, Mary and Shirley clasped hands and grinned at each other.

\* \* \* \*

From the top of the stairs, Mary saw Asa standing in the doorway to the parlor, nervously turning his hat in his hands, smiling up at her.

"Hello, Mary — Miss Lovejoy. My, my, don't you look a picture." The muscles in his face ached with the broadness of his grin. He couldn't take his eyes off this graceful vision descending the stairs.

"Why, thank you." She put her hand to her chest and took a deep breath. "You look quite elegant, yourself."

"Oh, Mary!" Shirley called, running down the stairs. "Don't forget your shawl, in case a breeze picks up and you feel a chill." She handed her a pale pink confection.

"Thank you, Shirley." Mary's eyes remained on Asa.

"Good afternoon, Miss Packard," Asa said.

"My, aren't we formal? I thought we had agreed on first names last night." Shirley laughed. "I hope you both enjoy the concert. Good afternoon, Asa."

Asa grinned. "Shirley." He tipped his hat. He ushered Mary to the car, and helped her in. As his hand brushed against her cashmere wrap, he thought how fine and soft it was. It suited her perfectly.

"What a grand car!" she exclaimed.

"Isn't it swell? One of the perks of working for Porter Motors. Don't tell Bill, Mr. Porter that is, but I'd work for free just to drive around in one of these. And the new model's even snappier."

The men were just finishing setting up chairs when Asa and Mary arrived at the common. Members of the orchestra were trickling onto the band stand; some of them had begun tuning up.

"Do you know what's on the program today?" Mary asked.

"Don't recall if the announcement said, just noticed the time and place," Asa said. "Don't they usually play some Sousa marches and a little ragtime?"

"Not with these instruments." Mary grinned. "Not a Sousaphone in sight."

Asa took his eyes from Mary long enough to look at the orchestra. There were violins, violas, a cello, flutes, clarinets, an oboe, and a bassoon. It was mostly wind and string instruments. The only brass was a trumpet, with nary a sign of tuba, trombone, or drum.

"No, I should say not!"

"We shall have to wait and see. Oh, look! There's a man over there with what looks like programs."

"Is this all right?" Asa seated Mary in one of the wooden chairs up front.

"Perfect," Mary smiled up at him.

"You wait right here. I'll just go over and get one of those programs for you."

He had a loose, easy stride, not the rolling gait of some sailors. Mary smiled as she watched him.

As they pored over the program together, the closeness of their hands and heads distracted them. It took a moment for them to grasp what they were reading. To their surprise, this was not the usual band concert, but a chamber orchestra performance. A note on the program told them that at the request of a wealthy patron, orchestra members vacationing on the Cape agreed to come together for this special concert of selections by Corelli, Vivaldi, Handel, Bach and others.

Although Asa had been meaning to go to the symphony, and maybe the opera, he hadn't got to it, yet. He was familiar with classical music, but only in passing. With the exception of attending a performance of Handel's *Messiah*, before the war, in London, he'd never taken the time to sit down and truly listen, allowing himself be absorbed by it. He liked music of all sorts, and enjoyed singing everything from hymns and folk tunes to old sea shanties and popular songs. In the port of New Orleans, once, he'd heard something even newer than ragtime, called 'jass' — a racy term. It had stirred him in a visceral way. He looked at the program again.

"Well, I recognize them as being from the Baroque period, but I'm afraid I've done more reading than listening. There aren't many concert halls at sea," he smiled apologetically. "The names of these selections fail to bring any melody to mind, though perhaps I might recognize a tune when I hear it."

She hummed a bit of Bach for him, pointing to one of the pieces. "I'm afraid I can't do it justice. You probably wouldn't recognize that, even if you had heard it before."

"Oh, don't say that, Mary," Asa protested. "It sounded good. I'm quite looking forward to this." He smiled at her with twinkling eyes.

As the chairs around them filled up, they settled back to listen. The chairman of the board of selectmen rose to announce their very good fortune and special privilege in having these musicians come to perform for them, thanked the orchestra and the people in attendance, and sat down.

"Unusually brief speech for him," Asa murmured in Mary's ear.

Mary smiled at him. Then the conductor raised his baton and Asa sat up, paying rapt attention.

As the concert progressed, he was aware of Mary dabbing at her eyes with her lacy handkerchief. He touched her hand. Bach's *Air* from the *Orchestral Suite No. 3 in D Major* so moved and entranced him that he saw the orchestra through a disconcerting blur of tears. He was spared further embarrassment when the concert moved on to Bach in his more mathematical mode. But then there was the Albinoni — oh, dear. After that were more adagios, more emotive violins and affecting oboes. At the end of the concert, they sat quietly after the applause had ended and other people left the common. They held hands, though neither of them remembered when they had reached out to one another.

"That was beautiful," Mary said softly.

Asa blinked and cleared his throat, but his voice came out in a croak. "I don't believe I have ever been so moved by a musical performance." He paused, cleared his throat again, and then said in a joking manner, "Was afraid I'd break down and start blubberin' in front of you and the whole world!" He turned to her and grinned.

"Well, I'm glad I remembered my handkerchief." Mary smiled at him.

"Oh, deah. I didn't mean to take you to something that would make you cry on our first outing." Asa looked at her with concern.

"Oh, but they weren't tears of unhappiness at all," Mary said. "It's just that when something is so beautiful, well, 'beautiful' isn't a good enough word — powerful, maybe, or stirring…"

"Ah, yes." Asa's deep voice was hushed. "Inspiring awe, such as seeing the stars that surround and almost overwhelm you on a moonless night in the middle of the ocean — so close you could reach out and touch them. Or when you look at a sky filled with color — a sunset, a rainbow, the aurora borealis, those dancing green and purple lights." He paused; his voice dropped to a whisper. "And out of the silence comes the music of the spheres… 'Tis almost like having the hand of God come down to touch your heart."

"Asa," Mary said in a low voice, "I'm about to cry again. Why, you're a poet!"

Asa shook his head as though rousing himself from a dream. "I've never said anything like that out loud before. I don't know why..." He looked at the ground, wishing it would swallow him up. He drew his hand down his face, as if to wipe away the blush. He cleared his throat.

Mary reached out and touched his arm. "I am moved that you would share those thoughts with me, would let me see your hidden depths."

The men putting the chairs away had reached the row behind them.

Asa cleared his throat again and stood up. "Let's go someplace, all right?" He took her hand and helped her rise. "Where would you like to go? What would you like to do? Do you want to go for a walk, or are you all done in? What about a ride in the car? We could take a ride over to Mrs. Brown's tea shop in Truro, if you'd like. Or do you have to go home and rest? I keep forgetting that you're convalescent, you look so good." He gazed at her appreciatively, his soft smile lighting up his eyes.

Mary smiled back. "I don't quite have the energy for a much of a walk, and these are definitely the wrong shoes."

Asa looked at the daring high heels and the shapely ankles they showed off. "Mm, *very* nice! I mean, uh, those are quite some shoes — very, um, fashionable." He could feel the heat rising to his face and tugged at his suddenly too-tight collar.

The pink of Mary's cheeks didn't come from rouge. She looked at the shoes and giggled. "They're Shirley's. I'll tell her how much you like them. Shall we take a ride in the car? You can show me how fast it goes."

Asa laughed. "I don't think you want to encourage me there. I warn you, Mary, most people are terrified at the speeds I drive."

"Oh, I don't know," Mary said recklessly, "I like to go fast." Happy, she thought.

"Well, if you say so." Asa helped her into the car. He cranked over the engine, got in, and drove off. "Hang on to your hat!" He laughed. Happy, he thought.

Mary clutched her hat and laughed gleefully as Asa set off at the breakneck speed of twenty-five miles per hour. On better roads, the car would go seventy miles per hour or more, theoretically, but there were no better roads, and he didn't want to wreck the undercarriage. He drove to a bluff overlooking the Atlantic. They got out of the car and held hands as they stood watching white sails against the deep blue ocean, gulls wheeling and calling against the azure sky.

"I haven't been this happy since..." Mary's voice dropped. "Well, since the last time I was with Father."

"I was just thinking — when's the last time I was truly happy? With Cap'n James, exploring Bombay, before he—" Asa shook his head, biting his lip.

"Our wonderful memories are tinged with sadness," Mary said. "But we should never push him out of our minds because of that. We must never forget him and the good times we had with him."

Their grief and longing for him brought fresh tears to their eyes.

"How I wish I had saved him!" Asa blurted out. "I should have prevented it."

Mary put her hand on his arm. "Asa, don't. You did everything you could have done, almost losing your own life trying so hard to save him. Mr. Slocum, Mr. Martin, and Dr. Coffin each wrote and told me what happened. Even if you had plucked him from the sea, the fever would have killed him."

"I'm so sorry he's never coming back home to you, Mary."

"And I'm sorry you'll never sail with him again."

Asa nodded, unable to speak.

After a few moments of silence, they spoke of James's generosity of mind, heart, and spirit; how much they'd learned from him, and what *joie de vivre* they'd had in his company. They told stories that brought tears and laughter to their eyes.

"He was…" Mary struggled to find just the right word to describe him.

"Electric," they said at once, then looked at each other and laughed.

"Ayup, he really lit up whatever place he was in. People just sparked right up around him," Asa said. "I'd never met anyone like him, and I don't think I ever shall."

"It's good to have someone to talk to who knew him the way I did," Mary said. "It seems to bring him closer, somehow. You remind me of him, in a way."

"Me?" Asa was incredulous. "Nunno. I could never approach his… I don't know what to call it."

"But you are like him in so many ways," Mary said.

"So are you," Asa said. "You have his strength of character and—"

"And you have his openness, his desire to understand and… and… Oh, I can't quite find the right words. Do you know what I'm trying to say?"

"Maybe… We remind each other of him, but it's more than just sharing memories," Asa said. "I think we each… how shall I put this? In a way, we embody him — his spirit — for each other. So he is closer to us, and we are closer to each other."

"Yes! Yes, I feel that, too," Mary said. "I wonder if he has—"

"If he has what?" Asa asked when Mary stopped speaking.

"I don't know. You'll think I'm being… silly."

"If you're silly, then so am I," Asa said. "Do you wonder if he has brought us together to console one another?"

"Yes. How did you know?"

"Well, now, that's a mystery, isn't it?"

They went to Mrs. Brown's Tea Shop. Following afternoon tea (coffee for Asa), they rode around enjoying the scenery, talking, telling stories, laughing, and, Asa thought, falling in love.

"I don't want to part from you, Mary. Have supper with me?"

"I'd love to, Asa, but the Packards are expecting me. I do wish I could stay with you, but I'm a guest in their home. I can't be rude to them when they've treated me with such kindness. You understand."

"Of course. I don't know what I was thinking. Yes, I do. I was thinking of myself, of not wanting to take my eyes off you. And here I've been wearing you out, taking you all over the place, talking your ear off, when you need to lie down and rest."

"Oh no, I'm fine." Mary grinned. "I feel better than I have in weeks."

They pulled up in front of the Packard's house. Asa shook his head. "I can see you're flagging. I should have noticed it earlier. I haven't been taking very good care of you, have I?"

"You've taken very good care of me. I haven't had so much fun since… well, in ages."

"Since your father? Neither have I." Asa's smile was bittersweet.

They both sighed, and reached out to hold hands.

"May I call on you tomorrow afternoon?"

"I should like that very much. Thank you for a delightful afternoon, Asa."

"Thank *you*, Mary, for agreeing to come out with me." Asa held her hand and gazed at her, entranced. He whispered, "You are so beautiful."

Mary squeezed his hand. "Your eyes are just mesmerizing, you know."

They laughed, blushing.

Asa walked around and opened the car door for her, helping her out. He escorted her to the front door. "See you tomorrow, then? What time?"

"After Sunday dinner. Shall we say around half-past two?" Mary said.

"I'm afraid I won't hear a word of the sermon, being lost in anticipation of seeing you."

This time, Asa did kiss her hand.

# Chapter 35

## *Love and War*

A s he polished his shoes that morning, Asa decided to make a concerted effort to polish his English as well. He'd noticed his accent slipping back into old patterns since he'd been home. He knew who he was and he certainly had no shame in his origins. He only hoped he could be as open-minded, openhearted, and honorable as his father had been, or as kindhearted and true as Si. Surely, enunciating more clearly didn't mean he was being dishonest about himself or disloyal to his family. No, of course not. If he could speak more than a dozen languages fluently, wasn't it about time to speak his native tongue properly? He merely wanted to make a good impression on Mary.

He gave himself a wry look in the mirror. Boy, did he ever want to make a good impression. He'd never been a dandy, but with the care he was taking over his clothes in the last two days, he could mistake himself for one. He'd chosen his other new summer suit today, the navy blue one, with matching vest, a blue-and-white striped shirt, stiff white collar, navy-blue tie with tiny white polka dots, four-in-hand knot perfect on the first try. He fastened spotless white spats over highly polished black shoes. He changed the band on his hat to navy blue.

As he entered the kitchen, Janet looked him up and down. "Where'd you get that suit?"

"Like it? Had it made in Boston a couple weeks ago. I know, I know — I already bought one last spring. What do I need another one for? Well, if I'm gonna be attendin' business meetin's with Bill, I can't very well go in my grease-stained coveralls, can I?"

"You already had two suits. I thought you hated new clothes. Did you get all dandified just to go to church? Ah you even goin' to church, or ah you just headin' straight ovah to see Miss Lovejoy?"

"I'm goin' to church, Janet." Asa sounded injured. Then he grinned. "I'm not seein' Miss Lovejoy until this afternoon."

"Janet, you make it sound like he skips church every othah week," Si smiled. "He only skipped once, when he was skipperin' Mistah Pawtah's yacht."

Asa laughed. "Thought you were gonna start singing."

"I leave the singin' to you; you've got a bettah voice."

"Skip, skip, skip to m' Lou / Skip to m' Lou, my dahlin'." Asa swung Janet in a circle as he sang.

Janet looked from Si to Asa and back again. "Stuff and nonsense. And *dancin'* on a Sunday!" She clicked her tongue and tried to scowl, but Asa saw the sparkle in her eyes.

\* \* \* \*

When he arrived at the Packard's house later in the day, he heard piano music, and paused on the front porch to listen. He didn't knock until the piece was finished. When the maid showed him in, he found Mary seated at the piano. She was wearing a pale blue dress of some lightweight material, with a tiered ruffled skirt and an ecru lace collar. Asa thought she looked lovely.

Mr. and Mrs. Packard, Shirley, and Edward Bellamy were urging her to play more.

"Miss Lovejoy, Mr. Mayhew is here," the maid announced.

He shook hands with Mr. Packard and Mr. Bellamy, said hello to the ladies, and presented Mary with one perfect red rose. He had picked it after dinner, painstakingly removing every single thorn.

"Oh, my, isn't that lovely! Thank you."

"I wish it could have been a dozen, but Janet would give me what-for if I picked all the roses in her garden." Asa grinned.

"Would you like me to put that in water for you?" the maid asked.

"Yes, please, Bridget." Mary handed her the rose.

"Please, sit down," Mr. Packard said. "Make yourself at home."

"Thank you." Asa took a seat near the piano and smiled at Mary. "Please, don't let me interrupt you. I listened from the porch and was enchanted. I'd like to hear more."

"Isn't it wearing a bit thin by now?" Mary asked. "I don't wish to bore you all to tears."

"If there are tears, I assure you, they won't be from boredom, but because your playing has moved us in your ability to express the emotion of the piece." Feeling the heat of a blush rising in his cheeks, Asa looked at the floor and cleared his throat. "What was that piece you were just playing?"

"One of Chopin's *Preludes*, number fifteen. Really, though, all of you must be tired of listening to me play." Mary blushed.

"No," Shirley said. "I could never tire of listening to you play."

"I wish you'd get your violin and play with me," Mary said.

"No, no," Shirley demurred. "You know I can't play in front of people. My fingers become all jangled with nerves and instead of music, they create the most horrible screeching sounds."

"Only to your perfectionist's ear. You play just fine." Mary sighed. "Shall I never convince you to try?"

Shirley shook her head. "I haven't your talent, Mary."

Bridget came in and placed the rose, in a bud vase, on the baby grand piano.

"Thank you, Bridget," Mary smiled at her.

Bridget, seeming flustered at being thanked, nodded and hurried out.

"Mary, you play beautifully," Asa said. "Will you play some more, please? If you're not too tired, that is. It seems that I'm not the only one who'd like to hear more."

The others all joined in, conveying their assent.

"All right, one more. I'll just play the *Adagio* of this sonata." Mary smiled. She took a deep breath, placed her fingers on the keys, and prepared herself. Then she went on to play the first movement of Beethoven's *Moonlight Sonata*.

When she had finished, there was silence for a moment, then the Packards began to applaud. Asa sat dazed and deeply moved. He gazed at Mary with brimming eyes. He vaguely heard someone suggest a game of croquet.

"I'm afraid I haven't the energy, but you go ahead and play. I'm sure Mr. Mayhew will keep me company," Mary said.

Caught up in a dream, Asa smiled at her. Despite his distracted state, he noted that Shirley seemed to have a glow about her, and that she and Edward were holding hands as they passed by. Shirley's diamond sparkled in the light.

"Well." He tried to recover his wits enough to speak in sentences. "I uh... I never knew music that had such power to... to do this to a fellah. Thank you, Mary."

She blushed. "It was my pleasure."

She was still seated, gathering the piano scores together. He rose and stood behind her. Unthinking, he placed his hands on her shoulders and began massaging them. Still bemused, he leaned forward and kissed the top of her head. He came to his senses and sprang back. "Oh! I... I didn't mean... I didn't mean to... uh... to take... liberties. Please fo'give... forgive me. It's just... I... uh..."

Mary swiveled around on the piano stool to face him. "There is nothing to forgive, Asa."

"Well... I, ah... was ovahcome." He shook his head and corrected himself. "Overcome... by the music, by your playing, by... ah, you."

"I'm rather sorry you stopped," she smiled. "Your hands on my tired muscles felt very good. And as for the kiss — well, a little peck on the top of the head is hardly taking liberties. Why, only a couple of days ago, I kissed a boy on the top of the head. He was sitting on my lap at the time. His parents thought nothing of it. Of course, he was only eleven months old. He was adorable, with his blond curls and big blue eyes." Her smile widened. "So are you."

Asa chuckled with nervous embarrassment. "Not as adorable as you are, my dear."

She reached out and took his hands in hers, looking into his eyes, murmuring, "So blue, like the ocean." She rose and stepped closer to him. He took her in his arms and breathed in the flowery scent of her hair. He tipped up her chin, and softly kissed her mouth.

*What have I done?* He thought. *I'm behaving like a rake! Any minute now, she's going to show me the door...*

"I... I shouldn't have... I simply couldn't... resist. But that is no excuse. Oh, what you must think of me..." If he'd been aboard ship, he'd have jumped overboard to put out the flames he felt burning up his face.

Her cool hand reached up to touch his face. "I think I like it," she whispered.

"Oh, Mary," he murmured, taking her in his arms again. She wrapped her arms around him. He drew her head onto his chest, and they stood with their arms around each other, his chin resting lightly on the top of her head. They broke apart when they thought they heard someone coming. It was only the maid, passing by in the hallway.

Asa cleared his throat, but only produced only a hoarse croak. "Ahem. Mary, I— ahem... Mary—" After a deep breath, he started again. "Is it possible? I mean, it's only been two days, and um... I think— No, I *know*—" His legs folded and he sank down on the loveseat. He looked at the floor. Mary moved to sit beside him. Taking her hand, he blurted out, "Mary, I'm falling in love with you. I think I've *been* falling in love with you since... well, as awful as it seems, since uh... that night, when I came to tell you..." He gazed into the distance. "I've kept thinking about you, all this time."

Mary held his hand in both of hers. "Yes," she whispered. "And I, you."

He gazed deeply into her brown eyes with their little amber flecks. He could bask in their warmth. "Your eyes," he paused, "have captured the sun."

She met his gaze. "And yours, the horizon of sky and sea."

Embarrassed at their romantic flights of fancy, they laughed, and then put their arms around each other again.

"Mary," he said. "I don't ever want to part from you, not for one instant. I wish I could see you again tomorrow, and the next day, and the day after that, until we run out of days."

"So do I," Mary said.

"You do?" Asa smiled. "Only trouble is, I can't very well ask Mr. Porter for time off when I just started working for him. I have to go back to Cambridge."

"Will you come back next Friday?" she asked.

"Come hell or high watah." He gasped and clapped his hand over his mouth. "Oh, I *am* sorry."

"For what?" Mary asked.

"My language," Asa replied. "I wanted to make a good impression on you, but I keep saying and doing things that— I'm behaving like a… like a bounder. Please, pardon me. I—"

Mary put her fingertips to his lips. "Sh, stop apologizing. I'm the daughter and grand-daughter of sea captains, remember? I have heard the phrase before." She grinned at him. "I confess; I've even used it."

"You're wonderful! The first time I looked into your eyes—" His smile vanished and he turned away, staring out the window. "When I looked into your eyes on that terrible night, I— I believed I could see into your soul." He paused again, catching and holding her gaze. "It was, and is, full of grace. Gracious and graceful Mary, I give you my haht."

She took his hand in hers, but did not speak. Her liquid eyes spoke for her.

"You must think I'm touched." He tapped his temple with a forefinger. "You have this effect on me. I open my mouth and these… these words… these emotions… come tumbling out. I… I can't… keep them back."

"I find your words — and your soul — beautiful, darling," Mary said.

"Darling," he echoed. Pulling her close, his lips brushed against her hair. "I shall write to you every day. May I?"

"I'd like that," Mary said. "I'll write back."

She leaned into him and listened to his heartbeat. He held her with exquisite tenderness.

"You smell so good," she murmured.

"You think so?" Asa chuckled. "It's just soap and watah — not even any aftah shave."

"And sun, salt sea air, and aromatic pipe tobacco," Mary said. "Like my father. You make me feel safe."

"I'd like to hold you and protect you forever."

They broke apart guiltily as the maid came in. "Excuse me," she said. "Mrs. Packahd has sent me to ask you to join them fo' tea on the back piazza." She led the way through the house.

The back porch was a large, screened-in, airy place. Straight-backed wooden chairs surrounded a table covered with a white linen cloth. On it were a pitcher of iced tea, thin sandwiches cut into fancy shapes, and tea cakes. The men rose as Mary entered. Asa pulled out her chair and seated her.

Mrs. Packard, pitcher and glass in hand, looked up and smiled. "Would you like mint or lemon in your tea, Mr. Mayhew?"

"Mint, please, Mrs. Packard." Asa smiled as he took his seat. "It's quite cooling in warm weather, isn't it?"

Edward smiled. "This is something of a celebration today, as Shirley has just agreed to be my wife."

"Well, congratulations!" Asa offered. He rose to shake Edward's hand. "And best wishes to you, Shirley. I thought I noticed somethin' glitterin' on your fingah — finger." Shirley held her hand out to him, proudly showing him her ring. "Oh, that's a dazzler. Very fine indeed." He looked from the ring to Edward and nodded.

To be polite, Asa took a tiny watercress sandwich. When Mrs. Packard pressed him to take more, he protested that he'd had a large Sunday dinner. In truth, his stomach was too full of butterflies to eat. He tried a sip of tea — too sweet. He succeeded in not making a face of distaste, but, unaware, he pushed the glass away.

Mr. Packard took a sip of his tea and did make a face. "This is dreadful! Why, it sets my teeth on edge! Sarah, where did you get this cook? Doesn't she know how to make a plain pot of tea, without adding a five-pound sack of sugar to it?"

"Sorry, dear," Mrs. Packard turned to the maid. "Bridget, would you please ask Mrs. Bridges to make a fresh pot of tea — with *no* sugar! Bring in the china cups. I'm afraid it shall have to be hot tea. Oh, and please bring in a pitcher of ice water and fresh glasses. We may wish for something cold."

"Yes, Ma'am," Bridget nodded. She was about to remove the iced tea.

Shirley said, "Leave it, please, Bridget. I've got a sweet tooth. I shall drink it, even if no one else does."

"I'll help you," Mary said. "I like it sweet. It just needs a little more lemon."

"Lemon," Bridget nodded, and went off to perform her duties.

"I'm sorry about this, Mr. Mayhew," Mrs. Packard said. "The cook is new. We certainly didn't mean to... well, set your teeth on edge." She smiled at her husband and returned her gaze to Asa.

"Oh, that's quite all right, Mrs. Packard. You're not to blame if your cook learned to make sweet tea the southern way. And please, call me Asa." Asa smiled.

While exchanging pleasantries and small talk with those around the table, Asa and Mary kept glancing at each other with blushing smiles, and looking away again. Their hands crept together beneath the tablecloth. Across the table, Asa caught Shirley and Edward looking at them, and then at each other with knowing smiles. It seemed to him Mr. and Mrs. Packard were smiling upon all of them.

Eventually, the talk became more serious, moving on to what was happening in the world. "What do you think, Asa, is the United States going to get into this war?" Mr. Packard asked.

"Well, though not official, I think we're already halfway in it. A lot of Americans have already volunteered to go over there: doctors, nurses, ambulance drivers... Manufacturers have been selling ammunition to the Allies for some time. There was the sinking of the *Lusitania* last year. Not to mention numerous suspicious fires and explosions on merchant ships as well as factories; saboteurs blowing up things such as that munitions dump on Black Tom Island — these things are changing people's attitudes. I think President Wilson still hopes to keep us out of it — at least until after the election, so his slogan won't be a bald-faced lie. But if the Germans keep attacking merchant ships and carrying out sabotage, I believe we'll be inexorably drawn into it. Especially if more people die as a result. What's your opinion?"

"I'm afraid I agree with you," Mr. Packard said. "Nobody wants to get involved in war, but when they're stuck in a stalemate over in France, when civilian ships aren't safe and your own citizens are being killed, what else can you do? The French and English boys over there are really taking a beating."

"Also the Belgians, Canadians, Algerians, Indians, and ANZACs. So are the Russians," Asa said. "The German and the other Axis lads as well. We might not feel sympathetic to enemy troops, but the Kaiser decided to go to war, and those boys had no say about being conscripted into it."

"Hmm, yes; I hadn't thought of it that way before, but I see what you mean," Mr. Packard said. "The loss of life is simply appalling, especially of the civilians who only happened to be in the path of this juggernaut of war. I don't see where it'll all end up. And now with this Black Tom Island explosion, I'm afraid our days of non-intervention may be coming to a close. Yes, I dare say we'll be in it before the end."

"I'll join the Army, if that's the case," Edward said. "What about you, Asa?"

"It'll be the Navy for me. When they passed the Naval Act, I tried to join the Navy Reserves, but they're not yet organized. I expect they will be before the end of the month." He cast a worried look at Mary. He hadn't mentioned any of this to her, and he was afraid of her reaction.

The color drained from Mary's face. "Doctor Stone was talking about joining up, too. His partner is already over there with the Harvard medical unit under Doctor Cushing. This is just dreadful! Don't you realize you could be *killed*? This isn't some great adventure!"

"What about us?" Shirley asked Edward. "What about our wedding? Do you want to go away and leave me a widow before we're even married?"

"But, Shirley," Edward protested. "We talked about this. It's not as if it's a surprise. I know you're against it, but if a man's country needs him, why, he's just got to go!"

"But I didn't think it would ever really happen!" Shirley said. "Didn't President Wilson say he would keep us out of the war?"

"He still may, dear." Mrs. Packard tried to console her, but Mr. Packard was no help.

"I'm afraid that if the Germans start torpedoing civilian ships again, President Wilson won't be able to keep us out of it," he said.

"Mary," Asa said. "I didn't mean to spring it on you like this. I spoke without thinking."

"That's the trouble. You men don't think! You don't consider how we women would feel if anything were to happen to you. Why do you feel you *must* go away to war?" Mary demanded.

"Oh, dear, now I've done it," Mr. Packard said. "I should have known better than to bring up the war with you girls present. You mustn't upset yourselves. This is all just talk. Perhaps the United States won't get involved, after all. Now let's forget all about it." But it was too late.

Shirley fled, crying, with Edward following. After she got herself under control, they slowly made their way back to the house.

Mary grew even paler. "Please excuse... need... air..." She went out and headed toward the Westport plank chairs facing the ocean.

"Air? We're on a screened porch," Asa said. "I must go to her. Excuse me." He hurried out.

"Mary!" Asa, alarmed at Mary's pallor, reached out to support her.

"Those chairs… were never so… far away," Mary said. Then she fainted.

Asa caught her. "It's all right; I've got you." He carried her into the house.

Shirley led him up to Mary's room, Mrs. Packard following.

"I'll telephone Doc Chandler," Mr. Packard said.

Climbing the stairs, Asa felt terrible. Mary hadn't recovered from her illness. He should have been more considerate. Here he'd spent the afternoon making love to her, telling her he never wanted to part from her, and then he turns around and tells her he's going off to join the Navy, to fight in a war, perhaps never to return. He'd have smacked himself on the forehead if he had a hand free.

He laid Mary down, trying to make her comfortable. Then he sat down in a chair at the side of her bed, holding her hand, chafing her wrist, and saying, "Mary! Wake up, Mary. I'm so sorry. Oh, please, dear, wake up."

Mrs. Packard brought a glass of water. As Mary began to come around, Asa supported her head and held the glass to her lips. "Try to take a sip," he encouraged. It didn't seem to help. "I think a spot of brandy might be of more use, if you've got any," he said to Mrs. Packard.

"Oh, of course," Shirley said. "Doctor Stone prescribed brandy for Mary to take before meals. It's right over here." She went to the bureau to retrieve it, and brought a clean glass.

Asa poured a little into the glass, and held it to her lips. She drank and began coughing and spluttering.

"Go down the wrong way?" Asa sat her up and patted her back.

She stopped coughing and took a ragged breath. Mrs. Packard plumped up the pillows to support her in a semi-recumbent position. Mary blinked and looked around, then looked directly at Asa.

"What happened?" Her voice was hoarse.

"Try another little sip of brandy," Asa suggested. "There, is that better? You fainted. How're you feelin', or is it too soon to tell?"

"Too soon." She sounded weary. "Oh, I remember now." She sniffed as tears began to trickle down her face.

"There, there." Asa felt helpless. He moved from the chair to the bed. He took her in his arms and murmured into her hair. "There, there. Don't cry." He blinked away his own tears. "Oh, my love, I'm sorry to have distressed you so."

Shirley and Mrs. Packard edged out of the room, leaving the door open.

Mary leaned her head against him. She took a shuddering breath. "No, *I'm* sorry, Asa," she whispered. "I ought to be stronger, but since I've been sick, I seem to go to pieces over the least little thing. I regret having caused such trouble for everyone."

"Hush, dear," Asa said. "I shouldn't have said anything about the war. I was very inconsiderate of your feelings, and I wish I could take it all back."

"No," Mary said. "I simply took a bad turn. The heat and humidity got to me, and I think I was too drained to cope with the possibility of anyone else — of any more — um..."

"Yes," Asa murmured.

"It's certainly not your fault if I'm too much of a goose to face reality," Mary said. "Father and Mother brought me up to be more sensible than that. Don't you dare feel guilty! Do you hear?"

"All right, love." Asa stroked her hair. "I'll try not to, if you'll try to forget what I said about going away. I'm not going anywhere — not yet, anyway."

"Who said anything about going away?" Mary's smile turned into a yawn. "Oh, excuse me. I'm so tired."

"You rest, now," Asa said. "Sleep, dear."

"Mm-hmm," Mary began to drift off. As Asa was about to settle her back against the pillows, she mumbled, "Don't let go. Not yet. I feel safe in your arms."

He cradled her, whispering, "Oh, my dear, it's all right. Everything's all right now, love." She was soft and warm. He wanted to hold her always.

Doc Chandler arrived. "What have you done to this poor young woman?" he demanded.

Asa eased Mary against the pillows before turning to Doc Chandler.

"Upset her with talk about the war," he said. "And I feel bad enough about it, but if you want to keelhaul me, go ahead. I deserve it."

Doc Chandler gave him a startled look. "Asa, I didn't mean… Well, I doubt you deserve to be keelhauled, even metaphorically. But for now, just get out of the way and let me see to my patient."

Asa paused in the doorway. "Oh, Doc, she was complainin' about the heat and humidity, said she couldn't get enough air. But it's not that hot, and there's a nice breeze. Maybe she's got a fever."

"Think so, do you, Doctor Mayhew? I'll be sure to check, don't you worry."

Asa shrugged. "Just thought you should know." He stepped into the hall, and Mrs. Packard went back into the bedroom.

"You look as if you could use some of that brandy, yourself," Shirley said to him.

"Oh, I feel just awful to have upset her like this." Asa felt knocked back by a wave of guilt and sadness, and leaned against the wall. "And to have upset you, too, with all this talk about the war."

"Oh, I'm all right now. It's just the thought of Edward—" She broke off, biting her lip and briefly closing her eyes before exhaling forcibly. "Well, I'll simply have to learn to accept it. But I'm serious about that brandy. Come on down to Father's study. That's where he keeps the good stuff. He and Edward are having a drink in there now, as a matter of fact."

Asa looked anxiously toward Mary's room. "I don't want to leave her."

"She'll be fine with a little rest," Shirley assured him. "She wouldn't have collapsed if she hadn't been so ill lately. She's made of tougher stuff."

"Still, I... I... wish I knew what to do for her." He rubbed his forehead as if to smooth away his worried frown. "I messed up, and I want to fix it."

"You look utterly dejected," Shirley said. "If you want to know what I think — and you probably don't, but I'll tell you anyway — you did *not* mess up. Sadly, you can't fix people as easily as you can fix a Porter engine. It takes time to recover from anemia. And grief, but you are well aware of that. Come and have a brandy before someone has to pick *you* up off the floor. When the doctor's gone, you can come back up to see Mary."

"You're right." Asa's eyes thanked her. "A little brandy might help."

"Buck up, Asa," Shirley smiled. "She'll be all right." She led him into the study, and asked her father to pour him a brandy, then went back to her mother and Mary.

"Say, Asa," Edward said, "You better sit down and drink that. You look as though something just hit you on the head. Cigarette?" He took out a silver cigarette case and offered it to Asa before taking one for himself. Mr. Packard was puffing on a cigar.

"Thanks." Asa took a deep drag, letting the smoke out slowly.

They drank and smoked in preoccupied silence for a while.

"I wish I hadn't mentioned the war," Mr. Packard said. "I never dreamt it would affect the girls in such a way."

"Neither did I. I should've known better. I hadn't even talked to Mary about my signing up, and with her bein' not fully recovered yet, it seems to have hit her like a ton of bricks. I shouldn't have said anything. I could kick myself," Asa said.

"Yes," Mr. Packard said. "I was just asking my wife why *she* didn't kick *me* when I opened my big mouth."

Asa leaned back in his chair and stretched out his long legs, taking another drag on his cigarette. "Wonder what's taking Doc Chandlah so damned long."

"Well, you know Doc," Mr. Packard said. "He can be as fussy as an old woman, but you won't find a better doctor around here."

"Ayup." Asa sat up, stubbing out his cigarette in the cut-glass ashtray. With a wry smile, he said, "You won't find *any* other doctor around here."

As Mrs. Packard came into the room, Asa stood. "The doctor's gone, now. You can go up to see Mary for a few minutes if you want."

"Thank you, Mrs. Packard." Asa covered the stairs two at a time.

Shirley was sitting with Mary, who had composed herself, but still looked wan. Shirley rose, giving Asa the chair.

"How are you, Mary?" Asa went to her, taking her hand in his. He looked into her eyes.

"Better, now, thank you. Asa, I'm terribly sorry I fell to pieces like that. I'm afraid I've been overdoing it a bit lately. I should have rested before your visit. It wasn't the talk about the war, although I must admit, that didn't help. I hadn't time to prepare myself for the thought of you going off to join the Navy. I'll be all right about it, now, much as I hate the idea."

"Are you sure about that, Mary?"

"I don't know about 'sure,' but whatever you feel you must do, I'll stand by you, rather than hinder you." Mary gave him a reassuring smile.

"It would be torture to leave you. I just discovered you're the love of my life, and... well, I wouldn't be goin' off with a light heart, that's for sure. Thank God we're not at war yet. I hope we never shall be, though I fear it's a forlorn hope." Asa searched Mary's face with worried eyes.

"Yes. I'm sorry I accused you of going off to seek some great adventure. I know you're well aware of the danger. Besides, you've already had plenty of great adventures, haven't you?"

"Yes, love. And perhaps too many that weren't by any means great." He looked away.

Mary reached up to touch his face. "Stop blaming yourself, Asa. It was simply a tragic accident."

Asa nodded, unable to speak past the lump in his throat.

Mary squeezed his hand. She tried to stifle a yawn, without success. Asa noted her eyelids at half-mast.

"You're exhausted." Asa's voice was hoarse. He cleared his throat. "Go to sleep now, dear. I'll stay for a while, in case you need me."

"If I could stay awake, there might be some point to your staying. But, much as I'd like to just sit here and look at your handsome face, I don't think I can keep my eyes open much longer." She yawned again. "Shirley and her parents shall look after me. But thank you for offering."

He leaned over and kissed her forehead. They hugged each other. It seemed as if they were holding on for dear life, as sad thoughts of the past and anxious thoughts of the future floated like specters in the room. Asa sighed, and Mary stroked his back. Then he leaned her back against the pillows and kissed her. She returned the kiss. Her warm smile was like a soothing touch. Again, he leaned forward and brushed her lips with his. When he straightened, she reached up to trace his lips with her forefinger.

His eyes were soft upon her as he held her hands. "I'll go, so you can sleep. May I telephone tomorrow, to see how you're feeling?"

"Mm, I'd like that," she said sleepily.

"Good night, dear, and sleep well." His lips touched her forehead once more before he left. She was asleep before he closed the bedroom door.

# Chapter 36

# *Doctor Stone*

D octor Stone sat at his desk, daydreaming over his charts, wondering how Mary was doing. Ten days ago, he'd picked her up in a taxi, and Mrs. Bird had almost made them late for the train. She'd fussed over Mary, asking if she had everything, did she want a drink of water before they left, telling her not to overdo, and generally hindering their progress out the door. When Doctor Stone finally extricated Mary from Mrs. Bird's clutches, they made their way to South Station, reaching the door of the railway carriage just in time to hear the conductor yell, "All aboard!"

He'd made sure Mary was as comfortable as possible, opening the window enough for some air, but not so much that it would blow soot on her. He'd told her to sleep whenever she was tired; she needn't think she had to keep up conversation simply because they were traveling together.

Although she had napped from time to time, Mary had proved to be an interesting conversationalist. They'd discussed literature and music, and discovered a mutual admiration for the novels of Henry James, regretting that had died last February. Sharing a love of Puccini's operas, they had each seen *Madama Butterfly* in April. To her piano, he played violin. They'd talked of current events. Much to

Mary's delight, he was in favor of women's suffrage. The war in Europe, looming over the horizon, was impossible to ignore.

Several of his acquaintances had volunteered with the Harvard Unit Doctor Cushing had set up, he said. He had wanted to join them, but so had his colleague. They couldn't both go; there was no one else to attend their patients here. Flipping a coin had determined that his colleague went to France, while he stayed home. If the United States did get involved, the Army would need surgeons.

She'd been anxious over this, saying surely it was dangerous, asking if the Army didn't already have enough doctors, and wouldn't he be needed here, to care for the men who would be returning. He had immediately regretted mentioning it, and apologized for causing her any distress, while at the same time he was secretly a little pleased that she should show such concern over him. There was nothing definite about it, he'd said, and he didn't want her to worry.

He had written to Doctor Chandler in Wellfleet, referring Mary to his care for the duration of her stay. Doctor Chandler had written to say he'd been Mary's doctor for most of her life. Doctor Stone had heard from neither the doctor nor Mary since he had placed her in Shirley's care at the Wellfleet station. He hoped this was a good sign. Surely, one or the other of them would have let him know if Mary had any setbacks.

Perhaps it would be more proper to contact Doctor Chandler to consult with him on Mary's — rather Miss Lovejoy's — progress, but he wanted to hear her voice. He called the operator, asking for the Packard residence in Wellfleet. She would ring him back when she had his party on the line. He was sitting at his desk, reviewing charts and updating his patient records, when the operator rang through.

After going through the operator and the maid, he spoke to Miss Packard. She told him that Mary had a bit of a setback yesterday, a fainting spell. Her color had improved today, her appetite had picked up, and she seemed much livelier.

"Oh?" Doctor Stone inquired, "What brought about the fainting spell?"

"I'll let Mary tell you." Shirley handed the telephone to Mary.

"Hello, Doctor Stone."

"Miss Lovejoy," he said, "I was just wondering how you're progressing. Miss Packard tells me you've had a setback; you fainted yesterday. Feeling any better?"

"Oh, yes, Doctor," she replied. "I feel quite recovered. The air is wonderfully reviving, and Shirley has raised my spirits tremendously. That fainting spell was nothing. I got over it right away."

"What brought it on?"

"Perhaps I overdid it a bit yesterday."

"Oh? In what way?"

"Well, I didn't take a nap after church, and after dinner I played the piano for about an hour. During afternoon tea, the heat and humidity made me feel as though I couldn't get enough air. Then the talk turned to the war. Shirley's fiancé and another friend said they would join up, and you had said you might go because they'd need doctors. Fatigue, the weather, the war — it all made my head spin, and the next thing I knew, they had carried me up to bed. So silly of me, really," Mary said. "But I'm quite all right now."

"I hope someone called Doctor Chandler." Doctor Stone frowned.

"Oh, yes, of course. He told me to stay in bed for the rest of the evening and gave me a sleeping draught, which was entirely superfluous. I fell asleep before I had a chance to take it, and slept soundly all night. I assure you, I'm feeling much better now."

"Oh, well, that's good. You've been resting, I hope, and not tiring yourself gadding about going to parties and such."

"Parties!?" Mary laughed. "No, no parties, but Shirley and I did go to the pictures on Friday, and I went to an outdoor concert on Saturday with A—," she broke off. "A friend. I felt no ill effects. Quite the opposite — I feel better than I have in weeks. One can't lie around doing nothing all the time, you know. It gets awfully boring."

"Well, I'm glad you've begun to get your energy back. I understand that enforced rest can become tedious, but I must caution you not to overdo. That includes emotional upsets. If you tax your system too much, you know you run the risk of a relapse, and then you'll have to go back on bed rest," Doctor Stone lectured. "Has Doctor Chandler been in regularly?"

"Yes, he came by three times last week; yesterday, of course; and he was here today. In fact, he only left about fifteen minutes ago. He seems to be satisfied, but it can often be hard to tell, with him." She laughed. "He can be rather funny at times, although I'm not sure he intends to be."

"Are you still taking your tonic? If you run out, Doctor Chandler can have more made up for you. I've given him the formula."

"Yes, but how much longer must I take it?" Mary asked. "It really doesn't taste very good."

He could almost hear the face she was making.

"Now, now. You know medicine isn't supposed to *taste* good." Doctor Stone laughed. "It's supposed to *do* you good. Keep on taking it until I tell you not to. You need to build up your blood. Your anemia was quite severe."

"Aye, aye, sir! I'll obey my doctor's orders like a good girl. I really am feeling so much better, though."

"Well, since you've had no adverse effects, with the exception of yesterday, I guess it will be all right for you to continue with some moderate activities such as picture shows and concerts, as long as you rest afterwards. It sounds as though you overdid it yesterday. You should have taken a nap either after church or after dinner, and perhaps cut the piano playing to half an hour — and no strenuous pieces. Don't try to do too much at once." He thought perhaps he was ordering her about too much, and changed tack. "How was the concert, by the way? Some friends mentioned that a chamber group we patronize had tried an outdoor performance, to see how it would be received. Was that the one you attended?"

"Oh, yes," Mary said. "It was wonderful. They played a lot of *adagio* movements from oboe and violin concertos. It was all Baroque — Corelli, Vivaldi, Bach, Albinoni, and… well, you know."

"Did your friend like it?" Doctor Stone wondered who this mysterious friend was. Male or female? Just an acquaintance or something more?

"Very much," she replied, giving him no information at all. "How was your sister's wedding?"

"Oh, fine, fine. It went off without a hitch. Well, not without *them* getting hitched," he laughed. "You know what I mean."

"Yes," she laughed with him.

"Perhaps—" Doctor Stone had thought he'd ask her to attend the symphony when the season began again in the fall, but realized it was too soon. He'd wait until she was fully recovered and no longer in need of his care as a physician. "Well, I'll see you when you get back in September. And if you have any problems or setbacks, don't hesitate to call me, or have Doctor Chandler call. It does seem from what you've said that your recovery is going well, although I don't like the sound of that fainting spell yesterday. Do take it easy. Continue to take that awful-tasting tonic and don't forget what I said about rest! Is that clear? Do you have any questions?"

Mary laughed. "Perfectly clear, Doctor Nag; no questions. I shall take my tonic. I shall rest after every activity. I shall eat well — plenty of red meat — and sleep well. I shall avoid emotional upsets. Those are your instructions as I understand them. Am I correct?"

Doctor Stone laughed. "Absolutely correct! I shall see you in a few weeks. Goodbye, Mary, uh, Miss Lovejoy."

"Goodbye, Doctor Stone. Thank you for calling."

# Chapter 37

# *Telephone Calls and Billets-Doux*

On Monday morning, Asa awakened thinking of Mary. When he got home from work, he'd call her. He couldn't wait to hear her voice.

As was his habit, Asa went in the kitchen door to the main house, where Martha filled up his thermos with coffee. She had already placed a thermos in their lunch basket, but one wasn't enough.

"Is Bill in the dining room?"

"Just finishin' breakfast," Martha said.

"Thanks, Mahtha," Asa said. "See yah latah."

In the car, on the way to the plant, Bill told Asa that they were going to begin construction of a new factory in New Jersey.

"There's no room to expand here, and we've got a site that will be closer to the Port of New York and New Jersey. I want you to look over the plans, to see if any modifications have to be made to turn it into an armored vehicle factory. They're calling them 'tanks'. To keep them secret, they were labeled 'water tanks' when they were shipped from England to France."

"We're really gonna build them then? Have we got orders from the Army?" Asa asked.

"Not yet, but I expect to get the contract as soon as Congress declares war," Bill said.

They had reached the plant, and Bill motioned for silence as they made their way to his office. Asa carried the lunch basket in, and placed it on a table in the back corner.

"Have a seat," Bill gestured to the chair across from his at the desk.

"Want some coffee?" Asa asked.

"No thanks, but you go ahead. We've got a lot to talk about," Bill said. "On second thought, I think I would like a cup of coffee, thank you."

Asa brought two mugs to the desk and sat down opposite Bill. "What's up?"

"A couple of things," Bill answered. "First of all, the tanks."

"I understand the first ones weren't very reliable. They stalled, tipped over, sank into the mud, were hard to steer — things like that," Asa said.

"They've made some improvements, but I think we can come up with better tanks that'll work in all kinds of terrain and weather." Bill's eyes lit up as he leaned toward Asa across the desk. "The new plant is in a fairly rural location, surrounded by woods. We'll have high fencing and guards, to keep out prying eyes. We're hoping the French will be sending someone over from Renault, and we're already in preliminary talks with the Royal Navy."

"Sounds like something we can really sink our teeth into." Asa was catching Bill's excitement. "But I'd like to see what problems the British and French have encountered. If something doesn't work, it'd be good to know about it before we start. No sense making the same mistakes twice."

"Right," Bill said.

"You said, 'a couple of things,'" Asa said. "What's the other thing?"

"Do you remember when we were out fishing, and I said the government might be interested in making use of your facility with languages?"

"Ayup. And?"

"They've been approaching those of us in business to... well, lend them employees who might have particular skills they need. It would seem they've been caught short-handed and without funding."

"I've heard something of the sort," Asa said.

"Along those lines, the Office of Naval Intelligence is sending someone over to talk with you today," Bill said. "In preparation for officially granting you authorization to work on secret projects, they've been checking into your background, as they have mine. But by some of the questions they asked me about you, I suspect they may want to ask you for additional duties I know nothing about. Now, I am aware that you dislike people prying into your private life, so I warn you: you may be asked some pretty personal questions that might get your back up a bit. If you want to keep working on this project, perhaps you shouldn't object or show your irritation. Just tell them what they want to know."

"No reason not to," Asa said. "I've got nothin' to hide. It's only the gossips I object to — people sticking their noses into things that don't concern them. But thanks for the tip-off."

"Good. I just wanted you to be prepared." Bill handed Asa a roll of blueprints for the new plant. "Look over the plans today. Then you and I will go down to New Jersey tomorrow to see the site. I've arranged with a pilot down there to take us up for an aerial view. We'll have to go up one at a time, but we can compare impressions once we get on the ground. Have you ever flown in an airplane?"

"Took a ride once at a county fair and liked it so much I wanted to have one of my own to play around with. Didn't buy one, though — no place to keep it." Asa grinned. "What about spies in airplanes, once we get this thing up and rolling?"

"Well, they won't be able to see through the roof, will they?" Bill asked.

"Not the plant, but the proving ground. Perhaps we should think about putting a roof over that, too."

"I hadn't thought of that. You see, this is why I need you. A roof or some kind of a canopy is a good idea."

Asa laughed. "I was just kiddin', Bill. A roof over the proving grounds is a completely untenable idea. Even with a dome, all the supports you'd need would interfere with the tryouts. Another thing — how could you test in rain and snow if you've got a roof or a canopy keeping the elements out? Nunno, a roof's no good. We need another way to prevent aerial spying."

"I'm sure you can come up with something after you've seen the site. I've got to make some telephone calls and dictate some letters, so I'll leave you to check over those building plans and make note of any changes you think should be made. Come over to my office when you're done, and we'll discuss it."

Asa was a bit unnerved by Bill's unquestioning confidence in his abilities. He went to work with the building plans, making notes on possible modifications and additions, thinking of ways to speed up production and to improve security at the new plant. He hoped Bill would see the need for more than just guards and a fence, as either could be easily overcome.

Most plant owners wouldn't have thought about any kind of security, other than a night watchman, perhaps. Only a few years ago, no one had thought of sabotage, and banks seemed the only places concerned with vigorously protecting their premises. Before the war, a lot of places, including military bases, hadn't even had fences, and people could wander all over the place, willy-nilly. One could even travel the world without a passport. That had all changed, but despite recent fires and explosions of suspicious origin, most manufacturers hadn't caught up to the necessity of protecting themselves against saboteurs. Asa would make sure *this* plant was secure.

\* \* \* \*

Just after lunchtime, Captain Robert Burns from the Office of Naval Intelligence arrived to interview Asa.

"Robert Burns? *But, Mousie, thou art no thy lane, / In proving foresight may be vain: / The best laid schemes o' mice and men / Gang aft a-gley, / An' lea'e us nought but grief an' pain, / for promis'd joy.*" Asa quoted, having no trouble rolling the Scots *r*. "I've always loved that poem. Imagine a fellah who feels such sympathy for this poor mouse that he sits down and writes a poem to it, after turning up its nest with his plow. Ancestor of yours?"

Burns was gruff. "Not as far as I know."

Asa thought Captain Burns probably saw him as a someone whose belfry was not entirely free of bats. He obligingly filled out forms and answered questions of a rather probing nature. He was glad of Bill's warning, so he was prepared when Captain Burns asked him questions such as: why had he left the merchant marine, what had happened during that storm at sea, and whether he was, indeed, healthy enough after his bout with malaria to take on what may be a difficult assignment. Asa raised his eyebrows at that last question, but then thought that in their background check, they would probably have questioned as many of the men aboard ship with him as they could find, including Doc. Secretly, he prided himself on bearing up under these questions without slipping into the past, into that state that virtually paralyzed him, even if his palms were deeply imprinted by his fingernails, and his cheeks were bloody from biting them to maintain contact with the present.

As Burns told him later, George Lovejoy had put in a bad word, and that had caused some minor difficulty until the Navy investigators had heard the real story. Besides, they'd seen that Lovejoy was under the influence of strong drink. As a counterweight to George's wild accusations, they had favorable reports from people of unquestionable probity. They'd questioned Captain Hookset and the men he'd sailed with, neighbors and townspeople, town officials, Hanson of the State Police, Josiah Mayo, Esq., and of course, Silas and Janet. Even Senator Cabot Lodge, whom Asa had met that day on Bill's sloop, gave an abrupt, but grudgingly favorable report. They'd had a good report from another congressman, with whom Asa had exchanged many letters regarding the wellbeing of sailors. They'd seen copies of the letters Asa had written, urging his Senators and Representatives to support Senator La Follette's Seaman's Act of 1915.

When the interview was over, Asa and Captain Burns got into a conversation about attempts to convince plant owners to be more security conscious. "The Office of Naval Intelligence, as you probably know, is engaged in preventing and investigating sabotage in the United States. It can be difficult to make owners see the necessity of taking some of the measures we suggest, largely because they're making money filling so many orders for munitions from overseas. They're more concerned about speed and volume. They'll hire just about anyone who walks in off the street." Captain Burns shook his head. "I understand Mr. Porter has asked you to come up with some security plans for this new plant."

Asa told him about his ideas, pointing out a few areas of concern. He said he didn't think a fence and guards would be sufficient protection against spies and saboteurs, and mentioned his disquiet about hostile aerial observation of the proving ground. He sketched out a few of the ideas he was formulating to circumvent sabotage and spying. Admitting that he was still thinking of the best ways to strengthen these weak points, he said he wanted to see the site first, and ask the architect and pilot some practical questions. He suggested thorough background examinations of job applicants, and identification badges for anyone entering the plant. Captain Burns agreed that he had some good points. "You'll be hearing from us in a matter of days," he said, and took his leave.

Asa saw him go into Bill's office. Looking out the window a few minutes later, he saw the captain sitting in his automobile making a few notes before driving away.

* * * *

Later in the day, Asa and Bill reviewed the building plans with an eye to the proposed modifications. They would meet with the architect at the site tomorrow.

Asa was still trying to come up with some solution to prevent aerial spying over the proving ground. Maybe something that would interfere with an airplane's ability to get close enough, so observers wouldn't be able to see or photograph anything more than vague, blurry shapes. He thought the pilot might know more about that than the architect. What would hinder an airplane? High structures like the radio tower Marconi had erected in Wellfleet? Wires strung across, with perhaps some netting or branches to conceal the grounds below, but not enough to interfere with precipitation?

As far as anyone climbing trees, that was easy enough. He sketched circles within circles. You just cut down the trees, like a fire break, around a perimeter wide enough to prevent anyone climbing a tree from getting close enough to see anything, even with binoculars. You erected a chain-link fence with barbed wire on top on either side of the cleared land. In the circle closest to the factory, you left thick woods, preferably of pine or fir trees that wouldn't lose their leaves in winter. Fir trees would not only screen the plant from view, they were nearly impossible to climb in order to take photographs. Aside from the outer chain-link fence and the inner one surrounding the cleared land, you could set up a high stone or brick wall between the evergreen forest and the plant. The wall could be topped with sharp objects, such as jagged stones, broken glass, or wrought iron spikes. Maybe the area beyond the wall and the fir trees should be littered with all kinds of hazards that would further obstruct anyone who had somehow managed to breach both fences and an ideally tangled wood from breaching the wall. He'd have to see if the site was large enough to support such measures, and if there were enough evergreen trees on it to screen the plant from view. Of course, two fences and a wall would require three gates, each to be manned with security guards, especially as the workers entered and exited for each shift, to check their identification badges. He sketched designs as he thought of these measures.

And then you had to contend with the workforce. You had to be sure they were trustworthy types who could keep their mouths shut. Even then, you had to ensure a saboteur couldn't get in by impersonating a worker. Identification badges wouldn't be enough, unless they included the worker's description — better yet, a photograph.

He continued throughout the day to have ideas for added security. He'd talk to Bill about it tomorrow, after they'd looked over the location.

When he wasn't thinking about work, he was thinking about Mary. He hoped she was better today, and that his talk of going into the Navy hadn't led to a recurrence of the more severe illness she'd been suffering in Boston. He remembered carrying her up to her room. How delicate she was, like a bird, light enough to fly. Her warmth and the flowery scent of her hair seemed to linger like an aura around him.

* * * *

When Asa was working in Cambridge, he stayed in what would have been the chauffeur's apartment over Bill's garage, had Bill ever wanted a chauffeur. It had running water and electricity, which was more than they had in Wellfleet. It even had a small kitchen, with its own apartment-sized stove, an icebox, and a closet-sized pantry. One thing it lacked, though, was a telephone, and he wished to call Mary. He wanted to know if she had recovered after her setback yesterday, and he needed to tell her about having to go away on business. As they left work for the day, Asa asked Bill how long they would be in New Jersey.

"Oh, no more than a day or two, I should think, unless something unforeseen comes up," Bill answered. "Why, did you have something you need to get back for?"

"Nunno. Just wondering. Say, Bill would it be all right if I use your telephone? I want to call Wellfleet. I'll pay for it."

"Of course, Asa, anytime! And don't worry about paying for it. I want you to consider my home as your home. I've told you that. You don't need to ask permission. Use the telephone anytime to call anywhere you wish."

The telephone was in Bill's study, where he left Asa, to give him some privacy.

\* \* \* \*

"Asa, hello!" Mary's voice conveyed her broad smile. "I was wondering if you'd telephone today."

"I said I would," Asa said. "Did you doubt me, Mary? How are you today, my love? Feeling better?"

"Much better, thank you," Mary said. "Doctor Chandler said my color was good, and he allowed me to take a short walk along the beach with Shirley."

"Oh, I'm so relieved to hear that. I want to apologize again for causing you so much distress yesterday," Asa said.

"Oh, Asa, please don't apologize anymore. I've told you, you weren't the cause of anything. It's my own fault for doing too much without resting. Then I allowed myself to lose control over my emotions, and I caused you just as much distress in doing so. I'm sorry."

"Nunno, Mary, it was what I said that brought about those emotions. But, lest we continue going back and forth like this, why don't we just say we're both sorry, and we're both forgiven. That way, we can move on to the next thing. Okay?"

"Yes, we could go around in this circle indefinitely, couldn't we?" Mary laughed. "I feel so bad for poor Mr. and Mrs. Packard, the way all four of us ran away from them like that. And I started it! Where were my manners?" she asked in a shocked tone.

"Oh dear me! We may never be invited to tea again!" Asa laughed. "Still, Mary, I'm glad you're able to have a sense of humor about it. I must say the picture of the four of us jumping up and running off in all directions does make for a mighty funny looking sight."

"Turn it into a moving picture, with all the jerky, speeded up movement, like a Mack Sennett film." Mary laughed. "Oh, it is good to make a joke out of it, isn't it? Takes away the sting."

"Mustn't forget to add the fast, staccato piano music! Oh, I must remember to bring Mr. Packard a bottle of fine Napoleon brandy for the next time he brings up an uncomfortable subject."

"Oh, you're too cruel!" Mary laughed again.

Asa delighted in the sound, joining in her laughter. "Dunno about that. Is the Saint Bernard with the barrel around his neck cruel? Just want to be prepared with the first aid."

"Asa, stop!" Mary giggled. "I'm already laughing so much Shirley's about to slap me. She thinks I've gone hysterical!"

"Me? Who brought up Mack Sennett?" Asa laughed. "Mary, I need to go down to New Jersey tomorrow on business. But it should only be for a day or two, Bill says. So I should be back in plenty of time to see you on Friday evening. Do you still want me to call on you after my train gets in? It'll be late — about 8:30."

"Of course I do! I can't wait to see you. Whatever would make you think I wouldn't want you to call?"

"I can't wait to see you either. I've been thinking about you all day, hahdly able to keep my mind on business."

"Don't let Mr. Porter hear you say that!" Mary laughed.

"I'm in his house and usin' his phone, too. Bettah watch what I say, huh?" Asa laughed. "It's mighty hahd not to think about you, though, Mary."

"I've been thinking of you all day, too. I was wishing I was walking along the beach with you, instead of with Shirley. Not to cast any aspersions on Shirley, mind you. She *is* my closest friend, and I *do* love her, but— Well, she's not *you*."

"Ayup, I know what you mean. I wish I would be spending the next couple of days with *you* on the train, *you* touring a building site, *you* riding in the car beside me, *you* sitting across the table from me at dinner, but I'm going to be stuck with Bill." Asa sighed.

"Asa, are you *trying* to get yourself fired? You better watch it. I hope he didn't overhear you."

"Nunno, he left me alone in his study and even closed the door behind him to give me some privacy. He's a good boss, and a good friend, too. I don't think he'll fire me." Asa smiled. "And when he meets you, he couldn't blame me."

Mary laughed. "Oh, go on with you!"

"Oh, Mary, I almost forgot to tell you — I couldn't get to the Little Store on Monday, since I had to work, so I asked Si to check the mail there, to see if they'd been holding any for you. Well, at least some of your mail is there. Did Mr. Billings give it to you?"

"No, and I've been going there almost every day. I must remember to ask him next time I'm there. I wonder why he... Oh, well. At least that solves part of the mystery. Now I only have to find out why I didn't get the letters you sent to me at Mrs. Bird's."

Crackling sounds began on the line, and it became more difficult to carry on a conversation.

"Mary? Mary, are you still there?"

"Asa? It's getting hard to hear you."

"Listen, I'll see you Friday, okay?" Asa shouted into the phone. Then he said quietly, "I love you."

"What was that? Asa, what did you say?" Mary tried to make herself heard over the static.

"I said I'll see you Friday!" Asa spoke loudly.

"No, I mean after that," Mary said. "Can you hear me? Are you still there?"

"I said I LOVE YOU!" Asa shouted, as the line crackled and went dead. "Mary? Mary? Operator? Hello, operator?" He jiggled the switch hook, but he couldn't raise the operator, either.

Bill knocked on the door and came in as Asa was hanging up the telephone. "Cut off?" he asked.

"Yes, we…" Asa looked up with his eyes narrowed suspiciously. "Say, just how much did you hear?"

"Only 'I love you.' I think they heard that all the way over to Harvard Square. I'd guess you weren't talking to Si." Bill winked.

Asa covered his open mouth with his hand, and turned it into a gesture of checking his beard. He could feel the fire in his cheeks.

Bill laughed and clapped Asa on the shoulder. "Have a drink, man." He went to the sideboard and poured them a couple of whiskies. "And a cigar." He opened the humidor on his desk and produced two richly aromatic cigars. He sat down on the other side of the desk, trimmed both cigars, handed one to Asa, and then lit it for him. Asa was still speechless with embarrassment.

"So, who's the lucky girl?" Bill asked.

Asa cleared his throat. "Well, I guess I might's well tell you, since it'll be all over the place pretty soon, anyway, and you being good friends with the Packards and all…" he trailed off.

"Not Shirley Packard!" Bill said. "I thought she was going with some other fellow."

"Hmm? Oh! Nunno. She's engaged to be married to the Bellamy fellah, Edward. It's Mary — Mary Lovejoy. She's staying with them for the rest of the summer while she gets her health back. You know, she's been ill."

"Why, you sly dog!" Bill smiled at him. "When've you had the time to meet her and fall in love? We've been working pretty full out in the city since she's been staying with the Packards."

"Waell, I knew her before, you know."

"Yes. Yes, of course." Bill shook his head. "Poor girl, to lose both parents within weeks of each other." He was quiet for a moment. "How long has this been going on between you and Mary?"

"Waell, not very long." Asa didn't really want to discuss it. "As a matter of fact, I haven't even told Janet or Si yet. I mean, they know I've gone out with her, but not— Waell, Mary and I— We just kinda— um, we just realized yesterday. I mean how we feel about each othah. You weren't supposed to— Ah, it's early days, yet, so just kinda keep it undah yah hat for a while, okay?"

"Don't worry, Asa. I know how to keep a secret. The government wouldn't have given me authorization to work on this project otherwise, would they?" Bill grinned. "Say, it's about time for supper. Why don't you join Emily and me tonight?"

"Thanks, Bill, but I think I'll just go on up to my own place. Have to throw a few things in a bag for tomorrow, and I've got some perishables that need to be eaten up if I'm gonna be away a couple of days. Thanks for the use of the phone, for the drink and cigar and all. I'll see you tomorrow morning." He just wanted to be alone to think of Mary, and to write her another letter, although he'd written one on the train early this morning, and mailed it from South Station.

# Chapter 38

## *Flying*

Trains and taxis took up a good part of the day. When Bill and Asa got to the town nearest the site, the sky was threatening showers. The pilot told them he would take them up tomorrow, providing the weather cooperated. They arranged overnight lodging at a small inn, and met with the architect. After reviewing Asa's proposed modifications, the architect agreed they were feasible. The three of them drove out in his Mercer touring car to view the grounds. A light rain began to fall.

Despite the steady drizzle, men continued to clear trees and erect a chain-link fence around the boundary line. Asa, Bill, and the architect, sheltered by umbrellas, walked around the area, noting the terrain. Asa viewed everything with an eye to security. As they walked, he discussed his ideas with Bill, who seemed to like most of them. He was still thinking of ways to prevent aerial surveillance. Tomorrow, he'd ask the pilot which theories might work.

He was also thinking of designs for tanks. When the United States declared themselves as allies and joined the war, he would able to speak with the British and the French. Until then, they wouldn't share any information, but he wished he knew a bit more about the failures they'd encountered. It would be such a waste of time to come up with a design, only to discover it had already been tried and failed.

The next day was clear. "George Wright," the pilot introduced himself. "No relation. Good day for it." He handed Bill a leather aviating cap and goggles and made sure he was secure in the passenger seat. He got into the pilot's seat, adjusted a few things, got out again, and swung the propeller. The engine coughed and sputtered into life, and he leapt aboard.

The De Havilland built speed as it taxied over the grass, then rose and began its climb. Asa felt a tingle of anticipation as he waited his turn from the side of the field, watching the biplane grow smaller as it circled away over the property. At last, he saw the plane circle back. Finally, Mr. Wright touched down and rolled to a stop. Asa ran to the airplane, grinning.

"It was great!" Bill said as he handed the goggles and cap to Asa, and they changed places. "What a thrill!"

"I can't wait!" Asa grinned and gave Bill a thumbs-up as George Wright taxied down the field. The engine ticked over beautifully. "Can you loop the loop?" Asa raised his voice against the wind.

"Sure," George replied. You want me to?"

"And a barrel roll, too?" Asa asked.

"You got a strong stomach?"

"In all the years I've spent at sea, I've never been seasick once," Asa shouted back. "I've flown once before — had a high old time. It was grand."

"All right, you asked for it!"

The engine roared, reverberating, powerful. They rose into the sky. The wind whined in the wires as they climbed. And climbed. And climbed. Vertically. When they were high enough and fast enough, Wright flipped them upside down, tail over nose, and looped the loop. Asa whooped with glee. Then they shot upward again, tilted to the side, and flipped over in a barrel roll. Asa shouted out his joy. "Bill was right," he yelled. "I love it!"

"Me too!" Wright shouted back. "Want to do it again?"

"You bet I do!" Asa didn't think he'd ever had this much fun.

This time, Wright flipped them over and flew upside down before making the perpendicular climb. On the way down, he added a spin. Then he climbed very high and looped very low, nearly brushing the treetops. He rolled them over three times, spiraled very high, and made one more loop, while Asa was yelling, "Whoohoo! Woweee! Oh, man! I gotta learn to fly one of these things!"

Although he couldn't stop grinning, Asa wrenched his mind back to business. He knew the square acreage, and had seen much of the area from the ground, but the aerial view impressed him with the overall size and scope of the site. A couple of times, he shouted to Mr. Wright and pointed at the ground, "Can you go a bit lower? I want to see..." Whatever he wanted to see, his words were lost to the wind. But George went lower, and after Asa had had a good look, he pointed up again.

"Seen enough?" George shouted.

"Yah," Asa shouted back.

George treated Asa to one more loop-the-loop before they landed.

Asa whooped with joy.

When they were on the ground, after thanking him profusely, Asa asked George about one or two devices he'd thought about to deter aerial espionage. Wright thought he was worried about nothing, but conceded that either towers or lofty masts with wires strung across would work. They would present an obstacle to flying low enough to take any detailed photographs. Blown up, they would be blurry, and a little camouflage netting would create indecipherable images.

Satisfied, Asa shook hands with Wright. "Thanks a million, Mr. Wright. That was great fun. Haven't grinned so much since I fell in love with my girl." He beamed.

"They're a lot alike," Wright said.

"What are?"

"Flying and falling in love." Wright grinned. "For me they're one and the same. I'm in love with flying."

"I can see that." Asa laughed and clapped Wright on the shoulder as they walked over to rejoin Bill at the side of the field.

"Thanks again," Asa said. "I may want your advice on aerodynamics. Can we keep in touch?"

"Dunno what help I'd be, but sure."

Asa and Bill exchanged cards with George Wright and bid him goodbye.

Asa glanced around to be sure they were out of anyone's earshot. "Let's walk," he said to Bill. He told him of his concepts for various devices to prevent espionage and damage by saboteurs.

"Asa, don't you think you're perhaps being overly — hmm, concerned?" Bill asked. "Do you really think we need to take all these steps to safeguard the plant?"

Asa put a hand on Bill's arm, and stopped walking. "Bill, if we are going to be at war soon, don't you think it's better to take precautions now than to regret not taking them if something should happen later? They had security guards at Black Tom Island, but anybody could walk — or row — onto the site. With adequate security, they could have prevented it. And what about all the rest? The explosion at the Anderson Chemical Company killed three people — not too far from here, over in Wallington. There were also explosions at the DuPont Plant and the New Jersey Freight Depot. Don't forget the fire at the Roebling Plant — all of them right here in New Jersey. You know the Germans don't want companies here to sell munitions — or anything else — to the Allied Nations. They've been trying to gum up the works in any way possible. There've been bombs found in the cargo holds of at least three ships that I know of, and fires of suspicious origin on other ships. I know some of the men on those ships, and their letters go into more detail than the newspapers do. One of them singed his eyebrows off and another one burned his right arm putting out those fires, and they've told me about men who've been hurt a lot worse. A saboteur even tried to blow up the *Eastern Trader* when we were in Liverpool, but luckily we found the bomb and defused it in time. Did you know five people died when that munitions dump blew up at Black Tom — including a *baby* a mile away? The concussion from the blast threw it from its crib. People get injured and die due to sabotage! I don't want to run that risk with you or the workers — do you? Nunno, I'm not paranoid. I'm paying attention, that's all."

Asa's intensity had riveted Bill to the spot. "Well." He contemplated Asa for a moment before resuming. "When you put it all together, I see what you mean. I read about these things in the paper, but it soon becomes yesterday's news. I don't see the larger picture. How do you remember all this stuff?"

"Certain things stick in my mind. They link together. It makes a pattern."

"I can see why Captain Burns wants you." Bill said.

"Oh, he does, does he? What makes you think that?"

"He stopped by my office for a word after your interview the other day," Bill answered. "Said you had some interesting things to say, and as you'd told him you'd made up your mind to go into the Navy if we got involved in this war, he wondered if he could borrow you for a while. He gave me a little speech, throwing in phrases like 'the good of the country,' and 'patriotic duty.' It will all depend on your background inquiry, which should be completed any day now."

"What do you think he has in mind?"

"Well, I wouldn't know, of course, but I might hazard a guess that he wants you to do a little espionage," Bill speculated.

"What about our work?" Asa scanned the area and lowered his voice. "What about the tanks?"

"If he offers you a job, I'll leave it up to you. I admit that I don't want to lose you, but I knew when I hired you that you'd join the Navy if we get into this war. I can see where your skills would be useful to them. Hell, I'm as much of a patriot as the next guy. Whatever you decide to do, you'll always be welcomed back at Porter Motors," Bill said.

Asa nodded, wondering how Mary would feel. "Dunno as they'd want me, though," he said. "Don't these intelligence guys usually look for someone more educated and high class than me? People like Assistant Secretary Roosevelt's yachting friends?"

"Asa, come on! You've got more native intelligence than most of the men in *my* Harvard class. Your thirst for knowledge and self-education shows that. I know you'll read anything you can get your hands on. You can hold your own in a discussion with any man, about any subject."

"But—" Asa tried to interrupt.

"And you can speak just as well as the senator, when you so choose. Don't think I haven't noticed how your accent and your grammar vary, depending upon whose company you're in," Bill kept talking.

Asa started walking. "Linguistic chameleon," he muttered.

Bill kept stride with him. "As far as class goes, well, you're in a class by yourself! You are the most original thinker I've ever met, and that may be due in part to your self-education. You haven't been stuffed into a mold!"

"Oh, please—" Asa didn't get any further.

"I know you speak several languages. Besides having heard that through the grapevine, I heard it for myself when you dropped that wrench on your foot last week!" Bill chuckled. "I'd imagine that facility with foreign tongues would come in handy in Captain Burns's business. You're a man of many talents, Asa."

"Cut it out, Bill! You're embarrassin' me." Asa's face felt hot. "And how would you know about the books?"

"I know you've read everything in my libraries *already* — in both Cambridge and Wellfleet. You read books like other people eat peanuts! One after the other, you just can't stop! Forget about a woman in every port! You bought *books* in every port."

"That's enough," Asa said. "I'm not listening to any more of this nonsense." He walked off.

Bill followed, his impish grin letting on that he wasn't going to stop. "Si tells me you built bookshelves for him, but the books are all yours. You've also got two trunks full crammed into your room, and the spare room is so full of your books you couldn't get another one in there with a shoehorn! Moreover, every once in a while you quote odd bits of poetry to him, and you've done it to me, too!"

"Oh, now you've gone too far!" Asa wished Bill would stop, but demurring only seemed to egg him on. "When have I ever quoted poetry at you?"

"Two weeks ago it was Wordsworth: *The world is too much with us/ late and soon/ getting and spending we lay waste our powers/ too little we see in nature that is ours.* We were talking about how the Cape is changing, all the rural areas being overtaken by tourist hotels and dance halls, the scenery spoiled by radio towers and telephone poles. Remember our discussion of industrialism and commercialism? Even though you and I are right in this rush of modernization and industry up to our eyeballs, you wondered what we were destroying in the process," Bill said.

"Okay, I remember," Asa admitted. "But you can't say I'm always going around quoting poetry from one example. I must've just forgotten myself for a moment, there."

"Is that so? Weren't you quoting Robert Burns to Captain Burns just the other day? And last Friday, I heard you at the shop sink, trying to scrub the grease from underneath your fingernails, and muttering, *Out damned spot!* Shakespeare, even!" Bill laughed.

"All right!" Asa threw up his hands. "I give up! I've got *a smattering of everything, and a knowledge of nothing.*"

"Dickens! There you go again!" Bill grinned.

"I'll give you the dickens, if you keep this up!" Asa's grin had an edge to it.

They got into the hired car waiting at the airstrip for them. The driver glanced back at them and then looked straight ahead.

"Well," said Bill, "I think that about concludes our business here for now, so let's just head back to the inn, settle up, and go catch a train back to New York." He pulled out his pocket watch. "If I remember the timetable correctly, there should be one along in about forty-five minutes."

"Sounds good to me," Asa said. "I hope we can get a bite to eat on the train. Dunno about you, but I could eat a hoss!"

"If we're lucky, we might catch the six… what is it? Six-fifteen? We might get to New York early enough to catch the six-something to Boston," Bill said.

"Fingers crossed," Asa said.

\* \* \* \*

Asa had picked up a catalogue from the Institute of Technology — he couldn't remember where — and was flipping through it on the train. He stopped at a page that caught his eye. "Look at this, Bill."

"What?"

"They've got a course in aeronautical engineering, starting in the fall. After being up in that plane today, gosh, I'd like to take that. Can you imagine? Designing airplanes?"

"You look so excited about it, how could I discourage you? Tell you what, if you get accepted into the course, I'll give you the time off and even pay for it. Can you imagine? Porter airplanes?"

Asa laughed. "Thanks, Bill, but I've got enough to pay for it. Now the only thing is to convince them to let me in."

When they got back to Boston, it was late, so they headed directly home. Bill invited Asa in for a drink, but Asa declined, saying he wanted to write some notes, and sketch out a few plans while the ideas were still fresh in his mind, which was true, but he was rather tiring of Bill's company. He liked him, but being together for two whole days was enough. Although he was pretty sure he was only teasing, Bill's excessive praise, despite Asa's repeated objections, bothered him. Besides, he wanted to write a letter to Mary.

He went up to his apartment and opened the icebox for a bottle of milk. He shook his head and laughed at himself. Bill's "brilliant man of many talents," he thought sarcastically, had forgotten the icebox was empty of everything, including ice. He went back down the stairs and in Bill's back door to the kitchen. Martha took pity on him, giving him a bottle of milk and a plate of sandwiches. When the iceman and milkman came tomorrow, she'd make sure they delivered to his place, too. "Thanks, Mahtha. You're a lifesavah." He went back up to his apartment, and sat down at the kitchen table to compose a letter to Mary while he ate.

*Cambridge, Massachusetts*
*August 9, 1916*

*Dearest Mary,*

*I have returned from my business trip, safe and sound. Going up in the airplane was interesting. What am I saying? It was WONDERFUL! Since I'm safely on the ground now, I guess it's okay to tell you: I got the pilot to loop the loop and do a barrel roll. I whooped with joy and told him I hadn't grinned so much since I fell in love with my girl. You see, I was thinking of you even while spinning upside-down in an airplane. (And why not? Since I met you, I have been spinning upside-down with love.) He said flying and falling in love, for him, were one and the same. He was in love with flying.*

*The view from the air changes one's whole perspective. I think you would have liked it. Everything looks so small from up there, but at the same time, so vast.*

*When I was a child, I remember watching the herring gulls soaring with such grace, floating on the air currents, then suddenly swooping and diving, only to soar upwards again in ever widening circles. Oh, how I longed to be able to fly with them! Though an airplane is noisy and not nearly as graceful, it's still thrilling to fly like a bird. I wish you had been there, flying with me.*

*Speaking of grace reminds me of you. I spent a good part of the day thinking of you. Indeed, I do so every day. In fact, you have so captured my attention that I can barely think of anything else, or perhaps it would be more accurate to say that I do not wish to think of anything else. (I do somehow manage to get my work done; ergo, there must be times when I'm thinking of that.)*

*Please write and tell me more about your childhood, and your life with your parents. I want to know every little detail about you.*

*What makes you happy? What makes you sad? What are your most vivid memories? What do you wish for the future?*

*Will you tell me more about the women's suffrage movement, too? I confess it hadn't taken up much of my attention until you brought it up. I have always believed, in a rather detached way, that women should have the vote. Because of you, I am no longer detached. I am angry that this right has been denied you. It is an insult to women, who are certainly as smart as men — or smarter. At the dawning of our democracy, the franchise used to be based upon ownership of property, and it was a rarity for women to own land back then. It is not quite as uncommon nowadays. Nevertheless, those property rules no longer exist. Excluding half of our society because of gender is just as unfair. The idea that politics is too dirty for the delicate sensibilities of women is balderdash! If politics is rife with moral corruption, shouldn't we be concerned with cleaning it up, rather than using it as an argument against suffrage? Besides, women are capable of holding their own, even in a dirty fight. Over the last seventy-five years and more, haven't suffragettes proved that? Brains, property, unsavoriness — what other fabricated impediments can men place in the way of women's enfranchisement? There can be none. Women's suffrage is long, long overdue!*

*Because you brought it to mind, I wrote a letter to my Congressman and Senators on the subject. (Although Senator Cabot Lodge doesn't like me much, so I'm afraid he may remain firmly against women's suffrage — if only because I've asked him to change his mind! Hah! As if he'll even read the letter.) I've spoken to Bill about it, and with Emily's encouragement, he has agreed to do the same. (She has written, but we believe that one's current ability to grant or deny approval at the ballot box carries a little more weight.) You are winning people to the cause! What was the name and address of that organization you mentioned? I wish to back up my words with more tangible support. You only gave me the initials, which were numerous. Must be quite a mouthful to say the whole name. I'd also like to purchase a subscription to the Women's Journal and Suffrage News. Please send me their address, as well.*

*You asked how I came to be named for your grandfather. I heard this story at my father's knee, and later at Captain Asa's. Mind you, sailors' yarns are known for their exaggeration, so it may not have been quite as dramatic as the telling. For example, I don't see how father could have been as high up as the topgallant crosstrees and survived. The way he told it, he didn't even break a bone. I suppose it's possible. Miracles have been known to happen, so I've been told.*

*Anyway, here's the story: My father, Sam'l Mayhew, was bo's'n on "Winged Mercury." It was a clipper — that beautiful old wooden ship Cap'n Asa loved so much. Remember her? Now, there was a ship that could fly with the grace of a gull. Father was high up in the rigging one day, replacing a clew on a topgallant sail, when a sudden, fierce wind kicked up, knocking him off balance. He could see he'd either fall to the deck, and probably shatter every bone in his body, or go overboard and drown. He knew hitting the water from that height would be almost like hitting the ground, unless he hit just right. All this went through his mind in a flash. He made a grab for the topgallant crosstree as he fell, but missed. He went overboard, all the way down praying the fall wouldn't knock him out, and that he'd learn how to swim in a hurry. Your grandfather seemed to be the only one who saw what happened. He threw a life buoy overboard, and yelled to the men to lower a lifeboat. He could see that my father was about to go down for the third time before they could even get the boat off the davit, so he grabbed a life preserver, jumped overboard, swam to Father, and held him on the life buoy, just in time to keep him from going under for good. Then he got him into the boat, which had finally been lowered. How I wish I could have done for your father what Cap'n Asa did for mine.*

Feeling a bit shaky, Asa got up and went to the sink. Splashing cold water on his face helped, so he sat down at the table to finish his letter.

> *My mother was expecting me at the time, and Sam'l was so grateful that his baby would have a father, thanks to Cap'n Asa Lovejoy, that he named his baby after him. (I wonder — if I'd been a girl, do you think he still would have named me Asa Lovejoy?)*
>
> *I shall be eternally grateful to your grandfather for taking me under his wing after my parents died, but I sometimes wonder if he felt responsible for me because of my name.*
>
> *Reading over those last two sentences, I seem to do an awful lot of wondering, don't I?*
>
> *I wonder if you are named after anyone, perhaps someone in your family, or some family friend. Perhaps you are named after one of the saints, for you are heavenly to me.*
>
> *I wonder if we shall marry some day and have a baby, and I wonder what we shall name him — or her.*
>
> *All right, enough with all this wondering, except to say that you are a wonder to me. It's a wonder that someone as lovely as you should love a wandering, wondering fool such as I.*
>
> *These lines keep running through my head whenever I think of you: "Shall I compare thee to a summer's day? / Thou art more lovely and more temperate."*

*I miss you more than I can say. The way your hair catches fire in the sun, and smells of flowers and lemons, those flashing golden glints in your melted chocolate eyes, the trill of your laughter, your dulcet voice. Preciosa, forgive me if I get carried away. I can't help myself. I'm besotted with you.*

*I hope I haven't made an utter fool of myself, but if I am a fool, it is for love. I wonder if I should start writing my letters on foolscap. Please forgive this fool's terrible pun. And there I go, wondering again. (I wonder if it's perhaps not such a good idea to write letters when I'm feeling silly with fatigue.)*

*I shall call on you as soon as my train gets in on Friday. (Should you happen to see the train come in, you'll know me. I'll be the one wearing motley and a fool's cap with bells on, doing handsprings and cartwheels all up and down the landing, for my lady.) How I wish it wasn't two whole days away!*

*With all my love, I remain,*
*Your constant admirer and besotted fool,*
*Asa*

\* \* \* \*

When Mary received the letter, she was struck by Asa's beautiful handwriting and... good heavens, was he really quoting *Shakespeare* to her? She laughed out loud at his playfulness with words. He was full of surprises. Pressed within the pages of the letter were some tiny yellow flowers with five roughly heart-shaped petals and three sharply heart-shaped leaves. She thought they might be yellow wood sorrel. Who would ever have guessed that Asa was such a romantic? '*Preciosa*,' what was that? Italian? Spanish? It sounds like precious. Was he calling her precious? She smiled dreamily and placed the folded letter and flowers within the pages of her book, then hugged the book to her chest.

She wrote back:

*Wellfleet*
*August 10, 1916*

*My darling Asa,*

*I received your lovely long letter in this evening's mail, and am counting the hours until your train arrives tomorrow. I laughed aloud at the image of you in fool's motley, cart-wheeling down the length of the platform!*

*What pretty little flowers! You are such a romantic, and a constant surprise.*

*No, my dear, I do not think you are a fool at all, or I am a fool also. I keep thinking of the lines:*

*"How do I love thee? Let me count the ways.*

*I love thee to the depth and breadth and height*

*My soul can reach…."*

*How is it possible that we have come to feel so deeply for each other in such a short time? I feel that I've known you all my life, or perhaps in another life, in which our love was so great, it fated us to meet again. Does that sound foolish? Well then, I am a fool for love, too.*

*I feel so safe and protected when you hold me in your arms. At times, I fancy I can still feel the warmth of your embrace, and my arms ache to hold you again.*

*I can barely wait until tomorrow, dearest!*

*I am sorry to cut this short, and will answer your questions in another letter, but I must rush to get this in the post in hopes that you shall receive it before you leave.*

> *With all my love, I am yours faithfully,*
> *Mary*

*(P.S. In answer to your question, I'm named after my maternal grandmother. I'm no saint, believe me!)*

# Chapter 39

## *Down the Cape*

Ten days later, Asa had the honor of driving the first new model Porter to its place of honor in the showroom. After he got out, he and Bill stood and watched the procession as the other motors were driven to their places. "Think we got all the bugs worked out of it?"

"With all the fussing and tweaking you've done, it should be perfect," Bill said. "Are you always this meticulous?"

"Waell," Asa drawled, "Both my father and Cap'n Asa taught me that if you're gonna do a job, do it right. Keeps you from having to do it all over again. Can't say I'm very successful at it. I often have to do it over and over and over again before I get it right."

"I've seen you keep at it long after other men would have said, 'Oh, hell, that's good enough.' But you won't quit until every detail meets your lofty standards. It's that kind of dedication that makes these automobiles a work of art." Bill thumped Asa on the back. "And you asked me if I wasn't worried that I'd be hiring a lazy lout. Hah!"

Asa sighed. "I wish you wouldn't do that."

"What? Pat you on the back?"

"It makes me… I dunno… uncomfortable," Asa said. "I'll never be able to live up to this inflated image you've created of me."

"Don't worry about that. I've never met a Jack-of-all-trades who has proven he *is* a master of them all."

"That's enough, Bill. Stop it right now. I'm not kiddin'."

Bill observed him for a moment, and then changed the subject.

"The workers are going to be busy putting together special orders with brass bud vases and all kinds of other foofaraw. You don't want to supervise the brass casting, do you?"

"Good God, Bill!" Asa snorted and shook his head. "I'll leave that to the men who know far more about it than I."

"Then things will slow down a bit for you and me," Bill said.

"Unless… Still no word from the Army or Navy?" Asa asked.

"They won't spend a plug nickel until we're actually in this war," Bill said. "So they won't commit to a contract."

"Right. Anyway, until the New Jersey plant is done, about all I can do right now is to get a few hypothetical designs down on paper. Ah, well… not much we can do about that." Asa shrugged. "We never talked about your quick trip to check the site day before yesterday. How's the construction going?"

"Trees are cleared from the perimeter; the outer fence is going up. They're still digging the foundation, but there are piles of bricks and lumber everywhere, so it looks as if most of the construction materials have arrived."

"You know, I was thinking…" Asa said.

"Uh-oh," Bill grinned. "How much money is *this* idea going to cost me?"

Asa laughed. "Nothing — at least not until after the war. In the long run, I think it'll make you lots of money."

"Okay, let's hear it," Bill said.

"Well, you're gonna have this great big plant with plenty of room to build a fast assembly line, like Henry Ford's. We could design and produce a more affordable line of Porter cars — not as big as touring cars, no fancy sports cars, but family cars with room for five or six. Wouldn't cost too much to build them, and you could sell a lot of them."

"Go into competition with Ford?" Bill asked.

"Why not?" Asa asked. "We could still build the luxury cars in Cambridge, but that's on a much smaller scale because they're out of reach for most people. Why shouldn't we build a lower-priced model, too? It would have the Porter name, and that stands for quality. People would jump at the chance to buy a Porter car if they could afford it."

"Yes, but could we maintain those standards in a cheap, assembly line car?"

"Sure," Asa said. "Don't think of it as cheap — that sounds flimsy. If I have anything to do with it, it will *not* be flimsy. Think of it as affordable. Now, the most important thing is the engine. It doesn't need twelve cylinders. Four or six will be fine. When you've got the kiddos in the car, you sure won't want to go seventy miles per hour. Not that we could do that anyway, except on the racetrack, until we get better roads. We'll make it reliable and tough, so it won't need a lot of repair, but if it does, it'll be easy to fix. Next, you want the chassis and body to be strong enough not to rust away when the car is parked out in all kinds of weather. You don't need fancy gewgaws that are just for looks. Not a lot of brass or nickel plating. Workin' man doesn't have time to polish all that brass, anyway. Keep it simple but solid."

"But it wouldn't look like a Porter," Bill protested. "Where are the sleek lines, the glamor, the class? I'm not sure I'd want to put the Porter name on it."

"We can still make them attractive with bright, shiny colors like red and yellow, with a high-gloss finish. Just the opposite of Ford — you can have *almost* any color you want, as long as it *isn't* black." He chuckled. "And they don't have to be boxy. I could design something a little more curved, and maybe put a... hmm... well, I have to think about it." Asa's hands illustrated the geometry. "Still don't want the Porter name on it? Then call it something else. How about something like: The Billy, a smaller, more affordable, no frills motorcar made by Porter, with that same great quality and reliability. Perfect for taking the whole family on a Sunday drive."

"So now you're an advertising man as well as a designer, mechanic, and at least half a dozen other things?" Bill laughed. "All right, I admit it's a good idea. Let's mull it over, come up with some kind of plan."

"Oh, I've been mulling it over, and I've got lots of plans," Asa grinned.

"Of course you do. Got the blueprints all laid out already, haven't you?"

"Bill, you know I wouldn't do anything without your consent. I hope I haven't overstepped—"

"Asa, can't you tell when I'm kidding?"

"Usually. But other times you're so straight-faced, and I sometimes suspect there's some underlying re—" Asa told himself to shut up before he made things worse. "Well, it can be hard to tell. I begin to worry that I've really made you mad this time."

"Relax, Asa. If I was angry, believe me, you'd know it in no uncertain terms. I tease you, but it's perfectly clear to me that you're the one who comes up with the fresh ideas. You're young; you've got an eye to the future," Bill said. "And people seem to want the newest, most innovative thing that comes along."

Asa inclined his head, feeling somewhat guilty for aiding and abetting this mad race into an uncertain and dangerous future. Designing tanks, for instance — what the hell was he thinking? Oh, well. Maybe it won't come to that. He brushed these clouds of doom away with a vision of Mary in his mind's eye — beautiful, lovely, dear Mary — an antidote to glum thoughts if there ever was one.

"Next time," Bill smiled broadly, gently socking Asa in the arm, "I'll try to remember to smile when I say that — whatever *that* is."

Asa smiled. "Say, Bill, I was wondering…"

"Not another idea! Where do you come up with them?" Bill made a show of wide-eyed surprise.

Asa laughed. "Nunno, not another idea — at least not yet." He suddenly felt shy, looking at his feet as the heat rose in his cheeks. "Um, since there's not… well not an awful lot of work… um, for me to do at the moment… do you think you could… that is, I, um, would like to… ah, go to Wellfleet… to see… well, to see Mary more often." He took a deep breath and rushed through his next sentence. "Could you maybe give me Fridays off until the end of the month?"

Bill gave him a concerned look. "I've never seen *you* shy and tongue-tied before. Did you think I'd refuse or reprimand you? Of course you may have Fridays off." Snapping his fingers, he grinned. "Aha! It's love, isn't it? That's what's got you all flustered, you poor fellah." He shook his head sympathetically. "Listen, until after Labor Day, take Mondays off as well."

"Gee, thanks, Bill!"

"You know what? I've got an even better idea. I'd like to see more of my family, too. Why don't we both take a week or two off and go fishing, sailing, walking on the beach."

"Oh, that'd be grand," Asa said.

"You look just like Billy waiting for Santa Claus." Bill chuckled. "Let's go home and pack our bags."

\* \* \* \*

As the train approached Wellfleet, Asa had his grip in his hand and was standing on the steps to the door before they pulled into the station. As they slowed down, bells ringing, he saw Mary waiting on the platform.

"See ya, Bill!" he called and was out the door as soon as the conductor opened it. Without a thought to propriety, he ran to Mary, dropped his bag, and enfolded her in his arms.

"Oh, Mary!" He breathed in her scent and sighed. "Mary. My dear Mary."

Hugging him back, Mary giggled. "Asa, must you keep repeating my name as though you're afraid of forgetting it?"

He chortled and released her, but reached out to take both her hands in his. "You have that sweet way of bringing me back to earth when I'm so happy I'm in danger of floating away like an empty-headed balloon. I am over the moon with love for you."

"I hope you've come to fetch me, then, because I've been over the moon about you for… gosh, I don't know how long. It seems like forever."

"Ahem," Bill cleared his throat loudly. "Good afternoon, Miss Lovejoy." He tipped his hat and bowed slightly. "Sorry to interrupt, but it seems to me that Asa is so bedazzled, he may forget my invitation, so I thought I had better ask you myself."

Asa gave Bill a sheepish grin as he and Mary released their hold on each other and stepped back a few inches.

Mary stood very straight, appearing to summon all of her dignity, despite her flaming cheeks. "Good afternoon, Mr. Porter. May I be so bold as to inquire what it is you wish to ask me?"

"Certainly. I wondered if the two of you might like to go sailing with Emily and me one day. What do you say?"

"To be out on the ocean again…" Beaming at him, she clasped her white-gloved hands together and took in a deep breath of salt sea air. "Oh, yes, thank you. It would be wonderful."

"Then it's settled. All you have to do is name the day. You talk it over and let us know." Bill grinned. "Be seeing you, Asa. I'll let you get back to your lovemaking now. Good day, Miss Lovejoy." He tipped his hat and walked away.

Asa looked at Mary, sure that the color of his face matched the shocking pink of hers.

"Oh, gosh," he said. "I'm so sorry for embarrassing you like that."

Mary tipped her head up, examining his face. "Embarrassing *me*? You didn't seem to have that sunburn when you got off the train. Could this be a case of the pot calling the kettle red?"

Asa chuckled. "I *do* love you, my precious darling." He offered her his arm. "Come on; let's get you home before it gets dark."

"There's no rush," Mary said. "Your cousin Silas brought me in your car. I thought we'd wait for you together, but he just smiled and said he had things to do, and he'd leave the car for you to drive me home. He also said we were welcomed to drop by to see him and Janet, and have a bite to eat, since you probably missed supper."

Asa beamed. "Good ol' Si. Could a man ever ask for a better cousin?"

Mary slipped her arm through his as they began walking to the car.

"Oh, Asa!"

"What? What is it?"

"Don't forget your valise."

He struck his head with the palm of his hand and dashed back to retrieve his bag. "I seem to recall this happening before…"

"The night you had to pound on the door to get Pete to let you back into the drugstore," she grinned at him.

"I'm only this absentminded when I'm around you, you know," Asa said. "I can't help it. I see you and everything else just flies right out of my head."

"Good thing I'm around to remind you, then," Mary laughed.

"I've got an idea…" Asa looked at her.

"Asa, if I didn't know better, I'd say you were leering at me," Mary smiled. "I have a feeling this idea isn't about motors."

"Oh, deah, was I that obvious?" He laughed. "Must be losin' my touch."

He opened the car door for her and helped her in. He looked down at her foot on the running board. No tango shoes today, more's the pity. Still, that ankle certainly was shapely. Instead of cranking the motor right away, he walked around and got in so they could talk.

"Big, bad sailor," Mary laughed. "All right, Lothario, just what is this immodest idea of yours?"

"Waell," he drawled, "I just thought that perhaps while it's still light, we might go visit Si and Janet for a bit. Then, after it's dahk, I can bring you home, stoppin' at some quiet, lonely spot along the way, so we can... you know... kind of, um, canoodle?"

"Hmm," Mary said. "What do you mean by *kind of* canoodle?"

"Um," Asa paused. "Spooning. That is, straight out kissing and caressing. I mean... I wouldn't want you to... ah, engage in anything you didn't want to. Just say so if you don't like the idea. Whatever you want, Mary. You know I'll respect your wishes."

"Asa, I was only kid— well, I wasn't altogether serious." Mary sighed. "I know you're not a rake. I *know* you'd never..." She heaved another sigh. "I didn't mean it as an affront to your rectitude."

"I'm sorry," Asa said. "I was afraid you'd think... Oh, damn. Oh! Sorry, Mary. I shouldn't use such language."

"Afraid I'd think what?"

"That I was trying to... well, seduce you. You know I would *never*—" He could feel the heat rising in his face as his erotic dreams of her came to mind. He *would* never — but he couldn't deny his desire. Feeling dishonest, unworthy of her, he turned to stare out of the windshield. "Now I've gone and ruined it, haven't I?"

"Ruined what?" Mary asked.

"The... um... the mood, I guess you could say."

"Not necessarily," Mary said. She leaned over and kissed him on the cheek. "Let's go visit Si and Janet, and then when it's dark, you can drive me home. We can stop along the way at some quiet spot..."

Asa's heart lifted. He looked around. There didn't seem to be anybody watching, so he put his arms around her and kissed her lips. "You're wonderful." He got out and cranked over the motor, beaming at her when he got back in.

\* \* \* \*

As Asa ushered Mary in the back door, Janet hissed in his ear, "Asa, you know bettah than to bring comp'ny in the back. You should've brought her in the *front* doah."

Asa murmured, "Too late now."

Si raised his voice to cover Asa and Janet's brief contretemps. "Miss Lovejoy, welcome. Please come in and sit down." He pulled out a chair for her.

The kitchen table was laid with plates of fancy tea sandwiches cut in diamond shapes, their fillings varied: chicken salad, ham and pickle, egg salad, tomato and cheese, and cucumber.

Asa's eyes widened as he looked at the elaborate display. Then he turned to Janet, winked at her, and said, "What, no watercress?"

Janet smiled and turned to Mary. "How lovely to see you again, Miss Lovejoy. I thought Asa mightn't have had a chance to eat somethin' before bo'din' the train. I hope you might be able to eat a little somethin', as well, to keep yaw strength up. Would you like coffee, or would you prefer cold tea ovah ice? 'Tis a little wahm today."

"Please call me Mary. 'Miss Lovejoy' makes me sound like… I don't know… the lady of the manor, or something, and I'm certainly not that. I think we know each other well enough to call each other by our Christian names by now. Don't you?"

"And I'm Si," Si extended his hand to her.

Mary grinned and shook it. "Pleased to be friends with you, Si."

"Janet," Janet nodded once.

"Happy to be your friend, too, Janet," Mary said, nodding back.

"Well, I'm glad that's settled," Asa said. "Let's sit down and enjoy these delicious sandwiches Janet labored over."

"'Twas nothing." Blushing, Janet bustled over to the stove and brought the coffee pot to the table, pouring a cup for Asa. He smiled his thanks, appreciating that she knew his preference without having to ask.

"I b'lieve I'll have some of that iced tea, Janet," Si said. He looked toward Mary.

"That sounds good," Mary said. "I'd like some, too, please, Janet."

Janet gave Si a warm smile as she poured the tea into tall glasses with ice chipped off the block. "'Tis black. Sugah and lemon's on the table, if you like, and there's some tall spoons to stir it in."

Mindful of Janet's attempts to make a good impression on Mary, Asa caught her eye, hoping she saw his gratitude.

He wanted to tell her she didn't have to try so hard, but wasn't he guilty of that, himself?

Here were the people he loved most, seated at this table. What were those confused emotions he was feeling? Ah, yes: ecstasy, tempered with trepidation. He wanted to hold them all in his arms, to protect them, knowing full well that was impossible. Reminding himself not to spoil the present with past grief or fear of the future, he took a breath as his eyes roamed around the table, then exhaled and relaxed. Let us enjoy this moment, he said to himself. Who knows how many more there may be?

Eating, talking, laughing, Asa knew that Janet and Si would come to love Mary as one of their own. He hoped she sensed the generosity of spirit they offered, and may come to feel comfortable as a part of his family when he asked her to marry him. He wondered how soon he could ask without seeming overly ardent and frightening her away.

On the way home, they did stop in a secluded spot.

When Asa leaned in to kiss her, the brim of her hat got in the way. When she reached up and removed the hat pin, it glinted in the light of the moon.

"That looks like a lethal weapon." Asa hoped Mary could see his grin. "I'd better be careful."

Mary put her hat aside. "I don't think I shall have to use it; the threat of it is enough." She laughed. "Shall we try that kiss again?"

He brushed her lips with his. "Oh, Mary," he breathed as he drew her closer. "You feel so soft and warm and precious in my arms."

"When you hold me, I feel so safe, Asa. Please tell me I am."

"Oh, my dear, if I were to kiss you on the lips and caress you amorously, would you still feel safe? Because that is what I should like to do. If you object, of course I shall refrain."

"Kiss and caress away, my dear."

Asa covered Mary's mouth in a passionate kiss. They murmured endearments to each other, their kisses becoming more fervent as they pressed against each other. When he slipped his tongue between her lips, she pulled away.

"What's this?" She sounded more curious than offended.

"It's called a 'French kiss' when our tongues converse with each other in a language beyond words. Would you like to try it again?"

"It sounds very European and sophisticated," Mary smiled. "You must teach me the ways of the world."

"I shall very much enjoy being your instructor." Asa grinned, and then turned serious. "But be assured, I respect you too much to—"

"Stop talking and kiss me," Mary said.

He kissed her, and her tongue met his.

He tentatively touched her breast. "Is this all right?"

"Mm," she murmured, turning her face toward his for another kiss. She slipped her hand inside his vest.

Feeling her hand on his chest, the pounding of his heart increased. His breathing became rapid. He gently squeezed her breast as she moved her hand, brushing the fabric of his shirt against his nipple. Drawing in a sharp breath, he heard Mary echo the sound.

For some time, their only intercourse consisted of wordless murmurs of pleasure and longing, heat and desire.

"Mary, we have to stop — Oh, God."

"Asa," Mary whispered. "I've never felt so — Ooh."

They both had to exert supreme self-control to break it off. Breathless and blushing, they straightened their clothing. Asa helped Mary hunt for hairpins as she attempted to repair her chignon.

"Oh, my love," he breathed as he held her softly once more. "I'm so… You have this… this effect on me… I hope I haven't gone too far."

Mary replied, "Heaven help us; I wasn't pushing you away, was I? Didn't you notice? You have the same effect on me, my dear."

"Oh, God, I want—" Asa took a deep breath. "Forgive me, Mary. I must take you home before I do something rash."

"If you'll forgive me."

"What on earth for?" Asa asked.

"For inviting you to… to proceed this far."

"Oh, my dear, there is nothing to forgive. You may not have slammed the door in my face, but I invited myself in."

As she opened her mouth to protest, he placed a finger on her lips. "Sh. We could go on asking for and receiving forgiveness all night." He sighed. "Shall we just say we are both subject to all the frailties of the human condition, and leave it at that?"

"Mm, yes, dear." Mary snuggled into his side.

"Don't get me started again," he whispered, leaning over to kiss the top of her head. "Speaking of starting, I'm sorry, my dear, but you have to sit up so I can get out to crank over the engine."

He drove her back to the Packard's, where they cuddled a little longer, murmuring and sighing. Then he opened the car door for her and walked her to the front door, where they engaged in one last kiss.

"Oh, my love, I hate to part with you," Asa said. "I'll see you tomorrow?"

"Yes, dear," Mary said. "At noon, for a picnic."

Reluctant, they let go of each other's hands, and said goodnight.

\* \* \* \*

All dressed up as if for a Sunday, Mr. and Mrs. Packard, Shirley, and Edward rode in Mr. Packard's car, while Asa and Mary followed in Asa's Porter. The dirt roads were rutted, bumpy, and sandy. Still, even if you had to drive less than ten miles an hour, a motor was such a convenience when you had a large picnic basket and a couple of blankets to carry. They were headed to a cedar grove on a hill, overlooking the ocean on the Atlantic side. A lethargic westerly breeze had kept the day warm.

"What do you say? Is this a good spot?" Mr. Packard emerged from his car with an armful of blankets. "Shall we set up in that small clearing?"

"Looks good to me," Asa said.

They spread blankets on the ground and opened the picnic basket.

Shirley and Edward sat holding hands and gazing into each other's eyes. Asa and Mary followed suit. With indulgent expressions, Mr. and Mrs. Packard looked on.

Asa and Mr. Packard caught each other's eyes and nodded. Though it loomed over them like an anvil cloud, there would be no talk of war today.

Mary took a deep breath and sighed. "Oh, isn't this a lovely day? The sky is so blue."

Beaming at her, Asa said, "Beautiful." He wasn't looking at the sky. "Did you know your hair glows like a radiant flame in the sun?"

Blushing, Mary ducked her head and smiled up at him.

As they ate lunch, they made pleasant small talk. Afterwards, they wandered about, admiring the trees and wildflowers.

"Is that cinquefoil?" Mary asked Asa. "Like the pressed ones you sent me, with those little heart-shaped flowers? Or is it wood sorrel?"

"Cinquefoil," Asa said. "I think the ones I picked were yellow wood sorrel, from the woods down in New Jersey. Cinquefoil has heart-shaped petals, but palmate leaves. Yellow wood sorrel has heart-shaped leaves. Look — forget-me-nots."

"Oh, what a lovely shade of blue."

They squeezed each other's hands.

The wind changed direction to come in off the ocean. Noticing Mrs. Packard briefly rubbing her upper arms, Asa went to the car to fetch her shawl. He admired its pattern and colors.

"Oh, Asa, thank you," Mrs. Packard sounded surprised. "How did you know I wanted that?"

"Thought you might get chilly when the sea breeze picked up," Asa said. "That's a lovely shawl."

"Mary crocheted it for me."

"She's an artist, isn't she?" he smiled, putting his arm around Mary.

"A talented musician, too," Mrs. Packard said.

"Oh, please stop," Mary said. "I'm no better than anybody else at these things."

"Oh, but you are, my dear." His eyes tenderly caressed her. "You are."

She blushed and leaned closer to him.

They walked into the grove, away from the others. Asa's heart was so full, he couldn't refrain from singing:

*O, my luve is like a red, red rose,*
*That's newly sprung in June;*
*O, my luve is like the melodie,*
*That's sweetly played in tune.*
*As fair art thou, my bonnie lass,*
*So deep in luve am I;*
*And I will luve thee still, my dear,*
*Till a' the seas gang dry.*

*Till a' the seas gang dry, my luve,*
*And the rocks melt wi' the sun:*
*I will love the still, my dear,*
*While the sands o' life shall run.*
*And fare thee weel, my only luve,*
*And fare thee weel awhile!*
*And I will come again, my luve,*
*Tho' it were ten thousand mile.*[33]

Mary was enchanted. "How romantic you are, my dear! No one has ever sung Robert Burns to me before. Has anyone ever told you that you have a glorious voice?"

"I don't know what came over me." Asa was abashed. "Yes, I do. You… Oh, Mary, I'm trying to say I love you. I love you so much, sometimes I think my heart will burst. Oh, gosh, I… Oh—" He clasped her in his arms. "Mary, oh, Mary," he breathed.

"Asa," she whispered. "You're trembling. Breathe, dear. You know I love you. I shall always love you. You needn't fear losing me."

"But we have… we have both lost so many we held dear. And sometimes I just— Oh, I just want to hold you close, to hold you tightly, to keep you from… from disappearing." He shook his head. "I'm sorry, Mary. I know that makes no sense and I sound mad as a hatter. Please don't be frightened. It's only a momentary… a momentary… um—"

Mary blinked away her tears. "I know, dear. I'm not frightened of *you*, but sometimes I'm frightened of *losing* you. I get those moments, too."

"You do?" Asa asked. "You feel the same way?"

"Mm. Here we are, clinging to each other like orphans of the storm… Well, I guess we *are* orphans of the storm, aren't we? It's a beautiful day, yet the world is in such… such turmoil…" Mary sighed. "But we have each other now. *Right now*. We are together. Although we plan for the future — as we ought — this instant is all we can ever be sure of, isn't it? So, let's savor it. All right?"

"You know, I was thinking along those lines yesterday, when we were sitting around the table with Janet and Si — all the people I love in one place. I was so happy, but at the same time, I wanted to wrap my arms around you all, to protect you. And then I told myself to enjoy that moment, because who knows how many more moments like that there may be?"

"You worry too much, dear," Mary said. "While I can understand your impulse to protect us all, you do know you've set yourself an impossible task. Don't you? You can't be responsible for me, and Janet, and Si, and everybody else you care about. Loving us is more than enough. Don't you see?"

"My brain understands that, my love, but I'm having a hard time convincing my heart," Asa said.

"Then give your heart to me," Mary smiled. "I'll take care of it."

Asa chuckled. "So, you're offering to be responsible for my heart, now? Talk about pot and kettle."

"At least I made you laugh. Feel better now?"

"Thank you, dear. Much better. Ah, you're wonderful."

\* \* \* \*

They chose a good day for a sail. On land, it was unusually sultry for the Cape; not a leaf stirred. Breezing along on the ocean, they were reinvigorated.

As Bill manned the helm and Emily the sails, Asa and Mary stood in the bow, reveling in the speed — and each other.

"The wind, the water, the snap of the sails," Asa mused. "Isn't this simply glorious?"

"It's wonderful to be out on the ocean again. Father and I used to…" She bit her lips.

Asa put his arm around her. "Mm. Good times, then, weren't they?"

Mary turned to him and smiled through the glint of tears. "And we shall carry his memory with us as we make our own good times."

"That's right, my love. We shall."

Little Billy came rushing forward. "Uncle Asa! Uncle Asa! Look! Is that a dolphin?"

After the stories, the moving picture shows, and the outings for ice cream, Bill and Emily had agreed with Asa that Mr. Mayhew was too formal. However, they objected to allowing Billy to use Asa's first name, thinking it not respectful enough. So they'd agreed on making Asa an honorary uncle.

"It *is* a dolphin, Billy. You know, dolphins are sailors' friends. They like to swim in the wake or in the bow wave, as though they're dropping by to say hello. See there! On the port bow — there's another one! Don't they look like they're having fun?"

Excited, Billy said, "They're jumping and playing. And they're smiling, aren't they?"

"Sure looks like it. They're pretty intelligent creatures. They have saved drowning sailors by buoying them up until help comes, and sometimes they've even pushed people to shore." Asa put his hand on the boy's shoulder and bent down, extending his other arm as a sight line for Billy to follow, pointing out to sea. "Can you see that? There's a whole pod of them."

"Oh, boy! I've never been this close to dolphins before!" Billy said. "They're just great!"

"That they are." Asa straightened up. "Billy, we mustn't exclude Miss Lovejoy from our conversation. It wouldn't be polite."

"Oh, Miss Lovejoy," Billy said as though seeing her for the first time. "I beg your pardon."

Mary grinned at him. "That's quite all right, Billy. Dolphins are so exciting, I was caught up in watching them, too. They're fascinating, aren't they?"

"Oh, yes! I wish they would stay with us all the way, but they'll probably swim after some other boat." Billy sighed.

"Well, then," Mary said. "All the more reason we should get pleasure out of their cavorting now, while they're still here. Oh, look! That one jumped right out of the water and did a back flip! I do believe they're showing off for us!"

Billy laughed delightedly.

Asa smiled, pleased at the interaction between Mary and Billy. He thought she'd make a good mother someday, and hoped they could make a family together. He'd have a dozen kids, if they could all be as bright and sunny as Billy. Well, maybe not as many as a dozen. Mary would certainly have something to say about that.

Later, he manned the helm while Mary trimmed the sails. After a while, they switched, with Mary at the helm and Asa managing the sails. And then Asa and Bill teamed up, so that Mary and Emily could get to know each other better.

After the dolphins had gone, Billy was playing with his toy trucks. "Oh, no," his voice wavered on the verge of tears.

"What's the matter, Billy?" Mary asked.

"I lost one. I think… I think it went overboard." Billy's lower lip quivered and he began to cry. "It was my favorite one, too — the American La France firetruck."

"Billy," Asa said, "I think if you'll look below, you'll find it. It rolled down the hatch into the galley."

Billy immediately dashed down the ladder, with Mary following.

"Well, lo and behold!" Mary said to him. "There it is!"

"Oh, Miss Lovejoy, I'm so glad!" Billy said.

"Now don't you think you'd better go thank Asa — Uncle Asa — for finding it for you?"

Billy scrambled up the ladder and ran to the helm, already such an experienced sailor as to duck automatically when the boom came around. "Uncle Asa, thank you so much for finding my truck for me."

"'Twas nothing, Billy. I just happened to see it roll down there while you weren't paying attention," Asa said. "But, you're welcomed to my help anytime I can be of assistance."

Billy looked down, shifting his weight from one foot to the other for a moment, and then blurted out, "You're my best friend!" Clutching his truck, he ran down to the galley.

Asa laughed as Mary smiled up at him, putting her hand on his arm. Then she took Bill's place.

Bill scooped up the rest of his son's trucks, and went below to talk to him, but not before a word to Asa and Mary. "You're both very good to my son. Don't think I didn't notice. Thank you."

The rest of the day passed without incident — no more lost toys, no sudden thunderstorms, no crises of any kind.

"Want me and Emily to take over?" Bill asked later.

"Oh, no, we're enjoying it too much," Mary said. "Unless, of course, you want to; she is your boat, after all."

"I want you to keep right on enjoying it," Bill said. "Asa, you want to sail her home?"

"You bet," Asa said.

As they disembarked, Bill said, "You're a fine sailor, Miss Lovejoy. You and Asa should feel free to use the sloop anytime Emily and I aren't using it."

"Thank you, Mr. Porter," Mary said.

"Call me Bill, if you feel comfortable doing so," Bill smiled. "I gather you and my wife are already on first-name terms, and as you've become such good friends with little Billy, I don't want to be the only one left out."

"All right — Bill," Mary said. "And you must call me Mary."

"It's a deal," Bill said.

\* \* \* \*

For the rest of his time off, Asa spent every waking hour he could with Mary, making sure she rested when she was tired, seeing that she ate red meat as her doctor had ordered. He presented her with a bunch of Swiss chard, laughing. "Other men bring flowers; I bring Swiss chard. Isn't that romantic? This is from Janet's garden. She says there's lots of iron in Swiss chard."

Mary laughed. "It *is* romantic. How many other men would be so attentive to my health?"

They sat in the Westport chairs behind the Packard's house, looking at the ocean, reaching across to hold hands, talking. They walked along the beach, avoiding the tourist areas. They dared to don their bathing costumes to brave the waves, and then lay basking in the warmth of the sun — and each other.

They rejoiced together, mourned together, and held each other close. At every opportunity, they escaped to be alone together, to kiss and cuddle under the moonlight.

# Chapter 40

# *A Proposal*

As August flowed into September, Asa accompanied Mary back to Boston and saw her safely settled at Mrs. Bird's.

The day after she returned, Doctor Stone paid a visit. "I'm pleased to see you looking so well," he said. "There are roses in your cheeks, and your hair is thicker and shinier than it was. You've gained a little weight, haven't you?"

"I'm afraid so. The Packards fed me all too well. Why, I've had to move the buttons over on some of my skirts!" Mary laughed.

"Well, it suits you. You seem to be well rested. I just want to draw a little blood to see if your red cell count is where it should be, and if it is, I'll pronounce you fit to return to work. I'll let you know the results tomorrow."

"May I stop taking that awful tonic, now, and the brandy?"

"The brandy, yes, but if your appetite goes downhill again, resume taking it. Keep taking the tonic for now. Let's wait until I get the results of your blood work. You seem to be fully recovered, but I want to remove all doubt." He snapped his bag shut and smiled at her. "I was wondering if you might like to attend a concert with me Saturday afternoon at Jordan Hall."

"Thank you for asking, but I'm afraid I must decline. I already have another engagement." Mary didn't know if he was inviting her as a romantic companion or simply as a friend. He'd always been perfectly proper in his treatment of her, but there had occasionally been a facial expression, a gesture, or an ambiguous remark that she'd dismissed as meaningless. Now she wondered if she'd been wrong.

"Perhaps another time, then," he said. "Would you like to attend the symphony when the season begins, or the opera?"

He *is* asking me on a date, Mary thought. She didn't want to hurt his feelings, but she couldn't let him go on thinking there was any hope.

"Um, Doctor Stone," she hesitated. "There's something you should know." She paused again, trying to find the right words.

"Yes, what is it? Have you had any more dizzy spells? Are you suffering any symptoms you haven't told me about?"

"No, no it's nothing like that. It's… um, well, you see…" She took a deep breath. "When I was in Wellfleet, I, uh, met someone."

"Yes?" He sounded wary.

"Yes — a man. And I… and he… Well, we're in love." She blushed, suddenly fascinated with the toes of her shoes, gazing at them intently.

"No wonder you've got roses in your cheeks!" Behind his forced good humor, his disappointment showed. "Who is the lucky fellow?"

The doorbell rang.

"He's the fellow ringing the doorbell." Mary had seen Asa walk past the window.

* * * *

There was an awkward silence as Sally ushered Asa into the parlor. He'd been fixing a problem on the production line. Too impatient to see Mary to go home and change from his work clothes, he was dressed in an old suit with baggy knees, fraying sleeves, threadbare elbows; a soft-collared work shirt with a faded tie; and a cloth cap. Mary swallowed.

"Doctor Stone, I'd like you to meet Mr. Asa Mayhew. Asa, this is the doctor who has been treating me for anemia."

The men sized each other up as they shook hands.

"So you're Mary's doctah. Thanks for takin' such good care of her." But it's my turn now, Asa added to himself; you can go.

"What is it you do, Mr. Mayhew?"

Asa thought he'd have a little fun with this Beacon Hill Brahmin who was looking down his nose at him. "Waell, right now, I'm talkin' t' you." He paused, grinning. "Oh, did yah mean for a livin'? Work f' Pawtah Motahs ovah t' Cambridge. Wheyah they make the Pawtah motahcahs, y' know."

"You're a mechanic there, I take it?"

"Waell, not exactly." Asa smiled broadly.

"What do you mean, 'not exactly'?" Doctor Stone sounded irritated.

"I'm not exactly a mechanic, although I do work on engines." Asa dropped the exaggerated accent and spoke in a relaxed, congenial tone. "But you're not really interested in what I do. You had already decided that I was beneath your notice, and you wondered what on earth Mary could see in a lowbrow like me. Have I got that about right?"

"Well, I— how did you— how *dare* you—" Doctor Stone spluttered.

"Read your mind?" Asa finished for him, grinning. "Well, 't was easy. You're as transparent as glass, you know. I saw how you took in my work clothes, and the disgusted look you gave to the remnants of grease under my nails when we shook hands. I also saw the green-eyed monster look out from behind your own green eyes when Mary introduced us. You're in love with her. Well, so am I." Though there was challenge in the words, his tone remained friendly and his expression bordered on mirth.

Mary had been turning her head as though she were at a tennis match, watching the men volley some other, unspoken communication back and forth.

"I don't know whether to be amused or appalled," she said. "You two are circling each other like… like… some kind of… Oh! I keep expecting you to lock horns!"

Asa snorted. "You hit the nail right on the head, Mary."

"How can you laugh?" demanded Doctor Stone. "You— you—"

"Bull moose?" Asa chuckled.

"How crude! And in front of Mary!"

"Well, I was the one who made the analogy." Mary grinned. "And it is the correct one, isn't it?"

Doctor Stone glared at Asa. When he turned to see Mary's laughing eyes, he smiled. "Well, it goes back to the beginning of time, doesn't it? Survival of the fittest, natural selection, and all that."

"Doc, may the best man — or the fittest beast — win." Asa offered his hand.

Doctor Stone shook it. "I'll accept the challenge."

"Although," Asa grinned, "I think the contest may already be over."

Still smiling, Doctor Stone shook his head in disbelief. "Well, Mary, I'll let you know the results of the blood test as soon as I've completed it. I think you'll be able to stop taking 'that awful tonic' as you call it, and return to work after tomorrow." He picked up his bag. "Good afternoon." He looked at Asa. "Mr. Mayhew." He picked up his hat, tipped it, put it on his head, and left.

"Do you think I was too hard on him?" Asa asked.

"The way he was looking down his nose at you, he deserved it," Mary replied, "But I do feel a little bad for him. Just before you came, he invited me to a concert, and I turned him down."

"Not a concert!" Asa put his hand to his brow, rolling his eyes in exaggerated consternation. "Anything but a concert! That's how things get started!"

They laughed. Then he took Mary in his arms and kissed her.

"Asa," Mary whispered. "Did you know your kisses always give me a thrill — a kind of fluttery feeling — way down deep?"

"My, my! They do? Do you know your kisses uh, stir me up... um, so to... ah, speak." Oh, geez, he thought. They also make me into an inarticulate idiot who may be prone to blurting out inappropriate things.

"You have such beautifully shaped, soft lips," Mary traced their outline with her fingertip, "and you taste of peppermints."

"Oh, my love. My love, you are the one with the beautifully shaped lips, and you always smell of lemons and flowers." Asa inhaled. "Aah... I wish I could carry your scent with me all day long." He smiled. "But perhaps it's best I can't, for I'd never get any work done, daydreaming of you."

Mary ducked her head and smiled, blushing.

They moved to the sofa and sat down. Asa angled himself to face her and took her hands in his.

"Mary, I've got something to tell you. That's why I rushed over here from work without taking time to change my clothes."

"What is it?" Mary looked worried.

"I'm afraid you won't like it." Asa took a deep breath. "The Office of Naval Intelligence wants me to work for them."

"But don't you have to be in the Navy, first?" Mary asked.

"No, they hire civilians. Anyway, you know I'm joining the Navy Reserve as soon as they get it organized. The thing is — they are desperate for men. They've been going around asking businesses if they'd be willing to lend employees with the skills they need. Ostensibly I'd still be working for Bill Porter — at least until the Director of Naval Intelligence can convince the Secretary of the Navy to loosen the purse strings."

"What do they want you to do?" Mary asked.

"To work here in the United States on plant security, ferret out saboteurs, screen personnel, that sort of thing. It seems they like the security plan I devised for the new Porter plant in New Jersey," Asa said.

"Does that mean you have to go away? How soon? How much longer do we have?"

He saw that she was trying to hide her fear and will away tears, and moved closer, putting his arm around her shoulders. "We'll have a little while. I'll be talking to Captain

Burns again. I won't know anything for sure until I get my orders, and it will probably take a while for them to come through. They didn't give me any details. In fact, it's all rather vague. I don't suppose they'll tell me more until I'm officially involved."

"Will you be involved in espionage? Will it be dangerous?"

"Well, as I said, it's not very clear, but the way it was described to me, it'll be more security operations than spying, although there'll be some of that, too," Asa admitted. "There'd have to be to uncover saboteurs and their plots. I think the level of danger would depend upon how well a fellow could keep his wits about him, keep his eyes and ears open. Don't worry too much about that, Mary. I know how to take care of myself."

"I think I've just seen a small demonstration of your powers of observation. All this time, I've had no idea of Doctor Stone's feelings toward me until he asked me to the concert today. Even then, I thought he may have been asking just as a friend. But right away, you saw that he was… um… attracted to me," Mary said. "I'm still astonished by it, but he didn't deny it. I suppose I would have caught on eventually, but it only took you about two minutes! How did you do it?"

"Well, that's a bit different than observing other types of behavior. Men have a kind of special sense about each other when they're in the presence of an alluring female such as yourself." Asa felt himself blushing.

"But, Asa, I've seen you notice things even when you appeared to be otherwise distracted. You knew Shirley and Edward were engaged before he announced it, didn't you? You saw Shirley's ring, even though we were all wrapped up in each other. Remember when Little Billy got so upset because he thought he'd lost his toy car overboard? Even though you were at the helm, you'd seen it roll down the open hatch into the galley. When we went on that picnic with the Packards, you were already coming back from the car with Mrs. Packard's shawl even before she said it was getting chilly."

"The one you crocheted for her," Asa said. "I have to confess, I just wanted an excuse to touch it and look at it again. That very fine yarn, those lacey stitches — you made it a work of art, Mary. What was that pattern? Wait — I remember. 'Grapevine,' is that right?"

Mary goggled at him. "Um, yes, that's what it was called."

"It was like a painting. Those colors — light to dark greens, violets to deep indigo."

"You astound me. All your life, you've been surrounded by men, and yet you notice and appreciate things like that — the way women do. Most men would neither know nor care whether it was a sweater or a shawl they were fetching, let alone what pattern and color it was."

"It was *art*." Asa shrugged, hands palm up. "I happen to like art."

Mary smiled at him, shaking her head. "To get back to what I was saying before, about your powers of observation."

"'Powers of observation,' indeed." Asa snorted. "Half the time, I'm wanderin' around with my head in the clouds."

Mary ignored his protest. "You're always anticipating my every little desire. Just as I'm about to ask you for something, there it is in my hand. When people dine with you, you've passed them the butter or poured them a glass of water just as they're getting ready to ask. Sometimes I think you *can* read minds."

"You seem to be a pretty astute observer, yourself. The first time we went to visit Si and Janet, you sensed right away that Janet was uncomfortable with physical contact and responded to her accordingly. You knew, didn't you, that she was no less warm and welcoming than Si?"

"Asa, those sandwiches were too fresh to be left over from an afternoon tea with the Ladies' Aide Society, and I know she didn't prepare such dainty things for you and Si. It was obvious that she was taking pains to welcome me and make a good impression, and she more than succeeded — because of herself, not her sandwiches. Although they were very tasty. I only hope I made an equally good impression on her."

"Of course you did, dear. How could you not?" Asa said. "But to get back to the subject of *your* powers of observation, you seem to be able to read me like a book, often to my consternation. Perhaps the government should recruit *you* as a spy." Asa laughed.

"Why do you laugh? Because I'm a woman?"

"Of course not! You know bettah than that. I laughed because of your exorbitant idea of my abilities. I *do* believe you'd make a good spy. You not only *notice* every little detail, you *remember* it."

"I'm only an astute observer of you, my dear. I'd be utterly useless at determining who may or may not be a saboteur. I can see why they want you; although, I'd far rather keep you here than let you go." She leaned against him. "Oh, I wish this horrible war was over, and I wouldn't have to worry about you or be without you."

"I wish I wasn't torn between my love of you and my duty to my country. I don't ever want to be without you." He took her in his arms. "Mary, oh Mary, marry me," he breathed.

He kissed her with such passion that she opened herself to him, returning the kiss with equal fervor, pressing against him. "Asa," she groaned. He buried his fingers in her soft hair, and leaned her back against the arm of the sofa, kissing her lips, her neck, caressing her breast. She clung to him, drawing him close, pulling herself up toward him. They felt each other's excitement, panting, bruising their lips, tongues entwined. They forgot where they were.

A loud crash from the hallway jolted them to awareness. They sat up and sprang apart, hurriedly straightening clothes and fixing hair, both of them trembling, blushing, and out of breath.

Far from being observant of anything other than each other, they hadn't heard the front door when Mrs. Bird had entered.

Asa looked at Mary with big eyes. "I'm so sorry," he whispered.

Mary smiled. "Don't be."

\* \* \* \*

"Oh, dear!" Mrs. Bird exclaimed. "Now look what I've done! Sally? Sally, please bring a broom and dustpan. I'm afraid I've broken that vase in the hallway. Sally?"

Sally came bustling in with broom in hand, and began sweeping up the mess. "I don't see how you managed to knock this ovah, Mrs. Bird. It was tucked away ovah theyah in the co'nah. You'd have had to…"

Flapping her hands in shushing motions to Sally, while glancing toward the parlor door, Mrs. Bird proclaimed, "Yes, yes, dear. Terribly clumsy of me, wasn't it?" Peeking in to see Mary hastily replacing hairpins, she deemed they'd had enough time to straighten themselves out and moved toward the parlor.

"Why, look who's here! It's Mr. Mayhew! How lovely to see you again!"

Asa sprang up, holding his cap in front of him, and tipped his head in greeting. "Mrs. Bird," he acknowledged, sounding strangled. He cleared his throat, desperate to recover his composure.

"Did you see Doctor Stone today, Mary? I imagine he gave you a good report. You seem to be quite recovered. I must say, your color is, erm, much improved." Mrs. Bird smiled, ignoring the intense blush on Asa's face.

"Oh, hello, Mrs. Bird, I didn't hear you come in." Mary flashed a smile. "Yes, Doctor Stone said I should be able to go back to work tomorrow or the day after, pending the outcome of the blood test he took this afternoon."

"I was just about to have a little glass of sherry before supper. Will you join me?" She hadn't been about to do any such thing, but felt she needed an excuse to insinuate herself into the position of chaperone.

* * * *

Asa didn't want to join Mrs. Bird in a preprandial drink, and he didn't think Mary did either. They looked at each other, unable to come up with an excuse to avoid a rude refusal. Still flustered, they nodded and stammered their acceptance. He hastily sat back down on the couch. Sally served them their sherry.

He held the glass's stem between thumb and forefinger with exquisite care. He thought it resembled a glass thimble perched atop a gilded toothpick. With painstaking precision, he placed it on a side table, untasted.

They made awkward, halting small talk. Asa and Mary were afraid to look at one another, though each would steal a veiled glance from time to time. When their eyes met, they blushed and looked away.

Beryl came in, giving Asa an opportunity to escape. "Well, I don't want to detain you ladies from your supper." He smiled at Mrs. Bird as he rose and picked up his cloth cap. "I bid you all a good evening."

Mary walked him to the door and went outside with him. He took a step down to be at eye level with her. They conversed in low voices.

"Oh, Mary, you must think I'm a libertine — heaven knows I behaved like one. I shouldn't have lost my head that way. I apologize. I put you in a very awkward situation. I don't think Mrs. Bird will ask you to leave, otherwise, she would have marched right in on us instead of going through all that rigmarole with the vase."

"You think she saw us?"

"Oh, I'm sure she did. I'm sorry, Mary. My 'powers of observation,' as you call them, failed completely. I was entirely too engor— engrossed to notice her arrival." By their heat, Asa knew even his ears were scarlet. He hurriedly went on, "That vase was tucked away in a co'nah, uh, corner, and she couldn't have knocked it ovah by accident. Nunno. She saw us, and smashed that vase on purpose to wake us up and give us a little time to pull ourselves togethah befoah she came in. Oh, Mary! It's a good thing she did. Another minute and I'd have just about... well, gone too fah… as if I hadn't *already* gone too fah. I don't know what's wrong with me!" Oh, yes, I do, he thought, hanging his head in shame. "I lost all sense of decorum and behaved like a boundah, a cad, a *beast*! Can you *evah* fo'give me?" His liquid, pleading eyes met her warm, understanding ones.

"Stop apologizing, dear. I wasn't protesting, was I? Far from pushing you away, I was just as... um, involved as you were, and I—" She looked down, blushing. In a nearly inaudible whisper, she confessed, "I couldn't control myself, either. You must think I'm some kind of a loose woman, to admit this to you. I've never, *ever* felt this... this... I didn't *want* to say no — not to you."

"Oh, Mary, *please* stop. I'm about to grab you and kiss you and make love to you right here on the front steps, in front of all of the Brahmins on Beacon Hill, in front of the whole world! Oh, my deah, I know we've only been goin' togethah for a month, and maybe it's too soon to ask, with the war loomin' and all, but I meant it when I said, 'Marry me.' This wasn't how I'd imagined asking you. I was going to go down on one knee, with a ring and everythin', but I just can't wait! Oh, Mary, will you marry me? Please say yes."

"Yes! Oh, yes! Of *course* I'll marry you, Asa. You know I've been over the moon about you since that night in the drugstore. No — even before that. Oh, let's not wait. I don't need — or want — a fancy wedding. Let's just go to a justice of the peace, as soon as we can, before you have to go away. Let's go tomorrow!"

"Oh, my love," he breathed, taking her hand. They gazed into one another's eyes. Asa shook himself out of his trance. "We'll have to get a marriage license. Do you have your birth certificate? I happen to have mine handy because I needed it to show to Captain Burns."

"I'm sure I have it somewhere. It's probably in my strongbox. I'll go right up and look," she answered, turning toward the door.

Asa stopped her, taking her arm. "Wait. I don't want you to miss suppah, and Mrs. Bird is probably wond'rin' what we're doin' out here." His words tumbled over each other. "Whyn't you go in an' eat, and I'll come back 'n about an hour. We'll need witnesses. I'll send a telegram t' Janet an' Si, an' call Shirley. I think we'll need blood tests an' there'll prob'ly be some sort o' waitin' period to get the license, but I'm not sure. I'll put off signin' the papahs f' the O.N.I. until I know, so we can be sure o' havin' time t' marry before I go." He took a breath and tried to slow his speech, to no avail. "Listen, you go in an' have suppah, an' I'll come back after I've sent my telegram. Oh, an' I've got to call Shirley and a few othah things. 'Bout an hour, mebbe two, dependin' how fast I can get everythin' done. All right, love?"

"Oh, yes, dear. I love you." Mary grinned. "You don't know how much!"

"I love you so much, I want to stand out here and shout it to all of Beacon Hill!" He flung his arms wide, laughing. "But Mrs. Bird would probably take a dim view of that." He looked around quickly, kissed her lightly on the lips, and held the front door for her as she entered the house.

She turned in the doorway, saying, "Asa, don't forget to breathe."

"Thanks fo' remindin' me," he laughed, then turned and leapt down the steps. He ran to Beacon Street, thinking he might find a taxi near the Statehouse or the Common. He didn't want to waste time waiting for the subway. He flagged a cab that had just dropped off a fellow he recognized as a state senator, and had the driver take him to Western Union and wait, while he sent the telegram to Silas and Janet. As he rode to Cambridge, he could barely sit still or refrain from singing. Halfway through the journey, he could contain himself no longer and said to the driver, "She said yes! I'm gettin' married! Can't you drive a little fastah? I've got a million things to do!" He laughed aloud. "Oh, I don't mean to be rude. I'm just so... I... um..."

The driver chuckled. "Yah think it's bad now, bub. Just wait'll you've been married a while. Wimmin! They get yah so yah dunno whethah yah comin' o' goin'! But I sure wouldn't wanna live without 'em."

Asa began singing, "Oh, Promise Me," and the driver joined in with harmony. By the time the cab pulled up in front of Bill's house, they were both laughing. Asa thrust money at the driver, dashed into the house to ask Bill for the use of his telephone. His grin could have lit up the eastern seaboard.

* * * *

Mrs. Bird drew Mary aside. "May I speak to you a moment, dear? In private?" She ushered Mary into the small sitting room across from the parlor, and closed the door.

Oh, Lord, thought Mary. Here it comes; she's throwing me out.

"Mary, dear, this is so difficult to say. You know I've always cared for you, and I rather took it upon myself to look after you when you first came here, since you had no mother or father to take care of you. And you have always behaved toward me as if you appreciated that and have treated me with respect. But... Oh, dear... How shall I say it? Ah... We have our reputation to uphold, you see," Mrs. Bird admonished. "You *do* see that, don't you?"

"Yes, of course," Mary said. "And I *do* appreciate your kindness toward me! Why, you went out of your way to take care of me when I was sick, and I couldn't have had better care from my own mother. I hope you know how grateful

I am to you and how much I admire you and value your friendship... Mrs. Bird, I think I know what this is in prelude to." Mary looked at the rug.

"Well, dear, I…"

At the same time, Mary said, "You see…"

They both stopped. Mrs. Bird said, "You first, dear."

"You saw us this afternoon, Asa and me, in the parlor, and I don't mean when we were having sherry. I'm terribly sorry for my behavior. It was unconscionable, I know. But you see, at the time, I just… we just…" She raised her palms in a helpless gesture, her eyes pleading for understanding. "You see, Asa — Mr. Mayhew — is joining the Office of Naval Intelligence, and we're going to get married as soon as possible, and… Well… I think we were both a little… how shall I put this? In the emotional intensity of the moment, we… um, just forgot ourselves… I *am* sorry. I assure you, Mrs. Bird, it won't happen again. Please know I meant absolutely no disrespect to you!"

"Well, dear, I'm glad you understand that that sort of thing really cannot go on here. This is a respectable house, and I won't have it. It's a good thing Miss Brooks left to attend nursing school this morning; although, I can't say I altogether approve of her wanting to go over *there* to nurse *men*. Well. It's just a blessing Miss Dickinson wasn't here to witness such a display. If you say it won't happen again, I believe you. We shall leave it at that. But I must warn you not to allow yourself to be overcome by any man, or who knows what might become of you? You must fight against it, dear girl," Mrs. Bird chided, shaking her finger, hinting of moral downfall and dark ends. "You don't want to get a bad reputation. As for Mr. Mayhew, why he placed you in such a position I'm sure I don't know. When I first met him, he seemed such a nice man."

"He *is* a nice man. He feels terrible about it. He's been standing on the steps apologizing most abjectly. That's why it's taken me so long to come inside. He's a *good* man, and I love him so!"

"Beware, dear, I wouldn't want to see you hurt."

"Oh, Mrs. Bird, Asa would never hurt me. Didn't you hear me when I said we're getting married?"

"Many a man has made promises just to get what he wanted, and then backed out of them. Oh, Mary, you are so naïve, so young. Please be careful."

"But Asa would *never...* He's not like that." Mary felt hurt and bewildered that Mrs. Bird didn't believe her. Nevertheless, deep down, she knew that if Asa *did*, she wouldn't want to stop him, and she blushed.

"Truly, I am not trying to spoil your happiness, and I shall be the first to offer you best wishes when you are married. I've simply seen young women have their hopes dashed before, and I don't want that to happen to you. I should be devastated if anyone crushed your spirit. You see, dear, I care about you as if you were my own." Mrs. Bird patted her sleeves, searching for a handkerchief to dry her tears.

"Oh, Mrs. Bird." Mary, her own eyes damp, took the plump little woman in her arms and hugged her. "Thank you for caring so much, but you're wrong about Asa. You'll see. You've no need to worry so! He *does* love me, he truly does."

# Chapter 41

# *All Aflutter*

Bill stood at the drinks cabinet. "Asa, come in. Have a seat. Emily and I were just about to have a drink before supper. Won't you join us?"

Asa looked ready to take flight. He glanced left, then right. In rapid succession, he bit his thumbnail, ran a hand through his hair, and frowned, putting two fingers to his temple as though trying to remember something.

When he didn't answer, Bill went on, "What a day, eh? So, that Navy chap is going to take you away from me. Looks like you won't be able to take that aeronautical engineering course after all. How much longer do I get to keep you, do you know?" He handed Emily her drink and turned back to fix his own.

Asa ran all his sentences together. "Sorry, Bill, I don't know. No thanks, no drink for me. Emily, how are you? Bill, may I use the telephone?"

"Of course, Asa. Is anything the matter?" Bill asked.

Distracted, Asa answered, "Nunno. Nothing's the matter. Everything's fine. Just fine." Then, with a huge grin, he blurted out, "I'm gettin' *married*!"

Bill fell the last few inches into his chair, his drink sloshing over his hand. He stared at Asa, open-mouthed.

Emily, more composed, said, "Why, Asa, congratulations!"

She got up and kissed him on the cheek and then handed Bill a napkin before returning to the sofa. Bill blinked, closed his mouth, and dried off his hand.

Asa beamed at them. He felt about to levitate.

"When did *this* happen?" Bill asked.

"Just now. I just asked her. You're the first to know. I'm so… I'm so…" Asa's grin was so wide, he felt his face would split. "Oh! I have to call Shirley. I'll be right back." He started out, then turned back again. "Say do you count any jewelers among your personal acquaintance? You see, it's past closing time, and I really need to get a ring. Today! Tonight!" He rushed off to call Shirley.

* * * *

Bill and Emily looked at each other, stunned, and then burst out laughing. "I've never seen him in such a state!" Emily exclaimed. "He looks about to go off like a Fourth of July fireworks display."

"If I remember correctly, from the time you said yes to me," Bill moved from his chair to sit beside Emily on the sofa, "I'm sure he *feels* he's about to go off like fireworks, too." They smiled at each other as Bill put his arm around Emily's shoulders.

In his haste, Asa had left the door to the study open, and they could hear snatches of his telephone conversation. "What size? Four-and-a-half? … When you call her, don't tell her I asked, okay? I want it to be a surprise… Oh, yes… Well, I don't know when, exactly. As soon as possible, that's why… Well, can you and Edward get away at a moment's notice? … Good… Say, do you know my cousin Si, or his wife Janet? …

Do you know where they live? ... Ayah, that's right. Do you have any way of gettin' ovah there? You see, they don't have a phone, and I've sent them a telegram, but... Oh, that's good of you... Yes, you can ring me back. I'm at Bill's... Ayup... Uh-huh... I'm sure she'd appreciate that... You do?... Say, I've got an idea. Would you be willin' to come out and help her get ready, if I can arrange it? ... You will? ... Oh that's great! Keep it a surprise, okay? ... Thank you, Shirley. You've been a wonderful help. 'Bye."

\* \* \* \*

Asa came back into the room and stood staring off into the distance for a moment. He blinked. "Oh, yah." He snapped his fingers. "Did you think of any jewelers who might be willin' to open up just long enough for me to get a ring? I'd pay extra, of course."

Emily said, "Let me call some of my friends. I'm sure we can find someone. Or are you expecting a call? I don't want to tie up the line if you are."

"Nunno, it's okay. Shirley's gonna call me back after she talks to Si and Janet, but not until later on tonight." As Emily went to the study, Asa frowned in thought. "Now, let's see. What was I gonna do next?"

Bill said, "Asa, sit down before you fly apart. And why is it so necessary to get the ring tonight?"

Asa paced back and forth, gesticulating as he talked. "Because I'm going back ovah to see Mary aftah she finishes her suppah. I've got to apologize to Mrs. Bird, and I've got to go down on one knee and ask Mary propah-like, and I have to find out if she found her birth certificate so we can get the license, and I have to... I have to..." Asa smacked his head with the palm of his hand. "I can't remembah what else right now."

"No wonder you look like you're about to split in two. Calm down, Asa. Why are you in such an all-fired rush?" Bill asked.

"Because we…" Asa threw his hands in the air. "We just can't wait!"

"You move at the speed of light, and I don't just mean your driving. A few weeks ago, you told me to keep your romance with Mary under my hat, and now you must have a ring immediately, or the sky will fall. What's going on?" Bill craned his neck to see if Emily was safely out of earshot, and lowered his voice. "You haven't got that girl into trouble, have you?"

Asa stopped in his tracks and stared at Bill. "*What?* Nunno, of coss not! What do you take me for? What do you take *her* for?" He began pacing again, chiding himself, *methinks thou does protest too much.* "No, no." For once, he separated the two words. "It's just this Navy thing. Mary and I… well, we want to get married before I have to go away. We need to be togethah, don't you see? We love each othah so much that it's just… it's just…" He spread out his hands, failing to find words. He abruptly sank down in a chair and gave Bill an imploring, soulful look. He blinked and cleared his throat. "I love her so much," he croaked.

For a moment, the two men were silent. Asa sat, elbows on knees, hands and head hanging down, staring intently at the pattern in the Oriental rug, trying to cover his embarrassment.

Bill looked concerned. "I understand," he said quietly. "But, Asa, you've hardly known the girl any length of time. Don't you think you need to step back a bit, and consider this? You're head over heels now, but are you sure it's love, and not just lust? I'm sorry to be so blunt. I know it *feels* like love, but don't you want to be sure before you rush into marriage?"

"God, Bill, people just don't talk about… *Oh*! Is this the fatherly talk?" Asa grinned. "Well, I *am* sure, Dad." He looked Bill directly in the eye and spoke deliberately. "I have never been more sure of anything in my life. It's not just physical. The more we talk, the more I love her. We have the same sense of humor. We like doing things together. We see things in the same light. We have similar principles. Of course, we don't *always* agree on things. It would be awfully boring if we did. But we respect each other's opinions and the right to have them. We're willing to listen to each other's viewpoint. We're both willing to admit when we're mistaken. And we introduce one another to new ideas. Because of Mary, I'm much more interested in women's suffrage, for example. And she's more interested in the safety and economic welfare of merchant seamen. Shall I go on?"

Bill shook his head.

"No, it's not just physical. I love her." Asa emphasized each word. "Bill, remember that conversation we had, when we were getting to know each other, out fishing on Gull Pond? Remember the 'girl in every port' reference? Well, I'll just say this. I spent about sixteen years at sea, the last several of which I was, shall we say, willing and able. Not that I was any Don Juan, mind you, but… I know the difference."

"Okay, you've convinced me," Bill said. "But I'm curious. When have you had time for all this talking? Except for that two week vacation, you've seen her only on weekends since you started working for me."

"Well, aside from billing and cooing and mooning over one another, we spent most of those two weeks talking, and we write. Sometimes two or even three times a day. I get letters from her in the morning mail and the afternoon mail. Of course, Wellfleet only gets the mail on the evening train, so Mary gets her two or three letters a day all at once. At first, they were just… well, *billets-doux*, but then we started writing about everything, anything that interested us. As well as how we felt about each other, we wrote about our lives, our memories, our families. We shared our beliefs and philosophies, our joys and sorrows. We wrote about what was happening in the world, and how we envisioned our future. We weren't always serious; we sometimes wrote silly, humorous things, too. Maybe we haven't been going together very long, but we *do* know each other," Asa said.

"I don't know why I ever doubted that you knew what you were doing. You always do," Bill said softly.

"Waell," Asa drawled, grinning, "I dunno about *that*!"

Emily came back into the room. "We're in luck. The Adamses were having a bridge night when I called, and Duncan and Jennie Cameron were there. Mr. Cameron owns Caledonia Jewelers on Washington Street, near Jordan Marsh and Filene's. They haven't started playing yet, and he's on his way to the store now, says he'll meet you there."

"Thanks, Emily!" Asa called over his shoulder as he dashed to the garage to get his car, but then he looked down at his shabby work clothes and thought Mr. Cameron would hardly open the store to someone who looked like him. He remembered he had to go up to his apartment to get more money, anyway, so he took the stairs three at a time, and hastily exchanged his old clothes for his beige suit. He left every other button on his shirt undone — it wouldn't show under his vest. He looked at his hands, and made another attempt with the scrub brush to remove the remnants of grease from beneath his fingernails. "Why is it," he muttered, as he got down on hands and knees to retrieve a cufflink that had rolled under the bed, "I never have trouble with collar stays and cufflinks except when I'm in a hurry." He was too impatient to tie his tie, and left it dangling; his hair wasn't plastered to his skull in the fashion of the day, but he hadn't time to mess around with brilliantine, so he grabbed his straw boater and leaped down the stairs to his car. He tore through the streets of Cambridge and Boston, alarming motorists and pedestrians alike. He slowed down in time to avoid being caught by a policeman directing traffic. While stopped, he tied his tie without the aid of a mirror. Mr. Cameron had just arrived when Asa got there.

"Thank you so much for agreeing to open up for me. You see, I really need an engagement and wedding ring tonight, so I can get married before going to work for the Navy. It just came about so suddenly, that I hadn't time to plan…" Asa heard himself babbling like a fool and stopped.

"Och, I understand. I was a young man myself once, going off to the Boer War with the Royal Scots, and I married my Jennie just the nicht before my unit boarded the ship. Tha' was seventeen years ago, but it may as well hae been yesterday." The *r*'s rolled off his tongue like little silver balls. "Weel, young man, coom in. Coom in," he said, as he unlocked the door. He turned on some lights and ushered Asa to a display case.

"Do you have anything in a size four-and-a-half?" Asa didn't want to wait to have a ring resized.

"Och, aye. Small hands she has," Mr. Cameron remarked. "But it does nae take verra long to make a ring smaller. Here are some lovely stones. What kind of stone do you want?"

"Hmm, I'm not sure. May I look at a variety?" asked Asa, leaning over the display case.

"Oh, aye. This is a lovely emerald, and over on the left, you'll see a very nice sapphire. We've some diamonds, as well. Of course, Cecil Rhodes with his De Beers Company makes a nice wee profit on those. Still, I suppose there's nothing wrong with a nice wee profit, is there?" Asa couldn't quite tell if he was being sarcastic about Rhodes, or if he was hinting at an extra nice wee profit of his own for opening up the store more than an hour past closing time. He'd get one, but if the hints got any broader, the extra profit would get smaller.

"Is that a ruby over there?" Asa asked.

"Aye, and rubies are for love." Mr. Cameron removed the ruby from the case so that Asa could get a good look at it.

"Hmm, it seems a bit large for her small hand, and to be honest, I'm not all that impressed with the quality of the stone," Asa said.

"You've a good eye, Mr. Mayhew," Mr. Cameron said. "It is less expensive than other rubies because it is nae quite so good, but less discerning customers care more aboot the price."

"May I see that one under a better light?" Asa pointed to one of the diamonds, already set in a smallish-looking ring.

"Aye. Tha's a bonnie one, is nae it?" Mr. Cameron was delighted with Asa's choice. Though it was smaller than some of the other stones, its flawless clarity, perfect cut, and brilliant color made it one of the pricier rings in his collection. "'Tis a size four-and-a-half, so nae need tae resize it. Ordinarily, the samples coom in larger sizes, since 'tis easier tae make a ring smaller than tae add gold tae the band. A gentleman was a bit too hasty in having this made for his lady. It seems he had nae asked her first, and she turned him down. I did nae hold him to the purchase, syne he'd already been dealt sich a blow, puir lad. Syne your lass has already agreed, there's nae misluck attached tae it. It seems tae hae been waiting for you tae come along. 'Tis a wee bit like fate, is nae it?"

Well, that story just made the jeweler's wee profit a bit bigger. His heart wasn't a hard diamond after all, but malleable gold.

"May I use your jeweler's loupe?" Asa examined the ring and found it to be flawless. When he moved it this way and that in the light, it seemed to contain tiny moving rainbows. "Do you have a wedding band to match?"

"Aye. This one is meant tae go with tha' ring, though many of the others would do. Will you be wanting a man's ring as well?"

"No, not right now. I do a lot of work with my hands, and I don't want to take the chance of losing a ring into a bit of machinery, or of having the ring get caught and losing my finger!" Asa laughed. "I'll take these rings, and please allow me to give you a little something for your time and trouble." He took a fat roll of bills from his pocket as Mr. Cameron looked on with a smile.

When Asa finished peeling bills off the roll, it was considerably thinner, but there was plenty more in the bank. He could afford an exquisite ring, but he would have bought it even if it bankrupted him, for Mary.

All those years at sea, he had been saving and investing his money. Although he gave a generous amount to Silas and Janet, he spent what he had only on the necessities of living. Books, of course, were as vital to the mind as food to the body, thus, were necessities in Asa's lexicon. He had intended to buy a house when he returned to Wellfleet, but hadn't had time to look for one. With the war looming, Si had told him it didn't make sense to buy a house now, especially since he'd been shuttling between Cambridge and Wellfleet. Now, Asa was glad he had agreed. He and Mary could choose a house together. Bill wanted to pay his salary even while he was working for the Navy, but Asa wouldn't hear of it. He had another proposal. Bill had been floored when Asa told him how much he wanted to invest, but readily welcomed him as a silent partner, as Asa wished.

As they left the store, Asa said again, "Thank you, Mr. Cameron. I do appreciate your coming out after hours."

Mr. Cameron shook his hand warmly. "It has indeed been a pleasure doing business with you. Congratulations, and I hope you shall be as happy together as my Jennie and I are. Guid nicht tae ye, Mr. Mayhew."

When they parted, Asa leaped into his car and sped off in the direction of Mrs. Bird's house. He paused to straighten his tie, and then leaped up the stairs in two bounds. He rang the bell, finger combing his hair as he waited. Sally answered and ushered him into the parlor. Mrs. Bird was embroidering and Beryl was knitting as they carried on a conversation. Mary was just coming down the stairs.

"I found it!" she called to him.

"Good," he answered, knowing that she referred to her birth certificate. They could go to City Hall tomorrow.

"Good evening, ladies. Mrs. Bird," Asa said, "May I speak with you for a moment, please?"

Mrs. Bird began to rise, but Beryl quickly finished the last stitch on the row, saying, "No, you stay. I'll go. I've letters to write and was just about to go up, anyway."

"Mrs. Bird," Asa began, "I don't expect you to forgive me, but I want to apologize for my appalling behavior this afternoon. I don't know what came ovah..." He faltered, knowing perfectly well what had come over him. He began again, "I lost all sense of decorum and polite behavior." He paused. "To say that I was completely overcome by emotion is no excuse." His voice had become hoarse, and he attempted to clear his throat. "I take full responsibility for my actions." Tugging at his choking collar, he cleared his throat again. "I have apologized to Mary." He turned to smile at Mary. The smile she returned melted his tension. Again, he looked at Mrs. Bird. "I can only assure you that it shall nevah happen again, um, in your home. I sincerely hope that you shall not always view me as a scoundrel. I certainly wished neither to dishonor Mary nor to offend you. I am truly sorry." Though he wished the floor would open up and swallow him, he did not look at it, or at the walls, or anywhere but Mrs. Bird's face.

"I appreciate your facing up to what you have done, young man, and coming to me to express your regret. You seem genuinely contrite. Perhaps I have misjudged you. When I spoke to Mary, I warned her against men who offer promises and speak sweet words, only to leave behind ruin and heartbreak. I accept your apology, but I warn you not to hurt Mary."

"Mrs. Bird, I'd like you to witness this." Asa knelt before Mary. "Mary, will you do me the honor of becoming my wife?"

"I've already said yes, Asa."

His eyes glowed like candlelight as he presented her with the ring. She gasped. "Oh, it's beautiful! How long... wherever did you..." Asa took the ring from its box and placed it on her finger. "It fits! How did you know what size? Oh, Asa!"

She stood up, tugged Asa to his feet, and right in front of Mrs. Bird, she hugged him and gave him a heartfelt kiss.

"Oh, my sweet." Asa enfolded her in his arms. "You have made me so very happy."

"Oh! Oh! I *am* glad for you, my dear!" Mrs. Bird was back to her fluttery demeanor. "Oh, Mary! You were right and I was wrong. Oh, Mr. Mayhew, how *could* I have thought you were... one of *those* men. Oh, my dears! How wonderful! A wedding!"

Asa and Mary stood holding each other, leaning back far enough to look into one another's eyes, beaming.

"You give me such joy," Mary said.

"My love, you give my heart wings," Asa said. "It ascends to the heavens, singing like a lark. It soars with the gulls, wheeling and laughing in the lofty blue sky."

Knowing Asa's habit of quoting bits of poetry, Mary asked, "Who said that?"

"Me." Asa sounded surprised. "Just now."

"My poet," Mary sighed.

"My inspiration," Asa laughed, blushing.

# Chapter 42

## *Surprises, Ceremony, and Sailing*

A s Asa let the doorknocker fall, Sally opened the door. Sounds of an argument drifted out.

"But I can't for the life of me understand why you're marrying *him*. You didn't even give me a chance! But you'll still come back to work, won't you?"

"I don't know, Jack," Mary said. "As I told you, I don't yet have the doctor's permission, and even if he says it's all right, I may not want to. At any rate, I won't be coming back until after I'm married."

Sally greeted Asa, "Good morning, Mr. Mayhew. Miss Lovejoy is in the parlor. She's expecting you."

"Thank you, Sally. I'll go right in."

Jack stood facing the fireplace with one hand on the mantel, the tension in his back revealing his indignation. "I don't see *why* you can't—" He spun around, flinging out his arm. Mary was standing behind him, to his right. The back of his hand, with its heavy gold Harvard class ring, struck her.

Mary gasped and put her hand to her cheek, shocked.

Jack's eyes widened as he gaped at her. "I didn't *mean* to— You *must* believe me, I didn't see you there!"

Asa felt the fire of fury in his face. In two strides, he was across the room, twisting Jack's offending arm behind his back. "Jack Chase, I presume." Asa's baritone had deepened to *basso profundo*. Though Jack was by no means short, Asa seemed to loom over him. "How dare you strike her!"

Jack talked fast. "Let go of me! I didn't mean to! It was an accident! Believe me, I would never—"

"Uh-huh," Asa interrupted. "Accident or not, you're leavin' now." He frog marched Jack toward the door.

"Take your hands off me!" Jack struggled against him in vain. "But Mary," Jack said, trying to twist away to look back at her, "Please, I really didn't—"

"So you said," Asa retorted flatly. "Run along, now, unless you want to start a new fashion in raccoon eyes. I'll give you two to match the one you gave Mary. Now, git!" He shoved him out the door.

"Who do you think you are, manhandling me like this?"

"Oh, didn't I introduce myself? Asa Mayhew, soon to be Mary's husband. I'd be lying if I said it's been a pleasure to meet you. Good bye, Jack." He shut the door on Jack's protesting squall.

Mrs. Bird had heard all the commotion, and was bustling into the hallway just as Asa ejected Jack. "What on earth?"

"Mrs. Bird, you wouldn't happen to have a beefsteak on hand, would you? Bettah yet, just chip some ice off the block, and wrap it in a clean tea towel for Mary, please," Asa asked.

Mary was standing agape. As Asa approached, she closed her mouth and blinked. Her cheekbone was reddened with an incipient bruise, and there was a tiny cut where the ring had grazed it.

"*Veritas*, indeed," Asa scoffed as he examined the ring's faint impression. "Come and sit down, dear. Does it hurt?"

"Just a little sting. Asa, you mustn't think he meant to do that! It really was an accident. He didn't notice that I'd moved—" Mary was interrupted by Mrs. Bird's arrival with the ice.

"Oh, that brute! Hear, dear, let me—"

"Thank you, Mrs. Bird." Asa took the improvised ice pack from her hand and gently placed it on Mary's face.

"Really, he didn't mean it," Mary said, muffled by the trailing ends of the tea towel. She took the pack from his hand and wrapped it tighter. "You're very gentle, dear, but I'd rather do it myself, thank you."

"What happened?" Mrs. Bird asked.

"I don't know for sure. I came in just as his hand struck her face. It could have been accidental, but…" Asa turned from Mrs. Bird to Mary. "What was he doing here so early, anyway? And why was he arguing with you?"

"He stopped by on his way into the office to see if I was coming in today. I told him it would be a bit longer, as I was getting married, and he was very… um, bothered. I think he had some idea… well…" Mary shrugged.

"Just before you went away, didn't he make some unwanted advances toward you in the garden? I remember it upset you so much you were ill," Mrs. Bird said.

"That was because of the ice cream. But he did say he wanted to court me, and tried to… well, he did kiss me." Mary dragged the back of her hand across her mouth, seeming unaware of the gesture. "I told him I didn't feel that way toward him. Then I had to make a mad dash into the house."

"Mary, my love," Asa reached for her hand. "I don't much care for the idea of you going back to work for young Mr. Jack Chase. I don't like his presumptuous attitude toward you. He may well believe that it was an accident that he hit you, but he was mad at you for getting engaged to another man, wasn't he?"

"Well, he… I don't know. The thing about Jack is that he tends to go about life charming people to get his own way. Dr. Stone called him a 'spoiled brat.' I don't think he's used to having his wishes thwarted, although his father has taken a firm hand with him lately. I truly don't believe he meant to hit me, though," Mary said.

Mary had lowered the ice pack, and Asa took her hand with it, gently guiding it back to her face. "You want to keep that on for a while, or you'll have a pretty good shinah. I don't want the ministah — minister to think I beat you into submission to get you to marry me!" He smiled. "It's up to you, of course, Mary. Just because I'm gonna be your husband doesn't give me the right to tell you what to do. I'm just lettin' you know how I feel, and I would rathah you didn't go back to work for that bas— um, boundah."

"I don't think I want to go back, either. It would be too… well, awkward after all this," Mary said. "But, Asa, what am I going to do with myself while you're off doing things for the Navy? If I don't have work to distract me, I'll sit around worrying about you all the time."

"How about finding a cause you're interested in, like joinin' that suffrage group you told me about? I remember you said you wished you had more time to devote to gettin' votes for women. You won't need to work, Mary. I've got plenty to support us, though I may not look it. And you won't need to pay rent." He turned to Mrs. Bird, "I'm sorry to be taking her away from your kind abode, Mrs. Bird, but as a married woman, of course Mary will be living with me."

"Oh… yes," Mrs. Bird said.

Asa turned back to Mary. "What was the name of that suffrage group again? B.E.S.A.G.G. or something?"

"Boston Equal Suffrage Association for Good Government," Mary answered.

"It would probably stick in people's minds bettah if they found a sho'tah — shorter name," Asa opined, grinning. "By the way, Bill and Emily want us to stay on at the apartment over their garage, if it's okay with you. It's a bit small, maybe, but I'll be away for much of the time, and you'll have the Porters for company while I'm gone. When the war's over, we'll find a nice place of our own." He hastily added, "Of course, if you don't want to live there, we can find another place right away."

"How kind of Bill and Emily," Mary said. "I think that would suit me just fine. And no matter how he pleads, I won't go back to work for Jack. I was getting fed up with his arrogance and slick charm, anyway. B.E.S.A.G.G. or something like it is a good idea. I'm sure I'll find plenty to keep me occupied."

"Good," Asa smiled. "Aftah we go to City Hall, I'll come with you to the office while you tendah your resignation, if you want. My presence might prevent Jack from givin' you a hahd time."

Asa took a deep breath. Ye gods, he thought, I mustn't let Jack rattle me so much it affects my accent to such a degree.

Before they left, another visitor arrived.

"Miss Lovejoy," Sally announced, "Doctor Stone is here to see you."

"Send him in," Mary said.

"Good morning, Mary — Miss Lovejoy. I came by to tell you the good news that your red blood cell count is back up to normal." He narrowed his eyes suspiciously at Asa. "Why the ice pack?"

Mary and Asa looked at one another. Asa tipped his head toward her.

"Well, uh… Jack was here," Mary began.

"That cad!"

"He didn't mean it!" Mary said.

"It's possible he didn't," Asa said. "When I came in, I just caught the tail end of it, but it didn't look good to me. I marched him out the door, but Mary insisted it was just an accident."

"He didn't notice I'd moved, you see," Mary tried to explain.

"Humph!" Dr. Stone said. "I wouldn't put it past him to strike a woman if she didn't comply with his wishes. He's exactly the type… Well, I suppose I shouldn't jump to conclusions. I wasn't here, after all."

"He was displeased, to say the least, that Mary told him she wasn't coming back to work right away," Asa said.

Dr. Stone seemed not to hear him, turning his attention to Mary. "Will you allow me to examine the wound?"

"Yes, of course, Doctor," Mary said.

Upon examination, he said, "No serious damage has been done. Since you applied ice immediately, I don't think you'll have a black eye — not much of one, anyway."

"We can thank Asa's quick thinking for that," Mary beamed up at Asa. "Right away, he asked Mrs. Bird to chop some ice off the block. Said he didn't want the minister to think he'd beaten me into submission to get me to marry him." She giggled.

"You… Am I hearing this right? You're betrothed?"

"Yes," Asa said. "Mary has agreed to be my wife. I love her very much, and I believe she feels the same about me."

"Oh, I do," Mary said. "You know I do!" She reached out and squeezed Asa's hand.

Stone was silent. Asa saw the disappointment in his face — more than disappointment — he looked crushed. He sympathized as the doctor made a visible effort to regain his composure.

Doctor Stone's smile lacked luster. "Well, apparently there's nothing left for me to say but 'Congratulations' and 'Best wishes.' Well, you're going to need blood tests for the license. Since I'm here, why don't I do them for you right now?"

"Thank you, Doctor Stone." Mary seemed subdued. "It's very good of you to offer."

"I'm sorry, Miss Lovejoy. I know you must be feeling rather like a pincushion after all the tests you've had to endure, but would you please roll up your sleeve just one more time?"

Mary nodded, blinking tears from her eyes and offering him a bittersweet smile as she rolled up her sleeve.

Asa looked on, struck by her compassion. Would Mary turn to Doctor Stone for comfort in his absence? He looked at her again and their eyes met. He knew he had nothing to worry about. She was his, just as he was hers, body and soul.

And then it was his turn.

"Thank you, Doctah Stone," Asa said as he was rolling down his sleeve. "I am sorry for your disappointment. I hope it doesn't hurt too much. But, you see… Mary and I are meant for each other. We really believe that. Perhaps you'll find some small consolation in realizing there's nothing you can do about fate." He paused, looking directly into Doctor Stone's eyes. "I'm sure you'll find the woman who is meant for you, too. I hope it will be soon."

Doctor Stone looked surprised. "Well, Mr. Mayhew, I have to confess that it does hurt, but I'm sure I'll get over it. Mary knows her own heart. I'll have to trust that you won't break it."

"I won't," Asa smiled.

"Congratulations. I mean that." Doctor Stone shook Asa's hand. "Well, at least it'll make it easier for me to volunteer to go overseas to serve as a doctor, now that I won't have to worry about her. Will I?"

"I'll take good care of her," Asa replied, wondering if he could truly promise this. He would be leaving soon, for God knows what. Well, he hoped his proxies, Bill and Emily, Si and Janet, would take good care of her in his absence. "Don't worry."

"I'll perform these tests immediately. I'm sure they'll be fine." Stone snapped his bag shut. "You can stop by my office and pick up the results before you go to City Hall."

* * * *

Later, test results in hand, Asa and Mary went off to City Hall to apply for a marriage license. As they were leaving, they met up with Mr. David Ives.

"Miss Lovejoy, what a pleasure it is to see you again, under much happier circumstances. I trust the business is going well?"

"What do you mean?" She looked puzzled. "I have nothing to do with the business. That's Uncle George's concern."

The lawyer frowned. "But didn't you know that a third of the business is yours? Your father left it to your mother, and after her death, it went to you. You don't mean to tell me that Mr. George Lovejoy has simply taken everything for himself! You hold equal shares with him, and the remainder is divided among the managing partners and Mr. Mayhew, here."

Asa was dumbfounded. "Me?"

"Why should that surprise you? Captain James Lovejoy thought of you as a younger brother, you know." Ives turned to Mary, "Why didn't you come to me? I would have seen to it that you were given your proper share."

"Mr. Ives, I didn't know," Mary said. "I suppose I couldn't take it in at the reading of the will. I was still in shock. I had no idea that I could be entitled to any part of the business. When Uncle George evicted me, I simply assumed he had the right to do so. I thought father had left the house to him."

"He did what?" Mr. Ives exclaimed.

"You didn't get my letter?" Asa asked.

"What letter?"

"I wrote to you as soon as I'd heard about George throwing Mary out of the house," Asa said. "I knew it couldn't be right."

"I received no letter." Mr. Ives shook his head. "Miss Lovejoy, I feel simply terrible that Mr. George Lovejoy has cheated you out of your inheritance in such a dastardly manner! I should have kept a closer eye on things, but at the time, my wife was undergoing surgery and, I must admit, I was distracted with worry."

"I am sorry to hear that. How is she?" Mary asked.

"She still has to be careful, but she is doing much better. For a time, I was afraid I'd lose her." Mr. Ives, the husband, seemed to soften and lose focus for a moment. Then Mr. Ives, the lawyer, briskly brought his attention back to Mary. "Still, that's no excuse. I must set about to remedy this situation right away. Will you come to my office? Let's see." He extracted a diary from his inside pocket. "Will Tuesday, the nineteenth, suit you?"

"I'll have to let you know later," Mary said. "You see, we're getting married in a couple of days, but we won't know exactly when until we've talked to the minister."

"Well, best wishes! And congratulations!" He turned and shook Asa's hand. "If Miss Lovejoy is about to become Mrs. Mayhew, perhaps I should be speaking to you."

"To me? Why? The business is Mary's, not mine. It's for her to make decisions. I would of course be happy to offer my opinion or assistance, should she request it. Nevertheless, she is an intelligent woman who is perfectly capable of handling her own business affairs."

Mary smiled up at him.

"Well, ah, after you marry, you shall have the right…" Mr. Ives was accustomed to men handling their wives' business affairs.

"Mr. Ives, please see to it that the business remains in Mary's name. Unlike George, I have no desire to steal her inheritance from her. It is rightfully hers and shall remain so," Asa insisted. "Moreover, I should like to give her my shares, so that she may have controlling interest in the company. Otherwise, George will drive it into the ground."

"If that is your wish," Mr. Ives said. "I shall draw up the papers. They shall need your signature, ceding any rights to Miss Lovejoy — Mrs. Mayhew, as she shall be."

"Mr. Ives, after I'm married, I'll contact you, and we can deal with this matter then. Surely, after all this time, waiting an extra week or two won't matter. I have no wish to be rude, but I'm afraid we haven't time for this right now, as we have several other errands to accomplish. We must bid you good day." Mary reached out and shook his hand, smiling.

"Well," Mr. Ives said, "You seem remarkably composed about this whole thing, and you certainly are decisive. Perhaps you shall prove to be a very good businesswoman. I'll see this put right, Miss Lovejoy." He tipped his hat. "Good day to you both."

Asa was rigid, his jaw tight, his hands in fists. Mary reached out and touched his arm.

"That *fils de chienne*!" He exclaimed through clenched teeth, sotto voce, so those around them wouldn't overhear. "I apologize for my bad language, Mary, but I'm so angry with Geo'ge for doin' this to you, I have all I can do to contain myself. No wondah he cast you out! He couldn't bear to look at you aftah he stole everythin' from you. That dastahdly thief! How could he *possibly* have been brothah to such an honest, upstandin' man like James? Such a… such a… *puerco, cochon, salopard, un salaud*, a changeling, a no good drunken cur of a yellow dog, a knave, a filthy lily-livered, action-taking knave, a calumnious, flap-eared, beetle-headed knave!" Aware that his voice was progressively increasing in volume, he took a deep breath and lowered it.

"I'm sorry for insultin' your uncle with such vehemence, but I simply *cannot* believe he could be the son of your blessed grandfathah and grandmothah. He *must* be a changeling. That… that… *crapule*! I'm sorry, Mary, but if I don't let off steam somehow, I'm afraid I might *hit* somethin'! Preferably Geo'ge!" He smacked his fist into his palm.

"Why offer apologies for the language of Shakespeare?" Mary softened his anger and soothed him by the simple act of slipping her arm through his. "And was that French? I've heard people say, 'Pardon my French' when they were cursing in English, but I've never actually heard anyone cursing in French before." She laughed, and Asa's thunderous fury dissipated.

"How can you laugh? Why aren't you seething with rage? I would be, in your position. Well, hell — I beg your pardon, yet again. Um… heck, I *am*, and I'm not the one he swindled!"

"More French!" Mary grinned. "Oh, Asa, if I allowed Uncle George's actions to get me into a state every time he did something like this, they'd have carted me off to the Boston Psychopathic Hospital a long time ago. I don't know if he can help being the way he is. He's… um, not quite right. There's something twisted and malignant lurking in his soul. I had to learn how to ignore him, simply to save my sanity. I have no desire for wealth; it doesn't bring happiness. And holding a grudge would hurt me more that it would hurt him. I'm truly not all that upset."

"My dear, you must be a saint," Asa said in awe.

"No, I'm not, and neither, by the way, was my grandfather." She shrugged. "I am, and he was, a mere human being, with all the usual flaws and failures. I think you're not only angry on my behalf, but because of the accusations Uncle George made after Father died." She leaned toward him and spoke quietly, "I know that hurt you to the quick. You loved my father as much as I loved him. You didn't know Uncle George as I did, so you couldn't simply dismiss what he said as the drunken ravings of a jealous fool."

"I'm just an open book to you, aren't I?" Asa smiled.

"Come on." Mary laughed. "Now that you've limbered up your glowering muscles, let's go see Jack."

\* \* \* \*

They stopped at Chase Imports and tracked down Jack in the warehouse.

"So, have you decided to come in to work after all?" Jack sneered.

"Quite the contrary," Mary said. "I've come to tender my resignation."

"But, Mary, this summer has been hell without you," Jack whined. "Please come back. I'll give you a raise, Friday afternoons off…"

"No thank you. After all that has passed between us, I would feel extremely uncomfortable continuing to work for you," Mary said.

"Can't we forget all that, Mary?" Jack said. "I'll change, I swear—"

Asa gave him a stony look. "Mr. Chase, this is *Miss Lovejoy* to you, and very soon she shall be *Mrs. Mayhew*. I suggest you remember your manners and address her properly from now on."

"Who are *you* to tell me to mind my manners?" Jack challenged. "Waterfront lowlife!"

Still smoldering at George, Asa hadn't any more patience to deal with Jack. His tone was hard, but he spoke clearly and evenly. "In case you've forgotten, I'm the fellow who threw you out of Miss Lovejoy's home this morning. I'm basically a pacifist who doesn't enjoy engaging in fisticuffs, but if you are really looking for a fight, I'll give you one."

Jack looked at him like a thunder cloud, forming his hands into fists.

"I'd advise against it," Asa went on. "I've got about two inches and at least ten pounds on you, and the muscles of a sailor against those of an office worker. It'd be a lot harder than hitting a woman."

"Why you… you…" Jack threw a punch.

Asa reached out and caught Jack's fist in his hand. "I really don't want to fight with you."

"You think I can't take you!" Jack started dancing around, shadow boxing.

Asa folded his arms, sighed, and stood back to watch.

Jack moved in and threw another punch.

Exerting no more effort than shooing a fly, Asa put up his arm and blocked it.

Jack's face was dark with anger, and he launched himself at Asa.

Asa hugged him, locking Jack's arms at his sides. "Stop it, Jack. I don't want to hurt you."

Still pinned in Asa's arms, Jack roared with anger.

"You're mad as thunder. But if you're thunder, I'm lightning. You can make a lot of noise, but if I wanted to, I could strike, and strike fast, with real damage. You're too slow, Jack; you'll never catch me."

"Oh, really? What makes you think you're so great?" Jack yelled.

"Experience. Experience that you seem to be lacking. You want to pick fights, you should take a few lessons at a gym," Asa said. "Now, if I let go of you, will you calm down and stop waving your arms around?"

"Damn you!"

"Watch your language in front of a lady," Asa said.

"Mr. Chase," Mary was stiffly formal. "Stop this nonsense. No matter what you do or say, I have resigned, as of this moment. Because of this foolish behavior, don't expect me to come back to train my replacement."

Asa slightly loosened his hold on Jack's arms. "Are you going to listen to reason?" At Jack's nod, Asa let him go.

"Get out, both of you!" Jack turned on his heel and walked into the warehouse.

"Whew!" Asa shook his head as they went outside. "How on earth did you manage to work for that little hothead for as long as you did without breaking one of those precious vases over his head?"

"Well, except for a few spirited arguments with his father, he didn't behave anything like this," Mary said. "He was more of a popinjay — a glib, shallow, party boy."

"Puffed-up popinjay or peppery pop off — I don't know which is worse," Asa shook his head. "Your forbearance is a wonder. It's a good thing, though. You may need it with me — always going off and leaving you behind."

"I come from a long line of sea captains, remember? I'm used to it." Mary hugged his arm, smiling up at him. "Nice alliteration, by the way. 'Puffed-up popinjay' is a perfect description."

"Why, thank you, Mary! I wish you weren't wearing a hat," Asa said.

Mary burst out laughing. "What a non sequitur! Why?"

"Well, in reply to your statement — not the popinjay, but the one about being used to it — I wanted to kiss the top of your head," Asa shrugged. "At that moment, I couldn't think of words."

Mary went into a spate of giggles. "Oh, you are precious."

Asa smiled at her. "More than words can say, I love you; more than all the water in the seven seas, I love you; more than life itself, I love you. 'Til a' the seas gang dry, my dear, 'til a' the seas gang dry."

Looking up at him with glistening eyes, Mary said quietly, "I see you found those elusive words. I wish we weren't on a public sidewalk."

"Now who's talking in non sequiturs?" Asa grinned. "I want to kiss you, too."

"There, you see? I must marry you; it would be indecent otherwise," Mary said.

"Indecent?" Asa asked.

"Because you can read my mind," Mary said. "I feel rather naked before you."

Asa laughed. "Well, then, we'd better go see if we can find the minister in his office."

* * * *

They went on to visit the rector of the Church of the Advent, which Mary had been attending with Mrs. Bird, and arranged to have a quiet wedding at the rectory two days hence. It was rather high church for Asa. On the other hand, he couldn't deny there was something about the pomp and ceremony he appreciated. It was something of an art form, like theater. And he loved the colors and workmanship of the stained-glass windows. If that was sacrilege, so be it.

It didn't go entirely smoothly. They agreed to use the ceremony from the Book of Common Prayer, but when the rector asked Mary who would be giving her away, she said, "Well, there isn't anybody but me, because I'm certainly not inviting Uncle George to the ceremony."

"I object to the question, 'Who giveth this woman to be married to this man?'" Asa said. "No one has the right to give Mary to anyone. She belongs to herself alone."

"But if you have an uncle…" The rector didn't get any further.

"No," Asa said. "He has no rights in this at all, and he is most definitely not invited."

The rector harrumphed. "I do not like that at all, young man. It is completely against tradition. A male relative or guardian should give her away."

"But Mr. Addison," Mary said, "There is no one. My so-called uncle simply isn't suitable."

"Aside from the fact that *no one* has that right, *this* male relative absolutely won't do," Asa argued. "He is a nothing but a drunken conniver who has stolen her inheritance from her, and I'm sure you wouldn't want a belligerent inebriate who holds a grudge against both of us ruining our ceremony. I repeat: absolutely no one has a right to 'give' her to me. She's not property. We did away with slavery with the thirteenth amendment. And if I recall the epistles of St. Paul correctly, there is neither slave nor free, male or female, for we are all one in Christ. If you insist that the formal ceremony be adhered to as it is in the prayer book, then I insist that Mary is the *only* one who has the right to give herself to me, as I shall give myself to her. Therefore, when the question is asked, she shall answer, 'I do.'"

"Well, I must admit, you do have a point, but to have the bride give herself away is quite unorthodox. Perhaps we should simply leave that question out of the ceremony altogether."

Asa sighed. "Thank you for seeing reason."

After the ceremony was sorted out, the rector asked if they had witnesses to stand up with them.

"Oh, yes. There shall be…" She looked at Asa, "Four?"

"At least four," Asa confirmed. "But we've asked some others."

"All right, at least four people in attendance, and possibly quite a few more," Mary said. "It depends upon how many have the time free, and how many can get here."

"Well, if there shall be many more, perhaps we ought to plan to have it in the Lady Chapel. The rectory may be a tight squeeze."

"That would be perfect," Mary said.

Asa beamed at her. "A church wedding after all."

\* \* \* \*

When they were outside, Mary took Asa's arm. "Thank you, my dear."

"For what?" Asa asked.

"For standing up for me, for saying that no one owned me," Mary said. "Do you know, you are more of an advocate for women's rights than many of the women I know?"

"Well, it's about time men started realizing how strong and capable women are. All they have to do is look around.

Look at how many years women have been fighting for equal suffrage, all the abuse they've been put through, including physical attacks — by the police, no less. And they've suffered through imprisonment and the torture of force-feeding. But you haven't said it's too hard and given up, have you? And in my travels, I've met women who ran their own businesses and supported whole villages, women who were intellectually and ethically far superior to the men around them, women who were braver in the face of danger than the men around them, too," Asa said.

"You're wonderful," Mary said.

"Waell, I dunno about that." He took out his watch and checked the time. "Let's go to South Station." He opened the car door for Mary. "I have a surprise for you."

"A surprise? At the train station? What is it?" Mary asked.

"Well, now, if I told you, it wouldn't be a surprise, would it?" Asa grinned. "You'll just have to wait and see."

\* \* \* \*

When they got to the right track, people were disembarking from the Cape train. "Looks like we got here just in time. Train's a little early," Asa said, craning to see over the heads of the crowd. "Over here," he said, steering Mary with a protective hand on her shoulder.

When the crowd parted enough for Mary to see, she crowed with delight. "Shirley!" They rushed into each other's arms as Asa picked up Shirley's suitcase. The two women immediately began talking about the wedding, extending their hands side-by-side, proudly comparing rings. They chatted on as Asa beamed at them, shepherding them toward the car and depositing Shirley's case in the back.

He was so happy he wanted to wrap his arms around the entire world.

When they'd arrived at Mrs. Bird's, Asa said, "I made arrangements with Mrs. Bird for Shirley to stay in the room that Miss Brooks used to have. I thought you'd like having her with you. You know — another woman to help you choose a dress and things like that. I figured you might need someone other than me to talk to about your worries, what with all the changes that'll be happening and, well... Who better than your closest friend?" Ever the perfect gentleman, he got out of the car and went around to open the door for her.

Mary blinked a few times, swallowed, and then said, "Oh, my dear, thank you for such a perfect wedding present."

He bent down, tipped the brim of her hat back, and kissed her forehead. Then he helped Shirley out of the car and carried her case inside.

In the front hall, Mary took her hat off. They stood holding hands for a few moments, giving each other adoring looks. Finally, Asa cleared his throat and said, "I'd like to stand here gazing at you all day, but I have an appointment with Captain Burns." He took out his watch. "Better get goin'. Don't want to get off on the wrong foot by bein' late for my new boss."

"And as much as I'd like to fall into the ocean of your eyes, I do have to pay some attention to Shirley," she said.

He smiled, bent down and softly kissed her lips, and then gently stroked her hair. Catching himself starting to turn misty and unfocused again, he cleared his throat. "Well, uh, see you latah, deah." He kissed the top of her head before departing.

\* \* \* \*

He left the two women cheerfully planning a shopping trip, and went on to meet with Captain Burns at the Boston Navy Yard. The captain congratulated him on his upcoming wedding and told him he could have a week's honeymoon before reporting for duty. So much was happening all at once that at times Asa felt caught up in a whirlwind. Far from feeling overwhelmed, he reveled in it.

# Chapter 43

# *A Wedding*

sa was happy that Si and Janet, Shirley and Edward, Mr. and Mrs. Packard, Bill and Emily, little Billy, Mrs. Bird, and Miss Dickinson could come to the wedding. Mary had said she'd wanted a quick wedding at the registry office, but he wanted to make it special for her. They had invited Martha, but she declined, saying she was too busy preparing the wedding dinner. In truth, outside the environs of her kitchen or of her own family, Asa knew that Martha was shy; still, he was somewhat disappointed. He had called Josiah Mayo to invite him, knowing it was such short notice that he probably wouldn't be able to attend. Sure enough, Josiah had to be in court that day.

"I wish I could have given you more notice, Josiah," Asa said. "I'd have liked you to be my best man. But you understand that I have to report to the Navy, and we just didn't have more time."

"I understand, Asa," Josiah said. "And I'd like to just drop everything and come. You don't know how disappointed I am to miss your wedding. After all, you are my dearest friend."

"Well, it couldn't be helped," Asa said. "I'll write to you and tell you all about it."

He went to talk to Shirley. "It's supposed to be bad luck for the groom to see the bride's wedding dress before the day, and God knows Mary and I have had enough of that. Well… you know what I… I mean, I hope you know…" Asa sighed. "Anyway, you helped her pick it out — the dress — so you would know… I mean, I want to buy her flowers. Can you tell me what color?"

With Shirley's advice, Asa presented Mary with a bouquet of pink and white roses and a corsage of pink rosebuds and white baby's breath.

On the day of the wedding, Asa wore a formal morning suit of black tails and striped gray and black trousers, with a pearl gray vest, a silvery gray and white striped silk ascot tie with a pearl stickpin, and a white carnation pinned to his lapel. His stiffly starched wing collar gleamed so whitely that it nearly gave off its own light. It was scratchy and uncomfortable, but he wore it gladly, for Mary. The toes of his black shoes shone like mirrors, his white spats immaculate. He stood at the altar waiting, with Edward by his side. They both turned to look as Shirley preceded Mary down the aisle.

Asa took in a deep breath as he caught sight of his bride. Mary wore a white dress with a froth of lace ruffles on the skirt and bodice. At the high neckline, she wore her mother's cameo brooch. A lace veil with pale pink silk rosebuds framing her face was pinned to her hair, done, as always, in a chignon. To make herself a little taller, she had bought the highest heeled white shoes she could find. Rather than a strap, a satin ribbon tied across the instep with a big bow. Asa knew feet must be killing her, but he suspected she wore them for him, and his heart went out to her. Her beauty took his breath away.

When Mary had asked him, Si said he would be honored to walk Mary down the aisle. Asa had smiled broadly, proud that she should choose Si, all on her own. She had already become a part of his family. "Oh, thank you," Mary had said. "Without you to lean on, I'm afraid I might break an ankle walking all that way in these shoes." They had all laughed.

Billy grinned from ear to ear. Dressed in his best Sunday suit, he strutted down the aisle after Mary and Si with his chest stuck out, carrying a small velvet pillow with the ring, proud as a peacock. Asa was so glad he had thought to ask Billy to be the ring bearer.

Asa couldn't stop smiling. He could hardly believe that the woman he loved, the woman of his dreams, had agreed to marry him. A bittersweet feeling came over him when he thought of James. He looked at Mary and knew she felt it, too. At that instant, a beam of light shone through the stained glass window and cast a rainbow of color over them. They looked at each other with glistening eyes, and he felt that James's spirit was there, blessing them both.

Gazing at Mary, wonder-struck, he was barely able to repeat after the rector the words that he solemnly swore to love and to cherish, forsaking all others, for richer or poorer, in sickness and in health, as long as they both shall live. Mary repeated the same words, her eyes on Asa's. They were pronounced man and wife, and shocked the rector with the passion of their kiss.

After the ceremony, they went to Bill and Emily's home. Before dinner, the wedding guests gathered in the parlor for champagne toasts. "To the happy couple," they raised their glasses. "Asa and Mary," another glass, and then another for "Mr. and Mrs. Mayhew." Asa raised his glass to Mary and sang:

*Oh promise me that someday you and I*
*Will take our love together to some sky*
*Where we can be alone and faith renew,*
*And find the hollows where those flowers grew,*
*Those first sweet violets of early spring,*
*Which come in whispers, thrill us both, and sing*
*Of love unspeakable that is to be.*
*Oh promise me. Oh promise me.*

She raised her glass to him and sang the second verse:
*Oh promise me that you will take my hand*
*The most unworthy in this lonely land,*
*And let me sit beside you in your eyes,*
*Seeing the vision of our paradise,*
*Hearing God's message while the organ rolls*
*Its mighty music to our very souls,*
*No love less perfect than a life with thee*
*Oh promise me. Oh promise me.*

Everyone oohed and aahed and clapped. Si sniffed and quickly ran a finger under his eye.

"What beautiful voices you both have," Emily said. "It's hard to stay on key when you're singing a cappella, but you were perfect."

Others chimed in with murmurs of agreement.

Asa and Mary spoke at once, "Thank you, Emily." They grinned at each other and hugged.

"I always thought there should be a verse that goes: *Oh promise me that we shall never part / That we shall hold each other in our hearts*, but I never got any further than that," Asa said.

"We shall have to sit down and write it together, then," Mary said.

"Maybe we could replace that line about hearing God's message while the organ rolls," Asa said. "Seems more like a sermon than a love song. Kinda takes the romance out of it."

Mary laughed. "I never really liked that line, either."

They strolled about, mingling with their guests, and then took their glasses of champagne to a quiet corner.

Edward and Shirley walked over to join them.

"That was a lovely wedding," Shirley said. "And you put it together so quickly."

"Would you like something like that, dear?" Edward asked her. "Or do you want a big wedding with hundreds of relatives and friends that takes months to plan."

"I think our parents are expecting that, but I'd be happy with a wedding like this," Shirley said. "For one thing, we could avoid all that squabbling over who gets invited and who doesn't."

"We could marry a lot sooner, and I'm sure your father wouldn't mind the money he'd save," Edward said. "It may not be tactful or courteous of me to say so, but who cares what the parents want? It's our wedding, isn't it?"

"Oh, you are bold," Shirley said. "Let's do it! Thank you, Mary. I should never have thought of it if it hadn't been for you, but it's perfect."

"Thank Asa," Mary said. "I would have been happy to get married at the registry office, but he wanted something nicer for me." She smiled up at him. "Didn't you, dear?"

"A gem such as you needs a much finer setting than the registry office," Asa smiled, putting his arm around her. He leaned over and kissed the top of her head. "I'm glad we had it in the Lady Chapel instead of the rectory. It was a perfect little jewel box, wasn't it?"

Mary put her arm around his waist and leaned her head against his chest. "You're such a romantic," she murmured.

Edward and Shirley smiled at one another. "Do you think they'd notice if we wandered off to talk to your parents?" Edward asked, sotto voce.

"I don't think they'd notice if the house fell down around them," Shirley said. "Look at them — they're just besotted."

Mary giggled. "I heard that."

"So did I, and you're absolutely right. It's a wonder we heard you at all," Asa said. "You know, Shirley, if you really want a small wedding, this is just the right time to go talk to your parents about it, before they forget how much they enjoyed this one, and while they're still basking in the glow of the wedding toasts."

"Good idea," Edward said. "Come on, dear. I think they want to be alone."

Asa chuckled. "Alone in a room full of people with a small child making a beeline for us."

"Uncle Asa! Miss Lovejoy — or, no, you're not Miss anymore, are you?" Billy said. "What should I call you?"

"Well, since I'm married to Uncle Asa, how about Aunt Mary?" Mary said. "I think Mrs. Mayhew is too formal, don't you? Besides, it would be too confusing with two Mrs. Mayhews."

"Two of you?" Billy's brow puckered in a puzzled frown.

"Yes, Janet is Mrs. Mayhew, since she's married to Asa's cousin, Silas Mayhew."

"Oh!" Billy said. He was about to say something else when his father interrupted with an announcement.

"Martha has dinner ready for us in the dining room, and she has outdone herself. Come and enjoy the feast!"

The first course was a chilled cucumber soup. Asa leaned over and murmured to Mary, "Thank heavens it's cold soup. I think I'd have melted had it been hot."

Mary fanned her face with her hand. "I know what you mean."

Next, there was a salmon mousse Martha had shaped in a ring mold. The center was mounded high with fresh green peas.

"Salmon and peas," Billy exclaimed. "Just like the Fourth of July! Can we have fireworks for your wedding, too, Uncle Asa?"

Asa laughed. "That would be grand, wouldn't it, Billy? But I'm afraid not. We'd have had to get special permission from the city, the state, and the fire department, and there wasn't enough time."

"There are fireworks enough with the sparks from your eyes," Bill said. "Both of you."

Mary blushed, and Asa leaned over and kissed her cheek.

There were murmurs of gastronomic ecstasy as Martha brought in the entrée: roast beef with roasted potatoes, green beans almandine, and buttered, herbed carrots, followed by a tossed green salad with vinaigrette.

Asa and Mary gazed at each other, smiling. Simultaneously, they rubbed their aching cheeks. Although Asa could barely tell what he was eating, despite his distraction, he couldn't help but notice that everyone else was thoroughly enjoying it. The babble of voices had hushed as they were too busy savoring every bite. Wordless sounds of pleasure alternated with, "This is so good," and "Please pass me some more of that."

Martha's crowning achievement, though, was the wedding cake. It took both Martha and Janet to carry it to the table after dinner.

"Oh, Martha, it's absolutely beautiful," Mary gasped. "It must have taken days to create."

"Just one," Martha blushed. "Wouldn't want stale cake, now, would we? Not for you and Asa."

"Mahtha." Asa was so overwhelmed he could barely speak. He cleared his throat and blinked tears from his eyes. "Deah Mahtha... All this... for us? How can we ever thank you?" He walked around the table to take her hand in both of his. He wanted to hug her, but knew she would be embarrassed and flustered if he did, so he refrained. "What a work of art. 'Tis a shame to have to cut into it."

"It's to eat, not just to look at," Martha said to him. "Have to cut into it to taste it."

Martha had created four round tiers, increasing in size from top to bottom, covered with satiny white buttercream frosting, elaborately piped decorations, and pink marzipan roses. Two red icing roses, complete with green leaves and intertwined stems, covered the top.

Asa and Mary cut the first slice from the bottom tier, holding the cake knife together. "Mm, strawberry cream," Mary said.

"Cut one from the second teah," Martha said, smiling.

When they cut into the chocolate cake filled with mocha cream, Asa nearly burst into tears. "Oh, Mahtha, Mahtha! You did this especially for me?" He fished in his pocket for his handkerchief, and dabbed at his eyes.

"Try the next one," Martha said.

Mary's breath caught. "Orange cream, my favorite. Oh, Martha you must really love us. You went to so much trouble. This is just— Oh! I hope you know I love you, and have since I was a little girl." Mary threw her arms around Martha.

"Now, now, deah." Martha patted Mary's back. "I didn't want to make you cry. I wanted to make you happy."

"But, Mahtha," Asa said. "These are tears of happiness. We're simply overflowing with gratitude and joy. Please sit down and have some cake with us."

"Oh, I couldn't—" Martha protested, blushing.

"Yes you could," Asa said. "Or else we'll invade your kitchen and sit at the kitchen table with you."

Bill went to fetch another chair.

"Sit heah by me. We've known each othah so many yeahs, you know *I* won't bite," Janet said. "Mr. Pawtah, you can put that chayah right heah, please."

Billy said, "I can hardly wait to have some of that yummy cake. Miss Martha, you give me treats for doing something good, and you worked so hard. You deserve a treat!"

Bill smiled. "Please join us, Martha. I'm not the lord of the manor, you know. And I don't bite, either, although I can't speak for Asa." He winked at Asa.

"Waell, I might, from time to time, 'specially if the moon is full, but I'm fah too happy to bite anyone today," Asa said.

Their laughter covered Martha's embarrassment.

"Now, what flavor would you like?" Asa asked her, knife poised over the cake.

"I should serve—" Martha began.

"Nope," Asa said. "You relax after all your hard labor. That feast is fit for the late King Edward VII!"

"Asa, befoah you cut any moah, you should take off the top layah. It's the traditional fruitcake prese'ved with brandy to save fo' yaw fust annive'sary," Martha said.

Asa got a plate and did as Martha instructed, continuing on with his fit-for-a-king praise. "This magnificent cake would make even starchy Queen Mary of Teck swoon! Why, that intricate decoration looks like you've draped her precious pearls and lace all down the sides!"

"Tsk. You always did exaggerate too much," Martha said.

Pretending not to have heard her, Asa went on, "You must be exhausted. You may not think so, but I'm perfectly capable of cuttin' and servin' a cake, even one as glorious as this."

He proceeded to do just that, going around the table, asking each guest's preference.

When he had served Mary, she said, "Well, will you look at that! Aren't I the luckiest wife on earth? I have a husband who will serve *me*, instead of expecting *me* to serve *him* all the time."

Emily, Mrs. Packard, and Mrs. Bird laughed the loudest.

Asa took a forkful of Mary's cake and fed it to her. She blushed and laughed. "He'll even feed me!"

She took a forkful of his cake and fed it to him. "Mm, with this ambrosia being fed to me by my stunning wife, I think I may swoon with ecstasy."

"If you do," Mary said, "I shall revive you with a kiss."

Asa laughed. "In a reversal of the fairy tale roles, you shall be the brave princess who rescues the sleeping prince. It's perfect, my dear, because you are so courageous."

Mary laughed and fed him another forkful. "Have some more cake, my dear. A full mouth may prevent you from spouting such nonsense."

After he swallowed his cake, he leaned to whisper in her ear. "But you *are*, my love."

After dinner, they tried to be sociable, but they were floating on air, ensconced together in their own iridescent bubble of joy. They held hands, stole kisses, murmured to each other.

"How long do we have to stay so as not to appear rude?" Mary whispered to Asa.

"I think after we go around and thank everybody, it would be all right to leave," Asa whispered back.

"Then let's do that. I want you to kiss me — I mean a real kiss — not just these quick little ones we can get away with in the company of our wedding guests."

"Oh," Asa drew the word out to a moan. "I want to be alone with you so much, it almost hurts."

"Mm." Mary leaned into him. "I can't wait any longer."

They looked at each other and simultaneously took a deep breath. Then, smiling and holding hands, they went around thanking each guest for coming and bidding them farewell. They went into the kitchen to thank Martha again. Mary kissed her on the cheek; Asa kissed her forehead. Martha blushed and wrung her apron.

As soon as they were out the back door, Asa wrapped his arms around Mary and leaned her back in a passionate kiss. Almost before she could get her breath back, he swept her up in his arms and spun around in a circle.

"Oh, Mary! I'm so happy, I feel as if I could fly! How do you feel, my dear?"

"I wish you would fly up those stairs with me, and bring me down for a soft landing — in your bed," Mary laughed.

"*Our* bed. Your wish is my command, m'lady. Hang on!" Asa ran up the stairs with her in his arms.

# Chapter 44

## *Alone at Last*

A t long last, they had escaped to their little apartment above the garage. Asa carried Mary over the threshold. He kicked the door closed behind them, kissing her with all of the passionate intensity he had been restraining since that afternoon in Mrs. Bird's parlor. Mary kissed him back with equal ardor.

He carried her into the bedroom, and gently laid her on the bed. He whipped off his collar and tie, flinging them away. They kissed again, shaking fingers fumbling with each other's buttons while their tongues sought each other's. Their hands were everywhere, stripping off frustrating layers of clothing, stroking and clinging to each other. Mary sat up, only breaking off their kiss long enough to pull her dress over her head while Asa dropped his trousers and yanked his shirt off. She pressed into Asa's kiss, holding him as tightly as she could, and fell onto her back, pulling him over with her. At last, they got down to skin.

He leaned back far enough to look at her. She was as pale pink as rose petals, and just as soft. He traced the outline of her face with his finger, and brushed a few curly tendrils of rich auburn hair from her forehead. "So beautiful," he murmured.

Falling into her liquid brown eyes, he leaned closer, kissing her gently. She put her hand on the back of his head and pulled him closer, pressing her lips into his. Their tongues danced and their kisses became more fervent.

His hand traveled from her breast and she moaned as he touched her.

"Oh, my dear," he murmured.

"Asa," she panted. "Kiss me some more."

She hungrily sought his mouth with hers again and they pressed together, lips, teeth, tongues, melding in the heat of passion. She pressed the length of her body against his.

Kissing her mouth, her neck, and sliding down to her breast, Asa took her nipple in his mouth. She moaned as he sucked on it.

Again, his hand traveled down to stroke her. She made small sounds of excitement.

She moaned, "Please, oh, please," as she raised her hips to him.

"Mary, oh, my love," he whispered. "Are you sure?"

"Yes, yes! Now, love, now."

He kissed her once more as he began to move over her. As he thrust into her, she uttered a sharp little cry. "Did I hurt you?" Asa held still, barely breathing.

"No," she gasped. "Don't stop. *Please* don't stop. Oh, Asa," she moaned, pressing closer to him, pulling him toward her.

He wanted to be gentle, he tried to slow down for her first time, but she seemed to be nearly as desperate for him as he was for her. She panted, pushing herself up against him. He moved faster. A low moan escaped her, and her breath caught. He continued to touch and kiss her as they rocked together. His breathing quickened and he came just as she did. She clung to him and pressed her mouth against his shoulder, trying to muffle her involuntary scream of passion.

"Oh, Mary," he groaned. When all the tension had gone out of her and she sagged beneath him, he withdrew and rolled onto his back, putting his arm around her and drawing her head to his chest. He buried his face in her hair and breathed in that lemon-flower scent he loved.

Asa wondered if he'd been too hasty, if he'd been selfish in not preparing her better. But he was so... God help him... he felt as though he'd been a starving man who was suddenly replete. He was ecstatic to have Mary in his arms. At the same time, he worried that she might be offended by his sweaty body, that she might find this behavior too... animalistic. But she had seemed to want him as badly as he wanted her. Fatigued, with shaky limbs, he turned a bit awkwardly to see Mary's face.

"How do you feel, love?" he asked.

"When I catch my breath, I'll let you know." She took a deep breath and let it out slowly. She snuggled into his side, draping her arm across him. "Mm."

"Are you sure I didn't hurt you? You cried out."

"It was just a little pinch," she said. "Isn't it supposed to be like that? Now I'm no longer a virgin."

"Oh, my *preciosa*," Asa breathed. He stroked her hair as they lay quietly together.

After a moment, he asked, "Do you know how you feel yet?"

"I feel as though my entire body were made of warm gelatin, and the only thing holding me together is my skin. I've never felt this relaxed in my life, dear. The only thing is — I don't think I'll ever be able to move out of this bed."

Asa's laugh was gentle. "Good. I'd like to stay in this bed with you forever, my love." He tried to move his leg, and felt it encumbered. He looked down at the foot of the bed, and laughed. "How would you like to try that again, only without our pants down around our ankles, and our shoes off?"

Mary looked down to see she was still wearing one shoe and both stockings, with their lacy blue garters, and her knickers remained wrapped around one ankle. Asa's trousers were around both of his ankles, impeded by his shoes. She laughed. "I guess we were in kind of a hurry."

Still, they didn't remove them, feeling too languorous to make the effort.

"This isn't how I planned it." Asa ran his fingers through her hair. He picked out the few remaining hairpins and deposited them on the nightstand. "I was going to be oh, so gentle, taking you step-by-step, being the wiser, older man who taught you about sex and coddled you through your first time. Hah! I guess my animal instincts overruled my higher brain. But you didn't seem to mind." He kissed her lightly.

"Mind? Quite the contrary, dear." Mary giggled. "'Wiser, older man.' What are you, five years older than I?"

"About that, I guess." She was so much more mature, Asa had to keep reminding himself that she was nineteen. "But I've had eons more experience than you. After all, I'm a man of the world, and a big, bad sailah, to boot! I don't understand why a sweet young thing like you wasn't quakin' in your shoes," he teased.

"'Big bad sailor! Man of the world!' Why, Cap'n Mayhew," she stroked his chest. "You may have a hard body, which I appreciate, by the way," her voice grew quiet. "But your heart's as soft and warm as lamb's fleece."

Asa laughed. "Nunno. The soft and wooly part is my head."

"That's only your hair," Mary giggled, tousling his curls. "Beneath the skull it's anything but."

"Hah! I wouldn't be too sure of that. I seem to do an awful lot of woolgatherin'."

Eventually, they removed their shoes and the remainder of their clothing, and did try it again, slower, gentler, and just as satisfying — perhaps even more so.

When Mary tried to stand up, she sat back down on the bed with a small thud. "Oh, my," she giggled. "My legs seem to have turned to jelly."

Asa laughed. "Need some help?" When he tried standing up, his legs trembled with muscle fatigue, refusing to support him, as well. They both collapsed in helpless laughter.

She succeeded on her second try, but her journey to the bathroom was a wobbly one. When it was his turn, Asa found himself hanging on to the furniture a bit, too.

They smiled sleepily at one another, kissed and snuggled, and fell asleep in each other's arms, only to wake up and do it all over again.

# Chapter 45

## *Honeymoon*

Asa and Mary were pleased that Captain Burns had given them a week, though they would have been happier with two. Bill offered them the *Emily* for their honeymoon. He asked Asa to put her in dry dock for the winter at the end of their sail. They drove to Wellfleet instead of taking the train, even though it took longer; they wanted to be alone and were not in any particular hurry. Asa had an air pump, extra tubes, and plenty of tire patches, and Martha had packed enough food and drink to sustain them for a month, should they find themselves marooned on some hitherto undiscovered island.

They sailed with no destination in mind, frequently dropping anchor near one of the outer Cape islands. They basked in the sun, made love, talked, made love, ate, made love, sailed, and made love.

Lucky in the weather, they went ashore only twice: once in Martha's Vineyard for fried clams, and once in Nantucket for a feast of steamers and corn on the cob, dripping with butter. They went to see if Doc Coffin was home, but he was out to sea.

"Ah well," Asa said. "I would have liked to introduce you to him. He's been a good friend to both your father and me."

"I would have liked to meet him," Mary said. "He sent Mother and me a heartfelt letter after father died."

One morning, they were perched on the gunnel in their bathing suits, basking in the sun. Asa's bathing costume was two-piece, a long black and white horizontally striped knitted thigh-length tank over matching shorts that came to his knees. Mary's was a short navy blue dress with a white belt, and matching bloomers peeking out beneath the three white stripes decorating the hem. She wore a white rubber bathing cap to protect her hair. On foggy mornings, both of them were so daring as to dispense with their suits altogether, and swim in the buff.

"Isn't it grand to be out here sailing alone? Just think, if we'd been at a public beach, they'd have probably fined you for going without hose." He laughed.

"Hah!" Mary exclaimed. "Under the guise of Puritanism, those officials who go around with measuring tapes to make sure our skirts are no more than nine inches above the knee are really just a bunch of dirty old men looking for an excuse to put their hands on girls' legs."

"Not a bad job to have." Asa teased. "Poor old boys probably have mean, prune-faced wives, and it's as close as they can get."

Mary laughed. "Better watch out, or it'll be as close as *you* can get!"

Asa grinned at her. "Oh, yah?" He drew her in with a one-armed hug and·kissed her.

"Mm," she murmured, kissing him back. "Want to go below?"

Asa laughed. "Oh, you bet I do! But, um, give me fifteen minutes, all right?"

"Oh, you poor fellow, did I tire you out this morning?" Mary grinned. "I don't know why we're so insatiable. Maybe it's because the war is coming, and we want to kind of…" Her grin had vanished. "I don't know… maybe store it up, somehow, for when we're separated. That doesn't make any sense, I know. But it kind of feels that way, as if I were trying to hoard something against leaner times."

"It makes perfect sense to me," Asa replied. "If we knew, or thought we knew, we were going to be together for a long, long time, and were going to see one another every day, there wouldn't be this sense of urgency… of having to grab all the life and love we can before…"

"Before you might get killed." Mary was so quiet that Asa wouldn't have heard her if he hadn't been looking at her. He drew her into his arms.

"That's not what I was going to say. I mean before we have to part. I'm not going to the front lines, love." He brushed a stray lock of hair from her forehead, looking into her eyes. "It won't be as dangerous as all that."

"But it will be espionage, and that's dangerous enough. No." She placed her fingers on Asa's lips before he could speak. "Don't tell me it's not. I'm not an idiot or a little girl that you have to shield from the truth. I know you don't want me to worry, but who wouldn't? Yes, I'll worry, but not to the point where it makes me blue and edgy all the time. I'll be all right. Don't *you* worry about *me*. I don't want you distracted by anything. I want you to be paying attention to what's going on around you, not to what's going on in your imagination back here. You'll need all your wits about you. Do you understand?"

"You've made yourself perfectly clear, my dear," Asa said. "I'll do my best, but like you, I probably will worry sometimes. I promise not to let it distract me, though. I fully intend on bringin' myself back to you in one piece when this is all over."

"You'd better." Mary teased. "There are men lined up waiting for a chance to wine and dine me."

"Waell, if you choose one of them, I suppose…" Asa pretended to think it over, rubbing his jaw. "I could always go back to havin' a woman in every port."

She pushed him overboard and jumped in after him. They laughed and splashed each other, then swam around to the stern and climbed back aboard. They wouldn't let somber moods spoil this week they had together.

Another morning, when they were anchored off a tiny island — it was more like a spit of sand that would disappear in the next storm — there was enough fog to shield them from passing boats. There was nary a breeze, so they thought it would linger for a while. The fore and aft lights were on so they wouldn't be struck, on the off chance that another boat had braved the fog. They padded the deck with cushions and lay down to make love. Out on the ocean, in a place that probably didn't appear on any chart, they felt safely removed from the world.

They took their time, gently exploring each other's bodies from head to toe, caressing, kissing, stroking. As their kisses began to bruise their lips and their breathing accelerated, they went further to excite each other more. When they came together in climax, they felt free to cry out their ecstasy without fear that the neighbors would overhear.

After their breathing slowed, they lay spent in each other's arms engaging in languorous, desultory conversation.

"Isn't it nice," Mary said. "Seeing what it's like to make love with the mist outside of us instead of inside."

Asa smiled. "Waell, I don't know about you, but that misty feeling is still inside of me. Outside and in — I'm just permeated with it. I don't think I'll ever be able to think straight again, since I met you. I'm just lost in this fog of love."

"You make it sound dangerous," Mary said.

"Not dangerous," Asa said. "More… soft, like a cloud. It's dreamy and comfortable, like waking up in a feather bed with a sweet, sleepy feeling."

"It might feel nice and cozy, but it *is* dangerous in the line of work you're going into," Mary said.

"My love, do we have to think about that now? Can't you just let me enjoy this feeling for a little while longer?" Asa drew her to him and wrapped his arms around her.

"Sorry, dear," Mary said. She snuggled up to him. "I don't know what I was thinking. I want to enjoy it, too."

They drifted into a doze.

Suddenly, Mary sat up. "Asa!"

"Wha…" He wanted to drift off again, but woke up enough to hear the panic in her voice. "What is it?"

"The fog has burned off, and I can't see that little island anymore! We're drifting!"

"How could we be? I made sure the anchor was fast." He stood up, looked around, and felt the motion of the boat. "By God, you're right!" He dashed to the cockpit to check the compass and get their bearings.

"Start hoisting the sails, while I raise the anchor, Mary, quick! We're drifting into a shipping lane!"

Mary sprang to the task, shouting, "I told you that kind of fog was dangerous!"

"This is *not* the time for 'I told you so,'" Asa said as he helped Mary raise the mainsail, and then jumped into the cockpit and took the helm. Tacking this way and that to catch what little wind there was, he had turned them around and headed in the right direction just as a freighter loomed on the horizon. "Pray for a following wind, m'dear. We've got to pack on sail!"

"Don't sailboats have the right of way?"

"Ayup, but not in a shippin' lane. We've got no right to be heah. Those big behemoths can't see us until they're right on top of us, and by then it's too late."

They were getting too close — close enough to hear the sailors shouting, whistling, and cheering. Just in time, the wind picked up and blew them out of harm's way. They let out sighs of relief and hugged each other, only then realizing that they'd been sailing in the buff.

Mary blushed scarlet. "Oh, gosh, do you think they were close enough to see us?"

By the sounds they were making, Asa thought they sure did, and they had been enjoying it immensely. "Waell, if they had binoculars… But don't worry, deah, we're complete strangers to them. Not a one of them would recognize us if they tripped over us on the street."

"Still…" Mary looked down at herself and then dashed below to put something on.

When she came back, Asa said, "Much as I wish we didn't have to, I suppose I'd better go put some clothes on, too. Take the helm, love, would you?"

"Of course, dear. Where are we going?"

"Thataway," Asa pointed.

Mary straightened up. "Helm is being relieved. Steady as she goes."

Asa laughed as he headed below.

Bearing cups of coffee for both of them, he came above and joined Mary in the cockpit.

"I've been thinking," Mary said. "How could the anchor have come loose when you'd made sure it was fast?"

"It's my fault. I should have dived down to check the bottom in this sandy shoal, but when the anchor didn't give, I thought it was set. The sands must have shifted with the tide, letting the anchor loose," Asa said. "Some sailor I am, eh? I've no excuse, Mary, and I'm so sorry for putting you at risk due to my negligence."

Although he thought his face didn't show it, internally, he winced. He'd never been able to shake the feeling that his negligence was to blame for Cap'n James's death, and now he'd put Mary at risk.

Mary put her arms around him. "Don't, Asa. I'm a good enough sailor to have known that, but it didn't even occur to me to check, either. I'm just as responsible as you are, so stop taking all the blame on your shoulders."

"But I—"

"Sh. You're human, and we humans are prone to distraction, especially when we're in love. You do have an excuse, and I'm it," Mary said. "I'm sorry, too."

Asa shook his head. "My dear, I do not deserve you. You are far too good to me."

"Don't be silly," Mary said. She stood on tiptoe to kiss him. "You are all I have ever hoped for, and I'm lucky that we found each other."

Asa clasped her in his arms. "Oh, my love. Oh, my love."

"Are you going to sing Robert Burns to me again?" Mary asked. "I wouldn't mind, if you are."

Blinking away his tears, Asa smiled.

"I am a fool, aren't I?"

"A fool for love, but so am I," Mary smiled, and hugged him.

* * * *

They sailed wherever their hearts took them. Moored in a hidden cove, they nearly got caught skinny-dipping. On a deserted island they made love and had a picnic. Once, they came across Si and Tony seining for mackerel.

"Hey, Si! Fancy meeting you here," Asa said, as they came alongside.

"Heard you just got married," Tony shouted from his boat. "Congratulations! And best wishes to you, Miss Lovejoy — I mean, Mrs. Mayhew. You're going to need them with this fellow!" He laughed.

The crew gave Asa a cheer, "Atta boy, Asa! Hip, hip, hooray! Hip, hip, hooray!"

Asa laughed as Mary blushed.

"Sorry, dear," he murmured to her. "They don't mean anything by it."

"Oh, I know, Asa. It's just somewhat embarrassing to be the center of so much male attention, especially knowing the connotation they put on it."

"We'll say goodbye and sail away now, all right?"

"Oh, I don't want to snub them," Mary said.

"They won't feel snubbed," Asa said. "They've got work to do, and we're interruptin' it."

"All right."

"Thanks, lads!" Asa shouted. "Nice to see you Tony. Si, we'll see you latah. Hope you get a good catch!"

"You comin' by for suppah aftah you put the boat up?" Si asked.

"You bet," Asa said. "Lookin' forward to it."

"As am I," Mary said.

Asa didn't think her voice carried across the water. "Mary says she's lookin' forward to it, too! See you tomorrow, Si!"

Mary waved enthusiastically as they sailed away.

Tomorrow. One more day — only one more day alone together.

## Chapter 46

## *Goodbye, Fare Ye Well*

W hen they returned to Cambridge, Asa left Emily and Mary to talk, and found Bill in his office. "Thanks so much for the loan of the *Emily*, Bill. We had a good time sailing her."

"I'm glad to have been able to contribute in some way to your happiness," Bill said. "Mary's a wonderful girl. I'm sorry I ever questioned your love for her. It's obvious that you belong together. It's too bad you have to rush off to join the Navy's fight against these saboteurs."

"Yah, well," Asa said. "I did volunteer, didn't I? More fool, me. Still, if my country needs me… Ah, well, it's the old conundrum, isn't it? Like that old Irish ballad where the lad has to choose between the old love and the new love — his country or his girl. It would be better not to have to make that choice, but in times such as these…" Asa sighed.

Bill put his hand on Asa's shoulder. "It's good you've had this time together, and I hope you shall have many more. Indeed, I wish you shall grow old together, just as I wish for Emily and me," he said. "You're leaving tomorrow?"

"Yah, on the early train from South Station. Say, I've got yet another favor to ask you."

"Anything, son. You name it."

Asa was surprised that Bill called him 'son'. He wasn't sure whether he was pleased or irritated. He had loved his father, and then Cap'n Asa had been his surrogate father. After him, James had been father, brother, and friend. Did he really need another father? Well… all his fathers were… gone. Yes, he was glad that Bill thought of him as a son.

"Mary wants to see me off, but I don't want her to be alone after I've gone. Could you or Emily be with her?"

"We'll both be there with her to see you off, and we'll see she gets home safely, with us to comfort her along the way," Bill said. "And we'll be here to help her in any way possible after you've gone."

Asa choked up. "Thanks, Bill. I couldn't ask for a better friend."

Bill hugged him, thumping him on the back. "Neither could I."

\* \* \* \*

That night, Asa and Mary took their time undressing each other in a ceremony of love and leave-taking. Unclasping Mary's necklace, Asa gently kissed the vulnerable back of her neck. She turned and removed his tie and collar, standing on tiptoe to kiss the hollow at the base of his neck. Slipping off his suitcoat and vest, she took the time to hang them in the wardrobe. Carefully undoing a row of pearl buttons that ran down her back from neck to waist, he paused, leaning down to kiss her spine. He lifted the smooth, satiny dress over her head and placed it on a hanger. She removed his cufflinks, turning each hand to kiss his palms. He removed the pins from her hair and brushed it in long, flowing strokes. In silence, tenderly removing each layer, they completed this ritual. With glittering, wide eyes, they studied one another from head to toe, memorizing the light and shadow as it defined each muscle and hollow, the texture and hue of each other's skin, as though they were to make sculptures of each other by heart after they parted.

They slid between cool sheets and turned to face each other. Asa traced the outline of Mary's face with his finger.

She touched his cheek beneath his eye. "My dear," she whispered.

Asa sniffed. "You caught me. I wasn't going to… I didn't want our last night to be sad. Oh, Mary, I don't want to leave you."

She drew his head onto her breast and caressed him. "I promised myself I wouldn't cry." Stroking his curls, she said, "I don't want you to go, either, but you no longer have a choice."

"I'm so sorry, love." He wrapped Mary in his arms and clung to her. "Can you ever forgive me?"

Mary hugged him tightly. "Asa, my sweet, there is nothing to forgive. I knew perfectly well what I was getting into when I agreed to marry you. The only one who needs to forgive you is you."

"But… I…" Asa sighed. "It's just that… I'm so torn. I want with all my heart to stay here with you, but… Oh, God help me… I feel it's my duty to go."

"I long for you to stay, but I understand why you have to leave," Mary said. "Truly, I do. It isn't simply duty. You are an honorable man and you must fulfill your promise."

"I want to say, 'To hell with duty and honor. Let's run away together — sail away to the ends of the earth, where no one will ever find us, and create our own Eden.'"

"That would be lovely, wouldn't it?" Mary smiled. "But we both know it's simply a wild dream."

"Oh, Mary!" He clung to her in a passionate hug. "I love you so much."

She clutched him back. "You know I love you."

They held each other and cried a little. Then they began kissing the salty tears from each other's cheeks. Soon, they were kissing each other's lips. Their lovemaking that night was exquisitely sensitive and devoted.

\* \* \* \*

They lingered over coffee in the morning, holding hands across the table, stalling until Bill knocked at the door.

"You'd better get a move on, or you'll miss your train!"

On the way to South Station, Asa was in turmoil. Although he was heartbroken to be leaving Mary, and feared that he may embarrass himself by shedding noticeable tears at any moment, another part of him was getting excited about joining the Office of Naval Intelligence. And then he felt that his anticipation was disloyal to Mary. Holding her hand, he watched her, trying to see how she was taking it.

"Are you all right, my love?" he asked.

Mary sighed. "I'm sad to be saying goodbye, of course, but I'll be fine. Just you be careful and make sure you come back to me; do you hear?"

"Loud and clear," Asa said. He leaned over to kiss her cheek.

At the station, they engaged in a long and passionate kiss goodbye.

Some of the other people on the platform tsk-tsked and gave them disapproving looks. They ignored them until a policeman came close with a loud, "Ahem." Emily smiled at him and mouthed, "Newlyweds." He tipped his hat to her and prowled off in another direction.

Asa was so reluctant to let go of Mary's hand, he had to leap aboard the train after it had started to move. When the conductor began to reprimand him, he smiled, embarrassed. "I'm sorry. I just couldn't bear to leave my new bride."

The conductor smiled. "Congratulations. But don't ever do that again or your new bride may find herself without a bridegroom."

He looked out the window and waved to Mary, watching her until she disappeared into the distance. Sighing, he hefted his sea bag and went to find a seat. He took out a book, but couldn't see the words on the page through the blur of salt water in his eyes.

His mind was a clamoring din. He didn't know whether to cry or grin or tear his hair out, but he couldn't very well do any of those things in a carriage full of people. Feeling melancholy, excited, and anxious all at once, he gazed out the window trying to calm himself with deep breaths as he said goodbye to the familiar sights of home, with its people he loved, as he traveled farther away.

\* \* \* \*

Mary smiled bravely for Asa, waving goodbye, but when his train disappeared down the track, she turned to Emily, tears running down her cheeks.

"Will he come back to me?" Her voice quavered. "Will he be all right? Dear God, let him be all right."

"If I know Asa," Bill said. "He'll come back to you come—"

"You can say it, Bill." Mary offered a weak chuckle that was nearer a sob. "I come from a long line of sailors, remember? Come hell or high water." Her smile got a bit stronger. "Yes, I believe you're right."

Emily put her arm around Mary's shoulders as they walked out of the station.

# Endnotes

1 Walt Whitman, "O Captain, My Captain!"

2 John Donne, "Holy Sonnets"

3 Walt Whitman, "Now Finale to the Shore"

4 *The Dead Horse* had nothing to do with old men or horses. It dates from the age of sail. The horse was a metaphor for the thirty to one-hundred days a sailor worked without pay when he first set sail, the pay going to the shipping company's boarding house. When the allotted time was over, the men made a "horse" out of odds and ends, raised it up to the yardarm with a long rope and threw it overboard, making a celebration of the day he'd finally get money for work, singing shanties and having a tot of rum.

5 'The submarines!' 'I understand. You are safe now. Are you from Quebec? Do you speak English?'

6 My name is Asa Mayhew, and yours?

7 Yes, but of course.

8 Agreed; all right; okay.

9 'Yes, of course! How could I forget? The American ship!'

10 'Do you see?'

11 'Please, do not go yet.'

12 'You are a good cat.'

13 Where is it?

14 Tell me or I will kill you!

15 Are there more bombs aboard?

16 No! No!

17 God will punish you if you're lying!

18 God is my witness; there are no more!

19 No more! There are no more!

20 That little shit.

21 That little shit.

22 immediately

23 Please. I am sorry.

24 Goodbye, Asa. Thank you.

25 Good luck.

26 Job 5:7

27 Psalm 69

28 Walt Whitman, "Passage to India."

29 Matthew 5:48

30 Walt Whitman, "Passage to India"

31 Juliana of Norwich, *Revelations of Divine Love*

32 William Wordsworth, Sonnet

33 Robert Burns, *A Red, Red, Rose*

# Acknowledgements

*Asa Mayhew* was inspired by the *Asey Mayo Cape Cod Mystery* series written by Pheobe Atwood Taylor in the 1930's and '40's. Wondering what Asey Mayo's back story was, while letting my mind drift one day, Asa Mayhew wandered in asking for his story to be told. Although he has a few things in common with Asey Mayo, he turned out to be very different.

My gratitude goes to Gabrielle Contelmo, who was an invaluable critique partner. Without her help and encouragement, this book may never have seen the light of day.

This series is dedicated to Uncle Harry, Mr. Burnham, and Percy, who all fought in the Great War, and whom I knew many years ago. May they rest in peace.